The Women
Of Woden

The Women Of Woden

Book I

Mystic Women of The Realm
Series

By
Robbie Collins

Gate Way Publishers
Vallejo, California

The Women of Woden
Book I, *Mystic Women of The Realm* Series
Copyright © 2005 Robbie Collins

All rights reserved, including the right to reproduce this book or portions thereof in any form whatsoever. No part of this book may be copied, stored in a retrieval system, or transmitted in any form or by any means without the expressed written permission of the publisher.

For information, contact Gate Way Publishers, 2801 Redwood Parkway, #219, Vallejo, California 94591 USA. Visit us on the World Wide Web at www.gate-way-publishers.com.

ISBN: 0-9635703-2-3

Cover Artwork by Javier Espinoza
Book Cover and Interior Design by DigitalWrite
www.digitalwrite.com

This book is a work of fiction. Names, characters, places and incidents are products of the author's imagination or are used fictitiously. Any resemblance to actual events, locales or persons, living or dead, is entirely coincidental.

To E.C., my High Queen.
"Wither thou, goest I."

Acknowledgements

*Thank you to E.C. who reminded me that I could,
and to Ann V. who provided the path.
Truth is ever more unbelievable than fiction.*

"Urgent: Woden's enemies are gathering their forces together. The warrior women of Woden must be told! We must find a way to inform them of their past so that they know they are not isolated. Their long-prior journals must be made available to them."

Unknown to the women warriors of Woden, their quiet community is about to become entwined into the mysterious and mystical realm of which they know so little.

As they prepare their community for battle, the women leaders learn of Woden's long-unknown past, their attraction for each other, The Realm's mystics, and the treachery that will lead them directly into the middle of The Realm and its struggles.

The suspenseful journey unfolds through a series of six books in a mystifying realm.

Come, let us pass through Woden's Gate together . . .

Chapter I
The Grassfields

The sentries had found her lying just outside Woden village boundary at what is called the Grassfields. She was semi-conscious, but was struggling to remain alert. Her dog had howled until someone came. The sentries had finally heard the dog and found the woman. They had then called for Meera, then for The Second, as a decision was needed about bringing the injured woman Inside. Not a decision lightly made in Woden.

When The Second arrived and saw the injured woman, she tried to mask her feelings. *So many moments have been wasted. I hope we are not overly late.* She had hurried to the site as quickly as possible, but it was an entire morn's journey from the Woden community. As she bent over her, the injured woman looked directly into The Second's eyes and blinked slowly as if it took great effort. Even this injured, her eyes seemed to speak to The Second with determination. The Second spoke tenderly to her. "You can rest now. I am known as The Second of Woden. We will take care of you and your dog. And we will tend to your injuries."

The injured woman nodded to The Second slightly, in apparent understanding, but didn't speak. She tried to recover something from an inside pocket. The effort must have caused her great pain as her face contorted into a cringe, but she remained silent. Meera's guards aimed their weapons upon her.

"Meera, have them place their weapons down."

"She might be armed, Second. She may be trying to hurt you, or worse."

The Second refrained from sighing. "She is overly injured to do anything, let alone hurt me."

Meera reluctantly motioned for them to back off. "Look, I think she is but trying to get something out of her garment."

The injured woman withdrew something small; some type of container. She held it up to The Second. Meera took it, then the woman slipped into unconsciousness. The Second tried to touch it, but Meera wouldn't let her near it. "Second, please touch it not; it could be dangerous. We will take it for study."

The Second knew that Meera was following procedure, but it still took all the patience she had to control herself. She just looked at Meera, who knew the look well, but Meera wasn't done with The Second yet. "Second, I think we should leave her Outside. We could make a shelter and tend to her here. We know not where she came from and know not if there is anyone else around with her."

As patiently as she could, The Second replied, "She is with her dog. If there were others, the dog would be looking for them. Have you never a dog, Meera?"

"No, I have not. But the woman could be dangerous, Second. And the dog will not let us near him. It is my duty to ensure that no harm comes to you or the community. How do any of us know that she is not here to hurt you, or The Highest? It could be but a trick."

The Second turned her gaze from the injured woman to look at Meera for the first moment since arriving. "If someone will do this much harm to one of their own people to trick us, then there is little in our power to prevent their kind of evil. No, I think her not dangerous. We will not leave her."

Pointing to the container that Meera was now holding, The Second said, "She came to deliver this to us, whatever it is. We probably cannot know what it is without her." Meera handed it to one of her guards. "The dog most likely senses that we are not going to harm her, and my guess is that he will follow wherever we take her."

The Second turned back toward the injured woman and bent down to examine her wounds more closely. "What be the extent of her injuries?"

"Her right knee was dislocated. We re-set it just before you arrived."

Ugh. The Second was glad she hadn't been here during that ordeal. *Painful moment*, she thought.

"She also has knife wounds in her left shoulder and arm, a deep gash in her left hand, and she has been hit on the head with something very heavy. Her dog is also injured. He has a knife wound on his hind end, but I cannot get close enough to see the damage. I think she will not live, Second. Her head injury looks overly severe."

"You and your guards have done well halting the bleeding and bandaging all the wounds. At least she is transportable. Did she carry weapons?" The Second stood up, yet looking at the woman. Her knee was dreadfully swollen, but well wrapped now.

"Thank you, Second. We have found nothing so far, except that object she but gave to us."

"Nothing?" She looked at Meera again and then surveyed the open grasslands. "Strange, is it not? Do you suppose her attackers took her weapons with them?"

Meera looked at The Second with surprise, "How did you but know it was more than one attacker?"

The Second laughed, "Just a guess. You have taught me well over the cycles." The Second had taken a quick look at the area Meera's guards had sectioned off, seeing more than two distinct sets of bootprints. "She looks strong, though. I bet her attackers look not much better."

"From the bootprints we think there were three, but one was dragged off. Dead or injured, probably. We can find no evidence of weapons, so they must have taken them."

The Second spoke softly to Meera so only she could hear, "I leave it to you to do your usual thorough investigation of the site. Make certain to check for how they got here. Her also. But be careful. We need not any more injuries. The healers have their hands full with The Highest. I also want to know how this happened at the boundary without the sentries but knowing it." She let the implications of that stand between them. Meera knew what The Second had meant in that statement. The boundary sentries were considered Woden's most important duty, as it was the first warning in case of threat or attack.

"Speak to me privately when you have your findings."

Meera nodded in understanding.

"Meera, do you think she walked here?" The Second hadn't seen any signs of a horse, but walking all the way from Apien or New Harborage was a formidable distance for anyone.

"From her clothing, I think she did. See her boots? They are heavy ones, and her long cloak was made for extreme conditions. The attackers must have shredded it. It is that pile of clothing over there at the edge of the woods. We have just begun searching for clues, though. I but think she came over the mountains." That meant a very long and dangerous journey.

"Has she spoken to anyone yet?"

"No, nothing. With her head injuries, I am unsure of her hearing ability."

Ever-negative Meera, The Second thought, knowing better. The injured woman had already acknowledged The Second's words. At least Meera was thorough, so The Second accepted her answers without argument. Besides, Meera was someone The Second respected. She took her duty seriously. Aside from that, she was The Second's closest friend. The Second hadn't really believed the object the injured woman had provided to be dangerous, but Meera had been correct - it was her duty to protect. She knew The Second well and knew when she could push an issue and when she couldn't.

They had been friends for over fifteen cycles. At one moment early on, some had thought that they would become more than friends, but those rumors died when Meera accepted another as a companion. During those fifteen cycles, Meera had prevented many potentially harmful attacks upon The Second, and they had remained close friends. She fully embraced that her duty was to protect The Second, and she did it well. The Second trusted Meera with her life.

The Second looked directly at Meera, "Take her and her dog to the healers and tell them to but heal both. I want no argument from them on this. Place her in my guest room when they feel they can move her, and assign a guard on her at all moments."

Both turned to look at the dog. He neither barked nor growled at them, but when the injured woman was moved to a litter, he followed. The Second wished that her purpose in life were so clear.

* * * *

Those few turns of waiting for the injured woman to regain consciousness seemed like forever to The Second. There was so much she needed to know that went unanswered. The injured woman remained unconscious the first two turns, only regaining consciousness slowly after that. In the interim, The Second spent her moments mostly with The Highest, her daily rounds, getting updates from Meera on her findings, and trying to appear normal to the community. She had gone to Meera and Caithas' dwelling this midturn for their usual updating session.

Caitha was Meera's companion and a master weaver and gardener. The Second loved going to their dwelling. Caitha always spoiled her, letting her sit in their patio, which was their private place. Caitha had decorated their dwelling and patio with peace, comfort and transcendence in mind. Given Meera and The Seconds' positions, they needed it. Meera and The Second were sitting on the patio discussing recent events while Caitha fussed over them, bringing them food and drink whenever she thought necessary. Their loving, but what they thought well-hidden looks between each other made The Second miss her own long-prior companion.

She laughed when Caitha poured Meera's drink. "Caitha, you spoil Meera. She lifts not one finger around here." Which was true, but Caitha seemed to relish in it.

Caitha smiled. "And she but deserves it!" She was always ready to defend her companion. "You work her overly hard, and that is all you two do, is work. Yourself needs a companion, as well!"

The Second ignored the suggestion, per usual, and asked Meera to update her while she ate Caitha's wonderful salad of goat cheese, lettuce, nuts, raisins, oil and vinegar.

"I have released the two sentries from their duties. I will need to deal with them later. They say they had become but bored, so had decided to sit together a while and talk. That is bad enough, but I also believe them not. The other sentries know nothing about the event, but those two tell the same story. Overly much so; same words and same details. We have confined them to their dwellings and placed guards outside their doors. That is not a popular decision, but I trust them not at all."

"Who is complaining about this decision?" If the two sentries had been neglectful, The Second couldn't imagine who would care that they had been placed under watch.

"The Counselors approached me. They said they were but certain it was an oversight on the sentries' parts."

The Second thought, *The controlling counselors.* She wasn't pleased. "And did they say how they came to know of the incident?"

"They said that the two sentries had come to them directly after the woman was brought Inside, to Woden. My fault on that one, as I did not cover it quickly enough. They also tried to give me grief about bringing the woman Inside."

The Second thought about that for a moment. It was apparent the Counselors knew too much.

But how?

Meera continued, "I would like to request Briggon over to but question them, as I have gotten as much as I can without using harsher measures. Perhaps he will even allow us to confine them over there for a while."

"Briggon? Drastic decision, Meera."

The Second considered Meera always a little hasty in her decisions. Involving Hengist, the men's community, was usually a last option, and one rarely taken.

"Why not just confine them to the sea for a while with Oisin?"

Sea Duty was one of Woden's vocations, but they also found it useful for those in need of closer scrutiny, watching, or general moments away from everyone. "Oisin told me that she is going over to Matah Island in the next few turns. She will be gone for over twenty turns, and has three ships going. These two sentries could be but placed apart, and we could let Oisin wear them down. At minimum, they will be away from here and the Counselors."

Oisin was The Second's counter-part on the sea. The Second knew that Oisin was much tougher than she was, being a strong, tall woman, with what some thought were brusque manners. The Second liked her and found her candidly honest. She never allowed anyone except The Second and The Highest to question her decisions, and always said exactly what she was thinking. The Second thought that she wouldn't allow any questioning of her decisions if she had the Sea Duty. It was rough and very dangerous. All in all, Briggon would probably be easier on these two women than Oisin. The Second didn't want to rely on Hengist, the men's community, unless really necessary. She just hoped that Oisin would bring them back. If they were guilty of being traitors, she knew that Oisin wouldn't bring them back at all.

"Oisin?" Meera wasn't questioning Oisin; she was questioning The Second's relationship with her. She knew that The Second and Oisin were involved with each other, but didn't know the extent of their relationship, and worried about it.

The Second just sighed, "Worry not. We are but friends, Meera."

"You and I are but friends, Second. You and Oisin are different than that. I cannot figure out your relationship with her. Why did you not accept her when she asked you?"

A few cycles prior, Oisin had asked The Second to be her companion. They had worked close together, out of necessity, for many cycles and had built a strong bond and trust with each other. For a few brief moments, they had discussed the possibility of becoming companions. But Oisin was a free spirit, and that's what The Second liked most about her: she was fun. After The Second lost her life-companion, Oisin had taught her how to laugh again. She would often bring The Second gifts from her travels and tell stories of her adventures.

The offer had been tempting. The Second was lonely, sad, and overly stressed at the moment. Woden had just been through four major attacks, and The Second worried about more. If The Second had accepted her offer, she could have stepped down as Second and traveled with her. But Oisin wasn't a companion. The Second thought her more a close friend, and was certain Oisin felt the same way. They both also knew that Oisin really didn't want a constant companion. She enjoyed her freedom too much. So they had become lovers, and The Second always found herself looking forward to sex with Oisin and their brief moments together. But she couldn't or wouldn't share this.

"We are but friends."

"Is she coming over?" Meera asked because she tried to watch The Second's dwelling more carefully whenever Oisin came over for the eve, for good reason: Both Seconds were in one dwelling. And since Oisin often brought strong drinks that The Second overly enjoyed upon a rare occasion, Meera was always concerned that they might end up wandering Woden's paths, naked.

"Next eve. Would you and Caitha like to come over to visit with her? You might as well. You will but worry otherwise. And it will give you a chance to speak with her about taking the two sentries with her."

Meera knew that Oisin's relationship with her own companion was just out of convenience, as neither of them wanted to be in a committed relationship, so Meera wasn't being cautious out of concern for Oisin's companion. The Second suspected Meera was instead worried about something else. She decided to wait and let Meera raise the issue.

"But what about the woman in your guestroom?"

"I have heard nothing about her being moved over yet. Have you?"

"She is being moved to your guestroom soon, at your request. The healers are complaining that she needs to spend more moments in the infirmary, but I think it not safe enough there."

"Instead of worrying, why not just come over and visit? You can have some fun, get to visit with Oisin, have but a few moments to talk to her about the sentries, and also keep me and Oisin controlled."

"A good idea. Do you really think Oisin can get anything out of them?"

"I certainly would not want to be in their position on Oisin's ships. 'No' is not an answer she permits. You but know the downside. If she finds they have betrayed Woden, we will not see the two again. They will become accidental fish-bait. Yet, it is better than involving Briggon and Hengist. I do not want them to know about this yet, if at all. I would rather keep this internal, if possible."

Meera nodded her acceptance of The Second's decisions. Caitha had returned as they were talking. The Second asked her, "Caitha, have you but seen or heard anything lately that seems a little suspicious?"

She nodded, "The weavers have seen the Counselors talking overly quietly amongst themselves for our liking."

The Counselors again.

With The Highest so ill, they were yet another problem for The Second to solve. Meera and Caitha could see The Second's concern about the Counselors. Their names were coming up all too often. If the Counselors were involved or behind this problem, then the problem ran deep, as they dealt more with Outside than any other of them. The Second wished she could ship the lot of them off with Oisin as well, but kept those un-leadership-like thoughts to herself. She knew Oisin would just as soon use them as an anchor. Oisin thought they were much too controlling and demanding, and spreading bad ideas inside Woden.

The Second had slipped into one of her usual long silences that always caused concern in Meera. Meera told her, "I will but assign someone to monitor their activities. Worry not, Second, we will figure this out soon."

The Second knew they would have to. She just didn't like all the underhanded plotting that was occurring. She knew that the only good in all of this, so far, was that whoever was behind this still didn't know that they were beginning to suspect something.

"When is your next meeting with Briggon?" Meera and Briggon met every few turns just to keep each other up-dated about the communities.

"In two turns. Do you wish me to go to the Bridge sooner to see if anything unusual is happening over there, as well?"

The Second nodded, "Yes. As soon as possible."

* * * *

The injured woman was moved to The Second's guestroom the next morn. The Second had informed Meera to place a guard outside her dwelling, but didn't think the woman would provide any immediate threat to her, knowing that she certainly wouldn't be able to move on her own for a few turns to come. One of the healers also remained outside on the patio, coming in periodically to check the woman's condition. When she could get it, which was seldom, The Second liked her privacy.

After she got up from bed, The Second went in to see the injured woman before meeting with her advisors. The injured woman had been placed in the guestroom that had its own entrance and outside patio. The room was more of a sunroom, so was a perfect place for resting, reading, and now, healing. As The Second looked upon her, she noticed that the woman's injuries were indeed extensive, but well tended. They had re-wrapped her knee, stitched up her knife wounds, and had been most concerned about her head wound. She would have many scars from this attack. The healers had been uncertain if she would regain consciousness, but she had. The Second didn't know why she hadn't seen them before, perhaps because of all the blood and dirt, but now noticed the tattoos on various parts of the woman's body.

Berth, one of the community's healers, walked into the room, bowing her head to The Second as she entered. "Good Morn, Second. How are you this morn? She is looking much better than when she first arrived." She didn't wait for an answer to her question. "The knife wound on her hand is quite deep and is yet leaking a bit, and I am but concerned about her head wound, yet she has regained consciousness. I have kept her heavy with potions for now. Did you but notice her tattoos?"

Berth removed the blanket a bit. The Second looked at the woman's hip. It looked like a word, but not one used in the community. "Jon." Nothing else. The Second wondered if it was the woman's name, but thought not. She didn't think someone would tattoo their own name on themselves. She looked at the coiled snake tattoo on the woman's ankle. Something about the snake played in her mind, but she couldn't place the reason. She then looked down at the dog. His hind end at been bandaged, which prevented him from moving around much. He was lying on the floor next to the injured woman in a bed the healers had made for him. Food and water had been placed close by.

Berth had seen The Second looking at the dog. She bent down to pet him, and his tail began to wag. "He will be fine and will recover soon. The wound was not overly deep, so he just has some stitches. He is a very friendly dog, and Jenna will be coming often to walk him around a little."

Jenna was Woden's main animal caretaker, and always made The Second laugh when she saw her. Every moment they happened to meet, she would say, "Hi, Second", and the bird who was her constant shoulder companion would do the same, "Hi Second; Hi Second". While she liked Jenna, she didn't need *another* person coming in and out of the dwelling. And she knew that she would end up wanting to do violence to the bird if she heard it more than once a turn.

She asked Berth, "Is there any chance the dog would go to but remain with Jenna for a while?"

She was desperate, and Berth knew it. "I am sorry Second, but the dog will not leave her except for a quick moment outside. I will speak with Jenna, though, to see if she can but wean him off her for a couple of turns." The Second gave her a look of hoped-for relief.

Lillon had entered the room searching for The Second, bowing her head to her as she entered, "Second?" Lillon was always formal with The Second. "All the advisors are assembled in your sitting room. Would you like me to inform them to begin the meeting?"

Lillon was The Second's assistant. The Second thought her to be a smart young woman who would make a fine leader soon. Lillon's patience with The Second was remarkable and was the only reason Lillon was allowed to spend her turns working with The Second. She had been made Second fourteen cycles prior and was to take an assistant then. She had resisted until two cycles prior, when Woden had grown enough to make the work impossible to handle alone. Besides, someone needed to be trained, as The Second didn't think she wanted this responsibility until she died.

"No," she sighed, "I need to be there. Have they but been provided with food and drink?" She always tried to soften the blows by filling her advisors with sweets before a meeting.

Lillon smiled knowingly, "Yes, Second. May baked some special orange sweets for them this turn. They have already almost emptied the plates, but May is bringing out more. She also told me to remind you that she has your morn meal ready for you."

The Second looked carefully at her. Lillon had just ended a relationship with a woman she yet loved but couldn't live with. The woman had been critical of everything Lillon did and of everyone Lillon came into contact with, often physically so. The Second could see that Lillon had been crying and knew that their discussions weren't yet over. She wished she could do more for her, but Lillon was embarrassed to speak of it. The Second was concerned that she had little personal experience to offer in regard to bad companionships. She knew that she would have to act soon regarding Lillon's companion, but hated to make that kind of decision. If Lillon's companion didn't admit to the violence by Festival, she was going to have to turn her out of the community. There would be protests, but the law was unmistakable. She mentally put aside these thoughts for later.

Turning to Berth, she said, "I will return to see her after the meeting. I would like a full report on her condition, then," indicating toward the injured woman. "I hope she will awaken soon. I must speak with her."

Berth was a good healer. She was patient and knowledgeable, but as with all healers, inclined toward healing the patient rather than The Second's needs toward communication.

"I am sorry, Second, but I have given her a potion to keep her quiet for a while. It is better that she rest for now."

The Second knew that, but was impatient to speak with the woman. There were many questions that she wanted and needed to ask.

Berth added, "I will be here, so will be able to give you the report whenever you are ready."

With that, she withdrew from the room. If The Second couldn't speak to the woman soon, she would have to insist that the potions be halted, but didn't want to force the issue until absolutely necessary. Instead, she hoped that Berth had heard her need and command, and would dispense with the potions until later. She turned to finish talking with Lillon.

"Lillon, would you mind not attending the meeting? I have something else I need you to do instead." Lillon nodded her acceptance, grateful that she wouldn't have to listen to the advisors, as her situation could be on the agenda.

"I would like you to begin finalizing the plans for Festival. Take special care to check out the bridge. Make certain it is in good working order. Oh, and please inform May that I will but eat later."

Lillon smiled, replying, "I already told her."

The Second thought, *When did I become so predictable?*

As The Second walked into the sitting room, she could hear her nine advisors speaking in softened voices. *Not a good sign.*

The Second knew that this usually meant they were speaking about her. She knew that they were a well-meaning group, but always nagged at her like mother hens to quit living her solitary life. With Festival approaching, she was certain her private life was the present topic of conversation. They wanted her to accept a companion at Festival. This was brought up at every Festival, so she considered the conversation wearisome, at best. She braced herself to have to listen to it once again.

The Second had loved well and been well loved once, but her companion had died defending her. Outsiders attacked the community and had tried to kill The Second. Meera had protected her, but hadn't seen The Second's companion acting as a distraction while Meera had taken The Second to safety. Even after all these cycles, The Second was yet haunted by those last moments when she caught one last frantic look at Brett. It took The Second many moons to recover from the loss to the point that she could walk in her realm again, and it had taken Meera equally long to get over her guilt. She had always felt herself to blame.

According to Woden's laws, The Second was required to have a companion, as was everyone. The Second always argued that she yet did, in her heart. Due to the nature of her loss, it was never pushed very hard. In her desperation to end the conversation and in her anger at her loss, she had once offered to leave the community, as prescribed by the law, if they truly felt she had no companion.

At that point The Highest had intervened. "Second, you know very well that this is not our desire. Of course you will always carry your companion in your heart. Your friends but believe that it would help you to accept another, though. I fear that this must be a premature discussion on our parts, however."

According to The Second, it was indeed. Her love had never ended. She yet carried her companion with her and would always love and miss her. No matter how entertaining and fun they were, every Festival served only to remind The Second at how much she had lost in Brett's death.

Per her usual fashion, she walked in and interrupted their well-meaning conversations, "Good morn, all. I am sorry I was a bit detained. I was just checking on our patient. There is nothing new to tell. She is yet sleeping, and her wounds have been well tended. Sephim, would you care to take over the agenda?"

They were all sitting in their favorite places. Over a long span, The Second had come to make this a comfortable room for them with Caitha's very artistic eye, even given its purpose. There were plants all around, trays and small tables for food and drink, rich but muted colors, and woven rugs to soften the sounds. She had experimented with the seats until each of the advisors had looked comfortable. Now the room contained all soft seating in various sizes, styles, and colors. She sat down in her favorite old chair.

The group was a bit jittery, but she passed that off to the new visitor. They each bowed their head toward The Second, "Good morn, Second. We have but a few items that require your guidance." Sephim always got directly to the point. "We feel that the patient should be more heavily guarded, and we but feel that she should be moved elsewhere."

The Second replied, "I knew you were going to raise this issue. You are concerned that this is a trap, and you are concerned that I am placing myself in jeopardy from those who might be trying to get into Woden. Clearly, we need to be more alert, but I do not want to give in to what-if's overly soon. I do, however, understand your concerns. We have been a closed community for over seventy cycles, closing our land and areas to prevent attacks and violence, and to maintain our freedom in a place of violent and un-benevolent rulers. Only a few—"

Tehna interrupted, "If I may, Second?"

She wasn't always this polite or formal. She was trying to be careful with The Second on this point. It was considered improper to interrupt The Second, but Tehna felt it important. The Second looked surprised, but nodded assent.

Tehna took a quiet sigh of relief, "You know why we are so protective of you, Second. You are the community's Highest at this moment, so extra caution should be but taken. On a normal turn, The Highest has more guards than you do now. Perhaps it is something you should get used to?" She hoped that she hadn't stepped out of line.

The Second knew that what Tehna had said was truth, yet didn't want to accept the fact that their Highest had become seriously ill since her last visit Outside. The Second was determined to remain in denial about The Highest's likely death.

The Highest had accepted an invitation as a show of diplomacy and trust from a very distant community to attend one of their sacred festivals. The Second kept hoping for a turn-around in The Highest's condition, but it didn't look good. If The Highest died, The Second would be losing her mentor, and the community would lose their beloved leader.

Meera and The Second had discussed the possibility of poisoning, but the healers had said that it was simply The Highest's cycles. Meera and The Second believed otherwise. Whenever The Highest's companion was unable to, The Second sat by her bedside for the past several turns just to spend some moments with her. The Highest slept most of her moments now, drugged to help with the pain. The Highest's illness, combined with the new concerns about the woman in the guestroom, had consumed all The Second's moments.

Meera added, "I have to insist, Second. Extra caution and protection must be allowed. There are overly many coincidences to proceed in a normal fashion. I know nothing yet, but there could be but a connection between The Highest's illness and the woman in your guestroom. Please understand the need for your increased protection. We must ensure your safety. Besides, there are overly many seemingly unconnected coincidences. I like it not."

The Second sighed in exasperation and struggled against just walking out. She looked around the room and saw each women nodding in agreement. She saw that she had been right—they had been talking about her before she walked into the room.

She stated what they knew she would, "The community will see the increased guards as but a sign of unrest. It will look overly suspicious," and immediately considered it a pitiful attempt on her part to fend them off.

Meera was prepared for it, "The community members already suspect trouble, and they are worried about you now. They do not want to lose you, too. They have already approached us and asked for extra alertness around you and your dwelling, Second."

Another sigh escaped from The Second, "If I agree to increased protection, I assume that you will do everything you can so that I feel or see it not."

Meera was patient with The Second, as always. "You will probably notice more women around your dwelling. I noticed that your gardens need tending and your patio walls need repair. And, you will be shadowed without you noticing it. In respect to your privacy, no guards will be placed in your library or bedroom. But I would like the woman out of your dwelling. You can place her in mine if you will not permit elsewhere."

The Second thought about their arguments for a moment, "I agree to the increased guards, but the woman must remain here. You may place one guard in her room if you must, but select her well. I want no words to leave this dwelling."

She knew that she hadn't needed to say that to Meera. Her guards were the best in the community. She thought that Meera probably made them swear death oaths to closed lips. No rumors were ever started by her guards.

Meera knew that The Second wouldn't allow the woman to be moved. She could tell from her actions. She simply nodded agreement to her proposal, but would take the issue up with her again later, privately.

The Second looked at Meera, "I feel like a trapped animal. This gives me even more respect for what The Highest has to put up with."

Meera just looked at her and patiently explained, "I know, Second, and I am but sorry this is overly frustrating for you. Yet we have to be very cautious now. We have gone through a lot in our cycles and we are overly experienced to let our watchfulness turn into carelessness. Thank you for allowing us to protect you."

Another sigh escaped from The Second. Meera was always good at instilling guilt in her.

The Second looked at her advisors, "These are very disturbed moments for us. The Highest is not expected to recover, as you know. This very sad fact along with the entry of our new visitor has raised many questions. I know you are trying to protect me, but I think that the real need for protection is of this woman. I cannot tell you anymore right now because I know not more. This woman is important to us and must be protected and given the moments to heal, if she can. I suspect we need her. She traveled a long journey to get a message to us. We must but help her."

She paused for a moment to gain strength for her next statement. She was about to give what freedom she had away for this woman, and hoped she was worth it.

"If I must make even more sacrifices to assuage your concerns, then I will, but I cannot allow her to be moved."

The Second seldom made such long statements to her advisors as she had this morn, so they understood her need for the woman to remain in her protection. They also knew from experience what a sacrifice she had just made.

Ghett said, "We understand, Second, but I had no knowledge of any urgency regarding this woman. Your permission to use guards as necessary will be but enough to calm the community for now." The Second considered her as good council regarding the community and was always on top of their concerns, especially the crafters. Ghett continued, "I assume you will inform us as you are able." They didn't like The Second keeping secrets from them, but she felt frustrated as she really wasn't. She hadn't had the moment or opportunity to tell them everything yet. "Then I will assume that we are but in agreement. The woman remains here, and Meera, you will do as you think best while protecting my needs as well."

"Of course, Second."

Meera was pleased that The Second had allowed more protection. This way she wouldn't have to be so secretive about it. She loved The Second and understood her need for some sense of space, but she also knew how extremely important The Second was to the community's future. She and a few others knew that The Second was the Spirits of the Falls' Chosen One. The Second had long forgotten that moment.

Sephim moved on to the next issue, "We would like to discuss the separation between Lillon and Hern. The laws are but clear and there are witnesses to the violence, but there has been no decision on this yet. We think it would be best if you made your decision well prior to Festival as possible."

The Second seemed surprised, "There were witnesses? I have not heard of this."

Tehna said, "Me, for one. Josin for another. And three other women and one child from the community. Josin, however, sees the event differently than the others."

Tehna was the Health advisor and had her ear to the community's self-appointed spiritual leaders, the Counselors. And most everyone considered the Counselors to be a difficult group. They were always distressing the women about what they should be doing rather than being true spiritual leaders. The Highest had discussed this problem with The Second just prior to The Highest becoming ill, and had agreed to offer them 'incentives for change', as she had called it. Clearly, she hadn't been able to attend to them prior to becoming so sick.

"Please bring me up to date on all this, Karan."

"Yes, Second. Hern struck Lillon repeatedly, with her fists, while on the path, yelling at her all the moments. Lillon has some severe bruising, but no other damage, yet the accounts differ somewhat. Josin says that Lillon incited the incident by purposefully infuriating Hern. The others saw Hern beating on Lillon. They know not why. Hern is making a political move to take over the community. She and the Counselors want a different form of rule. They thought that Lillon would act more as an inside agent."

The Second turned to Tehna for advice, "What do you think of this situation?"

Tehna motioned around the room, "We know the law is but clear on this. Hern must leave. But some Counselors will move to protest at Festival unless you make the decision prior to then. Hern is trying to convince others that she should be the next Highest. A small uprising at best, yet unfortunately, the first for our community. A small group believes her. All of us believe that you should evict Hern, and the sooner the better. The community but feels the same way."

Karan added, "That might cause more anger from the Counselors. They could use that move to tell others that if they do not agree with you, you have them removed and silenced."

The Second hadn't yet been informed about this growing situation. "What of her friends? Do they support her enough that they will but go with her should I evict her?" She was hoping the problem could be easily resolved, but knew better. "I suspect, as you do, that the Counselors have chosen this moment because they think I cannot make such a strong decision. Will they remain and try to create a turnover?"

"We know not." Meera was troubled that something had escaped her attention. "I will find that out. That is probably overly easy, though. Have you made a decision regarding Hern?"

The Second sighed deeply again, and was certain everyone heard her. She had a terrible habit of sighing whenever she was frustrated or at the end of her patience. She was trying to curtail the habit, but couldn't seem to halt herself at the correct moment. "Oh, I suppose I have, but I was hoping that Hern would but apologize and make an effort to continue their bond. From what I understand though, she has been changing; becoming more hostile against the charge of the community. I think we should know why. I am beginning to feel that there is more to this."

Ghett said, "I am concerned that the Counselors will get to the other witnesses and force them to change their minds about what they saw."

The Second was becoming angry, "What are we becoming? We have rules. Should we now not follow them? Decisions should not be based on popularity. This sounds like an attack from inside. Why did I not know about this rising problem? Why—?

Meera interrupted, "Second, if I may?"

She knew The Second was angry at not knowing about this escalating issue, but hoped The Second would yet continue to listen. Gratefully, The Second nodded in agreement.

"I have made certain that the Counselors cannot speak to the three witnesses without others being present."

The Second relaxed a little, "Good, Meera. Thank you. At least someone is on this. What does the community but say about this?"

Liley spoke up, "The large part of the community is angry at Hern for both reasons - Using physical abuse on Lillon, and for criticizing The Highest. Hern has not been very smart in criticizing The Highest while she be so ill."

Liley was the Farm and Garden Overseer, and spoke to much of the community daily. Everyone except for The Highest, The Second, Meera, Keets (Meera's counter-part advisor who worked with The Highest), Oisin and her crew spent some of their work-turn toward the community projects. The main project the women worked on was in the Farm and Gardens. Liley was primarily responsible for Woden's food production. Fortunately, her companion was as intent on the Farm and Gardens as Liley. If the community ever needed to find them, they were typically somewhere on the farms. Even their dwelling was located in the middle of the farm. It was like a two-in-one deal and the one of only two like that in the community.

"Most of the community feels Meera's move to protect the witnesses be a good one. But the Counselors are trying to sway opinion on that.

They are but trying to make it look like we control everyone's thinking. That be not a popular opinion, however."

The Second swallowed a sigh, "I will make a decision regarding the Counselors and Hern prior to Festival. Before that, Meera, do you have enough guards to do some detecting?"

"It would help if I could but use some of The Highest's guards."

The Second had just informed her advisors two midturns prior that The Highest had transferred her duties as Highest over to The Second, due to her steadily declining health. The Second hadn't wanted this and was hoping The Highest would choose another, namely Oisin, but the act was done. She had requested it remain quiet for now. Only The Highest, Oisin, the advisors and The Second knew. The Highest had wanted to transfer her position over to The Second as well, but The Second had talked her out of it. The Second had argued, "Moments enough for that later," and The Highest had momentarily conceded. Nonetheless, she had her wish placed in writing by Karan, Woden's resident Archivist and librarian, and was placed into Meera's protection. But all the advisors knew of her wish.

So Meera's request to use The Highest's guards wasn't out of line, but had potential of creating some ill will between the two groups. Normally, Meera's request to use some of the guards would have been a typical one. With The Second now overseeing both groups of advisors, the request would be seen as political posturing. All the advisors across the two groups wanted to know, "Who are going to be The Second's advisors?"

The request had created a silence in the room. They wanted and needed to know where they stood in regard to The Second's new position. She sat back and wished for better moments, swallowing another sigh.

"I have called The Highest's Advisors here for a meeting this after-midturn. I request your presence as well. I apologize for the short notice. They are not aware that you will be here. For the interim, I will be joining the two groups together until The Highest recovers, or the change has been formalized. Your patience will be most appreciated during this crisis."

There had been no opportunity to brief them on all the events, so this report had surprised most of them.

"Yes, Meera, you can have access to The Highest's guards. But please work with Keets. From your own guards, I want you to start doing some shadowing of each of the Counselors. Plus, I but want your guards to follow Josin and Jandra. I want to know all their activities. It is unfortunate that we have no insider in the Counselors."

"Consider it done, Second." Meera acted as if this was The Second's idea, but The Second thought that Meera was already doing this.

Sephim moved the agenda along, "We would like to remind The Second that now, since you have agreed to take over the duties of The Highest, the community appeals sessions are urgently needed."

These were sessions The Second had always hoped to avoid. Now they were staring her in the face. "Who is in charge of this?"

She really didn't know. The Highest had regular sessions with the community once every fourth midturn. The Highest would listen to the woman seeking assistance, take a few hints from her advisors, and then issue a decision. The Second could see her private moments diminishing even further.

Karan replied, "We had but thought that Lillon could manage this, as your assistant, but under the present circumstances, I would like to volunteer."

The Second caught herself in mid-sigh, "Thank you, Karan. That, at least, be but positive. Can we begin in four midturns hence? Please send a messenger around this midturn."

The Second suddenly shivered as she sensed a chilling foreboding that all their lives were going to change dramatically during the next few moons.

Sephim continued, "We have one other issue that needs your approval and understanding. We need to make certain that you are protected during your usual rounds. Although we but wish that you would discontinue your rounds during this moment, we know you will not. So, by letting us use guards, we but reach a negotiation."

The Second sighed and thought to herself, *Guards. On my rounds. What next?*

She said to them, "Under three conditions. One, I see them not. Two, there be no more discussion from you about me taking a companion at this festival. And three, there be no more discussion about the woman but staying in this dwelling. That is it. That is my compromise."

Her advisors nodded to each other. They knew to take the deal quickly before she changed her mind. Sephim said, "Done."

When bringing back the injured woman to the community, Meera and The Second had worked through a plan. They had agreed to share it with the advisors at this meeting. Meera rose and paced the room, a habit of hers. "The Second and I believe The Highest is poisoned with something our own healers cannot detect."

This would not be hard to do, The Second thought. *We need to provide our healers with more access to the Outside's medical knowledge, if any exist that are better than ours. Something for me to work on at another moment.*

Meera continued her pacing, "We know not if it happened while she was Outside, or if it be occurring within our community." The group shifted a little nervously. One of their own had just been accused as a possible traitor and assassin. "We do suspect a link, though. I have already replaced the guard in The Highest's kitchen with one of our own. And The Second has asked May to be The Highest's cook for a while."

"Who is going to cook for you, Second?" Zan asked and smiled. They all knew that The Second hadn't been allowed any moments to cook for herself for many cycles and were laughing at the prospect. They also all knew that May spoiled and protected her.

"Perhaps I can manage on my own."

She was dreaming too quickly of one less person in her dwelling, but Meera spoiled the moment, "No, May will but make meals for both of them. Security must be tighter and we can trust only May right now. But I need help. How can we get The Highest's cook out of there without looking like we are suspicious of someone?"

The Second interrupted briefly to ask Meera to meet her in the guest-room when the meeting was over, then excused herself to let them work out the details. The Second's advisors told her that they would be there this after-midturn and would do as expected. Given that there was another meeting later, The Second had enough. She walked through the dwelling to the kitchen. It was a hugely spacious kitchen and built to handle all the functions and affairs of The Second's position. May was The Second's cook and never let The Second do any of the cooking. May had inherited the position from her mother and was a wonderful cook. The kitchen always smelled inviting. The Second often found herself relaxing on one of the table's long benches, munching on May's sweets, listening to May chat about issues in the community.

As The Second entered the kitchen, May saw her, "Well, it is about the moment. Sit and eat. I have a delightful stew for you with some just-baked corn muffins, and a nice salad."

The Second really didn't have any spare moments, but it smelled so good that she thought she might eat while May spoke about The Highest.

"May, are you fine with doing the cooking for The Highest and me?"

"Oh, most certain, I can make enough for many, if it be necessary. Might give her the chance to taste some real cooking for a change."

She never liked the cook for The Highest and always told The Second not to eat anything when she went over for a meal with her. The Second thought the food fine, but May was convinced otherwise. The Second used to think May overly critical of the other cook, but was now re-thinking this position given The Highest's illness. She thought to herself that she was seeing conspiracy everywhere.

"You know that is not my meaning. Are you fine with the reason?"

"If you ask me, I would tell you that The Highest has been poisoned with that woman's terrible cooking for cycles. Her illness is but an accumulation of bad cooking." The Second was silent for a moment. May looked at her and said, "And you know you can trust me, Dear."

"I know. Thank you."

May overhead many secrets and private conversations in The Second's house, but The Second had come to trust her long prior. While May gossiped about the community (May said that this was a cook's prerogative), she never mentioned anything about what occurred within the dwelling. While The Second ate, May chatted on about the upcoming festival and reminded her that she should take a companion for her own benefit.

"May, why do you keep telling me that? You know I will not. I had my lifespan companion and but want no other."

"Because you are overly solitary. You need someone. You know, Second, you do not have to love a companion. But you could use a friend. I hear there are a few who will be asking you at this festival."

"Oh, no. Not again."

"Whatever you say, Second. But you yet need someone. I know you were but considering Jandra not so long prior. What but happened to that? Not to change the subject, Dear, but would you like to take your sweet in the guestroom? I know you are pressed for your moments. Please tell Berth that I made some broth for that poor woman."

"Thank you, May. The stew was delicious."

The Second thought to herself, *Jandra was not interested in me.*

She left the kitchen and went to the guestroom to check on the guest. As she entered, she saw that Berth was sitting next to her, talking, but she couldn't make out the words. Berth heard The Second coming, rose from her seat and bowed her head to her.

"Second. Our patient has opened her eyes," she said as she smiled at the woman. Turning to The Second, she said, "But she has not yet spoken. She is but confused from the potions we gave her. She will start to come around soon. I will be giving her more potions later, though, as she needs to sleep as much as possible."

"Can I but feed her? May made some broth for her."

"Good, she needs some nourishment and seems ready for it now. But nothing solid yet. We best put her in a more upright position first."

Berth told The Second what to do as they moved the woman to a sitting position. The Second didn't want to hurt her, but it looked like they caused her some discomfort. Again, she remained silent. The Second thought that most of the women in Woden would have been moaning from the pain.

Berth asked The Second if she could speak to her privately. They stepped outside. "I cannot tell if she be able to process conversation yet.

We will not be able to tell if there has been permanent damage to her thinking until she begins talking or showing signs of understanding."

The Second nodded her understanding, "I will be patient." The Second stepped back inside and sat down in the chair next to the bed.

She looked at the woman and was surprised but pleased that she was returning her gaze. Something about the woman looked very familiar to The Second, but she couldn't place it.

"I am glad to see you but made it through your ordeal. That must have been quite a fight on your part. Meera tells me that they must not have fared much better than you."

Meera had told her some preliminary findings the turn after the woman had been found. Their investigation had followed a trail of blood until they came to a river, where the trail ended. She had said that one person was carried to the river and another had barely limped their way to it. From the size of the bootprints, Meera had guessed that there were two women and one man. Meera had two scouts continuing to check for any further signs of the attackers.

"I hope that Berth told you your dog is fine."

The Second didn't see the dog, guessing that Jenna had taken him away for awhile. She silently fortified herself to be patient with Jenna's bird this turn, upon their probable return.

"You may not remember me from when we found you, but I am The Second of Woden. The women just call me Second. Terrible name, is it not?"

It had long ago been considered proper to call her by the title of Second as it was to refer to their main leader as The Highest. The Second had never really liked it, but had accepted it. She was seldom referred to by her real name and suspected that most had even forgotten it.

May walked in, "Here is your sweet, Second."

The Second looked at the injured woman, smiled and winked. *Point made, terrible name.*

May said, "I see that our visitor is ready for some food as well, so here be some nice warm broth I made especially for you."

She sat the sweet, tea and broth on the small table next to The Second. May looked at her, smiling, "She looks much improved."

The Second thought that a big stretch, but her bruises weren't so vividly colorful this midturn. The woman followed the conversation, but said nothing. She kept looking at The Second.

"Enjoy your food. I will return directly to pick up the dishes."

The Second decided to give the woman some background to Woden as she fed her, while trying to ignore the ongoing conversation in the meeting room. She was hoping that the woman would be able to speak soon.

The Second took the bowl of broth and began slowly spoon-feeding it to her, noticing that she seemed to want it.

"I know not if you are acquainted with our community. Perhaps a little background would help you as you eat."

The woman nodded slightly. From the nod, The Second assumed that she was easily able to follow conversation.

"The community used to be called The Town until we grew into a good sized place and changed the name. That was well long prior. It is an all-woman community. There are no men except during allowed visitations, festivals, or trading of goods. It has been a closed community since its beginnings."

She wondered if the woman understood what she was saying. Her eyes followed movements, however, so The Second thought she just needed more moments to recover from the attack as well as from Berth's well-meaning but overly done potions.

The Second kept feeding her the broth as she talked. "Women apply for entrance into the community, but can leave at any moment. Not many do, but there be a small of amount of turnover. We have many more requests of permission for entry than we take. We take only twenty-five new community members a cycle, but do have some plans for future expansion. It has more complexity than that, with the addition of children, but we do monitor our growth.

"We claim an area of twenty-two squares and presently credit a small part of it to a men's community. They pay us in trade items, security or labor. Most of our land be but unused, and we plan to keep a good portion of it in the more natural states. It is extremely good land. Three major rivers run through it and there is an abundance of wild grassfields. Our sides border the forest, mountains and sea. So we easily supply our need for wood and food. My archivist advisor but tells me that our founding women took two cycles scouting for this location. We have fought and won many battles over this territory. We also chose it because it be so distant from other communities, as you know from your long journey. Some think it odd that we work hand-in-hand with Hengist, the men's community, but it serves both of us well. We trade with each other, protect each other when attacked, hold five of our festivals together, and utilize one another for reproductive purposes."

Neither the men nor the women liked the notion, in general, but if someone wanted children, it was the only way they knew to conceive. Karan had informed The Second that some of the festivals had arisen out of a need to formalize the breeding process.

"In terms of leadership, there be The Highest, me, our Sea-Duty Second, Oisin, then our counsels. The Highest appoints all her positions, and the same with The Second. The Highest is selected either through appointment by the retiring Highest or by vote of the community. Hengist is governed through a Third, Briggon. They follow all our laws and rules, and whenever we change them, we include them in the discussion."

The Second paused, "That be quite a lot of detail for you at this moment."

The Second guessed that she was wearing the woman out with all this information. She had finished her soup broth, so The Second put the bowl down and picked up the sweet.

"Here, try one little bite of this. I love May's sweets."

The Second gave her one very small bite, mostly just for taste. She knew she wasn't to give her any solids, but thought that, "Sweets are, well, sweets". The woman smiled a bit at the taste.

The Second thought to herself, *Ah, sensual awareness. Good. She will recover quickly.*

She would need to eat again fairly soon, but this had been a good start. The Second imagined that the woman would be feeding herself with her good hand as soon as the potions wore off. She seemed to be more alert, and The Second guessed that the food helped offset the overly done potions.

"Our community has about 1,500 women and female children at present, and we have plans to halt expansion at 2,500."

The Second had wanted to halt it at 2,000, but it was a battle she didn't mind losing. She thought that they certainly had enough room for the growth.

"Every community member contributes toward the community projects such as the gardens, the farms and livestock, our sentries, sea-duty, building and maintenance, or whatever be needed. It is a good system and has served us well. But it does rely on the able oversight of a lot of strong and fair women leaders. Hengist has about 1,200 men right now. They have most recently decided to let in a few more numbers, but that is a change as they had closed their community to new entrances for a while."

The Second started to give her some tea to wash down the sweet, when the woman's right hand grabbed her arm. A surge went from The Second's arm to the injured woman's.

Nothing was said, but The Second suddenly was able to sense the woman's thoughts, *I'm here to help The Highest.*

She didn't understand how she sensed that. The injured woman held on tightly and tried to pull The Second forward as if trying to speak to her. The Second had no fear of her, so bent close to listen, "Highest . . . poisoned . . . anti-poison."

The Second was so shocked that she dropped the cup of tea as she stood up. What she sensed had been truth. The cup broke into pieces as it landed on the floor, causing much noise, while the woman's arm dropped back to the bed. Some facts were finally coming together for The Second. The guard, Berth and May all came running in asking questions.

"What happened?"

"Are you hurt?"

"Is she well?"

"Where did the noise come from?"

"Did she try to hurt you?"

The Second wasted no moment answering their questions but commanded the guard.

"Get Meera!"

May saw the cup and began to clean it up. The guard ran to get Meera, who was yet with the other advisors in the sitting room. Berth just looked perplexed.

"Thank you, Berth. Everything is under control."

Berth left the room without question.

"I am here, Second." Meera had arrived and the guard was with her.

The Second said, "Have your guard wait outside for a moment." The guard stepped outside without waiting for Meera's order.

"May, thank you for picking that up."

May understood that The Second was asking her to leave, and did so.

The Second turned toward Meera and indicated toward the injured woman. "Meera, remember the object she but gave us? It is an anti-poison. She said that The Highest has been poisoned. I believe this so. Retrieve it and come back. Before you go, though, get more guards around this place. I will tell you more upon your return."

Meera looked at the woman. The Second could see the cautiousness and concern in Meera's gaze. Meera went to her guard, "Get four more guards around this dwelling right now, and be very alert."

Meera turned to go, then looked back and almost whispered, "How do you know the object contains no poison? How do you but know that someone is not trying to poison her further?"

The Second didn't, for certain, and thought them good questions on her part. "I know not, but somehow I sensed the truth in her statements. For your benefit, though, get whoever of the healers you trust the most that might be able to identify an anti-poison, and bring her back with you."

That satisfied Meera for the moment, and she left on her mission. The Second sat back down and looked at the injured woman. The Second had pulled away from her as she stood up, so looked to see if she had hurt her some in the movement.

"You are certainly full of surprises. I fear that created quite a lot of commotion. How are you?"

The Second took the woman's hand in her own to examine her dressing. She wanted to see if she had caused her wound to open when she had stood up so suddenly. As she touched her hand, the strange feeling passed through it again. As it did so, the woman's eyes opened wide with the same feeling. She *felt* the woman say '*Thank you*' but knew that the woman hadn't spoken. The Second wondered what the feeling was, but let the feeling and voiceless message pass. She saw some new signs of blood on the woman's wound and called for Berth.

The woman simply whispered, "Fine," and let go.

The Second wondered, *Who be this woman?* then said, "No, you are not. I have caused your stitches to open. Lie still and Berth will tend to it."

The Second was glad to see her recovering though, and could tell that she would be able to converse soon. Then she could get their questions answered.

"We have been calling you the injured woman overly long that soon it will be your official name, unless there be a more appropriate name you prefer?" The Second was trying to provide a calm appearance, but a million thoughts were going through her head.

How does this woman know about the poisoning? Why would she have been sent to provide an anti-poison?

A soft, strained voice replied, "Keddi."

"Keddi? Well, Keddi, you may well be the hero of the turn." The Second was fairly certain that Keddi had indeed come to give them the antipoison. What she didn't know was why. The Second wondered how Keddi knew about The Highest's condition, and decided to talk to her about that later.

Berth entered and bowed her head. "Second?"

The Second informed her about Keddi's hand and blood, then left to dismiss the advisors before the next round of commotion began. When she returned, Keddi was asleep and Berth was gone. She sat down and waited for Meera and the gang to return.

Elsewhere, across The Realm

"Her powers begin to emerge, Highness."

The High Queen responded, "It has taken overly long. But she knows not what they are. She should have been told of them far prior to this moment. They have kept this overly hidden from her. I should rescue her from them. We will have great need of her, soon."

"You have vowed not to interfere, Highness."

She nodded calmly, "For now I will honor My vow. But I sense trouble. And I sense something else in this small human town. Some other power that is not human. Different than her, though. But I can't make it out. I will keep my senses focused on her development."

Chapter II
Woden

The Second had also fallen asleep while waiting for Meera's return. She had spent too many long eves with The Highest of late. Meera walked in and saw the injured woman awake and The Second sleeping. Since she didn't trust the injured woman, she was angry at herself for leaving The Second alone with her. Meera suddenly felt sorry for The Second. She hated to wake her, but knew she must. She also knew that The Second was shouldering the entire burden of the community now. As she shook The Second's shoulder lightly, she felt a sudden slight surge enter her body through her hand and wondered what it was.

"Second, I have returned with the anti-poison and Nill. If anyone can determine if it is an anti-poison, Nill will."

The Second awoke to Meera's talking and noticed that Keddi was awake.

"Give it to Keddi and let her tell us how to open it."

Meera and Berth just looked at Keddi in amazement, and both uttered simultaneously, "Keddi?"

The Second had forgotten that they yet hadn't learned of Keddi's name.

"We had a short discussion after you left. She seems to be doing better and is conversant. But I will let her show you that herself."

Meera held the object out to Keddi, but she just struggled to speak, "cup . . . " Meera called on May to bring in a small cup. With her good hand, Keddi moved one of Meera's fingers to the very middle of the object with the thumb on the opposite side, and said, "press . . . over cup."

Meera held the cup under the object with one hand while she pressed the center. Nothing. Keddi said, "Harder . . . " She did, and some liquid came out the bottom. Meera kept squeezing until nothing more came out. There was a very small amount of liquid in the cup.

"It seems not enough."

Keddi said, "It is." She turned to Berth, "Add same . . . amount . . . of sulfur, five drops of water." She paused for a moment. "Use needle . . . in hip."

She was fading quickly. The pain was returning, as could be told by her wincing.

Meera turned to Nill, "Will you be able to tell anything from this?"

Nill looked miserable, "No, because I know not the particular poison; unless she does," indicating toward Keddi.

Keddi shook her head slightly, *No.*

Meera turned to The Second, "We cannot just give this to The Highest. It could be more poison." It was a sound assumption, but The Second felt it a wrong one.

"Meera, just do it. The Highest will but die if we do not try. Even if this be an anti-poison, it may be overly late to create a reversal in the damage already done to her. Do you have but better options?"

They all looked at the liquid in the cup. The Second almost laughed, thinking that they hoped it would speak to them. She thought they must have looked quite stupid to Keddi, and expected that Keddi thought they might start chanting over it pretty soon.

Meera suddenly turned to Keddi, "Why should we trust you? Give me proof that you are here to do no harm."

Keddi looked at The Second and then at Meera. She also saw Berth and two guards. Meera wasn't taking any chances.

The Second could tell what Keddi wanted, "Meera, she wants to talk to us alone."

Meera thought about it for a moment. She looked around the room, and then nodded. She told her guards to stand just outside the doors to the room, not yet trusting the woman.

When everyone had left, she showed Meera and The Second her left ankle, "Tell Highest."

The Second thought, *The coiled snake tattoo.*

Meera asked, "You want me to believe that The Highest knows about this mark?"

Her answer was soft, but clear, "Yes."

"I bet she does, Meera. I recalled something about that snake tattoo the moment I saw it, but could recall no details. I know it but means something to us. We can ask The Highest before we give her the anti-poison."

The Second looked at Keddi. Keddi smiled slightly and collapsed back down onto the bed. The Second had started to go with Nill and Meera to The Highest, but Meera made some very persuasive arguments against it.

"Everyone will be but suspicious if we all go."

The Second argued that the women would also see her going with Nill as a problem.

"No, they will not. Nill has to check on her anyway, and I am going to give her a report on what we found at the Grasslands."

The Second felt trapped in her dwelling. "You are?" She wondered about this, as Meera only reported to her.

Meera grinned, "No. The Highest cares not about such things. It be just the story we are using."

The Second went to the sitting room to set it up for the after midturn meeting, but someone had already prepared it. She decided to get the report from Berth on Keddi and then prepare for the meeting with the advisors. She also needed to meet with Lillon, but Lillon hadn't yet returned. The festival was approaching, and The Second wasn't ready for it. She knew that she would have to begin concentrating on the details quickly, or it wouldn't go smoothly. She walked back to the guestroom through the long open hallway to find Berth yet in the room with Keddi.

"Berth, I would like that report now, if possible." She figured that Keddi might as well hear it if she hadn't already.

"She is doing well, considering the injuries." Berth was looking at Keddi but speaking to The Second. "The knife wound on her hand was quite deep. It was cut to the bone, so we had to stitch the muscles as well. It is healing nicely, but there is a slight infection in the cut. We will have to wait until it is healed to determine if there is loss of movement in it. Her dislocated knee has much less swelling now, but she will need to remain off that for a while. Her other knife wounds were more like slices. They were not as deep as the one on her hand, and they are all infected. And because of the infections, she has a small fever, but that be under control with the potions. And finally, her head. This be the major concern, and we will just have to see how that heals. She needs rest. She but needs to remain off her leg for a while, anyway. And we will begin giving her real food at the next meal, slowly. Most of all, she needs no more excitement."

The Second ignored the last statement, figuring it was an admonition for her to halt asking questions of Keddi. The Second could tell that Keddi's head must yet hurt quite a bit as she moved it very little.

"Thank you, Berth. How is her dog?" She hadn't seen her dog since early morn.

"Oh, Jenna talked him into remaining with her for the turn. It seems she has some very enticing food treats."

The Second sat down again in the chair next to Keddi, "I have questions to ask of you, but none that will not wait." She looked at Keddi and thought that if they did have someone in Woden trying to do harm, then Keddi was yet in danger. She looked outside and saw that her gardens were already being tended to, and the patio stones were being refitted. Meera's guards, she presumed.

"Festival?"

She looked back at Keddi, surprised that she had asked the question.

"I see we are being well-guarded," and nodded toward the new *gardeners*. "The festival, huh? Perhaps we can get you over there, if you are better by then."

The Second was preoccupied with all the need for increased security. She wondered if they should move Keddi to her bedroom. The guestroom was all windows on the patio-side and was too exposed for her to remain there. The Second knew she could make-do by sleeping in the library if necessary.

"Festival?"

"Oh, sorry. I fear my thoughts are but elsewhere."

She looked back toward Keddi. Although she looked frail lying in the bed, The Second could see that she had well defined features and muscles. She guessed that she must do something very physical. She also noticed her hair for the first moment. It was exceptionally short, black and shiny, but with some graying toward the left front side. A good part of her head had been shaved so the healers could tend to it better. The Second guessed her to be a little older than herself, but in imminently better shape. She assumed Keddi spent most of her life outside as she was quite darkened by the sun. Her green eyes were like jewels, and The Second found her very stunning to look at. That surprised her. But she also thought that Keddi looked vaguely familiar.

"The festival. Hmmmm . . . well, we hold but five festivals a cycle with Hengist, one at the beginning of each season. And then we have one more with just ourselves, at the Falls. This upcoming festival is the new growing season festival. It lasts but one full turn from sun's rise to sun's rise, although it really will not get started until well into mid-morn. There be entertainment, overly much food, dancing, music, our rebirth ceremonies, an evening fire, a ceremony for new companions, and a ceremony to request fertile crops and wombs. It be also at each of these festivals that a woman can ask another woman to become their companion, and it is at that same moment that those who have been asked accept, or not. The fertilization ceremony then ends with some of the women going back with the men to their community for the evening in hopes of having a fertile womb. All the women must be back by sunrise, though. A barbaric law, but one yet rigidly enforced."

She paused for a moment, thinking about this practice and about things she wouldn't say. Most women, as well as the men, reviled it, but it was a necessary practice if they wanted children. They had long prior conceded to this, as they knew no other way. The agreement was that the women's community would raise the female children and the men's community would raise the male children. The Second supposed that the practice worked well enough, but there were occasionally the men and women that wanted to be together as companions. There were other communities for this type of communion, but Woden and Hengist wished to protect their own practices. If the women didn't return by sun's rise of the festival closing, they weren't allowed back into Woden. Cycles in the past, well before The Second, the women who were late had been put to death. There was no exception to being cast out if a woman was late in returning, and sadly there were too many moments when women were late. It was a very unfortunate affair, and The Second hoped that it wouldn't occur during the next festival.

"I think you might be entertained at the festival. How about if I make some arrangements for you to be there for part of it?"

She nodded in agreement.

The Second then left as Keddi was tired, and she needed to prepare herself for the meeting with The Highest's and her own advisors. She didn't look forward to this meeting.

* * * *

The Second stood in her main doorway, welcoming all the advisors into her dwelling. She liked her doorway and felt safe near it. Brett had made it for her long prior. It was a short door, just a little over The Second's head, so some women had to stoop to enter. It was made of a red-tinted heavy wood onto which Brett had carved the Spirit designs. The Second smiled and greeted the advisors pleasantly, but apart from her own advisors, she considered them mostly droll and sour. She tried to fortify herself so that she wouldn't just toss them out the door. Several of them had already arrived.

"Welcome, Treena. We are about to begin."

"Second." She bowed her head, "What are your advisors doing here?"

"As you said, they are but my advisors. As you all are, for now."

"I oppose this."

It was as The Second had expected. The Highest's advisors expected not to work with her own advisors. She hadn't anticipated that all of them would be a problem, however. She just thought Treena dealt too much with the so-called spiritual leaders, so couldn't help herself from being a bother. The Second refrained from any further comments and turned to Jandra, the next advisor approaching.

She bowed her head. "Second."

Jandra was mentally a very strong woman, and was an exceptionally wonderful advocate for all the women in the community. The community loved her well, and enjoyed her endless determination, but also found her somewhat quiet. The Second considered Jandra excellent company, but seldom had the moment to enjoy it. And The Second considered Jandra the most beautiful woman in all of Woden. To all the women, Jandra was stunningly beautiful, but reserved.

"Hello, Jandra. It bodes a good turn for a meeting, does it not?"

It had begun to rain lightly, so The Second thought they might as well be inside.

"Thank you for inviting us to be your advisors, Second. I am most humbled and honored that you seek our counsel. I have long desired to work with you."

"And I with you, Jandra. The Highest has made much mention of the wise counsel you have provided her over the cycles."

"I have long wished to have a moment to speak with you about many issues."

She couldn't help staring at Jandra's dark eyes, thinking them the most beautiful in all of Woden. She struggled to remain distant from her feelings. "In truth, there never seems to be enough moments in a turn. I also would like such an opportunity to meet with you. There is much business between us that we but must guess about overly much. This separation of the advisors makes it most difficult."

"Second, I was but wondering if you would be interested . . . " Jandra then saw Meera. "What are *you* doing here?"

She stood in the path, fully surprised to see Meera, her body posture very rigid. She seemed almost hostile toward Meera.

"All my advisors are here this after-midturn. We need to work together now."

Meera walked up and tried to be polite. She nodded toward Jandra, "Jandra."

Jandra wasn't having any of it, "Your other advisors I mind not. But this one . . . " She looked angry at Meera, "You have interfered into The Second's affairs far overly long and have done her great damage."

The Second asked, "Damage? What do you mean? This be not like you."

She turned back to The Second, "My apologies, Second. I do not think Meera provides you the counsel you need, but that is your decision to make. Her presence startled me. Please forgive my actions. I would like to speak to you privately at some point, if I may, Second, but I fear I have just stepped out of line."

Jandra had controlled The Highest's council for the last few cycles. The Second had never learned of why The Highest allowed her do this, but assumed The Highest had her reasons, knowing that Jandra was very wise in her council.

She had never understood Jandra's outward dislike of Meera, but knew it had been that way for many cycles. The Second liked Jandra, and often found herself thinking about her when laying alone in her bed. At many of the social events, The Second often sought out Jandra's company for someone she could relate to. Two cycles prior, Jandra had lost her companion, and The Second had a passing thought of seeing if they could build more than a momentary relationship together, but never acted on it. She later learned that Jandra was committing more to Josin, so The Second never entertained the notion again.

"Let us forget this ever occurred, Jandra. I am more than happy to meet with you whenever you would like. You know this as truth."

"Thank you, Second. I will find a moment convenient for the both of us. I am sorry if my actions offended you."

Jandra turned to Meera and simply said, "Meera", and went inside.

"It would seem you have your own issues with these advisors, as well."

"So it seems with at least one, Second. Should I but throw them out already?"

The Second looked at her. Meera was smiling, so knew she was just trying to help make light of the situation. Jandra was challenging, but worth the effort. Treena was another challenge, but one in which The Second was unsure of. For many cycles The Second had surrounded herself with people she could trust. This was different, though, and was going to be difficult. She didn't trust all these women, and she didn't want to be at this meeting.

She stood and watched the rainfall for a few moments, thinking it peaceful and quiet. She liked the sound it made on the rooftops. The pathways needed the cleaning from the rain as it helped to settle the dust. Meera respected the silence. She knew this meeting was going to get combative, so gave The Second the moment she needed.

Eventually, The Second spoke, "Did you get to see The Highest?"

Meera nodded, "She said that she knows Keddi. She said that she trusts Keddi with her life and would tell you why later. She wants you and me to visit with her early this eve. We gave her the injection. I swore Nill to secrecy, but I do not think she be anything to worry about."

The Second looked at Meera for a moment and wondered if the community knew what a treasure it had in her.

"Well then, let us face the snakes."

Meera and The Second walked in together, closing the front door behind them. The room was extremely crowded, which is how The Second had wanted it, and everyone had divided themselves by group. The Highest's advisors sat on one side and The Second's advisors sat on the other. All were busy eating the food May had provided, though, so The Second silently laughed at that. Meera sat down at the far end, while The Second continued to stand.

"Thank yo—"

She had started to speak when Josin, The Highest's chief advisor, interrupted her, "Why did you invite your advisors? You have assumed The Highest's responsibilities now, so we are your proper advisors. This be not right. Dismiss them, now!"

"I refuse to work with these other women, too. I have earned my position and do not consider myself equal to these women," Treena added her say.

"And since we have Keets, we really don't need Meera." Josin considered herself The Highest at many moments and often issued such orders.

All eyes were moving back and forth between Josin and The Second. Meera felt sorry for The Second, but said nothing, well knowing that The Second could handle it. No one spoke. They were waiting to see what happened next. The Second knew Josin to be a troublemaker, but Treena was an issue that The Second couldn't understand. And Jandra just seemed to be angry at Meera for something even Meera didn't understand.

Yet standing, The Second faced Josin and Treena, well irritated at their outburst. In a stern voice she asked, "Are you so bold and disrespectful as to interrupt The Second of Woden?"

Jandra visibly flinched. Meera was stunned. She had never seen The Second be this forceful. Her usual style was to create negotiated stances. Meera wondered if The Second was overly strained from having to govern the entire community.

The Second continued, "And Josin, are you so insolent you dare to issue me commands? During my hopefully short tenure as acting Highest, I have been given the responsibility to oversee Woden. I hope that we can but unify during this stressful moment, but if you find yourself unable to participate as the position intends, then you are excused so as to be elsewhere!"

She took a moment to sit down, "I should not have to remind you that the two advisory groups were put together purposefully by our Highest so that there were task differentiations. I plan to uphold her wishes until her health improves. All decisions will go through me from this moment on, but I need this advisory council to help me make good decisions. I need and want all of you. *But*, I will treat you all as equals—there be no hierarchies within this group. And I will count on your respect."

She waited for the resistance to begin. Meera acted normally by reaching over for a sweet. Some of The Second's advisors followed suit, as did Keets, Meera's counterpart with The Highest.

Keets took a bite and then spoke up, "I, for one, am delighted you have but called us together as a group, Second. I know that Meera and I will be quite willing to work together. We have done so upon many occasions. I really do not understand your issues, Josin, but you are often as overly rigid. You know that The Highest would not like us to create dissension."

Keets was a good deal older than Meera, but capable. Her guards were no longer as good as Meera's, but this had occurred only through a long span and as Keets had gotten older. The Second would have to rely on Meera to pull these two guard groups together. Keets, for her side, had trained Meera and had done well for many seasons.

"Oh, shut up, Keets. Quit being such a simpleton. I know well that you hate working with Meera."

Keets didn't even seem perturbed, as if these attitudes were usual. "You make a fool of yourself, Josin, per normal. The only difference is that now it be in front of The Second's advisors. So much for a fresh start for you."

The Second guessed that she was well used to Josin's outbursts. She was tempted to let them battle it out between themselves, but thought better of it.

"Enough! This be not the moment. I will hear no more of this petty bickering. Fight between yourselves later, if that but amuses you. If I hear anymore fighting between any of you, I will permanently dismiss those responsible. We have overly many issues to take care of without bickering between ourselves."

She decided to cut the meeting short and just issue the tasks at hand. She had no patience for them and wondered how The Highest dealt with those two.

"I have reasons to believe that The Highest has been poisoned, in spite of what the healers say."

The Second had warned Meera that she was going to say this, and had asked her to pay close attention to everyone's reactions as she made the statement. They both suspected that someone in the room could well be behind the poisoning.

"That and the upcoming festival give me great cause for concern. Meera and Keets, please increase security for the festival without raising concern throughout the community. Give me a report on your strategy next morn."

They both nodded their agreement.

"Josin, Ghett, Fionn and Karan. Advise me on Lillon's companion by next after-midturn. I want advice on the laws regarding this, the concerns of the community, and the general feeling regarding what should occur. Josin and Fionn, if you are not up on the events around this, then Karan can fill you in."

Josin, Tehna and Karan all nodded in agreement.

Treena stood up, "We require no committee for this issue. I am the spiritual advisor and I know that this was an accident. Hern be a wonderful person and would not hit anyone. You are making overly much of this. Besides, Lillon be overly sensitive. In fact, Hern reported that Lillon caused it."

Tehna got up, stormed across the room toward Treena and almost spit fire, "You lie. Hern be a mate-batterer and you know it! She should be but expelled, as the law states. You are guilty of protecting one of your own."

Tehna obviously had lost her patience. The Second had hoped her advisors could keep it together, but Treena was quite challenging. They were standing face-to-face and Tehna's hands were clasped tightly into fists, "You are biased for Hern already and you have not even heard the facts. You should not be allowed on any such committee."

Treena turned, raging at The Second, "I DEMAND that you cancel this committee, NOW!"

"Sit down, Treena."

The Second had spoken. Everyone turned toward her and waited. Meera thought that she looked angry, for good reason.

"Tehna, excuse yourself from the remainder of this meeting. Treena, you are out of line. Speak to me after the meeting."

"Kandan, Lillon, Govan and Jandra, I need you to get this festival under control. Give me a report in two midturns, hence. I would be especially pleased if you four would just take this over for this season."

She had thought this would be a good team to work together on the festival and big enough to handle all the details. She wanted this off her hands for now as she had too much else to concentrate on. Lillon and The Highest's assistant, Govan, had both been working on it already, anyway, so she felt that this group could get this task done without her. She also knew that Lillon and Kandan would know what she wanted.

Once again, Treena interrupted, "But I am also the advisor for festivals. I should be on this committee as well. I am the one usually in charge of the festivals."

"Treena, you are to speak no more this meeting. I will speak to you after about your continued participation as an advisor."

Meera thought that Treena and a few others looked shocked at that statement. *So*, she thought, *The Second is making decisions about these advisors. Good.*

The Second then asked Alain, The Highest's advisors on accounts, and Ghada, her advisor on the same, to walk with her during her rounds for an update, following the meeting. They both agreed. Meera had already arranged with The Second that she would accompany her. The Second then finished distributing duties to the rest.

At the end, Josin spoke up, "I would like to be up-dated on this *mystery* woman you but keep hidden in your guestroom, and I would like to but know the reason for all the increased security that I see." Meera thought her tone was overly demanding. "I think that you are just building nothing to a crisis level. The Highest would not be so quick to instill such paranoia."

The Second looked at them slowly, studying them one-by-one. "I have no patience for this. Until this moment, I had decided to keep all the advisors together as one united group. After this child-like display, I will now reconsider my decision. The way in which you carry out your duties and the way in which you display attitudes needed during this moment in our community will but help me to determine which advisors I will continue to use. I will make this pronouncement at one of our upcoming community sessions. Consider yourselves on trial. Meera, would you please brief the advisors on Keddi?"

Meera and The Second had already worked out what The Highest's advisors should be told - not much.

"Meera, Keets, Alain and Ghada, please meet me in my guestroom when the meeting is concluded. I will see the rest of you at the arranged meeting moments. Please have your updates ready. Treena, come with me."

"Second?"

The Second turned to face Jandra. Her eyes glared and her lips were closed tight, "Jandra." Jandra bowed to The Second, "I apologize for my insolence, Second. You have my support, regardless of my feelings regarding some in this room."

The Second's eyes softened, "Your words and actions are accepted and most appreciated, Jandra." The Second slightly bowed her head to Jandra, then left the room.

Josin tried to get her to remain, "But, Second, you have not told us— "

The Second pretended not to hear her as she left, while Meera had jumped right up and began her briefing with them.

The Second went to the front door and went outside, willingly waiting for Treena to come. Of late, she noticed that she was quick to anger, and wondered if she were eating something that was creating some irritation. She prepared herself to be steadier when dealing with Treena, and guessed that Treena had decided to make her wait a bit. She didn't mind. Treena knew she had stepped out of line, so The Second wanted to give her a moment to recover. Treena came out rather hesitantly.

She bowed her head. "Second?"

"That was quite a show, Treena."

"I am sorry, Second. This entire event with Hern has been blown way out of proportion. It be not like that, Second."

"I understand that Hern be your friend. But there were six witnesses to the incident, and all the accounts but match except for Josin's. You seem to be neglecting the facts. That be not the issue here, though, is it?"

The Second waited a moment and then continued, staring directly at Treena, "I am the acting Highest now, Treena. You do not *demand* anything of me. I certainly hope that you have treated The Highest in a more respectful fashion."

The Second wondered how long this had been going on with The Highest, but would halt it now. Treena tried to look away, but The Second moved Treena's face back toward her, "Look at me, Treena."

As she touched Treena, they both felt a current pass from The Second to Treena. The Second was concerned about it, but became more so as she sensed Treena say, *They are going to kill me*. But Treena hadn't spoken.

Ignoring the feeling, The Second continued, "And you are never to address me in that tone. As one of my advisors, I expect you to remove yourself from all matters that may present a conflict. I also expect you to remove yourself from any discussion around Hern and Lillon. As *my* Spiritual Advisor, I expect you to display the situation in an unprejudiced manner. If I hear that you are convening with the Counselors on this, or taking any of their advice, I will remove you as advisor. I know that you can be an excellent advisor. I just think you have but fallen into a place you cannot get out of. You have been a valuable and respected member of this community for as long as I can remember. I am very disappointed to think that some women are making a move against The Highest."

The Second's words became very measured and carefully articulated. "Whatever is happening, Treena, know these two things: I will find out, and I will win. And when I do, all those that were out to cause harm to The Highest and to Woden will be punished; *severely*."

Treena's eyes had opened wide. The Second had surprised her with those statements. It also had surprised her that The Second knew something was happening in the community against The Highest. Treena was afraid of The Second now, and felt her feelings had been exposed when The Second touched her chin. She didn't understand it, but she knew The Second could sense her fear.

"I am confining you to your dwelling for the remainder of this turn. I expect you to talk to no one until you return to me in the morn to let me know which way you would like to proceed. If you want protection, I will arrange it so. If you no longer want to be an advisor, but wish to side with the Counselors, we can arrange also for that. But under no circumstances think that you can do both: You cannot have it both ways. If you want to remain an advisor, then do so with the knowledge that, as a group, we will look at the facts together. The facts and the laws. Make your choice wisely. It will follow you the rest of your life in this community. Be very, *very* careful now, Treena."

She looked at The Second, without menace, "Yes, Second. I understand. I agree to do as you say, for this midturn. I will talk to no one until after I meet with you in the morn. You but have my word on this."

"Go then, and think about why we have this community. Think about our goals and visions. Think about this community and all that we have built."

Treena turned and walked into the rain. The Second hoped that she would make the correct choice. She knew that Treena had been well manipulated and hoped that she would return willingly as one of her advisors. She looked at her hand for a moment and thought briefly about the feeling. She sighed and turned to go inside. As she opened the door, she found Meera waiting for her.

"Watching over me, per usual, Meera?"

She saw the look on Meera's face and knew that she had overheard the conversation.

"Have her watched."

"I already attended to it, Second."

"Just like you already attended to having the Counselors watched *before* I mentioned it in this morn's meeting?"

Meera just smiled at her, "That was good, Second. Treena is lucky to have you here at this moment."

"We will see next morn."

The Second always thought that she didn't give enough compliments to her own people. She felt lucky and grateful knowing that they were so good that they knew this was not one of her strengths. She also thought them secure enough to not need it often.

She put her hand on Meera's shoulder. "Meera, you know how important you are to me. I could not do this without—"

The current passed through her hand, again.

What is happening to me?

She felt Meera say, *It is beginning.* But like prior, no words had been spoken.

Meera saw the disheartened expression on The Second's face. "Worry not about it, Second. It must be something in the air. Let us attend to your rounds."

"What about the meeting?"

Meera grinned, "Not to worry. Karan is entertaining them with her vast knowledge of Woden's past. That will keep them silent and but contained for a bit."

"Rounds in a little while. I have something I need to do first. Come with me."

The Second left to find Berth, but knew she really needed to get out of the dwelling. She hoped that doing her rounds would make her feel better, but it was yet raining. She found Berth in with Keddi, who was now sleeping.

The Second turned to Berth and Meera, "I would like to move Keddi to my bedroom. I believe she will be safer in there."

"As do I, but it be not my first plan of choice. But it be better than what you have provided thus far."

"Good. So I will move to the library and sleep on the long chair. Can you arrange for that this eve, Berth? Perhaps the guards could but help you?"

"Oh, Second, the library be no place for you. Would you like us to move the guestroom bed to the library? We could put Keddi in there and you could but remain in your own room. You would be much more comfortable."

"Thank you, but no, Berth. The guards are going to need a place on their breaks, and the guestroom bed would be perfect for that. Besides, if I am to confine myself to one room instead of two, I would rather be in the library."

She turned toward Meera, "Have Keddi well-guarded. I bet that someone is going to try to get to her soon."

* * * *

The Second usually did her rounds around midturn so that she could wander in and out of the shops and community as well as speak to the women. It took her two turns to cover the entire community. She would normally do half of it one turn and the other half the next. She enjoyed the walking, and it let her keep in touch with most of the community, even if it was just to greet them. Since she was later than usual this turn, she thought she would just wander around without a pattern. The rain had halted for the moment, and the air smelled fresh. Alain was updating her about Hengist's payment for these past several seasons.

"The new ship be almost complete. It has but taken many seasons with work crews from both our communities to finish it. You should go see it, Second, as we are most proud of it. Since we had enough working resources to keep up with the Farm and Gardens as well as building and maintenance, it was decided to let Hengist help us with the construction as their land payment. They also had a crew working on the new dock for the ship. I would recommend, Second, that we have a celebration for it."

"This be good a good report, Alain. Will it be near enough completion to have it honored at this next Festival?"

She didn't want to hold any further gatherings until she had figured out their present problems. Combining the celebrations was the only other option. She hoped that it might also help uplift the mood of the community to let them take pride in something so big as this, but she had another reason, as well. *It might also help show the Counselors how much defense we have, now.*

Ghada liked the idea, "We could but begin the festivities at the ship and dock. It might provide the mood for the entire festival. Perhaps Oisin would even allow people on board."

The Second just thought, *Wishful thinking.*

"Perhaps she would allow them just on the top deck itself. Oisin is extremely protective of her ships. I will speak to her about this. Ghada and Alain, could you speak with the Festival Committee when they meet and suggest this idea? Alain, it might be best if you were the one to present it."

What The Second especially liked about Ghada and Alain was that they ignored the politics of anything; they just wanted to work with their accounts. And what most of the women tended to forget about them was that they were companions.

"We will be delighted to, Second."

"How are our stores of food and supplies?"

The Highest generally took care of these issues, so The Second was never well versed on them. Ghada handled the accounting for the work hours in the community projects and made certain that everyone did their fair share. She also made certain that all the projects got sufficient coverage. Alain handled the community's stores and supplies.

"We are fully stocked."

The Second didn't doubt that. Alain worried about the smallest of details, and knew that the community had gone through too many periods when the crops had failed for Alain to take chances. Woden tended to be very cautious with the food stores, now.

"I always make certain that we have our prescribed stock of six months, Second. But I do need your permission and advice on an idea we are considering."

She waited for The Second's permission to begin.

"Go ahead, Alain. You need not my permission to speak."

"Thank you, Second. Oisin met with Ghada and me and told us that she could trade three months worth of our grain supply for a new type of food product. I would not recommend it normally, but I consulted with Liley. She informed us that our early grain crop, which she is harvesting now, is larger than normal. The island Oisin be going to but needs the grain, and has a lot of other food stuffs they are willing to trade."

The Second asked, "Be there any risk?"

"Liley told me that Oisin needs to check to make certain that the produce will return safely and in good condition on the return trip. She also told Oisin that it must be isolated from any other foodstuff to prevent spread of disease. If it has seeds of any sort, Liley will but plant it apart from our food crops. Oisin will also be bringing back a new type of fruit tree stock."

"Liley has given her blessing to this trade?"

"Yes, Second. She is actually looking forward to it."

"Well then, go ahead and do it."

They walked down the main path past the shops. The main path provided the two main entrances to Woden, which was laid out in a square pattern. The town was a walled-in city. Each square and path was tree-lined, and each square contained twenty dwellings, except for four. A small park was in the middle of each square of dwellings. Visitors generally entered at one of the two large community parks. The Highest lived in the middle of the entire area, and both Meera and Keets lived nearby her.

The Second wanted to visit one shop and saw the woman who tended it, so went in. All of the shops on the main path were small two-level dwellings. The trade was conducted on the first and the women lived on the top part. They were getting better at building complex structures, but since these dwellings represented some of the first attempts, they were considered original structures and were thus well tended and kept in their original design.

"Good after midturn, Raitha."

Raitha made and traded pottery of all types. The Second particularly loved the colors she was turning of late. She had learned some new methods recently by going with Oisin to a relatively close island.

She bowed her head, "Second, good to see you again. I have not seen you on your rounds of late. Come in and look at some of my new pottery."

Everyone went inside her small and artfully designed shop. She had everything from bowls, to cups, to pitchers, to plates. The Second thought her new colors were wonderful.

"These pieces are stunning. These will be overly popular in the community. Will you be sending some with Oisin to be traded?"

"The men in the mines have found some wonderful minerals that produce these very intense blues. And I am sending eight complete sets with Oisin. I am also sending a set over to your dwelling. May told me that you have some pieces missing."

"Thank you, Raitha. I am well pleased." She paused for a moment, then asked, "Be there any new reports in the community?"

Raitha was quick to respond, "I hear that Hern is going to be evicted, if that be what you mean. I hear she beat Lillon almost to death. How is poor Lillon?"

Lillon also did rounds, and the community had readily embraced her. She had been resistant at first, as she was shy, but she saw the reasoning and purpose behind it.

"Her wounds are recovering, but her heart is broken. What are the shop keepers saying about Hern?"

"We wonder why she has not yet been banished, but you must have your reasons. I will remind you, though, that we are supposed to be a non-violent community. By the way, Second, when did Hern arrive here? None of us recall."

"Second, we best be on our way if you are to get through your rounds." Meera was helping The Second out of the conversation since she had no good answer to Raitha's question about Hern.

"We have witnesses to the attack and are discussing the incident now. While the law is clear, Raitha, we do need to make sure we hear all sides before making the final decision. Thank you for your visit. Regards to Afa."

They left the store and continued down the road toward The Highest's dwelling, the largest and finest in the community. The Second had done as much of her rounds as she could this after-midturn, and Meera and she needed to visit with The Highest.

"Alain. Ghada. Since we are near your dwelling, I have no need to detain you further. Thank you for walking with me to bring me up to date on our accounts."

Ghada and Alain bowed their heads to her and said their good-byes. The Second headed toward Woden's gardens with Meera beside her, sitting down to enjoy the season's flowers for a few moments.

"I need to gather my thoughts together before speaking with The Highest, Meera, so let us just sit here for a moment."

The garden was almost half as long as the entire length of the community, and there were two at this size, with The Highest's dwelling in the middle. One of the main rivers flowed directly through the gardens, and had been incorporated as part of the original design. Meera rarely accompanied The Second on her rounds so didn't know her patterns. The Second usually halted in the gardens for a few moments to enjoy the silence or to visit with others. Since other women generally surrounded her, there were few moments, except during the eves, that she had a moment alone for thinking.

Meera broke the silence, "I am worried about you, Second. You seem . . . distracted."

The Second looked at her but waited her out, really not wanting to hear about it, or to speak. She could tell Meera had more to say.

"I am worried that I am not seeing all the danger that is surrounding you right now. We have never had this much inside potential for harm to you. And I am but worried about how you are taking the duty of being The Highest. I know you have never wanted to be The Highest, but you are now. If The Highest lives, that be good, yet you know as well as I do that it will not be long before everyone wants you to become The Highest. Are you going to be able to deal with that?"

"Meera, you always worry about me." She smiled at Meera and laughed a little. "It be good that I never accepted your proposal to become companions. You would have but fretted over me every moment."

"I do now, anyway."

"But, Meera, I did you a favor. Now you have Caitha fretting every moment over you. And you deserve it."

Everyone had assumed that it had been Meera who hadn't accepted The Second's proposal. The reverse was true, but The Second never wanted anyone to know. Meera had honored, but not liked her request for silence on that. The Second had loved Brett too much and too well to take another companion. If she had, it would have been Meera. She hadn't wanted Meera to carry the burden of rejection when it was her own issue.

She looked around the gardens, "You know, Meera, I always wonder how I ever got to this position. All I ever wanted to do was to live a quiet life with Brett. Think not that I expect you to give your life for mine. Not even because of me being The Second. We are both in danger now. This community but needs you as well; perhaps more so. Use your guards more and you do less guarding. I want you safe. I could stand it not if I lost you also, to violence. We will have to deal with old cycles later, but allow not what happened to Brett happen to you."

She looked down the pathways. No one was in the gardens. It was almost too quiet, but she liked it this way. It was almost like she had willed it to be peaceful.

"I want not to become The Highest. I never have. Every moment I see The Highest, she tries to get me to take the position, permanently, not just for the interim. She be overly ill to continue, and she knows it. Even if the anti-poison works, I think she will not be The Highest for much longer. She is tired of it. Afterall, she has been The Highest for the longest reign of any of them. I have been doing a lot of thinking about the moment when I will really have to make that decision. What will I but do?" She looked at Meera. "The Highest told me that the Spirits of the Falls have spoken to her. Did you know about this?"

"No. What did they say?"

"That she can conclude her term. That she has served well and can step down. And that I am to be the next Highest."

"They told The Highest who is to be the next Highest?"

"According to her, yes. But there be something else that troubles me. They told her that they would hold a celebration for me at the Falls with both communities present, shortly after I become Highest. That is not our way, and it has left me concerned. Why are they but involved in our community after all these moments? I have never spoken with them, have you?"

"It is not my place to speak with them, Second. Perhaps you should speak with The Highest about this. She knows more than I on this issue."

Meera knew much more than she was willing to provide, but recognized that she wasn't the one to inform The Second. Apparently, the moment for the Chosen One was coming to pass, as the Spirit Mothers had foretold many cycles prior. She had begun to see changes in The Second during the past few moons, but hadn't connected the changes to anything in particular. She didn't think that The Second had noticed any changes in herself, however. If she had, The Second hadn't informed her.

The Second could sense that Meera wasn't telling her everything she knew. She placed her hand on Meera's, wondering if the current would pass through them again. She was surprised to learn that the current was even stronger, this moment.

Meera looked at The Second in surprise, so The Second knew that Meera had felt it too.

The Second felt, or sensed Meera say, *She is the Chosen One, as they said.*

No words had been spoken, but Meera somehow knew that The Second had heard her thoughts. Meera could also tell that each moment this occurred, it weakened The Second. She had seen it the first occurrence. The Second looked tired.

Defeated, The Second said, "The Chosen One, Meera? What do you mean by this?"

Meera shook her head trying to escape from the current that passed between them, "Please, Sam, do not make me do this. It is not my place to tell you."

She glared at Meera, "Not your place? Are you not my friend, Meera? What are you withholding from me?"

The Second hadn't noticed that Meera had called her by her given name. The Second's hand hadn't moved off Meera's, but the current had finally left.

Then The Second whispered, "What was that feeling? What is happening?"

She removed her hand and looked at it. Sadly, she said, "This is beginning to frighten me. And now I hear things that are not spoken."

"Perhaps you but need to know, after all."

"Know what?" and then she realized, "Meera, you but called me Sam."

"I am sorry, Second," and bowed her head.

"Oh, Meera, be not so," and unthinkingly reached out to Meera's chin to make her raise her head. The feeling passed between them again. This moment, she felt Meera's concern. The Second looked frightened.

"What is happening to me?"

Meera groaned, lightly. *Poor Sam. The burden is going to become unbearable.* But Meera knew that The Second needed to know what she was facing.

"Do you recall your Birth-Mother, Second?"

"Of course I do." The Second was yet looking at her hand.

"How far prior do you remember?"

"Not far. And I have always wondered about that. My earliest memory is just prior to my seventh cycle."

"No one ever speaks to the Spirits of the Falls, Second. No one, that is except for you. They only speak to those they wish."

"And you think they spoke to me?"

"I know they spoke to you. To my knowledge, they only ever speak to whoever The Highest is. But Second, they did speak to you once, and you to them."

"No, I did not. I would remember such a thing."

"No, Sam. They did. They spoke to you."

"How do you know of this, Meera? Who told you?"

"I was there."

Sam just looked at Meera in complete frustration. She had no idea of what Meera was talking about. She just wanted to return to her dwelling and go to sleep. She felt tired and drained.

"Then why do I not remember as such?"

"I have always wondered about that, as most our children can but remember easily from their fourth cycle. But now I believe they pushed that memory out of you until it was the moment."

"The moment for what? What are you talking about, Meera? You but make no sense."

"I am sorry, Second. I know this be confusing. I will explain, but you will need to get the remainder of the story from The Highest. When you were in your third cycle, the Spirits of the Falls summoned you and proclaimed you as their Chosen One. Your Birth-Mother, The Highest and her advisors were there. They all heard."

"And I am to believe this?"

"If not, then you explain what has been happening to you and the changes that you have been experiencing."

Sam couldn't, but the story jarred no memories for her, "The Chosen One? What be a chosen one?" She felt too exhausted to even care, but the need for answers continued to bear down on her.

"I have not these answers, Sam. You must speak to The Highest. She needs to explain."

Meera noticed despair in The Second's expression. Too many changes had been occurring, and this too was taking her energy. Meera wished she could help, but this was not something she knew about.

"Oh, Sam, I am but sorry. I wish—"

"Speak not about it anymore, Meera. It be already overly much."

* * * *

The Highest's dwelling was the largest one in the community, and it was the only three-story structure. The Highest lived in the back part of the first floor. The front portion of the first floor was the community's library. The Second floor was sectioned off into small meeting places, while the third floor was for large meetings and events. The Highest had been confined to her bedroom due to her illness, and that's where The Second and Meera headed. The Second noticed that Meera's guards were now at the doors and May was in feeding The Highest something that smelled wonderful. She realized she was hungry.

She went over to her bedside and bowed, "Highest," then waited to be acknowledged. She had never gone beyond the formalities with The Highest, as Oisin had done. Someone needed to set the example. Meera did likewise, but said nothing.

"Sam, come in. Come in. And Meera, you too. I feel a little better now. My stomach but seems to be settling down."

She seemed much more alert to The Second than she had prior, and was sitting upright in her bed.

May said, "It be my cooking that did it, of course," then left the room. The Highest was patting the side of her bed. "Sit down, both of you."

Meera sat on the side of the bed. The Second brought a chair over close to her.

"How did you enjoy your meeting with *your* new advisors?" The Second saw that she was chuckling.

"They are but a challenging bunch. You are looking much better, Highest. I am surprised. I knew not that the anti-poison could work so quickly. In fact, we were not certain that it would work at all."

"Well, May thinks it is due to her cooking. But you know, she be a much better cook than I am used to. Perhaps I should keep May on but permanently. She said that she would not mind cooking for the both of us."

The Second wanted to get to the business at hand, but had learned long prior to let The Highest control the meetings.

"Nill tells me that the anti-poison will halt the degeneration, but she does not think all of the damage will reverse itself. So, Sam, my turns are numbered as Highest. It is your responsibility now."

"If I may, Highest, I would like to return to this topic in a moment. I have some more urgent issues I need to discuss with you."

"I will listen, but I will make no vows."

Sam saw that she was in one of her non-listening moods, again. Whenever she had her mind set on something, it was all Sam could do to get her to listen otherwise. "Thank you, Highest. I will try to be brief. You were poisoned, and Meera and I believe that there are some on the inside who are the attempted assassins. This makes this a critical issue for all of us. Whether you like it or no, someone is out to kill you. Keddi's arrival with the anti-poison is but all the evidence we need."

"I know that, Sam. Do not be tedious. Have you but forgotten that I know Keddi?"

"No Highest, but you have not been able to supply me the details."

"Yes, yes. You are correct, of course. Meera, go get Karan for me."

Meera left while The Highest continued. "It be the moment I begin to tell you what you will need to know as Highest. Face it, Sam, this poison has taken many seasons off my life. I have not that many moments remaining to me. I can no longer fight these battles. I physically cannot do it. This has left me very weak, and I may never be able to get my strength back. And to think that one of my own advisors may be behind this . . . " She let the rest go unsaid. "But I know you will find whoever did this. You have always succeeded at the difficult matters for me."

Meera and Karan had just arrived. The Highest saw Karan.

"Ah, Karan, just the person we need."

Karan bowed to The Highest, and then bowed her head toward The Second.

"Karan, please inform Sam about our scouts." The Highest then looked at Meera. "Meera, wait outside."

Karan began, "During the seasons of The Battles, the former Highest recruited and trained twenty women to go Outside and be scouts for Woden. Woden was in jeopardy of continued attacks unless we knew what the other communities were planning. A single mark was placed on each scout for identification purposes: The coiled snake. Only the current Highest, Oisin and I know about these women and who they are. Oisin needs to know because these women may seek passage home on one of her ships. Two women have come home prior to Keddi. Some of the others have found ways to send messages to The Highest as they thought needed. We have never heard from one. Now these messages will but come to you."

The Second was stunned. To her, it seemed that Woden had a hidden society.

The Highest halted Karan, "That is only the beginning of what you need to know. Karan will meet with you to inform you of our background and everything else you will need. Karan, please see to this, give her some reading to do so she will learn of our background. And thank you for dropping in."

Karan bowed to The Highest, bowed her head to The Second, and left.

The Highest continued, "You may have forgotten this, Sam, but your Birth-Mother had also been a scout for Woden for many seasons prior to having you."

Sam had forgotten her Birth-Mother's snake tattoo, but now remembered. Her Birth-Mother showed her the tattoo upon only a few moments. She had died when Sam was a young girl, but the memory stunned Sam. *My Birth-Mother was also a scout, like Keddi.* She realized that Woden seemed to have a long background of scouts and wondered why she had never known about them.

"Sam, I would like very much to give you the opportunity to reflect on becoming The Highest, but I cannot. Think about it. Do *you* know of anyone else who would really want to be The Highest? Your answer, of course, is 'no.' Oisin is but overly controlling for the position. You have been well groomed, the community loves and respects you, and you make sound decisions. Besides, you are hand-selected by me, and I know I have made a fine decision on this. This be your destiny, Sam, so quit the sliding. It be the moment to embrace the position. I must quit. I will work with you for a short while to help eradicate some of these problems. I am sorry I was unable able to fix my advisors or the Counselors for you, but we will work on that together, too. I think Jandra the only good one of the bunch. I think you will find her quite special. I am sorry Sam, but it be the best I can do. Besides, you are ready to do this. I expect you to now take the position over. Thank our Keepers for Keddi's safe return. Not for my life, but for the continued safety of Woden. Karan will update you more on Keddi, as you are ready, and you will come to know how critically important our scouts have been for our continued safety. They have but given and risked their lives for us, so treat Keddi well."

As The Highest spoke, Sam had quit listening, wondering instead about why she seemed to be the last to know about anything in the community. She couldn't know if she interrupted The Highest or not, but said, "Highest, I need to talk with you about something personal."

"Why, Sam, you looked troubled. What is it? Are you afraid of being The Highest? You should not be—"

"No, Highest. It is not that. I fear that I cannot even explain it." She thought about it for a moment and then realized what she should do. "Forgive me, Highest." She then touched The Highest's hand, feeling the current passing through both of them.

She *felt* The Highest think, *So, it has begun. And I have not had enough moments to tell her of the advisors, The Realm, or the Spirit Mothers of the Falls. Or of her sisters—*

"Yes, Highest, so it seems. I just know not what *it* is."

She was yet touching The Highest's hand, and could hear her thoughts, *You are The Chosen One, Sam.*

"Yes, Highest. I sensed that much from Meera, too. But what does that mean? And . . ." She removed her hand from The Highest's, and looked at it. "What but happens to me?"

"Oh, my poor Sam. You must but feel so confused right now."

She opened her arms, inviting Sam to come to her. She did, and The Highest just held her.

Sam could feel her thoughts, *Be not afraid, child. If we fear what we do not know, we will always live in fear. Your destiny is greater than you will ever come to imagine.*

She let go of Sam and motioned for Sam to sit down next to her. Sam did so, but was getting increasingly tired.

"I thought your change would not occur until after you were The Highest. I saw the prophesy in a dream, but now I am proven as wrong. It would seem the Spirits of the Falls as well as The Realm need you now.

She touched Sam's arm. The current once again coursed its way through both of them.

Be at peace. You will receive your answers at the proper moments. Trust the Spirits of the Falls. They will protect you.

She let go and said, "I am sorry to say that we have overly few moments or resources this eve to tell you the entire story. Come by next after early eve and I pledge to enlighten you and to answer your questions. Go in peace and be not afraid. I do have one thing you should hear, but will not understand as yet. Should anything happen to me, Sam, know that I am but sorry for what you will learn."

Thoughts raced through Sam's head, yet even the thoughts made no sense to her, *Keddi and The Highest. My Birth-Mother. I am the Chosen One. The Spirits of the Falls. The Realm. Meera. My destiny. I sense thoughts. Sisters?*

"Yes, Highest." She bowed and left the room.

Meera was waiting for her, "Oisin sent a message. She said she is leaving for your dwelling in a few moments and will meet you there. Can you tell me anything The Highest said?"

In shock, exhausted, and not knowing where or how to begin, she simply said, "You will find out soon enough, I suspect."

"I will walk you back and then come back and get Caitha."

"No need, Meera. One of your guards must be around. It will but take me a few moments.

"Second? May I walk back with you?" Jandra had appeared out of nowhere.

"Of course, Jandra, as long as you mind not the guard."

"Jandra." Meera said as much of a greeting as she could to Jandra.

"Meera." Sam found the air tense between them, but thought that they needed to work it out between themselves, as it was most likely a personal issue.

"I will catch up later, Second." Meera left to find the guard to walk The Second back to her dwelling.

Sam was delighted to see Jandra. She always found her heart racing a little when they were together, but knew her hopes of long prior would go unheeded. "Jandra, this be certainly a surprise. I am most glad to see you. What is on your mind that you need to meet with me personally? Is everything well with you?"

"Oh, yes, of course, Second. I am well. It be a beautiful eve, is it not, Second?"

Sam was confused, but didn't want to rush Jandra, so just went along with the conversation.

"Yes, it is. Meera and I were just enjoying it prior to my meeting with The Highest."

"How is The Highest?"

"She is much improved. Have you been updated on the reports about the anti-poison and Keddi?"

"I have heard the rumor, Second. So it be truth, then?"

Sam nodded, "It is. The Highest was just sitting up in her bed and but eating her late eve meal."

"So Keddi is one of our long-lost daughters, returned home."

"Do you but know of this, too, Jandra?"

"You but mean our scouts, Second?"

"Yes. I was told it a secret."

"Oh, it is. Secrets but float on the winds. The Highest talked a lot in her very disturbed sleep, recently. I hope the anti-poison will prove to be but lasting."

"I as well. I want not The Highest to leave us." She looked at Jandra as they walked, wondering what Jandra wanted. She wished she could touch her, but refrained. "But Jandra, be this why we meet this eve?"

"No, Second, I just have difficulty discussing the personal issues."

"I do as well, Jandra. Just pretend I am not here."

Jandra laughed, "Yes, Second. I have done that many moments in my dwelling when I am alone. And I must tell you that you received the information very well."

Sam laughed too, enjoying Jandra's laughter and humor, "Well, there you are. So just pretend you are in your dwelling and I am but a glimmer of your imagination."

"You know that my companion died two cycles prior."

"Of course I do. I attended the ceremony."

"The community now wants me to take another companion."

Sam turned to Jandra and faced her, "Oh, Jandra. I know the feeling well. Prior to every festival, my advisors but nag at me like a bunch of old women to do the same. I am so sorry."

As they approached Sam's dwelling, Jandra continued, "I was but wondering if you would grant me the permission to take—"

Sam watched May come out the dwelling's front door and knew that she was waiting for her.

"Of course, Jandra. Whoever you select is fine with me. Just make sure she makes you happy, as you certainly deserve as such. That, and you are most beautiful." And she meant it.

May came over to meet Sam, "Your guest is here, Second."

* * * *

Sam had wanted to return before Oisin came, but found her waiting in the front meeting room. Being too exhausted from the turn's events to deal with Oisin, she had wanted to cancel the eve.

As she entered her own dwelling, Oisin met and embraced her, "It has been but overly long. I have missed you."

Oisin never was subtle or shy, and Sam usually liked her aggressiveness when it came to sex. It was no different for Sam this eve, as it helped her to forget the turn's all-consuming events. As Oisin embraced Sam, giving her a long, urgent, and passionate kiss, the current surged through Sam into Oisin. Oisin mistook the feeling for passion and urgency from Sam, and kissed her even more passionately.

Sam *felt* Oisin thinking, *By the mothers, you feel so good.*

Sam laughed a little, feeling somewhat comforted in the ordinary feelings that Oisin was unknowingly sharing with her. She knew where this was heading and hoped that Meera had sense enough to wait a little while before coming over.

Oisin was extremely used to being in control, "I have but thought about you all this turn and cannot wait longer."

Oisin undid Sam's buttons and slowly traced Sam's breasts with her fingers. Sam no longer perceived Oisin's thoughts. She was too busy feeling her own needs and desires to notice. The current was there, but it had now turned to passion.

Sam gasped for breath, "Not here, Oisin. I have the guest in my bedroom and she will but hear us. We need to move to the library. Besides, Meera and Caitha will be here in a while, and we need them not walking in on us, do we?"

Oisin laughed, "They would probably learn something useful if they did." She let go of Sam, "Wait here, I have a surprise for you."

She left, but quickly returned with some new type of chair. It was all wood but had curved runners at the bottom. Sam thought it beautiful.

"I found this on my last trip and knew immediately it was for you." She set it down in front of Sam, "Sit in it."

She did, and it rocked back and forth. At first it was an unsettling feeling, but after just a short moment, she began to like the feel of it. "This be wonderful. A new type of chair. The other women will want one as soon as they try this one out. I will have to let the wood crafters have a look at this."

"No. That one be yours. I brought another for the woodcrafters. They have already taken it apart and be but busy making patterns. Everyone will have one soon enough. You have the original. I find it much like the feeling of sailing."

Sam continued to rock in her new chair, enjoying the feeling.

Oisin held out her hand to Sam, "Come with me. I need you before Meera and Caitha come over. While they be here, you can but rock all the eve."

Sam took Oisin's hand and rose. The current surged through both of them as Oisin pulled Sam to her and gave her another long and very urgent kiss, but Sam didn't notice. Oisin explored all over, kissing Sam's neck, lips, mouth, breasts and lower, slowly at first, then with a steadily increasing desire. Sam had no moment during the turn to think about Oisin's visit, but instantly fell into the passion and need, desiring the moment as much as Oisin. They finally went to the library.

May worried about Sam as much as Meera, and had placed a small bed in the library for her. Sam wouldn't have to sleep on the long-chair, and now Oisin and she could use the bed. Sam thought she was getting too old for these types of physical maneuverings anymore, anyway. As they entered the library, Oisin again pulled Sam to her and kissed her. Sam could feel the current run between them, but now it was more a part of their need for each other. She returned Oisin's passion, and they soon urgently began undressing each other. When their intimate moment was over, Oisin lay exhausted and spent. Sam laughed. It had been a much-needed release for her, as well.

Oisin wanted to meet Keddi, and decided to visit with her before Meera and Caitha arrived. Sam was exhausted, but forced herself to get dressed so she could entertain this eve. She saw that Keddi was awake when they entered, and that May had provided some more for her to eat. She looked a little stronger to Sam, and was feeding herself.

Sam sat down next to Keddi, "Good eve, Keddi. Let me but introduce Oisin, our Sea-Duty Second."

Oisin hated formalities and just began talking, "I hear that you be one tough woman. I like that. Held your own. Good for you. I but hope you gave them as bad a moment as they gave you."

Keddi smiled at Oisin's comments.

"What community did you come from?"

"Fornaith to New Harborage."

"Long way. And then you walked over from New Harborage? Quite a trip. Trying to avoid suspicion? That be but a difficult journey, and through the mountains, too. How was the community of New Harborage? Last trip I was there, they were but having problems within the community."

"Same. The women and men are leaving for other places. Disorganized and corrupt."

Keddi was speaking much better after her last rest, but very softly. Sam could tell that her strength would take a while to return.

"I will not go there anymore due to that. They but try to steal everything off my ship. I had to have my weapons out in sight last trip just to keep them away. Wasted trip. Where are the women and men going?"

"To Apien, if they could not afford passage elsewhere. Some women want to come here."

Apien and New Harborage were both communities on the same landmass as Woden, but on the furthest opposite shore. The ship captains from the various communities had charted four landmasses so far, but hadn't yet covered the entire known realm. It was guessed that all the communities combined covered only a very small portion of the total landmass.

Oisin looked at Sam, "You know, we should provide shelter to these women. Some of the communities have not enough women for their men, so are capturing and enslaving them. What crafters do we need? If I find any, I will but bring them back."

Woden had provisions for this. "They will have to get here, first, though. We have no other way to find them, unless you pass by there on your next trip. We need any crafter and artist you can find, but especially good healers. Do you need more ship builders or crew?"

Sam halted, wondering, "I thought that Apien was a men's community."

Keddi responded, "Was, but it was taken over. It is now a combined community, but ruled by a tyrant. I fought my way out of there."

Sam looked back at Oisin, "How are our ships compared to theirs?"

Oisin smiled knowingly, "With this new ship, good luck to them. We have but many more ships than they do, unless they have stolen the ones from New Harborage. I had better leave my assistant behind, guarding the coastline while I am gone, though."

Oisin continued to ask Keddi questions while Sam quietly just listened and observed. Oisin had recognized and admired Keddi's strength right from the beginning, and Sam wondered why she hadn't seen it. Keddi seemed an extremely confident and capable woman. The graying in her hair only added experience to her beauty. Through the conversation, Oisin remained fixed on Keddi, as was her usual style, but Sam often caught Keddi looking directly at her.

What does she want of me?

Berth interrupted the conversation, "What are you two doing in here? The poor woman needs some rest, after all! Besides, Meera and Caitha have arrived, and May put out some treats for you."

That reminded Sam that she had missed her mid-eve meal, so the treats would have to suffice.

"Berth is telling us to get out, Oisin."

To Berth, Sam added, "We will leave her to you. But I will speak with her again in the morn."

* * * *

The eve provided a brief escape from reality for Sam with Oisin, Meera, and Caitha, but had contained no rest, which she had desperately needed. When Meera and Caitha left after late-eve, Oisin spent the remainder of the eve continuously desiring and needing Sam. Sam hadn't felt emotionally up to it, and had drunk more wine than she should have, but her body continued to crave the physical passion and release. Oisin had left just before the sun's rise, so as to miss seeing anyone. But morn came early now that Keddi was staying there. May came just at sun's rise to begin the cooking, just after Oisin had gone, and Berth came shortly after her to check on Keddi. With Oisin gone, and she physically and mentally spent, Sam quickly slipped into a deep sleep.

May came in just few moments later with her usual positive early morn announcement, "Good morn, Second. It is a lovely morn to be up. You have much to do this turn, and already Meera, Keets, Berth, and Keddi are all awaiting your presence. Since they are all here, I decided you would like to take your morn meal with them."

She couldn't wake her up, so sent in Meera.

Meera was standing next to Sam's bed, looking down at her, and shaking her shoulder gently to try to wake her.

"Second, wake up." As Sam woke from the feeling of the current flowing from her as Meera shook her shoulder, she *felt* Meera thoughts, *She is so beautiful.*

Sam had no clothes on, and her breasts were exposed from the eve.

But that I could have touched her breasts just once.

Sam hadn't opened her eyes yet, but said, "Go ahead Meera. They will not bite." Meera's thoughts had amused Sam.

"Oh, Second, I am so sorry. I should not have touched you, but I forgot that you could read my thoughts. You should not have heard that, and I should not have thought that."

"It be overly late for that now, Meera."

She opened her eyes, yet very tired, and smiled at Meera, "I am the one that is sorry, Meera. That was inappropriate of me. But it made you blush."

Meera was fully embarrassed. She had forgotten that Sam could now read some of her thoughts when there was a physical contact.

"Be not so embarrassed, Meera. I knew that much anyway, from our past. Neither of us is used to whatever is happening to me, so we will have our embarrassing moments. Help me to get dressed. I am overly tired to even move. Oisin left but only a few moments prior."

"You have not been to sleep?"

"No, and I am so tired I know not if I can even function. Perhaps some of May's tea might help."

Meera helped The Second get dressed and ready for the turn, then they went to the kitchen. Even Keddi had been helped into the kitchen and was sitting at the long table, although Sam thought that she looked quite uncomfortable.

As Sam entered, she said, "I would welcome you all to my dwelling for this morn meal, but it would appear as if you have all made yourself comfortable already, so I will not bother. May, I need a cup of tea as soon as you can manage one."

Her mind was asleep, her head felt heavy, and she thought she should just turn around and go right back to bed. She couldn't imagine how she was supposed to do the work of The Second, as well as The Highest's, feeling this way. She sat down next to Keets and across from Keddi.

"Keddi, you look most uncomfortable. Are you certain you be up to this, or is Berth controlling your life like May be controlling mine?"

"Oh, listen not to her," May said to Berth and Keddi. She turned to Sam, " . . . and you should be but grateful that Berth and I know what is best for you and Keddi." She laughed and got tea for Sam.

Sam thought, *How can I complain when someone but waits on me all the moments?*

As Sam ate her first meal in over a turn, she realized how hungry she was and hoped the food would help to restore some of her energy. Meera and Keets detailed the beginnings of their security plans for the festival.

Keets seemed proud of their new idea, "We are going to be trying out a new security idea: security that does not look like security. We will just let the guards be on duty even though it will look like they are not. Of course, all our guards are always alert, but during this festival, they will all be on-duty and not just on alert."

Meera added, "And we will have Briggon but do the same with his guards."

Sam was uncertain if that would be sufficient, "That be a good start, but I would like to see more detailed plans for the areas the festival will not be held in, like the dock, the grasslands, and the perimeters. Perhaps you can recheck with Briggon and work more on that plan. There will be no need to hide the security in those places, though, so it should not be as difficult."

She hadn't given them many moments to make their plans, but had hoped for better. "I know this be difficult, especially since everyone wants to attend the festival, yet we need increased protection. Consider using shifts of guards so that everyone can participate in the festival at some moment."

Keddi added, "Any attack will have to come from the sea. While New Harborage is the only town that has enough people to mount such an attack, the distance and their own internal conflict will prevent that, for now. My best advice is to loosely guard the perimeter for the turn, but be more careful on the seaside. They have been preparing ships for battle, as they are better at short, quick surprise attacks than large-scale ones. I suggest to Oisin to have all the ships ready for any surprises. Perhaps part of the festival could also be held at the dock."

Meera and Keets listened to Keddi with surprised interest. Once they found out that Keddi had been a well-trained scout for Woden, their opinion shifted to one of intense respect of Keddi and what she had accomplished.

May changed the subject, "So, Second, what did you and Oisin *discuss* last eve?"

They all laughed.

Meera just added, "They did not *discuss* anything, May."

And they all continued to laugh.

"Wonderful. I am so delighted that my sex life be such a happy topic but for your merriment. However, you may be interested to know that Oisin gave me a present last eve that will please the entire community. It be in the sitting room. Go find it and try it out."

Everyone but Keddi, Meera and Sam left the room to see the new chair.

"You provided some good advise to Meera and Keets about security. Your input will prove to be invaluable for us. I am glad you have returned home."

Keddi grinned mischievously to Sam, "Where else could I go to hear about The Second's sex life?"

"Since you are my guest, I am delighted that I am so entertaining for you."

Meera and Keddi just laughed, but Keddi looked as if she was tiring.

The Second asked, "Have you had enough of sitting up yet? You look like the pain is settling in for a long stay."

She nodded.

Meera called for Keets, and they carried her back to her bed. Sam decided to sit with her a while to discuss what The Highest had told her.

They got her settled into the bed, then Meera said, "I will come to escort you over to the Community Sessions this midturn, Second. I will also go to get Treena in a while, but first I will find out if we should even waste your moments with her."

Sam had forgotten all about Treena. She knew she was much too tired to deal with her, but realized she would have to, for Treena and the community's sake.

"Meera, you will need to be patient with her for now. If she makes the decision to remain with the Spiritual Leaders, we will deal harshly with her later."

Meera nodded, "Also, Second, forget not that you are to but meet with Karan, Josin, Ghett, and Fionn later this after midturn."

Sam had indeed forgotten that, too.

Where be Lillon? Lillon helped her organize her turns, and Sam missed her. She knew she definitely needed some sleep. As everyone returned to the kitchen, they all exclaimed that they wanted one of the new chairs. They had brought it in for Sam to sit in while talking with Keddi, and then went about their duties.

Sam sat down, "I visited with The Highest last eve. She informed me that you were one of twenty women from this community to be scouts. She also reminded me that my Birth-Mother had also been a scout. I had forgotten about her snake tattoo, but thought yours looked familiar when I first saw it. My Birth-Mother never talked about her experiences as a scout."

Keddi nodded, "Your Birth-Mother helped train me. Only six of her group returned. She told me that it had been overly difficult to remain alive during that moment. Like me, she had been very badly injured prior to her return. She birthed you shortly after."

"She told you all this?"

"She did."

"What else did she tell you?"

She paused, then continued, "There is so much you know not, Second, but that you should not know." She looked pained.

Sam was irritated that she had been left out of so much for what seemed her whole life up to this point. But it wasn't Keddi's fault, so she tried to be patient. "Should that not be my decision to make?"

Keddi just looked at Sam. She so much wanted to be with her; to be near her. She had noticed that Sam was very unaware of her beauty; of herself. At this moment she knew she was going to disappoint Sam, and would have done anything to prevent it. But since Sam had touched her and they both had felt the power that was now building in Sam, Keddi knew the prophecy was beginning. It saddened her as Sam was so unaware of who she was. That would soon change. But The Second had been right; it was her decision to make.

"She told me so that I would know how dangerous it was to be a scout for Woden. She was very skilled in self-defense; the best of the group, and yet she barely made it back alive. Your Birth-Mother loved you but knew she was not to live long. You never knew your Mother. Your Birth-Mother watched while we trained with others, and then selected two of us to be trained by her. She refused to train anyone else. She made the two of us vow to watch over you. She knew that you were to be announced as The Chosen One, and knew that you would need protection. She only agreed to train the two of us so we could . . . would, act as your protectors."

Sam didn't, couldn't answer. It was simply too much information to fully process. She was unsure of how to feel. Anger was there, but at whom? She felt betrayed, but by who? Her Birth-Mother? She felt like a juvenile, kept out of everything, and everything withheld from her for her own good. She just looked at Keddi and waited.

Even Keddi knows that I am the Chosen One. Am I the only one who knew not?

Sam's mind suddenly cleared. Her voice became strained, "So, you heard that I am to be The Highest now and have returned to protect me, as you had vowed my Birth-Mother you would."

Keddi didn't need to say anything. Sam could see that this was truth. She was becoming more frustrated, "Why now? You did not think I needed protecting prior to this?"

Keddi just winced. Sam couldn't tell if it was from her wounds and pain, or the thought of having to provide the answer. And she didn't know how close to the truth she had accidentally come.

Keddi simply said, "You had Brett."

Sam stood up, shocked, "Brett?"

Her mouth was too dry to say what was left unsaid. She glared at Keddi, "You are *not* telling me that Brett was a scout for Woden too, are you?" But as she had said the statement, she saw Keddi's face, and saw it was truth.

To herself, but spoken aloud, she said, "Oh, please, not Brett, too." She suddenly remembered Brett's coiled snake.

Sam was angry; and hurt. She felt deceived, even by Brett. But now she was angry with Keddi no matter how unreasonable she knew that was. Her tone was more enraged than she ever remembered, "So you think that what? That I but *want* you here to protect me?"

Keddi just let her speak. She knew that The Second had cause for anger, and just hoped that it wouldn't end whatever relationship they might have known.

"I loved Brett, and now you tell me that she was *protecting* me and became my companion only because of my Birth-Mother?"

Keddi reached for Sam's arm in an effort to provide some comforting, but Sam was so angry she just snatched it away from her. The current had now taken on Sam's anger. It surged from Sam to Keddi, throwing Keddi off her bed, as if it were obeying Sam's command to reject her. Sam had kept talking, not yet realizing what had occurred, "*Dare* not assume you can touch me. *Dare* not assume I want you to protect me."

Then she realized what had happened. Seeing that Keddi had bumped her head in the fall and was bleeding, she rushed over and helped Keddi back into the bed. Tears began to roll down Keddi's cheeks from the pain. Sam was unsure why Keddi was crying.

Keddi managed to look at Sam, and snapped, "Brett loved you more than you know. She *wanted* to be your companion. That she was your protector was just convenient."

Sam was now both angry at and concerned for Keddi, but was yet enraged. "And how would *you* know about that? That was *my* life. Mine and Brett's!"

Keddi just closed her eyes. Tears rolled down her cheeks. Quietly she said, "Brett was my sister."

Sam's head spun out of control and everything went black. The next thing she knew, Berth and Meera were standing over her, and she was in her bed in the library. She looked around, searching for answers. But her realm had changed. Everything that she had known about her life had changed. She wanted back her other life, prior to Keddi, prior to The Highest being poisoned. *I want not this life.*

"Second, how are you feeling?"

"Go away. Leave me be."

She was crying, silently. She couldn't face them, or anyone. Keddi had been right after all; she really shouldn't know all Keddi told her. Everything just felt . . . dark.

"Second, what happened? You need to tell me."

Meera didn't know what to do. Keddi had refused to tell her what had occurred.

"If Keddi hurt you in any way . . . "

"Leave."

She hadn't cried since Brett's death, many cycles prior, and it now caused Meera to panic. Sam knew she needed to say something, or Meera wouldn't leave.

"I cannot talk about it right now. I will be fine. And no, Keddi did not hurt me. Now, go away." Then she remembered that she had hurt Keddi.

She bolted straight up. "Keddi?"

As she sat up, her head began to throb with pain, and her arm felt bruised. She lay back down.

Berth answered, "I had to re-do the stitches in her head. She said she bumped her head. She was in terrible pain, but refused any potion to help her. What happened to her, Second?"

Sam didn't answer. She didn't care if Berth knew or not. Berth had tended to Keddi, and that was all that was needed from her. Sam put her hand to her head. It hurt so.

Berth went over to her, "Second, you need to rest for a little while. You must have hit your head on the ground when you fell. You might have a concussion from the fall. You need to rest for the morn so I can watch over you and make sure you are fine. Let me take a quick look at your head."

"Not now, Berth. Let her be, for now." Meera intercepted Berth before she could touch The Second's head. Sam sighed with relief.

Meera said to Sam, "I will escort Treena back to her dwelling, and bring her back later."

Sam could hardly breathe, yet now she had to deal with Treena. She was angry anyway, so thought she might as well. "No, Meera. Please just give me but a moment to recover. Have her wait in the sitting room."

Meera nodded and left, taking Berth in-hand to make sure she left with her. Sam tried to get her tears under control. Her heart ached more than her head hurt, and now she had hurt Keddi, too.

She remembered what Keddi had said: *Brett was my sister.*

Her head felt like spinning again, but on this moment she didn't blackout. She forced herself to face the reality. *Keddi and Brett were sisters.*

How am I supposed to deal with that? Why did I not know this?

As selfish as she felt regarding Brett's death, she now realized she had failed to understand what it had meant to Keddi. She too had faced a great loss.

Sam got up slowly, feeling like a very old and stupid woman. Her whole body hurt, her head ached, and her mind was weary.

How have I been so blind? Why has The Highest not told me of this?

She tried to put it aside. She knew that she should return to Keddi to see if she needed anything.

How can I face her after what happened?

She was uncertain if she even wanted her in the dwelling anymore. She couldn't trust herself to keep from harming others, and she didn't like what was happening to her.

She quietly went beside Keddi's bed. She seemed to be resting now, and her eyes were closed.

She is lovely, but so different from Brett.
Does she look like Brett?

Then she saw the resemblances to Brett. Her hair coloring was the same.

The eyes; the outline of her eyes. They are just like Brett's. This is why I have thought her so familiar looking.

She wondered why she had missed it. She caught herself from reaching to touch Keddi's mouth, to trace the outline of it, something she had often done to Brett's.

"Looking for Brett in my face?"

Keddi's eyes were closed, yet she knew Sam was there, and what she was doing. There was no malevolence in her tone. Sam was too tired to be embarrassed. She waited to answer.

She sat down and finally responded, "Yes." She paused, then added, "I knew not that she was your sister."

Keddi opened her eyes and turned her head to Sam, with a flinch. Her head and eyes pounded and her eyes were tearing from the pain.

"How did you know I was here?"

"The energy must flow about you. I could feel your presence."

Keddi's face contorted again in pain. She looked like she was about to become ill. Sam didn't understand what made her do it, but she placed both her hands on Keddi's head, feeling the strange power surge through them as she had guessed it would. The power was so strong that Keddi's head tilted back from the force and Sam's hands jerked away from Keddi's head. Sam was suddenly violently ill. She ran outside, knelt down and wretched for what she thought an eternity. Afterward, she struggled to rise, but couldn't and decided to wait there a moment.

Keddi helped her up, "Your power grows stronger."

She helped Sam inside to the chair. Sam sat down before she fell down.

"Yet I grow weaker."

She couldn't think of a moment she felt so weak and drained, and thought, *This must be the feeling of death.*

She looked up at Keddi, confused, "How is your pain? How is it that you are able to help me?"

"You seemed to have healed my head. My other wounds are yet present, but far less severe than my head wound was. I limp with one leg very well. How did you know to do what you did?"

"My body seems to know what to do while my mind remains witless."

She leaned back in the chair and tried to rest.

"Thank you for healing my head, Second, but are the consequences worth it?"

Sam just closed her eyes and thought, *Would I but knew the consequences of living, I would not have wanted to come into this land. Oh, Brett, I so desperately need your strength.*

Keddi wished she could take away some of The Second's burdens, but also knew that many more, outside Woden, would face her in her future.

"Brett loved you, Second. She was your companion because she loved you. That is all you need to remember about her. I have returned because you and Woden need me now, and I want to be here."

Sam could no longer react to Keddi or even comprehend what she was saying. She would think about all of it later when she was better able to think through it. She just sat there, eyes closed, resting. She found some peace in knowing that a part of Brett was yet with her.

"I am sorry you lost Brett, too."

* * * *

The Second forced herself to find enough energy to face the meeting with Treena. As she arrived, Meera was standing outside the meeting room, waiting for her.

She bowed her head, "Second. Would you like me to come in with you during your meeting with Treena?"

"I think not, Meera. I do not want her to feel we gather forces against her."

"Yes, Second. I will be outside the door if you but need me."

Meera was deeply concerned about Sam, but felt helpless in preventing further burden. She was upset that The Highest was so quick to unload her burden onto Sam. Because The Highest was almost giving away her long-standing role so easily, Meera had begun to wonder if The Highest had another reason for doing so.

Sam walked into the room to find Treena looking down at the floor. When Treena heard Sam enter, she quickly rose, bowed, and said, "Second." She looked as if she had been crying all the eve and hadn't gotten any sleep. Sam felt no sympathy for her.

"Good morn, Treena. I am glad to see that you have agreed to come to speak with me." She sat across from Treena. "I find myself wondering how to begin. Perhaps I will just let you say what it is you want to say."

Treena nodded, but looked like she had no strength to begin.

She started to cry. Sam just waited.

"Oh, Second, you were correct. I have gotten myself into a place I know not how to get out of. And I know not what to do. Lives are being threatened; The Highest is dying, and all because I have been but weak to report anything. I have been a terrible advisor and but a worse community member."

Sam wasn't interested in soothing her feelings. She knew that Treena was correct; she had been weak, and she had allowed herself to be manipulated.

"Why not begin at the beginning, Treena, and tell me the whole story?"

She looked at The Second, wiped her eyes, and nodded, "Yes, it be a good idea, but I hope you have a while, because this be a long story."

Sam thought a long story wasn't what she needed, but resigned herself to listen.

The story went back two full cycles.

As Treena told the tale, Sam kept fretting, *How could we have missed all these clues? How could they have gotten away with all this sabotage?*

Treena told how, at first, the Spiritual Leaders manipulated her by making her feel important, and telling her that she would be an excellent Highest. They gave her gifts. They told her how important it was to turn the community into a mixed community, telling her until she began believing it herself. The Spiritual Leaders argued how weak The Highest was as a leader, that Sam, The Second, was just The Highest's shadow, and that it was Treena with the real leadership ability. And they told her that they could turn this community into a mixed community of thousands, and she could be the leader of a kingdom. They had even arranged mixed marriages for her, her companion, and all the Spiritual Leaders to men from Fornaith and New Harborage. Treena had told how she was betrothed to some prince of Fornaith.

Sam thought, *Prince? Now we have princes?*

Treena told of how when she questioned them once, they began to tell her how they would remove all her power; how they would abduct Treena's companion, Persane, and keep them apart forever; how they might even be forced to violence. It was then that she became frightened and decided to follow along, out of fear.

At the end of the story, she said, "I know they will but kill me, Second. And Persane, too. And once they find out I have told you all this, they will kill you, too. And, Second, I do not want a mixed marriage."

She gave Sam all their names and told of all their meetings places and schedules. Then she really surprised Sam, "Second, you should know this: There be a man behind all this. A man they want to rule as the Very Highest."

Sam wondered about this. *A man. A mixed community. Who put them up to this?*

She thought it not anyone from Hengist, as they were as loathe toward a mixed community as the women were. She thought it the moment to bring in Briggon and group.

When done telling the story, The Second thought Treena looked exhausted. Sam felt defeated. External enemies were hard enough, but to have internal sabotage was new for Woden. And that their Spiritual Leaders wanted them to be a mixed community was sabotage.

"Second? Are you going to say anything?" She waited while Sam just looked at her. "I assume you will punish me, but please let Persane and me remain in the community. I will do anything to make it up to you and the women. I do believe in this community's mission and vision, as you said prior midturn. And I realize that I have been but listening to the wrong women. I am so scared."

Sam thought, *That is fine, but the damage has been done.*

"Well, Treena. That be quite a story. I can see well why you are afraid of being killed by our Spiritual Leaders. We will but protect you and Persane for your willingness to come forward and but share this information. I need some moments to decide what to do with you, and I also need some moments to ensure that you have not lied to me and set us up, further. You used to be a very good advisor. I hope the moments come to be so you can be as such, again. I will require you to tell this story to Meera and Keets so that they can check out the facts and question you about the details."

"I understand, Second. I will help all I can to save this community. Can I but tell just Meera?"

Sam considered Treena's grieving wearisome, as it had provided much damage to Woden. She had to persuade herself that Treena was telling the truth, so got up and walked over to Treena.

Since I seem to have this strange force in me, I might as well use it to our advantage. Even though it will tire me more, at least it will be purposeful . . .

Sam placed her hand on Treena's shoulder. Treena felt the current from Sam, and froze in fear. Sam felt her say, *I am so sorry. Please let them forgive me.*

Satisfied that Treena had told the truth, Sam called for Meera and sat back down. She was too tired to stand. The use of the current now seemed to be affecting her heart as well, her heart now beating most irregularly. She could feel the change in it.

"Meera, I need you to listen to Treena's story and but confirm the details. She asked to not have to tell this story to Keets. I did not ask the reason. She gave me all the names and places of what has been occurring. You will need to move quickly on this, though. The community is being sabotaged, internally. But you already knew the Spiritual Leaders were up to something."

Treena looked surprised at this.

"I also am wondering if this, too, be but another trap on the Counselors' part. Be careful on this. Treena informed me that the Spiritual Leaders want to make this a mixed community, and that this all involves a man they are referring to as The Very Highest. After you confirm the story, arrange a meeting for us with Briggon. There seems to be a prince from Fornaith who is but betrothed to Treena. I suspect that is where our problems are rooted."

Meera nodded, holding her thoughts to herself, "Yes, Second."

"I gave my word to Treena that we will protect her and Persane in the meanwhile. Please have them moved to a safe location, out of the community, so that the Spiritual Leaders will be unable to find them or communicate in any fashion with Treena. I have no idea how you plan to get her out of here unnoticed, but please get Persane out of her dwelling at the same moment, and both as quickly as possible. The Spiritual Leaders must already know of this meeting."

Sam thought that Meera had probably already made preparations to remove Treena and Persane out of the town, as she usually was ahead of her own thinking in regard to these matters.

"You are correct, Second. My guards already saw them watching your dwelling. They have already begun to publicly protest."

"Create a diversion, then, elsewhere. But get Treena out of here, soon."

Treena looked frightened.

"Meera, one other item. Once you determine this story's authority, could you arrange a meeting with my advisors, with Oisin, as well?"

"It will be done."

"Oh, and Meera?" Sam looked at Meera.

"Yes, Second. I am here for you."

"I would like you to remain near by. We have much in need of attention. Have your assistants attend to these details. You are needed here."

"So it will be, Second. Treena, come with me, please." Meera looked at Sam. "Not to worry, Second, I have this under control already."

* * * *

Sam was exhausted but felt that if she lay down to sleep, she would be unable to get up for many turns. She sought out one of the guards.

"Margeria, when Meera returns, would you please inform her that I will be in the meeting room?"

Margeria bowed, "Of course, Second."

"Could you also send someone to find Lillon for me? I have not seen her in over a turn, and she was to report back to me late prior turn."

"Please consider it done, Second."

Margeria bowed slightly and went to the task. Sam went and retrieved one of the books that The Highest wanted her to read, and checked in with May.

"May, is there anything that I could eat?"

May looked very concerned for The Second, but tried to hide it from her. She had heard from the guards that The Second had been sick.

"Oh, Second, yes I do. I have been hoping you would have some moments for the midturn meal. I made something very special for you to give you some energy."

May winked at her, "I know how busy you have been. And I was so terrible to you this morn, getting you up before you even had moments to sleep." She began to prepare the food for Sam.

"Will you be taking your meal here?"

"If it does not inconvenience you, May, I would like to take my meal and rest in the meeting room."

"Of course, Second. I will also bring you some nice strong tea to help you remain alert. I have some very nice sweets to—"

"No sweets, May, please. The sound of sweets is unpleasing to me right now."

"Not a problem, Second. Please just go sit wherever you wish, and I will be right in with your meal."

Sam left, book in hand, and went to the meeting room. She was sorry that her new chair was in Keddi's room, but thought it a good thing, as she would probably go to sleep in it. She chose another and sat down.

Margeria walked in, new chair in-hand. She bowed to Sam, "I apologize for the interruption, Second, but May asked me to bring this in for you."

"Thank you, Margeria." Sam looked at it. It seemed almost a lifespan prior that Oisin had given this to her. She had no energy to get up, though, so decided to remain in her chair.

"It be called a rocker. I saw one like it in another village, and that is the name they gave for it." Keddi had entered the room, hobbling on one leg. Her statement had startled Sam, but she was surprised to see how much better Keddi looked. "Do you mind if I join you, Second?"

Sam was unsure. She needed some moments alone to sort through the recent events, but was curious as to why Keddi came in.

"Why not try out the new chair? What did you call it, a rocker?"

Keddi nodded and sat in the rocker, and then propped her hurt leg up onto another chair.

"I think I may have scared Berth into believing she was seeing a spirit. She came in to check on my head and found it completely healed. She asked me how my head could have healed so quickly. I just said, 'My head? There was nothing wrong with my head.'"

Sam laughed with Keddi, "Poor Berth." Sam laughed again, imagining how Berth would explain this to the other healers, when May finally came in with Sam's meal.

"Oh, Keddi. I knew not that you were going to eat with The Second. I can but run and get your food, too. Second, I have brought you food to help restore your energy. And you are not to worry about it at all, because it will be easy on your stomach."

Sam wondered how May knew about her being ill, but let it pass. May knew everything. It was annoying, but at the same moment, comforting. She looked at the bowl and noticed that May had given her a rich broth with noodles and vegetables in it. It smelled wonderful, per usual. She started to eat and for a moment forgot that Keddi was there.

She looked over to her, "I am so tired and hungry that I forgot to be a good host."

"You need to rest, Second. Your use of your power is draining your energies."

Sam didn't feel the need to be lectured to by Keddi, "That along with everyone telling me everything I should have known a lifespan ago."

She halted eating and just sat back. She liked Keddi, but was now growing tired of the problems that had come with her. She knew that under different circumstances she could be attracted to her, but now that she learned Keddi was Brett's sister, it was too complex to even consider. Sam wanted to avoid comparing Keddi to Brett, and realized that in a close relationship it was inevitable.

"I suppose I deserved that, Second."

May returned with Keddi's meal. It was much more substantial than The Second's, but food no longer interested Sam. May looked at Sam and became concerned, "Second, you need to eat your soup. It will help you to feel better."

"Thank you, May."

Sam knew she was being dismissive, but she was too tired to fight anyone off. She laid her head against the chair and tried to rest, hoping to sink into unconsciousness. Keddi got up and came toward The Second.

"Please, Keddi, touch me not. I have no energy left to allow anymore of that current, or whatever it is, to occur. It drains me too much. I do not want to get sick anymore. My stomach is already sore from the first episode." She decided not to tell Keddi about her heart.

"I have been thinking about that. Try folding your hands together, Second."

"Keddi, what are yo—"

"Second, please place your hands together so they touch each other."

Sam looked at Keddi, questioning what Keddi was saying.

"I have done a good deal of thinking about this problem since I saw you become so ill this last moment. I have a guess that if you can control the channeling back onto itself, then you will not experience the drain when you wish it to not occur. I have seen another, with powers, do as such. Do you wish to attempt my guess?"

Sam clasped her hands together, with equal amounts of reluctance and hope. Keddi went in back of Sam and touched her shoulders. Sam tensed, expecting the current to release itself into Keddi. Nothing happened.

"I have not felt any current, Second. Have you?"

With relief, Sam said, "Nothing. Thank you Keddi. That gives me some hope."

"For now, try to remember to keep your hands together when with others. At least until we can invoke a better solution."

Keddi began to massage Sam's back and neck. At first, Sam mentally resisted the feeling, but slowly relaxed into it. She could feel her muscles beginning to loosen, and also noticed that she was feeling better. Keddi watched intently for signs of improvement from Sam. She noticed that Sam's breathing evened out and that she was giving into letting go her tension.

"Your Birth-Mother used to tell me that I do not have to own the problems, I just have to act on them."

"That sounds like something my Birth-Mother would say. But, Keddi, I really do not expect to have to deal with you as my Birth-Mother." After a few moments, Sam asked, "Who followed you back here, Keddi?"

She shook her head slightly, "I am sorry, Second; I cannot remember. Berth says that I have a memory loss due to the head wound. She says it might return, or not. It be very frustrating. I can remember getting ready for the trip and hiding the anti-poison, but I cannot remember anything after that. Even given that you but healed my head wound."

Sam hoped her memory would return soon. They needed to know who followed her and what became of them.

"You seem to be feeling a little more relaxed, Second. Do you think you might want to finish your meal?"

"I think I can do that now, Keddi. Thank you. Now if I could just get some undisturbed sleep for an eve or two, I might feel like my other self."

"You go ahead and eat and rest, then, Second. I will just sit here and eat my meal."

Sam was used to women watching over her, so thought little of having someone else in the room with her while she read. She began eating, and picked up the book and started to read.

> Journal #4 – Settlement Two; 7th cycle – Spring II; Entry #1
>
> I've just found the rest of the journals, but start this one in despair - the experiment has failed. We've become nothing more than a barbaric hoard, fighting over everything. Our governance has failed, and everyone's splitting up into small groups and going their separate ways to begin their own idea of what the experiment was meant to do. Everyone is fighting over the supplies and equipment, and with everyone leaving, there're very few left to do any of the repairs on the energy sources. I can't keep up with the repairs, so our main generator has died. I couldn't train enough others to help, so the solar generator is also gone.
>
> I should've left with the first groups as now we've been taken-over by Burn who has turned into nothing more than a mean tyrant and despot. No, he's not just mean, he's evil. I think he's gone mad, and is so paranoid that he threatens to kill anyone who looks at him. Now I'm unable to leave. He keeps most of us prisoner in the compound. He forces us to listen every morning to his sermons about god. I hate him so. If I could, I would kill him. He's destroyed everything and all our dreams. The philosophy I had to study in college always talked about our penchant for violence. I never believed it, but now I've seen it. I wouldn't have come if I had known we would degenerate so far. I hate it here. I want to go home.

Sam studied the language. It seemed so strange, so old sounding to her. They used words she didn't know, and other words seemed joined to others in some bizarre fashion, but were confusing. She wondered who god was, who the generator that died was, what a sermon and a Spring II were, and what happened to the first three journals. Woden had a dictionary of sorts, that had been handed-down, but Sam decided to look up the words later. She also wondered where Settlement Two had been. She guessed that whatever the experiment had been, it had failed by their seventh cycle.

"Keddi, have you ever heard anyone say the word can't'?"

"Can't? What is can't?"

"How about should've?"

"Are you saying *should've*, or should *have*?"

"Hmmmm . . . " She thought about it for a moment, then added, "Perhaps you are correct, Keddi. They may be saying should have, but combined it. Perhaps it was the more proper language. Try it out for me."

"You *should've* slept more last eve, Second."

"And you *should've* minded your own business." She started laughing.

"And you *should've* been more quiet." They both laughed.

"And you *should've* closed your ears."

"And you *should've* halted after three moments, Second."

They were both laughing hysterically. It sounded so funny to The Second, and she was enjoying the game.

"And Oisin *should have* left after the third moment."

"No, Keddi, you said *should have*. It is hard to get used to. Is it for you as well?"

"What was the first one you said? Can't? How is it used?"

"They say, 'I can't keep up with the repairs . . . So I think it correct; they did combine the words. We would say 'I cannot keep up with the repairs'. I cannot was I can't. Do you suppose I am saying it correctly? Try it out."

"I *can't* believe you had sex all eve."

"I *can't* believe you are yet talking about this."

"I *can't* imagine how tired you must be."

"I *can't* think."

"I *can't* believe I heard you each of the four moments."

"Oh, Keddi, you embarrass me," and she continued to laugh.

"Be there any more of these combined words?"

She looked, then nodded, "Yes. Try one more. Ah, here is one: *wouldn't*. They said, 'I *wouldn't* have come if ' This seems very strange to me. *Wouldn't*. Would not. I think it be the same amount of wording. I wonder why it was used so."

"*Wouldn't?* It does sound strange. Okay, here it is. I *wouldn't* have been able to keep up with you last eve."

"Then I *wouldn't* have been pleased in the morn." Sam grinned, then laughed.

"Then I *wouldn't* have been invited back."

They laughed uncontrollably for a long while. May came in to retrieve the dishes, smiled, and left quickly so as to not interfere or halt them. She thought that The Second needed a good laugh.

Drying her tears from laughing so hard, Sam said, "How funny their language was."

"What are you reading, Second?"

"Our background. It be our first writings."

"Well, I *wouldn't* think that very interesting," and they began laughing all over again.

* * * *

Sam began to read again but was interrupted by Margeria. Bowing, she said, "Please, Highest. Your presence be requested on your patio."

"By who?"

"Your advisors, Highest. It be urgent."

Sam looked out and saw many of the community around the patio. Oisin was there as well. She looked at Keddi, wondering, "Is there a full moon, or have I done something to offend our mothers?"

Keddi knew it was just a comment on the overly many events that had been occurring, so said nothing. Sam followed Keddi out to the patio.

Oisin stepped forward and guided Sam to the middle of the patio. All the advisors were present except two. Oisin spoke softly to Sam, "Sam, I am sorry to inform you that The Highest has died."

"Died? The Highest?"

"Yes, Sam. And you must now become The Highest."

Sam staggered slightly from the report, and a momentary thought came into her head that Margeria had addressed her as Highest. Oisin and Meera grabbed her arms and held her upright. The energy force flowed through them. Sam's heart halted for a moment as she sensed their concern, but their thoughts were too difficult to untangle.

Her own thoughts raced through her mind, *Oh, no, not The Highest . . . dead. My heart. I am dying. What did Keddi say? Think! Something about my hands together. Put my hands together.*

Sam did as she remembered, and was able to halt the drain from the energy enough to stand on her own.

She asked weakly, "How? Why?"

Oisin answered, "We are under a small siege, Highest, but one we will be able to halt. A few Counselors tried to kidnap her, but she chose to swallow her poison, instead."

"Swallowed her vial of poison?"

"Yes, Highest. And now we have great need and few moments to establish you as Highest, informally until the morn. We must but act quickly. You be aware of the laws."

"Now?" She tried to compose herself. She needed Lillon.

Karan answered, "Our laws provide that when The Highest dies, another must be but immediately instated by the leaders of the community until the morn after, when the formal ceremony is to occur in front of all."

"But why? The Highest has already passed her duties to me."

Karen shook her head, "It is our custom, Highest. Our laws are such so that there be but no absence of a Highest for any moment longer than necessary."

"But now? I have not had any moments to think of this. Where is Lillon?"

"She has also been captured, but is alive."

"Captured? Lillon?"

Oisin looked at Sam, "Sam, why do you but hesitate?"

Sam shook her head, "Hesitate? You just now tell me that The Highest has died, by her own hand, and then tell me that Lillon is being held captive, and yet you expect me to make sense of this? It be overly sudden. It can but wait until the morn."

Karan came forward, "I am sorry, Highest, but it cannot. You need to be instated by all the advisors and leaders, and then begin the process. You are to remain in isolation from mid-eve until the sun rise, at which moment you will be escorted to the formal ceremony."

"Why isolation?"

Oisin replied, "Sam, you but hesitate. Why?"

"I know not if I can or should do this, Oisin. There is overly much occurring at this moment."

"The Highest said that you were to be made Highest, and all these advisors in front of you say as well."

Sam looked around and saw that Josin was missing.

"Where be Josin?"

"She be with Hern, holding Lillon."

"Josin? A traitor?"

Oisin just nodded her head, "She be the one who tried to kidnap and murder The Highest."

Meera came over to Sam. "Highest. You must do this. We all stand with you."

Sam whispered to Meera, "Meera, if I do this, I must choose a Second—"

Meera shook her head, and took her aside for a moment. She spoke softly to her so no other could hear, "It cannot be me, Sam. Do not even think it so. I am and will always remain your protector. I want no other position. You must select another." She hesitated a moment and then continued, "Sam, Woden needs you. We have much in front of us and we need you. There is not one advisor here that could hold this position. There is not a woman here that wants other than you."

"But, Meera, if Josin be a traitor, then some of the other advisors could be, as well."

"I have already recognized this as a possibility, but we cannot know this at this moment. And at this moment, all these women here stand with you and have pronounced you as the next Highest."

Sam lowered her head, thinking, *Why is this to be? Has not enough occurred in our lives that this should but occur, too? I know not the laws, the background, and all the items The Highest wished me to know. How am I supposed to act as the leader of this entire community? Oh, Brett, where are you when I need you? Where are these so-called Spirit Mothers of the Falls that are supposed to provide us with guidance? Who am I to do this?*

Unknowingly, she nodded her consent, looking at Oisin with sadness in her eyes. Oisin thought it was a terrible moment for both of them, as she would have to be the one to invest Sam as The Highest.

Oisin faced Sam, and began the proceedings, "Kneel, Second of Woden."

Sam knelt in front of her advisors, and bowed her head. She was in shock, but knew she wasn't to be given the moments to prepare for this.

"Sam of Woden, Second of our domain, do you accept our need of you as Highest?"

Sam looked at her advisors, and then at Oisin. *How can all this occur in this span of turns? Am I to bear all this alone? Mother of the Falls, I need you now.*

Everyone was waiting her answer.

Softly, "Yes."

Oisin turned to Meera, "Meera, I but need your sword."

Meera unsheathed her sword and handed it to Oisin. Oisin took it and rested the tip of the sword upon Sam's head. "Then I, Oisin, Sea Duty Second of Woden, the next in command, ask your solemn oath for our community: Do you agree to uphold the bonds, mission, and laws of our community?"

"Yes."

"Do you agree to provide us your best guidance until your death?"

To herself, she thought, *NO! I cannot!*

But she knew she had to take the responsibility, for Woden. She sighed deeply, then mustered as much strength as she could to provide her quiet response, "Yes."

"Do you agree to be loyal to our mothers prior to us?"

"Yes."

"Do you agree to treat us all as your lineage?"

"Yes."

"Do you agree to fight to the death our ways, beliefs and customs?"

"Yes."

"Do you, Sam and Second of Woden, pledge your life to Woden?"

She sighed and nodded, "I pledge you my life and loyalty. They are but yours to command."

Sam didn't want to be The Highest. She was fighting every muscle to run away, to hide. She wanted to shout, *NO, I want not to be The Highest. No, you have chosen the wrong leader.* But she couldn't. She felt her mother spirit walking her to her destiny. Sam thought, *Here I am, surrounded by women who think I can lead them and this community. I feel worse this turn than ever in my life. I look terrible and feel worse. And I may now have a power that will kill me before I get past one turn as Highest.*

"I, Oisin, your Sea Duty Second, pronounce you as The Highest of our dominion." She helped The Highest to stand. Sam had remembered to keep her hands tightly clasped together. Oisin knelt before her and bowed her head, "Highest."

Each advisor knelt before Sam and recognized her, "Highest". Apart from Brett's death, Sam couldn't recall ever having been so sad.

Softly, and just to Sam, Oisin explained, "Sam, you need to select a Second. We are under conflict situation, and without leaders. I know you have had no moment to consider this, but one must be chosen and Lillon will be but a most difficult choice. I suggest you choose another."

Sam nodded. She hadn't needed to think of this. She turned to her advisors and saw who she was looking for.

"Jandra, I request your presence."

Jandra came up to the patio, "Highest?" and bowed. "Have I done you a disfavor?"

"No, Jandra. I have need of you and all your experience. I need you to attend Woden and me, now. Would you be willing to do that for your community?"

The Highest had just asked Jandra if she would become The Second. The question had stunned Jandra. Sam thought that there was not one woman in the community who would have guessed her choice. But she had heard upon many moments from The Highest how she respected Jandra's council.

"Me? As Second? I believed you not to even respect my knowledge and ability."

"You overly assume much, Jandra. We have other issues that we must deal with first. Please provide your decision."

"Yes, Highest, I will honor your need."

"Thank you, Jandra.

Sam turned to Oisin and nodded.

Oisin faced Jandra, "Jandra, please kneel."

Jandra did so, and bowed her head.

Oisin lay the tip of the sword upon Jandra's head, "On your oath to me and the community, will you attend The Highest?"

"Yes."

"Will you uphold all that The Highest would wish for the community?"

"Yes."

"Do you agree to provide The Highest with your most honest, wisest, and direct council?"

"Yes."

"Do you agree to treat all members of our community with respect and fairness?"

"Yes."

"Do you understand that upon The Highest's death, you may become The Highest?"

"Yes."

"And should that occur, do you agree to uphold the bond of this community and protect it to the death?"

"Yes, I do. I swear my undying allegiance to The Highest and the Woden community."

Oisin pronounced, "Then, in the presence of all that here attend, I, Oisin, Sea-Duty Second of Woden, pronounce that you, Jandra of Woden, are henceforth to be known as Second, with all the respect and expectations therein."

Sam noticed tears in Jandra's eyes.

Jandra went to Sam and knelt before her, "I pledge you my undying loyalty."

Sam placed her hand upon Jandra's head, "Thank you, Jandra, Second of Woden. Rise. We have much work to do." Jandra felt a strange power surge from The Highest's hand into her body. As the surge passed from Sam, she sensed Jandra's loyalty and devotion, but she also sensed herself growing far weaker.

The community bowed their heads and echoed, "Second".

Sam turned and went inside. As she did, she said to Jandra, "Second of Woden, before I but begin my period of isolation, please assemble the leaders and advisors in the meeting room immediately, and please include Keddi and Margeria."

"As you bid, Highest."

* * * *

Sam went to the meeting room and sat down in her rocker. The word tired no longer expressed her physical state, so determined to keep her hands clasped together. Once everyone entered, the room was full. Oisin looked beyond serious and Sam could tell she was indeed worried about attacks from the seaside.

"Meera, Keets, please update The Second and me."

"Lillon is being held hostage by Hern, Josin, and four of the Spiritual Leaders."

"Hostage? Why?"

"They say they will trade her, in safe condition, in return for Keddi."

"Keddi? Why Keddi?"

"They must think she knows something we know not."

Looking at Keddi, Sam replied, "Yes, and something Keddi cannot remember." Turning back to Meera and Keets she said, "Only four Spiritual Leaders and two advisors? Have the others abandoned their cause?"

Oisin answered, "The others stole a small boat and escaped to the ship that is presently in our harbor. My crew saw no reason to halt them. This way all those traitors will be in one place."

"So, these events have all been well coordinated?"

Oisin said, "So it seems, Highest."

"And there is a ship in our harbor?" Sam was displeased about this event.

Oisin nodded and frowned, "We had left for our journey out, but came across the ship in the early morn. We overcame it and escorted it back here. The captain requested safe passage and safe harbor in port. Over my dead body will they but enter the harbor. We have them under heavy guard just outside the harbor."

"You have that ship under good guard, so I am unconcerned about that matter. Have you found any other ships nearby?" Sam knew that this would have been Oisin's first plan of action.

"Not as yet, but we remain searching all the coves and hiding places."

To Meera and Keets, she said, "Can you overtake Hern and the others?"

Keets nodded, "But not while ensuring Lillon's safety."

"Do we know of Lillon's condition?"

Meera replied, "I demanded to be shown Lillon. She is presently unharmed. Jandra has seen her, too."

"Jandra, you knew of this?"

"I was trying to get Hern to release her, Highest."

"It be truth, Highest. We had to halt Jandra from throwing herself at Hern. She kept calling Hern a traitor and threatened to kill her."

Sam turned to Jandra and smiled, "I knew I made a wise choice. We need to free Lillon quickly, but I will not hand over Keddi to those wom—"

"Highest, I may have an idea that can return Lillon to you unharmed."

"Keddi, I wish you not involved in this. They will kill you the moment they get you on board that ship. You are overly weak to fight anyone."

Keets intervened, "Highest, we might be able to use her council. You said as much, yourself."

Sam just looked at Keets in frustration, "Yes, I know, Keets, but I also know she will seek to put herself into the middle of it." She looked around and saw that they all looked disappointed, "Oh, go ahead, Keddi. Tell us your plan."

"It involves what occurred with my head wound. Do you wish this to be known?"

As The Highest thought about that, it dawned on her what Keddi needed. "I understand what you will need, and what it requires of me. But you also said that the consequences are overly great. However, can you ensure safety for the both you and Lillon?"

"Yes, Highest. I can make it so."

Margeria entered the room. She bowed, "Highest. Please excuse my lateness in arriving, but I have been attending to a request of you."

"A request of me?"

"Yes, Highest. A delegate from the ship requests an audience with you to deliver a message from the leader of Fornaith."

"Is this delegate of any authority?"

"He says that he is the king's assistant."

Sam was surprised, "King?"

"Do not do this, Highest." Meera didn't want Sam risking herself.

"This should not occur, Highest."

"It be a trap."

"We cannot permit this."

"It is overly unsafe, Highest."

Sam waited for them to finish voicing their opinions, then, smiling, said, "I am well amused. They think they can play with us."

Oisin, not smiling, said, "Sam, this be no game."

"You think not, Oisin? I think this the biggest game of all. Margeria, send a message. Please inform this delegate that we have received the message and are delighted. We welcome him into our community to deliver his message. We would be pleased if they would honor us with their presence this late before mid-eve for sweets and drinks. We guarantee them safe passage."

"Yes, Highest." She bowed and was beginning to exit.

"Margeria, please just send the messenger and return here to me. We have need of your expertise."

"As you wish, Highest."

"And please inform May of the treats and drinks needed for this late eve."

"Yes, Highest. It will be done." She was pleased but nervous to be so closely connected to the needs of The Highest. Her goal was to become the next Second's Meera. Meera had known this about Margeria, and had informed Sam many turns ago that Margeria would be a good woman to begin training for a leadership position. Now with Sam as The Highest and Jandra as The Second, there would be a slight shifting in the advisors. Sam liked to keep a natural progression through the ranks if some women were so inclined, and this newest event would help to determine Margeria's abilities. Sam tried to always be one step ahead, knowing that as battles occurred, some women might be lost. It was always good to have more prepared, as the community had just seen.

Oisin said, "Highest, I do not think you should entertain these men. They bring malice."

"Did I not just give my solemn oath to protect this community, Oisin?"

Jandra spoke, "I think The Highest correct. We cannot know our enemies until we meet with them. We will just have to ensure that The Highest be well protected."

"Me only, Jandra? I think you as well, as you will be here, as will all of you. This will be a busy turn for us. We must first rescue Lillon, capture our traitors, and then don ourselves in our finery."

"Highest?"

"Yes, Meera. Me included, in our best finery."

Karan reminded Sam, "Highest, you must be in isolation by late mid-eve."

"I understand Karan. I will make it so."

Meera knew that Sam had never worn her finery. She let The Highest tend to such events and thought finery to be uncomfortable, so laughed quietly to herself.

May came running in and interrupted, "You are overly tired, Second. You cannot entertain this eve."

Jandra stepped up to her, smiled and said, "May, forget not, you speak to The Highest now."

"Oh. Yes. I am sorry, Highest, but you cannot entertain this eve. You must rest. I know you were ill this after midturn."

"May, I am overly tired to fight unneeded battles, such as this. Unfortunately, this is one meeting to which I must attend, since I am Highest. I will rest this eve."

"Yes, Second, I mean Highest. But please tend to your own health. You push yourself overly hard."

Meera asked Sam, "You were sick this turn?"

Oisin was concerned as well, "You are ill? Why did you not but tell me so, Highest?"

Keddi intervened, "Perhaps I could provide you my plan. It will answer their concerns about you at the same moment, if you have decided to agree to it."

Sam thought again what it might mean to share the information with everyone. She guessed that they would find out soon enough, anyway.

"Oisin, would you be able to overtake the ship and capture our traitors at a moment's notice?"

"Our ships are at your command and will take but few moments to overtake that pitiful excuse they call a ship."

"Can you do this and yet keep everyone alive."

"It can be made so. We can always kill them in the morn, as needed."

"Keddi, I accept the plan. To be done by early eve."

Keddi explained how Sam had healed her head, but also what it had taken from Sam to do it.

Oisin looked quizzically at Sam, "But what about prior eve?"

Sam smiled knowingly, "I cannot explain it Oisin, but it seemed to work with that instead of against it."

"Ah, that is why . . . uh, well, uh, never mind, Highest. We can but discuss this later." She blushed because of what she almost had said aloud in front of everyone.

Meera didn't find the solution suitable. "But, Highest, the same thing will likely occur, will it not? If it hurts your heart and makes you weak and sick, then what be the gain? This is unacceptable to me."

Karan nodded, "I agree with Meera, Highest. We cannot afford this risk. It be overly great. Meera's and Keet's guards are well trained and will be able to overtake those traitors."

Jandra disagreed, "Not without losing Lillon, however. And they clearly want Keddi. Since I seem to be the newest to these events, I think my stance a bit more objective. If we give them Keddi in her present condition, the chance be great we will lose her. If we attack them with no one inside to protect Lillon, we will most certainly lose her. The Highest curing Keddi seems to be our best risk, although I like it not the prospect of harming The Highest further."

Keddi looked at Sam, "Highest? What do you wish to do?"

"The safety of the community be my first priority. If I can but heal Keddi, she can rescue Lillon while Keets and Meera's guards capture our traitors. Then, when the delegation comes to our little party, Oisin and crew can overtake the ship and capture the other traitors. If I do not cure

Keddi, we will probably lose her and/or Lillon during the battle. Losing one is better than losing two."

"Please excuse me, Highest, but your thinking be most disturbed. I like not your logic." Oisin could care less about losing a few women if necessary, but losing Sam was out of the question. "You are The Highest and must be more respectful of the position. The Highest should not be risked for such."

Oisin turned to Keddi, angry, "And you are wrong to ask this of The Highest. You place her at risk and use her good nature to better your own cause."

"Oh, nonsense, Oisin. Keddi is just trying to help the community. Besides, I am not going to die. I will just need rest. I even wonder if I can do anything at all right now, with my sorry tired state. Keddi, what do you need healed most?"

Meera was angry with Keddi and upset with Sam, "No, Highest. You must not do this. You have already grown weak. We can all see it in you."

Sam rose and went over to Keddi, and looked at Meera and Oisin, "Do you have another way?"

They shook their heads.

"Keddi, let us begin."

"Good, Highest. I know you can do this. But remember what I said about your hands?"

She nodded.

"As you touch my knee and hand, I want you to first visualize your hands clasped together. Can you do that?"

"Do you think it will halt me from becoming ill?"

"I am just hoping it will halt from effecting your heart, Highest. It is only a guess. As Oisin says, there be a risk."

She nodded again.

Keddi moved close to The Highest, "Look at your hands, Highest. Memorize them. Then close your eyes. Can you see your hands clasped together?"

"Yes."

"Good. Now open your eyes, but keep the visualization in your head. Can you do that?"

"Yes."

She put her hands on Keddi's knee and hand. The power jolted through her into Keddi. Keddi fell off the chair from the force of it as Sam crumpled in her chair.

"Highest!" Meera was frozen with fear.

"Sam." Oisin ran over to Sam. She saw a small trickle of blood run out of her nose. "SAMMMM!!!"

Oisin had howled at Sam being hurt so. No one had ever seen Oisin care about someone before.

Keddi got up and walked, without a limp or hobble, over to Sam. She bent down to try to help, but Oisin raged at her, "Touch her not. This be your doing. If she be harmed, I will hold you to the blame."

Jandra was shocked by what The Highest had just given with so little thought to her own well-being. She had no idea what Sam had been going through, or how much she was willing to risk. Even Meera and all Sam's other advisors had impressed Jandra. It had been a very long while since she had seen the former Highest's advisors act as a group so well. She knew she had too harshly judged these women. Even Oisin hadn't been high on her list as a serious leader. Her respect for them had grown immeasurably during these events, and she meant to make right her previous annoyance at them. The Highest had trusted her and given her a high position. She must now earn that trust with all of them.

Jandra went to Sam, kneeled down and spoke to her, "Highest, the community needs you now. We all need you. You must return to us." Jandra thought to herself, *There must be a way for her to take my strength. There must be a way. She cannot hear any of us this way. She be overly weak to hear us.*

Oisin looked at Jandra and roared, "What are you doing?"

Jandra ignored Oisin and, without warning, suddenly took hold of Sam's hands, clasped them together and then surrounded them with her own. She couldn't feel much, but she could feel some of her own energy being drained from her. She wondered, *How is this possible? This is the stuff of children's stories.*

She held strongly onto the connection, trying to make it stronger. Her head was bowed in deep concentration, although it looked to the others like she was showing reverence to Sam by kneeling. They had no clue what Jandra was up to. Jandra then remembered what had been told: *Sam could hear one's thoughts.* With that, she began trying to send her thoughts, while mostly feeling dimwitted and useless.

Sam, we need you. Take my strength. Feel my energy. I have enough for both of us. Leave us not, Sam. Return to us. Fight through my strength. I have always needed you, Sam. I have always been angered at Meera because she denied you, while I so much wanted and needed you. Now I am your Second, yet you begin to leave us. We need you, Highest. Do not give in to this force. Fight!

She waited and began to lose hope. It felt odd to try to speak through her thoughts, knowing them to be scattered, like most thoughts. Then she realized that a steady energy was leaving her, going into Sam. She tried sending her thoughts again, thinking that she was doing something wrong, or not sending them hard enough.

She didn't know where her thoughts and ideas were coming from. *How is this even as possible, sending thoughts to another?* She couldn't know that within some short moments in the future, this thought would be well remembered: *Have I seen this done, long prior, somewhere?*

She continued to send her messages to Sam, *Use my strength. Come back. You must give me some moments to earn your trust and respect. Take my strength. Please, take my strength.*

Finally, very faintly, she heard, sensed or felt, she was unsure which, The Highest reply, *I am here . . . tired . . . I denied Meera . . . could not accept Brett's death . . . get traitors . . . Wake me when Lillon and eve . . . your strength helped.*

Jandra removed her hands and looked around smiling, "She be with us. She has spoken."

Keddi needed to know, "How do you know? What did she say?"

Jandra was yet smiling. She hadn't smiled this much in very many cycles. "She said she is overly tired, and to wake her when you have rescued Lillon."

How was this accomplished? What be occurring amongst us? How did I know what to do? She wondered how, amongst all these others, she knew what to do, yet without knowing of it.

Keddi's knee and hand were unbelievably healed now, along with her head that was healed just prior. No one could believe it, but they accepted it for knowing not what else to think of it. Nothing like this had ever occurred in Woden. These events were not within their understanding, yet they had no choice but to accept them as truth. The rest of Keddi's cuts and bruises would have to heal on their own. And Keddi knew that she would now have to deal with Oisin. She guessed Oisin to be partly correct about her motives for getting healed, but hadn't really believed that Sam could die from this strange power. She hoped she hadn't been wrong, thinking that Sam was strong.

Jandra took over the session, "Oisin, would you please take The Highest to her bed? Margeria, please have May get Berth to tend and watch The Highest. Meera, would you please assign some guards to The Highest's room until we return?"

Jandra was slightly afraid that everyone would turn against her and not listen to her, so was pleased to see everyone quick to action.

When everyone returned, she said, "Meera, Keets, and Keddi, please quickly work out the details of your plan. The Highest wants Lillon back by early eve. Can you get this done for her?"

Meera responded, "We have just the last details to work out, and then we will get her back. Will you be coming with us, Second?"

"Do you so request it of me?"

"I do, if you would so oblige. We could use your leadership." Jandra thought it a tenuous beginning, and knew she had a lot to account for with Meera.

"Thank you, Meera."

* * * *

Oisin had very tenderly placed Sam in her bed. She noticed that her breathing had returned to a somewhat normal state, so was not as worried as she had been. She wondered how Jandra had known what to do, but thought that Sam had always been an excellent judge of character, herself included. She reminded herself to thank Jandra at some near point in the future. She was yet angry with Keddi, but Sam was more important to her at this moment.

May had been outside the library, but had overheard Oisin say to Sam, "Sweet Sam, you are well loved. Rest, and return to me; to us all. I have not done as much for you as I have wanted to, in my heart, but that does not mean you are not well loved and not thought of every moment of my journeys."

May looked in and saw Oisin kiss Sam on her forehead, and fix her hair ever so slightly. She had never seen a tender side to Oisin, so was surprised. But she had guessed that although Oisin had a very tough exterior, there must have been some tenderness inside or Sam would never have allowed her into her bed. She watched as Oisin just looked at Sam. When Oisin moved to take her leave, May walked in as if she had just happened in.

"Oh, Oisin, you be yet here? How be Sam?"

"She rests, May. Please watch over her."

"No one will disturb her, now, Sea-Duty Second. I vow you this."

"Two of my crew be just outside. If anyone tries to but interrupt her rest, please have them do as they have been ordered. They are here to protect Sam. I will have them respond only to you."

"Thank you, Second. I hope they will not be needed."

Meera, Keets and Keddi detailed the plan to Jandra and Oisin. Keddi was to be placed on a litter as if yet gravely injured. Oisin rewrapped her head with bandages. Keets suspected that Hern wouldn't let Lillon go, as she had vowed, when Keddi was given to them. Keddi was to let them take her inside, and then the attack would proceed. Meera and Keet's guards would take over the outside, and it was up to Keddi to find and recover Lillon and get her safely away from Hern. Meera and Keets had informed their guards to try to take the traitors alive. Oisin would prepare her crew so that when the delegation entered The Highest's dwelling, Oisin and crew would take over the ship and capture the traitors. Oisin had informed them that losses might occur.

Jandra then asked them to prepare for any surprise attack while the delegation was at The Highest's dwelling. Meera, Keets and Keddi informed Jandra that they were well prepared for any surprise, while Oisin said that the harbor would be more than well prepared for attack. They told her that Briggon would be in attendance this late eve with The Highest, and his guards would serve as greater support for any surprise attacks. All of the Hengist community was prepared for battle. Jandra felt much better knowing that there were so many that could hold Woden safe from further harm.

She didn't yet know of the events across The Realm. None of them did. None of them could, as yet.

Jandra asked Meera and Keets, "Where will you hold the traitors?"

Meera responded, "We have a secured dwelling we will use. The Highest and you will have to make a decision regarding the traitors by mid-turn next. That be all the moments the law allows."

Jandra nodded, somewhat surprised that she would need to make a decision with The Highest regarding the fate of the traitors. She never had the heavy responsibility of making a decision on someone's life. Her respect for Sam continued to increase.

Keets added, "I personally think hanging be overly good for them."

"From what The Highest told me, Oisin would like to make them but fish-bait. Right Oisin?" Meera was laughing.

"Fish bait? That be not enough. I would keelhaul them until their eyes popped out. And then I would use them for fish bait."

"Let me at them and I would gladly rip out their eyes." Jandra had lost her former Highest, and almost lost all these women that she was now pleased to work with.

Keddi said, "A man has begun this. It is typical that what begins by men must end by women."

Meera laughed, "Keddi, I think you have spent overly many moments in a mixed community."

Keets arose and announced, "It be the moment. Let us be about our brutal business."

Meera was observing Keddi, "You need to look more pained."

"Not to worry. I will moan as we arrive."

Oisin went to Keddi, "You used Sam to heal you, and told her that you could save Lillon. Make certain you do, or you will account to me." She turned to Keets, "I expect to be informed of this outcome when it be but complete. And I expect it to be successful. I will be at the ships."

"Yes, Second. I will send a messenger."

All the guards were in ready as Keddi was carried to Hern's dwelling. Women were gathered around at a distance, but overly close for Jandra's liking. She was unaware that Meera's guards were in the crowd as onlookers, remaining close by in case they became needed.

Meera walked close to Hern's dwelling.

Hern said, "That be close enough, Meera."

"Hern, we have brought Keddi in exchange for Lillon. Bring her out and we will but begin the exchange."

"I will show you Lillon, but she goes no further than the door until I can see this woman who has caused us so much trouble."

Under normal situations, Meera wouldn't have agreed to Hern's terms, but she wanted to get this over and knew that Hern was set to a single path.

"Hern, I must ask you once again to give this battle up. It is no good. You will lose. You know that we have more strength in numbers than you do. What do you but hope to gain from this?"

"Halt the lecture, Meera. You but waste my moments. These women about us see who the real traitors are. They want me for their highest."

Keets came over to Meera, "You talk for naught. She is deranged. Let us get this over with, Meera. She is not going to listen to you."

Meera knew that Keets was correct and nodded to the guards carrying the litter. She silently wished Keddi well, but knew enough about Keddi's background to let her be about her affair.

When the guards got to the door, Hern said, "Set the litter down. I wish to speak to this woman alone for a moment. I will then hand over Lillon."

"That was not the agreement, Hern."

"Take it or leave it, Meera."

She nodded, knowing what was to come next. Hern did as expected. She had her women take Keddi, who was sufficiently moaning at this point, inside.

"Hern, we upheld our bargain. Give us Lillon."

She just laughed, "You are such a foolish woman, Meera."

At that moment, Keets gave the command to attack. Four-dozen women led by Margeria, surrounded and subdued the traitors outside the dwelling. Inside, as soon as she heard the attack and saw a few of the women run outside to help against the intruders, Keddi got up off the litter.

"Hern, where be Lillon?"

"What? What are you doing up? You are supposed to be injured. Even the healers have said how badly inju—"

"As you can see, I am not. Where be Lillon?"

Hern made a move to fight Keddi, but was no match against her. Using Hern's momentum, Keddi grabbed onto Hern's clothes and guided

Hern directly into the wall, headfirst. Hern dropped to the ground, unconscious. Keddi tied up Hern with her bandages, then stepped outside. She felt somewhat unsatisfied thinking, *This was too easy.* She felt robbed of being able to take out her anger on Hern. She then went out the door.

"All clear in here. Has anyone seen Lillon?"

"Look inside for her, Keddi. We have gathered all the traitors together. Is Hern alive?"

"Yes. We will watch her die later."

Keddi went back inside and found Lillon under a bed, unconscious, but alive. She pulled her out from under the bed and moved her to the litter.

"Second, I have found Lillon. She be alive."

Jandra smiled. It had gone well. All the traitors were captured, no deaths occurred, and only three guards had minor wounds. She didn't care that some of the Counselors were more seriously hurt. She suspected that midturn next, their pain would permanently be gone.

"The Highest will be pleased."

Two of Keets' guards were dragging Hern out of the dwelling. It looked like Keddi had done all but kill Hern, and Jandra began to understand the discipline that Keddi must have had to not do so. It looked like it was something exceptionally easy for Keddi to do. Jandra then saw Josin trying to talk to Margeria. She hadn't seen Josin during the short fight, but knew that she had been somewhere near Hern.

"Your words are wasted on me, Josin. You are no longer of this community."

"Margeria, is Josin giving you trouble?" Jandra hated Josin and couldn't stand to think she might talk her way out of this. She had argued bitterly with Josin of late about her recent stances against The Highest. Josin had tried to turn Jandra against The Highest, Sam and the rest, and that was when their relationship had ended. Jandra was deeply loyal to the community and would have no part in Josin or Hern's plans.

"Not to worry, Second. Josin is but hot air." Margeria nodded to the guards to take Josin away, and shoved her harshly toward them.

Josin screamed after Jandra, "You are the traitor, Jandra. You have crossed over to Sam's side. This be only the beginning of our battle with you, Jandra. I may die, but you will too."

"As we all well, Josin, eventually."

Standing by, Meera nodded her head toward Josin, "It is not overly soon to lose that one. How did you put up with her?"

"There are a lot of things that I wonder about now, Meera. The Highest's advisors have been out of line far overly long. It be good that Sam is now The Highest. Many things that are wrong will now be put right."

Meera nodded, "Yes. Sam has seen this to be true. But at what cost to us all?" She studied Jandra for a moment, wondering if Jandra could fill The Highest's place as Second.

"Let us see to Lillon."

Keddi was standing near Lillon, trying to awaken her. Lillon was coming around but seemed confused.

Meera, Jandra and Margeria went up to her, "Lillon?"

"Oh, hello, Meera. Jandra. What are you doing here?"

She was indeed confused, but it appeared she would recover soon. "Keddi, please take Lillon to The Highest's meeting room and let her rest there. You might look in Lillon's chests to see if she has any appropriate, what did The Highest say, finery?"

"I will look for some 'finery' for me and Margeria, as well. Come, Margeria, we must go shopping for our finery," Keddi said as she laughed and went to do so.

Jandra looked around and saw that all was in order, "We should go back to The Highest's dwelling and help prepare for the delegates.

"Second, begging your patience, Keets and I must see to our women and make our guards and sites ready for any surprise attacks. Keets and I must also meet with Briggon's guards briefly to outline the plans. With your permission, we will meet you back at The Highest's dwelling this late-eve. I have guards already posted, so you need not worry about The Highest or the dwelling. She and the dwelling are well safe."

Having been Second for only a short while, Jandra was unused to knowing the duties and roles in these events. "Of course, Meera. I am certain that you and Keets know your duties well. I mean not to interfere with them."

"I understand, Second. It will take all of us many moments to accustom ourselves to all the new changes."

Jandra had never known that Meera could be so gracious. Perhaps what she had heard from The Highest had been correct, and she had been angered at Meera all these cycles for no reason.

"Thank you, Meera and Keets. You should be proud of your guards."

"It is not yet over, Second."

* * * *

Jandra had returned to The Highest's dwelling as soon as she had gathered together her own finery. She was concerned about The Highest and wanted to be there if there were any word. Throughout the late after mid-turn, she had gone in and out of The Highest's room, checking in with May. May was allowing no disturbance of any sort, but sensed that Jandra only wanted quietly to check on The Highest. Everyone was stepping gently all throughout the dwelling.

Since May had seen that Jandra wasn't going to disturb The Highest, May had left Jandra in-charge and had gone off to supervise the cooking and preparation for the eve's affair. Jandra knew Lillon was in the sitting room but was overly concerned about The Highest to check on her. She also knew that Lillon would be attended to by others and thought that May would have seen to it. Jandra just sat next to The Highest, reflecting on her life and that of The Highest's.

Why are these feelings toward The Highest coming so strongly forward? This is not usual for me. I have never desired her, prior.

She looked at Sam and realized how glad she was that Sam was now The Highest. She hadn't realized how the former Highest had slipped in her ability.

Then she realized, *Just a few moons ago, I thought Josin a good advisor.*

She came to realize that Josin had been responsible for much undoing within the community. *Why have I not seen the harm that Josin has caused? I might have prevented all this. And how could I have but allowed her in my bed?*

Jandra studied Sam's face. Sam had made no movement since Oisin had brought her in, but her breathing had been steady. She thought Sam a beautiful woman. Jandra knew that everyone thought so, but Sam never indicated that she knew or cared about such things. Her hair, as disheveled as it was, yet looked beautiful. It was smooth and shiny, her eyebrows as blond as her hair, and Jandra thought her eyes so deeply blue that one could see all the skies in them when she smiled.

Noise outside the room was beginning to filter in as everybody began assembling for the delegates' visit. Jandra didn't know whether to wake Sam or to wait for May, and without thinking, began pacing.

As she paced, Sam stirred and rolled over. It was the first movement Jandra had seen from her all late midturn and early eve. Sam moaned a little.

So soft it could hardly be heard, Sam said, "Thirsty."

Jandra went to the guard at the door and whispered, "The Highest be thirsty."

The guard quietly left. Jandra went to sit by The Highest in case she awoke. Sam had turned on her side but not yet opened her eyes.

Again, softly, "Thirsty."

"Yes, Highest. Drink is coming."

Sam opened her eyes. She just stared at Jandra, not speaking. She looked about the room and seemed extremely disoriented. Jandra thought she had good reason to be.

May came in, drink and nourishment in-hand, "Jandra, this be a good report, indeed. I never thought I would be so glad to hear that The Highest be thirsty."

Sam focused on Jandra. In that same soft voice, Sam said, "I owe you my life."

"Then it is as it should be, Highest. I am your Second."

So loud that it caused Jandra to jump, May said, "Jandra, I mean Second, would you mind going out to entertain all those who await The Highest? I will just give her some drink and nourishment, and make sure that she gets into her finery. I will send her out when I receive a message that those awful delegates have arrived."

"Huh? Oh, yes. Certainly May. I should have thought of that myself." Jandra left the room to go settle and organize the advisors and other leaders. She was delighted that Sam was waking, but was concerned enough to know that it would now take a long while for a complete recovery. She knew that she must work to help protect The Highest, now.

May looked at Sam, "Can you move, Highest?" She started to help her sit up.

"Thirsty, May."

"Here, drink this. It will help you regain your strength. Everyone is worried about you, you know. They hover around like bees, creating chaos in my life." She held the cup up to Sam's lips and helped her drink.

"Drink slowly, Highest. It will feel better that way."

Sam began to hold the cup by herself, and finished the drink.

May gave her a bowl of soup, "It seems that all I am feeding you of late be soup. But never mind that for now. Eat this down, slowly, and I will attend to your hair. Then we can get you ready for your delegates."

Sam nodded. May's constant talk helped Sam regain a hold on her own existence.

Yes, I am alive.

I am in my library.

I have been asleep for just the after midturn.

Yes, I will yet be able to meet with these delegates.

Something was missing, though. She couldn't place what was wrong.

"Lillon is here and safe, Highest. They had knocked her a good one on the side of the head, but she is quite well and awaits you in the meeting room."

Yes, that be it. Thank you, May. Sam had thought the statement, but May hadn't heard it.

"Hern?"

"Hern, Josin and four of the spiritual leaders have been captured. Meera holds them in the holding cell. Only a few guards took minor injuries and none were lost. Meera considers that part very successful. Oisin's crew and Briggon's guards be all on watch. Your hair seems to shine even more this eve, Highest. Finish your soup, and I will assemble your finery. Sarra spent all after midturn making certain that it will present you well this eve."

"Thank you, May. I feel somewhat improved."

"Oh, Second, I mean Highest, I am so glad. You are speaking." May had tears in her eyes.

"Why must everyone cry when they see me? It is beginning to make me think myself dead."

May just smiled at her as wiped her tears.

Although the event had been scheduled to occur at the patio of Sam's dwelling, much arguing had taken place over the event's location. Keets had argued that it should be at the former Highest's dwelling as it was the official Highest's dwelling. Meera said that it should be outside at the patio so there could be increased protection. Margeria noted that Sam's dwelling was the furthest for the delegation to have to come. The arguing had halted when Karan reminded everyone that it would tire The Highest further to have to go even that short a distance.

May had overseen all the preparations for the eve's affair. She had made sure that the food and drink were well prepared, the flowers were fresh and placed in the appropriate locations, and that the tables were all set up. The patio had been constructed so as to be able to host large numbers. On this eve, it was a good setting. The weather had remained pleasant, the flowers picked were at their peak, and the guards that had been assigned to help guard Keddi had done well refitting the patio stones.

As the advisors and leaders of Woden gathered in the meeting room, there was much talk over each other's finery. It had been several cycles since anyone in Woden had a need to wear their regal garments. The former Highest had all but closed the community to help ensure safety. Regardless of the seriousness of the affair, the women couldn't help be somewhat excited simply because of the festive nature. And each woman's colors only helped to provide a sense of pageantry.

When Briggon and two of his advisors arrived, the sense of excitement increased. Only recently had Hengist given in to the notion of finery, so this was their first affair in it.

Tehna asked, "Meera, do you know what The Highest will be wearing?"

"I have no clue, Tehna. She has always refused to wear her regal garments and has always let The Highest do this type of entertaining. I am sure that whatever she has will be attractive, though."

As Jandra came out from Sam's room, everyone wanted to know The Highest's condition.

"Is she well, Jandra?"

"Second, tell us how The Highest fares."

"Jandra, is The Highest awake?"

Meera looked at Jandra, thinking to herself, *Here stands the most beautiful woman in all of Woden, and now she is our Second. But what is it about her? She looks not like those of Woden. But by the mothers, she is striking.*

Jandra finally found a space in their questioning to explain that The Highest had woken, and that May was in giving her nourishment and drink. "May has requested that we inform her when the delegates arrive. The Highest will attend at that moment."

A guard walked into the meeting room. "The delegates have just left their ship."

Meera said, "Perhaps it be the moment we move to the patio."

They did so and began enjoying some of the treats. Some musicians were performing to help make the event more festive, the torches had been lit, and Meera noted that all the guards were in place. At some point, a messenger whispered to Meera that the delegates had landed and were now walking to the community's gates. Meera knew that if all went well, Oisin would be on her way to the eve's events by the moment the delegates reached the patio.

Shortly following that message, another messenger arrived announcing that the delegation had just arrived at the community's gate.

"How many delegates come, Meera?"

"We hear that there are seven. Seven men."

Jandra was nervous. She would be the main greeter, yet had no desire to welcome any of these men to her community. She knew that their cause was selfish and had no idea why The Highest chose to welcome them, but accepted that she must have her reasons. She recalled that The Highest and Oisin had argued over this issue, and that The Highest had said this was the biggest game of all. She didn't understand what The Highest had meant by that, but knew whatever it was, it was about to begin.

As the delegation arrived, Jandra welcomed each one to their community and introduced the advisors and community leaders. Meera had sent word to May that the delegation had arrived.

"We thank you, kind and most beautiful lady, and you are indeed most beautiful. I be Sir Devin, King Buron's assistant. Accompanying me are my kinsmen Sir Gowan, Lord Estray, Knight Notren, High Knight Medwin, Sir Glain, and Lord Umbar." He had indicated to each one, and each one bowed. The visitors were entertained and provided with food and drink and entertainment while everyone waited for The Highest. Each of the advisors took turns helping Jandra serve as host.

The patio doors from Sam's room finally opened, and Karan stepped out, beautiful in her finery.

She announced, "The Highest of all of Woden Falls."

With that, she knelt and Sam slowly walked out. In truth, Sam couldn't move fast, but the appearance of regal bearing had been created by Karan so as to help mask Sam's weakness. As Sam walked out, everyone knelt. Unknown to Sam, most everyone also gasped. Sam, dressed in her fine garments, was breathtakingly beautiful. Her light-colored tunics served only to accentuate her natural beauty, but they were striking in themselves. She wore a full-length tan colored gown with the royal tunic over it. The royal tunic was white with soft-gold trims in the Spirit circle designs. While her garments were elegant in their simplistic beauty and softness, it was Sam's overall bearing, grace and beauty that surprised everyone. Keddi and Meera were staring at Sam's splendor. Never prior had Meera seen Sam so striking. Jandra was most of all affected and almost frozen at such majesty. It was if Sam glowed, to Jandra. Keddi noticed that the visitors were awe-struck as well.

As she got to the center of the patio, she halted, "Please rise. There is no need of such formalities," and then she let the game begin.

As she came to Sir Devin, he bowed with a flourish, "M'Lady. I am Sir Devin, assistant to King Buron. You do King Buron and I great honor this eve. King Buron sends you gifts and words of great love and admiration. Give me leave, M'Lady, but you do but take a man's breath away. Pray you to hear thy message."

"Gifts, you say? And I have taken away your breath as well? Sir Devin, you flatter me, yet I am but a servant of my people. I think perhaps you mock me."

"Oh, nay, M'Lady. It be not so. You are as my Liege has said. You are the fairest in all the land. He will be most pleased to know that the rumors be true. Pray, M'Lady, give me your leave to deliver thy message."

"I will hear your message, Sir Devin." She sat down in the chair that May had provided for her.

"M'Lady, you are most gracious." He bowed again and then said to Sam and all, as if in a theater:

"King Buron sends you his most admiring and devoted love.

"He bids you know that his heart has halted beating until he can behold your beauty.

"He knoweth you as the fairest in all the land, and that you would doeth him the greatest favor by returning his great love and admiration.

"He sends you great gifts as demonstrations of his deep love, and he asks that you permit him to court you onto marriage.

"He exclaims how happy you maketh his heart in knowing that this fair union will be happily productive in his heirs.

"And he bids you know how greatly his lands need such a Queen as thou.

"Pray, by your leave, M'Lady, these are my Liege's words. May I now present you with my Liege's gifts?"

Sam had noticed that Oisin had shown up and was presently speaking to Keets. She wondered how the plan had gone, but had to first play the game out with this Sir Devin man. She found his use of language tedious and difficult. Karan came up to Sam and whispered a message to her from Oisin. Sam looked over to Oisin and nodded that she had understood. She dismissed Karan and let Devin continue.

"I will see your Liege's gifts, Sir Devin."

"M'Lady, you are a good and kind gentlewoman. My Liege will be most pleased. Kinsmen, bring forward the trunk."

"First, my most gracious Lady, King Buron gives you this necklace to adorn your most stunning chest, as a show of his deep love."

It was a necklace of beautiful green stones that shone like brilliant stars. Sam thought it beautiful, even though she had no need for such ornaments. Woden's life was one of simplicity, and such trinkets, while nice, had little usefulness.

"He bids you wear it so that I may tell of your most gracious pleasure and beauty."

"If it pleases you, I will put it on."

May came over and placed the necklace of green stones around Sam's neck. Everyone thought the necklace beautiful, but knew that Sam thought little of such items. Sam thought nothing of the necklace until it was placed around her neck. She felt something troubling about it, but held the thought until later.

"It pleases me well, your Highness, but it pleaseth my Liege a 1,000 fold." Devin turned to his kinsmen and waved his hand. Gowan went around the corner of the dwelling and snapped his finger. A guard came forward holding onto the reins of four very handsome horses. Sam could barely contain her laughter.

"King Buron sends you four of his finest horses, M'Lady, so that you might ride into the countryside with him to take your pleasure of him in leisure and entertainment away from the castle."

"The horses are beautiful, Sir Devin, but tell me, what is a castle?"

"A castle, M'Lady? You knoweth not? Please forgive me, Highness. I should have but known. It be but my fault."

"Sir Devin, you would do me great pleasure to just answer my question."

Quickly he said, "I am sorry, M'Lady. Of course. As you bid. You are most gracious. A castle is the house of stone, built to withstand siege."

"A house, Sir Devin? What is a house?"

"Why, M'Lady, it is what you live in."

"Ah, yes. Thank you, Sir Devin. Then I take it that King Buron lives in such a castle?"

"Oh, yes, Highness. A large and great castle. The largest and best in all the land."

"Yes, I am certain it must be."

"You are a most gracious and kind kinswoman. My Liege will dance with pleasure of this knowledge of you. May I present the next present, M'Lady."

"As you will, Sir Devin, as you will." Sam found the entire affair very humorous, but also embarrassing.

Does he not know this is a woman's community?

She had seen Briggon holding himself so as to prevent his laughter from escaping. Oisin was standing slightly apart from anyone, staring at Sam and smiling slightly. She enjoyed watching Sam play this man's hand out.

Oisin thought to herself, *So, our Sam is but a master of deception, too. Now I understand why she thinks this the biggest game of all. And she plays it well.*

"Next, M'Lady, my Liege sends you four courtly gowns. They come from a most special of all places, from deep within a Queen's Valley." He clapped his hands and his kinsmen brought forward each of the gowns. They were indeed beautiful, sewn with jewelry embedded into each. And each was very, very low cut in the front, in a deep 'V' shaped pattern.

"King Buron, M'Lady, would liketh you informed that he aims to pleaseth you in the private moments of love, and that he is well endowed. He will be most pleased to learn that you are as equally endowed in the regions these gowns have been made to display."

"Sir Devin, please excuse my ignorance of your language, but are you saying that your King thinks himself as a lusty and large sort, and that he prefers women with large breasts? And please know, I mean no disrespect." She could almost not contain herself from shrieking with laughter. *Such arrogance these men display.*

Oisin had started to laugh at Sam's statement and had to place her hand over her mouth and turn from the events.

"And none is taken, my Highness. Language barriers can be most difficult to forge. It is as you say, M'Lady, thus ensuring many happy unions and many heirs. With your beauty and, as you say, breasts, M'Lady, it shall be that the King never leave court again."

"Well, we couldn't have that, could we? I am certain that the King has many affairs outside his court he must attend." She had hoped Keddi had heard her say "couldn't", one of the new words they learned this turn, and felt it a fine addition to this other old language she was hearing. She looked at Keddi to see if she had, and saw Keddi silently laughing.

"Yes, M'Lady, but your presence and beauty would hold him tight, as it would any man."

"Your tongue is glib indeed, Sir Devin, but you flatter me overly. I am just a woman like any other."

Sam had heard upon many moments how beautiful she was, but had always felt herself the same as any other woman in her community. She couldn't figure out what all the fuss was over some physical attributes.

"Nay, it not so, M'Lady. I have sought beauty such as yours for my Liege for four cycles. There be none so fair and beautiful as what we have seen here. And pray believe me, you do taketh away a man's breath."

"Do I take your breath away, too, Sir Devin?"

"Yes, my Queen, for my Liege, my breath hath but been stolen in your singular beauty."

Jandra thought, *And this woman's breath, as well. You are truly beautiful.* Jandra knew she would always keep such thoughts to herself, as she knew that Sam had so many others she could consider for companions. But she thought them, nonetheless.

"You do over-flatter, Sir Devin, and we thank you for these gif—"

Sam was growing tired again and was glad that the charade was almost over.

"Oh, M'Lady, I beg your forgiveness, but I be not yet finished. There is one more gift my Liege wishes you to have. As a show of his undying love for you, he has sought that which means much to you. Please take this gift as a show of his true and generous love in hopes that he may soon have an heir. He wishes to know one item of privacy first, my gracious Queen."

"I do not yet think me your Queen, Sir Devin, but what is this information your liege would know of me?"

"Oh, most kind and gracious Highness. The King wishes to know if you hath lain with a man."

"Lain with a man, Sir Devin? Our community shares our societal functions in bond with a men's community, as I am sure you must know. Is this your reference?"

"Nay, M'Lady. The King requests to know if you be, pardon me, M'Lady, but this is a most difficult of question, if you be chaste."

"Chaste? What does this word chaste mean, Sir Devin?"

"This language barrier doth make it ever the most difficult, M'Lady, and I apologize for my inability to make myself clear. The King wishes to know if you hath lain with any man, most gracious and beautiful Lady of all the land, or have you been chaste for our Liege?"

"Oh, Sir Devin, I think I understand. Do you mean have I been with a man before, as in communions to have children?"

"Oh, most smartest of Queens, that is what the King asks. Hath you lain with a man and hath you produced children?"

"This is a most private and quizzical question, Sir Devin, but I will answer it. No, I have not lain with a man, and so I have no children."

Oisin almost began to laugh out loud. *This Sir Devin is such a simpleton. Can he not see how Sam plays with him? Of all things,* chaste. *Ha! Sam chaste. Not if I were to have my way, Sir Devin, and believe me, I have. Chaste is not a woman's quality, Sir Devin, and Sam is most of all, a Woman.*

"Oh, most Highest and Pure Queen of all the realm. My Liege, King Buron will no doubt have a celebration that will last for endless turns at such knowledge as this. I know I have but chosen well. Pray allow me to present you with this last gift."

He held out a package for her.

Karan came forward to accept and open it. As it was opened, she handed it to Sam. It was a book. One of the *first* books. This took Sam's breath away. This was something that Sam had asked Oisin to search for on every trip. It was known that the First Ones had books. A few were in Woden, but had been obtained in very poor condition, and all missing pieces and sections. The dictionary that Woden had was also one of the original books, but several complete sections were missing from it. Here in front of her was one of the original books, in beautiful condition, completely intact, and with a beautiful cover. Sam opened it and read the title, *Le Morte D'Arthur* by Sir Thomas Malory. This was indeed a highly prized possession, and King Buron was giving it to her.

"Sir Devin. This be a gift of superior merit, but as such, I find it very difficult to accept."

"M'Lady, it pleaseth me and my Liege that this gift hath done its purpose. It hath given you the pleasure that the King cannot until you are in his arms."

"These gifts are remarkable, indeed, Sir Devin, but I know nothing of your countryside and ways. And are you not aware that you are standing in a woman's community?"

"But, M'Lady, we too have women's communities. We call them convents, or nunneries, but they are such as this - women living with other women. What is done in such communities hath no meaning to a man's realm, as a woman is not truly a woman until she lies with a man."

At this statement, every woman in attendance had to withhold her anger. Even Sam, but all held their tongues.

Meera cringed, *Such belittlement of women. Who do they think they are? We could easily overtake their sorry selves.*

"I thank you for that explanation, Sir Devin. It does serve to explain. But tell me, Sir, what of your community, or should I say, castle?"

"No, M'Lady, the castle is the dwelling. We hold many villages, and it is a feudal dominion. Our people are taxed to gain the King's protection, but all live happily in the Kingdom."

"Ah, so it is called a kingdom."

"Yes, my most gracious and intelligent Queen. But have you not heard of this?"

"I am but a simple person, Sir. I have no such knowledge."

Sam was tiring quickly. She needed to rest for longer than half a turn.

"It be not so, M'Lady. Our lands be far distant from yours, and your ignorance of our ways is no shame on your part."

"How large are your lands, Sir Devin, and on how much protection may I count on?"

"Oh, Highness, yours and King Buron's lands are large indeed. We have nearly 1,200 souls in our kingdom. And you may count on well trained armies for your protection."

"Armies, Sir Devin? Could those be what we call guards?"

"Yes, most gracious, kind and purest of Ladies, those would be the same."

"And what of your ships? Would my coastline be well attended?"

"With the best and most ships in the land. We have over six fully rigged ships, your Highness."

"We are pleased by these gifts, Sir Devin, and by the graciousness and generosity of King Buron. But you have not spoken of the terms of this union. What might we have to offer your liege?"

"My most wise and gracious Queen, but yourself. You are the most prized possession in all the realm."

"And why would that be, kind sir?"

"M'Lady, pray give me leave of these words, but you are the fairest and most beautiful in all the realm. Your beauty is such that it shineth many leagues from here. Your blond and silky hair shineth like the stars in all the sky. Feasting one's eyes on such as you is akin to sailing through the heavens. With a woman such as you at a man's side, no man could fail in their quest."

Keddi thought, *And I know why Brett fought for you until her death.*

Sam looked at him with her eyebrow raised and asked with a slight, but hard edge in her voice, "That, Sir Devin, *and* that I am The Chosen One?"

He bowed his head and spoke softly, "Yes, your Highness, as you say. It be the prophecy."

There were many murmurs and loud gasps in the crowd. Sam had wondered how far this legend had spread.

Now she knew.

It has spread throughout The Realm. How is it that everyone knew of this before me? If I am to be The Chosen One, then why am I the only who did not know?

She shook her head clear of these questions for later. She had to concentrate on this overly wearisome man and his ridiculous words. She was tiring, and she had much to attend to on the next morn. The traitors would face Sam's sentencing, and the former Highest would have her funeral at midturn.

She frowned at him, "I think you flatter me overly, Sir Devin. It is The Chosen One you want, and not me."

"Nay, M'Lady. Pray say it not so, as it be not so. You are a chaste lady, are you not?"

"By your definition, Sir Devin, I suppose I am. But I am also not a young woman. I think that your King Buron may want whatever it is The Chosen One to have. Is that not true? By all accounts, should he not want a young and beautiful woman with her whole life yet to live? One that could give him many heirs to his kingdom?"

"Nay, M'Lady. King Buron loves you and is most devoted to you. He will shower you with love, devotion and any material item your heart may desire for your entire life. He wishes nothing else but to lie with you, M'Lady, produce strong heirs so that your union may live forever, and to giveth you much pleasure. He thinks a young woman to be silly and frivolous. It be only you he desires, M'Lady. And M'Lady, while you not a young frivolous thing, you are not old, either, and you hold the beauty of experience. As I most sincerely sayeth before: You taketh away a man's breath. Any man would fight legions for you, my Queen, and I speak this most truly and honestly, and from my Liege's heart."

As would this woman, thought Oisin.

"I am certain it is as you say, Sir Devin."

"You are but the wisest of all, my Queen."

"Being a chaste, kind, wise, gentle, gracious, pure, intelligent gentlewoman, I cannot step into this union so quickly, Sir Devin."

"Oh, my Queen, Your Liege would have it as you wish. He would have it to maketh you to swoon. He would like to present you into a courtship, M'Lady."

"Sir Devin, please explain this word, courtship."

"My most kindest of gentlewomen, courtship is a period prior to the union."

"And what does this courtship entail, Sir Devin? What would you require of me?"

"My Queen, to be as beauteous and chaste as you stand here. My Liege would have me return, with your leave, in two moons hence. The courtship would proceed with more gifts, by your leave, and more vows from my Liege. He wishes to win your good graces over fully, so that your first union with our Liege would be one as the shooting stars."

"It is acceptable, Sir Devin. But we are a simple people. What does your Liege expect in return from me? As a simple woman, I have no idea what your King may want from me that would be acceptable, so please just tell me and save me the guessing."

Meera thought that Sam was definitely tiring. She noticed that Sam's tone was becoming impatient. Yet, she didn't think that Devin could tell.

"Oh, M'Lady, you are the most noble of all the realm. My kindest and gentlest of Queens, your Lord would hath only a piece of what you wear with your own perfume."

"Karan, please retrieve my shawl."

May ran out to Karan with it and Karan presented it to Sir Devin.

"My most wondrous of Queens, my heart beats with joy for your Lordship over this gift."

"Sir Devin, please give a message to your liege."

He knelt before Sam, "I will memorize faithfully your words and carry them in lightening speed to my Liege so that he may know your kindly and most gentle of thoughts, M'Lady."

"Please tell King Buron that we accept his most gracious gifts and we are most pleased by his message. Tell him that he makes this chaste and kind gentlewoman blush in anticipation of this courtship and union. Tell him that we are most happy to consider his request for my hand in this union, that we will give him our decision at the cycle-end's solstice."

Sam paused for a moment, and then said, "Sir Devin, please be honest. Will this message please your liege or is my requirement of overly great length for him. I wish not to offend."

"Oh, nay, M'Lady. You are the most intelligent of all. The King will be most pleased that you will begin the courtship. That you have considered a moment for the union will bring joyousness throughout his realm. The amount of moments prior to the union will be most needed by us to begin the preparations needed for such as you, my Gracious Queen. You have made my Liege's, and mine as well, heart a happy friend."

"I have one parting issue to share, Sir Devin."

"Whatever it be, my good and gracious of all Queens, if I can but solve the dilemma, it will be so."

"You will notice, Sir Devin, upon return to your ship, that we have well supplied it for your voyage, with fresh foods, drinks and harvests."

"We are most sincerely pleased, my Highness." He bowed. "We had not wanted to ask strain on your supplies, but am not surprised after having met your most kind, gentle and generous nature. We will hold a portion of these supplies out for our Liege so that he may see and taste of your unasked generosity and kindness to his men."

"I think you as kind and noble as you say of me, Sir Devin."

"How so, M'Lady?"

"As we supplied your ship and gave a feast for your crew so that they too may celebrate this eve, we saw that you are so kind as to try to help those poor very diseased women."

"Diseased, M'Lady?" He looked surprised, and a little frightened.

"Oh, yes, Sir Devin. They have a bloodsucker in their brain that has caused them to go mad. They have gone throughout our realm speaking of things that have never or will be. And they go about slashing their families' throats in the eve."

Devin looked very concerned, "M'Lady, is this bloodsucker catching?"

"Oh, yes, Sir Devin, almost immediately. But you need not worry. So that you may have a successful journey back, we have rid you of these vermin infested women. Once we informed your crew, they knew not what to do. By their graciousness and gentle manners, they helped us to remove these poor but ill-fated women to the deep forest so that they can bring no harm to your men. We hope they have not, already, Sir Devin. If your King be half as kind and good hearted as you, kind sir, he will be a most gracious companion. I fear for your safe journey, though, Sir Devin. I would quietly warn you to beware of disease that you cannot see. I hope you see this as a happy accident, kind sir."

"M'Lady, I had no idea of such bloodsuckers. We most happily thank you for our safe return. If you had not intervened, I shudder at the thought."

"Yes, Sir Devin. As your ship arrived, your King would see nothing but crazed men or slashed throats throughout the ship. But fear not, Sir Devin. We have learned well how to prevent this disease from spreading and have given your men the needed potions. They were most kind and gracious in their willing acceptance of it. We will provide you and your kinsmen with the same this late eve, if you would be so kind?"

"We are indebted to your great nature, M'Lady and thank you most sincerely for casting your eyes to our well being."

Sam rose and Sir Devin stepped in front of her and knelt. Not knowing what to do, everyone else knelt as well.

"I keep you and yours from this festive affair, Sir Devin, and I wish you to have your leisure at what small entertainment we can but provide. With that, I wish you and your kinsmen fair winds, good speed and safe return to your realms and Liege, and please remain a while longer to enjoy our ladies' company. We will provide you with safe passage back to your ship."

Sir Devin, yet kneeling, took hold of Sam's hand and gently kissed it. The current that Sam had hoped to avoid for a long while surged through her into Devin. She staggered while he looked shocked.

"It is as they say, M'Lady. You *are* The Chosen One."

"Good *eve*, Sir Devin."

Elsewhere, across The Realm

"Highness. Buron has sent his messenger to her."

"Really? Such as this, then? He didn't go himself?"

"No, my Queen. Just his assistant."

"Is there any sign that Buron knows of what I did?"

"None, my Queen."

"Or the Spirits. Do they know of what I did? Any sign from them?"

"None, my Queen."

Taking a deep breath, she relaxed a little, hoping her messenger was correct, "Then perhaps The Highest will win her fight against him. I should interfere, though, so as to protect her."

"The Spirits would remind you of your vow."

The High Queen nodded. "I remember, for now. Does she gain her powers?"

"Yes, my Queen. But there is a problem. She grows weakened by them instead of stronger."

She became instantly angered at the report. "The Spirit Mothers are fools! Do they not see this? They need to teach her the powers so she is not harmed by using them in this fashion. Her powers could kill her if the Spirit Mothers don't do as such, soon." She paced for a moment, then added, "I will give them a short while to repair their harm. If they don't, then I will break My vow so as to save her. The Realm has great need of her."

"Yes, my Queen."

"Watch over them carefully. Once this battle begins, Buron must not win."

"To your will, Highness."

Chapter III
The Highest

Sam returned to her bed. She was exhausted before Devin had deleted more of her energy by touching her, but was now thoroughly drained again. Oisin had helped Sam go back into her room while May shut the doors. Having no energy to do otherwise, Sam left her advisors and Second to the entertaining, then ridding the community of these men.

"They will be escorted out in the very early morn, Highest."

"Please, Oisin. Call me not by Highest. May? Will you please get Jandra for me?"

Sam gratefully sat down on the side of the bed.

"Yes, Highest, and then allow me to get you back into your bed for more rest."

"I like that plan, May." She smiled. This part was over and she had liked what Oisin had done. "Oisin, that was a stroke of genius on your part. So no blood was shed and you have all our traitors?"

"I do, Sam, and am most pleased. I too thought it a masterful plan, but I have to give credit to Margeria. She approached me, hesitantly I might add, and suggested the plan. I liked it not, but my assistant said to listen again, and when I did, I but saw the merit in it. It was not quite as you detailed to Devin. We had gotten the crew drunk and then scared them to death with that tale of disease. They were so frightened they were pushing those traitors out of their holds. It was a sight to see, and no weapons were needed or raised. My crew were somewhat disappointed, but enjoyed the trick. I liked your telling of the story, though. You are a master deceiver. One note, Sam. We also retrieved five young women who had been abducted. We are tending to their wounds and such. They have been most abused, from what my crew has but told me."

"Where are they now?"

"The healers are tending to them."

Jandra entered the room, "Highest?"

"Oisin, take your leave but be sure to be back in the morn. We will speak about these other women at another moment. Please keep them well separated until we learn of their desires. Will you return for the ceremony?"

"I need not go with the ships to escort them, Sam. I will have three ships escort them to the sound. I have no fear of them now. First, they have few arms. We saw that for ourselves. And Second, they are overly afraid from the disease to return right now."

"Good. We have much to do on this next morn and midturn. We have traitors to attend to, a Highest to the funeral, and five women to tend."

"And the sun rise ceremony for you as Highest, Sam. You must not forget this."

"Have all of Woden and Hengist been notified?"

"They have."

May intervened, "Highest, we must get you into bed, then you can finish your discussion."

Sam nodded to May, standing up so that they could help prepare her for sleep.

"Oisin, take her tunic off her. Jandra, take that silly necklace from her neck."

They did so, and Sam just stood in compliance, wanting to lie down. As the necklace came off, she felt a slight unnerving feeling.

"That necklace—"

". . . be ridiculous, Sam."

"No, I know that, Oisin. But there be something about that necklace."

"Do you think it but charmed?"

"Charmed?" She thought about it for a moment, then added, "We know of no such things as this, but I am unsure. It felt strange when I first placed it on, and then when Jandra removed it, the same feeling returned."

Oisin raised her finger to her lip in consideration of what Sam had said. "Let us take no risk until we understand more. I will take the necklace elsewhere just to keep it away from you for now."

"What if it helps her, Oisin?"

"It could be, but now is not the moment for that risk." Oisin took the necklace and placed it into one of her pockets. No more was said of it.

"I am overly tired, May."

"I know, Highest, but you first need to eat."

"Then go and get it before I fall to sleep. Jandra can attend to me. We must speak, anyway. Oisin, go about your affairs. I will see you in the morn. Please extend my sincerest thanks to your crew."

May left the room, and Oisin bent down to Sam to kiss her. Jandra was surprised, but Sam enjoyed the moment. Oisin had been careful to take Sam's hands, as Jandra had done earlier, place them together and quickly cover them with her own. Sam felt some energy flowing from Oisin, and it made her feel better. Oisin then gave her a tender yet passionate kiss, Sam suddenly remembering that Jandra was in the room, "Oisin, Jandra is present. You embarrass me."

"You are overly beautiful to let go, Highest. It was not just Devin's breath that was taken away with your beauty. I thought my heart had halted."

"Oh, Oisin, that is so absurd. What be beauty, anyway?"

Jandra spoke, "But it be true what Oisin and Sir Devin say, Highest. You truly are a most beautiful woman."

"Enough of this. It be tiresome. Oisin, please go now. I will see you in the morn. Jandra, please attend me so that I may lay down before I fall down."

"What would you have me do, Highest?"

Sam was struggling with her gown, but was too tired to lift it off.

"Just help me take off my gown. I am well tired of these garments."

Jandra raised the gown over Sam's head and placed the gown onto a chair. As she turned to help Sam further, she saw that Sam was standing there fully naked. Sam began to sink into the bed, tired from all her prior events. Jandra had thought she was falling so she reached out to hold her. As she did so, the current went through Sam into Jandra. Jandra ignored it, realizing it was overly late anyway, so just helped Sam to sit up safely in the bed. Sam had, unknowingly, reached into Jandra's thoughts.

She is so beautiful. Devin was correct. She takes my breath away and makes me feel like I have never prior felt. She gives me urges I have not felt in many cycles. But what about Oisin? No, Sam could never want me. Besides, she is most attached to Oisin.

And then, Sam sensed sudden fear and embarrassment, *Oh, no. Please let her not have heard these thoughts.*

Sam acted as if she had heard nothing. "Jandra, we must speak about our plans for the midmorn."

"Yes, Highest. But I must say, your game, as you called it, was magnificent. Highest, do you really plan to make union with this king?"

Jandra took the bed covers and started to cover The Highest. She noticed that Sam seemed to feel no immodesty at all with her nakedness.

Nor should she with such beauty as this.

Sam sighed, "My first duty is to our community. If through such a union we are guaranteed safety from harm, then it is a consideration a Highest would have to make. But no, Jandra, I desire not as such, and have no intentions to do as such. I was but trying to uncover the length of their holdings and their mannerisms so that we know how much to prepare for battle. We discovered their legions are no match for ours, given Hengist's involvement, too, which I feel would be most certain."

May had entered with Sam's meal. More broth, and much of it.

"May, am I not to have any more food in this life?"

"Highest, dear, you have become dehydrated. If you finish this, I will bring you some food that will be easy on your stomach. Here Jandra, help The Highest to eat her soup. She looks overly pale for my liking."

She looked at Jandra trying to cover The Highest, "Oh, Highest, where is your bed shirt?"

"I know not, May. I was overly tired to fetch it, and Jandra knows not my room."

May went to the wardrobe and took out Sam's bedshirt. "Here, Jandra. What are your trying to do, let The Highest catch a fever?"

"I am sorry, May. I know not your custom."

Sam laughed, "Do not let May beat you into submission, Jandra, or you will but live to regret it."

"Eat your soup, Highest. Jandra, place on her bedshirt before she catches a fever. What would The Highest do without me?" She shook her head and walked off muttering, "Just sitting there without her bed clothes on. I know she is trying to—"

Sam laughed again, "She be so bossy, that May of ours. But she cares well for me."

Jandra placed Sam's bedshirt on her, then finished covering her with the bed covers, "I think that will keep May's fever away from you now, Highest."

"It is a little warmer. Thank you. May I have my soup now so that I can have something of substance, or would you be so kind to throw that into the bushes so that I may just eat my other meal?"

She shook her head while laughing lightly, "No, Highest. As May said, you do look pale, and you are dehydrated. You need the liquid."

"You are as bad as May. Let us get this part over with, but I am tired of soup. And Jandra, if you would rather be out enjoying the festivities, please go and do so. I can feed myself this soup."

"Thank you, Highest, but no. I have had enough of that for one eve."

"If you would rather be in your own dwellin—"

"No, Highest. I am where I should be."

"Then let us to our plans for the midmorn. Are all the traitors captured?"

"Yes, Highest. Meera, Keets, Oisin, Keddi, and Margeria provided brilliant campaigns. All our traitors are secure. Meera tells me that you are aware that we must pronounce their sentence in the morn."

The Highest sighed, "It be true." She shook her head. "This be a sad way to begin your term as Second, Jandra, and I am well sorry for it. It will be overly difficult to but watch and pronounce."

"We must place them to their death according to the laws, be that not correct?"

"It is, but it be the manner in which we must do it. You may not know the law on this. They killed The Highest. The pronouncement is grim indeed for the act, and it is about that which we must speak. I could allow it that you need not be there, Jandra, if it will be overly difficult for you."

Sam watched Jandra's reaction, knowing that while Jandra had lost her companion two cycles prior, Josin had since been visiting with Jandra through the eves. She also knew that while Jandra had kicked Josin out of her dwelling, permanently, witnessing such an execution of someone she knew in such a way would not be easy.

"My place is beside you, Highest."

"Do you know of this manner of death that we are so obliged by law?"

"No, Highest, but they are traitors and must face their fate."

"Jandra, I wish not to interfere into your private affairs, but I do know that having to watch Josin face this type of death may be other than what you can face."

Jandra looked surprised, "You know that Josin and I had been together?"

"It is my duty to know the women I serve. And I know that you also have been split from her for at least three moons, now. But Jandra, this be not a pretty sight and you have not been a part of these events, ever. Death be never pretty, but killing and torture are most vile."

"Whatever it may be, Highest, I choose to be at your side, as is my duty."

Sam nodded, "So be it. Are we prepared for The Highest's funeral?"

Sam had finished her soup so leaned on her pillow and set about listening to Jandra. Jandra reset Sam's bed covers for her.

"All is arranged. I have organized the musicians, the singers, and sent a message to the entire community, as has also been done for the morn." She could see that Sam was beginning to fall asleep. "Please worry not about the ceremonies, Highest. They are fully organized."

Sam's eyes were beginning to close, but she struggled to remain awake awhile longer. "Jandra, there be something we must talk about."

Jandra got a chair and sat next to The Highest's bed, "Yes, Highest. I am here."

"Do you remember when I lost Brett?"

"Yes, Highest. We were under full attack and had almost lost our community. Brett had been killed as Meera took you to safety."

Sadly, Sam replied, "Yes. This be truth. Were you also aware at how much I had loved Brett?"

"There are songs to that love, Highest."

Sam didn't know about these songs, so was surprised. She thought that she might like to hear them, at a later moment. "It took me a long while to be able to see our realm again, Jandra. I lost track of all that was around me. Meera took constant care of me, almost eve and turn. I refused to eat. I refused to listen to anyone. And I refused to even care. It was Meera who kept talking to me and who kept letting me rant and rave in my anger at my loss."

"Meera is a good woman, Highest."

Sam's eyes were closed now, "She is, but that is not the point, Second. Meera was with me all the moments. She fell in love with me and asked me to be her companion. In my concern over her and what others might say of her, I told her that I could not, but that the rumor was to be that she rejected me. I wanted not that Meera carry the burden of rejection with her. She liked it not, and argued with me fully, but I would not relent. You have hated Meera these cycles because you but believed she had rejected me. It is an honest mistake of my doing. I would now ask you to embrace Meera for the full gift she is to our community. You will know no better woman. You can trust her with your life, and you will now learn that you will need to do so."

"I know this as truth, Highest. I will make it right."

Sam nodded and began to settle in for the eve.

"Highest? Is it an increased burden for you to hear other's thoughts? It seems to double your concerns."

"It does, but at other moments I find it amusing."

"Amusing?"

Sam opened her eyes a bit and smiled a small but mischievous smile, "I have learned that I take others' breath away besides Sir Devin's, and that seeing my body gives others urges they have not felt for a long while. Possibly, Jandra, this might help to increase my sorry sex-life."

Jandra blushed, "I am embarrassed, Highest. I never meant for you to know of these thoughts."

"And I never wanted to know of others' thoughts and desires. But it be not all bad. I have always known and respected you, and always knew you to be The Highest's best advisor. She told me so upon many occasions. And because of this unwanted gift that weakens me by the turn, some happiness comes of it. I know your true feelings that you have deeply hidden from all, including yourself."

"A question, Highest. Why did you choose me as your Second when you have trained Lillon to take this position?"

"You are the more qualified woman. Lillon is not yet ready, and I trust you to be my best counsel, as you were for The Highest."

"Has it anything to do with Hern and Lillon making a bad judgment?"

"No. We all make bad judgments. It is how we come out at the other end of those judgments that make us the women we are. You chose your path in full understanding and have remained steadfast to the community."

"Has Lillon not done this, as well?"

"She has done it in her own way, but will face some scolding from the community. You learned of your mistake and acted quickly and swiftly to solve the situation. In a moment of chaos, a good leader is able to focus, make a plan of action, and carry it out. You but showed that ability."

Sam began to laugh quietly.

"What is so humorous, Highest?"

"You know, Jandra, your advisors will now pester you to take a companion as they do me prior to every festival. Keddi is available. She would be a good choice for you. Strong, lusty, fun. And Lillon is also now available, but a little needy for you, I think."

Jandra groaned, "It be good you can laugh about this. Perhaps, I too, will be able to laugh about it, soon."

Sam's eyes were closed again, and Jandra just studied her face as she thought about all that Sam had said.

Sam spoke quietly, "You are thinking overly hard. I can hear your thoughts."

"But I have not touched you. Can you now hear thoughts when there is no contact?"

"I jest. But I could tell that you are thinking."

She nodded, even though Sam's eyes were closed, "I am. It be truth."

"It is difficult to drop the events of the turn. Are you thinking of them?"

"No. I am merely wondering of your words."

Sam opened her eyes, slightly, and smiled again at Jandra, "Go now, Second. May will watch over me for the eve.

"My apologies, Highest, but May asked if I would do this for the eve. I agreed, but could find another if that be your desire."

"No. This is fine. I will need someone to wake me in the morn."

"I will be here to do so, Highest."

"I will rest better knowing this. Thank you. Now, Second, tell me of your needs."

Jandra did, but noticed that Sam had fallen asleep. She thought her words fell on deaf ears. Jandra thought it all the better and talked to the sleeping Sam for most the eve. And Sam missed out on the meal that May had brought in.

* * * *

The before-sun morn came too soon for both Jandra and Sam. Jandra had slept only slightly, watching over Sam all the eve, and Sam had yet recovered from her exhaustion. May entered the room quietly.

She whispered, "Thank you, Second. I needed a good sleep after all that fussing. How is our Highest? Did she sleep well?"

"She sleeps like the dead, May. It be most distressing."

"She does? I often come in to a bed that looks like a huge wind storm came blowing through the room, and when she has been alone, too!"

"I think it the moment we wake her, May, but how should that be done?"

May ceased whispering, "Oh, I think us talking will do it. She sleeps not as deeply as you think. You should be but forewarned. She also has many bad dreams that pull her wide-awake. This be a troublesome position you take on, Jandra. I think you know not the stress our sweet Highest has had as Second. It is enough to kill a horse, but now with these strange things happening to her, it is as if she is cursed. She thinks of all the women and their needs constantly. Walking around daily on her rounds listening to their complaints. And what does she get in retur—"

"May, hold your tongue. You have managed to wake me."

"See, Second. Just start talking about how badly she takes care of her own life, and she wakes up without me having to worry. It be like magic. So, good morn, Highest. As always, it be good to hear you so pleasant."

Looking at Jandra, she winked and said, "You know, Second, The Highest's best moment of the turn is the morn. She loves to wake up in the very early morn just before the sun's rise."

Sam ignored the jest, "Tea, May. And please, no more soup."

"Tea it is, and porridge."

She groaned, "You will kill me."

"Jandra, please ignore her early morn comments. They do but make the birds fly away. Please help her to get up and prepared. This morn's events are grim, and she must be ready. I will return in a moment."

In a serious tone that May often heard, Sam said, "May, one thing before you leave."

"Highest." Her smile had left.

"Attend not the mid-morn's events. You need not see such a thing as this. It will haunt you, and I wish you not those types of dreams."

"Yes, Highest. Thank you."

Jandra looked surprised. "Do you not want the community there?"

"That is difficult. I will respect those who wish to be there, knowing that some of the women will seek to see for themselves the end of these women who murdered The Highest. But it will be most brutal, Jandra."

"They did not really murder The Highest."

"You argue their intent? You would spare their life?"

"No, of course not, Highest. It is just that The Highest took her own life. They had not the opportunity to murder her."

"The intent when it concerns The Highest, as by law, be the same as the act."

Jandra nodded understanding and changed the topic, "Did you sleep well, Highest?"

"I am weak, but seemed to have found my tongue, at least. I hope the weakness will leave me. It is fine to sit, but I have little energy to move. Perhaps May's morn meal will give me enough to get through this turn's events. Did you hear that we have five new women that Oisin's crew found on the ship?"

"Do they desire entrance into the community?"

"There has been no chance to speak with them. Meera and Keets will no doubt perform that function soon. It is always difficult if they have come from a mixed community and wish to keep to that type of companionship. Oisin can take them to such a community if that be their choice, however."

Sam looked distant, "Attend to yourself, Jandra. We must get ready for this which I have tried so hard to avoid."

May came in and helped Sam prepare, and to make certain that Sam ate and drank enough. Few words were spoken by any of the three women, and regardless that Sam had little energy, there was no question in anyone's mind that Sam must attend the turn's events. As May helped Sam get dressed, Jandra attended to herself. She knew that she would have to help walk The Highest to the various sites. May helped Sam dress in The Highest's ceremonial gown. Sarra had worked all the previous eve on it so that it would fit Sam. She had to take in many hems, but the gown was now a perfect fit for Sam. It was an off-white gown with vivid blue trim, in honor of the Spirits of the Falls.

May noticed Sam's eyes, "Highest, your eyes have grown much bluer of late. Have you noticed this?"

Sam just shrugged, "No. But I have not looked into any mirrors in a long while. Perhaps it just seems so due to the blue in the gown."

Jandra looked at Sam's eyes and noticed the same. They were almost an unreal blue: extremely bright and the color and intensity of a deep clear pool of fresh water. She knew that Sam's eyes were blue, but remembered them as a soft pale blue. She also noticed that Sam's hair, even for its continual lack of tending by Sam, was shiny and very alive looking.

Jandra added, "I but guess that it has something to do with this new power of yours. Have you noticed any other changes, Highest?"

Sam shook her head and tried to avoid the conversation.

Jandra was focused on the executions. She had, as Sam knew, well avoided any such prior event. Although Sam had excused her from this one, Jandra felt she needed to be there for Sam, for the former Highest, and for herself. She felt that Josin had sabotaged the community, and she felt to blame for not informing anyone. But the event yet troubled her, wondering as to such harsh executions.

May said, "Jandra, is it yet with clouds outside?"

Jandra looked outside, "It is, but it will not rain. The clouds are patchy. It remains a gray turn. I can see the women starting to prepare for your ceremony, Highest. May, are you attending as well?"

May nodded, "Most truth. All will attend The Highest's ceremony."

Jandra went to the patio to wait for Sam.

May started to leave, then turned, "Highest. Please take care this turn. I have set your other garments out for you so that you may change following your ceremony. It will not be proper for you to wear your ceremonial gown to the executions. Your other gown for The Highest's funeral has also been prepared and be laid out for you to change into following those gruesome events."

Sam nodded her understanding and went to the patio where Jandra was waiting, "Jandra, may I but use your arm to help me walk more securely?"

"Whatever you need, Highest, it be yours."

Sam looped her arm through Jandra's and held her own hands together. Jandra could help stabilize her while not causing any unbroken connection that would drain Sam. Jandra nodded to their escort of guards and were led to the ceremony, with Keddi and Margeria in the lead. No words were to be spoken from this moment. The ceremony to bestow a Highest, along with the funeral of a Highest, were the most spiritual and formal in the community. Not having any spiritual leaders from Woden to rely on this turn, the formal ceremony fell to Oisin and the spiritual leaders of Hengist. Sam had been but a young girl when the former Highest had been bestowed, so remembered little of the ceremony. She knew that the ceremony itself would occur at their Sacred Rocks, a natural amphitheatre of stone that had been carved by the river eons prior to Woden's settlement.

Long prior, one of the rivers of Woden, on its downward path to the sea, had formed huge waterwheels that served to pound out other rock areas in the river into low-lying pools of water. As the river shifted course, the pools eventually drained dry. The Woden Sacred Stones was a naturally formed arch of three enormous rocks, the top cross one being flat, like a table top. The arch was large enough for ten people to stand under and be sheltered. Surrounding the Sacred Stones were nine natural circles, each higher than the other, that formed the amphitheatre appearance. The stage was the arch, in the middle of the circle, and the lowest part of the amphitheatre. The women, through the cycles, had built stairs down to each tier and enhanced the tiers so that all the community members could fit. Each tier stood easily one woman's height to the next tier. Many cycles prior, Woden held plays in the amphitheatre, but those had been long forgotten by many. Although made orderly every moon, the Sacred Stones had gone unused by Woden for many, many cycles. This turn, the women of Woden and the men of Hengist would find themselves twice to their sacred site.

Sam was escorted to the procession line. Oisin and the Spiritual Leaders from Hengist led the procession. The drums, instruments and chorus were next, followed by all the men of Hengist and then by all the women of Woden, half holding torches to light the way in the predawn moment. The advisors of Woden and Hengist were just prior to the procession of guards in which Sam was placed in the middle. As Oisin gave the signal to begin, the chorus, instruments and drums began a song that Sam could only imagine she knew from the ceremony so many cycles prior. It was both eerie and reverent in its tune, a tune that recognized the deep responsibilities and graveness of the ceremony itself.

The procession walked to the Sacred Stones, a location outside the community's walled community, but inside Woden's boundary. To Sam, each step taken seemed to tire her more. She was unsure if it were the changes occurring within her to cause this, or the silent weight that this new position held. As the procession reached the Sacred Rocks, the musicians descended to the Second tier up from the rocks, Oisin and the Spiritual Leaders from Hengist descended to the Sacred Rocks, the women and men from the communities filled the tiers, the advisors descended to the main ground tier, and the guards lined the stairs, at full attention. Sam was held at the top by Meera and Keets. Just prior to the sun's rising, Oisin unsheathed her sword and held it high above her head, signaling the guards to unsheathe their swords to form an arch, sword tip touching sword tip. It was under this arch that Sam followed Meera and Keets down to the Sacred

Stones, as the drums and musicians played their ceremonial tune. Sam was directed by the Spiritual Leaders of Hengist to go to under the Sacred Stones arch.

Fornan was the Spiritual Leader who would bestow Sam as Highest this turn. He was well known to Sam, and had been considered as a selected partner when Brett had wanted a child. He was, as was all of Hengist, especially exultant this turn to have Sam become The Highest, as she was someone they truly admired and respected. But he also recognized the sadness of the moment, given the former Highest's death. Sam was relieved and pleased that Fornan had been the one selected to lead this turn's ceremony.

He looked at Sam, and in a voice all could hear, said, "Sam of Woden, kneel before your community."

She knelt under the arch, and bowed her head. Fornan began the ceremony as the sun could be seen rising, still under the mountains. He gave a prayer to their Spirits of the Falls. He told of the background of Woden and Hengist. He reminded all of the duties and responsibilities of The Highest. Just as the sun was about to rise over the mountains, Fornan nodded to Oisin, Meera, Keets and Briggon. They each laid the tips of their swords upon Sam's head, a symbolic gesture that served to remind all of the past: If The Highest betrayed the oath, the swords would be used to behead her. Fornan began the final part of the ceremony.

"Sam of Woden, are you prepared this turn to become The Highest of all of Woden?

Sam answered, "Yes."

"Do you understand the duties and responsibilities of this position?"

"Yes."

"Do you pledge your life to all of Woden?"

"Yes."

"Do you pledge all of your loyalty to Woden?"

"Yes."

"Then, Sam of Woden, repeat after me: "I, Sam of Woden.""

"I, Sam of Woden."

"Give my life and loyalty to Woden."

"Give my life and loyalty to Woden."

"Swear to obey and uphold the customs and laws of Woden."

"Swear to obey and uphold the customs and laws of Woden."

As the oath went on, Oisin looked down at Sam and hoped that soon, she would be glad of having taken this position. Meera looked down at her own sword tip on Sam's head, feeling sadness in knowing how Sam had never wanted this position, yet knowing the seriousness of this moment.

As the sun was mere moments from rising over the mountains, Fornan could see that his calculations had been good. "I, Sam of Woden, pledge you my life and loyalty. They are yours to command."

Sam looked up to Oisin and Meera, and then to Fornan and Briggon. "I, Sam of Woden, pledge you my life and loyalty. They are yours to command."

Fornan then addressed the community, "Do you, as members of all of Woden, accept Sam of Woden's pledge?" As custom, the women and men all held their thumbs straight up as a sign of acceptance. The guards held up their swords.

"Do you swear your loyalty and allegiance to Sam of Woden?"

They repeated their gestures.

"Do you swear that Sam of Woden is your chosen Highest?"

They again repeated the gestures.

The sun finally rose over the mountains and shone on Sam. Fornan said in a loud voice, "I, Fornan, Spiritual Leader this turn of all of Woden Falls, pronounce Sam of Woden as The Highest. All kneel before our Highest."

He held out his hand and motioned for Sam to rise. Oisin, Meera, Briggon and Keets removed their swords from Sam's head and re-sheathed them. She rose and saw that everyone in the community had knelt before her, and all the guards held their swords above their heads as a sign that they were hers to command. As each woman and man knelt, they each said, "Highest."

The ceremony now over, Meera and Keets motioned for Sam to lead the way back up out of the Sacred Rocks. She followed Meera and Keets as they ascended their way back through the archway of guards. The others followed, beginning with the advisors. The procession made its way back to Woden's entry accompanied by the choir, musicians, and drums. It was a solemn affair from the beginning to end, in acknowledgement that while they celebrate a new Highest, they must bury another. When Sam was back through the entry, she began to make her way to her dwelling in order to change her garments and prepare for the executions. She hoped that May had left out some food for her. She felt exhausted and depressed, but the turn had just begun and she knew that this had been the highlight.

Meera came up beside her and saw that Sam was walking very slowly. "I but think our community needs you as Highest, Sam. I think much has been allowed to erode of late, and I know that you will now make it right."

"You give me but overly much credit, Meera."

"We shall see, but I think not. Has May left out food for you?"

"I hope so."

"We will find something."

Jandra came up to them. "Highest. Meera. Highest, may I help you prepare for the executions?"

Sam looked at Meera and hoped she was not disappointed. Meera nodded to Jandra, "This be but an excellent moment, Second. I must attend to my guards in preparation for the executions. Will you but see that The Highest make it out to the site? The Highest be also hungry."

Jandra nodded to Meera, and Meera left to her duties. Jandra opened her arm to Sam without saying a word. Sam took it gratefully, saying nothing.

"It was a good ceremony, Highest."

Sam nodded.

"The women and men are well pleased. The sun rose just as you were pronounced Highest. They think this bodes well for the community and you. And they be most pleased with you as Highest."

Sam sighed once again, and nodded. She held back the tears that so desperately wanted their release.

Jandra noticed Sam's sadness, "Perhaps it be best if you not think about this turn and all that occurs within you. It but overwhelms, I think. Perhaps we should but talk about who you should take as a companion."

Sam just rolled her eyes and laughed, "And that is supposed to cheer me, Jandra? You are but a funny one. I need not one more thing to think about this turn."

"Perhaps they would take excellent care of you."

Sam shook her head and just smiled.

As they reached the patio, Jandra motioned that Sam should sit at the patio table. "Let me find us some food and drink, and then I can help you to change your garments."

Sam shook her head again, "I need to change from these garments first, Jandra. They are most uncomfortable and overly remind me of who I must be, now." Sam turned to go to her bedroom but saw Jandra waiting.

"Come, attend to me, Jandra. I could use your help."

Jandra nodded and followed. She helped Sam change and noticed that Sam was remaining very quiet. "Highest, when this eve comes, will you regret being alone?" As she asked the question, she frowned, wondering, *Why did I say that?* She shivered and felt suddenly quite odd, but had no understanding of it.

"Perhaps. I am but overly weary to consider it."

Jandra finished helping Sam change, "Go sit in the patio. I will bring out some food and drink."

Sam nodded and left to the patio. She noticed that there were now twice as many guards around her dwelling. As she had been told by one of her advisors, perhaps it was something she should now get used to. She could hear the river flowing and let the sound comfort her. Jandra came out with a platter of food and drink.

"May had it prepared for you. She has enough for a small party. Are you expecting company this eve?"

Sam shook her head, "I cannot imagine anyone wanting to be with me right now. If I look half as bad as I feel, it would scare the children away."

"It is but that you are overwhelmed. If you looked into a mirror, you would see that what you say be most untrue. I know not what occurs within you, but outside, you grow more beautiful, if that be at all possible."

Sam just looked at her as if she were crazy, and smiled, "I think you have been alone overly long, Jandra."

* * * *

They ate their meal in silence. As they were finishing, one of the guards came to inform them that they should leave for the executions.

"Perhaps we should not have eaten, Jandra. Our stomachs will have difficulty with this event."

They began walking to the site, the guards following at a small distance.

"Where is it to be held?"

"Out at the border, Highest. It is a mid-length walk, but we will arrive soon enough."

"Out where we found Keddi?"

"No, Highest. Straight out from the gate; out by the river."

"On the open flattop, then?"

"Yes. The Highgrounds. Keets wanted them on the Highgrounds for all to see."

"A beautiful place. I have always liked the view from there with the valley just below. It will be but sad to leave those memories on it."

"Do you go there often?"

"I make the attempt to see all our lands at least every moon. It is most enjoyable up there when the early flowers take bloom. There are great boulders there, and at moments, it is as if they speak."

Jandra thought about her moments at the boulders, far prior when she had once been there. They called to her in a way she didn't understand, but let the thought fade. "You have done more than I can even suspect. It be no surprise to me of the length and depth of the respect for you in the community. I know of your daily rounds, but that you watch over our entirety . . . we owe you much respect. I should have done as well. We all should. I will speak with the community about this."

Sam listened to Jandra, but chose not to respond. Jandra was good with the women, and it would only help to have more women watching over the lands.

"How did you think I fared with Sir Devin prior eve?"

"Oh, Highest, you were magnificent. But I must say, it was all I could do to keep myself from laughing."

They continued to talk about the eve's events through the walk. Sam tried not to lean on Jandra overly, not wishing to tire her. She knew that she would need increased assistance for the return, so planned on getting Oisin or Meera to help, too. The walk wound through some of the food and herb gardens. What were always pleasant walks in the past were now but grim reminders of the cycles of life and death.

Meera met them as they arrived, bowing to Sam, "Highest."

"Meera. Is all in ready?"

"It is, Highest. I have also made certain that Treena be but present to watch the executions. I think it her due punishment."

Sam nodded, "Yes. She needs to see. Who is to be the executioner?"

"Keets. She says she is doing this for The Highest."

"I hope we do this for no other reason."

"We will execute the counselors first, then Hern, and then Josin."

"It is as expected." She looked around. "It be sad to leave these memories on this place."

Meera nodded, "Let us hope it be but the last place we must leave such memories on."

Meera looked at Jandra, "Second, please take no offense of this, but should you attend this morn's events? Josin's execution will be difficult for even me, and I do not think you will be—"

"Thank you, Meera. But I want to be here. Josin will meet her due. She has done more harm than you know. I take the blame for not telling you before it be overly late."

"This be not the moment for regrets, Second. Josin knew well what she did, and knew well the consequences. What any of us knew or not would have made little difference in her scheme."

Sam nodded, "Well said, Meera. We all will be here for Jandra should she need, but she has told me that she needs to be here for the community, for us, and for The Highest. Meera, has anyone attended to these traitor's poor wretched companions?"

"Tehna and Liley have, Highest. They meet with them now at The Highest's dwelling so that they would not attend these proceedings. Fortunately, most of these counselors were but companions of each other. Josin's companion is well rid of her, from her own mouth, and Lillon, I doubt, will not miss Hern. But Lillon attends, Highest. She be over by

Karan." Sam looked over and noted that Karan was speaking with Lillon. She could guess the topic.

"Keets is bringing them over now, Highest. I am sorry your beginning as Highest is filled with such acts as these. Will you know when to begin the proceedings?

"Give me word, Meera, and I will do my duty."

Meera left to help Keets.

"Jandra, I know your heart be in the right place, but I ask you once more: Will you not leave this place of our vile revengeful deaths? Even the dark realms visit not with us this turn."

"My place is by your side, Highest."

"So be it, and may our Mothers be with us this turn."

Sam went over to where she must make the decrees. She noticed that about 400 women were here to observe the executions. It was the amount she expected, and about the amount she thought effected in one way or the other by The Highest's death, Hern's acts, and Josin's sabotage of the community. Jandra remained by her side.

Margeria was in charge of the traitors, but Sam didn't know if Margeria were ready for this turn. She hoped that Meera had spoken with her about this. She saw that Keddi was at Margeria's side, and thought that wise on her part. Keddi was well used to the harsh realities of executions. Keddi's dog was also in attendance, sitting where Keddi had told it to remain.

The traitors were a depressing lot. Josin stood firm and tall, defiant in her stance. Sam didn't think she would be able to hold this act when she finally was to hear of her particular execution. The Counselors were mostly crying, showing much fear about their impending deaths. And Hern was, unsurprisingly to Sam, shouting at everyone. Sam knew that she too would face a grim reality, momentarily.

Meera nodded at Sam, and Sam said only loud enough for Jandra to hear, "Let us get this unnatural act done."

Sam stepped up to the hill, directly facing the traitors, and began the worst duty a Highest could face. "I, Highest of Woden, as required of me, now pass sentence on you. You have committed acts of treason against all of Woden, and you have attempted murder on The Highest. Woden law commands that such acts be punished through execution within one turn. I now uphold this law. You have committed these acts in full awareness of these sad consequences. You, as Woden's daughters, have brought shame and most grievous sorrow to Woden and our Mothers. There be no compassion for you this turn. Because of your actions, we are all shamed this turn. May the mothers hold you in their thoughts. I do not."

She nodded to Margeria and Keddi, and they brought the Counselors forward.

Sam tried to block her ears to the wails and cries of the counselors. Their fear filled the air. As she nodded to Keets, Keets' guards, one-by-one, tied the women to their stakes. One had fainted, while all the rest were begging and wailing for mercy. None would be given this turn.

Jandra watched, paralyzed by the sounds. She looked at the boulders, trying to distance herself from the scene, wondering if they felt anything. She wished she could touch them.

Oisin stood with torch in-hand, "May the Mothers be with you."

Oisin handed Keets the torch, and at Sam's nod, Keets lit each mound of straw and wood. Sam hardened herself to withstand the screams, the smells, and the most unholiest of visions. It was her duty to stand and watch as if justice was better than the evils done. She tried to block her mind of all thoughts so that she may continue these fateful, awful, hideous and frightful sights. She knew well that her eves would be those of revolting dreams for long to come. The odors of burning flesh and hair permeated the air, but Sam refused to weaken. Woden had been through many battles in her short life, and each ended with some event as this. Through each one, Sam thought of the severity Woden's laws exacted on the guilty. There had never been enough peace to permit leniency. She hoped to live long enough to know that type of peace and justice.

"Highest, this be most gruesome. These poor wom—"

Brusquely, from her own sadness and frustration, Sam said, "Harden yourself, Second. Toughen your soul and think of The Highest. Let not these acts or these traitors catch you soft. They felt no such compassion for The Highest, or for those of Woden."

The screams of the burning women had all quieted after many moments. Now the piles of wood burned but dead flesh. The executed would be left in place until the fires burned out and until the carrion eaters had cleaned the bones.

When the fires began to merely burn instead of rage, Sam nodded once again to Keets. Hern was brought forward. Sam had a swift reflection that Lillon was here, but would leave Lillon to Karan.

"I want neither your pity or mercy, Sam. May you be struck dead."

"As I will be one turn", and nodded to Keets. Oisin came forward with sword in-hand. Keets made Hern lean over a rock so her kneck showed, then moved her hair.

Oisin said, "Your remains will be untouched and unburned so that you will return not to our Mothers."

With that said, Oisin brought down the sword, and as suddenly, Hern was dead. Meera thought it overly fast a death for such as Hern, but didn't deny its grace considering what Josin was facing. The body was left where it lay and Hern was permanently silenced. Oisin felt the sentence fitting for

Hern. Hern had sought much attention and had been overly loud. The quick and silent death provided a stunning contrast to Hern's noise.

As Sam nodded to Keets, Margeria brought Josin forward. Two guards brought forward a narrow table with a cross bar. They laid and strapped Josin to the table, and strapped her hands, legs, and arms to stakes in the ground. Josin's eyes were wide open in the now-known horror of what she faced. She screamed, and wouldn't halt, calling Jandra's name as Sam resigned herself to this hated moment. She had seen this particular execution but once in her life, and yet recalled it through overly vivid images. She felt deeply saddened to be The Highest at this moment.

She turned to Jandra and softly pleaded, "Jandra, you know not this horror, and I would wish it so. I implore you to leave before you watch this event. I know that she tried to murder The Highest, but this woman was your lover. By the Mothers, Jandra, save your mind from this torture."

"The hate in my heart will not allow me to withdraw from this justice."

As she made the comment, Jandra instantly felt the profound and overwhelming truth of it and knew fully of its meaning, *It is my fate.* But how and why remained as an impossibly unsolvable mystery to her.

Sam nodded to Keets and Oisin. Meera and Oisin stood on the opposite side of Keets, each equally trying to harden themselves before they began this act. Margeria was looking pale, but Keddi moved her slightly away. Keets drew up a knife.

Oisin looked down at Josin, "There be no mercy for you, Josin. Your death will be slow and tortured, as is required by our law. Your screams and cries for mercy will fall on deaf ears, as you heard not our pleas. Your body will lie where it dies. We will not return you to the Mothers through the fires. May the Mothers have mercy on your soul, Josin, because none do here."

Josin's eyes were ablaze in fear. She mentioned Keets name as she yelled her terror, but made no sense. Sam had no understanding of how Keets was able to do this act, but Keets began at Josin's stomach and made her way slowly to the heart, piece by piece, as if no screaming or torture were occurring; as if she were a healer performing an operation. Sam thought herself to be sick as Keets pulled out the sections one-by-one. Meera stood by staunchly, but looking pale. Keddi watched as if she had seen this horror a hundred fold, and Margeria had moved away to be sick. The screams of Josin persisted. Keets was doing as the law had intended. This would be a slow, horrible and painful death.

Sam turned to look at Jandra and saw that Jandra had knelt to be sick. She placed her hand on Jandra's head.

The current went through into Jandra, but this moment, Sam sent the message, *Be strong. It bodes well that we be sickened by such events. Take my strength and stand.*

Sam had used a great deal of energy to send that message and help heal Jandra, and Jandra knew it. Sam had made her stronger. She stood and watched the horror of this turn, knowing the strength and courage of these women. The sound of Josin's screams calling to her had caused the pain Sam had forewarned. She looked at Sam and saw a determination she hadn't prior seen. A determination that spoke of sadness so great that it had no seeable end, and a resolve to rid the realm of such for all. And she saw tears on Sam's face.

When Josin had finally taken her last breath and scream as her heart was removed, Keets let the knife drop, bent over, and got sick. Meera went over by her side and just held her shoulders. Keddi went to help Margeria, as did her dog. The women who had attended the executions all turned to leave. They would leave Josin and her parts on the ground for the birds and beasts. This gruesome event was over and Sam turned away from the remains of the executions. She well knew that while she might physically leave this dark site, her memory wouldn't.

* * * *

Oisin helped Sam as they walked to the garden benches where Sam could rest. It would be only a short while before The Highest's funeral was to begin, and Sam needed the moments to rest. Jandra walked alongside while Meera, Keets, and Margeria prepared the guards for the funeral procession. Keddi came up to walk alongside them.

Oisin and Sam turned to look back at the remainders of the turn.

Jandra was surprised, "How can you look back at such a site?"

Oisin had seen many such events during her life, "How dare we not? We are not yet done with these traitors, as they have cast the seeds of war across our land. I will burn these memories in my eyes so our next foes will shake with fear."

She softened just a bit at Jandra, "The darkness just begins, Jandra. The acts we do this turn should serve to harden our souls to our fight; not soften them. When we have executed the last traitor, I will then weep from sadness at the things we do. You are a Second, Jandra. Such things will be expected of you, now. Follow well Sam's steps. While I know these acts place great burden on her, she shirks not from these loathsome killings."

Jandra was surprised at what Oisin had called the executions, "Killings? This be justice."

Sam shook her head, "These most assured murders are merely cloaked in the shroud of justice. We know full well we do no better than they. Perhaps we do far worse."

Keddi added, "But what we do here as an occasioned event occurs daily without reason throughout The Realm. Peace is a hard-won battle from merciless and barbarous leaders and their followers. What sickens us this turn is but standard entertainment anywhere else."

"It is truly such as you say, Keddi?" Jandra was in disbelief of The Realm's reality.

"It be such as this. As Oisin knows. Perhaps this explains well why Oisin remains as she does."

"In truth, it is so, Jandra. I see it with my own eyes on every voyage. That be why my crew seem so distant to the rest of the community members. There can be little understanding of the evils we see."

Oisin had noticed that Sam had spoken but once and was now walking very slowly, only step-by-step. "Sam, need you rest here?"

She gasped for a breath, "I cannot seem to find enough air to breathe." She kept fighting to breathe. "How much further are the gardens?"

Oisin frowned, then picked her up into her arms, "Not far, Sam. Just a few moments," and carried her to the nearest bench.

Sam looked pale but smiled as she looked into Oisin's eyes. She laid her head on Oisin's shoulder, wrapped her arms around Oisin's neck so as to create an unsevered connection, and rested.

Keddi said to Oisin, "I will run ahead and bring water for her."

Oisin was a strong woman, and taller than most, but it was not easy carrying a woman any distance. She had noticed, though, that Sam had lost much weight of late, and became even more concerned.

Oisin nodded and replied, "And find food. We might as well have a meal before the funeral."

When they finally reached the gardens, Oisin set Sam down to rest on a bench. Oisin sat on the ground while Jandra sat next to Sam.

Sam finally rested enough to breathe more easily, then asked Oisin, "When do you take leave on your journey?"

"After the funeral."

"Need you so quickly? Why not in the morn?"

"I cannot afford to waste the moments. I want to return more quickly than planned. Events are not stable enough here to take a good part of our defense for long. We will return for the festival, winds willing. I think it safe here for that long, though."

Sam nodded, "Yes, I think it will be quiet for a short while, now. Whoever is behind this will have to reorganize first. Get much information from those two sentries you take."

Jandra wondered what Sam had meant of the two sentries, but said nothing of it. "How do you know of these things in all The Realm, Highest? I sat with The Highest for many cycles and we knew or spoke of not."

Oisin looked up at her and laughed, "Ah, Jandra. We knew The Highest and her advisors remained in ignorance, but it was by their own choosing, you included. They seemed more concerned about the turn-to-turn events in the community. Someone had to take care of the larger occurrences, and The Highest's advisors were not interested in our knowledge. The Highest was fully aware of our undertakings."

"I have much to be ashamed of."

"It be not so, Jandra. Sam and I knew that The Highest had lost her quickness and that one or more of the advisors had begun to take over. For a cycle, we thought it you. You are Second this turn because of your courage to stand fast against the storm of betrayal. We understand now why you often acted as Highest."

Sam nodded at Jandra, "This be truth, Jandra. We were not allowed to meddle, as I believe you had once said to me, into The Highest's affairs. We then began to act as an independent group so as to protect the community. It be why Meera's guards are so superior in their training to Keets'."

"I am ashamed, Highest."

Oisin tapped Jandra on the knee, "Look over there, Jandra. Some women beckon to you."

Jandra left to attend to the women while Oisin looked up at Sam. Sam was holding her hands together and touching Oisin's side with her legs.

"I will miss you, Sam. Take care while I am gone. You will not see me leave as I will do so directly after the funeral. Please mind to your health. You know I need you. And I love you well."

"Oh, Oisin. What are we to do with this relationship? I cannot take you as a companion, and you need your freedom. And now I must find a companion. But it is you that I love."

"Our bond will always be close, and I will always protect you. After last eve's show, Sam, I think you not need as much protection as I would have you need. You ran Sir Devin around with your words, and he knew not. It sounds much like we can win this battle."

"If they do not join forces with another. That is what we must find out from Sir Devin."

"You will not lay with this King? I do not think I could stand the thought of it, and would not like it so."

"To protect our community, I would bear his heir, Oisin. But I think we can prevent the union."

"A child, Sam?"

"I know not, Oisin. The Spirits begin to call, and I sense things. I now have short visions. But there be a child somewhere in the future. I know not to who it belongs."

"Some moments, Sam, I think I should let another be Sea-Duty Second, so as to remain with you and enjoy your beauty. You certainly made Sir Devin have lusty dreams last eve. And me, as well."

Sam laughed, "You would tire of me in ten turns and seek for another."

"Never!"

Sam frowned, "I will not ask you of what you do on your voyages, then."

"It be not the same and you well know it. I think only of you."

It was a topic with much disagreement, so Sam dropped it. "Did you think Devin had strange language? I found him tedious and dimwitted. Why do you think they talk so?"

"The crew told me that this King Buron fashions the community from the book he gave you."

"From the *Le Morte D'Arthur* book?"

Oisin nodded. She was enjoying the feeling of Sam's legs resting against her. "The same. Devin's crew said that the idea for knights, lords, and all those peculiar words were from the book."

"How strange. Why would they do such?"

"I know not, but as you say, he was a dimwitted fellow. He knew not your jesting."

"I wanted it that way." Sam saw Jandra returning.

"Be safe on your journey, Oisin. We need you. I need you."

Jandra bowed to The Highest. "Highest, some of the women would have a word with you."

"Of course, Jandra. I am here for them to command. Bid them to come over."

Oisin moved so that the women could speak to Sam without having to step over her.

Five of the community women approached. Sam could see who they were and called to them, "Good early midturn, Emma, Anselet, Jehanne, Nichola, Lora." Sam knew most of the women from performing her daily rounds.

They knelt before Sam and bowed their heads, "Chosen One."

Sam looked questioningly at Oisin. Oisin just shrugged her shoulders.

"Chosen One? Please just call me Sam. And please rise. There is no need for kneeling."

They rose, but kept their heads bowed. "Oh, no, Highest, that be not possible. We cannot call you by your given name. The Spirit Mothers forbid such."

She ignored their statement. "Is there something I can do for you, Emma?"

She held out a bouquet of flowers and three shawls. "These are gifts for you, Highest."

Sam smiled as she inspected the gift, "Thank you. I had occasion last eve to give my shawl away. This is much needed."

"Yes, Highest. We heard the story. We have also heard that as the Chosen One, you are weak from not yet learning how to use our Spirit Mothers' power they give you."

Sam looked at Oisin again, and once again Oisin shrugged her shoulders.

"How do you know of these things, Lora?"

"It be the prophecy, Chosen One."

"What prophecy?"

"You know not, Highest?"

"No, I have not been informed."

"Then you will need to hear it from your Spirit Mothers. They will tell you soon. In the meanwhile, Highest, please use the shawls to remain warm. You must not grow weaker before your role comes due to you."

"Thank you. I will treasure and wear your shawls. The flowers will remind me of your generosity."

"Will you yet do your rounds, Highest?"

"Would you but have me do so?"

"Oh, we would. We look forward to those visits with you."

"Then it shall remain so."

"Thank you, Highest. Please mind you to your health. Your community needs you." They bowed and turned to walk away.

Sam looked at Jandra, then Oisin. "Does everyone know of this Chosen One except for me?"

"So it would seem."

"How is it that everyone knows of this strange power?"

Jandra sat back down. "The rumors have spread throughout Woden. Such should be expected."

Keddi returned with food and drink. Sam was relieved, as she was thirsty.

Oisin took some of the food, "Sam, I must go prepare for the funeral. It be but a short walk to your dwelling from here. Do you think you can make it, or should I remain to give you assistance?"

"No. You are correct. It be a short distance from here, and I am feeling improved after the rest and this drink. I will manage."

She looked at Keddi and Jandra. "You must also prepare for the funeral. Go and get yourselves ready. I will be able to manage by myself."

Oisin just looked at her. "That is not acceptable, Sam."

"I can go to my dwelling and retrieve my tunic, and return to assist The Highest."

Oisin shook her head, "I think not, Jandra. The Highest needs you to tend her. Keddi, I saw you a swift runner. Run to Jandra's to retrieve her tunic and deliver it to Sam's dwelling. Jandra, you can help The Highest return to her castle."

Sam smiled, "You make me laugh, Oisin. Must you go?"

She bent down and said gently to her, "I must Sam. I am sorry. I have much to see to prior to the funeral. I must make certain that the crew has prepared the ships. But know that my heart is with you."

"But these are such sad turns, and they will now be sadder for your departure."

"I will bring you back a fine gift."

"I am not interested in gifts. It would seem to me I have enough riches to wear and horses to ride."

"I will return safely, then, Sam."

"Then it will have to do. Safe journey and swift winds, Oisin. I love you, Sea-Duty Second."

Oisin bent down and tenderly kissed the top of her head, and then departed. Keddi left with Oisin, and Sam got up to begin her slow walk back to her 'castle'.

"Let me help you, Highest."

As they walked back, Jandra asked, "What is your relationship to Oisin, Highest? It be most confusing to me."

She laughed lightly, "To me as well, Jandra. You are not the only one to ask this question. I love Oisin, but not as a companion. She would tire of me in a moon's passing, and she well knows it."

"No woman would tire of you, Sam. Not one."

"This is not truth, and you do not know or understand not Oisin. She would tire of me, and does now. On this voyage of hers, she will take many lovers. I would wager that she has someone in her bed this eve."

"What about commitment? Why does she not remain loyal to you?"

"Me, Jandra? We are not companions, remember. And what of her own companion? I cannot complain. She is but my lover and my protector. She is feeling closer to me right now because I am so soft and fragile. When or if my strength returns, she will not like it as much."

"But she loves you. I can see that. It is for all to see."

"She loves the idea of me. The idea she conjures in her head during our absences. That, and she loves my body."

"It be a most excellent body, Highest. But would you not like her as a companion?"

She shook her head, well assured of the answer, "No. You know I turned her down in prior cycles. It be not a good match. I could not have Oisin around for longer than an eve. And I remain uncertain of commitment, anymore. I don't think it is for me."

"Would you not like a companion, Highest?"

Sam paused to stand still and look at Jandra, "Yes. I very much would like to have someone that loves me for me, and I them. But it does not seem meant to be. I seem to have but a series of one-eve relationships. And perhaps that is for the best. And I am uncertain if I could remain loyal to anyone."

She resumed walking again, "So I enjoy my dalliances with Oisin as I may. There is deep friendship in this, but I do miss the feeling of having someone truly love me, and having someone to speak with in the eves. But I fear I might also tire of them."

"I think more would do this with you than you know."

She laughed, "You just think they would. Like Oisin, sadly, they would only like the notion of me, not the actual woman." She looked over to Jandra. "I mean not to be negative. It is the way it is. I understand and accept it, but will not settle for that in a companion. Brett loved me for me. She took the moments to know me. This makes no sense?"

"But I saw love in your eyes to Oisin."

"It is not safe to assume what you see, Jandra. Looks can be too deceiving. But she does, as you say, love me well enough. For the moment only, though."

"But I have seen the tenderness between you."

"That is the confounding part of it, and the part that makes me let her back into my bed. That, and she is but a most excellent lover. But I have learned long prior that things are different in the morn. But I do love her."

"We are almost returned. Do you need rest?"

"No. I think I can make it. Please slow up a bit. But what of you? Do you not want a companion?"

"I have wanted one, but gave up hoping. I, like you, have overly many demands and expectations. I expect to be able to talk together, make plans together, laugh together, and have intimacy. I would like to grow together, but others seem to want their freedom and moments in bed. I, too, like the moments in bed, and I like freedom. But why have a companion simply for sex? I think it not meant for me. All I see now is that they try to bend me to their ways. There is little compromise. I would like someone who is certain of themselves, and committed."

She looked at Sam, "Are you disappointed that Oisin will not spend this eve with you? I would be."

Sam looked confused, "Disappointed? I do not want Oisin this eve. What do you speak of, Jandra?"

"You asked her why she could not leave in the morn. Was she not to be your guest this eve?"

"Oh. That. No, I cannot have Oisin with me right now. I am overly tired and weak. I could not entertain her energy this eve. While I much like her ways, she is overly demanding."

"Then perhaps you would choose another, as it is as I said, Highest. There are many that would have you. There would seem to be a line from my point of view."

She nodded and grinned, "Maybe it be truth, Jandra. In truth, I know not these things and have seen no line out my door. But would I have them, is the question, and I think not. Yet, I must find a companion. As Highest, this now weighs even heavier on me."

"Perhaps your lover this eve might become your companion."

"I have asked no one. And no one has volunteered."

"Be there someone you would ask if it a better moment?"

"Yes. Perhaps. There is. But it is not the moment."

"So there is someone you like. But it seems not enough to move you beyond your fears."

"No. I like this woman well enough, but it is complicated as I am now The Highest. I must take a companion, but I fear of making a bad relationship. As Highest, I must hold a steady relationship to me, as a good example for the community. And there is one that I like but I know not if this woman feels anything toward me. But I have heard her say so herself. But she has had another. But she—"

Jandra couldn't believe what she was hearing. Sam was so unsure. "Highest, hold. You cannot solve this problem in your mind, as it is someone else's mind. You are a beautiful, intelligent, and witty woman that provides excellent company. It is only you that holds back the possibility. What would you expect of this woman this eve if you had asked and she accepted? Are your expectations so outlandish that this be as impossible?"

"I expect this woman to be very good company. Everyone usually just wants the thought of me or just wants my body. Some moments I just like to sit with someone and talk. I am around women all turn, but often very alone at eve. And I would but hope that they would understand my mistakes and weaknesses, especially of the flesh."

Jandra laughed, "But you said you had a sorry sex-life. It sounded as if you like sex and want more of it."

Sam laughed, too, "In truth, it is so for both: I do like sex and I do have a sorry sex-life. It be a shame!"

"You? I would think someone with you every eve, like Oisin."

"Oh, Jandra, you do make me laugh. Be not so naïve. Once every three moons is more the truth of it. Some moments I get so desperate I think of inviting a guard in. I do not, of course."

"You, Highest?"

She shook her head, "Yes, me. I would better prefer good company, anyway. It is always overly rushed. I would like to perhaps take a meal, talk, laugh, and allow for intimacy if it should occur, or not. A one-eve moment and sex are always a given with me, it would seem."

Jandra nodded, "I agree, Highest. It is very lonely for me at moments, too, but I would rather remain as alone than deal with such relationships. I, too, long for good conversation at moments, so I know well what you mean. It is often difficult for someone my cycles to go in search of a new companion, as required. It seems so graceless. I do not do well with this searching for a companion undertaking."

Jandra helped Sam to sit on one of the patio chairs, "We are finally arrived. Would you like to rest for a few moments before we prepare? I could get you some drink."

"Just a drink, Jandra. I had enough when we ate prior."

"This be not a good eve to be alone, Highest. You should have invited someone over. Even Meera and Caitha would have come."

Sam nodded, "I know this as truth, Jandra, but there are moments that they too must be allowed their privacy. I know what these events do to Meera, and she needs her moments with Caitha this eve, as Caitha will make it better for her."

"And who will make it better for you, Highest?"

Sam just shook her head, *Oh, Brett, where are you now?*

Sam had changed from her daily garments to another high regal tunic, this one a dark blue in representation of The Highest transforming back to the Spirits of the Falls. Jandra did likewise with the tunic that Keddi had dropped over. Keddi was waiting for Sam in the meeting room.

"Keddi. I know not you were here."

"Highest, I have need to speak with you."

Keddi's dog came up to Sam. "Your dog seems much improved, Keddi. Is he well now?"

Sam bent down and petted the dog.

"His name is Rundle. He is healing quickly. I am glad of his safe return to me and owe The Healers and Jerna many favors."

Rundle seemed very happy with Sam, and was licking her face. She laughed, "Rundle, I am pleased you are here." She stood back up. "What did you wish to speak with me about, Keddi?"

Keddi kept shifting on both legs, "Highest, when I first arrived, I sensed you cared for me a great deal."

"Yes, of course, Keddi. I yet do."

"In what way, Highest?"

"In what way? Whatever do you mean, Keddi? You are a wonderful woman highly skilled in defense, and a great asset to Woden. You have risked your life for us, and came back to save The Highest. You are a brave and honorable woman, and Brett would be proud of you. I am proud of you, as is all the community. You are but an excellent role model for all our daughters. I hope you remain in the community, as we have great need of you. And you are my beloved sister by companionship, and daughter, as I am Highest."

"Yes, Highest. But is that all?"

"All?" Sam thought about her question for a moment, and then guessed her meaning. "Ah, I see where you head."

Sam sat down. "Please sit with me, Keddi." She waited for Keddi to sit. "You ask me if I care for you as a companion."

"Yes, Highest. That is my question."

She shook her head, "No, Keddi. I will give truth. You are Brett's sister and it would be unfair to the both of us. I would only compare you to Brett. You need someone who wants you for yourself. You have wonderful attributes and I am most certain you will make a fine companion, but I do not think it is for us. In truth, I thought of it for a moment. I have noticed your beauty, and I do much admire your abilities, but hope I offend you not, Keddi."

Keddi looked relieved, "No, you do not offend me, Highest. I might have been offended prior midturn, but since you healed me, for which I will owe you much and will repay in several fold, I have met someone who excites me very much."

Sam smiled, also relieved, "Ah. Would that be young Margeria, Keddi?"

Keddi looked surprised, "It would, Highest, but how did you know? Oh, through your senses."

Sam knew just by watching Keddi with Margeria, but had no need to tell her that, "Then I am happy for you. It will become an excellent match."

"I will have no need to remain here any longer, Highest. But if you would like me this eve, for increased protection, I would be pleased to remain."

"No, Keddi. It be not necessary. I am well guarded."

"Then I will move you back into your proper bedroom."

"That would be most appreciated as I have sent May home for the midturn and eve. Thank you for thinking of it. Do you need me to find you a place to dwell?"

She smiled, shyly, "I think not, Highest. I have found a place."

"Then we will see you at the funeral." She turned away so that Keddi wouldn't see her beginning to laugh.

"I will take but a few moments to return your bedroom to normal, and then I shall go to prepare."

Sam went back to her library where Jandra was waiting. Jandra had overheard the conversation and was all but laughing, herself.

Whispering, Sam said, "Did I not tell you? These women think they want me, but are overly frivolous for my liking. I must be getting old, as I like a little more stability and a little less lust." She looked away as if in a dream, "Although lust is not always a bad motivation."

Jandra covered her mouth so as not to laugh.

"It has been good to laugh a bit after the early midturn's sad events. Now we must attend to the last event."

They began walking to The Highest's dwelling. "Keets informed me to gather at The Highest's dwelling. From there the procession will continue to The Sacred Stones."

"At least it is not so far as this midturn's distance."

"How are we to get you your strength returned to you? I am most concerned for you."

"I hope to relax and rest this eve."

"How do you get the memories of this midturn away from your thoughts?"

"They never go away, Jandra. It be the sad fact of these positions. They just ease a bit. If I sit alone this eve, I will surely think overly much on this turn, but it is the price of choosing so. I should just take a distraction for one eve to keep my mind from such."

"I think you would have to have a companion that would be willing to hear of such things, as well. It would help to be able to speak of them with someone, but in truth, I don't wish to place these thoughts on anyone."

She nodded her head, "I do not think you know how very correct you be."

"Will you be moving over to The Highest's dwelling soon?"

"I have decided to remain where I am. The community can use it for other purposes. Meera will fight me on this decision, as will my advisors, but I will listen with closed ears. You know, Jandra, you will need to think of your advisors. You will need to select them soon."

"I will wait for you to select yours first."

"Perhaps we might reconsider how we form our advisors. Perhaps we can speak of that at a more relaxed moment."

"Will we ever have such?"

"I hope so, and I hope it will be soon."

They had arrived at The Highest's dwelling, seeing that all of Woden and Hengist were also there. Tehna, Karan, Lilley, and Jenna had lined everyone up so that the procession might begin. The musicians with their drums, horns, tambourines, and flutes were in the front. The Highest's banners followed, the former Highest atop a raised litter was next, and her now widowed companion directly behind her. Sam followed, along with Oisin and Jandra, the advisors, Briggon and his leaders, and then all the women and men. It was a quiet and solemn procession that began as the musicians started to play. The drum led the mournful tune, and some of the women sang along with the musicians. The tune was primal and somber, as was usual for the funeral processions. What was unusual for this turn was the lack of any spiritual leader from the Women's community.

When they arrived at Woden's Sacred Stones, the former Highest was placed atop the large, raised platform, the rock that formed the top of the arch that now had wood piled on top of it. She would be cremated, as was custom, so that her spirit would be released back to the Spirits of the Falls. The many women and men had returned to their spots in the tiers with no room to spare. Oulin, one of the spiritual leaders from Hengist, had volunteered to lead the ceremony, while honoring the women's ways.

"Let us sing our departure to our Highest."

It was an extremely sad song that began with a lone woman's voice sounding as a lost soul. The other women gradually entered the song, and finally, so did the men. The song ended as it had begun.

The Spiritual Leader from Hengist stepped forward and began, "It is to the Spirits of the Falls our Highest now returns. She has graced our communities with her wise counsel for many cycles. Our communities have grown because of her. If we look around us this turn and see our communities and each other, we can see her work and know that it will continue. We lose our heart as we lose our Highest. But the Spirit Mothers have called her to their service, and we are asked to move on without her. She will be gone from our presence as of this turn, but will live in our memories, stories, songs and hearts forever."

He knew it was awkward for the women to have a man lead the ceremony, but the women had welcomed the intervention, as they knew him to be a truly spiritual person.

"All those who would, let us say our final leavings to The Highest."

The procession came down, one-by-one, and walked past The Highest where she now lay, one last moment. At the end, Mandra, The Highest's companion, went up and bowed her head, touched the stone, and returned to the circle. Sam then went up and knelt down onto her knees, bowed her head to the ground, and placed one hand upon one of the three large stones. She gave her thoughts silently, and all waited with much patience.

I come now to bid you my farewell, Highest. So much is left unresolved. Why did you have to take your vial of poison? I would have found a way to save you, and you knew as much. You know this as truth!

As vowed, the traitors were captured and executed. Their deaths were overly easy for the loss of you, for now we truly have no mother. I have no mother. And you left me as The Highest. I have not the abilities of you, Highest. You were the community's mother. I am but a solver of problems. How could you leave me with this disarray? You knew I was to be the Chosen One, and yet you never told me. You knew that I was to get this strange power, and yet you told me not. You always told me that it is lonely to be a leader, but did you make certain that I listened? Oh Highest, you were right. I will most apparently become The Chosen One only after having been made Highest, as you saw it as so.

I am angered at you. I am angered at your death. We need you. Who will I now turn to for counsel? Who is there for all of us now? I am but a pitiful excuse of a leader. I am selfish. I am needy. And I am immature and tedious, as you had told me countless moments.

While you were indeed well loved, it is not until this sad moment that we now recognize the strength, courage, and patience you possessed. I am afraid now, Highest. I have this strange power that seeks to kill me. I have visions, and I fear that I will have to bed or battle a man, and birth a child. I am well afraid. You have always been there for me, for the community.

We just executed twelve women this turn. We murdered them as they were to murder you. Would you have done as we did? I think not. I think you to place them on a deserted island and left them to their own devices. You were not as I. I act overly quickly. You have said so yourself.

I am afraid for me, Highest. And I am afraid for my communities. We but scarcely mete out a living on our lands, and have just managed to get ahead because of you. You were wise in the skills of negotiation and what you called politics. I am naïve and brash. I will offend where you made liaisons.

What will become of us, Highest? You were our map. You were our counsel. You were our mother. Will we become lost now without you? Were we ready to be cast out on our own?

I will miss you, Highest. This is truth. As I speak with you now, my eyes tear from the sorrow. All are here to give their final respects. I do not . . . no, I cannot let you go. I do not want to let you go. I need you as I need Brett. Why did you go when you knew I would find a way? You had said as much yourself. You knew I would find a way, Highest. And you did anyway. Now we must become whole in a new way.

We return you to your mothers now, Highest. The winds are gentle this turn and will carry you in a safe journey. We pay homage to you and all that you were. You were a woman we all modeled. We now turn to the winds, the sky, the waters to speak with you. Please hear us, Highest. Please do not abandon us. We are well afraid of the dark, now.

As is my duty, as you so oft told me, I give you your leave to return from which you came. Safe journey. Keep us safe and watch over us now.

Sam struggled to get up and did so slowly. She had been sending her final thoughts to The Highest longer than she realized, but everyone had waited. She stood by the platform awaiting her next duty. The spiritual leader waited to see if anyone else would come up, but none did. He removed the torch from its holder and gave it to Sam.

She held it high, "Highest of all of Woden Falls, I return you to your mothers. May the Spirits of the Falls guide you in your journey, and may you watch over us and protect us."

More softly, she added, "We will miss you, Highest." She put the torch to the wood pile and stepped back.

The gathering watched the fire roar. It was a good fire and would burn hot and true. When the fire slowed its forces, the gathering began to return to their communities. The turn was done, the traitors executed, and The Highest given her funeral.

Sam waited until most the women and men had left.

Meera came near, "Highest, do you need company this eve? Caitha and I would be delighted to remain with you."

"No, Meera. Jandra and I may talk about our advisors. I must tend to that. I have long wanted to improve that practice."

"Back to the community affairs so quickly? You need to rest."

"I will, Meera. Meet me on next after midturn and we can have our meal together. It feels so long since we have spoken, yet it has been but a short moment."

"Overly many events, Highest. Please rest. You look well exhausted and pale."

"Until the after midturn, then, Meera."

Jandra came up to Sam, "I will walk you back, prepare you for the eve, and then leave you to your rest."

She looked at her, and then turned to begin walking, "May I lean on you but a bit? I feel myself growing weak yet again."

Jandra nodded as she opened her arm to Sam. "It has been a long two turns. I am weary from all the chaos and sadness. I will miss The Highest most deeply. I have worked long with her and will miss her leadership. She has seen us through many crisis. It is turns such as these that make me wonder if I should retire to the gardens. But you are tired for even many more reasons. You grow weak from using this extraordinary energy you have. You need to rest and take care of yourself."

"Weary is a good term for it. It is turns such as this that make me want to sit on the patio and breathe in the fresh scents of the flowers. I need to get the smells of the morn out of my lungs. It seems I will smell those foul odors evermore. It would be good to just relax."

"Yes. That would be good, to just relax and let down our emotions. They be overly vast on turns such as these. But those moments are hard to find."

"It be true. I have decided that one must make such moments rather than wait for them to come along."

* * * *

"We have arrived, once again. Would you have me prepare you?"

"Please just help me remove my tunic. The rest can remain for now."

"You are overly weak to remove them later."

"Then I will sleep in them. I care not."

Jandra did and Sam moved to the patio.

"Do you have the moment to share a drink, Jandra?"

She nodded, "I could use one."

"Can you get the container of wine over on the ledge for me, and those cups as well?"

As Jandra retrieved them, Sam asked her, "Would you like some wine so that we may rest for a moment?"

"That would be most appreciated." She sipped the wine, enjoying its taste, "The wine makers did well with this crop. Does this woman you like enjoy wine?"

"In truth, I know not. I think she might. Do you?"

"I do. I cannot get much of it, but I do like it. It is difficult to obtain, as our supplies are short. Have you ever spent many moments with this woman that you like?"

"Such as?"

"Oh, say, a meal."

"No. I have never had her over for a formal meeting."

"No? Do you know what she likes to eat?"

"No. I can but guess. I think it matters not, though. What is it you like to eat?"

"I am not a picky eater." She laughed, "If someone likes to do the cooking for me, I will not complain."

Sam smiled as she nodded, but just sat and relaxed. Neither had the need to hurry the conversation.

"It be a beautiful eve. I can hear the river from here. I was unaware of this."

"I have always liked that sound, but find few moments to enjoy it."

Jandra got up, "I think is sounds romantic," and then laughed. "Perhaps you should use it to improve your sex-life."

Sam smiled at her, "You think my sex-life amusing?"

"You surprise me with your lack of it. I would not have thought you to have to search for company or intimacy."

"Intimacy?" Sex is distant enough for me, but intimacy is non-existent."

"Oisin be not intimate?"

"That be not a word to describe Oisin, I think. Needy. Lusty. Aggressive. Desirous. Strong. But certainly not intimate."

"I understand. I have had such. As you say: sex-life, not love. Intimacy is unimportant, so it seems."

"I think we just have to find the right companion for such, do you not?"

"I certainly dream and hope for such. But I think you more correct when you say the eves become very different than the reality of the turn. Thank you for the cup of wine, Highest. I will take my leave now. Are you certain you would but spend the eve alone? I could have a guard send an invitation to this woman."

"I have not the courage or energy this eve to ask this woman. And I know that she is not interested at these moments. She has much else on her mind, as it should be. But that is not your worry. Be about your own business. I will be fine. I have many things I must read, and I must tend to my health, as everyone prescribes. Have a good eve. I thank you much for all your tending. Let us meet for the morn meal as we have much work to discuss."

For a moment, Jandra had thought Sam had been thinking of asking her if they could consider a relationship. Now she saw it was not so, and was disappointed.

"As you say, Highest. And you do look tired. Might I retrieve your meal for you before I depart?"

"No, Jandra. Leave me now. I will be fine. I know where the food is if I want it."

Sam poured herself another cup of wine, then watched Jandra as she walked off the patio in the direction of her dwelling. *She is a most beautiful woman. So small compared to Oisin, and yet so strong.*

She listened to the sounds of the river for a moment, then to the skies, beginning to wonder if she could keep Woden safe from the likes of Buron. She looked back in the direction that Jandra had left, seeing her finally turn at the edge of the dwelling. She felt lonely, and took another drink.

Look at how pathetic I be. I just let her go, once again. It be so much easier with Oisin.

I do not have to consider the relationship. I must only spend the eve. Oisin cares little about talk unless it is about battles or the sea.

I love Oisin, but not. And Jandra is attractive to me. She is a most beautiful woman and not hard, such as Oisin or Keddi. Nor be she as forceful. I could enjoy more the company and not rush the eve . . . or the morn.

But I put pity on myself because of myself. I am weak and courage-less when it comes to facing relationships.

I sit here thinking of Jandra's most wonderful face. I like her voice. And her hair. And her eyes. She is most intelligent. She is quick and kind. She is harder of temperament than I, but will treat me as The Highest now, and this be not good. But I would so love to touch her.

She took another drink, wondering what Jandra had seen in Josin. She thought about Jandra's body for a moment, then Oisin's, then laughed aloud at her own thoughts, "This certainly be no fair comparison."

She knew that she, more than ever prior, needed to take a companion, but didn't think she had the energy to be The Highest as well as enter into a new companionship.

"And she is my Second." She took another drink.

No, this will not work. She wants her solitude. She said as much. And I must be more careful of our positions. If it did work, how could a Highest and a Second be in the same dwelling? No, see? This is wise and good. This companionship should not be. And I do not love her as I do Oisin.

But I do so like her looks and her company. I would like so much just to touch her and feel her; gently, not forcefully. And I do not have to have sex. Just feeling her hold my arm was enough. It was strong, but gentle, and aware.

But enough of this! Be to your reading or bed. I am so pathetic regarding relationships. I will just have to find a rock for a companion, or perhaps Keddi's dog. But Jandra did help to relieve me from the events of this turn. And it felt . . . nice.

Sam had decided to rest and finish the wine, listen to the sounds of the eve, and then go to rest. She was more than exhausted, but the events of the turn had created a sort of awakeness that she couldn't understand. She knew she avoided sleep because of the inevitable evil visions that would haunt her this eve. It had been another reason she had thought of taking

Jandra up on her offer. Now she knew she would need to face this eve alone. She could do it, and knew that she could, but she didn't want to. She listened to the river and heard that it ran full from the recent rains.

Sam was hungry but too tired to retrieve the meal May had left, so she sat, avoiding movement. She was sad. The recent past events had indeed, as Jandra had said, been overwhelming. She momentarily thought it would be good if Jandra had yet wanted to be with her. But she knew that desire had passed two cycles prior with Jandra. It would have made the eve far removed from the turn's events. And she knew that she wanted Jandra, but knew it was also best to not think of these things. And she knew that she would eventually desire Oisin, even with Jandra in her bed.

I have wanted her prior and let her go. So be it. Perhaps it is for the best. She is my Second now, and I should leave it at that. I would probably tire of her in the moments to come, like I do with the others.

Sam ignored the tears running down her cheeks, and lost track of the moments; so she just sat. The sun had set long prior, and the guards had lit the torches.

Jandra appeared with two plates in her hand, having arrived from the kitchen entrance. She laid one in front of Sam, and placed the other on the table for herself.

She handed Sam her handkerchief. "Wipe your tears, Sam. It be not good to cry alone."

Jandra sat down at the table, then smiled at Sam, and began to eat. Sam just looked at her, wondering what Jandra was doing.

"I am most hungry, are you not? Eat. May has prepared a most excellent meal of roasted fowl."

Sam wiped her tears and began to eat. She was surprised at how hungry she was.

"What are you doing here?"

"Eating. What does it look like?"

She turned her head sideways and looked at Jandra for a moment, then ate a little more.

Jandra acted as if nothing were strange in her being there. "May is a good cook."

"Yes. I enjoy her meals. Jandra . . . would you . . . "

"Do you have something you would like to ask of me, Sam?"

"Well, I do . . . but . . . "

Jandra just waited and ate the food. She got up once to get Sam more of the meal, then returned.

"You know, Sam, I have fears, too."

Sam nodded, "I would expect as much.

Both ate a bit, and enjoyed the sounds of the eve.

"It is not easy for me, either."

"No. This I would expect as well."

Jandra got up and returned with May's sweets and cups of tea.

"And perhaps it may not be as we hope."

"Yes, Jandra, this be truth."

They ate their sweets, and Jandra was glad to see that Sam had eaten everything she had given to her. She had noticed this turn that Sam had lost weight, so had determined to make her eat.

"And I am not strong and lusty as Oisin or Keddi."

"I know this not but would thank you for it."

Jandra rose and took the plates and cups back to the kitchen. She brought back another sweet for Sam.

"I have many hopes and expectations of a relationship."

"I do as well. Perhaps overly many."

Jandra poured more tea for Sam.

"And we must both find companions, soon."

Sam nodded, "This you speak most truly."

"And it may, in fact, not work between us."

"Yes. This is a possibility."

She at last took the remaining plates into the kitchen. When she returned, they both just sat at the patio table for a long while, enjoying the late eve smells of the flowers and the sounds of the eve.

After a while, Jandra stood, "Sam, I think it overly chilly for you to be out. You need to be inside."

Sam had very much enjoyed the meal spent with Jandra. They had spoken very little, but it had been most pleasurable. And she enjoyed being taken-care of by Jandra, but felt that overly selfish.

"Unless you have anything to say to me, I will help you inside, and then I will take my leave."

Sam didn't want her to go so struggled for conversation.

"I have noticed that you changed your garments."

"I have. These are much more for comfort, and are easy to remove."

"I like them much."

Jandra stood and waited. She provided no smile or frown. She simply waited.

"And I have noticed that you smell overly fresh."

"I cleaned to rid myself of the turn."

"I did not."

"It matters not and can be taken care of."

She waited more.

Sam just bent her head. "I cannot do this. Good eve, Jandra."

Jandra looked disappointed.

She began to go, but something inside of Sam wanted her to remain. "This be most difficult for me, Jandra. I am divided."

"You are afraid?"

Sam nodded, "Yes."

"Because of Brett, and since then, you have avoided intimacy."

"Yes, and more."

"You love Oisin, but cannot take her as a companion."

"This be truth."

"But we must both take companions."

Sam nodded.

"Are you afraid of me?"

She lowered her head, "I am afraid of losing another as I lost Brett."

"We cannot control these events, Sam."

"Yes. You be correct."

"Might you not lose more by never taking the risk?"

"It be truth, but facts are easier than reality."

"Your ghosts are embedded deeply."

Jandra made a move to help Sam rise by taking hold of the back of her chair. Sam rose and began to go inside. As she got to the patio doors, she turned and saw Jandra yet standing at the chair. Jandra made no show of emotions or any attempt to move. Sam stood for a moment without speaking.

"You want to remain?"

"I am the one who returned, Sam."

"I cannot predict the future for us."

"Did I ask it of you?"

"You are an insistent woman."

"I know what I want and what I expect."

Sam nodded, "It has been what I like about you."

"Oh? I cannot see that now."

She continued to remain at the chair, "You know, Sam, this be not the first moment for either of us."

Sam wanted Jandra to remain, but couldn't find the words.

"Jandra . . . I need you this eve. And I do not refer to my pitiful sex-life."

"That is not acceptable, Sam."

Sam halted to think what she had said, knowing she had said something wrong.

"I feel like I have done this all wrong."

"So? Make it right, then. I am yet here. I cannot decide this for you, Sam. You are but The Highest and any relationship will have issues because of it."

"You are correct, but I am not so brave."

Jandra turned to leave.

"No, Jandra, do not go. Give me but a moment."

Jandra could see tears in Sam's eyes, but continued to stand at the end of the patio. Her heart raced but she showed no emotion or movement.

"You are a most beautiful woman, Jandra. I like much the moments we have spent together and have often thought we are enough like-minded to see ourselves into . . . intimacy. I fear such, as you have said. It is easier with one-eve moments that come and pass in the eve, as they make few demands on me. I also fear my selfishness. I liked much the attention you provided this meal. I was much amused by your style and mannerisms. And I would like to touch you. Your body is exceptional."

Sam held out her hand to Jandra, "You make my heart race with anticipation, Jandra, not for sex, but for the togetherness. I have not felt this way in overly many cycles. I want you to remain this eve, next eve, and the next until we can no longer count them, if we can but make it work. I am a demanding woman, as are you. I am also The Highest, which makes its own demands."

She moved closer to Jandra, but kept her hand out.

"When I sent you away this eve, I broke my own heart. When I saw you return, I thought I had but seen a glorious vision. I had wanted to ask you two cycles prior to spend some moments with me, but others came into your life. As you said of me, I but thought you with someone every eve, for your beauty. I think much of you. What it would be like for us, together, in the eves, in the morns, in the midturns. I think of touching you, of holding you, of laughing with you. I find you most pleasurable to look at, and I much like your gentle but firm, no, stubborn counsel. I have not shared these thoughts with even myself.

"I need you this eve, and am, in truth, desperate for you this eve. I ache for you with a hurt I cannot understand. I fear more of letting you go than of you remaining. If it will help, I will throw myself down on my knees and beg if you will but remain here this eve. But I will then need you desperately in the morn, then the midturn, then—"

Jandra had come over and placed Sam's hands together and then held her arms.

She tenderly smiled at Sam and placed her finger against Sam's mouth, "Hush. You made it right many words ago. Let us go inside where it is warmer."

****

After they had entered into the bedroom, Jandra had removed Sam's garments and helped her to bathe. Then Jandra placed her into bed, removed her own clothes, and joined her. There was no hurry in Jandra's movements. Together, they well explored the meaning of physical intimacy, talked, and slept some throughout the late eve. After awhile, Jandra made Sam go to sleep so that she might get the rest she so badly needed.

In the early morn, Jandra had heard May enter the dwelling, check in on Sam, and return to the kitchen. Jandra looked over at Sam and saw that she was sleeping. She softly touched her cheek, got out of bed, dressed and went into the kitchen.

May heard her coming, "Would you like a cup of mint tea, Jandra?"

"That would be most welcome, May. How goes the morn?"

"It seems quiet. There was overly much sadness prior turn. How is The Highest?"

"She is sleeping. She ate very well last eve. Two helpings of the fowl, and two sweets."

May nodded, "She has lost much weight of late. Will she be ready for her morn meal soon?"

"No. I think not quite yet."

"I will have your garments moved over this turn."

"Thank you. I will need them."

Jandra returned back to the bed next to Sam and just sat in bed enjoying her early morn tea, waiting for Sam to awake.

Finally, Sam moved and Jandra saw that her eyes had opened. "Have you finally woken?"

Sam studied Jandra. Unlike most her previous lovers, Jandra was yet here. It was a strange sensation, but one that Sam hoped she would enjoy getting used to.

"Please say you are unlike May and not an early riser."

Jandra smiled at her and moved a bit of hair off her face, "Someone has to tend to you. I can do so while you sleep. But I am here for you. Be there something you would need from me?"

"Just hold me. Let me deny the turn for a few moments longer." Jandra held her closely. "Thank you for remaining for the eve, Jandra. And the morn be much improved with you in it."

Sam finally rose from the bed and looked for her garments. Jandra came over to her.

"Here, allow me to help."

"Jandra, last eve when you returned, how did you . . . "

"My slow-minded brain finally put it together."

"Then I am much grateful to your slow-minded brain."

May knocked on the door and then entered, "Good morn, Highest, Jandra. I heard you speaking so have brought your morn meals to you. Highest, you stand naked again. Do you try to worry me to an early death? Jandra, I hold you to blame for this."

Jandra blushed and laughed, "Yes, May. I suppose it is my doing."

Jandra began helping Sam get dressed while Sam looked at Jandra and felt quite pleased in the moment, "May, please see that Jandra's garments are moved over this turn."

May winked at Jandra, "Yes Highest. It will be done by eve. What else do you require—"

A guard knocked and entered the room, bowing, "Highest, there is *something* out here that seeks your company."

Jandra wasn't pleased at the interruption, "Explain yourself. What do you mean by something? Who wishes to see The Highest?"

She bowed her head to Jandra, "I am sorry, Second. I am unsure as to what it is. It must be a person as it stands and walks on two legs, and it speaks our language, but it smells of dirt and it remains unknown to me be it man or woman."

Sam had finished dressing, "Be this person with weapons?"

The guard shrugged her shoulders, "It has no weapons, but some of the young guards fear it to be a witch. It has asked for food while it waits."

Jandra turned to Sam, "You cannot just see this person. We need to call over Meera or Keets."

Sam thought about it, then responded to the guard, "It is perhaps a better idea. Please summon Meera, or Keets if she is unavailable. Jandra, go ask May to give our guest some food."

Sam went to the kitchen to eat with Jandra before Meera came. When Meera arrived, she entered, "The guard be correct, Sam. It is something, but I know not what."

"Did you speak with this person?"

"I spoke to something, but it demands to speak only with you."

"Then it is moment for me to see what this be about. Meera, join me."

Jandra had been listening, but didn't expect to be left out, "I need to see about this, Sam."

Sam looked at her, then Meera, "Then let us speak to the guest."

As Sam left the kitchen to the patio, she could see what the guard had meant. The guest was extremely short, very hunched over, smelled of dirt and grime, and very, very old. She or he was dressed in layer upon layer of rags, and wore only animal hides on its feet, tied on with sinew, Sam guessed.

Sam went over the table that May had set the food upon for the guest, "I am Sam, Highest of Woden. You have summoned for me?"

It looked at Sam and hissed, "You only. No one else."

Sam sat down across from the old person. She motioned her hand so that Meera, the guards, and Jandra would all move back so that the old person could deliver his/her message. Jandra and Meera watched as Sam listened to whatever this person was saying. Sam apparently asked a question that the guest didn't like.

They heard the ragged one spit out, "NO. It is not meant that . . . " and they could hear no more.

Jandra thought this out of line and began to go over.

Meera grabbed her arm, "No, Second. You must learn to trust Sam. She has an instinct like no other for what is needed in these situations. My guards and I are here. If you look about, you will see that they are at the ready. No harm will come to Sam."

Jandra was upset and stubborn, but knew that Meera was correct. She looked around and saw that the guards had their bows and arrows at the ready. "It be difficult to wait. I am overly used to commanding others for The Highest. But you are with truth."

After what seemed a long while, the Old One rose from its chair and began moving over toward Sam. The guards quickly drew their bows.

Sam looked over at Meera and made a motion to have them relax their weapons. Meera didn't like it much, but did as she was bid. She signaled to the guards to be at the ready. Jandra and Meera watched as Sam rose, then knelt before this Old One, and bowed her head. The Old One, after removing them from the multiple layers of rags, placed her hands on Sam's head. When Sam finally stood, it shocked all to see how very short the Old One was. Sam wasn't a tall woman, average in height, but stood as a giant over this old ragged one. Sam smiled kindly down at the woman and helped her back into her seat. The old raggedy one yelled out, "Wine."

Sam came over, "Jandra, have May give food, as much as needed, to our guest, and wine. Also, please see if our shoe maker can but provide a pair of boots for our guest."

Sam went over to a guard and talked to her privately for a few moments, then came back to Meera.

Meera noticed that the guard left on an errand.

"Meera, go prepare yourself. We ride this turn."

"You and me, Highest? I think it not enough."

"Add who you would then, but keep it small. We must fly like the wind."

Meera nodded, "Keddi and Margeria. Keddi is the best archer I have yet seen."

"We might have use of our weapons."

Meera nodded and sent a guard to retrieve them.

Jandra had returned and overheard part of the conversation, "I go too, Sam."

"I know this will be most difficult, but it cannot be so. Where we go has the potential for danger. With me gone and Oisin to sea, you are the acting Highest." She shook her head, "I am sorry, Jandra, but you cannot go. Besides, I could not risk both of us. Did I not say that the demands of The Highest would be our issues?"

Meera silently watched the interchange, but saw that the relationship had somehow changed between them. She observed them carefully. Both of them beautiful, standing almost the same height with not much weight difference between them. Sam was stunning, being more pronounced in her features, but Jandra had the grace and movement of a dancer and was the more striking and stunning of the two. Sam had the blondest of blonde hair, wildly straight to her lower neck, while Jandra's hair was as dark as a the raven, wavy and flowing down like rippling water to the middle of her back. Meera knew that Jandra was a few cycles older than Sam, but noticed that the age on Jandra added dignity and softness instead of the usual hard lines in others.

"No, Sam. It cannot be so. I too must go. I will not come as far as we have and accept this with a wave of your hand. Did you not say that if you but knew my expectations, that they could be so met?"

"If our relationship were as it was in the prior turns, would we be having this argument?"

Jandra stood looking at her, well frustrated in the argument. "No. But that does not make it the more fair for it. You cannot cast off our relationship this easily."

Sam looked to Meera, "What think you of this, Meera? Would you have The Second to go with us?"

Meera frowned. "Thank you much, Sam, for this opportunity to make you both enemies of me. Has Jandra not hated me well for long enough?"

Jandra looked at Meera with surprise, "Oh, Meera, that has been but my mistake. But allow me to tend to that later. Go ahead, Meera. What say you in this matter?"

Meera looked at Sam, "She is The Second, and is needed in the community, as you say. And she does not ride or wield weapons, as we are so able. But, Highest, would it not give her the opportunity to see a side of Woden she has not? Would it not give her the opportunity to learn to ride as we must? It would mean more watchfulness on our parts, but I can see no reason why she should not attend. Briggon can be enlisted to be more mindful of the borders while we be gone. And there have been such occasions in the past when all the leaders had been absent for a full two moons."

Sam shook her head, sighing. She was already feeling slightly trapped in the relationship. "Add another horse and weapons. I will speak to May about our nourishment needs. Meera, send for Karan, Tehna, Lillon, Briggon and Keets. I will speak to them as we take our leave."

Sam went to speak with May, "May, we leave for three turns. Please prepare carry meals. There be five of us. And I will require six flasks of wine."

Sam dressed herself and Jandra in appropriate riding garments. They were of leather, and Jandra found them odd feeling. Leather was not a material the Woden woman wore, except in battle. Sam was busy searching for something she couldn't find. Finally, she rose up from a chest and handed Jandra a knife in its sheath.

"Here. Tie this around you. You may as well learn to use it."

Then Jandra watched, surprised, that Sam opened a tall cabinet, reached into the back, and pulled out a sheathed sword. Jandra had never seen Sam with such an unwieldy and heavy weapon.

"Be this your sword, Sam?"

"It is. I was trained with this for many cycles."

"You were? How is it I know not this side of you?"

Sam looked over to her, "Perhaps Meera correct in that you need to see another side of Woden, of me, and of you." Sam walked over to Jandra as she put on her sword. "Please say you be not like Oisin and like only the gentle and soft side of me, Jandra. A leader is complex and there are moments when all of us may need to know the use of these weapons."

"It makes no difference to me, Sam. It is merely difficult to view The Highest with such a weapon. It bodes not well for the community. And I never saw our former Highest lift any weapon."

Sam thought about Jandra's statement for a moment, realizing that she also had never seen The Highest lift a weapon. "Does it make you sad?"

"No, in truth, it but provides more intrigue of you."

Sam smiled, "You please me well. Let us to the horses."

They went out of the dwelling where everyone awaited. Keddi and Meera dispersed the weapons. Sam strapped on her bow and arrows across her shoulder, and Meera, Keddi, and Margeria all did the same. Sam noticed that Keddi had a special bow and several more arrows. May delivered the carry meals to Meera, and Meera, Keddi and Margeria strapped them to their backs. Margeria helped Jandra up on her horse while Sam watched her mount, seeing that the horse responded well to her.

Unusual, thought Sam. *This is typically a nervous horse, but it stands as if pleased by Jandra.*

All the others but Meera and Sam mounted. Sam went over to where Karan, Tehna, Lillon and Keets were waiting. She saw Briggon running up. They all knelt before her, and she made her usual show of not desiring it. As they stood, she spoke to all of them for a short while. They nodded and all turned to their business, except Briggon. Sam spoke to him for a longer moment. When she was done, he knelt before her again, then rose and left. Sam went to mount her horse.

Meera asked, "Are we to take the Old One with us?"

"Only to the gorge river. She will ride with me."

Meera helped the Old One walk over to Sam, and then lifted her up onto the horse. Sam placed her in front of her and put her arms around her for safety.

Sam led the group as they rode outside the community, past the gardens, and out into the grasslands. Sam kept them at a steady but normal pace.

Meera came near, "Where is it we head, Sam?"

"To the valley of the caves. Do you know of them?"

"Not well, but well enough. It is thought to be a dangerous area. We do not much attend to it."

"So it would seem."

"What is it we seek?"

"The Woman in the Woods has summoned for me."

Meera made no show of her surprise, but was well displeased about it. She now knew the extent of the possible danger they faced. It was in the legends that all those that sought the Woman in the Woods would face much resistance. She looked around at their small group once more, wondering if they should add more weapons and guards. She saw that they were fully loaded and hoped that Margeria was as good as she had been trained.

As they arrived at the grasslands, they halted a moment for Sam to speak with a sentry.

The sentry had heard them coming and waited for them to come up to her.

"Anicia."

"Oh, Highest, forgive me. I could not recognize it as you." She knelt.

"Is all well?"

"This is what I have come to ask you."

"I am gladdened for this. I could not retreat my position, but have a strange sighting to report. Please come this way. If it had made a move to come closer, I would have sounded an alarm, but it has remained there."

They all dismounted, except for the Old One, and followed the sentry.

"What is it you see, Anicia?"

She pointed, "Look far off in the distance this way."

Jandra instantly saw it. "Smoke."

Sam looked at her, well surprised. *How could she see such a distance as this?*

The rest of them tried again but saw nothing. Meera asked, "What is it we look for?"

"It is most difficult to see, and I have but wondered if I have imagined it to be there. But look; there. Look way out, down in the river valley. Do you see the curve?"

They kept looking for a long while, when suddenly Keddi cried out, "Yes, I see it. Look where she said, Highest. There is smoke. At first I thought it to be mist, but it be smoke, as The Second said."

Sam saw it. Jandra noticed that she had an overly determined and concerned look on her face. Sam began to remount. "You are an excellent sentry and have done much for your community this morn. You will be rewarded for this excellent attention to our lands. You need say nothing of this to anyone, Anicia."

"I understand, Highest."

"We will go there, now. When is your duty completed?"

"I will be reprieved in the early morn."

"Visit me upon my return."

She turned to Jandra, the least practiced of the riders. "Hold tight, Jandra. We must make our horses to fly." She turned to Keddi, "Guard the rear, Keddi. Meera, you lead us from here." To the Old One she held in front of her, she asked, "Is this where we head?" The Old One nodded.

Meera, a skillful rider and the best of the group, made her horse take off like the wind. Throughout the morn and midturn, the horses and their mounts descended to the valley where the smoke waited, the horses running in a pack as if trained to do so. Jandra hung on desperately to her horse, determined not to become a concern for the others. She had never seen any of these women in such weapons and attitudes. It was if a whole realm of knowledge existed that Jandra had never known. That Sam had donned weapons had taken her by complete surprise. She studied closely at the way Sam carried her weapons and immediately knew that Sam could also well use them if needed. Jandra again wondered why Sam had chosen her as The Second. She knew now why not Lillon. But now that she had seen how imposing and capable Meera was, Jandra knew Meera to be the better choice. And the way these women sat on their horses well showed their experience. By early after midturn, the horses finally descended to the gorge.

Meera turned back toward Sam, "We must slow now. The way becomes but a path. I think what we seek be around the next bend or so. It looks like we will need to walk the horses in but a moment."

Sam nodded, and Meera continued to lead. Jandra noticed how silently the women rode. Not a word had been spoken the entire turn. She looked back at Keddi and saw her looking about, as if on guard. She noticed that Margeria did likewise. And she admired how well and straight Sam rode her horse. Sam's movements were so subtle that it seemed as if the horse could sense the direction Sam headed.

When did Sam become a warrior? When did she learn to ride, so? And then thought, *No wonder The Highest spoke so highly of her.*

When they finally reached the river, Meera halted her horse and dismounted. She went to Sam and reached up for the Old One while Sam helped place her into Meera's arms. Sam dismounted, retrieved two flasks of wine from Meera, then walked with the Old One a short distance.

In a hiss and whisper, the Old One said to Sam, "It is dangerous for you from here. Walk downstream to the caves. But be careful. Others will be about you. You must wait until morn. At sun's rise, you will see a cave entrance. It will not be visible in the eve. It will have a torch. Look for a symbol on the handle. You will know when you recognize the correct sign. Trust no other. There are many who seek to halt your passage to the Woman of the Woods. Your friends will be unable to accompany you after the cave's entrance."

Sam gave her two flasks of wine, then watched as the Old One ambled upstream, keeping to the river, until she was out of sight.

She went back to Meera and the others, "Remain watchful. It to be dangerous from here."

Keddi and Margeria readied their weapons, and Meera began to walk her horse by the river's edge. There was no path, but to Jandra, Meera seemed to know where she was heading. The others followed Meera's lead, but no words were spoken. Jandra was uncertain of the need for silence, so guessed that the women were silent to remain alert. She had noticed that Meera had not needed to signal to Keddi or Margeria to be ever the more watchful.

At one point they had followed the river downhill to where they walked between a steep ledge and the river. Meera turned to Keddi and motioned to the top of the ledge. Without a word or acknowledgement, Keddi sheathed her bow and arrow, and quickly but silently ascended the ledge. There she remained, walking alongside the group from atop, while Jandra was placed in-charge of Keddi's horse.

The constant sound of the river at her left and the steady thump of the horses' hooves droned Jandra into a hypnotic state. The scenery was spectacular, and she had never seen such sights. Without warning and but a small sound of the arrow landing, Keddi had let fly an arrow in front of Meera. Meera readied her sword and looked far up at Keddi to determine the danger. Keddi signaled that there were seven waiting for them around the next bend. Sam tied the horses to a bush and readied her bow and arrow while Margeria ran just ahead to prepare.

Meera backed up to Sam, "Seven-to-five. And they know not we know. Is this but a good turn for a fight then, Highest?"

"Sounds like good odds to me."

Jandra took out her knife and swore that she would learn to use a bow and arrow at the very next possible moment. She was sorry that she had insisted she come. She was not afraid of a battle, but realized that these four would have to fight for her too, and felt as a bother. Sam and Meera went up to just behind Margeria, then waited.

Whispering, Meera pointed across the river, "We begin when we see Keddi over by those rocks. She makes her way there now."

Sam studied the gorge, seeing that they had little room for a fight on this side of the river. She was glad that Keddi would be able to shoot from the other side.

She then went over to Jandra, whispering, "There are but seven, and they know not we have arrived. They wait like fools for us to come to them. They think us witless enough to be unguarded. Be prepared, Jandra, but our arrows will get most of them, so the fight may be but contained before it reaches you."

Sam stroked the horses' noses, softly whispering soothing sounds into their ears so that they wouldn't become excited. "Keep the horses calm as you can. A surprise attack will be our best hope."

Jandra nodded and began to do as she had seen Sam do. She was angered at herself, *How do these women know of these things? How is it that I am so sheltered? They have done much to protect our community, and no one knows of this bravery and selflessness. It will end upon my return. They will know the bravery and deeds of these women.*

Sam walked quietly up to Meera and Margeria. When she heard the enemies' voices, it suddenly dawned on her. She looked over to Meera and whispered, "Men."

Meera nodded. Margeria, kneeling on one knee and in readiness to snap her arrows into her bow, looked up at Sam and Meera. Very softly, she said, "It sounds as if they have been drinking overly long. They brag about who they will take to their beds this eve, already."

Sam whispered Meera, "Try to save one to question."

Meera looked around for Keddi. She saw her over on the rocks, beckoning for them to move forward a few paces. Jandra remained with the horses to keep them calmed, but would move up as the battle began. Keddi moved forward slowly on the rocks, remaining well hidden from the men.

Meera watched Keddi carefully, "We attack on Keddi's signal."

Margeria nodded and rose. She would have to go around the bend to attack from this side. They would have to wait for Keddi to send across the first arrows before they would move. Keddi moved slowly in the rocks, yet remaining well hidden. Meera could see Keddi studying the men. What she was waiting for, Meera could only guess. Jandra was staggered that these women could wait with such apparent ease and calmness. She felt like being sick.

Suddenly, Keddi jumped up high on a rock, yelled, "You, over there," and let loose two arrows. Jandra watched as Keddi had two more arrows in the bow just barely as the others had left it. Sam and Margeria turned the bend and let loose their arrows, and Meera had moved into what was left of the group with her sword. Jandra ran up to help and found Sam and Meera in sword fights with two of the men. Keddi was yet sending arrows, and Margeria was throwing her knife. As Meera dispatched her prey, she turned to help Sam, but saw that Sam had her sword pointed to the throat of the only man left.

Meera went right up to his face and removed his weapons. "How many other groups are you?"

He spat in her face and she brought up her knife to his eye. "How many, or lose it now."

"One."

"How many in it?" She began to push the knife forward to pierce his eyelid.

He screamed, "As many, maybe a few more."

"Are they drunken pigs as this group?" She kept the pressure applied.

He yelped, "You she-bitch. You torture me."

Meera kicked him in groin and he fell to the ground. Sam moved the sword back to his throat.

"Answer."

"I die anyway."

Without another word, Meera sent her sword through his heart. She looked at Sam. "We know there be at least one more group such as this."

"They possibly camp where we must this eve."

"Do you think they expect us?"

"No. They are lazy. They send their worst to slay us to avoid the exertion. They think us dimwitted fools and soft women."

Sam went to see to Jandra. She was standing over one of the dead men, and Sam could see her knife in his back. Jandra looked shocked.

"He was injured but got up to attack Margeria from the back."

Margeria came over, smiling, "Many thanks, Second. Well done."

As Margeria spoke, Jandra went over to some bushes and became sick. Margeria looked surprised. Sam looked at Margeria, shrugged and said, "It is her first killing, and it but surprised her."

Margeria nodded knowingly, "Then she will be fine, as she did not hesitate. She should be most proud."

Sam gave her a smile. Margeria wasn't the type to understand Jandra's heart, but she had spoken wisely.

Sam went over to Jandra and touched her, *I am most proud of you. You have acted as the finest Second, without hesitation, and the reason you are well chosen for it.*

Jandra smiled up at Sam, then turned and became sick yet again.

Keddi found a way across the river, while the others engaged in gathering the men's weapons and horses. Keddi and Margeria began collecting and cleaning their arrows to place back in their sheaths, fully knowing that they would have need for them yet, up ahead, while hoping they hadn't been bent.

Meera tied up the horses so that they could get water and eat from the grasses and bushes until their return. They would take the extra horses and collected weapons back to Woden when they were able to return.

Meera spoke to all, "It will grow dark in this gorge quickly. We must find this other group soon."

They began walking ahead again as Keddi went across the river and Margeria climbed to the top of the ledge. Sam and Meera both guessed that they would hear this lazy group and see their fires well before they arrived to them. Keddi and Margeria had agreed with them. Their concern was the number the group might have.

As they walked, Meera kept close watch on Keddi and Margeria. Margeria had gone far ahead to scout for the group. As before, the group remained silent. Jandra now knew the need for constant alertness and remained ready. She had taken a spear from the assortment of weapons gathered and thought it a good weapon for herself. She hoped she could keep the fouled knife sheathed.

As the sun began to set behind the gorge, Keddi sent an arrow across the river in front of Meera. Its message was clear: *Hold.*

Meera looked for Margeria but could no longer see her, so was forced to trust in the young guard's abilities. Meera motioned to Keddi, *How many?*

Keddi didn't look pleased. She signaled back, *'thirteen'*, that she could see. She indicated that some were resting around the campfires, some were eating, and only two were on guard, nearer to Meera. Meera yet saw no sign of Margeria and signaled such to Keddi. Keddi shook her head, *No.*

Meera motioned to Keddi, *Begin the fight at dark.* Keddi nodded. They all waited until the sun's set and the shadows had disappeared. All weapons were readied, and Meera hoped that Margeria would be close by to help. Suddenly, Meera heard the rushing sound of arrows released, and then heard their targets scream in pain. More arrows were released. More sounds of the arrows making their target. Meera couldn't tell where the arrows had come from and wondered if Margeria were assisting. She moved forward, along with Sam, and they also released their arrows. Meera was pleased that Sam had been correct. These men were fools, standing about the fires so that they were excellent targets. Jandra moved forward and speared a man, then discovered that it was difficult to remove the spear. Sam was quickly beside her, fighting off the next man heading toward Jandra as she yet struggled with her spear. Sam slashed his torso, then moved on. Jandra, in desperation, left the spear in disgust, and picked up the man's sword. He made a move to grab her arm and she sent the sword through him without thinking. Removing the sword was far easier than removing the spear.

Sam yet heard arrows flying but couldn't tell their targets. She feared they might be from the men's group.

She yelled to Meera, "MEERA! Overly many arrows fly."

It was Sam's signal to move away from the fires. Sam made a motion to Jandra to back up to the gorge's wall, out of the shadows. Meera and Sam did likewise, watching for the remaining moving shadows. They heard two voices whispering, and Sam and Meera jumped out from the wall and overtook the two. With swords at their throats, they remained still. It was too dark to see far, so Sam hoped that Keddi and Margeria covered the edges.

No sounds were about except the moaning of the injured. The dead were silent where they lay.

Keddi came up and said, "All clear. One went running, but he knows not that Margeria is waiting for him. She will return with him, directly."

Meera was trying to count, "How many do you see?"

Jandra looked around and counted, "I see but eleven."

Sam had been afraid of that. One missing, not counting the one heading toward Margeria. She listened. Nothing. An arrow raced by Keddi and slit across her arm. Her arm bleeding, she made no notice of it as she unsheathed two arrows, knelt and sent them flying from where she heard the arrow. As soon as the two were released, she released two more, slightly moved to the right. Two more, slightly removed to the left, then two more until she heard the impact of an arrow into her target. An arrow returned, way off target. She knew she had hit him. She drew one more arrow and aimed to where the last one had hit. She pulled back hard and let it swiftly fly. She once more heard the soft thud of it hitting her target. She was on her feet and running before Jandra even realized that Keddi had unsheathed her first two arrows, for Keddi was surprisingly quick.

Meera looked down at the two yet alive and put her sword to one's eye, "How many more groups be there?"

The other one tried to spit on her. Meera moved her sword swiftly into his heart. She moved it back to the other and placed it against his eye. "You have but one moment to answer."

"You will kill me anyway."

Meera nodded, frowning, "You speak the truth. I will. But I will do it slowly or swiftly. It be but your choice."

The man had already been well injured and was in much pain. Meera could see that he wanted no more suffering.

"There is a group on the way. They should arrive two turns hence."

"How many in this group?"

"Perhaps ten. Perhaps twenty. I know not. My own group began with twenty, but many died on the way here."

"Where do you come from? Who sent you?"

"I come from Apien and am but a hired fighter. I know not the leader of this."

He closed his eyes for but a moment, and Meera swiftly and quietly put her sword through his heart. He didn't even know he died. Margeria entered the camp with a badly limping and much wounded man. She kicked him over to the fire.

"This thick uncouth makes the thirteenth."

Meera was glad to see Margeria but saw that she too had been wounded, as Margeria limped slightly over to Sam and Meera.

"You are injured."

She shook her head, "Worry not about me. It is twisted and cut from climbing the rocks. A turn's rest will see it better. Where be Keddi?"

Meera looked across to the rocks, but could see nothing. "She finds her target."

Meera moved over by the injured man and sent her sword through his heart. She would allow no survivors this journey.

Sam was with Jandra, laughing, "So, Jandra, how did you fare with the spear?"

Meera laughed as well, knowing that spears, when embedded in bone, were difficult to remove. She had seen Sam save Jandra from the man taking the advantage as Jandra struggled with the spear.

Meera went over by Jandra, "Do not let her jest with you. You did well and are most courageous. I am proud you fight with us, Second. We must teach you to use more than one weapon. As you saw, they are often needed."

Keddi came back into camp. "How many arrows did you let fly, Margeria?"

"All. I have none left. We must recollect them."

Meera had been amazed at the sheer volume of arrows that had been used in the battle. "Between you two, it was as if legions were letting fly their arrows. Keddi, how does the wound fare?"

Keddi also wondered about the number of arrows that had flown during the battle, thinking that there far more than she could account for, but having no logical answer for it, let it go, "It will need purifying, and will scar, but what is yet another scar? Margeria will tend to it."

Meera looked around, "Let us remove the bodies to beyond the bend, and we will make camp here. The Highest believes that the cave entrance is across the water."

Jandra started unloading the food, "We must eat. It has been all turn and you have all worked well for your meager meal."

Margeria laughed, "It be not so meager. Look here," as she held up the men's rations.

"No wine for us this eve. Jandra, you will take first watch. Keddi, Second. I, third, and Margeria fourth."

"Why not me as well, Meera?"

"You have much work in the morn and will need your strength. Let us tend to the fires."

They put out all the fires, knowing that they were nothing but targets and signals. Jandra made a move to gather the weapons, but Meera halted her.

"Rest for this eve, Second. The Highest gives us moments in the morn as we wait for her. We will find their horses then, too. They will not have strayed far."

* * * *

They talked for a while before resting. Meera noticed that Sam no longer grew weakened through contact. She guessed that the little old person in the rags had done something to her when Sam had bowed before her.

Jandra was thinking the same, "Sam, what did that old ragged one do to you? You no longer grow weaker from your power."

Sam shrugged, "In truth, I know not. I know only that she said she would make it right until I met with the Woman in the Woods."

Keddi asked, "Who was the old person? Be it woman or man?"

"Also in truth, I know not. It was certainly older than all of the eons, though. And he/she was a most kind soul and has lived beyond our dreamings. She/he was of the earth itself. She came to summon me to the Woman in the Woods."

Meera asked, "And who would the Woman in the Woods be, Sam?"

Sam sighed, "This makes as much sense to me as for you. I know not. I wish that I but did. I cannot even imagine having a power. It be far too distant from our lives and realities to think of such a thing. What be this magic? I know that it is not of us. I know that I am to meet with the Woman in the Woods. Become The Chosen One at some point in the future. And that they were here prior to all humans, as they refer to us."

Jandra was sitting beside Sam, holding her arm to her, while Sam laid her head on Jandra's shoulder. Meera saw that Sam was well weighted by all this.

"Sam, I grow well concerned. You are The Highest now, and that of itself is enough to bear for the community. But this has added strain beyond measure to you. I like it not."

Sam sighed, "There have been moments these few prior turns when I but wished I was no longer of this realm. I have noticed, though, that life gives one the bad along with the good, and for this I try to remain strong."

Meera pressed a little, "Are you concerned for yourself in these next events?"

"I think our main test outside the cave's entrance. Be well prepared for surprises while I be gone."

Jandra laid her head lightly onto Sam's.

Meera smiled at Sam, "The next festival proves to be a happy one for the both of you."

Jandra frowned, "It did until that old person appeared. Now I will worry until Sam's return."

Meera nodded, "It be what women are set to do in this realm."

Keddi had been thinking about what Sam had said. "Highest, the Old One told you that these spirits are not of us?

"The Old One did. It said that this had not meant to be a realm with such as us. It was their realm, free from our kinds."

"How can that be so? What does that mean?"

"I know not. It said that perhaps we might know, but that the clues were there for us."

Jandra asked, "Clues? What clues?"

Sam laughed a little, "If we but knew, we would know the answer to our questions."

Margeria asked, "Highest, what is the use of this power and why is it being given to you?"

Sam looked at Margeria, shook her head, and sighed, "I wish I but knew."

Meera had said they should all take to their rest. Given the events of the turn, they all did so willingly, except for Jandra who stood first watch.

* * * *

Margeria woke The Highest just before the sun's rise.

She bent down and spoke softly to her so that Jandra might sleep through Sam's exit, "Highest. It be the moment for you to watch for the cave entrance."

"Is all quiet?"

"All through the eve, Highest."

Margeria handed Sam a cup of tea, "Compliments of the slain."

Sam rose and began to prepare. She donned her weapons, freshened herself, and watched for the sun's rise to hit the cave's entrance, wherever it was.

"Do you know where the entrance lies, Highest?"

"No. Help me to look, Margeria."

As the sun raised its rays onto the rocks, Margeria saw a small cave opening. She pointed to it.

Sam nodded, "Look after my friends and companion. I know not how long I be."

Margeria nodded and placed her hand firmly on Sam's shoulder, as all guards did when facing battle. Sam returned the gesture and walked to the cave's entrance. Margeria saw her examine the torch, take it, and enter the cave. Margeria went back to watching over the camp until the others awoke. She would deal with Jandra's anger later at having not been awoken as Sam left.

Sam yet had her weapons but decided to keep them sheathed. She followed the instructions but wondered why the Women of the Woods couldn't just meet with her by the river. This all seemed overly mystical and magical, something not of Woden. She walked for what seemed like all the morn. She thought that this power and magic weren't for such as her kind. As she neared the end of the cave, she felt and saw great fog. The torch lit very little now, so Sam had to check the path carefully to make certain she yet followed it. After what seemed an eternity of walking, she began to see a clearing. She was glad as she was growing tired. Too tired to be some place this dangerous, alone.

At long last, she entered the clearing and waited. For what, she knew not. *Is this a hoax? Then how might I dream such a thing and meet the woman/man in the rags?* She tried to place out of her mind her concern for her growing weakness, as she knew it would be most difficult to do the return trip back to the river. If she met anyone dangerous here, she knew she would likely die.

She walked around the clearing slowly, looking for signs of any life. Seeing nothing, she decided to rest upon the path for a short while, and then head back. As she rested, a movement occurred in the fog surrounding the clearing. Sam hadn't yet seen it. It was as if a forest tree shaped itself into a woman. The woman began to walk out of the fog, and Sam caught her movement. She stood and watched, seeing a very old but beautiful woman, with silver hair hanging to the ground. The air shimmered around her.

Sam, startled, knelt down, "Woman of the Woods."

So, you have finally come. I have called you upon many moments, but finally had to send my old friend.

"I came with greatest haste."

Come, walk with me through the Woods. I will show you our realm.

Sam rose, and the Woman of the Woods held out her hand to Sam.

"I am for some strange reason, overly tired, so will be unable to walk far."

Never mind about that. Take my hand and you will be comforted.

They walked into the fogs, and into the Woods. They seemed to walk a great distance, but Sam noticed she no longer felt weak or tired. She saw no path or clearing, and noticed that the trees just seemed to part for this Woman.

Do you not recognize me, Sam?

Sam studied her very closely. She had never seen anyone with such beautiful but long flowing hair. She thought it must never have been cut. She had a fleeting yet vague memory of when she was young.

"At the Falls? Your haired flowed about as the water."

The woman smiled and her face shimmered as she did. It looked like the sun shone upon her, but Sam could see no sun through such deep fog.

Yes, Sam. This is good. The memory is returning. We had removed it from you until it was the proper moment. Life is difficult enough for you creatures, so until you were needed and ready, we kept it from you.

"Why are you known as witches?"

The Woman of the Woods laughed, and then looked upon Sam sadly, *This will happen to you, too, my young one. When you have gained your power, many will shun you. Unlike us, however, you are partially of the human sort, so will not have the same or equal powers. We hope you will be able to mask them. Ours fly about us as they are part of us. Yours you will learn to summon. Your kind cannot understand mystical abilities, so think of us as witches.*

Sam saw a great dwelling in the Woods. The dwelling looked like the trees, but not. From what she could tell, they were trees, as she knew them to be, but then they would suddenly appear as a dwelling. It was a dwelling, most certainly, but one that looked of the Woods. It was open, but closed, and Sam noticed that as the wind blew around, the leaves would move to shelter the dwelling's openings. The Woman of the Woods led her into the dwelling and had her to sit at a table. The table was a table, but also a tree. Sam could see one, and then the other, as if the shapes merged into the other, but not. She began to notice there were others moving about. They were not people, such as Sam. She could almost see through them. They seemed to almost hover, and then she saw that they were looking at her.

"What am I seeing? What is this place?"

Oh, but I am so unused to your type. You always hurry so. Here, Sam, drink this. Your sisters are about you, but you know them not. Look at me, Sam. Who do you see? Look very hard into my eyes.

Sam drank from the cup handed to her, then looked in the Woman of the Wood's eyes. She felt hypnotized by the effect, but began to clear her head.

Sam opened her eyes wide in understanding but disbelief. *You are my Mother of the Fall's mother. You are my grandmother. But you are so—*

The Woman of the Woods laughed. *Old? Are you trying to say that I am old, Sam? Indeed I am old, as is your Mother of the Falls. It is alright that you say so as you know nothing of cycles.*

But how can that be? How can I be a daughter of spirits?

* * * *

It was morn of The Second turn and Meera was beginning to worry. It had been one more turn and eve, and she was now facing an enemy group descending on them of perhaps twenty men, or more. Jandra tried not to bother Meera or the others, but was overly worried for Sam. They had rested and eaten well, but the moments were quickly becoming a concern for each of them. They had built traps in case the men came. It had taken a half-turn to build their ambush, but knew it would be worth the effort if the men arrived. Even Jandra had made an ambush of her own design. In the prior eve as they waited for Sam, Jandra explained to Meera why she had long hated her.

"I but thought that you had denied Sam, and could not understand it."

Meera shook her head, "All these cycles, Jandra. At least it now be over."

"I am so sorry, Meera."

"It is of no importance now. And I had asked Sam overly soon after Brett's death."

"You have remained the closest of friends to Sam. How could I have not seen the devotion in your eyes for Sam, even after all these cycles?"

"I am a warrior, and you saw that part."

"Perhaps. But I am sorry for it, all the same."

During the same prior eve, Keddi had asked Meera if she should go in search of Sam, but Meera remained steadfast. If Keddi asked now this morn, she was uncertain if her answer would be the same. Meera was deeply worried about Sam. She knew that whatever Sam faced beyond the cave was not of what they knew.

Jandra came up once again to her, "Meera, we need to go find Sam. It has been overly long, and I am well concerned. As are you. I can see it in your behavior. You but pace."

"Perhaps you be right. It has been overly long. But let us wait until midturn to begin."

As they all prepared to wait a little longer, Jandra yelled out, "Sam!"

Meera looked to the cave's entrance and saw Sam. Her hair shimmered, and her eyes but glowed and shone like deep pools of water. Meera noticed that they were becoming almost unnatural looking, but deeply compelling. Her eyes no longer looked as if they could see in the same ways as others.

Keddi began to smile and wave at Sam, but a distant movement caught her eye, "To your weapons. Quickly."

The group of men was upon them and had seen them. Margeria went to the trap they had prepared and waited for the right moment. Meera saw that there were at least twenty-eight men, all on horses, and all well prepared with weapons. Jandra gasped as she saw them racing toward them, wondering how any of them thought they would come out of this alive. Unknown to Jandra, both Keddi and Meera thought the same.

Keddi knelt and prepared her bow with arrows. Sam moved quickly into the rocks and prepared her bow and arrows as well, not yet having seen the trap lain for the men. As the men came into the trap, Margeria released her rope, and Keddi shot at one across the river. It missed. She shot again and hit the target. Both ropes finally loose, rocks came tumbling down upon the men and horses. Sam busied her bow, as did Keddi and Margeria, upon the remaining men. Quite suddenly, many arrows were flying. Sam thought there were far too many arrows, even with Keddi's great skills, and from the direction of the high cliffs. She wondered briefly over it, wondering which of them had been on the cliff top. Meera had seen the same and had also wondered about the arrows, but didn't have the moments to look up to the cliffs.

As the men came charging toward them, Jandra released her rope, and up swung a barricade of spears. Several men and horses found their deaths on Jandra's spears. The few men remaining quickly dismounted and ran toward the women while waving their swords. There were six remaining. Keddi's arrows found their target in two of the men. Meera and Sam were fighting with two others, and Margeria had sent her arrows into another. Sam's blade had found her target's neck and she turned, thinking that all had been well dispatched. She saw that Meera had won her battle, but had received two wounds. As Sam turned toward Jandra, she saw that Jandra was being held by the last man, his knife blade was upon her neck.

He was laughing, "What say you now, Sam of Woden?"

Margeria had seen the man take Jandra, so began to move silently behind him, as he hadn't yet seen her. Keddi knelt and drew her bow.

Sam looked carefully at the man and his knife. She closed her eyes. *Focus. Focus on the knife. Focus as the Woman of the Woods taught you.* She choked away any self-doubt as Jandra's life was at stake.

Meera saw the man suddenly struggling as if fighting with his own knife. She looked at Sam and realized that Sam was doing something with her newly-found powers.

Focus. Move the knife. Summon and focus the power.

The man looked shocked. Suddenly, Sam's eyes opened and her arm raised straight out to the man.

"NOOO!" The man's hand opened and dropped the knife. In his surprise, he accidentally let go of Jandra, and Keddi and Margeria instantly took the advantage. Within an eye's blink, Keddi sent two arrows into his chest. He staggered momentarily, then fell dead to the ground. Sam fell on her knees, violently sick. She cared not, though, as Jandra was alive and safe.

Jandra and Meera went to help Sam, Keddi left to check for survivors and Margeria began to collect the remaining horses. Sam tried to waive away Meera and Jandra, but they insisted on remaining close by, feeling helpless.

Meera tried to lighten the moment, "Who needs weapons when you are around?"

When Sam was finally done being sick, she looked wearily at Meera. "Fine, Meera. We will but hope for an enemy of one from here on."

Meera laughed and thought it good that Sam yet had her sense of humor. Jandra just held Sam's shoulder for lack of knowing what else to do.

Meera looked at her, "Let The Highest rest but a bit, Second. Would you mind collecting the men's weapons? We need to make haste from this place."

Jandra nodded, kissed the top of Sam's head, and left to collect weapons.

"That be most amazing, Sam. As soon as you learn to control that power, you will be a most frightening enemy."

"I think the emphasis be on the word 'if', Meera. 'If' I can learn to control this power."

"Rest for a moment. I will help the others. You will need what strength you have to ride."

They had found ten horses from the Second group, removed their reins, and released them into the wild. They did the same with the remaining of this group, save two. Onto one horse they packed all the collected weapons.

"Meera, do you think any others await us?" Margeria was growing tired, as were they all.

"I hope not, but we must remain on our guard. If we make haste this morn, we might yet make Woden this eve."

Keddi came back into camp with one survivor. The man looked weak and scared, not like the others who were more tough and rugged. This one seemed almost gentle.

Keddi kept moving him forward to Meera, and then made him move to his knees in front of her.

"What is this Keddi? I want no survivors."

"I think his story interesting. I believe he was not part of this group."

"Oh, no, Highest, I wasn't. I belong not to this band of ruffians."

"I am no Highest. Address me not so."

He sniveled, not knowing what to say.

Meera grabbed his hands and looked at them. "They are hard as a fighter's."

"He says he is a blacksmith."

"Then why be you with this group?"

"I was walking to Hengist, and they came across me and made me join their group."

"Walking to Hengist? And you expect me to believe such a story as this? There be no roads."

"Facing death in the wilds is better than what waited for me in Apien. It is but a bed of corruption."

Meera looked at him, wondering what to do with him. "And why should I believe this story? I think you but try to save your own life."

"Let me prove it to you, Highest."

"Call me not Highest or I will slit your throat." She looked at him. "Prove this to me, then."

"May I borrow your sword?"

Her answer was quick, "You jest."

"No, madam. Just hold it out and I will but point out its features for you."

Meera held out her sword. "Keddi, be ready to cut this one's head off if he but makes the wrong move." Keddi nodded. The man rose and looked at the sword.

"See here?" He pointed to where the sword met the handle. "This be but a weak connection. I can do much better to make this sword stronger. Look at the blade. It is uneven in its weight. The weight is all wrong for you. Each sword should be made for its owner. I see you have some of the men's swords on that horse. Can I but show you one of them?"

He didn't wait for an answer but shuffled over to the horse. All of them were now looking at him, and hiding their laughter from Meera. "Look at this one." He pointed to one tied onto the horse's side. "See how this one is tapered in its weight? Yours should do the same. And see the beveling from the middle of the sword out to its sides? Yours doesn't do that. I could make you a wonderful sword. I am a very skilled blacksmith." He smiled at Meera. "You would be most happy with one of my swords in your hand."

Keddi smiled at Meera, "He does not seem a fighter. And he speaks like The Highest has read in her journals."

Meera looked at Keddi, "What?"

"He says the old words like doesn't and wasn't.

Meera had enough of this jesting. She looked at him and raised her sword to him as if to cut off his head. He fell to the ground, whimpering with his hands raised up in fear and weak protection. Meera saw that he was no fighter.

"Why are you walking to Hengist?"

"I heard it a peaceful life that needs skilled crafts-folk. And I want to live in a men's community. I have heard of it many moments along with the women of Woden. Be you the Women Warriors of Woden in the stories?"

Meera looked at Keddi. Keddi simply shrugged her shoulders.

"Women Warriors of Woden?"

Margeria overheard the conversation and laughed, "Yes, good sir, that be us. We are the Women Warriors of Woden and have just killed all the men in these three pitiful groups."

He begged, "Please take me to Hengist. Keep me in chains if you like, but see for yourself my skills. Let me make you a sword and you will see. I can shoe your horses. I can make you the finest door hinges in all the land. I can make you body armor."

"What be body armor?" Margeria wanted to know.

"Plates of metal that help protect you from arrows. Plates that fit to your body."

Meera nodded to Keddi, unhappy that they had a prisoner. She hoped he wasn't lying. Woden and Hengist could certainly use another blacksmith with the skills this one seemed to have.

"Tie him well. I want no trouble from him. We will give him to Briggon to deal with upon our return."

"Oh, thank you, madam highest. You will not be sorry. I am a most excellent blacksmith and will make you the finest sword in all the land. All of you. I will make each of you a special sword made just for you. I will tend to all your personal blacksmith needs. Oh, madam highest, I will but make you the finest—"

Meera looked at him with a frown, "Your mouth overflows as this river. Keep quiet unless you would like to call more enemies to us. And then I would have no choice but to think of you as a trick from the enemy."

He made a motion as if to seal his lips. He was smiling.

"I hope he can ride."

Keddi laughed, "I would wager against that."

"Let us leave quickly for Woden. I want The Highest home by eve."

It was enough of an incentive to quickly complete their duties. They helped Sam onto The Second's horse. Meera took its reins and began leading them back upstream toward their first battle site. Keddi guarded the rear and watched the prisoner, and Margeria volunteered to run along the ledge top as a lookout. Per Meera's desire, she also checked on top for the arrows from the unknown sender. Jandra walked alongside Sam's horse, holding onto Sam's leg, as Sam drooped on the horse, her energy exhausted.

They made it back to the site of the first battle, and found their horses and gear waiting as they had left them. They took but a few moments to gather all the horses together and head out away from the gorge. Within a short while, Meera motioned for them to mount their horses and tie the rest to a lead. They waited for Margeria to descend from the ledge top. As they waited, Meera mounted Sam's horse and sat behind her so that The Highest wouldn't fall on the ride to Woden. Sam was too weak to fight against Meera's protective behavior. When Margeria descended, she shrugged as to the unsolved mystery arrows.

"Nothing? You found no other bootprints?"

She shook her head, "Nothing, although I was certain there would be."

"Nothing? This could not be so."

She shrugged, "I examined everything carefully, but found nothing."

Both Keddi and Meera knew that the sheer number of arrows had been far more than they could have provided, but now saw that the mystery would remain unsolved. Meera led them out of the gorge, finally on horseback. Jandra had been sore from the first turn's ride, but was grateful to finally be leaving the gorge of death as quickly as possible. As they reached the gorge's exit, Meera had Keddi help her move Sam to a fresh horse. Meera then mounted behind Sam and made the horses to race toward home. All through the morn and midturn, the only rest Meera provided was when she changed horses.

As they entered the grasslands, a sentry approached and asked them to hold. Meera jumped off the horse and spoke briefly to her. She then remounted, and the group returned to inside Woden.

As they rode up to The Highest's dwelling, they saw torches lit around it. They all dismounted and helped Sam off her horse. The guards came forward to help, seeing how injured the group looked. Jandra knew them to be dirty, exhausted, and well bruised and injured from their battles.

May came rushing over, "What is wrong with The Highest?"

"She will be fine. Take her to her bed." May followed.

Meera saw Keets and nodded slightly. Keets said, "You have returned from what looks like battle."

Meera nodded, "We killed around forty men these prior turns. They come from Apien. I could not learn of the leader."

Keets put her hand on Meera's shoulder, "All is well here, for now. Go rest. I will have the horses tended to. I see you bring back many weapons and a few new horses." She looked at the blacksmith. "And one prisoner. That be most unlike you, Meera."

"We collected the weapons. I saw them of worth to study and copy. The prisoner is a long story, but he be not a fighter. He was running away from Apien to come to Hengist. He is a blacksmith. I will take him with me for the eve. He can but sleep on the floor, well-tied up. I will take him to Briggon in the morn since I have business with Briggon, anyway."

Caitha came running up and gave Meera a hug. She was crying. "You are hurt. Let me take you home to mend your wounds."

"It be good to see you, Caitha. I have but missed you. We have a prisoner for the eve. Have you enough meal to share?"

Caitha eyed the blacksmith. "A man? In our dwelling?"

Meera whispered to Caitha, "I think him harmless. He be like a pet dog."

Caitha laughed. They then left, arm-in-arm, with the blacksmith trailing behind them.

Jandra turned to Keddi and Margeria. "You have served The Highest and the community well. You will be well rewarded. Go rest. I will send for you in the next turn."

Keddi said, "I owe The Highest my life and have repaid her very little. I devote my life to her safety. Good eve, Second. Rest well."

As Keddi and Margeria left together, Jandra went to Sam's bedroom and found that May and the guards had gotten her safely onto the bed. Jandra saw that she looked to be asleep. It had been a long journey and Jandra had gained much respect for these women. She knew not how to think of Sam, though. No Highest had ever risked so much for her community as this woman, but this woman was her lover, and Jandra didn't wish her to risk so much. She knew that Sam had been correct—the demands of being The Highest would provide much strain on the relationship.

She went to her and moved some of her wild but beautiful hair from her face. Sam was so small, in truth, when standing next to Oisin. Even Meera was much more powerful and taller than Sam. Yet Sam faced her enemies as if she were a giant. Lying here in bed, Jandra thought her to look like a half grown woman. Her face was young in appearance, almost child-like in its innocence, yet Sam had seen more killing and death than the entire community had in a lifespan. Jandra was amazed and delighted that they had become lovers, wondering if their relationship would last.

May came in and startled Jandra out of her reflections, "Second, dear, we must get you prepared for bed. You look to be sleeping on your feet. Let me tend to your wounds."

May helped Jandra out of her riding garments, washed Jandra, tended to her cuts and bruises, and helped her into one of Sam's bedshirts.

"I know not what you wear to bed, Second, but we can sort that out in the morn. All your garments and articles have been moved over. We will speak of where you wish them to be next turn."

May helped Jandra into bed, "I have made it so that you will be undisturbed until you summon me in the morn. Many guards watch over you this eve. If you have need of anything, one waits in the meeting room. All you need do is call. I will return in the early morn."

Jandra laid her head on the pillow and moved her arm to drape across Sam's side. She remembered that May had said something, but couldn't recall the details. She was asleep almost before her eyes closed.

Sam woke in the morning to find herself in her bed, in her bedshirt, with Jandra's arm draped over her. She turned and looked at Jandra, her lover. She touched Jandra's cheek and felt its softness. She saw that Jandra's hair flowed about her, and enjoyed its beauty. She had selected her Second well. Jandra was untrained, but a natural leader and fighter. She reacted quickly and decisively when needed, and Sam felt proud of her. And she had been a most skilled lover in the brief moments they had enjoyed, which delighted Sam even more. And she was unbelievably beautiful, yet somehow slightly different than all the other Woden women.

She unbuttoned Jandra's bedshirt and admired her exposed breasts. She circled them with her fingers, touching them lightly. She bent down to kiss them and gently suck on them. Jandra half-awoke to the strange sensation. She too, like Sam, had very few lovers who had remained through the morn. To awake to such enjoyment was arousing. Jandra moaned softly and moved into the feeling.

In a morn's soft voice, Sam said, "I like your breasts. They are full and soft, and enjoy being caressed."

Jandra thought, *They do indeed.*

She moaned again, softly. She woke enough to move to kiss Sam, pressing her own hands hard and urgently against Sam's breasts. Jandra moved on top of Sam, and lay upon her, kissing her. Sam enjoyed the feeling and gave in to it. Yet half asleep but determined in her focus, Jandra kissed Sam's face, her neck, her breasts, her stomach, and slowly moved down between Sam's legs. Sam protested and tried to move Jandra back up to her, but Jandra acted more forcefully, caressing Sam's breasts while remaining between her legs. Sam quit protesting and began to moan. Jandra had guessed right: Sam was used to more aggressive partners than herself. Jandra thought that she would much like this. The morn went on undisturbed as May had vowed, while Jandra and Sam went in between their intimate physical explorations and sleep, only waking to the touch of the other.

As they lay together, tired but content from their passions, Sam moved so that Jandra lay on top of her, a feeling she well liked. Sam put her arms around Jandra. "Thank you for returning that eve. You allow the morn such that I can face it."

"You are the one who saved my life, Sam, remember? You are the strong one."

Sam laughed, "No, you are the strong one, and you but lied to me. You said you are not as Oisin. I think you perhaps more forceful and strong in my bed."

"*Our* bed, Sam."

Sam touched Jandra's hair and face again, "You are most beautiful. You make me to need you again."

Jandra laughed, "You are a hard one to tire."

Jandra began to move away but Sam pulled her back down. "But it is your fault that you make me desire you. You are overly beautiful. In truth,

I think you have hidden your beauty. And we have had but a short moment together."

"As are you. You make me melt at the sight of you. Your beauty and looks make it so that I can deny you nothing. Your eyes have become mesmerizing. I would find it near impossible to say no to these eyes."

After, while Sam was sleeping again, Jandra rose, tended to her needs, placed on her garments and went into the kitchen to see May.

"Jandra, how do you feel this early midturn?"

"Tired and sore, May. The Highest but wears me out. And be it midturn already?"

May laughed, "I had no chance to forewarn you. Her lovers all have the same complaint."

Jandra also laughed, "Oh, I think I might be able to handle the attention."

Jandra made arrangements for The Highest to visit Hengist, meet with the advisors, and begin the community sessions, and she had arranged with Meera to come over for after midturn meal with Sam. The advisors would be here this after eve meal, and Jandra found herself nervous about the meeting. She went to wake Sam for her meeting with Meera. She saw Sam yet asleep and hated to wake her. From May and Meera, Jandra knew that Sam had little chance for sleep over the prior moon.

As she looked down upon Sam, she yet thought her to sleep like the dead. Sam hadn't moved from the position Jandra had seen her in earlier.

"You need to wake up now, Sam. Meera is coming to join you for the after midturn meal."

She rubbed Sam's head and hair a little, trying to wake her.

She opened her eyes and looked at Jandra, "You are already risen?"

"Long prior. I had many arrangements to tend to. You are meeting with Meera for your midturn meal, and with the advisors after the eve meal."

Sam sat up, "It would be a happier rising if you were but here with me in bed."

"Then we would not be rising but making more a mess of the bed."

"And I would be much more the glad for it."

Sam rose and began to tend to her needs.

"May I attend to you?" She was concerned, seeing Sam as somewhat distant.

"No. It be fine. I can tend myself. Perhaps it will help to clear my head. Be it midturn, in truth?"

"You have not had much sleep of late and well needed it. It be a little beyond midturn and have much to do."

"And I have a Second that could do all this for me. I am not needed. You are The Second and can tend to the advisors, the festival, and Briggon. Are Meera and Caitha yet here?"

"Caitha? I arranged it for you and Meera."

"Not you as well? Why is this, Jandra?"

"Have you not the need for private communication?"

"I will but have to inform you later, would I not?"

"I will tend to it." She began to leave, somewhat perplexed at Sam's foul mood.

"Jandra. Hold but a moment. You need not make my arrangements for me. There are others to do these things."

She sat Jandra down on a chair and sat down next to her. "When I first became The Highest's Second, she would tell me, 'Sam, do not assume what I may or may not want.'" She closed her eyes for a short moment, then looked at her. "You are now The Second of this community and must stand on your own. You have well earned this position and although I am The Highest, you are not my assistant. Lillon and Govan are our assistants and should be here now attending to the issues at hand."

"May has kept everyone away for the turn."

"Then May also assumes, as May will do. Have Lillon attend to your needs the remainder of this turn. But for this meal with Meera, I would much like you and Caitha present."

"Would you like me to cancel the advisors for this eve?"

"No. You are correct; they need to meet. I am certain they have many questions they would like answered. I hope you are ready."

"Are you no longer happy, Sam, as you were this morn?"

"The reality of the turn sets in, and I am just weary. Perhaps a meal would be most beneficial. It has been long since I last ate."

"I will send a messenger for Meera and Caitha and have May prepare for two more. Go sit and wait on the patio. I will be there directly and we can but enjoy the solitude for a moment."

Sam watched as Jandra left the room. She had much enjoyed the morn, but the reality of becoming The Chosen One was beginning to emerge much too soon. The responsibilities the Woman in the Woods told her of were laying with dread on her shoulders. She finished tending to her needs and went to wait on the patio, sitting at the small round table. May had placed some bread and drink there, and Sam guessed that it was for her. She looked around and noticed that everyone was at a distance from her. She focused on the cup as the Woman in the Woods had taught her. *Focus. Concentrate. Think of where you want it to go. See nothing else. Think nothing else. Move the cup.* Sam summoned her power and focused. Slowly, the cup moved a little. Sam raised her hand up off the table and focused on the cup again. The cup began to rise to her hand.

"Sam!"

The cup dropped back to the table and Sam picked it up. Jandra had completed her errand and was coming to meet her, and had seen the cup rising.

"Look at what I have done. What a mess I have made." Some of the wine in the cup had spilled onto the table. "I will get a towel from May," and she got up quickly to do so.

Jandra knew what she had seen and wondered why Sam was trying to keep it from her. She sat down and waited for Sam to return. She thought that they did indeed have much to work out between them.

Sam returned with the towel and began to wipe up the spill. "Jandra, can I but pour you some wine?"

Jandra just looked at Sam with an eyebrow raised, "If you cannot trust me, Sam, perhaps I should return to my own dwelling."

"It be not an issue of trust."

Jandra waited and finally said, "Then explain it to this poor witless brain of mine."

"It be not about you, or about you and me."

She yet frowned, "Does it concern you?"

"Yes."

"Then how does it not concern me as well, then? Do you wish to have a companion or no, Sam? If you do, then we must work through each other's issues together."

"You will have enough burden as Second to carry without me adding to it."

"You are but selfish and witless. And you are overly used to having your own way. May has spoiled you. But you wanted me to remain, Sam, so what will it be?"

"Why do I do this all wrong?"

"Because you *assume* I cannot, should not, and do not want to hear your issues."

Jandra rose and went across to Sam. She put her arms around her and gave her a long and fully passionate kiss. Her tongue explored Sam's mouth so that Sam instantly became aroused. Sam responded and held Jandra in return.

In a seductive voice, Jandra asked, "Would you like me in your bed this eve, Sam?" and she kissed her again in the same way.

After the kiss, Sam was left gasping for air, much surprised, and wanting more. "Of course I would."

Jandra again raised her eyebrow and frowned, "Then, you will begin to work out the other parts of our relationship too, Sam."

Sam sat down, heavily. Jandra could see the burden increasing for Sam, but she knew she needed to help Sam to share more of her burdens with her.

Jandra placed her arms around Sam's neck and held her from the back as Sam was sitting. "I respect you more than any woman I have ever known, even The Highest. I remain in awe of the sacrifices you give to this community. But your burdens are now *our* burdens. If you cannot share them with me, then our relationship cannot work. I am strong, Sam. You have said as much yourself. You must learn to trust me."

Sam reached up with her hands and held onto Jandra's arms. "You are correct, of course. I have been overly solitary for overly long now. You speak wisely. I am selfish and witless, and you are strong. I have long faced—"

Just as Sam was beginning to speak about the burden she so heavily faced, Meera and Caitha walked up. "We have caught you at a tender moment."

Jandra removed her arms and went to sit down. "Welcome, Meera, Caitha. Please sit with us."

Caitha went and hugged Sam, "I am so happy you have finally after these many cycles found someone you want to share your life with."

Sam looked over to Jandra guiltily. Caitha then went and hugged Jandra, "And Jandra, I never dreamed you would finally gather your courage to speak to Sam about becoming your companion. I be so proud of your bravery."

Jandra looked over to Sam guiltily, and they burst out laughing.

Sam looked at Meera, "Sit, my friend. We have much to speak of this turn. Tell me of your blacksmith. Be he a real smith?"

Meera nodded, "I took him to Briggon this morn. Briggon gave him one chance or it was off with his head. Briggon took him to Hengist's smith, Raynod. Do you know of him?"

"I have seen his work and have spoken with him but a few moments."

"Raynod looked at Ivers, our man from prior turn, and told him to make a door hinge. Ivers went straight to work at the bellows and hammered and heated, and hammered and heated, and then produced a fine door hinge. Then Raynod told him to make a horseshoe. He did. And this went on until I left. As I left, as I became most bored, Raynod declared our new man an excellent smith. Had Briggon informed you that Raynod lost his companion but less than a cycle ago?"

"No. I had not heard of this. So, be this a match?"

"So it would seem." Both Sam and Meera laughed. "Then it worth the effort to bring him back. And we can but use another smith."

Jandra looked at Meera, seriously for a moment, "Meera, why is it you want no prisoners?"

Meera looked at Sam, but responded to Jandra's question, "I allow nothing in Woden that could cause potential harm."

Sam also replied, "Meera allowed a prisoner once. That prisoner almost killed me."

Jandra knew that she had asked enough about this and could see it an uneasy issue.

Caitha asked Jandra, "Jandra, may I bring out this new chair to sit in?"

"Oh, you mean the rocker? Certainly, Caitha. It is in the sitting room." She looked to Sam. "We will return quickly."

As they left, Meera took the opportunity to ask Sam, "How did this come to be? Are you well pleased at this companionship?"

Sam nodded, "I had thought of asking Jandra two cycles prior, but had not the courage. She has told me that she did the same. As I am now The Highest, I knew all of you would place much pressure on me for a companion. It is sad, though, that a highest and a Second live in the same dwelling. Do you see this as a problem?"

Meera shrugged, "Both ways, I think. It is easier to guard, but we must remain more alert. If it but makes you happy, then I will but find a way to make it safe for you. Is she attentive to you, Sam?"

"Thank you, Meera. I have enough burdens these turns to not add safety to them." Sam nodded mischievously, "And yes, Meera, she is most attentive and most forceful. I just hope I can manage a constant companionship."

"Meera dear, I would much like a rocker." Jandra and Caitha had returned with Jandra carrying the rocker. "Jandra says that I may rock in it out here. Sam, do you but mind?"

"Of course not, Caitha. Enjoy it much."

Caitha sat in the rocker, "I have long thought you two should be companions."

Jandra was in disbelief. "That not be the truth, Caitha. How would you but know?"

"It be most true. Ask Meera. I have said this upon many, many occasions. Have I not, Meera?"

Meera nodded, "She speaks truly, but then Caitha tries to be Woden's matchmaker."

Sam laughed, "Why not tell me prior, Caitha? Perhaps I would not have remained so dimwitted."

"No, poor Sam. You be The Highest, but of these things you are, in truth, witless. Poor, poor Jandra."

May came out with the meal. "Here be your meal. Eat and enjoy. Remember Highest, your advisors come in but a short while."

They ate their meal and as she had been of late, Sam was famished. She ate everything and got more. The prior turns had left her with even less weight and even she knew she would have to be more careful, so set about eating.

Caitha was surprised at how much Sam could eat. "You eat like a horse, Sam. How do you remain so thin?"

Jandra answered for her, "She eats only once every few turns."

Meera laughed and asked Sam, "Are you certain that you are but ready for a companion?" and then told Jandra, "You know, Jandra, Sam has a past of much rumor."

"Oh, do tell me, Meera."

Sam just looked at Meera with a sneer, "What bad lie do you now spread of me?"

Meera ignored Sam and told Jandra, "It is rumored that no one has been able to fully satisfy The Highest in the bed."

Sam just moaned and Jandra laughed. "May informed me of that same rumor just this turn. So Sam, be this true?"

Sam just blushed and the others laughed.

They ate their meal, laughing and talking throughout, and Sam was glad to have good friends. She knew that Jandra had been correct. She would need to confide more in her, along with Meera and Caitha.

She hoped that their lives would remain calm for a while, but had a dark foreboding that she should enjoy this moment. May returned with plates of sweets and after-meal drinks, and finally informed them that all the advisors were present and waiting.

Elsewhere, across The Realm

She knelt and bowed her head, "My Queen."

"Good, you return. Rise. Tell Me your report."

"She was summoned to the Woman in the Woods."

At first the High Queen said nothing, but looked displeased. After a long moment, she finally spoke, "Pity, as that one is far from The Realm. I will have to deal with that one upon one turn. But at least she will have increased her powers. Did the Spirit halt her weakening?"

"Mostly, Highness. Some remains. She made a male warrior to drop his knife by using her powers, but became sickened directly after. She is a strong warrior, my Queen, and her companions are also strong and most capable. But she thinks of herself as human only."

"Male warrior? She was in battle?"

"On the way to the Woman in the Woods."

She looked angered, "The Woman in the Woods again. She conjured up that legend on her own."

"Legend, my Queen?"

She waived her hand as if dismissing the topic's importance, "The one that tells of great resistance to those that seek entrance into her lands. Stupid legend."

"Yes, Highness."

"How many were in this battle?"

"There were three separate battles, Highness. I counted thirty-nine men against the five of them."

She raised an eyebrow, becoming more interested, "Only five? Are they such strong warriors as this, then?"

Her messenger blushed, "With a little help, my Queen. By the way, Highness, she is The Highest now."

She turned, looking fully at her messenger. "The Highest? What happened to Woden's Highest?"

"She drank from a poisoned vial, Highness."

"Why would she have done such as this?"

"I know not, my Queen. There is some sort of inner conflict within Woden. The new Highest has had many traitors put to their death."

"I met the former Highest once, did I not?"

"Yes, my Queen. You thought little of her abilities. You said that she was overly connected to the Spirits of the Falls."

"Ah, yes. I recall her. A slow thinker, and overly cautious. They will do better without her." She paused for a moment, "So she is now The Highest of Woden. And she is learning of her powers. Tell Me of her companions in this battle of theirs."

"Her force leader is called by Meera. She is most capable and strong. She could serve The Realm most excellently, Highness. The others I know little of, as yet."

"Watch them. Tell Me more of them upon your next report."

"Yes, my Queen. There is something else, Highness."

She raised an eyebrow, waiting.

"She has taken a lover."

She laughed, "So? Can one not have a lover?"

"It is much more complex than this, my Queen. The lover seems different than all the others."

"Why do you say as such?"

"Well, my Queen . . . the lover is exceptionally beautiful. And she has no fear of anything, yet she is untrained. She is as an innocent, but overly intelligent and observant."

She was amused, "Does beauty not occur in Woden, My messenger?"

"Yes, my Queen. It is just that she looks somewhat different."

"Different? In what way?"

"Her beauty is astounding, and her looks remain apart from any other in Woden. And there is something with her and the animals, but I will learn more about this."

"Watch it carefully, then. You know My expectations."

"Yes, my Queen. It shall be as you say."

"Did that awful Buron return safely to his lands?"

"Yes, my Queen."

"Pity. We should have interfered. An accident would perhaps have gone unnoticed. He will take up battle against her soon, I think."

"The Spirits of the Falls already didn't trust you, my Queen. They accompanied him back to his lands."

Chapter IV
Hengist

Meera, Jandra and Sam went to the Meeting Room to find the room full, and everyone eating May's sweets and drinks. As Sam entered, all the women rose and bowed, "Highest," and then nodded to Jandra, "Second." Sam noticed that all the advisors were there except for Treena and Josin.

Sam decided to begin the meeting. "Good eve, all."

"Good eve, Highest."

"I am sorry to say that there is no agenda for this meeting as I had not the chance to prepare for it, formally, but I do have some items for your consideration. The first being the advisors. I know that you have all waited patiently for Jandra and me to but name our new advisors. In truth, Jandra and I have not had a chance to make this determination, but I have an idea I would like to put forth. For many cycles we have had a system of separate advisors with very little contact between them. I would like that practice to halt and to put all the advisors into one group and have a shared system. I would even like you to consider bringing in the Hengist advisors once every moon. What say you on this?" Sam sat down. In truth, she had no idea of what any of them would have to say about this, not even Jandra.

Liley stood up, "In regard to adding the Hengist advisors once per moon, I think this an excellent idea. We are facing potentially dangerous turns before us and we will need to have better, quicker and more assured communication and support from Hengist if we all are to survive. I believe that Hengist would also welcome this change."

Zan asked, "Would all of us be needed, or would some need to leave?"

Sam didn't answer. She had determined to let the group work this out. She just took a cup of tea, then sat back.

Meera looked at Sam and figured out what she was up to, so added, "Woden is growing enough to need all of us, and it would be but good to have Hengist in once per moon. We could but know our needs better across the two communities."

Karan stood, "I have always seen that one thing has influence over every other thing. So if we but make a decision about the gardens, it affects our trade, which affects our supplies, which affects our health, and so on. So I think it better that we all sit together as one. As for Hengist, we need each other, and this way we would avoid over-duplication of produce that we currently have."

Vining looked less agreeing, "I think it a bad idea for both. I believe The Highest should have only advisors that understand that level. Placing all of us together will create far overly many problems. And the number of advisors be way overly high. Bringing Hengist into our meetings would allow just mere *tenants* to have a say in how our community is run."

Fionn agreed with Vining, "We should not allow the power we have be given up."

They argued back and forth over the issue for many moments, when Jandra finally got up, seeing that Sam wasn't going to. She looked at Sam, "I *assume* this would have to be held in another meeting room as there would not be enough room here." Sam said nothing but sipped on her third cup of tea. "How shall we show agreement on this. By vote?"

All the advisors agreed and Jandra held the vote. All but three voted for the ideas. Sam was surprised that there was some dissension, but said nothing of it.

"Thank you. The majority votes yes, so it be done. I would like all of you to think about your duties as advisors. Should we keep the same designations, add more, or reduce? Please bring your ideas to the next meeting. One more item: Festival be upon us and will be here most directly. I had asked a group to handle this, but much has occurred, so, I would like Kandan, Lillon, Jandra and Briggon to work this out. Would anyone else like to volunteer to help?"

Govan raised her hand, as did Tehna.

Sam nodded, "Fine. I will no longer tend to this chore. Jandra, since you are Second, you are now in charge of the festival." She smiled as she sat down, thinking that being The Highest was good in one regard—she no longer had to worry about the details of the festivals.

Sephim stood up and bowed to Sam, "Highest, I would like to raise but two issues once more."

"Go ahead, Sephim. We will all be equals while in our sessions."

"Thank you, Highest. First, I need to remind you about the community sessions. The women need these, and it has been but a long moon since the last one."

Sam chuckled, "It is good, Sephim. I have thought much about this and my place in it. I am The Highest now, but every highest has her strengths and weaknesses and likes and dislikes. The community sessions are but both my weakness and my dislike. I have seen Jandra as a fair-minded and objective judge when it comes to such things. So I am giving this duty to The Second of Woden. Be there any objections?"

Sam looked at Jandra and raised her eyebrow. Jandra would feel free to counter Sam anywhere in their personal life, but never in their professional life. She knew Sam had won this one. And, in truth, Jandra knew that she looked forward to this duty. No one raised any objections.

Jandra said, "I will take this duty, Highest, and it will be my pleasure. In truth, I like such challenges as these complexities. Lillon, will you send a messenger around for two turns hence?"

Sam looked at Sephim, "Sephim, you had one more issue?"

"I do, Highest, but am afraid to mention it again."

Meera laughed, "She growls worse than she bites, Sephim. And besides, she is yet our Sam."

Sephim didn't look certain, but continued, "The festival arrives, Highest."

Sam looked at her and sighed, "And?"

"Highest, it be long past the moment that you consider taking a companion. The women all say that you need one. Your, well, your . . . "

"My what, Sephim?"

"Well, your evening activities are becoming, well, shall I say, most legendary and not as we might need in a Highest?"

Sam looked straight at Sephim with her mesmerizing eyes. Sephim thought that Sam was going to become very angry with her. The women in the room also thought the tension overly much. Finally, Sam laughed while Sephim looked at her, wondering if The Highest had gone crazy. The advisors, in truth, knew not what to think of Sam now, given her eyes and almost glowing appearance.

"I will give it strong consideration, Sephim. Would that but do for now?"

Much relieved, she said, "Oh, yes, Highest. Would you like us to tell you of the available women?"

Sam laughed again, "I will make note to visit with these women on my daily rounds, Sephim. Meera, perhaps Caitha would like to go with me on these rounds?" and she laughed again. Only Meera and Jandra knew why Sam was laughing, and why she had wanted Caitha to go with her. Caitha could match all of these women to each other.

Lillon stood up and bowed, "Highest, Govan and I would like to know if we are to remain as assistants, and if so, which of us is to be your assistant or The Second's?"

Sam shook her head and looked at Jandra, "Jandra, I know not. What say you?"

Jandra took Sam's lead and looked at Lillon and Govan, "What be it that you two might want?"

It was apparent that Lillon and Govan had discussed this issue prior to it being raised. "I am uncertain about remaining an assistant after what occurred with Hern. I know not what others think of me now or if they can but trust me."

Sam saw the courage this took from Lillon and felt sympathy for her. She and Lillon had discussed that the women would need their opportunity to say things to her previously left unsaid.

"Lillon, I cannot speak for others but I can say this: Hern betrayed your loyalty and love. It is a difficult thing, as you and I spoke often about, to care deeply about someone and learn that it is not returned. You have felt it your fault that she hit you. You have felt it your fault that she did not love you. You felt if you had loved her more, she would have remained a true companion and loyal member of the community. You are young and could not see the evil Hern had in her heart. I do not like saying this, Lillon, but I do not believe Hern ever loved you. I believed she used your position to steal her way into the advisor circles. The community knows this as well. They wanted you to act more forcefully against Hern, but I spoke with you often and I know how difficult that would have been. It be not within your character. We all learn from our experiences, and I hope you learn much from this experience about mutual and shared relationships where both companions trust each other." Sam looked at Jandra and wondered how she could ever live up to those words with her, silently hoping she would never betray her, so. "But you did not betray the community in any fashion, and you are an excellent assistant. If I but had the last word, I would tell you to remain as assistant. But this be between you and this group. What is it you would like to do, Lillon?"

Lillon was all but crying, but trying to remain strong, "I would like to prove myself, Highest. And I very much enjoyed working with you prior. If I am but given the opportunity, I would like to be your assistant and prove my loyalty."

Sam sat down. It was the moment Lillon faced the advisors' words on this.

Meera stood and looked at Lillon, "The Highest is our most revered figure in Woden. Sam is my most revered friend in all The Realm. I want an assistant for her that would throw herself into danger rather than see The Highest harmed in *any* fashion." She sat down, but looked angered.

Keets stood, "The assistant to The Highest must be strong and must be able to face down adversity for The Highest. You did not betray the community, but did you face down adversity?" She sat down.

Karan stood, "Lillon, The Highest has done much for this community. She too has lost a companion, but she remained strong and steadfast. How will you demonstrate that you are worthy of this position?"

Liley rose, "I will speak for Lillon. It be truth that Lillon stood by while Hern betrayed all of us. But did we act any faster? When it came the moment to for justice, Lillon attended the execution and spoke not for Hern. All of you were there. You heard Hern crying for Lillon to speak on her behalf. She did not. She has learned, and will prove a worthy assistant to The Highest or The Second."

Govan rose, "I know Lillon well. I know of the many moments she tried to speak to Hern, trying to halt her betrayal. In her way, Lillon fought against what Hern was doing. None of you may have been able to see it, but Lillon fought with all her might to keep her companionship, as be our way, and to halt Hern from betraying the community. I would like to be Jandra's assistant, as we have worked together as the prior Highest's advisors and assistant and know each other well, if she would so accept. And I believe that Lillon was an excellent advisor for The Highest when she was Second." Govan was the oldest woman in the room, and all thought that she had much wisdom and patience. She seldom spoke, but when she did, all would listen.

Jandra looked at Sam and could see that Sam wanted her to make the decision, as Second. Sam thought that since Jandra was going to run the community sessions, this would be good practice.

Jandra rose, "You all speak with much wisdom. Lillon, I myself would have wished more from you in this instance with Hern, but I have also been through many bad relationships that I should have removed myself from sooner. It be not an easy thing. Govan, you are but a light in the fog for us and I think you most patient. Since The Highest seems to be letting us make this decision, I think we should allow Lillon the opportunity to continue with The Highest and prove herself. Govan, I am most indebted to you for offering to be my assistant, but I feel, in truth, the roles will be reversed."

Sam rose, "Then so shall it be. Lillon, please attend me beginning in the morn."

Lillon smiled slightly, "Thank you, Highest. You will not be sorry for this decision."

Meera rose, "Lillon, know this. I will give this my leave without malice and will accept The Highest's and The Second's decisions gracefully. And I will willingly work with you. But if any such thing occurs that endangers The Highest and you have not acted with the most profound haste, you will face me but once."

Sam thought these overly harsh words but also believed it good that Lillon heard what the women had been thinking throughout the event but had remained silent.

Lillon nodded to Meera, "I understand your words. And know that if I cannot do as I need, I also accept the final punishment. But, Meera, I will prove to you my worth and thank you for your truth and acceptance."

Meera nodded and sat down.

Sam thought they had accomplished enough for one eve, "I have but one last item. All of you well know of my daily rounds. I am uncertain if they will remain daily, but I will continue these rounds as The Highest. I also expect Jandra to do rounds. I have learned much from these rounds: I have met with each woman in this community and know their needs, desires and fears. I know who gets along with who, whose dwelling needs repairs, how the water system is working, and every detail in the community. But I am concerned: You, as my advisors, know not these things. And I believe it vital to our community for our leaders to hear of our women's needs and concerns, first-hand." She stood up. "I would like each of you to begin doing rounds. It need not occur every-turn, but I would like you to have a solid presence in the community. I would like our decisions based on the community's needs. You will learn many good things along the way and you will be given many excellent meals and products. I need not Liley or Jenna to do this, however. They see all the women in the gardens and the animal farms. Any objections?" She knew that no one would object to her wishes, but hoped they would want to do this.

Karan said, "I do this but slightly, Highest. I did not wish to take your "rounds" from you in any fashion, so am well pleased you would like all of us to do this."

"Thank you, Karan. I hope all of you will enjoy this as I do. If it comes to be that it is a wasted effort, I hope that you will find a way to share this truth with me. Thank you all for attending on such short notice. We will meet when Jandra sends notice of the next meeting. I will see all of you in the morn as we go to visit Hengist. Good eve."

Everyone said good eve to Jandra and Sam. Sam was amazed that the advisors yet remained unknowing about her and Jandra.

After the last advisor left, Jandra turned to Sam, "So be the rumors true?"

Sam was confused and couldn't remember any rumor mentioned during the meeting. "Who spoke of a rumor this eve?"

"The rumor, Sam. That no one has been able to satisfy The Highest in her own bed."

Sam looked puzzled, and then slowly smiled, wickedly, "Oh, it be not a rumor but highest truth indeed. And it be a grave and sorry tale it tells."

Jandra smirked, "Even Oisin?"

Sam looked at her again, even more impishly, "Even Oisin could but last until early before sun's rise and had to retire to her own bed. Many have tried, but all have failed." Sam shook her head as if in dismay. "It be a sad, sad tale indeed."

Jandra took Sam's hand and began to lead her to the bedroom. "I think this tale of woe and this rumor end this eve."

"Oh? But it be a standing legend I be most proud of."

"Then you must create yet another legend," and Jandra began to unbutton Sam's shirt, "as I aim to satisfy your every need this eve."

"And how will you know?" Sam began to unbutton Jandra's shirt.

"You will finally tell me to hold," and she began to caress Sam's breast.

"Me? Say hold?" and she leaned into the caressing.

"It will be a safe wager," and she made Sam to step out of her garments.

Sam moaned as Jandra pressed harder on her breasts. "What wager would you place?"

Jandra put a hand between Sam's legs. Sam moaned again. "I wager that if you say hold, you will vow to *always* tell me your inner most concerns," and she pinched Sam's breast lightly.

Sam closed her eyes, wanting only to feel what Jandra was doing to her. "And if I do not say hold?"

Jandra kissed Sam long and fully. "You tell me, then," and she moved her hand more in-between Sam's legs.

Sam was dizzy with pleasure. "You will not accompany me into battle."

And Jandra moved Sam to the bed, laid her down and slowly moved her own body between Sam's legs. "It is a deal. Too bad you will lose it, Sam."

Sam moaned and could hardly speak, "We shall see."

The morn came too early once again, but Jandra was sleeping well, as she had won her wager. Sam had finally told Jandra 'no more'. Sam woke first when it was yet early morn. As Second, she had gotten used to many late eves, so morns were not moments Sam did well. As Highest, she thought the same pattern would hold true. She sat up and looked at Jandra. She thought it astonishing to have someone in her life now. *This will take much getting used to.*

She bent down and kissed Jandra's cheek, "Jandra, are you glad you are here?"

Jandra looked through a half-opened eye, "Most likely not at this moment, Sam. Be it the moment to rise already?"

"No. We have a few moments yet. I was but thinking on life."

"You are just regretting that you lost your wager last eve."

Sam ignored her jest, "Do you become concerned over being here, with me?"

"Sam, you are so serious. What be this about?"

"I am not perfect, Jandra. I have lived long alone and have developed most independent ways. It is difficult, I think. Perhaps not so for younger ones, but it be a strange feeling. I worry about being able to be a good companion."

"You mean it feels strange to wake and see someone here yet in your bed?"

"Yes."

"Do you want me to leave?"

"No. I like you here in my bed, our bed. That be not the issue. I most like you being here. It be just strange. There will be much to learn, but I keep doing it all wrong. I thought I used to be a good companion, now I but wonder. It seems to be much easier to give advice than to do the thing yourself."

"It is much change for me as well. You, at least, have remained in your dwelling."

She hadn't thought of that, "Oh, Jandra, do I but make you miserable?"

"No, Sam, I like your dwelling much. It will just take me some moments to get but used to the strangeness, and for you as well."

Sam held Jandra and kissed her gently. Jandra began to touch Sam. "Hold Jandra. I can take no more. I think I will not walk straight for a moon."

Jandra smiled, then laughed, "I jest. Let me help you prepare for our visit to Hengist. This is exciting for me as I have never been to a Hengist community talk."

Sam tilted her head sideways, "Be that the agenda? I knew not of this."

Jandra was startled, "My apologies. I thought I but informed you. The men of Hengist would like to honor you at a town meeting this turn."

"It be not a problem. It is only that I knew not. I thought we were just visiting their craftsmen this turn. It be good, though. We can but tell them that we would like to make them more a part of our advisors."

* * * *

Hengist was joyous with excitement, much of the community waiting at the gates for her arrival. As she came, several could no longer contain their excitement.

"The Highest comes."

"She has arrived."

"She is here. The Highest is really here."

It had been long since the former Highest had visited Hengist. Sam had known that The Highest seldom visited Hengist, but thought it due to Hengist's wishes. Sam, Jandra and all the advisors had walked over across the bridge, and were now waiting at Hengist's gates.

They were met by Briggon, "Highest." He knelt, then bowed his head to Jandra, "Second."

"Briggon, this is a fine turn for a visit. Thank you for allowing us this opportunity."

"Highest, it is our pleasure, indeed. Please follow me through the gate and you will but see. We hope this begins a new era for us with Woden and but hope you will come more often."

The gates were opened and Sam saw the path lined by the men, many holding banners. When they saw The Highest, they knelt and the musicians began a welcome fanfare. Sam was fully surprised, as were all the advisors.

She leaned over toward Jandra and whispered, "Why all this ceremony? It be just us."

"We have not visited Hengist in a very long while."

Sam looked at Jandra with surprise, "I but thought that The Highest and her advisors visited every moon."

Jandra shook her head, "No. The Highest had some difficulty with Hengist, so chose not to visit with them often."

"How did I not know of this? Hengist be our friend and ally, are they not?"

"Of course, Sam, but The Highest had her desires that we followed."

She saw Briggon looking at them with concern, "We will speak of this later."

Sam wasn't happy with this knowledge, and upset that she hadn't known of it, but decided to wait until later to pursue it. Sam bowed and smiled slightly to the men and followed Briggon down the path. She saw that the men were dressed in their finery as if this a celebration.

Briggon turned to Sam, "Your presence has made this a special turn for us and we have many events planned for you. I hope you will but like and enjoy them."

As they continued down the path, the men began to follow after them. Sam wondered why The Highest had chosen to ignore Hengist.

Briggon led them to Hengist's outdoor theater and showed them their seats, "Our actors would like to present this play for you in your honor. They have worked hard on it and hope you most enjoy it."

"A play, Briggon? I have not seen a play in a long while. I will most enjoy this."

"I hope so, Highest. The former Highest disapproved of plays."

Sam held her tongue but thought that also the reason why there had been no plays presented in Woden for many cycles. She hadn't ever seen a play presented in Hengist's theater and began to wonder as to why.

The play was a reenactment of the recent betrayal by the spiritual leaders in Woden, the attempted murder, The Highest's suicide, Sam's rise to Highest, the execution of the traitors, and a concluding speech of Sam speaking to a return of benevolence between Woden and Hengist. Sam recognized the play for what it was: Hengist's view of Woden's most recent events and a political message, but she had enjoyed it and thought it an excellent way for her people to have voice. As the audience was clapping and shouting their approvals, the actors, Hengist's advisors and Briggon all watched for Sam's reaction. They went unnoticed by her, but were well pleased when she clapped and genuinely smiled at the actors.

Briggon came up to Sam, "Highest, did you enjoy our play?"

"It was wonderful, Briggon. I would like it much if your men would perform it again for the Women of Woden. Perhaps it could be done at this next Festival?" She looked at Jandra for approval since Jandra was on the festival committee.

Jandra nodded to Briggon, "Briggon, The Highest would like this to happen. Would this be acceptable to your men?"

Briggon was delighted. He ran down the stairs to the stage and asked for the audience to hear him for a moment, "The Highest was so delighted with our play that she has asked if we would but present it for the Women of Woden at this next festival. What say you?"

The men stood, clapped and shouted their approvals. It was clear they were extremely pleased with The Highest's wishes. Briggon went back up to The Highest and led her to their next event. Hengist had set out all their crafts and wares in their park. The musicians were playing, storytellers were telling stories, and in general, it was a celebration. Sam went from table to table, inspecting and enjoying the many crafts so different, and generally much better than Woden's. She once again wondered why there seemed to be a closing down between these two communities. She had assumed, wrongfully, that there was an open exchange of crafts and products.

"Jandra, some of these craftsmen are most talented. Why do we not have them teaching our own women?"

"The Highest wanted no open trade between Woden and Hengist."

Sam looked with frustration at Jandra, but chose not to respond with so many people standing near her. She could see that even her own advisors were clearly puzzled by things they were seeing. They had all been given wine as they walked around enjoying all the tables of pottery, weaving, artists, candles, soap makers, garment makers, medicines, and all the others, including some new foods that Sam tried and liked. It was as if it were a festival.

After visiting at all the tables, listening to all the musicians and storytellers, and watching all the jugglers and such, Briggon asked, "Would this be a good moment to begin the town meeting, Highest?"

"Of course, Briggon. We are here at your schedule. You but tell us what to do and we shall be glad to please."

Briggon led them to a prepared place in their park where all the men began gathering. Sam and her advisors were asked to sit on a wooden stage, very low to the ground. The men sat on the grass in front of the stage.

"If it meet with your approval, I can but begin the session, but the men have many issues and questions."

"That be fine, Briggon."

As soon as Sam and her advisors were all settled on stage, Briggon began, "Men of Hengist. Our Highest of Woden and Hengist, of all of Woden Falls, is here this turn to hear you. As do you, I too hope this marks the beginning of a new era for us between Woden and ourselves. The Highest and her advisors are ready to begin our town session."

One man rose, meekly, then knelt, and rose again, "Highest. We thank you much for coming and hope you have enjoyed yourself. But we would like to know why there is not open trade between us and Woden."

As he sat, another man knelt, rose and asked, "Why have we been shut out of Woden?"

And on and on it went for many, many questions, "What can be done to improve our relations to Woden?" "Why can we not share more plays and entertainment?" "Why can we not have a voice in the politics?"

Sam was deeply surprised. She had no idea that the former Highest had closed so much between the two communities. She felt enraged but masked her feelings for fear the men would think her angry with Hengist.

She looked at Jandra, "Is what they ask be true, Jandra?"

Jandra looked embarrassed, "Yes, Highest. It be most true."

Sam frowned, "Then it be a wonder that they help us at all in battle. These are good men."

She looked at her own advisors and found them amazed as well. She wondered what The Highest's advisors had been doing these past few cycles and was regretting including them all as her advisors now.

Sam rose and went to the front of the stage and stepped off onto the grass. The men were all shocked and all got up to kneel, for they didn't know what else to do. No Highest had gotten this close to most of them prior.

"Please sit. I have little, but much to say."

She waited for them to sit. "Thank you, Men of Hengist, for your most gracious warmth you have displayed this turn. I have had a most enjoyable turn and hope you will invite us often. As I stand here as Highest, I am taken by surprise at many of your questions and issues. I will but attempt to answer them all. As Highest of all of Woden, I think of Hengist as part of Woden, a counterpart to our women. I see no reason we should not share in our entertainment, as it be an excellent way to provide voice to the communities. That open trade has halted occurring be but a surprise to me. As of this turn, I assign Ghett, Ghada and Alain to the task of opening the trade between us. They will meet with Briggon next turn to ensure this within five turns. You have my word as Highest on this. And as of this turn, I assign Lillon, Govan and Sephim to the task of opening entertainment between our two communities."

All the men cheered and clapped.

"Woden and Hengist share lands, rulers, produce, trades and strength. You give and provide much to Woden, and we are deeply indebted to your display of loyalty and courage. As my advisors and I meet, once per moon, so shall Hengist attend. Briggon has agreed to come with his advisors to join together with Woden's so that we are all informed. Woden and Hengist will decide our future, together."

Once again, the men cheered and clapped.

One man stood up, and knelt. He waited to be recognized.

Sam walked over to him and placed her hand upon his head, "Rise, gentle man. You have no need to kneel so on my behalf. I am but your servant. What be your name?"

He continued to kneel, "Oh, no, Highest. You are most deserving of this recognition. You have made me but a happy man. I am called Gerild. It has been long since we have seen happiness and promise in a highest's face."

"Rise, Gerild, and speak to me as a community member of Woden Falls."

He rose but kept his head bowed, "Highest, if it would please you, you would do us great honor to visit us at least once per moon. We would celebrate each visit and make you feel most welcome."

Sam looked at him with sadness, "It be an easy enough request, but it makes my heart sad to think you yearn for so little and receive much less. Briggon and I will make it so, Gerild. Let me but ask you a question, if I may?" She turned to Briggon, "And I will count on Briggon to assure your honesty. In order for me to know my women and their lives and needs, I walk around the community visiting so that I may know them each. Would you be open to this type of visit? Briggon, perhaps you might accompany me in such rounds? And perhaps my advisors may do as well?"

Meera rose and walked over to Sam, "Highest, we must ensure your safety on this."

Sam looked at her and smiled, "Then you will attend with me, Meera, along with Keddi and Margeria." She laughed, "Is this acceptable to Hengist, or would it be best to keep the visit more formal such as this turn?"

Another man rose to kneel, then another, and another until every man was kneeling before Sam. Briggon knelt and said, "Highest, it be beyond our hopes and dreams that you speak of such this turn. We have never prior been recognized in this most pleasing of fashion. You do us but great honor."

Sam turned to Lillon and Govan, "Please make this so. To begin in no more than ten turns." They nodded in agreement.

Briggon came forward, "Highest, we have a gift for you and Meera. Should your other advisors wish such a thing, we will arrange it so."

The blacksmith whose life Meera had spared came over. He carried two swords. He knelt before Sam and Meera and held out the swords.

Sam said, "Ivers, rise and present me my sword."

He rose, smiling, "Highest, I have made this special for you. It is of a size and balance that fits your height and strength. You will be able to wield this mightily." He gave it to her and Sam admired its beauty. He held out the other to Meera, "Meera, who spared me my life, this be a most special sword. I hope you find it worthy of your ability as a Warrior Woman of Woden." Meera took it, turned to Sam, and they played with the swords for but a moment, trying out their weight and balance.

All the men were astonished, but began clapping, cheering, and showing approval of the playfulness between them in such a setting.

Meera turned to Ivers, "It be well your life was spared. This be a most excellent sword and I thank you for it."

Sam nodded to Ivers, "Thank you. I will treasure this gift." She turned and gave it to Meera to carry for her.

Briggon stepped forward once again, "The community of Hengist has had a most productive cycle in its wine yards. As a show of thankfulness to you and all your advisors, we are sending over to each of you twelve flasks of our best wine. We have heard that your crop was not as productive so know that you are low on supplies. We will also be able to supply the wine needed for the next festival. Highest, we send over fifty flasks for you and your affairs."

"We thank you much Briggon and Hengist, and as you know, we will most enjoy your wine. We must now take our leave, but as vowed, we will visit to walk our rounds most frequently. We will no longer be strangers."

Briggon and all the men accompanied them while the musicians played all the way to the gates, and the men danced and shouted in merriment over a most successful visit. As the gates closed behind them, Sam's advisors chatted with each other, including Jandra who was speaking with Ghett about trade. Meera noticed that Sam was walking alone and not much pleased.

"Sam, you be unhappy, yet this seemed a most successful visit for us, did it not?"

"Oh, Meera, you surprised me. Yes, I am most pleased at its outcome. It is good to strengthen this relationship I think."

"Then why be you sad?"

She looked at Meera as they walked, "I am not sad, Meera. I am angry. How has this come to be that Hengist has been so excluded?"

"We could ask the former Highest's advisors. They should but know."

"Yes, Meera. I agree with you. I *know* they know, and that be what bothers me."

Meera halted briefly because of the thought in her head, "Sam, you are not but thinking that there is more to this recent betrayal than we know?"

Sam shook her head, "I know not, Meera, but I continue to wonder why The Highest was so quick to take her own life. It makes not any sense to me. She well knew that we would be able to save her."

"You could ask Jandra."

"You are correct, I could."

Meera saw hesitation in Sam, "But you know not if you be yet able to trust her?"

"Oh, Meera. I am a most awful companion. If I cannot but trust her, then why am I with her, and why then would I have chosen her as Second?"

"Perhaps it was because she was with Josin for a short while that you have some hesitation?"

"I think the former Highest's advisors will have to earn our trust. Until then, we cannot trust any of them."

"Perhaps that be wise, Sam. Could you not use your strange power on Jandra to ensure of her loyalty?"

Sam looked doubtful, "And how would you feel if I but did this to you, Meera?"

"I would understand, Sam."

Sam nodded slowly, "Yes, I think you would, Meera, and that is why you are my best and most trusted friend. We fight together and trust each other with our lives."

"Perhaps you should think about that, Sam. Perhaps it might be but a good discussion to hold with Jandra. You might consider giving her the opportunity to tell you of this. Perhaps there have been no good moments to do as such."

Jandra had come up and overheard her name and asked in jest, "What bad things are you but saying about me, Meera?"

Meera simply nodded and said, "Second," and dropped back with the other women.

Jandra looked at Sam quizzically, "Sam, be something wrong?"

Sam smiled at Jandra and took her arm, "No, Jandra. All is well. It has been but a long turn and I have many thoughts in my head. Do you think the visit a good one?"

"It was wonderful, in truth. It will mean much for the women, also. And some of their crafts were much improved from ours. It is good to begin a new era."

As they reached the community's gates, Sam bid good eve to all her advisors, and she and Jandra went to their dwelling.

"Would you like some tea?"

Sam nodded, and they went to the kitchen. As Jandra began to prepare their tea, Sam stood at the window, looking out toward the river. As Meera had suggested, she had decided to give Jandra the chance to tell all she suspected of the prior Highest's advisors.

"Jandra, I have been but wondering about The Highest. Do you not think it odd that she killed herself so quickly when she but knew that we could save her?"

Sam turned slightly to see Jandra's reaction but saw nothing.

"Tell me why this be puzzling you, Sam."

"Because it was done overly quickly. There must be another reason for The Highest to have done as such. It makes little sense."

There was a long silence between them, and Sam thought she could feel the tenseness between them grow.

Sam turned around and looked at her, "Have you not found it strange that Hengist had been shunned by The Highest?"

Sam saw Jandra sigh and hang her head slightly.

She waited another moment, then asked, "Jandra, why do you hesitate?"

Jandra turned away from the counter and looked fully at Sam for a long moment. Sam saw that her eyes looked deeply burdened. Jandra's words were slow, "Although I had hoped Woden's troubles were finally over, I see that my prior suspicions lie deeply within you, as well. Sit down, Sam. I think it the moment I tell you of why I took over the prior Highest's advisor meetings."

Sam sat on the long bench and listened as Jandra told the amazing tale. When she was done, Jandra again lowered her head and sighed, "I am sorry I did not prior tell you this. It has been hard to determine the amount of damage that was done, but more than this, it is hard to determine if it continues. I keep hoping that the others who were involved have reformed."

She looked up at Sam, her face showing her sadness, "I should have told you this, prior. I am sorry, Highest, for not doing so."

"There be no need, Jandra. You knew not who to trust in all those moments, and surely could not have come to me, for even I could have been part of that corruption. I had guessed that The Highest might have been blackmailed, but could find no evidence to this. But now we must undo all this treachery, fully."

Jandra was deeply troubled, "I wanted to inform someone, but as The Highest stepped down, I didn't think such knowledge would benefit the community to know of her betrayal of them."

"I would have done the same, and you are most correct in this. This knowledge will fall most heavy on all of Woden. She was well respected. But now we must repair all the prior deception. I must but speak to the guard for a moment."

Sam went and spoke to the guard. The guard nodded, replaced herself with another nearby guard, and went off on her errand.

When Sam returned, she saw Jandra sitting at the table, her head propped-up in her hand, looking like all the burdens of Woden had crashed fully upon her.

* * * *

She placed her hand on Jandra's shoulder, knowing it wouldn't remove her defeated feeling, but hoping to supply some support, "In truth, Jandra, given the depth of the deception, I also would not have told anyone. In your position, who could I have told?"

She looked up at her, her eyes moist, "Oh, Sam. I was hoping you would never have to know." Sam saw that she looked beaten.

Sam went suddenly cold at the thought of what Jandra had told her. "Prepare yourself, Jandra, for I have summoned for the advisors."

Jandra thought Sam looked sadder this moment than when she had lost Brett. She could see that Sam was indeed deeply saddened to learn that the betrayal of the community had also included The Highest. And she knew all the others would be, as well.

Sam went to the meeting room to find the advisors and assistants present. Meera stood on the side, knowing fully that if Sam called a surprise meeting this late, it was for good reason. Sam noticed that Meera had brought her sword, but had hidden it behind herself. She nodded to Meera, a sign to be on alert. Jandra came in after Sam, looking deeply burdened. Meera took quick notice of it. The guard Sam had sent had awoken the advisors and told them it was a most urgent meeting.

"What is wrong, Highest?"

"Are we under attack?"

"Did someone die?"

"Are you ill?"

Sam raised her hand for silence, "Thank you for coming. I will explain why I have summoned you here."

She sat down, "As you are aware, we visited with Hengist this turn. During the visit, many questions were raised that I could not answer. "Why had The Highest not visited with Hengist, as be our agreement?"

Meera looked around the room, watching the women's reactions to Sam.

"And why do we no longer have open trade with Hengist, as is our law?"

Sam watched the women she suspected. "Why has entertainment between the two communities been halted?"

"And why did The Highest kill herself overly quickly when she knew we would but save her?"

Jandra kept her head bowed, ashamed that she hadn't told this tale to Sam well prior to this moment. Sam was The Highest and should have been informed, perhaps even when she had yet been The Second. Jandra felt she had let down the community.

"Keets, can you but answer those questions for me?"

Meera was shocked, but held it in. She saw that Sam knew something she didn't, and had learned not to trust many women long prior. She would trust Sam over Keets any turn, *But Keets?*

"Why, Highest? What do you mean? Why do you but ask me?"

Sam looked at Fionn, "Fionn, would you care to answer these questions for me?"

"Perhaps The Highest was overly ill to continue, so killed herself instead of being taken hostage."

Sam nodded, "That be exactly what I had thought, Fionn, but then I remembered a conversation of late that I had with her. She said she was looking forward to stepping down and spending her last cycles in peace. She knew she had not long to live, but she had some things she yet wished to accomplish."

She looked around the room slowly, then settled on one advisor in particular. "Vining, perhaps you could answer these questions for me?"

Vining shook her head nervously, "No, Highest. I know not of what you ask."

"If Treena be here, I would but ask her as well. But I will ask one of my own advisors instead. Kandan, what can you tell me of my questions?"

Kandan suddenly began to cry. Meera was surprised at how many Sam was pointing to, but toward what, she had no clue. But Meera was stunned. *Even Kandan?*

Sam turned to Govan, "Govan, since I know you as all-knowing, perhaps you would answer my questions?"

Govan turned white and shook her head, "No."

Meera began to worry. There were no guards inside the meeting. It would be only her if something were to occur.

Even though no one was answering Sam's questions, and everyone was claiming innocence, Sam waved her hand as if it didn't matter, "While I would much like these answers, I know that Oisin will get them from the two sentries that say they found Keddi at the grasslands."

There was a momentary silence, then suddenly, Fionn jumped up and rushed toward Sam, trying to get close enough to kill her with her concealed knife. "Noooo!"

As Meera moved to halt Fionn, her worse eve visions came true. She had moved slightly so as to intercept Fionn, when she suddenly saw Vining draw a knife and move toward Sam.

Pandemonium abruptly ruled the room.

Meera drew her sword and moved to intercept Fionn while hoping to halt Vining with her body. But as suddenly, Lillon threw herself in front of Vining, while Jandra hurtled herself upon Fionn. By the moment Meera and the others halted Vining and Fionn, Lillon and Jandra were lying on the floor, well injured. Meera's guards had been alerted through the shouting, so were now inside holding Fionn, Vining, Keets, Kandan and Govan at sword point.

The remainder of the advisors were looking to Sam for an explanation, but Sam was more interested in tending to Lillon and Jandra. Liley, who was with Lillon, told Sam that Lillon would live, but would require much care, as the knife had entered her ribs deeply.

Sam looked at Jandra, seeing the knife deep within her midsection. She knelt down to her, "Why did you do as such? Woden needs you, Second."

Jandra knew she was dying, but cared little over it. She smiled weakly, "At least you know my tale of guesses to be but truth, now. At least you have allowed me to see that all of Woden's deception is now fully over, before I die."

"You cannot die as yet, Jandra."

Jandra placed her hand on Sam's arm. She was beginning to see only darkness, and tried to hold tightly to what she could yet see of Sam's blue eyes, "Worry not over me, Sam. You are The Highest, and Woden clearly needs such as you."

Sam rose and went to Meera. She placed her hand on her shoulder, "More than any prior moment between us, I now trust you will know what to do, my friend. Forget not my prior meetings with the mystic ones."

Meera looked at her questioningly and had absolutely no notion of what Sam meant.

"I am sorry to put this burden on you, but it must be done. Act quickly, but hold steady to that all my trust is within your great abilities."

Sam then returned to Jandra and sat down on the floor next to her. Jandra looked at her, but as if she could no longer see her, "Sam? Is it you? I am sorry."

Sam said, "I know this as truth, Jandra. But you will not leave me as soon as this. We yet have a lifespan before us." She placed her hands on Jandra's stomach and focused, well knowing from the Woman in the Woods that using the power to save a life demanded a life.

Focus.

She heard Jandra speak to her, "No, Sam, it will kill you. I can hear it in your mind, and my life is not worth yours." Everyone heard Jandra say, "NO, Sam!"

Focus. Sam blocked out Jandra's thoughts.

Sam's hands suddenly jumped away from Jandra, and Sam passed out, falling to the floor from where she sat with Jandra. Jandra, all but healed, moved to pick up Sam and hold her head in her lap. She knew Sam was now dying, and thought it should be her. She just rocked Sam back and forth, crying softly. She kept crying, "No. Not Sam."

The eve was a long sad vision to Jandra and Meera. Meera was unsure what to do or think about Jandra, but focused more on Sam. She loved Sam to the very core of her heart and couldn't stand the thought of losing her.

She went to Jandra, "This is what she told me prior to healing you."

Jandra listened intently to the tale, then nodded, "Then that is what must be done."

Meera nodded, finally understanding, then called for Keddi and Margeria.

When they came, she told them the errand, "Find the old raggedy one, or the Woman in the Woods. Find one of them and bring her back, quickly. Tell her their Chosen One be dying. Run like the wind."

Keddi and Margeria didn't hesitate, and took two guards with them. Meera hoped they could find one of the Spirit Mothers, and quickly so. But she knew it would be more than difficult to find either, if not impossible.

They moved Sam to her bed, where she lay barely breathing. It was the most lifeless Meera had ever seen in a living one, and could barely contain the rage she felt inside. Jandra couldn't move easily, but no longer cared. Sam had healed most of her wound, and the rest could easily heal itself, but Jandra wished it were her dying instead of Sam. Meera could take no more.

Leaving Sam in May's capable care, Meera went to Jandra, yet in the meeting room, "Tell me what you know of this, Jandra. I must know."

Jandra looked slowly up to Meera, her mind yet numb from the recent occurrences. She didn't feel she could even breathe, but nodded.

"I only guess much of this, but have pieced the following together. In truth, until this turn, these were but guesses and suspicions in my mind. About four cycles prior, Fornaith, what we now know as the place with King Buron, came to meet with The Highest. They asked The Highest to give some of Woden's women to them, for their men, in exchange for her own dwelling and many servants. At that moment, she must have said no to the offer. Then, according to Josin, another leader came, from yet another community. But this leader was someone from another race than ours, and someone with mystical powers. I prior thought this foolishness, but now after seeing Sam's powers, see it far differently. At first I thought these were two separate events, but that did not come to be as so.

"The Highest called her the High Spirit Mother, and said that she came from fire. Josin told me that this Spirit Mother wanted The Highest to also give her the women in Woden. Josin said she offered a very high price and gave The Highest many presents. According to Josin, The Highest took the presents, but yet said no to the offer. At the moment, I thought Josin was lying. In all ways, the story sounded unbelievable, as it yet does.

"But Josin said that Buron and this High Mother became angered that The Highest would not agree to their bargain, and Buron then threatened war upon Woden if The Highest did not comply.

"They must have met again, I know not when or where, and the High Spirit Mother said she would take but one child from all of Woden, and that this would be enough to save Woden, if The Highest but agreed to the exchange. It was at this moment that I became confused, as another tale told of a High Priestess who said that she would prevent war on us if we would only give to her a long-lost sister. Josin spoke of each of them, but seemed to have little regard for the High Priestess woman. I know not of either of these and never met them.

"The Highest, apparently well worried, told Josin of this, or so Josin said. She also made the mistake of telling Josin that she had already accepted many gifts from this High Spirit, thus obligating herself and all of Woden to them.

"Josin has long wanted to be The Highest, so used this knowledge against The Highest. I never knew this, but it was my guess that The Highest was being blackmailed. And now this eve, I just learned that Sam also thought this." She hung her head, "I wish I had been able to make sense of all this, but yet have overly many questions remaining."

She took a deep breath and began again, "I knew not that Josin wanted to be The Highest until she told me of such, but then it made much sense. That was the eve I kicked her out of my dwelling. She must have told the Spiritual Leaders of this story, and together they must have devised their takeover of Woden and Hengist, thinking that this High Spirit Mother would help them once they gained control. Josin had long wanted a mixed-community for all the riches the women of Woden would bring as slave trade, as well as the men of Hengist, also as slaves. She now saw her opportunity. Buron, apparently, just desires the women for his men.

"Josin must have then made her move on The Highest. Instead of killing her directly, with some secret arrangements through Keets, a message must have been sent to Apien and New Harborage saying that Woden was now open and receptive to providing women to their men.

"That must be how the plot for poisoning The Highest began. Josin must have asked in exchange for the Women of Woden, that Apien and New Harborage provide a way to kill The Highest and make it look an accident. I know for truth, as you must also recall, that they invited The Highest to a ceremony. I know that Josin encouraged The Highest to attend, and The Highest did. I argued strongly against it, but The Highest listened not to me. This must have been when The Highest was poisoned.

"Vining and Fionn are involved as well. To what degree, I know not. Keets supplied the messengers and sentries for Josin's needs. For what reason, I know not. Kandan had been friends with Vining, who must have shared the story with her, but I know not to what extent Kandan was involved. I do know that Kandan supported the idea, agreeing that The

Highest a weak leader. I heard her say as such. Treena never wanted such a betrayal, but knew not how to go against Josin.

"When The Highest discovered she had been poisoned, she must have guessed that Josin was trying to kill her. It would have been the only logical choice, but I think it may have surprised her to think that her favored Josin was turning against her. My guess be that she then wanted to publicly and quickly place Sam in as Highest so as to seek revenge on Josin and the Spiritual Leaders. She probably thought that Sam might be able to stand against this Buron and the High Mother, especially knowing that Sam was the Chosen One. I know this not for certain, but I did see a change in The Highest toward Josin around the same moment she began to make Sam The Highest.

"Two cycles prior, I began to see something wrong between The Highest, the Spiritual Leaders, and Josin. Josin, rather than risking me finding out, decided to act as if she but wanted me as her lover. I believed her and we began our affair." She hung her head again, shaking it heavily from side to side, "I cannot believe that I took that woman to my bed."

She sighed, then began again, "Slowly, each moment we spent the eves together, she would tell me these stories of how much more was out there in The Realm, awaiting us. Of how many riches there were for the taking, in The Realm."

She looked up at Meera, "In truth, Meera, for all my lifespan, I but believed that Woden Falls was the largest and strongest community in all The Realm. And never did I know of such things like these mystic powers they speak of." She shook her head again, "And now we learn things such as the Woman in the Woods, and this raggedy one."

She placed her hand to the knife wound, feeling it throb, but ignored it, "Josin kept telling me that should we agree to this partnership with Buron and the High Mother, Woden would become the main center in The Realm. She often invited Woden's Spiritual Leaders to my dwelling so that they would tell me of the same things, and that this mighty Buron and High Priestess but wanted us and needed us as their appointed leaders in The Realm. She told me that we needed to unite with this High Spirit Mother and Buron to stand against some evil queen of some valley, but I know not who they spoke of. Yet another mystery.

"The eve I finally kicked Josin out of my dwelling, she had threatened that if I did not follow her ways, I would be considered as a traitor. I told her that if she continued on this path that I would have no choice but to inform the community."

Meera remembered well the yelling and the words spoken, but knew not the context at the moment. She had been there, summoned by her guards, to ensure that the breakup between Josin and Jandra remained unphysical. She hadn't needed to intervene, but now recalled the words Jandra was saying.

"It was at that moment that I began trying to control the advisor meetings so as to prevent their takeover. They had nothing over me, so could not control me, and I kept threatening to inform the community of their plans. I knew not, though, that they were but blackmailing The Highest. Through their threats, The Highest began to cut-off communication and trade to Hengist, more-or-less enslaving the men prior to a takeover, or protecting them. I never could figure out which. I can only guess that Keddi had learned of the plot and came to tell of it and to bring the antipoison. I later learned that Josin had prepared some of the sentries, and that three from Apien had followed Keddi to prevent her from reaching The Highest."

Meera interrupted, "So Keets volunteered to remove Josin's heart to silence her."

Jandra nodded, "I know this not, but so it would seem. I should have informed you and Sam of this story, but knew not who to trust. And in all truth, it sounded overly crazy to believe. When The Highest died and Josin and the Spiritual Leaders were executed, I thought it but over. I knew not that Fionn and Vining would make such a move now that Josin be gone."

She looked up at Meera, "And I have no idea of what to think of this Buron, the High Spirit Mother of Fire, or this High Priestess. It would seem, as Sam has said, that the betrayal of Woden runs most deep. I can only guess as to what this means for Woden, though, for if there are truly this many in The Realm, and with such powers and abilities, we are well unprepared for such."

"What of this story of a child?"

"The High Spirit Mother wanting one of Woden's children? Is this your meaning?"

"Yes. Why a child from here?"

Jandra shrugged, "I know not, and I know not who."

Meera placed her hand on Jandra's shoulders, "That you held fast speaks well for you, Jandra. It be not easy to know who can be trusted through such events, and you knew us not well enough to do so. This is a most complex tale involving many more than we have guessed. And, in truth, you should not have informed Sam as you knew not the depths of her abilities or commitment."

Jandra held in her sobs, but cried quietly, "But I should be dying instead of Sam. If she had but known all this, she would have removed all those involved. I but thought they had changed and fixed their ways now that Josin was gone, and perhaps they have. In truth, I know not about Keets, Kandan and Govan."

Meera had the hard look of a warrior in her eyes, "Nor do I, but we will soon find out."

Meera looked out to see the sun's rise, "It is finally the morn, and we have traitors to which we must now tend. One of them will tell me who be this High Spirit Mother, and whatever else there is to know, if you will but give me your leave to do as I must."

Jandra didn't hesitate, "Do as you must. I will come with you." Jandra looked sadly into Meera's eyes, "What will we do about Sam? We cannot lose her, Meera."

"May is tending to her, but let us hope that Keddi's search be successful. I will not give up easily, Jandra. But for now, let us tend to her would-be assassins."

Meera walked with Jandra out to the grasslands where Keddi had been found. Meera had already arranged with her guards to have the prisoners taken there. She carried her sword and offered Sam's for Jandra's use.

"Fionn and Vining die this morn."

"Be this why you give me Sam's sword?"

"No. Unless that be your wish. They will die through torture until I find out what we must know. Then we will cut off their heads and leave them for the animals."

"What about Keets, Kandan and Govan?"

"That depends on what we learn from them. I will torture them until I learn this truth. This be a deep betrayal of Woden. To learn that the former Highest was involved will shock the community. We need Sam at this moment, as she will be a great Highest. Your story explains much to me, though. It explains why Sam was kept so distant from The Highest's advisors."

"It was almost as if she were protecting Sam, and perhaps Hengist, through isolation."

"I also thought as much as I listened to your story. I know she thought much of Sam. How be your wound?"

"It hurts some, but I will not complain. It will heal and at this moment the pain reminds me of Sam."

They walked the rest of the way in silence. As they came to the site, Jandra saw all of Meera's guards present. She knew this to be unusual.

"Meera, are all your guards here this turn?"

She nodded, "They have risked much lately because of these traitors. It be their right to this. These are very loyal women to this community and have much rage from what has been done. You cannot know how much these guards respect Sam. That Sam lies dying, they blame on these traitors. I will allow them their due this turn. I hope your stomach be strong. These women will expect it so and will want no mercy for these traitors, especially Vining and Fionn."

"What think they of Keets?"

"They will kill her this turn. Whether it be quick or slow, I know not. I have stepped aside from Keets and will allow justice to occur. It is overly sad for me, but so it must be. Keets should have known better, and I am ashamed for her. She has shamed all our guards."

"Should we not have called for the community?"

"Due to the torture, the guards asked it to remain private. They did not want the community to witness such evils. The rumors will but be bad enough for the others."

Meera's guards had already prepared Fionn since she was the first to make a move to murder Sam. They had suspended her between two trees and removed most her clothes. Her arms were fully outstretched as she hung from the trees, but Meera could see that Fionn was acting defiant.

One of the guards approached Meera, "Be there anything you would like to know?"

Meera gave her the information she wanted, to obtain in whatever fashion they had to use to get it. The guard nodded when Meera finished.

"Do we have your leave to do as we must, then?"

Meera looked at Jandra, "You have my leave."

Jandra nodded to Meera and the guard, "Obtain the information Meera needs. We will remain here."

The guard bowed her head to Jandra, "Second," and went off to inform the others.

One of the guards went close to Fionn, "Tell us of this plot. Who be this High Spirit? Make it easier on yourself, as you will but die this turn. Slow or fast, it is your choice. We care not."

Fionn continued to look defiant, "Even if I knew, I would not tell you."

Anyst just shrugged, "We shall see."

Another guard came over with a torch and handed it to Anyst. She stood near Fionn and placed the torch just under her arm, holding it there through Fionn's screaming. Jandra wanted to look away, but the guards would test her this turn, so she remained steadfast and unflinching. She hoped Fionn would quickly tell them what they wanted to know, and was surprised for how long Anyst held the torch to Fionn's flesh. The odor of burning flesh made Jandra feel ill.

Anyst halted and asked again, "Who be this High Spirit Mother?"

Fionn no longer looked so defiant. She was in great pain as the torch had burned much of her arm. Meera thought the pain would be most intense, but Fionn hadn't yet passed out, although she had continued to scream.

Fionn looked wide-eyed at the torch in great fear. She spoke quickly in hope of avoiding further torture, "Vining knows. I know not. All I know is she wants one of Woden's members. I know not who it be. She says it be a future leader."

Meera spoke softly to Jandra, "The child?"

Jandra shrugged, "I cannot make sense of this."

Vining, being forced to watch Fionn, yelled, "Traitor. You traitor."

Anyst remained unphased, "Three more questions for you. If you but answer them truthfully and quickly, we will relieve you from your pain. If you do not, we will continue throughout the morn. Either way, you will tell us, Fionn.

Fionn nodded slightly, her head sagging from pain and lost hope.

Anyst nodded, "Good. First question. Who be this High Priestess?"

Fionn groaned her pain and looked beyond frightened, "I met her once, only. She is not of Buron or the High Mother. She wants her long-lost sister, only this, and has vowed she would help us to battle against Buron and the Spirit Mother if we gave the sister to her."

"Who be this long-lost sister?"

"In truth, I know not. She also knew not."

"Second question. What was Keets role in this betrayal?"

Fionn was in agony, so speech was difficult, "Keets followed along with whatever The Highest or Josin said." She paused for a moment to regain her strength, then added, "She was stupid and easy. And she followed all our orders without question if they came from The Highest or Josin."

Anyst nodded, "Answer this next question, Fionn, and you will have no more pain. "What was Govan's role in this betrayal?"

Fionn looked at Govan with rage, "Oh, so sweet and so innocent Govan. Everyone believes she be so wise and pure. Just look at her. Even now she hides behind her mask of sweetness and old cycles! She was Josin's main supporter. She wants more power, and Josin vowed her that she could be Second. Govan has longed for power for many, many cycles and has long resented The Highest. After Josin, she be your main traitor. But she will never show it. I but hope she gets her due as she has betrayed us all. Every one of us."

Anyst looked up at Fionn, "If this be true, Fionn, and we will find out, then I but vow to you that this turn, Govan will get her due."

Fionn looked back at Anyst, "I have told you true."

Anyst asked, "Do you have any last requests?"

She breathed in and closed her eyes as if tired of living, "One. Please give my daughter to a good home that be safe and protected from all this. And tell my daughter that I love her."

Anyst nodded, "It shall be done, Fionn."

As Anyst nodded to the other guards that had been waiting and prepared with their arrows ready, twelve arrows went straight into Fionn's heart. She felt no more pain.

Two guards lowered her as Anyst asked the guards, "She showed truth and courage until the end even though she betrayed Woden. Do we burn her, for her final truth telling, and send her to our Mothers, or let her rot as a traitor, forever remaining apart from our Mothers?"

The guards voted through a show of thumbs. All but three voted no—Fionn wouldn't be sent home to her mothers. When Fionn was laid on the ground, two guards dragged her body but a short distance away and chopped off her head. There they would leave her remains. Two other guards began to raise Vining, who had continued to make an equal show of defiance.

She shouted, "You will get nothing from me, Meera."

Meera came forward to Anyst as they were preparing Vining, "Anyst, I wish not to interfere, but I would like to get the first words out of Vining. I have great need of this."

Anyst nodded and bowed her head to Meera, "I well understand. I know the pain you must be in with our Highest in her deathbed. It would be our pleasure. Please make it slow."

Vining continued to struggle against the ropes and continued to shout in anger at Meera, "I hope your precious Sam dies."

Meera didn't yet speak. She took her sword and raised it to Vining's elbow, whereupon she sent the tip of the sword into the bone, breaking it. Vining screamed . . . and screamed . . . and screamed until she was so weak she could do so no more. Since Vining was suspended on ropes by her arms, Meera knew that such a break in the joint would cause excruciating and unending pain. She waited for a short while before speaking, allowing the moment to get the better of Vining.

Finally, Meera began "Do *not* speak to me, Vining, unless you but answer my questions. I have no sympathy for you, unlike my guards displayed for Fionn."

She noticed that Vining was beginning to look scared, and that tears were streaming down her face. *Good*, she thought. *Let her be afraid of me.* Meera raised her sword again, to the other elbow.

Vining screamed her pleas, "NO! *Please*, Meera," before Meera even touched her elbow. "I will tell you what you want to know."

"Who else is involved in this betrayal, and make your answer quick."

Her speech was frantic and halting, from the pain that had been inflicted on her, "Kandan and Govan . . . three sentries . . . the two that Oisin has plus Amara, five of Keet's guards, I know not their names . . . two men from Hengist, Govan knows their names, and one scout, Bentan. There may be others . . . I know them not." Her groaning was increasing.

"Where be this scout now?"

"In Apien . . . but it be only a guess."

"Who be this High Spirit Mother?"

Vining was struggling to speak, her pain great. She groaned and cried as she tried to answer, "A most powerful woman in The Realm . . . She fights against a queen of a much larger community. She wants one of Woden's children, but we never did learn which one . . . She uses Buron to fight against the queen she speaks of, as she needs more forces. Buron be one of the leaders of her forces."

"Who be this High Priestess?"

"A powerful woman from The Realm. She looks for a long-lost sister. I know not who this is, and as Fionn has told, neither did she."

"Is she with this High Spirit Mother?"

"She said that if we but found her long-lost sister, she would help us to fight against this Buron and the High Spirit Mother."

"Who be this Buron? Why be he so important to this High Mother?"

"He be part human, and part of another sort . . . I know not." She groaned, then tried to continue, "It be rumored that he but laid with the queen they all fight against."

"Human? What be this, about?"

"This Realm is mostly of others . . . not our types. At least this is what the High Mother has said to us, through Buron . . . He be only half human."

"So, you just wanted power and riches."

She raised her head to look at her, looking well defeated and in deep pain, "Meera, believe me. There be so much in The Realm that we know not of, and we should have some it. We be so poor compared to others . . . When you see this, you will understand." As she answered, Meera could see that Vining fully believed her own words.

"You have seen this for yourself?"

"I saw their treasures, and they be wonderful. And I saw The Highest a weak woman. I only went to kill Sam because she had found out."

Meera pointed her sword at her, "Where be this High Mother?"

"Never meet with her, Meera. She be evil, truly and has many forces, beyond our abilities."

"How much was Govan involved?"

As she tried to answer, she accidentally moved her injured elbow, and screamed. After a few moments of screaming and pleading, she finally could scream no more and just hung her head, fully exhausted from the effort. Her words were quietly spoken; her defeat abundantly clear, "It is as Fionn has said."

"How is Kandan involved?"

Her voice was now all but a whisper, "She is stupid as Keets, and flies as the wind in any direction. She is of no use to you or Sam as an advisor."

"Do you have any final requests?"

"Give my two daughters to good homes."

Meera nodded to the guards and 12 arrows went straight into Vining's heart.

Meera turned to Anyst, "She will remain unburned. We will not send this traitor to the mothers."

"It will be as you say."

"Have a guard bring Amara here, quickly. She will also die this turn."

"It shall be so, and has already been tended."

Meera looked tired and put her sword back into its sheath, "The rest are yours. Secure the information in any way you need. I know that there must be more involved. Get the two names of the men of Hengist from Govan. Then have a guard inform Briggon that he has but two men involved in this betrayal."

Anyst put her hand on Meera's shoulder, "I know that Keet's was your teacher. Perhaps it be best that you—"

Meera interrupted her, looking suddenly well angered, "Sam be my friend and Highest. Keets made her own decision and I will not feel pity for her. If Keets or any of you wants pity on her, look not my way."

Anyst nodded and motioned to the guards to prepare Govan. As they began raising her up by the ropes, Govan struggled, yelling, "I have done nothing, Meera. Anyst, you know me well. Jandra, you know me to love Woden. Please, halt this. I have done nothing!"

Anyst went up to Govan, ignoring her comment. "You saw Fionn and Vining. You know you face the same. If you tell us truth, we will end it swiftly for you. Who else is involved in this betrayal of Woden?"

"I am not a traitor. It is you, poor Anyst. It is you who will die the death of a traitor. All of you. The High Mother be great and all-knowing. She will have no pity on those who do not follow her. And Buron be a leader of leaders. Please, hear me. It was The Highest who betrayed Woden. Not me."

A guard handed Anyst the torch and Anyst did the same to Govan as she had done to Fionn. This was most difficult for Anyst as Govan was an older woman, but one who had betrayed Woden. As she knew would occur, Govan screamed and begged for mercy, like the others.

"So these *friends* of yours permit killing of a Highest?"

Govan was suffering from the pain and moaned and cried for a long while. As she became exhausted, her screams quieted and any hope she held had vanished. Finally, although crying, she answered, "She lied to them, and showed her weakness. And she thought she could keep Woden isolated from The Realm. But Woden will be destroyed as The Realm now faces battle. Only this High Mother and Buron can but save us. They know of the evil queen and fight against her."

Anyst just shook her head in disbelief, "I think you crazy, old woman. Enslaving our women be not saving them. Who are the men involved from Apien and New Harborage?"

"You refer to Manthar and Rolnen."

"Be they also the leaders of these towns?"

She nodded lightly, "They provide the leadership the High Mother commands."

"Who else be involved, Govan?" and she held the torch up so Govan could see that her patience was ending. "Who be the two traitors from Hengist?"

Govan hesitated. Anyst didn't. She took the torch to Govan's other arm and held it for a while.

After she removed it, and after Govan halted her screaming and wailing, Anyst tried again, "Give me the names of the two men from Hengist."

She moaned, then whispered her response, barely able to speak or breathe from the pain, and barely conscious, "Jaspun . . . Bortrun."

Anyst had heard enough and nodded to the guards. The arrows flew into Govan. The guards did another changing of the ropes, placing Kandan up. One guard went running to Hengist and Briggon.

Anyst came over to Meera, "What else would you wish to know from this one?"

"See if she can but add to these stories. And remind Kandan that she was perhaps a traitor to both Sam and me, as well. Kandan may be stupid, but she was one of Sam's advisors and I want all to know this as unacceptable. I want this one not easy."

"But Meera, she be weak and not one of the leaders of this."

"She was one of Sam's trusted advisors. It be enough."

Anyst bowed her head, "As you say. It will so be."

Anyst turned to go toward Kandan, but Jandra interrupted, "I will do this."

Meera and Anyst turned to Jandra. Anyst said, gently, "Second, we respect that you remain here through these events, but to perform the act itself is for a guard. It be a most difficult thing, and we have all watched it overly much."

"I am not here to prove myself to any of you. I am but here for Sam. Kandan betrayed Sam. I will learn why."

Both stepped aside and Jandra went up to Kandan. Kandan was crying, as she had been since the advisor's meeting prior eve.

"Kandan. You have disappointed all of us. It was enough to know that The Highest's advisors were betraying Woden, and that The Highest herself was as well. But Sam's advisors had remained true and loyal, except for you."

"Just kill me, Second. I meant not to hurt Sam or the others."

"Stupidity is not a part of Sam's advisors. You knew that. You *knew* what you were doing, Kandan. You are just sorry now because you have been found out. Tell me of this story."

Kandan told of what she knew. The stories remained much the same.

"Who else is involved?"

"I know no others."

Jandra took Sam's sword and held it up to Kandan's stomach. She sliced across it. As the blood and various stomach parts came rushing out, Kandan screamed in pain.

"Who else is involved?"

Gasping, her eyes wide with terror, and in full shock, she half-spoke, half-screamed her desperation, "None."

"Why did you betray Sam?"

She was sobbing, yet screaming, but her voice was going quickly weaker, "Please just kill me, Jandra. I beg of you. Please . . . "

"You will have no mercy this turn from me or these guards. You will die where you hang."

Her voice was now even softer, but her effort great, even as she accepted her pending death, "My daughter and companion. Have them taken care of."

"I will have your daughter given to Apien. Since you were involved in wanting to have our women enslaved, so shall be your daughter, Kandan. Others will know of this betrayal of Sam."

She wailed her desperation, "*Please* . . . not my daughter!"

"It be what you wanted for the Women of Woden."

Jandra walked away, trying to block out Kandan's screams for mercy of herself and pity for her daughter. By the moment, though, her screams and pleas became softer and less able. Her strength and life were leaving her as quickly as her blood was flowing out of her.

She walked back to Meera, "Leave her to die. Have her daughter sent to Apien to be enslaved."

Anyst responded, "Her daughter be but thirteen cycles."

"Have it done. No one will ever betray Sam in this fashion again."

The guard nodded, "As you say, Second."

Kandan died shortly from the deep gash Jandra had made. The guards then switched from Kandan to Amara, who two guards had just returned with.

Given the suddenness of the event for Amara, she was in shock, "But I know nothing about this. I only was given things for a small service."

The guards wasted no moments on Amara, simply executing her on the spot with the arrows. It was done very quickly, and was meant to unnerve Keets.

They brought Keets up and began to prepare to raise her ropes. Keets was a well-trained warrior and had many cycles of being hardened against pain and death. She watched the guards do their duty as if she were a mere observer, then looked at Meera, fully knowing well her weaknesses, "Meera, do I deserve no respect?"

Meera stared at Keets, surprised at the statement, but understanding Keets' intent to disturb her. Meera steeled herself. "Give us the name of your guards in this betrayal."

"Make me a deal, Meera."

"I will listen to it."

Anyst warned Meera, "Second, she but uses you for a quicker death."

Keets kept talking, trying to get Meera to ignore Anyst, "I will tell you all I know if you will but let me die as a warrior. Let me fight you. You know you will but win, anyway. This be between you and me, Meera. Not all these guards."

"I will first hear what you have to tell, then I will make that decision."

She looked straight at Meera, ignoring the guards around her, hoping she could convince her. Beyond all else, Keets wanted to avoid being tortured. She raised her eyebrows, as if trying to look sincere, "It be as Vining and Fionn have said. I was stupid and ridiculous. I knew The Highest to be weak, and I questioned Josin and The Highest about this High Mother, but I saw no harm in it. I was trained to follow The Highest's every command, as you do with Sam, and The Highest spoke not against Josin."

"You be wrong, Keets. Sam expects me to question her when I think her wrong."

Keets nodded, and tried to look understanding, "Then it be good and you have done well. Follow not my example, for I have been weak. I knew Josin to be evil, but I thought The Highest would take care of it, and when Jandra began to run the meetings more, I thought it all might be well."

Meera was more than suspicious—she now knew Keets to be manipulative and conniving. She could barely contain her anger, "And you thought nothing of bribing sentries and sending secret messages to Apien and New Harborage? A message that wanted nothing but slavery for our women? A lifespan of slavery? How stupid be you, Keets? In truth, I think you wanted more power and have long been jealous that my guards were better. In truth, you wanted to control all the guards in The Realm, Keets, and were most likely vowed this by this High Spirit Mother of yours. You can go ahead and act stupid if you wish, but I know you for who you are. And you are nothing but a coward. You have not just betrayed this community, Keets, but you and I go long back, and now you have betrayed me. You make me sick, Keets. Give me the names of your guards."

Keets hung her head and gave her seven, and not the five they thought. Meera was sickened from the information, but held it in.

Meera turned to Anyst, "Get these guards, and loan me your sword."

Anyst nodded, handed Meera her sword, and sent out a group of Meera's guards to get the now seven of Keet's that had helped betray the community. Anyst had seen Meera angry often, but had never heard Meera say so much. She saw that Meera shook with anger. Anyst motioned for two guards to come close by.

Meera noticed, "They will not be needed, Anyst, for Keets is as weak in body as she is in the brain. She has grown fat with laziness and arrogance, but she displays herself as strong and kind."

She looked at Keets, "I will but give you your fight, Keets, but you would have more dignity dying as the others. I will shame you to death as we fight, for you have shamed all of us; all my guards. You are nothing but a loathsome embarrassment to all our training and all of our community. You will rot before I give you any dignity, Keets. I asked Anyst to keep me out of your death. Not out of pity but knowing what my heart wants to have of you."

Meera raised her sword toward Keets, and Keets screamed, "No, Meera! Please." Meera's eyes narrowed as she shook her head, dismayed, "You disgust me, Coward." With a quick movement of her sword, she cut the ropes from Keets, then tossed Anyst's sword toward Keets, who was too slow to catch the movement. Meera watched the sword drop to the ground, disgusted in her prior teacher.

"You are nothing but a pitiful and shameful disgrace, Keets. Pick it up and try to fight. Try for just one moment of your pitiful existence to act as a warrior."

Meera held her sword firmly and focused on Keets as her target. Slowly, she circled around Keets, while Keets just remained motionless, but holding on to the sword.

"Are you overly weak fight, Keets? Do you want my pity, too?"

Meera waited for Keets to take the first swing. Finally, Keets raised her sword and lunged toward Meera. Meera thought it a pitiful attempt and ripped across Keets' shirt and front. A small cut in the flesh had occurred, and the shirt hung open.

Meera laughed, "You look like a little girl when you swing your sword, Keets. How did we ever allow you to become as you are? We should have retired you many cycles prior."

Keets lunged again. This moment, Meera cut Keets' upper arm. Keets was showing a great deal of blood but no major wounds.

Keets was becoming angry at her own inability against Meera. She knew she looked the fool and resented Meera for it.

"Be this the best you can do, Meera?"

Meera sneered at Keets, "Oh, I know, Keets. I meant only to remove your shirt, but instead caught some of your flesh. My error." And she refocused and waited.

Keets suddenly raised her sword and swung down toward Meera, but the sword was too heavy for Keets, and it swung uncontrolled. Meera met it with her sword and sent it flying out of Keets' hands, then took another swing of her sword and cut off Keets' pants.

"Get your sword, you old stupid woman. You embarrass me in your fighting."

Keets picked up her sword and came running at Meera. Meera waited until the last moment, then swung her sword and cut off Keet's left arm. Keets howled liked a trapped injured animal in pain, but held onto her sword.

"Tiring of your cruel game, Meera?"

"I tire of you, Keets. You no longer belong here."

Keets lunged again and Meera countered, cutting open Keets' upper leg.

"You are not worth this effort, Keets. In truth, why did you help Josin?"

Keets continued to circle, as did Meera. Meera never lost her concentration, but looked as if she had relaxed. Keets tried to catch Meera off-guard, and struck again. Meera easily knocked the sword from Keets' hand.

Keets went to retrieve it, while Meera waited. Keets was bloodied everywhere, with one arm missing, and could no longer hold her bitterness aside, "You are correct, Meera. I do resent you. You think you are better than me."

They began to circle again. "So this be all about control, Keets?"

"Now who is the stupid one? Of course it be all about control, Meera," and she moved toward Meera again. Meera sidestepped her advance and swung across Keets' leg and cut it off. Then she did the same with the other as Keets fell to the ground. Meera moved closer and cut off Keets' sword arm.

Then she bent down and retrieved Anyst's sword, walked over and handed it to her.

"Thank you for the loan of your sword. Leave her there to die. She will bleed to death in but a short while."

"The seven guards are here."

"Kill them as you will. Be there anyone with any difficulty in doing this?"

"No, Meera. It will be our pleasure."

"Question them about others' involvement, but I think we but have all that be in our community."

Meera could yet hear Keets' screams and howls, but chose to ignore them. She saw Briggon come with some of his guards and the two men who had been accused as traitors.

Briggon went to Meera, "The traitors say no, but the guards have said that they think they saw them re-entering Hengist from Woden late one eve."

"Give them to Anyst if you would like. She will find out for us."

Briggon nodded and took Jaspun and Bortrun to Anyst. Anyst had Jaspun strung as the women, while Bortrun was held tight.

When Jaspun was prepared, Anyst turned to Briggon, "Would your guards but want to do this torture to find out what he knows?"

One of Briggon's guards came forward - Andren. "Third, I would most like to take from this traitor's lip all he knows."

Briggon nodded and Andren unsheathed his sword.

He went up to Jaspun. "What have you to do with this betrayal in Woden?"

Jaspun tried to kick Andren, but couldn't, due to the ropes. Andren took his sword and cut under Jaspun's arm, into the muscle, from elbow to arm pit . . . very slowly. Jaspun first screamed, then passed out from the pain, but Anyst provided Andren with some water to throw upon Jaspun's face.

As Jaspun came to, Andren said again, "Tell me and spare yourself more of this."

"I want to live as a man. With a woman."

"Then why did you not leave for Apien or New Harborage?"

"I was vowed a woman from here. We were going to take over Hengist and rid ourselves of your scum."

Andren took his sword and cut Jaspun's other arm the same. Jaspun's screams echoed through the forest, making every living thing shiver from fear.

Andren ignored Jaspun's agony, "Who else is involved from Hengist?"

Jaspun's muscles were coming out from his arm. Meera had never seen such a thing and thought the pain must be beyond bearable, yet Jaspun continued to remain conscious.

"I know of no other."

Andren took his sword once more and held it up to Jaspun's sex parts.

"Speak truly or the pain will become much worse."

Jaspun whispered, moving beyond consciousness, "I speak truly."

Andren took his sword and cut Jaspun's body in half. The guards let down the ropes, removed Jaspun and began to raise Bortrun. Bortrun was fighting it, completely frightened from what he had seen, "No, Andren, *please!* I will tell you, but torture me not."

Andren turned to him, "Then speak quickly."

"As Jaspun said, there are no others from Hengist. Josin gave of herself to me and vowed me more. It be the truth. My companion will tell you so. He has not yet forgiven me."

Andren said nothing, but picked up his sword and cut off Bortrun's head as he stood. Briggon nodded to Meera and went to stand next to Anyst. "It is done."

Meera nodded, glad that it was finally over, then walked back to Jandra.

"Meera, you look but tired."

"The thought of Sam weighs heavy on me. We lose many from our community this turn. It seems as if we have done nothing these prior turns but kill our own. We face many broken companionships caused by this. We will need much healing in our community and yet we have but killed our spiritual advisors. Our community be both strengthened and weakened through our acts."

"It is so. Sadly, you speak truth."

"I speak with experience and sadness, only." She looked back to her guards. "My guards will take care of their own betrayers. Let us leave them to their own vengeance. I wish to check on Sam."

"How is Caitha able to comfort you after so much killing as this?"

"Caitha and Sam be my life. I live and fight for them. They give me purpose. If Sam dies, many others will die for it. If someone hurt peaceful and loving Caitha, no rock would be left unturned until I found them."

* * * *

They walked back to The Highest's house, both silent in their worry for Sam. As they entered, they saw May sitting beside Sam's bed.

Jandra could see that May was crying, "May, be there any change?"

"I think her heart is slowing down. I think she be but dying," and she began to sob.

Meera placed a finger on Sam's neck to feel her heart rate, noting that May was correct. It was much too slow from normal. Meera checked Sam's breathing and found it shallow and sporadic. She tried placing her hands over Sam's as Jandra had done what seemed so long prior. She felt nothing, but just continued to hold them and tried to send her thoughts.

SAM! You cannot leave us. SAM!

I have sent Keddi for the old raggedy one—hold on.

Breathe, Sam. Make your heart beat stronger. Hear my heart. Hear it. Make yours do the same. Breathe, *Sam!*

She didn't know what else to do so just told Sam the story about the High Spirit Mother and Buron, what Josin had wanted to do, and the secret notes to Apien and New Harborage selling Woden's Women into slavery. She told Sam that she was confused about these issues in The Realm, and didn't understand what was happening. She spoke long to Sam, and held Sam's hands together tightly in case it would help.

Jandra tapped Meera on the shoulder, "Meera, you must rest for a while. You have been with Sam for most of midturn. If you but help give her power, then you now lose overly much. I will take your place for a while. Go into the sitting room and lie down. May will wake you for a meal soon, and Caitha has come to be with you."

Meera felt overly tired, so went to lie down as Jandra had suggested. Jandra did as Meera had, holding Sam's hands together and telling her, through her thoughts, all that had occurred this turn and what they had learned.

Sam. We need you. Woden knows not of such things as powers and High Spirit Mothers. We need you, in highest truth, as there must be some connection between you and them.

Jandra's thoughts were broken when she felt Meera pulling her up, "Jandra, you need to rest now. May has our meal ready for us. I have sent out guards with fresh horses in hopes they but meet up with Keddi and Margeria. Enough moments have passed that they could now but show up at any moment. All the women of Woden and the men of Hengist stand outside in vigil, all with candles."

Jandra nodded and followed Meera. They ate their meal together in silence, with May and Caitha, then went back to check on Sam. Meera tried to check her heart rate, but could find nothing. She checked her breathing. The same. She found nothing. She beat upon her chest to scare Sam's heart into starting, but felt nothing.

Meera knelt down on her knees and began to cry. Not knowing what else to do, Caitha just tried to hold her. Very few had ever seen Meera cry, but knew it well as a sign of primal loss. May went through the house wailing in the pain of knowing that Sam had died. Jandra just sat in disbelief, *How can we possibly go on now?*

A guard outside yelled the message, "The Highest is dead."

It resounded throughout the community, and all the women and men outside began to cry their grief of losing Sam. All grieved until early morn.

By early morn, Meera had given up. The advisors had come and finally convinced Meera and Jandra that Sam must be given her funeral and Jandra must be made as Highest. Caitha just tried to comfort in what little way she could, but was also devastated at this loss. May prepared Sam for her funeral, and the guards came in and placed her on a litter for her final journey. Meera and Jandra were both in such shock and mental anguish they could hardly move. They stood by as if frozen into perpetual statues of sadness. May hadn't halted her wailing and sobbing from the eve prior and moved about in a state of loud mourning. As the guards began to carry Sam out of her dwelling to the Sacred Stones, Meera again fell to her knees in total despair. She was so consumed in her grief that she hadn't heard when the horses finally arrived.

Keddi came running in, "Meera, I have returned with the old raggedy one. She comes now. She wouldn't let me carry her inside."

Meera shook her head, with no hope remaining to her. "It be overly late, Keddi. Sam has but died a while ago. We but begin her funeral now."

Keddi looked at Jandra and Meera and knew it to be true and just knelt and cried.

The old raggedy one came toddling in, accompanied by Margeria, and went over to the guards who were holding Sam. She motioned for them to place Sam down upon the bed. Meera nodded to them to do so, but thinking the effort was for naught. They did, but looked with wonderment at the old raggedy smelly thing. She jumped up onto the bed, felt Sam's neck, as Meera had, and checked her breathing. She opened Sam's eyelids and looked into her eyes. Then she reached over and hit Meera on the side of the head.

"Help me, you stupid thing.".

Meera was too startled to strike back, as was her first instinct, "What do you but require of me?"

"Sit her up in the bed."

"She has died, old raggedy one."

She hit Meera on the side of the head again, "Don't be so stupid. If she were all-human, like you poor stupid thing, she would be dead. But she is not and will but live if you will listen to me."

Meera didn't wish to be hit upon the side of the head again, so moved Sam as well as she could to a slight sitting position.

The old raggedy one then slapped Jandra on the side of the head, "You are but stupid, too. Get me some water."

Jandra also was too stunned to question this old smelly earth creature, so left to retrieve a pitcher of water for her.

The old raggedy one began speaking a chant that no one could understand. The language wasn't of theirs. Meera motioned for the guards to leave the room, and the advisors as well, while the old raggedy one held some clods of moss over Sam's head, dropped water on her head from them, and continued to chant. Her chanting grew to a half-chant, half-song and Jandra thought it the most beautiful thing she had ever heard. A thought came into her mind that if a waterfall could talk and sing, it would sound like this, for it reminded her of flowing water.

It is as if I have heard this song, long prior. But from where?

The old raggedy one continued her half-song and half-chant through half the morn. Meera thought her crazy and was about to send her away, but this earth-smelling bag of rags was her only hope to save Sam. Finally, around midturn and after what seemed far too long, the raggedy one opened Sam's mouth and poured some water into it, saying different words. Most of it spelled out. She continued this three instances, then titled Sam's head back a little to let the water go down her throat. Jandra thought that if Sam had been alive, it would have drowned her.

The raggedy one then clapped her hands together once, grabbed Sam's hands and held on tightly. Suddenly, Sam breathed in a breath so deep it was as if she hadn't breathed in over a moon, then bent over and began coughing.

As she did this, the old raggedy one climbed down from the bed and looked at May, "Get me some wine."

May, fully surprised, went to do so, and the raggedy one followed after her, chortling with glee.

Sam was yet coughing and trying to breathe. Meera, in disbelief and paralyzingly stunned, tried to help Sam to bend forward a little more.

Jandra just kept saying, "You are alive. Sam, you live."

Meera was in full disbelief, "You but died. I know this as truth."

Sam's coughing began to slow down, but she continued to take huge breaths, as if trying to fill air into her body. She finally opened her eyes.

Yet slightly coughing, "I am sorry to have done this to you, Meera."

She placed a hand on Meera's shoulders and Meera could feel Sam's strength flow into her. Instantly, Meera was relieved of her deep worries and felt as if everything would be fine. Sam smiled at her, in between her coughing and breathing, thankful for her good friend. As her need for coughing halted, she began to breath in more slowly but yet fully, as if her lungs held volumes of air. Meera was unable to move, but wouldn't leave Sam's side.

Sam looked to Caitha and smiled, "Come nearer, Caitha."

Caitha did as Sam asked, and Sam placed a hand on her shoulder. Caitha felt the power that Meera had spoken of to her in their private moments, and felt Sam thanking her for taking such good care of Meera. She also felt Sam's love for her. Caitha smiled and touched Sam's cheek in return.

Sam then looked at Jandra and smiled, "Jandra. So sad," and she touched Jandra as well. Like with Meera and Caitha, Jandra could feel the strength flow from Sam, but saw that Sam was unaffected. Jandra felt comforted by Sam's touch and knew the community would be safe for a while longer. Sam wiped a tear from Jandra's face and looked at it. Sam cried but one tear, took her tear and joined it with Jandra's, placed it in her hands and rubbed them together, and then placed her hands within Jandra's. Jandra had no idea what that was about, but Sam seemed to know something she didn't.

Sam then looked at Keddi, "Our sad and loving scout."

She touched Keddi's cheek and Keddi also felt Sam's strength flow into her, and instantly felt the love that Sam and Brett had shared. She was glad that Sam now knew for certain that Brett had loved her deeply, in truth, and not because she was a scout.

The old raggedy one came back in with a flask to her lips, "Are you not out of bed yet? I must be back and you must provide me with supplies. They listen not to me!"

Sam laughed, got off the bed, knelt down to the old raggedy one, and placed her hands on the old raggedy one's head, and they both remained in that position for a long while. Meera and the others just watched in disbelief, not wishing to interfere.

When done, Sam removed her hands and kissed the old raggedy one's cheeks, "I will see to your provisions."

She looked at a guard, "Please make certain that she has all that she requests, and double it."

Sam began to go with the raggedy one to her horse, but Jandra halted her, "Sam, you cannot go out dressed like this."

Meera laughed, "That would certainly prove your reputation," and then began to cry. "Oh, Sam, I am so glad that you be alive." Sam went over to Meera and hugged her. She said nothing to her, nor did she send her any thoughts. It was just enough to hold her for a moment.

Finally, Sam said, "I knew but to trust your instincts, Meera. I am sorry to have done this to you. I but knew that I would die, but I also knew you could find the old raggedy one."

Meera being Meera, pulled away and said, "I am sorry. I should not have allowed such emotion. But thank you, Sam. Now, you must dress as you are completely naked, again."

Sam looked at Keddi, "Who will take the Old One back home?"

"Margeria and I will. She is a character and I think Margeria has taken to her as one would a pet."

After seeing that the guards could see to the Old One's provisions and wine, May came back in to see Sam. Sam saw May and went to her, placing her hands upon May's head. May couldn't understand what she was feeling but could feel a strength enter her body and make her feel younger. Sam let go and then hugged May to her, gently, for a brief moment.

After placing on her garments, Sam went to the patio where all the Women of Woden and the Men of Hengist were waiting a report. They had first heard she was dead, and then heard that the strange old person in the rags brought her back to life. They didn't understand this, but accepted it, as there was certainly no way for them to understand how such could occur. And they had waited throughout the long eve.

Sam began to speak to them. She told them of the betrayal. She told them of Meera and Jandra's turn and what they had to do with the remaining advisors, guards and sentries who had betrayed Woden. She told them of how Hengist had become isolated from them. And she told them, in length, of the High Spirit Mother and the evils she had caused. She told them how Josin and The Highest had betrayed the community. She then told them of their return to their original practice with Hengist and that trade, entertainment and an open exchange of ideas would become an accepted practice between the two communities.

And finally she said, "Many of us have lost our companions these prior turns, but we must now grow back our strength and community. We will discuss our issues and questions together as we have done prior. We will grow and learn together as a community, as we have ever prior done. And we will relearn to trust and respect each other for our strengths, our weaknesses, and our differences. Thank you for your good wishes. Return to your dwellings and let us begin in the morn with a renewed community that now includes Hengist. Our festival approaches, and I vow that it will be a grand one. Good eve."

All the women and men knelt, "Highest". "Chosen One." "Highest." "Chosen One." Her community then rose and turned toward their dwellings, and Sam returned to her own. She told May to go to her own dwelling and rest, had Meera move the guards outside her dwelling, kissed Meera and Caitha a good after midturn, what was left of it, and got everyone out of the dwelling.

As all were leaving, Sam saw that Jandra was leaving as well.

"Jandra, why do you leave me?"

Jandra turned to her, looking well saddened. "Sam, I know I have done wrong to you and the community by not telling you this knowledge sooner. So I am leaving, as I know you must no longer trust me. I understand, though, Sam. I have broken your trust and what love you could have for me."

"No, Jandra. This be not so. You have done no wrong. In truth, you held true to Woden. How could you know who to trust in all these moments of such deception?"

"Perhaps it is as you say, but I am yet sorry for such occurrences."

Sam nodded knowingly, "It is so, as am I, but it is not of your doing. Come, you must rest. It has been but a long vigil for you. I will hold you while you sleep."

Jandra followed her like a puppy and could think of nothing better than to fall asleep being held by this most wonderful woman, no matter how strong and strange her new power now felt. Jandra had no fear of Sam, and that was strange enough, but as she had felt the power, she also felt it as a familiar and safe moment, from far long prior.

* * * *

While Jandra slept, Sam began reading the diaries that The Highest had wanted of her. She had much knowledge to put together and felt that some of it was in these diaries. She knew that Woden had much to learn, so began where she left off what seemed like so many turns prior:

> With his army, as he calls that motley and disgusting group, he is now forcing all the women to get pregnant so that his community continues to grow, in what he calls "the ways of the lord". So, he rapes us daily to ensure that we get pregnant as soon as possible, although he calls it as doing his duty. Yeah, right. The only good thing to come of all this is that we are being well fed so that we can continue his precious birth cycles.
>
> This morning, he forced us to listen to him read an entire chapter from his bible. If we show we don't listen, he has us whipped. He is now forcing us to memorize passages from his sermons. Like I care. All our knowledge, and we have come to this. All of us have our Ph.D.s and yet we can do nothing. How stupid I feel.
>
> He had been keeping all us women apart so that we couldn't unite against him, but without the proper maintenance, the housing sheds are beginning to fall apart out of neglect, and the forest encroaches daily. He's no choice now but to keep us all together in one of the last two housing sheds. The men fare

no better. Those that choose to follow him must deal with his insanity, and those that dare go against him are being hung. If we women speak out against him, he whips us until our backs are bloody pulp, but goes no further until he achieves his ideal community numbers. Of course, he is the only one allowed to touch us, so all the children will be closely related. I personally hope this baby dies. If it doesn't, and I'm still here, I will be forced to kill it just so Burn doesn't get his hands on it.

What have I become?

We women have united together now, and whenever he isn't in the shed doing things to us that I thought existed only in horror stories and preaching to us, while the other men watch (and I'll never forget that they just stand there!), we have begun a plan. Three evenings ago, we helped six women to escape. They have stolen some equipment and promised that they will return for us when they find us a spot to live, and a way to get there. In the meantime, we steal what goods and weapons we can and wait until we have enough supplies to begin our revolt. In return for services, some men give us weapons and supplies. We have buried them in the ground for now.

From the reading, Sam could tell that this had been a shared community where women and men lived together. She remembered from the first journal entry that the writer referred to this trip as an experiment. She wondered what type of experiment the community had been. She read through the next several journal entries, which seemed to get worse for the women with each moon. She read that some of the women died in childbirth, and some died from what they termed a venereal disease, an unknown term to Woden. Sam thought that the experimental community's medical knowledge seemed far more advanced than Woden's. She read that the imprisoned women had asked Burn for a medical kit, but he had refused. Sam noticed that according to the journal-writer, Burn was getting increasingly more insane from this venereal disease, and then saw that events suddenly changed greatly in Entry #9.

We did it! We escaped this last eve and are holding-up in a makeshift shelter. We have enough weapons and ammunition to hold off Burn for a while, especially now since some of the men escaped at the same time. We are hold-up about two miles north from the original site. He knows where we are, but we will stay and battle it out from here. Some of the men have asked to stay with us, but we've decided that they will not after the treatment they have shown us. We no longer trust any of them. We would be stupid to do so.

It's a bittersweet victory, though. We have lost five more women, and I dropped two of the journals during our escape. I will make an attempt to retrieve them at some point, but fear Burn will destroy them if he finds them first. He's systematically trying to destroy all the last remnants of our ways of living and our history. At the mention of Earth, he kills the one who says it. How very sad for us.

Entry #10:

We begin to build our own community now. We've distributed chores so that everyone takes care of the gardens, everyone helps to build the buildings, and we trade off with the guarding duties. We do this so that we all will learn. If we become specialists, we stand the chance of losing our basic skills if the specialist leaves or dies. We have learned this the hard way with all the technology, which is now useless.

Our gardens are really pitiful. I would trade my Ph.D. for a gardening book. We saved what seed we could but have only potatoes, tomatoes, green beans, cabbage, one type of lettuce only, and onion. We'll have to learn to cultivate wild vegetables from the jungle even if these do produce well for us. Four of us go out daily to hunt for whatever we can find. If I'm ever out hunting and run across Burn, the women better watch out if I'm also cooking, cause I'll serve him up for dinner. I hate him. I really, really hate him.

An interesting thing is happening to us. We no longer want or need men. Some of the women have begun to pair up with each other. While not so unusual back home, I have a feeling that this may soon become our norm. Some of the men that we haven't allowed into our community have settled near us, but follow our rules. They keep to their own but have promised to help protect our new communities. We don't like it, but it makes sense for now.

I wish I knew how long we'll have to wait. The waiting for our scouts to return seems never ending. I'm constantly reminding myself of the Shackleton Antarctic journey, as he came back for all his men, after a really long time, too. But for all I know, our scouts may get killed or die with disease and never be able to come back to us. I think we should begin to build a boat, just in case. Yeah, right. Like we're boat builders, too. Dream on, Kimi.

I miss home and wish I'd never come. This was supposed to be the biggest moment of my life. I had qualified to come here, to this new place. And while it's much like home in its flora and fauna, we have become barbarians, and all due to Burn. Whoever wrote that Lord of the Flies book was right on the money.

Sam halted her reading and thought about the new book in her community: *Le Morte D'Arthur*. She wondered briefly where it might have come from. Nowhere in all the realm could such a book be produced in this fashion. She noted that most of Woden's books resembled the journals that she was reading. She was curious about the journal writer and her reference to home.

Finally tired after reading, Sam went to sleep with much on her mind regarding the recent events. She woke early, but Jandra had already woken and was waiting for her.

"Have you been awake long?"

"For but a little while. I just wanted to be near you and watch you breathe. We all thought you had but died."

Sam yet lay upon her pillow, just looking at Jandra and choosing not to reply.

"Why did you so easily trade your life for mine? Your life be much more important than mine."

"You are wrong, Jandra. No one life be more important than another. I chose to save your life because your life means much to me and Woden. You did the same for me when you jumped in front of Fionn."

"But I owed you that. It was my fault that Fionn and Vining tried to kill you."

With her finger, Sam traced Jandra's frown, "No, it was not. As Second, you will learn that you cannot take the blame for other's actions. It be enough we tend to our own. You did as you thought best."

"You were so serious when I told you the story. I know that it upset you."

Sam sighed and began to touch Jandra's hair, "Certainly it upset me. It upset me because the betrayal was deeper than we had but imagined and I had not trusted my instincts. I knew The Highest took her own life overly quickly."

"I wonder who be this High Priestess' sister that she says be in Woden."

"How might this be so? None of us is mystical."

"You are."

Sam looked at Jandra quizzically, beginning to think the same, ". . . but what do you think this means to—"

May entered with the morn meal, interrupting Sam's thoughts, "Good morn, Chosen One. Good morn, Second. I but overheard you speaking so knew you were awake. Both of you need to eat, as you both grow much overly thin. I cannot have sickly looking ones under my roof when I am but the cook. It bodes badly for my reputation."

Sam smiled at her, "It is good to see you too, May. Thank you for this meal. We will take the moment to eat and enjoy it so that we grow meat upon our bones once again."

Sam rose from the bed and held out her hand to help Jandra, "Would you give me the pleasure of walking with me on my rounds this turn, if you but have the moment?"

Jandra took Sam's hand and rose. Holding hands, Jandra kissed her. She hoped that their relationship was changing from passion to love. She liked the thought of it, but didn't yet believe that Sam could truly love her, knowing that Sam loved Oisin.

"Of course. I would like this much. I must first attend to the community sessions this turn, and then a short meeting this eve with Tehna and Briggon to attend to the festival. It seems to be a duty I inherited. We can take our late eve meal together. Perhaps you would consider attending the community sessions with me but this once?"

Sam nodded.

"Sam? Why do you but ask me to go with you on your rounds? Is that not your moment alone with the women? Are you certain I will not be interfering? Or are you just trying to teach me how to do rounds so I do not offend others overly—"

"Hold, Jandra. You make me dizzy with all your questions. In truth, I ask you as I would like the women begin to see us as together. As Highest and Second, and as companions. It be the moment this be made known. This community has had but overly many secrets."

Jandra wished that Sam had said 'as lovers' instead of 'as companions,' but settled well for whatever it was that Sam could give. Through the turns, she hoped that Sam could learn to love her.

* * * *

Sam walked arm-in-arm with Jandra to the park where the community sessions were to be held. She didn't wish to take away from Jandra's duties or esteem with the women, but knew that the women were glad to see their Highest alive and well. As she and Jandra arrived, the women knelt before them.

"Highest."

They would acknowledge Jandra as they went up to her so left the greeting with just Sam.

"I will but wait for you nearby. The guards have informed me that they would like to keep me within their watch. They are yet nervous on my behalf, so I will just speak with the women while you be Second. Who tends to you this turn?"

"Karan has volunteered. I see her coming now."

Karan walked up and knelt down. "Highest." She took Sam's hand and kissed it. "I am so grateful for your life. My sadness at your death took me stronger than I had but guessed. All the Women of Woden felt the same."

Sam placed her hands upon Karan's head and allowed her power to flow through her. Karan felt gratitude from Sam, but knew not how. And it made her feel loved and needed.

"Have you any word on Lillon?"

"She be in great pain, Highest. But she will recover."

"Does she remain in the infirmary?"

Karan nodded.

"Thank you for volunteering to help The Second with the community sessions. I know you will give her your usual most excellent counsel."

Karan smiled, bowed her head and motioned for Jandra to take her seat at the benches. A small crowd of the women were awaiting The Second's presence.

Karan stood beside Jandra and bent to her ear and whispered, "The women are ready when you are, Second."

"Thank you, Karan. Let us begin, then. You take care of the order."

Karan motioned Evane and Kilna to come forward, "This will be an easy one for you, Second. Do you know Evane and Kilna?"

Evane and Kilna walked up and bowed their heads to Jandra, "Hello, Second. Thank you for seeing us this midturn."

"My pleasure, Evane; Kilna. What is it you are requesting?"

Karan whispered again into Jandra's ear, "Evane is one of our herb gardeners and Kilna works on building our dwellings."

Kilna responded, "Two items for your consideration, Second. First, Evane is a very good herb gardener, but she wants to open a shop and provide herbal creations. She has some ideas for herb soaps, herb arrangements, herbal remedies, dried herbs in bunches, and quite a few other items, but it would mean she would have to work less in the herb garden out in the gardens."

Karan whispered once again into Jandra's ear, "We could allow her to plant and tend new herb gardens in this main park section. It will yet supply us with needed plants from the gardens. It would just extend our gardens into the park. And we do have a few vacant shops, so it would be a good idea."

Jandra turned toward Karan, "Oh, Karan, that is a very good idea. Evane, we could move you and Kilna into one of the vacant shops that Karan just informed me about, and you could move your herb gardens to the park. Of course, I would want them to fit into the surroundings, so they would have to be both functional and pleasing. The Highest but loves the gardens, so we should keep them beautiful. What do you two think about this?"

Evane seemed well pleased, "I think it be perfect, Second. I could grow a magnificent and beautiful herb garden in the park, with places to sit in it for The Highest and the women. It will be beautiful. And, I would be but close enough to the shop to manage the trade and do the herbal arrangements. Thank you, Second, Karan."

Kilna added, "Yes, thank you, Second. And I can help build those sitting areas Evane wants."

As they walked away, chattering happily about their new plans, hand-in-hand, Jandra looked at Karan, "I hope they are all that easy and fun."

Karan just shook her head, "I would not count on it, Second," as she motioned to the next two women. "These are Lenore and Bertun. They have a difficult issue for you."

Lenore and Bertun walked up. Neither spoke to Jandra but they did bow their heads. Their daughter waited, but didn't come up with them.

"Lenore; Bertun. What can I help you with this midturn?"

Lenore spoke first, after a pause, "The Highest gave us permission to split our union."

Jandra looked at Karan, who nodded in the affirmative, then looked back at Lenore.

Lenore continued, "But she told us not who Berlen will go with."

Jandra looked at the two unhappy women before her, *Ah. It is my happy duty to determine who Berlen will live with. But I am not so happy about having to make this decision.* "Have you both found new companions?"

They both nodded, "Yes."

Bertun spoke, "We will both take our new companions this next festival." Then, with anger, "But Lenore has been having an affair with Todra for a long while now, even while we were yet companions, and told me not. I think Berlen should remain with me."

Lenore nodded her head, "Bertun speaks truly, Second. I fell in love with Todra while with Bertun, and I know I hurt her, but that is no reason to take Berlen away from me forever. I am the Birth-Mother."

Jandra looked at Karan and quietly asked, "Why did The Highest not deal with this when she allowed the split?"

Karan spoke softly to Jandra, "She did. She told them to try to work it out themselves. If they could not, then they needed to come back."

"Karan, please bring Berlen up here for me."

Jandra looked at Bertun and Lenore, "I am going to speak with Berlen. Please go aside for just a moment."

They did so and Berlen came up with Karan. She looked in middle young-age. Jandra guessed her to be around eight cycles.

Jandra smiled at her, "Hello, Berlen."

She looked scared, and whispered, "Second." She looked only at the ground.

"Berlen, I need to ask you some questions about your family situation. Would this be acceptable to you?"

She nodded.

"Would you come sit by me for this talk?"

Jandra could tell that Berlen didn't want to, but Karan led her over.

"Berlen, your mother and Birth-Mother would each like you to live with them in their new dwellings. Do you know what that means for you?"

She just nodded, but Jandra prodded, "Can you tell me about those discussions?"

Berlen didn't answer, but Jandra out-waited her, "Mother wants me to be with her and Ata, and Birth-Mother wants me to be with her and To-dra."

"Yes, you are correct. That is exactly what they want. I am going to ask you a very important question, and I really need to know your most honest answer. Can you do that for me?"

She nodded.

"Berlen, you have probably thought about this some, but I need to know. Who do you want to live with?"

"Both."

Jandra nodded to Karan to get Lenore and Bertun. "I can arrange that, Berlen. You go back and wait for them. And worry not. This will work out for you."

Berlen left and Lenore and Bertun looked a little surprised that Jandra had consulted with Berlen instead of them.

"Berlen wants to be with the both of you, and given the size of our community, there be no reason she cannot go back and forth from dwelling to dwelling until she reaches her majority, or until some other arrangement becomes necessary. She is to live one moon with each of you, and then move to the other for the same. This arrangement will begin with Lenore, her Birth-Mother. I expect each of you to display respect for the other to Berlen."

Lenore looked at Bertun, "It is acceptable to me. You?"

Bertun looked sad, but said, "It seems a fair solution. I can live with it as long as you speak no ill of me while she is in your dwelling."

"Go now, and try to make this a positive experience for Berlen."

Sam listened to the first two community sessions and thought once again that she had chosen well. Jandra was going to make a fine Second.

She went over to one of the guards, "I am going to visit with Lillon in the infirmary. Would you please see to it that Jandra is informed of this if I am not returned by the moment she finishes?"

The guard knelt in front of her, "It would be my pleasure, Highest. But Highest, may I please assign two guards to accompany you until you return? Meera will but have my skin if I make this not so."

Sam laughed and nodded consent. With the two guards in tow, she went to the infirmary. She guessed that she would be back well before Jandra was finished. As she entered the infirmary, she met up with Berth.

Berth knelt down, "Highest. It is good to see you alive and well, in highest truth. What may I do for you?"

She took Berth's hand and made her to rise, "I would like to visit with Lillon. How many women be in the infirmary this turn?"

"Only two others. Patrice is ill with a fever, and Morane is very ill. Her insides seem to be decaying on her."

"I will visit with them after I see to Lillon. Can you but show me where she be?"

Berth took Sam to Lillon's bedside, then left.

Sam saw that Lillon was most weak and had lost much blood from her knife wound. Lillon had been sleeping, but now struggled to sit up. Sam placed her hand upon her shoulder to keep her lying down.

"No, Lillon. Please remain as you were. You will cause yourself pain if you but move. I came by to thank you for trying to halt Vining. You helped to save my life."

Lillon cried, "Oh, Highest. You are alive! I am so glad. I wanted to prove so desperately to you that I am loyal to you. I am but glad that Vining gave me the opportunity. But she angered me so that she tried to kill you."

"Let me see your wound, Lillon."

"No, Highest. You must not try to heal me. I will be fine in a while. You must not misuse your energy upon me."

Sam ignored Lillon's protests and moved aside the bed cover. She saw a very inflamed and angry knife wound, somewhat infected, and with many angry looking stitches. She placed one hand on the wound and focused her power, slowly. She restrained from providing too much, as Lillon was correct - she shouldn't both heal and lose her power. The old raggedy one told her to focus with restraint. After a short moment, Sam removed her hand and saw that the wound would now heal well and much of the pain wouldn't return.

Sam smiled down at Lillon, "It be just a little I do, Lillon. It be not enough to completely heal your wound, but it now be no longer inflamed or as painful. Try to not speed the healing by moving overly now. Take the moments to heal well so that you can return to me as my most needed and prized assistant."

Lillon looked surprised, "Oh, Highest. Is it possible it can feel so much improved? I can but rise and return to my dwelling now," and she began to do so.

"Then take a command from me Lillon. Remain here for two turns hence."

Lillon looked a little sad about it, "As you say, Highest," then smiled, "It be a much shorter moment than it would have been. Thank you, Highest. You have my word."

Sam rose and went back to Berth, "Please allow me to see Patrice."

Patrice was asleep when they arrived at her bed, so Sam merely placed her hand upon Patrice's head and healed Patrice's fever. Sam noted that it was a minor fever, so was relieved.

She nodded to Berth to take her to Morane's bed. She looked down at the sleeping Morane and saw a dying woman in her older cycles. She placed her hand upon Morane's head and focused. After a few moments, she removed her hand, feeling sad. She could do nothing to save Morane at this stage of the disease. But she had given relief to Morane from the pain that she would be facing, and felt comforted in knowing that Morane would have a peaceful death.

"Thank you, Berth."

She bowed, "Highest."

Sam returned to the park and found that Jandra yet had two more companions to complete. She just sat and waited on one of the park's benches, with her two faithful guards directly in back of her. She enjoyed just watching the activities of the park and overhearing Jandra's decisions, and was delighted she had thought to pick Jandra as her Second.

Jandra walked over when she finished, sat on the ground, and leaned against Sam's legs, "I now know why you gave me this duty. Thank our Mothers for Karan. She be overly good to believe. She knew every woman's name and all but one of their issues before they came up. She whispered everything into my ear and made me look much better than I should have. I could have done this not without her."

Sam took Jandra's hands into her own, and laughed, "Karan be a wonderful advisor and I am most grateful for her, but I chose you because I knew you would but do it so well. And you have proven me correct."

Jandra moved her hands and laid her head on Sam's lap, "I knew not that so many women have so many intense problems. It but saddens me."

Sam lightly stroked Jandra's hair, "Then they are fortunate you are Second. You will help to make things easier for them, and more just. We should consider doing the same for Hengist if Briggon provides this not."

Jandra reached up and held Sam's hand, yet keeping her head in Sam's lap, "I know he does not. He has but three advisors so they have not the moments. And it is not an easy duty, Sam."

Sam hadn't noticed that all the guards standing nearby had quizzical, but smiling faces. None had yet known about Jandra and Sam, so had been surprised.

She helped Jandra to stand, then looped her arm through Jandra's and smiled as she looked directly into Jandra's eyes, "You will feel better as we do our rounds together."

Elsewhere, across The Realm

She knelt and bowed her head, "My Queen, I return."

She turned around, surprised, "You return with yet another tale of Woden? As soon as this?"

She saw The Healer was also in attendance with the High Queen. "Yes, Highness. She met with the Most Honored Spirit Mother of the Falls."

"And the Woman in the Woods? Both?"

"Yes, my Queen."

She frowned, "This is not a good report, Force Leader. You know well what this means."

"Yes, Highness. They have joined forces, against us."

"And they now seek to bring her into their fold."

"Her lover saved her life, my Queen."

"Her life? Tell Me more on this."

"More traitors in Woden, Highness. Two tried to kill her, but her lover took the knife. She used her powers to save her lover, then died, but the Most Honored Spirit Mother of the Falls then returned her life."

She raised an eyebrow as her eyes narrowed, "The Spirit Mother returned her life to her? Without dying? She doesn't have this power." She frowned, "I like this not. Watch them well."

Chapter V
The Boundary Lands

Sam chose to do rounds in the other half of Woden, the half she didn't live in. She was seeking general feelings from the community regarding the recent betrayals. As she and Jandra approached the first section of dwellings, Morian and Jardua approached with their two daughters, one but a small child.

They knelt, "Highest", then waited for her to respond.

Sam touched their shoulders and motioned for them to stand, "There be no need for you to kneel to me. How be your children this turn, Morian?" She had asked her specifically as she was the Birth-Mother to both of the girls.

"They are well, Highest. Would you like to hold little Morija?"

Sam let go of Jandra and held out her arms to see if Morija would come. She did, and laughed at Sam, "Play." Sam twirled her around a bit and then touched her hand to Morija's head, briefly. Morija laughed and laughed and laughed. Sam smiled at her and gave her back to Morian, then bent down to the other daughter. "What have you been doing all this turn, Mordua?"

"My Birth-Mother let me help in the gardens this turn. And then I got to pet a horse. Have you ever ridden a horse, Highest?"

"Oh, yes, many moments. Would you like to ride a horse? She held out hand to Mordua who instantly took it and held it, and together they walked away a little.

"Can I, Highest, really?. I would like that very much. Can I? Can I?"

Sam placed a hand on Mordua's head while yet talking and walking, "I think that can be arranged, if your mothers would but allow it. How many cycles have you now?" Sam frowned for a moment. She placed both hands on Mordua's head and was silent for but a moment. Mordua, being but a child, didn't notice that Sam had focused on her thoughts.

Mordua began pulling on Sam's sleeve, "Highest? Did you hear me?"

She smiled at Mordua and laughed lightly, "Yes, Mordua, you said nine cycles, which is more than old enough to begin to learn to ride. I will speak with your mothers to arrange this. But you will have to do your chores, as this will be a most special treat."

They returned and Sam asked if she might arrange some riding lessons with Jenna for Mordua.

"Oh, Highest, she has been after us long to do this, but we were unsure if there were moments in Jenna's schedule. That would be wonderful."

They spent the remainder of the after midturn and early prior eve completing Sam's rounds. Jandra noticed that Sam felt compelled to see as many children as she could this turn, to see if the betrayals or executions had effected any of them. At the end, Sam was exhausted and went to the park to rest for a while. Sam sat near at the bank of the river and played with some river birds. She was hungry, as they had missed their midturn meal, but felt she needed some moments to her own thoughts. After a while, Jandra came over and sat down on the bank next to her, but as soon as she sat, all the birds waddled over to her and sat down beside her.

"What did you do to them to make them do that?"

Laughing a little, but as surprised as Sam, she said, "I have done nothing. Do they not do this to you?"

"Ha! They come to me looking for food. They see you, these little traitors, and go to you as if you were their Birth-Mother."

Jandra stroked the birds' heads, taking some comfort in the feeling. "They have done this to me for as long as I can but recall."

"Jandra, were you but born in Woden?"

"It was told to me that I was an orphan, left at the gates."

"When is your first memory?"

Jandra thought about it for a moment. "On my sixth or seventh cycle, I think."

"Not earlier than this?"

"No. I cannot recall my overly early childhood."

"Are you ready for our early eve meal?"

"I thought you would never ask. We missed our midturn meal and I am but famished. How do you do so much walking on so little food? You are getting overly thin. You will not be able to lift your sword anymore if you do not eat. And I have a meeting with Tehna and Briggon this eve about the festival, so we must get back."

"I need to speak to the guard. I will return in but a moment."

Jandra had learned to worry whenever Sam spoke to a guard, so hoped it was about nothing serious.

Sam returned quickly, "Worry not. I have just sent a message to Meera and Caitha. I have need to speak with them. Your meeting provides me a good opportunity. Would you mind if they joined us for our meal? I just hope May has made enough, but I have asked Caitha to bring extra, in case."

Jandra would have been disappointed in past relationships about not having a quiet meal alone, but knew Sam was The Highest and needed some freedom in her decisions. "Of course, Sam. If you need or want to see them, then we will have a good moment in their company."

She suddenly sensed Jandra's disappointment, "I should but have asked first. I am sorry, Jandra. Let me just cancel the message." Sam went to talk to another guard.

"Hold, Sam. There is no need. I speak truly. It will be good for you, as I will be busy with my meeting."

They walked back to the dwelling arm-in-arm, chatting about the women they had spoken with, and the children. Jandra could hear in Sam's voice that she was concerned about the children. She made a mental note to have all the advisors tend more to the children that had suffered from the executions.

"Sam, what did you sense in the children that made you frown so?"

Sam shook her head, "A worm. An overly dark insidious worm. They know of this High Spirit Mother, and are now fearful."

Jandra changed the subject so that Sam might become less stressed, "I saw that you were reading from the journals. What have you learned?"

Sam sighed deeply, "That there always be an overly dark insidious worm."

Jandra once again wanted to change the subject so began telling Sam about one of the requests she had this turn, "It was very humorous, and I tried desperately not to laugh. Karan kept pinching the back of my neck, as she was afraid I would start laughing. But I saw her try not to, as well. Do you know Bernare and Lorian? They had this fight . . ."

By the moment they had arrived at their dwelling, Jandra had succeeded in making Sam laugh at her stories, "Thank you for those most wonderful stories. I think I am quite ready for our meal. I hope Meera and Caitha arrive soon. I am starved."

When they arrived to their dwelling, Sam went to change her garments and tend to herself while Jandra went in to see May.

"Good eve, May. Was the guard able to deliver the message to you yet?"

May was upset with Jandra and Sam, "Yes, they did, and of course I have enough, and both you and Sam should but know this as you both missed your midturn meal so there is much for all of you to eat, and yes, I know that Meera and Caitha are arriving too, but if you two do not start eating more, and more often, you are—"

"MAY! It be enough. I know. Sam needs to eat and she is not. I will tend better to this. But she is most hungry this eve, so will perhaps eat enough to help fill out her bones. I have a late meeting in the sitting room with Briggon and Tehna, but Sam will remain with Meera and Caitha out on the patio, so perhaps you could keep providing her more food. If I could but find a way to get Meera and Caitha in helping us to feed Sam more . . ."

"I will tend to that, Second. Now go and get ready for your guests and let me tend to our thinning Highest."

Jandra went to find Sam, and found her out on the patio, looking off into the distance. She hoped that May would bring out some food for Sam, quickly.

"What are you thinking, Sam?"

She turned and looked at Jandra, "I was wondering about life, and our future in it. That be all."

Jandra had noticed that Sam had changed her garments. "Your garments suit you well. You look most beautiful this eve, Sam."

"They are just comfort garments."

May brought out some food for Sam even knowing Meera and Caitha were not yet arrived, "You two can begin with these refreshments. I will bring out the main courses when Meera and Caitha arrive so that Second will have a moment to eat prior to her meeting."

Sam began to eat, "May, these are wonderful. They taste like the little foods I had at Hengist this prior turn."

"I had learned that there were some foods you liked much over there, so I asked a messenger to get one for me. I have recreated it for you so that you can enjoy it more."

"May, you spoil me." Looking at the other items, she asked, "Are these little things the other ones I liked?"

"Yes, Highest. Go ahead and eat them all. I have lots more."

Caitha and Meera arrived and greetings occurred. Caitha and Jandra went inside to get the rocker so that Caitha could sit in it.

Sam poured Meera a drink, "Have you heard anything about the five new women from the ship?"

"I know that Karan placed them in dwellings of volunteers, and all five have but requested to enter into our community."

Sam sat back and waited for the meal, "Why do you think our advisors became traitors?"

Meera also sat back and drank her wine, "It is but a puzzlement to me. They had everything that all the others do. They had enough to eat, to wear, nice dwellings, responsibilities, leisure moments. They wanted for nothing of which I am aware. They had positions of importance and some esteem, if that but mattered to them."

She looked at Sam, "I have thought much on this and remain confused. They wanted more power, but to what purpose? Why would that be important to them? I have not satisfied myself with an adequate answer. And who be this High Spirit Mother and Buron?"

Sam listened intently but also could find no answer.

May came out with the meal, "Here are you meals. Where are the other two?"

Meera looked around, "I thought they left but to get the rocker for Caitha. Where could they have gone?"

"I will find them. You two go ahead and eat. Meera, I expect you to make certain that our Highest eats plenty this eve."

Meera nodded and laughed, "Do you ever get any peace, Sam?"

Sam just laughed and began to eat, "It be difficult to complain when they but tend to me so well. Meera, have homes been found for Fionn and Vining's daughters?"

"Karan is tending to this, as is her usual. She is but an excellent advisor, Sam. It is Kandan's daughter that but worries me. Jandra has ordered her to Apien as part of Kandan's torture - trading her daughter into slavery as she wished to have done for our women. Be this something you would approve of?"

"What do you think we should do with her?"

"It be a harsh punishment for but an innocent victim."

"I think it will take care of itself. Hold her, for a while."

As Sam ate, she saw that it was one of her favorite meals - vegetables layered and baked with cheese and long thick noodles. May always provided at least two types of cheeses in this dish. And Sam saw that there was a bowl of fresh lettuce.

The gardens must be producing heavily once again.

"In truth, Sam, Caitha is a good cook, but May is the best in the community. I can boil but an egg and would not do that unless needed."

"Ah, but you wield the best sword in either of the communities."

"But Keddi is a master with her bow and arrow."

"We should make her teach us."

Meera nodded, thinking that a good idea.

Caitha and Jandra finally came out with rocker in-hand, but followed by May, "Just as I thought. These two were up to no good. They have been rearranging the bedroom furniture."

Caitha sat down in the rocker next to Meera, and tried to look innocent, "It is just located all wrong in their room, Meera. I could not but help myself. It called to me."

Jandra went over to Sam, "I am sorry, Sam. I know it to be your bedroom, but it does not look like it is well cared for, so we just began to make it more, well—"

Sam interrupted, "It be fine, Jandra. Caitha. Whatever you wish to do be but fine." She went back to eating her meal, "May, this meal is my favorite and is most delicious. Thank you for making it for us."

"Would you like more, Highest?"

Sam nodded, "Is there enough?"

May didn't wait to give an answer but went to bring more back for Sam.

Caitha brought her meal to the rocker, "Sam, I have heard that you but visit with the children. Did the executions do much damage?"

Jandra frowned, not wanting such a topic raised, but saw that it was too late.

Sam also frowned, shook her head, and halted her eating, "Everything I do or touch of late seems to be involved with betrayal. The children have been infested with the idea of evil. I but tried to replace some of their thinking with other notions, but I fear the ideas are with them. We will have to work hard as a community to rid them of such."

Jandra noticed that Sam had quit eating, when May returned, "Here is another helping, Highest."

"I have changed my mind, May. I will settle for just some tea."

May glared at Jandra, and Jandra glared at Caitha. Caitha saw that she had raised a bad topic that had caused Sam to halt her eating. "Sam, you but get me into trouble by not eating."

Sam looked around and saw that May wasn't going to leave until she ate some more, "Are you all certain that I am old enough to be The Highest? You but treat me as a child."

Meera laughed, but Caitha hit her gently on the arm, "Do not side with her. Look how thin she gets."

Meera moved away, in play, "She be correct, Caitha. She can live her own life quite well. If you but saw her with a sword or a bow and arrow, you would understand. When we fight together, I know that my back be but well tended."

Jandra shook her head, "That be fine, Meera, but it be not enough. She may be a decent warrior, but she tends not to herself at all well. Eat, Sam, or May, Caitha and I will have to force it down you."

Sam laughed and looked at Meera, "Sounds like a bet, to me. Should we take them on?"

Meera shook her head and continued to eat, "You are on your own. I like this food much and will not waste my moment on this bet. Given their frustration with you, we may lose as we will not pull out a sword."

Sam grinned and held up her hands, "You win, May and Jandra. I eat."

Sam sat down, and finally all were eating their meal.

After her Second helping, Sam sat back and drank her wine, "Meera, I want to tend to the boundary."

Meera looked well surprised, "During these moments, Sam? Now?"

Sam nodded, "It has calmed down some, and I haven't been at the boundaries in well over a moon. I am past due. And, unless someone else arranged for it so, Betten and Anja, and Sumi and Nodda need supplies. They haven't recently come to the community."

"I have not seen or heard from them either, but I think it better that I but send someone else, Sam."

Sam looked at the gardens, "Meera, I go."

"Who goes with you?"

Jandra noticed Sam's funny use of language, "What be this word you use—haven't?"

"I read it in the diaries of old. Does it not sound old to you?"

"What is it?"

"Haven't for have not, I but think."

"The First Ones used such a word?"

"Many such words. Shouldn't. Can't."

"Can't? What does this mean?"

"Cannot. I can't go to the boundary because Meera is overly mean to me."

Meera laughed, "I say again, Sam, who goes with you? You cannot go alone."

"Who would you have go with me?"

"All our guards would please me well."

Jandra interrupted, "Who are these people you speak of? Are these women of our community?"

Meera looked at her, "You know them not?"

Jandra shook her head, "No."

"They are of our community but wish to be self-reliant. We trade goods with them and Sam takes out needed supplies to them when she but goes."

"How do I not know of this?"

Sam and Meera both shrugged but said nothing. It was becoming obvious to both Sam and Meera that there was much that went on in their small communities that had been hidden.

Sam sighed and changed the subject, "Speaking of your guards, Meera, and I am but sure you have already tended to this. Will you re-train Keet's guards for us?"

"It has already begun. They are but lazy. We have them on a training schedule that they but complain about."

"Should we have a replacement for Keets, or would you be willing to provide leadership to all the guards?"

Jandra interrupted, "Make her a Second of Defense, and have her be the advisor to all the guards."

Meera shook her head, "Keddi could replace Keets."

Sam shook her head, "No. We have other uses for her. We must consider beginning the scouts once again. I need you to take over the command of all the guards. Will you do this for me?"

Meera looked hard at Sam. "Who but goes with you on your boundary round?"

Sam laughed, "Must I always get one thing by giving away another?"

Meera raised her eyebrow and said nothing. She waited, smiling her wily smile.

Sam thought about it a moment, "I have gone alone prior, Meera."

"You were not Highest then. And you also left before I but knew."

"I could do so again."

Meera shook her head, "I would warn you not to place a wager on that statement. You are well watched these moments."

Sam sighed again, "You have imprisoned me, then."

Jandra didn't want the eve to deteriorate, "Sam, what if we turned it into an adventure? I have never been to the boundaries and much enjoyed the scenery on our last journey to the Woman in the Woods. What if we took Meera and Caitha, Keddi and Margeria, and you and me? It would be fun. You would be well guarded, and I would get to see the boundaries. Caitha, what do you but think?"

Caitha was yet eating. She loved May's cooking. "Meera tries to keep me but safe and secure in the community. But for myself, I would love to see the boundaries. I have not yet seen them prior, either."

Meera looked at Sam, "Be this what you want?"

"You?"

"That and two more guards and I will but agree."

May brought out sweets for all, "Highest, I think you will but like this. It is a new type of cake I make. Try it and let me know."

Sam took a bite, "This is wonderful, May. What is in it?"

May winked, "I will not tell. The more you eat of it, the more familiar it will become."

Sam ate and enjoyed her cake. It tasted of a spice cake but looked like it had some vegetables in it. She cared not. It was a sweet and delicious. She asked for another piece after she finished her first.

"I agree, Meera. Four guards and four of us."

Jandra looked suddenly troubled, "Sam, perhaps I should not ride with you. I must tend to the festival."

"We will be gone but two or three eves. Can you not have the others tend to it during that moment?"

"If it be no more than three. That will leave me three to tend to the festival, and it will be enough."

Meera arranged the trip for them to leave the next morn. The horses, supplies, guards, and weapons would all be ready by early morn. Meera and Caitha then left as Jandra had her meeting to arrange for the festival. Since she had some moments of peace, Sam retrieved the community's diaries so as to continue her reading. She returned to the patio to read since the sun was yet up, and since Jandra had taken the meeting room.

> Entry #11:
>
> After 2 cycles here, our scouts have finally returned with good news. We have our land. We've been saving provisions in preparation for the move, but it's been a hard battle to keep them. The colony keeps raiding our temporary community, but we keep holding them off – thankfully, not for much longer. I have buried the original diaries in order to keep them safe, in a small box. We have marked the site with a large stone, 250 paces in from the sea, in the middle of our temporary community. The large stone sits among four nut trees. We will try to take the diaries with us, but I believe we'll have to fight our way out of here, so will probably have to return at some point to retrieve them. And I don't think we have enough room in the boat for everything.
>
> Some more women from the colony have risked coming over to join us. We now have 44 women who will make the move in just a few days. Most of us have never been on the sea so are fearful of the voyage, but would rather face the sea than risk further enslavement from the colony.
>
> Many women and men leave the colony now. People are put to death daily for an infraction of any rule. While some men seek refuge with us too, we will accept only women from this point on. After the rule of silence imposed on all women, mandatory laws to birth five children each, and the loss of all personal freedom, we can no longer stay here. We have lost many lives in this battle, but we now leave soon. The colony will be unable to follow us, as we have sunk most of their boats.
>
> As a community we fight hard, but have few skills. We hope our gardening and building skills, as miserable and pathetic as they are, will allow us to get through our first cycle. Our scouts tell us that we will be able to sustain ourselves through fishing, if necessary, until our crops are successful. While I don't

wish to eat fish for longer than necessary, I would eat raw worms for many terms than stay in this place any longer.

Entry #12

We prepare to depart. We have managed to steal another boat. Our own attempts at building one were disgraceful, but since we don't want Burn and the likes of him to follow us, we stole one of his. It isn't as good as the others cause we had burned his good ones, but it's the only other alternative we have.

We've saved some garden seeds for replanting, have made some leather hides for blankets, but they don't smell too good, and we have a lot of dried food. We're hoping we can stop to fish and catch some game along the way. Our scouts have told us that it will take us at least 3-4 weeks, perhaps longer.

I'm excited about the new land. Our scouts have told us much about it. It has three very large rivers. It borders the forest and the sea. It has grasslands for good crops. And it is well sheltered and far away from all other communities.

It'll mean having to rebuild everything, though, as we can't take everything we have made during our wait. It's all we can do to carry enough food, water, supplies, tools, our tamed livestock, and weapons. We've finally decided to let the men come in another boat and build a community next to ours. They've volunteered to have only a men's community, follow our laws and offer their assistance and protection. Like us, they've begun to pair off within themselves. They no longer need or want women. There's been far too much abuse between us to try to get along anymore. There's been too much abuse and control on their parts for us to ever trust them again, at least in my lifetime.

I can't go back to retrieve the diaries I buried. Burn has taken over that area and camps right on top of them without knowing. Perhaps in time I can return to retrieve them, but I fear they are gone from us forever.

It's strange, now. I have come to see this as my home and this violent life as my life now. Once upon a time, I was a noted scientist. Now I'm becoming a gardener, builder and woman-warrior; and perhaps, lesbian – if such a label even applies. I still think of home, so many light years away, but no longer think of it as home. Now we will begin a new life. One I hope more from. We have begun to talk about a system of governance and have agreed we need a leader, but we haven't decided if it should be voted like we did back home, with elections every so often, or if we should just have a monarchy and be done with it. We leave in the morn, winds willing.

Entry #13:

It's night of our first day at sea. Most of the women are sick on board the boat I'm on. Only two know how to sail and give orders to the rest of us. We had a very difficult leaving. Burn had his men watching us well, so knew that we were planning to leave soon as they saw all our activity to and from the boats. So we had a major battle this morning. We lost three more women in battle, but we seem to keep getting more and more. We now move with 87 total woman and 45 men. Burn's numbers are about the same, but all they've eaten these past months is game, so they don't fare as well as we do.

The men we take with us are all on two boats. We have five. They know we don't want them, but they have managed to persuade us that they'll be useful and peaceful. That's what we fear most from men, now; their violent nature. Too many of us have suffered by their dominant strength. Some of us think that they are traitors and will but give us away to Burn. I don't agree with this, but I guess we'll see. No matter what, it's easy to become very paranoid from all this violence.

We have 14 children with us, too. All Burn's, would be my guess. He yells to us from a distance that he wants his children returned to him. I'd rather kill them, first. [and I would, too!] My child didn't live through its full-term. A boy. I don't know what I think that it has died, but I just try to forget about it and not think on it. Too much of this is way too depressing. We have no doctors, no nurses, no medical experts. All our technology is gone except for what's in our heads. Our tools and weapons are all homemade now, and while we know the concept of guns, we've not the skills to make them. We've tried to learn blacksmithing, but without books or manuals or others to teach us, it seems hopeless. But we're on our way now and will be safe for a while, anyway. At least until Burn finds us.

Entry #14:

Burn has followed us and tries to engage us in fight. We outrun him but will have to stop him at some point, as we don't want him to know where we head. We have taken a divergent route so that he doesn't know the direction we head. Elaine, our ship captain, says that we've added an extra two weeks to our journey, but since we don't want Burn to know, then we show him a different route. He thinks we head north. Elaine is hoping for a fog storm so that we might slip away from him. She also thinks he'll stop following us in good time if he thinks he knows where we head.

Most of the women are still seasick. The children seem to be faring better, thank goodness I lose track of days and years now, so no longer know what season, day, month or whatever it may be. I threw my watch away long ago, as it seems so ridiculous and useless here. We tell time by the sun. I can't even believe that in my former life I drove an Audi to work every day, 30 miles, and it took me only 20 minutes each way. Now, 30 miles seems like an impossible distance. We brought horses with us from home, but on this trip we can't take any as there is no room. 30 miles will now mean a very long walk of 2 or more days.

Sam halted her reading in order to reflect on it. She thought about the very beginnings of Woden and how the women had been treated so badly that they separated from the men.
So, wherever they had come from, they had but come as a mixed community.
But she also read that it was not uncommon in their former home to have all types of companionships, apparently all living together in a community. She wondered how many books they may have had and thought it, once again, to be quite a lot. Woden had no such book making ability as with the likes of *Morte D'Arthur*. She thought that so much in the journal readings was confusing due to the terms.
What be a mile?
What be a year?
A watch?
A car?
An Audi?
She wondered if she might ever know the answers to her questions.

It was getting too late to read on the patio any longer, so she decided to take a walk. Sam knew that she couldn't really walk alone anymore, that guards would shadow her, but she would try to deny that piece of knowledge and just pretend she was alone. She walked down the main path, the one with the shops. As she left her patio, the guards became startled but remained quiet. She went past them and halted herself from looking back to see if they followed. She knew they would. In the recent past, she might have tried to elude them, but this eve she just wanted to take the walk whether they were there or not.

From sensing the children's thoughts, she knew that they were thinking much on the notion of betrayal and death. This disturbed her greatly as she knew this might instill fear into them, a concept Woden couldn't afford in their own. Death seemed to be part of the nature of their lives, but inflicting the notion of betrayal onto children just seemed evil to her.

Sam walked over the bridge, then turned down the path to the shops. She noticed that the path was well tended and had been planted with more flowers. Berga was out cleaning the window of her shop. It was a tea specialty shop, and often during the turns she would provide cups of teas for the women, or men, to try before they traded. She had three small tables out in front of her shop where women could sit while they drank their tea.

She waved to Sam, "Highest. Would you like a cup of tea?"

Sam turned toward the voice and recognized Berga, "Yes, Berga. That would be wonderful. What type do you have warmed this eve?"

Sam went over while Berga pulled out a chair for her, "I have two types. Mint and blueberry."

Sam sat down, "Mint, I think."

Berga went inside and returned quickly with two cups. She sat one down in front of Sam. "Mint is a good soother for your stomach. How is it to be The Highest for you?"

"I think not enough moments have passed to answer your question. What is the community thinking of all these events and traitors?"

Berga frowned, "I always knew that Josin to be but a bad one. She never had a good word to say to any of us shopkeepers, and not once would she visit with us, as you do. She felt herself better than all of us. I have not spoken with everyone, but my friends are very saddened to hear that The Highest had let things get so out of control. And to hear that she was betraying Woden in a small way is but a sad report indeed. But my Birth-Mother used to tell me that for every sad event, there is a happy one waiting. And it be true as we now have you as The Highest. So I think the community to be well-pleased. All the killings of these traitors have been hard, but was necessary, I think. We are glad you did it. It would be unwise to keep these traitors with us. We cannot afford to be weak or we will become slaves like so many of our sisters. Do you like your tea?"

"The tea is most soothing. Did you have Oisin take some on her journey?"

"Four barrels. Four types. For trading. I am hoping for some different spices and dried fruits or herbs in exchange. We will see what she finds."

"Where is Inma this eve? Why is she not with you?"

"She worked late in the gardens this late after midturn so will be but back soon. She has been pruning some of the fruit bushes."

Sam finished her tea, "Thank you for this late eve tea, Berga. It has been a treat for me."

Berga nodded, as if they were old friends, and smiled at Sam, "I hear rumors, Highest. Be they true?"

"What do you speak of, Berga?"

Berga smiled again, "We hear that you might but have a companion, finally."

"Perhaps. We shall see."

If I can but figure out how to have a companion yet not lose all my freedoms.

"It has been a long moment for you, Highest. You but carried Brett with you for many cycles. The songs about that moment are yet but sung."

"I have never heard those songs. But I think it perhaps the moment to accept a companion."

Berga smiled, "I think so, too. You need someone Highest. It is not good for you to just have one-eve visits. While the legends can make us smile of your pleasures, the realities are that you remain but alone overly long."

Sam rose to leave, "Many thanks, Berga. I have enjoyed this eve with you. Please give my regards to Inma. I am sorry I missed seeing her."

Sam began walking down the path again, noticing that all the shops were now dark. The only sounds she could hear were the river sounds, and the sounds of the guards quietly following her. She turned and decided to return to her dwelling. As she arrived, she saw that Briggon and Tehna had just left through the front of the dwelling. She went around to the patio and sat down at one of the long chairs and just enjoyed the solitude and quiet. She thought much of Jandra, but having someone around all the moments would take much getting used to after all these cycles of living alone.

Jandra came out, "Sam, you need to come inside. It be but chilly out here. Are you not cold?"

Sam hadn't noticed the chill and looked up at Jandra, "How was your meeting? Is the festival all arranged?"

"I feel a little guilt over my decision, but I handed the festival over to Briggon and Tehna, mostly. Briggon and Hengist are very excited about this next festival now that we are but re-opening our gates with them in trade and entertainment, so had much to offer for the festival. And Tehna was excited about the play and all the new arts and crafts that Hengist will have to share at the festival, so will work with Briggon. This festival is going to be but a gift from Hengist, and I am glad to let them have it. How have you tended to this most awful chore all these cycles?"

Sam laughed a little and motioned to her seat, "Sit with me, Jandra."

Jandra noticed that Sam wasn't yet ready to go inside. She sat down right next to Sam. It was a little overcrowded but helped to keep her warm. Sam took one of Jandra's hands and just held it as she gazed into the dark eve sky, "Look at the stars, Jandra. Do you not wonder about them?"

"What are you thinking, Sam? What do you but see?"

Sam hesitated, yet looking at the stars, but then said, "I think the First Ones come from up there somewhere."

Jandra looked at Sam with some dismay, "What are you talking about, Sam?"

Sam looked back to Jandra and just smiled patiently, "It be unimportant for now."

Jandra rose and started to pull her up, "Come, Sam. Come inside and hold me. I am cold and we need our rest for the next turn's adventure."

Sam resisted and gently tried to pull Jandra back down, "But, Jandra, it be a beautiful eve, is it not?"

Jandra sat down next to Sam, then began to unbutton her own shirt. She opened it part way and placed Sam's hand on one of her breasts, "I think we should go inside."

* * * *

Sam was awake early, even prior to Jandra. She was preparing their garments and weapons for packing and had heard Jenna bring up the horses. She also packed one of the diaries so she could share it with the group in the eves while they were gone. She wanted their impressions of them.

Jandra awoke to Sam's packing, "Are you up so early?"

"I thought that I would but prepare us for the trip. I have packed the garments you will but need."

Jandra got up and began to dress into the garments Sam had laid out for her for the turn, "Is anyone here yet?"

"The horses are ready."

"Do you always take the horses on this trip?"

"No. At some moments I but walk the boundary. But we have not the moments for this now. It but takes me a moon or a little more."

May walked in. "Oh, Highest, you are up early. Meera and Caitha have just arrived. I have your early morn meal ready for all in the kitchen."

Sam nodded and began to stuff their items into the leather pouches. "Jandra, I will meet you in the kitchen. I am but taking our items to the horses to pack."

"You have walked the boundary?"

Sam nodded.

"Alone?"

Again, Sam nodded, but said nothing.

Jandra shook her head and began to get ready, *She be more independent than I first thought.*

They all met in the kitchen and began eating their early morn meal. Finally, Keddi and Margeria arrived, along with Rundle, and they too ate the morn meal.

"Thank you, Highest, Meera, for inviting us. This be most exciting to me. Keddi and I are most delighted to guard for you during this trip." Margeria was pleased by the invitation.

Keddi nodded, "And I have brought an extra bow so that I can teach The Second to shoot in the eves, after we have halted for the turn."

Meera looked at Keddi, "Good. Then you can but teach me to shoot two arrows at one moment, then."

May prepared all their food, while the two extra guards, Anyst and Anicia, began packing the gear, weapons and food. By the moment Sam had finished her early morn meal, the horses were ready. Anyst and Anicia distributed the weapons, and then everyone mounted.

Sam watched, once again, with quiet surprise, while Jandra's horse seemed to take great interest in her. Sam watched, seeing that Jandra took it as normal that the horse would show such attention to her. But Sam knew otherwise. Each of the horses given to Jandra to ride all did the same. She let it go, shaking her head in dismay, knowing that one of the horses that had come up to Jandra to be petted was well-noted for biting its rider.

Meera rode over to Sam, "I assume we but ride the entire perimeter. Where do you desire to begin?"

"Let us take the supplies first to Betten and Anja, then Sumi and Nodda. I wish to speak with them. We can leave the extra horse with them, then pick it up on the return. You lead. Have Keddi and Margeria bring up the rear."

Meera nodded and dropped back to speak with Keddi and Margeria, and then told Anyst and Anicia to ride flank, leaving Jandra and Caitha surrounded by guards. Meera would guard The Highest.

They rode out toward where the rivers met, past the farms and gardens and into the wild grasslands. They would ride the horses easy on this trip, as there was no need for hurry. Rundle ran alongside Keddi or Sam's horse as they went, enjoying the moment of excitement. As they reached the rivers' fork, Meera took the left branch and rode on, keeping the river to her right. By early midturn, they reached Betten and Anja's dwelling and farm. While they were yet a short distance away, Sam had them halt so that Betten and Anja could see who came. Betten and Anja saw them, waving their greetings and excitement.

Sam rode up first, as she knew them best, then dismounted. "Betten. Anja. How fares your farm?"

They knelt before her, "Highest. We but heard the report. We never thought you would but come to visit with us again."

Sam took their elbows and helped them to rise, "There be no need to kneel to me. We be but friends. Come, allow me to introduce you to my escorts. You know Meera."

Meera dismounted and went to give them each a hug.

"This be Caitha, Meera's companion." She motioned to Jandra, "This be The Second."

They bowed their heads toward Jandra. She returned the gesture.

Betten looked closely at Jandra, as if studying her. "You look as the old ones tell in their stories. Different, yet the same. Are you one of the old ones, from across The Realm?"

Jandra cocked her sideways a bit at this, wondering, but let it go. She thought she might raise this with Caitha later, as Caitha knew most of the old stories.

Sam laughed a little at the comment, but also wondered about it, "She came to Woden as a babe; found at the gates in a basket. She knows not of her background." Then she motioned to the guards, "This be Keddi, one of our Scouts. Margeria, Anicia and Anyst, our guards."

Rundle moved forward and wagged his tail, hoping for a friendly hand. Keddi laughed and introduced him, while Betten and Anja knelt down to pet him and let him lick them all over their face.

"Please, come inside. What we have is yours. Please share our mid-turn meal with us."

As they went into Betten and Anja's dwelling, Jandra was surprised to see such simple living. It was a one-room dwelling with very little accommodation for comfort. In one corner, Jandra could see where one of them weaved blankets and clothing, and in another corner, the other one made and repaired their tools and weapons.

Sam nodded, "We have brought supplies for you. And I have two flasks of wine for you. May also sends two sweet cakes."

Anja smiled, "Thank you. We have our items for return trade. Are you but able to take them back for us?"

Sam nodded, "We are riding the perimeter, but with your permission we will leave one horse with you for three turns. When we return, we can pack your trade items then."

Betten and Anja fed them some soup and fresh bread. Keddi and Margeria, like Jandra, hadn't known that they had women of their community who lived apart. As soon as Anyst and Anicia had eaten, they began to unpack the supplies and feed the horses. They repacked the supplies for Sumi and Nodda onto their own horses.

Keddi was curious, "Do you find it dangerous out here all alone?"

Anja shook her head, "No. The sentries come by every few turns to check on us. And your Highest comes by once per moon. We love her visits. But we have had no danger from men or women until of late. We saw some fires down the valley, so Betten traveled to the sentry and informed her."

Anicia nodded, "Yes. They be the same fires I saw, Highest, but they had come a little closer."

Meera frowned, "Have you seen them since?"

Betten shook her head, "No. Not since."

Everyone prepared to leave and exited the tiny dwelling. Sam remained inside with them for a moment. When she came out, Meera saw that she was frowning. Sam looked up and saw Meera looking at her. She shook her head slightly, but said nothing.

Sam gave Betten and Anja a hug, "We return in two or three turns."

The others had already mounted their horses and just awaited Sam.

As Sam mounted, Meera asked, "Is all well?"

Sam just shook her head, but smiled at Anja and Betten. They then waved and rode off toward Sumi and Nodda who lived a half-turn's walk away from the river. Meera once again took the lead, but kept Sam within her eyesight.

Jandra rode up closer to Sam, "Why do these women but live so far removed? Are they not overly old to do so?"

"It be but their choice. They have done so since they took each other as their companion. It has been over forty cycles of which I am but aware. They have no sense of cycles in that regard, so would not be able to say. They enjoy the quiet life and think Woden overly busy and stressful. They have been most successful in their gardening and crafts. And they eat no animals of any kind, except for the fish they can catch from the river."

"How long have you but visited with them?"

"I began when I became Second. Over fourteen cycles prior."

Their ride to Betten and Anja's had been mostly over the grassland area. As they began to travel toward Sumi and Nodda's, the terrain became hillier and they could begin to see some mountains off in the distance. Meera saw smoke in one of the valleys of the mountains. She had decided to wait until after their visit with Sumi and Nodda before raising the alert. Keddi rode up next to Meera and, saying nothing, nodded toward the smoke.

Meera nodded, "I have seen it. We will investigate after we unload the supplies."

Keddi nodded and returned to her position. Sam had also seen the smoke and had seen Keddi warn Meera of it.

She rode up to Meera, "I think we should begin a regular visit of the perimeter with fully armed guards."

Meera nodded, "Let us hope it be but a small group. I think we should investigate after we drop off our supplies. We could leave Jandra and Caitha at Sumi and Nodda's until our return."

"We can try, but do you plan to tie up Jandra to make her do so?"

Meera laughed, "Look near those trees, Sam. I see their dwelling."

Sam knew their dwelling well. A very small dwelling, much like Betten and Anja's, but made of logs from the forest. It had only two small windows and one door. Nodda did the hunting while Sumi tended to the garden. They lived next to a small river from which they caught some fish. One item they regularly traded with Woden was their leathers and furs Nodda cured from her hunting. As Sam's group got within shouting distance of the dwelling, Meera gave a warning signal.

"Sumi. Nodda."

After four tries with no response, Sam began to worry, "Sumi be not responding. She be always about. Something must be wrong."

Meera signaled to Keddi, Margeria, Anyst and Anicia, "We go in on foot, quietly. Be mindful of an ambush."

Keddi gave Rundle a hand signal to go to the forest and check for sounds. Rundle ran off quickly but quietly, somehow knowing not to bark.

Meera gave directions for how each should approach the dwelling, noting to all that she would ride up as soon as she had but given them a moment to arrive on foot.

"Sam, you wait here with Jandra and Caitha. "

Sam nodded, wanting to go but leaving it to Meera. Meera looked at Sam quizzically.

"What?" Sam asked.

"You argue not with me?"

"It must be your lucky turn. Now go, before I change my mind."

Jandra nudged her horse toward Sam's, "What be wrong?"

"No one responds to our calls. It is unusual, so we be but cautious. It is probably of no concern." But Sam knew better. Sumi was always around the dwelling.

She watched as Meera began to ride up. She could see the others moving forward quietly, but remaining as hidden as possible in the trees and bushes. As Meera arrived at the garden, she dismounted and called again, "Sumi. It is Meera, from Woden. Are you here?"

Yet no response.

Keddi and Margeria had arrived at the dwelling, coming up on one side of it. They crept their way forward to the door, one on each side, their bow and arrows pulled and ready. Meera had her sword unsheathed.

She called again, "Sumi. Nodda. It is Meera, from Woden."

Nothing.

Finally, Keddi kicked the door open and moved in, dropping to a stooping position, her bow readied. Rundle came running in beside her. She saw nothing in the dwelling, so got up and looked around.

"No one here, Meera. There looks to be no sign of fighting, either. Everything seems to be in its place. The fire in the fireplace is cold, but there are warm embers at the bottom."

Meera waved for Sam and the others to come up to the dwelling. Anicia and Anyst came in from the forest. As they arrived, Sam, Jandra and Caitha dismounted, then went inside.

Sam looked at the garden, "It looks to be well tended, so I do not think they have been gone for long."

Meera nodded, "I saw as much."

She began walking around the dwelling and the gardens, looking at the ground. She kept enlarging her circle. After a few moments, she halted and looked off into the distance.

Sam walked over to her, "Do the bootprints lead off to the smoke?"

Meera bent to the ground and studied the bootprints more. "Two sets of bootprints. They go voluntarily, on their own. Sumi must have gone along with Nodda. The bootprints look deep. Perhaps they take supplies with them. They must have left this morn. It is but a long journey on foot. If we left now, we would arrive just shortly after them, around mideve."

Sam looked at the trampled grasses, "It looks like they have gone this way but prior."

"You be correct. Perhaps three or four other moments."

"What be your suggestion, Meera?"

"We could but scout it out. If there be overly many, we could send a messenger back for more guards."

Sam nodded, "Let us go, then, before it becomes dark."

Meera called to everyone to mount up. Anyst and Anicia unloaded the supplies for Nodda and Sumi, and then mounted. Meera had Keddi and Margeria scout the way. Rundle now felt a sense of purpose and kept his nose in the air. She cautioned that they must give no warning to their arrival and also to watch for Nodda and Sumi. Keddi and Margeria left at a fast gallop and would slow and dismount as they came closer to the smoke.

Meera rode beside Jandra and Caitha, "When we but arrive toward the smoke, I will leave the two of you behind until we know it but safe."

"But I am Second and I deserve to—"

Sam interrupted and smiled at her, "There are moments when even a Second must obey the commands of Meera."

"But, Sam, if you get hurt or—"

"Then someone must be able to get back to warn Woden. And someone must remain back to protect Caitha. She has but no skills in weapons, and you do."

Jandra rolled her eyes at her, "This is a reason? My ability with weapons?"

Sam laughed, but turned her horse toward the valley. Jandra thought it a weak excuse, but knew that Sam was partially correct. Someone had to remain with Caitha, and Caitha wouldn't be able to go in with them until it was clear. They rode at a normal pace toward the smoke. Anyst and Anicia had taken watch positions, one in front and one in back, with their weapons ready. Sam and Meera waited to draw their weapons until closer. As late after midturn arrived, they came upon Keddi and Margeria's horses. They had gone on foot from this spot. Rundle was not to be seen, so must have gone in with them. Meera decided that this is where Jandra and Caitha would wait until their return, so had all to dismount.

Looking at Jandra and Caitha, she pointed to the trees and quietly said, "Go into the forest with the horses and wait there. Jandra, have your weapons at alert. Caitha, listen for sounds until we return. You must both remain on alert, quiet, and on watch. If anyone comes by, hide behind the trees and keep the horses quiet. We will be back to get you shortly. Move not from this spot, and make no fire."

Jandra nodded and took Caitha into the woods. Meera and Sam watched them go, and then Meera motioned to Anyst and Anicia to scout ahead for them. All four left quietly. From this point on, they held their weapons on the alert. Sam and Meera walked upon the freshly trampled path while Anicia and Anyst trotted alongside in the forest, making sure no one was ready in ambush. As they arrived within hearing distance of the smoke area, an arrow landed in front of Meera. It came from her right. She waited, knowing it was either Keddi or Margeria's.

Margeria came over from her left and whispered, "It be but a small community. Perhaps eighteen or twenty men and women, including a few small children. There could be a few more in their dwellings that we could not see. I know not Sumi and Nodda, but saw two older women who looked liked they had but just arrived. They looked rather wild and unkempt, both with hair that needed much tending. Be that Nodda and Sumi?"

Sam nodded. It was.

Margeria continued, "It looks to be but a small town and very poor and desperate. The people look as if they starve. We saw no weapons. And some look to be quite sickly. Keddi and I think that the Nodda and Sumi women give them food."

Meera nodded, "How far from here?"

"But a few moment's walk straight in."

"You and Keddi go around and be prepared to defend us. Anyst and Anicia will do the same. Surround the town without being seen, but make certain that you can protect The Highest at all moments. We will give you a few moments to get into place prior to us leaving."

All four nodded and left.

Meera looked at Sam, "We go straight in."

"It sounds like a mixed community of desperate men and women."

Meera shook her head, "I have longed feared and thought that men and women from the mixed communities would seek us out for refuge."

"I as well. I fear we will have to create a third community under Woden Falls if we are to maintain safety in the realm. This moment, a mixed community."

"It will take Hengist and Woden many moments to get through their thoughts on this, but it is most certain that this group will not be able to remain here if they are to survive. This be but a most pitiful place to attempt a community. The storms blow through this valley with force, and the land be overly poor for good crops."

"Do you think Margeria correct in that they have no weapons? How do they hope to survive?"

"I think they but escaped from Apien or New Harborage and sought to try to reach Woden. If that be true, then they escaped but to survive."

Sam nodded, thinking the same. They began to walk up toward the smoke, slowly so as to give Keddi and the rest the moments needed to get into position.

As they entered the small cluster of shacks, Sam saw that the dwellings were nothing more than temporary shelters, with no doors, and none with windows.

They walked into the camp and Nodda and Sumi finally saw them, "Highest!" They turned to the rest of the camp men and women, "This be The Highest. This be who we have spoken much of."

Nodda and Sumi knelt to Sam. The small community also knelt. Sam saw that they looked frightened, hungry, and wretched condition. She saw that that the women looked particularly worn and miserable. Meera motioned for Keddi and Margeria to look through the dwellings. Anyst and Anicia stayed on alert just on the outskirts of the dwellings, but now within vision. Rundle remained near Keddi, on full alert. Sam went to one the palest looking of the women and saw that the woman was but crying.

Sam said softly, "You have no reason to fear us. We are here in peace."

The woman nodded but said nothing and kept her head bowed as she knelt.

Sam tried again, "Do you know who I am?"

Meekly and softly, the woman replied, "Yes, Highest."

"Then why be you afraid of us? Do you think we will harm you?"

As Sam spoke to the woman, Meera looked around at all the men and women. To a one, they were all kneeling and had their heads deeply bowed to Sam. They shivered as frightened hares and looked hungry as starving orphans.

Again, the woman nodded.

Sam went close to the woman, "May I lay my hand upon you, frightened one?"

The woman nodded, and Sam placed her hand upon her head. She sensed the woman so frightened that it affected her heart. Sam also sensed that she was with child, but that this woman was in danger of dying from starvation and her child was dying at this moment. Sam focused and gave the woman a little of her energy, and also sent a soft message of safety to try to calm her. She couldn't save the child.

Sam looked to Meera, "Send Anicia for Jandra and Caitha. Have them bring the horses. Have Keddi and Margeria hunt for what food they can but find prior to the eve."

Meera nodded and made it so.

Sam looked back to the woman, "Rise, and look at me."

The woman rose but kept her head bowed. She no longer was crying.

"What do they call you, young one?"

"Tedra of Bolden. He be my mate."

Sam looked around, "Show me Bolden, your mate."

Tedra became nervous all over again, "Oh, please, Highest. Please do not harm Bolden. He be a good man. He does not deserve to die."

Sam looked surprised, "I am sorry that your life has had such misery in it for you to be this afraid of me. I will not harm him, Tedra. Please, introduce me to your mate."

Tedra yet looked frightened but motioned Sam over to Bolden, who Sam saw to be a young man also close to dying from starvation.

She placed her hand upon his frightened and bowed head. Once again she sensed sheer terror in these people, and complete hopelessness. She also sensed from Bolden that he had no skills in farming, building or hunting.

She saw that he also cried. "What is it you do, Bolden?"

"I was a musician and instrument maker. I also made paper."

"Rise, Bolden, and tend the fire. We will eat well this eve. Bring out what serving bowls or plates you but have, and let us prepare."

She turned to the rest of the camp, "Rise. You have no need to bow before me. I am The Highest of Woden, and we will now tend to your hunger, safety and wellness. Come and sit around the fire so that you may introduce yourselves to me as my guards prepare our meal."

Sam went over to Nodda and Sumi, "It be good to see you well. How long have they been arrived here?"

Nodda answered, "They but told us they walked from Apien. They lost many along the way. We bring what supplies we can. We saw their fire a few turns prior and have been trying to teach them survival skills, but they be overly hungry to even fish. They have been here no more than that."

"Excuse me but a moment. I must tend to a duty."

Sam walked over to Meera, "Send one of your guards back to Woden. Have Karan send enough horses for these men and women so that we may bring them back to Woden for care. They but die here. Have Briggon return with some of his guards and horses, as well. Also, have May send another pack of food, enough for four. You, Keddi, Margeria and I will complete the perimeter duty."

"Sam, we have found but not one weapon in this place. How do they but plan to protect themselves?"

"In truth, I have never seen such terrified men and women. I read Bolden's mind and sensed that he was abused much in Apien. The child his mate carries is not his, but of another. What has Apien become?"

"It would seem Apien has become but a plague. I will send Anyst back to Woden and will have her return with guards, horses and food. I will also have Anyst inform May to prepare the healers. She can but return by early midturn next."

Sam nodded and returned to Nodda and Sumi, "It is good of you to try to help these men and women. We will take them into Woden and heal and care for them. If they be willing to follow Woden's laws and ways, they can rest under our protection."

Sumi smiled at Sam, "It is as I have told them you would say, Highest. You are the best of women in all The Realm and I but knew that your heart would go out to them." Then she frowned, "But they be overly frightened to believe us. They fear you mightily and have been told many stories of your terrible powers."

"I will make it right for them, Sumi. Help to prepare a meal, if you would, and then we must begin to prepare them for departure at midmorn next."

Nodda went right up to Sam and hugged her, "Thank you, Highest. On our way back, please halt by our dwelling. I have prepared a most magnificent floor piece of animal fur for you. It be the best one I have done, and you deserve it."

Sam looked again at Sumi, "Sumi, could you look around this area to see if there but be any wild plants that could be prepared to the meal?"

Sumi nodded and headed off toward a small river. She knew what she was looking for and Sam knew that she would bring back armfuls of wild vegetables for their meal. Sam walked over to the fire where the men, women and children were all sitting, yet looking at her in fear.

She went up to one of the female children and sat down next to her. "What be your name, little one?"

The child was also crying. Sam was frustrated at all the crying, but knew that they were overly hungry and scared to be emotionally stable.

The child looked up at her, "Sansa."

"A pretty and most unusual name. How many cycles have you, Sansa?"

"Eleven cycles, Highest. Are you going to kill us?"

Sam laughed, "No, Sansa. I am going to feed you, take care of you, and try to make you a nice new comfortable dwelling, away from this most difficult of spots. Would that be fine with you?"

Sansa nodded her head vigorously, "Are there other children, where you are?"

"There are, Sansa, but I know not if you will choose to live in our community. But in Woden, you shall have many wonderful things to keep you occupied."

Sam placed her hand upon Sansa's head. She sensed the child hungry, but otherwise well, and like the others, afraid. Sam sent Sansa an image of comfort and safety and noticed that Sansa seemed to relax a little.

"When do we get to eat?"

Sam laughed, "Soon. We prepare the meal now. You will have all you desire this eve, and hereafter. You no longer need to worry about food."

Anicia arrived in camp with Jandra, Caitha and all the horses. As Jandra came into camp, all the women, children and men went to her, bowing before her, trying to touch her. Sam watched in disbelief, also seeing the surprise upon Jandra's face. But she also saw that Jandra's presence comforted them, so was pleased that at least something calmed them.

Sam went from person to person, placing her hand upon their heads and trying to comfort them. She was able to heal a few of some minor ailments, but found that a few had ills overly large for her powers. Jandra saw what Sam was doing and also went to each of them, trying to comfort them. All the men, women and children responded most favorably to Jandra. Caitha did likewise, telling wonderful stories about Woden, Sam and Meera. Sam went back to Tedra.

Tedra saw her coming over to her and knelt down, "Please, Highest. I will do what you want, but please do not kill Bolden."

Sam sat down next to Tedra, "You may remain in that ridiculous kneeling position if you want, but I have need to find some information from you."

Finally, Tedra saw that Sam meant what she said. She rose from her kneeling position and sat down next to Sam, "What be it you need from me, Highest?"

"Why did you come here?"

"We have heard stories of your greatness."

"Did you not know that we are but an all woman community?"

"Yes, we know. And we know of Hengist, too. But we want to live our lives peacefully, as your women do of Woden and your men of Hengist."

"Do you not know that we have no mixed community?"

"We know this, Highest, and are willing to abide by your laws and split our unions so as to live peacefully. Our lives are certainly not worth living, at this moment. We will be but happy to see our mates at the moments of the festivals. It will be enough for us, Highest, but to have this peace and safety. We will do anything you ask of us, with no complaint."

"It has been that bad for you, then?"

Tedra nodded, "All our children are raped by their sixth or seventh cycle, regardless be they girl or boy. There is no way to halt the abuses. *Those* men are evil and want only power over everyone. And all the women are raped daily to keep us with child. The men . . . " She hesitated, "Well, they are also well abused, perhaps even more than the women."

"Who does these acts on you?"

"Manthar says that he is to be the father of all our children, in the name of High Spirit Mother."

"How is it that all the women and men do not revolt?"

"We have tried but are enslaved, so it be impossible."

"Then how did this group escape?"

"One of the guards wanted to escape and began the plan. He but died as we came here."

"How many be there in Apien now?"

Tedra shook her head, "I know not, Highest. We are not allowed to see much of Apien. I would but guess 400 children, men and women."

"Do they have ships and guards?"

"They have three ships, but one is rumored to leak. They have many guards, but all can be bribed."

"Are all the guards men?"

Tedra nodded, "And when Manthar doesn't look, they rape the women and children as well."

Sam smiled at Tedra, "Rest, Tedra. All is well for you now."

Caitha began singing, and everyone listened. She had a beautiful voice and it helped to calm the camp. When she was done, she began telling more stories of Woden. All the children gathered around Jandra, so she held them as she could. Sam saw that they looked as if they had found their long lost mother.

Rundle came over to the children and Jandra, wanting attention. At first, the children were afraid of him, but as he wagged his tail and waited, they began to pet and embrace him. Sam went to help in the preparations of the meal. Keddi returned from the forest with some wild fowl draped over her shoulder, and three hares. Margeria returned with seven large fish. Nodda took charge of the food and prepared the meal while Margeria plucked the feathers from the fowl and Meera cleaned the fish.

Nodda and Sumi had brought some potatoes over from their dwelling, and Sumi returned to camp as Sam had predicted—her arms full of wild but edible plants. The women, men and children of the camp just waited, amazed at the amount of food they were seeing. They hadn't known so much was available.

When the food was ready, Meera served it to the children and women first, a little, so that they would not over-stuff themselves. The men came next, and Meera did likewise. Then she nodded to her own group and they came over to get their serving. As all completed their meal, they waited to see if there was more, and Meera kept going around refilling their portions until all were full.

She said to the group, "There will be food in the morn enough for all. Rest this eve. We will but guard you and keep you safe. In the morn, you will need to pack. We take you to Woden for care and rest."

During the meal, Sumi went to Jandra, bowing her head, "Second? A question, if I may?"

Jandra rose, "Of course, Sumi."

"Are you of the old ones, as the stories say?"

"Old ones? What do you mean by this, Sumi?"

Sumi looked surprised, "You know not of this? But most certainly you are. You could not have been born in Woden, as you are not of Woden. Have you not seen this as so?"

"You have seen this? How?"

"The animals and the children, Second. The way they love you, even upon first meeting you. It is as in the stories of the old ones. And you resemble them, from what I know of the tales."

Sam had overheard the conversation, but didn't know what to think of it. Jandra was very surprised in Sumi's words, but could say nothing either way, "All my life is of Woden."

Sumi nodded, "Perhaps it is as you say, Second. Perhaps the stories have not come to be."

Sam and Meera watched as the group went to their pitiful shelters for the eve. Sam had counted nineteen in all, plus two women with child, not including Tedra. Sam knew that at least two more would die from overly long starvation. Jandra and Caitha went from dwelling to dwelling to ensure that the people were warm and comfortable. Keddi, Nodda and Margeria had gone off hunting and fishing again for the morn while Sumi had gone in hunt of some roots that she could pound to flour for some bread.

Anicia was tending to the fire, "Meera, do you wish the fire to go through the eve?"

Meera shook her head, "No. Put it out. It be safer without it, and the eve is warm enough. We need it not until early morn."

Sam began attending to the horses, tethering them so they wouldn't wander off. She then began to undo her group's bedding so that they too might rest before the morn's events. She guessed that Anyst would return with guards and horses by midturn, at the latest.

Meera walked over and began to help, "It seems that Woden grows."

"We need to think about Apien. Has the moment come when we should protect others and take the innocent out of Apien?"

Meera frowned, "Perhaps. It will but increase our battles here, also."

"Are we prepared to defend Woden as well as do battle elsewhere?"

Meera nodded, "We can make it so. We will need to be prepared to but kill the leaders, though, so that they do not do this elsewhere."

"Woden has never battled so distant."

"Perhaps it be the moment."

Caitha and Jandra returned to the fire ring, each with several of the children.

Jandra smiled at Meera and Sam, "Highest, these five children are orphaned and wish to spend the eve with Caitha, Rundle and me. They have been frightened and want to feel safe."

The children went up to Sam and knelt before her, "Highest."

Sam rose so that she stood before them. She saw that one of them was Sansa. "Sansa, who be your friends? Rise and introduce them to me."

Sansa and her friends stood while she motioned to each as she introduced them, "Highest, this be Jemera. She has eight cycles and lost her Birth-Mother on our way here. Her father is yet with us."

Sam silently recalled that Jandra had said the five children were orphans, so wondered why Jemera had presented herself as such. She let the issue remain at rest until a more proper moment. Sam bowed her head to Jemera, "Jemera. Do you but ride a horse?"

She bowed her head and shook it looking sad, "No, Highest. Does this but mean I will have to remain here?"

Sam laughed lightly, "No. We will teach you to ride next turn."

"Highest, I want to live in Woden with the other women. I no longer wish to be raped."

Sam nodded but chose to say nothing. She wondered how a child of eight could know of such things in this realm.

Sansa continued, "This be Alduth. He has twelve cycles and came with us, alone. He knows not his Birth-Mother or father."

Sam bowed her head to Alduth, "Alduth. You are a brave young man to come so far alone. What is it you seek?"

He knelt before Sam and bowed his head, "I wish to be knighted by you, and fight in your name against all The Realm's evils, Highest. I have long sought to come and be your champion. I know you to be but the Chosen One, along with another."

"Another? What do you mean, along with another, Young Alduth? Who be this other?"

"I know not, Highest. But another, such as yourself. It is in the stories."

Sam took Alduth by the arm and made him to stand before her, "What does this word you use mean? What be a knight? And where did you hear such a word as this?"

"Manthar but met with some prince from Fornaith and he had knights with him. He called them Knights of the Round Table. The Queen or King gives this title to their most noble and brave warriors."

"And why would you but fight for Woden or Hengist?"

Tears came to Alduth's eyes, but he fought them back, "Because I hate all those evil men. They have hurt and killed everyone. They will pay for what they have done to my people."

"Well, Young Alduth. Be you aware that Woden is a Woman's Community and Hengist is a community of men?"

"Yes, Highest. I but saw Briggon with Oisin, your Sea Duty Second, three cycles prior when he visited Apien from a ship. I most want to be like Briggon, and he told me much of Hengist. I have longed for this since that moment."

"Then you shall have your wish. You will see Briggon again next turn, and he will find a dwelling for you. He will then prepare you to be one of our young warriors. Have you but ridden a horse before?"

"No, Highest. I wish to, but have had no horse to learn on."

She touched his shoulder, the warrior-to-warrior greeting, "You will learn to ride at midturn next. And Briggon will have a sword made for you so you can begin to learn to wield such a weapon."

Alduth's eyes shone in excitement. He knelt before Sam again and touched his lips to her hem and kissed it, "You will not be sorry for this, Highest. I pledge you my loyalty and my life. They are but yours to command."

Sam startled at these words, "Where have you heard this oath prior, Young Alduth?"

"It is known throughout The Realm as the oath of warriors, and the oath you but pledge to your kingdom."

Sam heard Meera laughing. Meera walked over to Sam and Alduth, "So, you but wish to be a warrior, do you?" Meera removed her sword and held it out to Alduth, "Take my sword and help guard our camp this eve, then. Remain alert, boy, or I will but have the hair off your head. Guard to the east of the fire ring, just this side of the trees. Listen well for any strange sound."

Alduth's face broke into complete happiness, "Yes, Meera. As you command. I will guard you and The Highest well this eve. No one will get past your sword."

Alduth took the sword, his hands shaking in nervousness and excitement, and took off to his assigned duty.

Meera turned to Sam and winked, "That was your sword, but I will not tell him that. I will need my sword this eve."

Sam laughed ad turned back to Sansa.

Sansa motioned to her next friend, "This be Lorquist. She is but fourteen cycles and hates all men."

Lorquist bowed her head to Sam and said quietly, "Highest. Thank you for helping us."

Sam raised Lorquist's head by her chin, "You are with child, Lorquist."

Lorquist winced at that statement and sneered, "If you were raped twice per turn, you would be with child, too!"

Sansa nudged Lorquist gently, "Lorquist, be polite. You but speak to The Highest."

Lorquist's expression turned to fear as she fell on her knees, "Please forgive me, Highest. Please kill me not. I come to live in Woden away from all evils and torture, and to raise my child in peace and kindness. I will work hard, Highest. I am sorry for my outburst." She began to cry.

Sam made her to rise and wiped the tears from her face, "You speak truly, Lorquist, and I take no offense. Have you heard of the laws of Woden, Lorquist? The laws of companionship?"

She nodded, "I have, your Highest. I had but a companion on our way here, but she died in journey. I be but alone now."

"You had a companion at fourteen cycles?"

"Yes, Highest."

Sam asked her, "Have you ever ridden a horse?"

"None of us has ever been allowed away from our compound for fear we would escape. No, never, Highest."

"I will check with Meera and Keddi, Lorquist, but I fear you may be overly far with child to ride. Either way, you will be in Woden soon and will deliver your child into safety. Is your Birth-Mother yet alive?"

Lorquist lowered her head, "I know not. We were separated two cycles prior. Father Mantas separates all children from their Birth-Mother at least by their twelfth cycle, if not sooner."

Sansa motioned to the last of the four, "Highest, this be Wigrad. He has but seven cycles. He is alone, so we brought him with us so that he could grow up in a safer community. He be scared."

Wigrad was trembling like a frightened rabbit. Sam bent down to his level, "It be safe, Wigrad. I will not harm you." She picked him up and held him close, trying to comfort him. She sent a message of safety and love, noticing that he calmed down a bit.

"Wigrad, would you like to ride with me next turn on my horse?"

He wiped his nose with his arm and nodded his head vigorously.

"We will find a new family for you, and you will have many friends soon to but play with."

Sam placed him back on the ground and felt him grab on to her clothes and not let go. She let him be, and he kept wiping his nose with his arm. She heard Meera laughing again, this moment joined by Jandra. Caitha was smiling overly, but came over and gave Wigrad a cloth and showed him how to use it to wipe his nose. He took and used it, but wouldn't let go of Sam. When Caitha tried to take him away, he howled.

Sansa took Wigrad's hand, "Leave her be, Wigrad. She has vowed that you will ride with her next turn. She is not leaving you, and we will sleep near her this eve."

Wigrad looked at Sansa, and as if in considering the truth of her statement, then looked up at Sam.

Sam laughed lightly, "She speaks truly, Wigrad. You may sleep near me this eve."

He nodded, but didn't smiled, and went off with Sansa.

Caitha smiled at Sam, "It seems you have a new friend, Sam. I will go help them settle." And she walked away laughing.

In the late eve, after Keddi, Nodda and Margeria returned with what food they could find for the morn meal, they all settled around the now quiet fire ring. Sumi had returned with her root vegetables and was busy turning the root into a mashed mess of some sort. Meera thought it not appetizing looking, but complained not, knowing that any food these people would get would be most appreciated.

"Anicia, you take first watch along with me. Go now to relieve Young Alduth. Tell him he will take the early morn watch. Get back my sword for me and tell him that he can but have it on the next watch."

"Keddi and Sam, you but take the next shift. Wake Margeria, Nodda and Sumi toward early morn so that Nodda and Sumi can but get the fire and food prepared. We will need to rise early so as to dismantle this camp.

I want no sign of it having been here. We will burn the shelters and then cover the ashes."

"Meera, you have not assigned me to a watch." Jandra wanted her fair share of the duty.

"Me either, M'Love. I can but listen to the sounds as well as any one of you." Caitha was tired of being left out, but also felt sorry for those on watch all the moments.

Sam looked to both of them, "Then enjoy it as you will have much to do in the early morn helping to prepare all of them. They will need your patience and guidance. The rest of us will have to dismantle the camp, and that will take most of the morn. We must be ready when the guards come so that we may return to Woden by late eve."

The eve passed quietly except for the brief moment when Alduth had to be convinced that even guards had to sleep. With the re-told vow that he would meet Briggon on the next turn, he went to rest. The watches went according to plan, and Nodda and Sumi had Margeria wake the camp when they had the morn meal prepared. Even Meera had been pleased with the meal. Sumi had made a thin flat bread from the root flour, had placed the meat and vegetables in it, then rolled it for easy eating. She had made an herb sauce from the meat drippings, and the meal was well received. Most went back for more, even given the large size of the meal. Sumi had made enough for the return journey, so that this group had food to eat whenever they became hungry, as the stuffed bread meals were easily packed and carried.

Keddi, Sam, Margeria, Anicia and Meera set about clearing the camp while Jandra and Caitha helped the women and men to pack their meager belongings. Sam had Alduth guard again, giving him something useful to do, but also setting some mild protection to the camp. Keddi sent Rundle to watch over Alduth. As the people moved their belongings out of their shelters, Meera and Keddi broke the shelters up and set fire to them. Nodda destroyed and covered over the fire ring, and Margeria and Sam began to hide or burn all other signs of the camp. They then brought in much leaf cover so as to make it look more natural.

Meera told Sam to cover the trail with as many leaves as they could, knowing that this many horses would create a noticeable trail. Sam looked over to the women, men and children and saw that they were ready to leave.

"All of you that are able, collect twigs, leaves, small logs and such from the forest and help to cover the trail. The horses will trample it down, but the trail must not be seen."

When all was done and inspected by Meera, the group rested for a bit. Sumi and Sam both noticed that many of the camp people were eating their stuffed bread meals. Sam saw that, even in one turn, they were looking a little better and seemed less nervous.

Keddi looked at Meera, "Horses come."

Rundle ran to the sound. Meera had everyone take shelter in the forest, just in case. They had been told what to do and where to hide, and everyone scattered quickly. Meera and her guards all readied their weapons.

Anyst came up first, "We are returned, Meera. Should I have them come up now?"

Meera nodded and Anyst went to get the rest. She, Keddi, Margeria, Anicia and Sam all stowed their weapons. There were enough guards now for them to not have to remain on alert. Sam saw the guards ride up and noticed that each guard brought two to three other horses each. She also saw that Briggon, Karan, Lillon, Sephim and Jenna all came. She walked up to them as they dismounted.

They knelt before her, "Highest. We come as you have bid."

"Rise. We are glad you have are arrived. I knew not that so many of you come."

They rose and bowed their head toward Jandra, in acknowledgement, "Second."

Karan gave her horse reins to Jenna and came close to Sam, "Highest, we thought you might have need of all of us, and I have a report. One of our ships has returned. There has been a battle at sea, and Oisin but wins, but she sends message that she goes to Apien to retrieve some women and children and to do further battle with Apien's ships. She has destroyed two of them and sails after the other two that run in defeat. She has been angered."

Sam nodded and looked at Meera to see if she had heard. Meera just nodded in acknowledgement that she had, well understanding the consequences.

Karan continued, "And Oisin but sent you a message. She says that 'The sentries were traitors. They are no more.' She now goes after the leader in Apien; the one they call Manthar."

Sam turned to Meera and asked quietly, "Does Oisin have enough weapons and guards?"

"Her ship guards are quick and steady, and she has more weapons than she needs. If she remains cautious and bides her moments, she will but win her goal."

Karan added, "She adds that she apologizes for not waiting for your command, but felt there no moment to wait."

Sam turned to Meera again, "So we be without full protection from the sea-side."

Meera nodded but said, "We have enough. Remember Highest that Briggon's ships are yet in port."

Briggon came up, "My guards but protect the harbor, Highest. We will remain on alert until Oisin's return."

"It be good to see you, Briggon. I have a young warrior here that has met you prior and wishes to be a knight in Hengist."

Briggon looked surprised while Sam motioned for Young Alduth to come forward. He did and knelt before Briggon.

Briggon was embarrassed that someone would kneel to him while in the presence of The Highest. "Kneel not to me, young one. You kneel only to The Highest."

Alduth stood, embarrassed, but smiling the widest smile Sam had ever seen.

Briggon was yet surprised, "We have met prior?"

"Oh, yes, Sir Briggon. You and Sea Duty Second visited Apien a few cycles prior. You probably recognize me not as I have but grown into a man now."

Briggon smiled at Sam as she nodded, "He has pledged his life and loyalty to Woden. He is now yours to command."

Briggon nodded and took Alduth aside with him, and gave him one of the horses. Meera had Jandra and Jenna distribute the horses, assigning a person with a guard if they were uneasy about riding. Everyone else began packing the gear onto the extra horses.

Sam went to Karan, "I know not of these things so am asking you. We have a young girl of fourteen cycles that is far along with child. Should she but ride a horse?"

"Be this her first child?"

Sam motioned for Lorquist to come over.

Karan asked Lorquist, "When be your child due?"

"Two more moons."

"Have you any pains or other disturbances?"

Lorquist's face went red, and she whispered into Karan's ear. Karan laughed softly, "That be but normal."

Karan looked to Sam, "Let her ride a short while to see how she fares. If the horses go slowly, she should be fine. She is overly thin, but the unborn one yet remains high in her."

Wigrad came up to Sam and held tightly onto to her clothes.

Sam looked down at him and placed her hand on his head, "I have not forgotten you, Wigrad. You will but ride with me this turn."

He wiped his nose with the cloth that Caitha had given him, and Sam noticed that it had been well used through the eve.

Sam heard Karan and Sephim laughing quietly, "It would seem you have but another new young warrior that has pledged his loyalty and life to you."

Sam just rolled her eyes and nodded, "So it would seem."

As everyone was prepared, they mounted their horses. Sam saw that the Woden guards, if not riding with a member of the Apien group, kept their horse aside one of them. All of Sam's advisors had also placed themselves strategically amidst all the Apien group so as to maintain calmness.

Meera and Keddi came over to Sam, "All are ready now, Highest. Should we leave?"

Sam looked around. Wigrad was yet holding onto her. She nodded to Meera, "Help Wigrad up to me."

Sam mounted while Wigrad stood and stared. He then raised his arms up to her so that Meera could lift him up. Even Meera couldn't but help smile at this young one. Both had noticed that he hadn't spoken since they had arrived.

Meera and Keddi mounted their horses. Rundle was at Keddi's side. Meera asked, "Who rides rear guard?"

"Briggon and his guards. Margeria rides on the right flank and Anyst rides with Anicia on the left. I will ride with Margeria. You have the front?"

Meera nodded, and Keddi left to go to her position.

Sam made sure that Wigrad was well adjusted, "Are you ready, Wigrad?"

He nodded heartily, and wiped his nose, yet unsmiling and unattending to those around him.

Meera just shook her head and laughed. She led the procession of horses back to Sumi and Nodda's dwelling where they would rest a bit and let the Apien members have another meal. Sam let Wigrad hold onto the reins a little. He said nothing but petted the horse and held the reins lightly. By early midturn, they had reached Sumi and Nodda's dwelling. Meera told everyone to take a short rest and eat a bit. The Apien group had never ridden on horses before so were sore from the long ride, yet they had another half-turn's ride. Along with the food Meera's guards had brought from Woden, Sumi's stuffed bread meals, and the short rest, the Apien group was feeling better.

Sam went to Jandra, who had been busy tending to the other children. "Jandra, I have need to speak with you."

"We have had few moments together this journey. Be everything safe, Sam?"

"Jandra, I have need to complete the journey around the boundary. I think it best that you take this group back to Woden while Meera, Keddi,

Margeria, Anyst Anicia and I check the boundary. I have become concerned and have need to make certain that Woden be safe. I know that you approve not of me going without you, but Woden needs one of us there, and this group needs to see a leader. But one of us must see to the boundary. You have seen for yourself that it must be overseen. I will be but two turns."

"Why not just let Meera, Keddi and Margeria go for you? You are The Highest, and Woden needs you more. Why must you place yourself in danger such as this?"

"It is who I am, Jandra. I know that I am but The Highest, but I am also Sam. It be important to me that I know all of Woden, that I know every part of it so that I might protect it better. I cannot be Highest if I must sit inside Woden every turn. And I cannot be made a prisoner of Woden. I was Second for fourteen cycles, and I have been Highest for but a few turns. I have been trained this way, Jandra. I mean not to upset you."

"I like it not, Sam, but you are correct in that one of us needs to be back in Woden. And you are The Highest and I am The Second. If we were not companions, I would not be making this argument with you. I will return and make the arrangements for these people, and I must tend to the festival. What would you like done?"

Jandra wasn't pleased about Sam's pronouncement, but had decided to give Sam more freedom. She knew that Sam wasn't the sort to want or need to be near a companion at all their moments. She wondered if Sam would ever come to love her, but was pleased that, at least, Sam had thought about her feelings.

Sam informed Jandra of where she would like each of the Apien women, men and children.

"Also, have the advisors meet and create a plan to increase our guards. We might be going to battle against Apien, unless Oisin takes care of Manthar first. And have Briggon begin work on another ship. And one more item, Jandra. Speak to the advisors about beginning a new community, a mixed community that will follow Woden's laws, as does Hengist. I continue this journey to scout for a location. This be something I would much like, Jandra, and I think Woden has turned its head to this need. The Realm is but a dangerous place for most women and men now, and Woden Falls be the only safe place. They will come whether we have a place or no, as has now occurred. We need to begin to break our shackles of fear of this. There will be tensions, as we had with Hengist, but Hengist has worked well for and with us, and has made us both stronger."

"You are the one that should but tell this to our advisors. But I will do as you bid, Highest."

Sam nodded and then brought Jandra close to her and hugged her. "I know I am difficult, but I do this for Woden. I will return to you in two turns. Have some quiet moments set aside for us. I will miss you."

Sam kissed her, and Jandra blushed, "Sam, halt. Everyone watches."

"Let them watch, then. I be not ashamed of it."

"Be safe. I will worry while you be gone. And May will also worry."

Wigrad came up to Sam and held on to her clothes. Sam and Jandra both looked at him, as he looked straight to the horse and acknowledged no one.

Jandra bent down to Wigrad, "Wigrad, I have a request of you. I am not such a good rider as The Highest, and I need help with my horse. I saw how well you commanded The Highest's horse and I am wondering if you might ride with me to help me."

Sam saw that Wigrad considered this for a moment, and looked up at Sam, "It is fine, Wigrad, if you would want to help Woden's Second. I would consider it a favor from you. The Second means much to me, but she needs much help with her horse."

He toddled over to Jandra, hugged her briefly, then went to Jandra's horse and had a guard lift him up to it.

Jandra laughed, "That settled that problem."

Sam shook her head and laughed too, "I think that he will go with no other though, Jandra. See if he but will. If not, keep him around for a few turns and we will get Briggon to but find someone that can do as much for him. I was but thinking that Ivers, our new blacksmith in Hengist, might be the best person for this little one."

"I will speak to Briggon and have Ivers come to your dwelling for a few visits. Ivers also needs such."

Sam held Jandra closely once again, and then helped her to mount her horse behind young Wigrad. Sam put her hand on Wigrad's dirty little knee and in a serious tone, said, "Wigrad, as Highest of Woden, I expect you to take good care of Woden's Second."

Wigrad nodded, but didn't look at Sam. He held the reins correctly and waited for the signal to begin. Jandra shrugged her shoulders and just wrapped an arm around Wigrad, "I hope this bothers you not, Wigrad, but I need something to hold on to. I fear falling off the horse."

Wigrad nodded again and wiped his nose with the cloth. Sam just shook her head and silently laughed. Jandra smiled.

Sam placed her hand upon Jandra's leg. She nodded to Briggon to begin the procession and Sam waited with Jandra until they left. Sam waved as they left, noticing that the Apien group was waving to her and Meera. She watched as Meera said her farewells to Caitha, who now had four other children beside her.

Elsewhere, across The Realm

Bowing her head and kneeling, she addressed her Queen, "Highness."

"You arrive again so quickly? Is something wrong?"

"No, my Queen. All is well. Her powers grow. She can heal others now, slightly, by touching her hand to their head."

She nodded, "Some powers, but not many. But at least they grow. Does she yet become ill upon using them?"

"No, my Queen. That seems to have left."

"A good report. Keep Me informed."

"There is more, Highness." She waited until her Queen acknowledged her, seeing her as somewhat impatient.

"Tell Me."

"Yes, my Queen. Her lover is well loved by all the animals. They come to her like no other. And two of the women from Woden said she looked as the old ones, as told in the stories."

The High Queen listened, thinking on this report. "The Old Ones. Interesting. What else?"

"The new humans to Woden that she has been rescuing have reported to her of a High Spirit Mother and a High Priestess."

Her eyes narrowed at the titles, highly displeased, "Who are these?"

"I know not, nor do they, my Queen. The report is that this High Spirit will not destroy Woden, through Buron, if she is allowed to take a future child."

"Ah. The legend of the Promised One." She turned suddenly to her, angered. "But who demands this child to them? This child is vowed to The Realm."

"Yes, Highness. It is as you say."

She sighed, "Yet another issue. But what of this High Priestess? Is she involved in this corruption, as well?"

"I think not, Highness. I think she comes alone. She is searching for a long-lost sister who apparently lives in Woden. She has vowed her forces if Woden helps her to find this sister."

"Who is this long-lost sister of this mysterious High Priestess?"

"No one knows, Highness."

She nodded, but wasn't pleased. "Anything else?"

"They prepare for battle against that other human town of Apien."

She shivered at the mention of the town. "As they should. A vile place. I should have ordered them all dead long prior. Does she go?"

"No, Highness. Their Sea Captain has taken over this battle."

"Ah, yes. I forget that they travel in such a fashion. Is this captain a good warrior?"

"Most capable, my Queen."

"Have you learned more of her companions?"

"A warrior named Keddi is most excellent. Her skills with the bow and arrow are exceptional, perhaps more than ours. She has been one of their scouts, and has just returned from being gone for many cycles. She is the sister of The Highest's long-dead companion."

"They all seem overly connected in that small place. Were they all born in Woden?"

"Know one seems to know where her lover was born, Highness."

"The one who seems different than the rest of them?"

"Yes, my Queen. The one all the animals and children wish to be near."

"And you say she is beautiful?"

"Forgive me, my Queen, but she is the most beautiful woman I have ever seen, in all The Realm."

"Really? Such as this?"

"She takes my breath away, Highness."

She smiled softly at her, "A rare compliment from you. What else of her?"

She blushed, "She is The Second of Woden, as they call her, Highness."

"The Second? As The Highest was just prior?"

"Yes, my Queen."

"And now a Highest and Second live together, as lovers?"

"So it would seem, my Queen."

"Thank you. You have My leave."

"Highness? There is one more item."

The High Queen looked at her, just waiting.

"Her relationship seems to be troubling her, my Queen. She seems to desire more freedom."

The High Queen raised an eyebrow, but said nothing. She placed a hand upon her messenger's cheek, "You have done well, Force Leader. Keep Me informed."

As she left, the messenger bowed her head, "Yes, my Queen."

Chapter VI
The Green Stones

Sam went to Nodda and Sumi after the group left, "We take our leave now. Many thanks."

They both bowed, "Our pleasure. Please return soon. We gave your floor fur to one of the guards to take back for you."

Sam hugged both and then mounted. The other five were ready.

Keddi asked, "Which way do we head, Highest?"

"To the southern boundary, then east along the sea" as Sam motioned the direction. "Meera, you but lead. We look for a site for Woden's third community."

Meera nodded and began to ride. They rode without speaking, with Rundle running alongside Keddi. They arrived at the sea at early eve, just prior to the sun's setting. Meera kept them moving, riding their horses slowly on the beach.

When Meera found a sheltered cove, she halted and dismounted. "Let us camp here for the eve. It has been a long turn and we need the rest."

She had Anicia and Margeria check out the site for safety, Sam to make the fire, and Keddi to catch some fish. Meera tended to the horses, while Rundle remained in camp near Sam. After Sam got the fire started, she helped Meera undo the bedding, then brought in five stumps and logs for them to sit on around the fire. Meera had retrieved the food bags and began preparing some of the dried food they had brought with them, as Anicia returned with no sightings of others. Keddi returned with two large wild fowl, and Margeria finally returned with another report of no sightings. They all sat around the fire while Keddi first scalded the fowls, and then plucked off their feathers. Margeria prepared the spit for the turning and roasting.

As they sat around the fire, waiting for their food, Sam retrieved her sword and turned to Meera. "Practice with me, Meera."

Meera unsheathed her sword and ran to Sam as if attacking. Sam countered and they practiced until they could no longer hold their swords. When they were done, they returned to the fire, re-sheathing their swords.

Sam turned to Keddi, "In the morn, you will teach us this fine two-arrow trick of yours."

Keddi nodded and reached over to pet Rundle, who looked exhausted from the turn's journey. Margeria sat on the other side of Rundle, also petting him. As they sat around the fire, finally able to eat their meal, Sam told them the stories of the diaries. They all listened intently, amazed at how similar the story of the First Ones resembled what was now occurring in Apien.

Anyst replied, "I think it be but men. Every moment they are in control, this type of abuse occurs."

Keddi laughed, "Oh, Anyst. And what do you know of men? But perhaps you be close. They could be from those same first ones."

Margeria asked, "Highest, where did these First Ones but come from? Do the diaries make mention of this?"

"No. It just mentions something about Settlement Two. The diary writer refers to their community as a failed experiment. And she seems to miss what she refers to as home. There are many words that I recognize not." Sam looked to the stars, "I think they came here from elsewhere. Out there somewhere."

Anicia shook her head, "Highest, forgive me, but how do you but think this? They did not fly, as we cannot."

Sam smiled, "I know not, Anicia. You speak truly. I only know that if they be, in truth, the first ones here, then it but makes me wonder how they got here."

"I know not these ideas, Highest, but as you say, they had to come from somewhere. Could they have come from somewhere else in our realm that we have not yet explored?"

"It be a possibility, Meera. I too know this not, and I guess it to be a large realm, indeed. It is but a guess on my part."

Anicia braved herself to ask, "Highest, can you but read us a part from the diaries? I would like to hear their language, as you mention it to have strange words and words we use or know not."

Sam nodded, "Place another log on the fire so that I can see. It be overly dark to read much, but I can read one entry."

Sam opened the diary to the section she had finished and began reading from the next.

Entry #15 – still at sea

We've been at sea now for 5 days. Most of the women are still seasick, but some improve. We lost Mary. She was just too sick and couldn't deliver her baby. The death I've seen since coming to this place is almost too much for me to bear at times. Back home, I would watch the daily news every night at 10:00 p.m., but was never this close to it before. I've never delivered a baby before we came here. I never killed an animal, either. I just bought my meat at the store. Now I can catch and clean fish without a wince. My mother would be amazed. Me? I'm just sickened at all this death. If we had a decent medic, Mary wouldn't have died.

We think we've lost Burn. We watch carefully for him and sail well out of our way so as to lose him. What I wouldn't give for a pair of binoculars or a scope of some type. Speaking of scopes, eyeglasses have become a major problem. I wonder what we'll do about people's failing eyesight. We need to learn to make glass and lenses. And do metallurgy. And mine some minerals. It just never ends, the list of what we need to do. I spent 12 years getting my Ph.D. Twelve years of specializing in solar engineering. Geeezzz. How's that supposed to help now? Why didn't I take basket weaving instead? At least it would've come in handy. We don't even know how to make bowls or flat wear. We're having to eat with our fingers. *We've become barbarians!* It's so depressing. And yet, much of it's exciting. I sometimes feel what I think Columbus must have felt like: an explorer. It's exciting in a weird way. It's a new land. Some new plant life. Some new kinds of animals to us. And we're like the explorers of old times, before motors, before technology. I feel like I'm back in the middle ages. Some of us even begin to name our children from that era.

I remember watching some sci-fi flicks about some space explorers that went to a new planet to build a whole new civilization. At the time, I thought it sounded like the perfect life. I wish I'd taken it more to heart and learned more basic survival skills. But if nothing else, we're sure learning them now. It's just sad we have to learn them at the expense of some lives.

The coastline is beautiful. We've just passed a section yesterday that looks just like the inland passage of Alaska. But I don't want to live in a rain forest. And I hope we go to a place with little or no snow. I feel like I have been cold my entire life. Our settlement was encased in fog more days than not.

As we sail, mammals swim with us. Some look like dolphins and whales, yet have different markings and different fin structures. The whales don't seem as large as our own big ones. They all seem around the size of the killer whales. I have seen no sign of seals or puffins, or sea lions. I remember the first animal I saw when we arrived, and had to laugh. It was a sea gull. They seem to be everywhere, even here.

Elaine tells me that we now head toward our destination. She's been teaching me to sail. I'm finding myself attracted to her. Funny, back home I was attracted to men, but here, I find Elaine very exciting. The women on my boat are thinking that Elaine may be a natural leader for us. I tend to agree. Back home, she was a microbiologist, but here, she seems to be a natural born explorer and do-it-all person.

"That is the end of this entry, and it be overly dark to read further. It be interesting, is it not to you?" They had listened intently, enraptured with the story.

Meera nodded, "They do, as you say, use language strangely. They used those words that you spoke of - don't; didn't; wouldn't; I've. And there are many words I recognize not. What be solar engineering?"

Sam shook her head, "I know not, and most these words be not in our pitiful dictionary."

Anicia was confused, "So these be the women that began Woden? I but thought it all different than what this says."

"Karan has told me that Woden's first Highest went by the name of Elaine. Elaine the Wise. So this must be but the same person the diary writer mentions."

Keddi said, "Highest, have you thought that we should try to retrieve these original diaries?"

"I have. I think that the very first diaries would tell us how the First Ones arrived here and where they came from."

Anyst sat up suddenly, "Something just came to me. Do you think it coincidence in names with this Burn of the first community and King Buron?"

Sam and Meera both nodded. Meera responded, "I thought as much, also. It could be but a coincidence."

Sam added, "Possibly. It but seems he had enough progeny."

With the thoughts of the First Ones on their minds, they went to sleep. Sam wanted to rise early to begin the check of the boundary. Meera woke with the sun's rise and woke the rest. After they ate their morn meal and broke camp, they rode east along their southern sea boundary. They moved the horses slower on the beach, and Rundle ran alongside, going in and out of the water, playing. The weather was perfect and they enjoyed the peace of the ride. As they neared the southeastern boundary, the terrain began to change to that of rocky cliffs. Keddi, Anyst, Margeria, and Anicia had never seen this side of Woden prior, and were amazed at the quantity of landmass that Woden took. They noticed that the forest also changed from seasonal trees to more evergreens the higher they went. So far, they had seen no sign of any one else having landed within the Woden boundary.

As they rested their horses, Keddi looked down the cliff, far below to the sea, "I had no notion that we rode so high. If we fell, we could recite a full poem prior to hitting the rocks below."

Anicia laughed, "Cheerful thought, Keddi."

Meera looked at Sam, "Those are dangerous tides on this point."

Sam nodded, "Indeed. Ships would most likely go aground. Oisin could probably tell us much about this point. I know that when she heads this way, she goes far out to sea to avoid it."

Keddi noticed some different sorts of trees that she hadn't yet seen. "Look at these trees. They have a reddish bark on them, and look how tall they be."

They all looked straight up into the sky toward the tops of the trees.

Sam said, "Tell Oisin not of these, or she will be over here cutting them down for her masts."

Meera laughed, "That be most correct. I hear her always grumbling about the lack of straight enough trees for her masts. She will be most interested in these."

Sam smiled, "Perhaps. But some things are better left just to the enjoyment of them."

They continued their ride, now heading north toward Woden's harbor, yet more than a half-turn's ride away. The route heading north on the western boundary also followed along the sea, as Woden's land bordered the sea on two sides. The route headed back downhill and the terrain began to change to more grasses and rolling hills. As they arrived at the junction of the sea and the river that came down from Hengist, Sam turned inland toward Hengist, keeping the river on her right. There was no path to Hengist from this part of Woden Falls.

"I was thinking that a third community could be placed somewhere upstream, but close to the sea."

Meera was uncertain of the location, "It be but a long walk to Woden from this spot."

Sam nodded and they continued their ride inland for a short while. When Sam arrived to where she thought would be a fair town site, she halted the group. They were southwest of Woden and Hengist, and closer to the sea, but at an unvisited part, even given its proximity to them. From here, if a third community was begun, the towns would form an off-center triangle.

"Walk around this site for a short while. Tell me the good and bad aspects of placing the third community in this location."

They left their horses to graze on the grasses while each looked the area over.

When they had all reconvened, Meera handed each their midturn meal and began providing her views, "It is downstream from Hengist so the water may be but overly used."

Keddi said, "There are but good grasslands here. As good as Woden's."

Margeria added, "There be but another river, although much smaller, that feeds into this river. It is upstream a bit but might be able to supply a new community with their water. The size of the community might be limited by the size of the river, though."

Anyst had drawn a triangle in the ground, "It be easy access to both Woden and Hengist. If we move to the northern side of Woden, it will be a long distance from Hengist to the third community."

Sam considered their concerns, "Be there but another spot that would be close to both Hengist as well as Woden and yet have their own water supply, and with good grasslands?"

Meera nodded, "There is, but it be inland. Do you wish to see it?"

Sam nodded and they all remounted and began to ride. Meera crossed the river upstream at the junction of two rivers, and they were all drenched as the horses swam across.

Anyst tried to shake off the water, "Cold!"

Meera kept them heading in a northwest direction toward the path between Woden and Hengist. Once they arrived to the path, she kept going in the same direction until they arrived at the river that crossed half of Woden's lands, headed straight down toward Woden's harbor, but was used by neither Hengist or Woden. When they arrived at the river, Meera found that they once again had to swim their horses across. It was as large a river as Woden or Hengist's.

"Here, Highest. This be the spot I was but thinking of."

"Nice spot, Meera. I had not thought of this area. I had forgotten about this river. I seldom enter into this part of Woden on my journeys."

Sam dismounted and asked all to scout the area once again.

When they all returned, Keddi began, "A good site, I think. Close to both Woden and Hengist. Good water. Good grasslands. Much like Hengist's terrain. The spot we stand on be flat enough."

Meera agreed, "I thought this might be the best spot. We could but ride to one other location, but it will be, as Anyst has said, far from Hengist. Perhaps that not all bad, though."

Anyst added, "And this would be close to the path so all the communities would share the same paths between them, with little added effort, and each would have their own water source."

"Good grasslands. The grass be sweet here. Look at the horses. They have not halted in their eating since we arrived." Keddi thought it a perfect location for a new town.

No one else had anything to add so they remounted and continued their ride. This moment they rode in a northeast direction, beside Woden's farms and gardens, and straight down again to the sea. They arrived to the sea by early mideve and began preparing their camp. They were now northeast of Woden, which seemed to be a sheltered side. Each went about their prior eve's duties without Meera having to repeat the orders. Sam noticed that the sea was much calmer on this side of Woden than on the south side. She thought that it also felt warmer even though there was a small wind. The shoreline was also much more gentle with mostly large boulders and sand. They had camped once again where a river met the sea. It is from this spot that they would head inland at next turn to examine yet one more site for a third community. Rundle had enough traveling for one turn and instead of scouting for food with Keddi, he remained near Sam's side as she built the fire.

When Meera was done with the horses, she began preparing the dried food. "Did Jandra mind you coming on this journey?"

"She did. She understands not the stress for me in staying inside Woden. Many moments, I feel but a prisoner. I am uncertain as to this companionship, also. I don't know if I have it in me to be as she needs. I have been alone overly long, I think."

Sam went over to the beach and began to look at the rocks and shells. She collected some beach wood for the fire and brought it back and then returned to the beach for more. As she bent down to pick up more wood, she saw a green stone. It was just like the bright green stones in the necklace. She picked it up and held it in her hand. She went back to the fire ring and sat down. Rundle nudged in close by for warmth.

Meera looked at the stone, "That stone looks much like the ones in the necklace Devin brought you."

"I thought as much."

She closed her hand around it and felt some power enter her body. As she undid her hand, she and Meera saw that the stone had turned dull. Within a few moments, it began to turn bright again.

"How did you but do that?"

Sam shook her head, "I know not. I felt some power move from it into me, though. So perhaps the brightness is the power within it."

Sam tried it again, and as prior, she felt some energy move from the stone to her. It made her feel tense and restless, and a little irritated, but stronger. She held it longer this moment. After a while, when the energy felt drained from the stone, she opened her hand and saw that the stone was lifeless and dead looking.

Sam gasped, "What be this stone?"

Meera cocked her head sideways, "It does strange things to you. Your eyes have taken on the color of the stone."

Sam shook her head, trying to clear the new energy from her thinking. It felt to her as if it were taking over, yet she got up and went in search of another stone. She felt the need of more of this energy. It made her feel stronger and more powerful.

Meera followed and found one of the stones, first. She picked it up and held it in her hand as Sam had. She felt no energy from it, so tossed it into the sea.

"Meera, hold. I but need that stone."

"No, Sam. It takes over."

Sam shook her head violently again, "You are correct. It tries to make me find more."

Sam felt dizzy, yet stronger. She stumbled on a log. Suddenly angry at it, she bent down, picked it up and tossed it into the forest, a good distance away. Meera couldn't believe what she had seen. Sam suddenly realized what she had done.

She whispered, "What but happens to me?"

Meera went to Sam and guided her back to the fire ring, away from the stones. "Those stones cause you to be extremely strong, Sam. And they make you want more of them, and quickly so. You have had but two in your hand yet your craving for them grows a hundred fold with each one. It is like an obsession. You gain much strength from them, which be good, but at what cost? It is like they give you the gift of strength in return for you."

Sam looked stunned, "Meera, the necklace. Where be it?"

"Oisin took it with her."

"Do you think it does the same to her?"

Meera shook her head, "I held one of the stones such as you did, but nothing happened. It must have something to do with you being but the Chosen One."

"How would King Buron but know about these stones?"

"It is an assumption that he does, Sam. He may not. It may be coincidence."

"As you have said prior, Meera, there seem to be but overly many coincidences of late."

Meera looked at Sam and raised her eyebrow, "Remain apart from those stones, Sam. They could but turn you into a one of those evil leaders, like Burn."

"I but agree." She looked at her, "Meera, you do not suppose that they also held these stones, do you?"

"And that is what made them evil? Is this your meaning?"

She nodded, but Meera only shrugged, "Perhaps the Old Raggedy One could but tell you about these stones."

"Or my grandmother, the Woman in the Woods."

"I see someone but returning. Sam, for your safety, please tell no one about this, but remain vigilant about remaining away from these stones. We will inform Oisin upon her return. These stones should be cast back into the sea or buried whenever we find them. You will have to will yourself against them, Sam, as they call to you like sirens."

"I will try, Meera, but I could not halt myself. It was as if they forced me to pick them up. Are you certain that they had no effect on you?"

Meera went and found another stone and closed her hand tightly around it for a short while. She felt nothing and when she reopened her hand, the stone was yet a bright green.

"No, nothing. Remain away from them, and tell no one. Not even Jandra. The fewer that know, the fewer that could be but forced to tell of this thing."

"Do not throw away the necklace, though, Meera. I want to speak to the Woman in the Woods about these stones, first. I think Buron knows. And now that I but think about it, there are some of these green stones in two of the gowns he sent."

"This be good that you have but found out. Keep thinking, Sam. Was there anything else? We will place them in a safer spot from you upon our return. You must not have contact with these stones. They will make you do things that are not of your nature. It is almost like they force you to be exactly who you are not. They seem to hunger for more power; your power."

Sam yet felt restless, "Come, Meera. Help me to burn off this feeling of uneasiness within me. Teach me new sword moves."

Meera laughed, "Be this but a good moment? You will cut off my head with the power you now have."

Sam looked at her but didn't smile, "Perhaps there can be a good use to these stones. We will but have to learn it first, though."

Sam unsheathed her sword, as did Meera. Meera began to teach Sam some new moves and their practice went on until all the others had arrived. As they were practicing, the others made the eve meal and watched. No one in all of Woden had the skill of the sword such as Meera, and Sam was almost as good, so it was fun to watch them practice together. When they finished, they all ate their eve meal. Sam then wanted to learn how to shoot two arrows at one moment, such as Keddi. All of them practiced until the sun's setting, and then returned to the fire ring, exhausted.

"Thank you, all. I had great need to work off much unused energy. Riding on a horse releases not the stress within me. And I have wanted to learn about this two-arrow shooting. I can see that it will take me many moments to even come close to your skill, Keddi. It be most impressive."

"Your Birth-Mother is the one who taught me. I saw her use three arrows, but only once did they all land where she wanted them. She was highly skilled in the bow craft."

Meera arose, "All of you. Come with me but for a moment."

They followed Meera over to the log that Sam had tossed into the forest so easily.

Meera motioned to the log, "Let us pick up this log and move it over a little. Sam, you but watch."

They all began to try to lift the log, but couldn't.

Keddi suggested, "Let us all try to lift just one end."

All came to Keddi's end and tried to lift it off the ground. They managed slightly, but couldn't hold up the log for very long, and let it back down.

Keddi asked, "Meera, why do we do this?"

Sam looked stunned and looked back to where she had tossed it from.

Meera replied, "It be of no matter. I was just checking on something. Thank you."

They returned to the fire ring and Margeria settled down next to Rundle, who was helping to keep her warm. "Highest, will you read one more entry from the diaries for us this eve?"

Sam nodded and retrieved the diary from her carry pouch.

> Entry #16:
>
> It's been three days since I last wrote in this diary. A storm came up and we've been busy trying to keep everything and everyone on board. We almost swamped the boat three or four times, but we've all survived, at least in this boat. When the storm had cleared, we saw that we were missing two boats. One of the women's and one of the men's. We hope they've just become separated from us but fear that they've sunk in the storm. Some of our tools were in those boats, so our beginning has been made even the more difficult now.
>
> Elaine takes us directly to our new home. She guesses that it will take us about 2-3 more weeks and hopes for clear sailing. One of our sails is beginning to rip, so we have been trying to mend it during the non-wind periods. Some women continue to be seasick, and they grow even weaker as they can't eat anything.

In contrast, I find myself enjoying the trip and the sailing. I've never sailed before and dreaded the journey, but I love the feeling of the wind and riding in the boat in full sail. It's like floating. I watch Elaine all the time. She's a master sailor and almost reads the winds. She's most beautiful when standing at the helm with the wind blowing her hair. She's a natural leader and isn't quick to anger, but is able to make quick and accurate decisions when needed. For those of us who don't get seasick, she makes us train with our swords everyday so that we become better warriors. When we aren't busy sailing and practicing our weaponry, she teaches us to repair the rigging, the sails, and mend and make fishing nets. We should've had her as a leader since we left Burn. We would be more prepared had we listened to her from the beginning. The other boats watch us but don't follow our daily habits. It's sad, as they just sit there doing nothing. Elaine says that she's going to speak to their captains to make certain the others exercise and prepare as we do.

Elaine let me take the helm today, and I got to steer the boat. I was so excited I felt like a kid at Christmas. I haven't felt this happy since we left for here. I feel like Amundsen exploring the South Pole or Perry at the North Pole, or Magellan sailing the world. I want to travel forever, away from all our past horrors. I haven't felt this free since my last vacation over 10 years ago when I went to Norway for five weeks. It was like heaven. But this is even better. Now I no longer want to land. I just want to keep sailing, off to the sunset everyday. Elaine says I have become a true sailor and laughs. Perhaps she's right.

Burn is nowhere to be seen. With any luck, the storm sunk him in his boat and this world will never have to see him again. At least he doesn't know where we head, so with any luck, we'll never see him again in my lifetime. My mother used to tell me that everything has a silver lining. I believe her, but I just wish I could see it.

Elaine says that we'll look for a small sheltered cove tomorrow to give the women and men a rest and to gather some food and fresh water. I've no desire to step foot back on this evil land, but Elaine says that if I don't get off the boat now, I'll never have land-legs again. She also teaches me new rope knots whenever we have a moment to spare. And our dolphin and whale-like friends have returned now that the storm is over.

Sam closed the diary. It had been a long entry.

Margeria asked, "What be a vacation?"

No one answered, but Keddi asked, "What do you think happened to the two lost boats?"

Sam shook her head, "They could have sunk like the writer of the diary guessed, or they could have survived the storm and landed elsewhere and began a new community there. There are many small communities in our known realm. Not big enough to prosper, but big enough to survive. Unless, of course, the leaders of Apien and New Harborage had but captured and enslaved them and brought them back."

Rundle got up from Margeria and went next to Sam. He laid down right alongside her and moved her hand with his nose, signaling to Sam that he wanted her to pet him. She laughed and did so. He seemed a good dog and she enjoyed his quiet company. Sam wondered why they didn't have many animals such as this in Woden.

Perhaps it would do the women good to have such a comfort as this.

"Keddi, do you know where we can get more like Rundle?"

"Rundle was another refugee from Apien. Both Apien and New Harborage have dogs such as Rundle. I could ask Oisin to bring some back on her next trip."

"You would need to help train them."

"I could train those who wish to have such as Rundle. Their trainer should train the dog. They also had another animal in Apien and New Harborage that we do not have here. Cats. They are smaller animals, mostly for the dwellings, and like to sit in their people's laps."

"Something for us to think on. Have you ever had such an animal prior?"

Keddi shook her head, "No. But I have seen them and petted them. They are mostly worthless, but do seem to catch mice and little rodents."

Meera doused the fire, and all went to sleep for the eve, trading off watch shifts, with Meera taking the first. They arose a little later than the prior turn, but had no need until Anyst had teased them awake with the morn meal and cups of hot tea. No one had woken Sam through the eve for her watch. She was going to reprimand them, but then thought better of it. They had done her a favor and she decided that she should be grateful.

* * * *

She yawned, stretched and then smiled at all of them, "You spoil me and I thank you much for it. There is nothing better than to be gone from the every-turn strains of Woden. We return this turn, but it has been a welcome journey and brief reprieve for me."

Meera nodded, "We could send a message that we will return in one more turn."

Sam considered the possibility, "Perhaps. Let us see what this turn brings for us."

Keddi looked around the beach and the forest, "This be an attractive side of Woden—tame, yet wild. The winds are mild, the waves be more gentle, and the trees be less dense. Our mothers' mothers did well in finding this site for Woden. I have seen none fairer in all my journeys. I like much the inland passage from Apien, but had little moments to enjoy it. But it be not as fair as this."

Sam looked into the forest, "I have ever felt that there was something special about this location." She laughed for a moment, "But then, what would I know? I have never prior been elsewhere."

"What did you see on your passage over that caught your eye, Keddi?"

"I saw one valley that was wonderfully deep. I tried to find a passage down into it, but could not. On the other side of it though, I saw such a passage. A river runs through the valley. I also saw huge forests, such as these. Large lakes. And the largest of mountains. They reach well into the sky and when I stood on top of one of the smaller ones, I found them so high that it was difficult to breathe. And strange animals that I know not of. But Woden seems to have much of what I saw, and more."

They finished eating their morn meal, broke camp and began their journey along the northern boundary. They began their journey by crossing the river and then following it upstream. When they had journeyed to about the same distance Woden sat in from the sea, they dismounted to look for a possible settlement site.

When all returned to the horses, Meera provided, "It be a good site, but far from Hengist." All the others agreed with her.

"Is that it, then? Just that it sits far from Hengist?" They all nodded.

"We could give them but a choice, if we choose to move in this direction of beginning a third community. Let us go up to the boundary corner from here, and then we can but head back to Woden."

They rode up to the northwestern boundary, riding along the northern boundary and along the forest. As they came up to the site where Keddi had been found, they saw a sentry and dismounted.

The sentry knelt as she saw Sam, "Highest. I was not aware you come this way."

Sam bent and touched the elbow of the sentry, Surrien, to make her rise, and the sentry did so. Suddenly, Rundle began to bark in the direction of the forest. Everyone instantly went on high alert. Keddi made a hand motion for Rundle to go see the problem, and Rundle ran off into the forest. Margeria and Keddi ran after him, drawing their weapons as they went. Meera unsheathed her sword, and Sam readied her bow and arrow. Surrien, Anicia and Anyst all did likewise but began to broaden the watched area. The horses acted nervous, so both Sam and Meera knew that something or someone was out there.

Meera and Sam followed in Keddi and Margeria's direction, but remained close to the forest edge. After what seemed a long while to Sam, Keddi reappeared, carrying a very young girl. Sam guessed the little girl to be about four cycles. She looked very thin, very dirty and very tired. She was also crying.

Keddi handed the girl over to Sam, "She calls for her mother, so we look for her. We are trying to follow this little one's bootprints, but she made only a few light ones."

Sam nodded as Keddi left to rejoin the search. Sam looked at the girl, "Do you have a name that you are called?"

The girl nodded, "Gretlen."

Sam knew it was hopeless to ask questions of Gretlen, but she tried anyway, "Gretlen, have you but been walking a very long way?"

"Birth-Mother says many moons."

"Do you know what town you but came from?"

Gretlen shook her head, "But there is a mean man there that hurt my mother."

"Where be your Birth-Mother?"

Gretlen pointed back in the forest.

"Be there anyone else with you?"

Gretlen nodded, "My mother and Verdith. Can I pet the horse?"

Sam walked her over to her own horse and let Gretlen pet the horse's nose.

"Can I ride her?"

"As soon as we finish here, you will ride with us back to our town."

"Is this Woden? Did Birth-Mother find Woden?"

Sam nodded and hoped that the child's Birth-Mother had lived to see her goal.

Meera had seen Keddi run up with the child and run back into the forest, so had followed her. Rundle was nowhere near Keddi, so must have gone in search of other smells. Off in the distance, after what seemed a long while, Meera heard Rundle give a bark, and then another. Meera went toward the sound. As she arrived where Rundle was, she saw that Keddi and Margeria were coming in from different directions, and she also heard what she hoped were Anicia, Anyst and Surrien. After a moment, she saw that it was, and they all went closer to where Rundle was patiently waiting. As Meera walked up she saw Rundle waiting near two women who looked sick and exhausted.

Keddi was bending down to one of them, but the woman looked in shock, "My daughter. Where is Gretlen?"

Keddi tried to reassure the woman, "We have her. Worry not. She wandered up to us, and Rundle heard her." What name do you go by?"

The woman was concerned, "I warned her not to wander off, but she went off in search of help. I could no longer follow." The woman grabbed Keddi's arm, "Is she well?

Keddi nodded, "She be fine. What name do you go by?"

"They call me Ronaith."

Keddi nodded, "Come. We will take you to your daughter."

The woman began to cry, "Where be Hanya? Have you found Hanya?"

Meera saw that the woman near Ronaith was lying on the ground. She was unsure if the woman was alive. She went over and felt for a heartbeat. There was one, but it was weak. She knew fully that this woman would have to be carried.

Keddi rose and motioned once more to Rundle. The dog began to use his nose and sniff for the trail. He followed it back more, and Keddi and Margeria followed. Meera motioned for Anicia, Anyst and Surrien to carry the woman on the ground back to the horses. Meera helped Ronaith to rise, and then helped her walk to the place where Sam and the child waited.

"Highest. This be Ronaith. She is Birth-Mother to the little one."

As Meera settled Ronaith onto a grassy spot, Meera heard a faint bark and knew that Rundle had found the third woman. She hoped there were no more, and she hoped the woman would be alive. She saw Sam holding the child and letting her pet the horses. Sam saw them return and held on tighter to Gretlen, who she thought would want to run over to the two women being brought back.

"Birth-Mother! Verdith!" Then Gretlen looked at Sam, "What be wrong with Verdith? Why be she carried?" She began to cry.

Anyst went to her horse and mounted so that Surrien and Anicia could help her get Verdith up to her. They all knew that the woman needed immediate care, so Anyst was riding directly back to Woden while the others looked for the third woman. Sam placed Gretlen on the ground and the girl instantly ran over to her Birth-Mother. They both hugged and cried.

Meera went to Sam, "There is a third, also, named Hanya. She was but back further, though. Keddi's Rundle be a good search dog."

"Gretlen informed me that they left a town that she knew not the name of, but a place where a mean man hurt her mother."

Meera shook her head in frustration, "So, now the women but leave in any fashion they can so as to escape and try to reach Woden."

"If Oisin goes to battle with Apien, I wonder but how many women she will return with?"

"And men. It but seems that they all want to leave that place of violence."

Rundle ran up to Sam, and Sam looked to the forest and saw Keddi and Margeria returning with the third woman. Meera went to help.

Sam walked over to see if the woman was yet alive. She placed her hand upon the woman's head and sensed a strong will to live, but a next-to-death heart. Sam then placed both her hands upon the woman's head and focused. She sent her powers into the woman, giving her some strength and healing of the heart so that she may be strong enough to recover. She felt the woman questioning if they had arrived to Woden. Sam sent her a message: *You have but arrived and are now safe. We will take care of you.*

Meera motioned for Anyst to mount her horse, and the others helped give Hanya up to Anyst. When Anyst had settled Hanya upon the horse so that she could hold on to her, she turned her horse and headed toward Woden. Meera then motioned for Margeria to take Gretlen's Birth-Mother with her on her horse, and all helped the Birth-Mother up on the horse, to Margeria. Keddi mounted then, and Meera handed Gretlen up to her.

Keddi and Margeria then turned their horses also to Woden, "We will deliver them to the healers and then inform you of what we have learned." Rundle ran alongside Keddi's horse.

Meera turned to Surrien, "Perhaps we should get a Rundle for each sentry. He is able to smell things you cannot."

Surrien laughed, "And he but hears much better, also. It would provide needed company, as the watch can but drag on the quiet moments. Rundle is well trained by Keddi, though." She looked back into the forest. "I wonder how long they have but been there, waiting. The child must have been wandering around for a while."

"It is with luck that we had Rundle with us. We would not have seen anything, either. Rundle must have heard or smelled the child."

Sam nodded her farewell, "Thank you for your assistance, Surrien. It is good to know we have such sentries as you on our border. We will try to find more like Rundle so that you may have such on your duty."

Sam and Meera mounted, waved their farewell to Surrien and headed back to Betten and Anja's to pick up their extra horse. From there, they would head straight back to Woden.

"It seems that Woden is facing great change, Sam."

"Indeed. You speak truly. I wonder, though, how the other communities fare. Woden cannot be the only one these women and men wander toward."

"Perhaps our builders should build but a few more dwellings?"

"I think we can manage for now. It will be the third community that will need building, and I was but thinking of another ship or two. We must be prepared to defend all of Woden. Do you think that reinstating the Scouts a good idea for Woden?"

"It does and not so. It seems but servitude for those who volunteer. And so few of them return. We should seek Keddi's advice as she has done this for Woden for many cycles."

They rode in quiet for most of the way, pushing their horses fairly hard.

As they arrived to Betten and Anja's, Meera asked, "Be they dying of old age?"

Sam shook her head, "They have some type of disease that is much advanced. I could slow it down, but it will consume them. They are ancient as it is. I think I should not interfere with their chosen life. Do you think I make a wrong decision?"

"Who can know? These types of answers are not for us to know. They wanted a more natural life, so I think you probably correct in your decision."

Betten and Anja saw them coming and greeted them, "Highest. Meera. It be good to see you once again. Your horse is well and is ready to return home."

Sam and Meera dismounted and told Betten and Anja of the women, men and children they had found along their perimeter ride. Sam noticed that Betten was having more difficulty getting around and thought her to be in some pain. As they were eating inside the small dwelling, Sam got up and placed a hand on Betten's head, providing an excuse of seeing something in her hair. Sam provided enough of her power to help with the pain. She asked them if they thought that they might be getting old enough to need to move back into the community. The two resisted, as Sam had thought they would.

As they mounted for their return to Woden, Anja came up to Sam, "Worry not, Sam. It be but our choice to live and die this way. Our illness be not secret to us and we be not afraid."

"I will make sure the sentries come by more often. If you need me, send them to me and I will be here within a half-turn."

Meera took charge of their extra horse as they went back to Woden. They rode back at a leisurely pace, Meera thinking that Sam took a slow ride so as to avoid the return.

* * * *

Sam went to Meera and placed her hand on Meera's shoulder, "Thank you for this journey. While it was not as expected, it was with good company. We will have an advisor's meeting next turn. Perhaps we should consider making Caitha an advisor. We are but short a few these turns."

Meera placed her hand on Sam's shoulder and nodded, "I will speak with Caitha of this" and then left for her own dwelling and to Caitha.

May came out of the dwelling, "Welcome back, Highest. Jandra is over at the community park completing her town sessions. She but left just a few moments ago. Come inside. I have a nice meal prepared for you."

"Let me clean myself first, May. I have a few turns of dirt and dust on me and smell like the farm animals Jenna keeps."

Sam went and bathed herself. She noticed that her skin was more tanned than when she began the journey. When she looked in the mirror to fix her hair, she noticed her eyes for the first moment since all this began. They were shockingly blue. She remembered that several had commented on her eyes, but thought they embellished the truth. Now she knew them to be speaking truth. They looked like deep liquid pools of water. The blue eyes against her wild blond hair created a stunning appearance, and one that no one could ignore.

Even Sam was bewitched by her own looks. She had never seen herself look as such, and wasn't sure she wanted eyes such as this. Knowing that she could do nothing about them, and Sam being ever practical, she fixed her hair the best she could, placed down the mirror and forgot about her eyes. She knew her hair to be wild, but now at least it was clean from the ride.

She put on clean garments and went to the kitchen.

When May saw her, she said, "Your eyes are getting bluer every moment I but look at you, Highest. What causes this to be so?"

"I know not, May. They are a bit overly blue, though, are they not? I am going over to see Jandra. Be there some food I might take with me, or should I but wait until I return?"

May gave Sam cheese and bread pieces and some fruit to take with her, and Sam walked over to the community park where Jandra had held her prior town session. Two guards followed Sam, but she cared not to notice. As she reached the park, Karan was with Jandra once again, acting as Jandra's assistant. Sam noticed many women waiting, so knew that it would be but a while before Jandra was finished. She sat down by the river and began to eat her bread and cheese.

One of the guards came up to her, "I am sorry to disturb you, Highest, but some women ask your presence."

Sam nodded and rose. She saw three women come up to her: Eeda, Draigen, and Eimhear. She knew Draigen and Eimhear to be companions.

The women came up to her and knelt before her and bowed their heads, "Highest."

They waited for Sam to acknowledge them, "Please rise. There be no need for you to kneel so. What may I do for you this turn?"

Eeda spoke for the three of them, "Highest, we but wonder if we may sit with you to discuss the idea of a third community. We have drink with us that we can but share so that your bread and cheese go down easier. We will not take much of your moment."

"Please, sit." Sam motioned to the ground and sat so that they did not feel awkward.

"May I offer you a little bread and cheese?"

"No, Highest. You eat. You but look overly thin. Is May not feeding you well?"

Sam laughed, almost choking on the question, "If she but heard that question from you, she would slit my throat. She has been after me for turns now to eat more. It has been an overly busy moon, has it not?"

Eimhear nodded, "And but a sad one. Overly many traitors. Overly much death."

Draigen spoke up, "Highest, do we hear true about their being but a third community, and that it be a mixed one?"

Sam chose her words carefully, "It is something I would like Woden to but consider."

Eeda asked, "But why? Do we not have enough people now in our community? Would that not bring in more troubles?"

"Have you been informed of all that occurs in The Realm?"

They all shook their heads. They hadn't. Sam told them the story of Apien, of New Harborage, of the three women and one child they had found just this turn, of the others on the beach that they had sent to Woden. Of Manthar and Rolnen and what they were doing to people. And of the diaries. They listened, well-amazed.

When Sam was finished telling the story, Eeda asked, "You think many women, men and children come, then?"

Sam nodded, "I think they will try. The ones we found this turn had walked from Apien. So desperate to leave, they had few supplies. They are in the infirmary now. So desperate for a more peaceful life that they risk their lives to get here. What are your thoughts? Should we keep Woden as it is? Should we expand our own communities? Should we open a third community for a mixed one?"

Draigen offered Sam some drink, "Highest, are these mixed community people different from us?"

Sam shook her head and put down her drink, "They do not appear to be so. I would be concerned about increased companion abuse, but we have rules for such and would require the same consequences."

Eimhear shook her head to Sam, "But Highest, they *think* differently that we do. They raise their boy and girl children together, as one example."

"You speak truth, Eimhear. But does that mean different is bad? Did we not have the same issues with Hengist when we but allowed it? It is written that we had a few beginning difficulties. And has this union not been beneficial for the both of us?"

Eeda agreed, "You speak truth, Highest. Hengist has offered much to us, and they think differently than us, too. They have but followed our rules, though, and that has made the difference. Would we require the same from the third community?"

Sam answered, "The land is of Woden, so all the laws and rules be the same. If they wish different rules and laws, they can go elsewhere. There is much to consider prior to making it so. I have questioned much on this myself. I wonder why we even have a bridge, at moments. Have you ever wondered about this?"

Draigen nodded, "Often. We have our own companions, so why is it that we have to maintain this bridge between us? If we use the men only for breeding purposes, then why be there fear that we would not return? Many of us wish not to be there for any longer than necessary. And yet, the festivals do not always correspond to our breeding cycles, although for the most part, they do. What do you think would occur, Highest, if we opened up the gates between Hengist and Woden so that passage be free as desired?"

"I have thought much on it, but know not. I would hope that life would go on the same, but only freer and without the confines of this process. I hate the closing morn of the festival when but a few of the women are late. I wish not to banish them, but it be the law. But why do we banish just the women? Are not the men also a part in this? So why banish them at all? Why be there this law, at all? And to where do we banish them? Certain death?"

Eimhear nodded, "If you agree not with this law, and we do not, and we know that many of the others do not, why do we but continue this practice? I want my own companion, so if one of us chooses to but mate with a man so that we can have a child, I will remain as little as possible in Hengist. I want to return to my companion. Can we change this law, Highest?"

Sam agreed, "I think much will change soon in Woden. Perhaps this is a natural progression in our practices. Our laws were made long prior for reasons we know not, now. It is good we question them, though, and perhaps it be the moment to change some. I hope the community speaks of this between themselves and lets me know what it thinks. I much appreciate you coming to me and discussing all these issues. Perhaps the other women will see they can do the same with me."

Eeda laughed softly, "You think yourself an ogre, but the community knows far better, Highest. We but give you space and quiet. We know you would see us if we asked."

"It be good, then. Do you think we should hold a town meeting with all invited, including Hengist, to discuss the idea of a third community?"

"And besides, Highest, it is good for all of us to hear your views, at moments. We rarely get to hear you speak and we much enjoy it. Please come and see us on your rounds. We have a small gift for you."

"Eeda, how goes the winemaking?"

"It will be much improved this cycle, Highest. I helped Liley mix some grape vines a few prior cycles, and they bear well, now. Their taste will be unlike any wine we have had so far. I am most excited about it. And they are yielding much more than our other vines, which is as hoped. I tried a new technique in the processing this cycle, and removed the skins of the grapes a little sooner than prior. It made a light red wine you might enjoy."

Sam nodded, "And Draigen, have the furniture makers had a chance to begin building the new chairs for the community; the ones that Oisin called by rockers?"

Draigen frowned, "I blame myself for not thinking of this model prior to this. It be simple enough, yet a much useful design for our women. Many thanks to Oisin for bringing back one for us to use as a model. The women have supplied their orders. We will be busy making these for many moons to come. Do you but like it, Highest?"

"I do, but at moments I prefer a more padded seat."

"That gives me an idea, Highest. We could make a padded rocker. Perhaps just some small pads on it. I will speak to the garment makers about this. It will be a joint project. I will deliver some of these small pads to your rocker when we have them perfected."

Sam smiled and then asked Eimhear, "And are the candle works going well?"

"Overly well. We have more than enough for another cycle or two, so we have begun doing other duties. I take up building in the off-moments. I have created scented candles now, though. Scented with some herbs and some of the flowers."

They rose to leave, and Sam did as well to see them off, "Thank you much for the good conversation and drink."

She looked over to see Jandra yet engaged with a few more women, and sat back down to wait. She took the leisure moment to think about what it would mean to Woden to bring in such a third community. She remembered that the diary writer had mentioned that they hadn't wanted the men to accompany them on their journey to their new land, but had relented. Sam assumed that those men became the beginning of Hengist. She wondered that if people had such needs to be with the opposite, then why should it not be so?

She wondered if that would be so bad and thought that perhaps it would create a more open culture. Her Birth-Mother had always told her that Woden's women always had a difficulty accepting difference, but that they had a good and gentle nature and would soon seen the benefit for all.

But why do we need this separation at all? Why can we not live together as but one community? Or perhaps even three communities, not separated by this thinking?

What Eimhear and the other two had said to Sam had interested her about the thinking of Woden. If the women of Woden thought the bridge not needed, then it was useless to them as a community. Sam sensed much change coming to Woden, and not all of it bad.

Sam watched Jandra work with the women of Woden and saw her patient but firm. Jandra was a good companion, and Sam wondered if she would come to love Jandra as she had Brett, or now Oisin. Sam was yet amazed that Jandra had returned that eve, and thought she was grateful for it. It had been a long while since Sam watched and waited for anyone, surprising even herself.

She looked at Jandra carefully, seeing her astonishing beauty.

Why is it I remain as such with her? Her beauty is profound, and she is most kind and giving, and yet I question her presence in my life.

Finally, Sam saw that Jandra was finishing up her final session. She went over to a guard, "Please send a messenger around. There will be an advisor's meeting next turn, early midturn. And have them invite Briggon and his advisors as well. Please have the messenger inform Briggon that I will be doing my rounds over there after midturn. Also have the messenger inform May about the advisor meeting."

The guard knelt before Sam, bowed her head, and said, "As you say, Highest.". Sam then walked over to Jandra, who yet hadn't seen her. She noted that Jandra was overly busy as Second, as Sam had been. She also noticed how attractive Jandra was in her gown. She thought that Jandra had a beautiful regal stance. Unlike Sam, Jandra paid attention to her appearance, and Sam was glad of it. She looked at Jandra's hair and thought it was the most beautiful in all of Woden. She examined Jandra carefully, wondering as to her background. In all of Woden, no one appeared quite like Jandra did. There was something just a little different in her overall appearance. But Sam couldn't place it. But to almost everyone in Woden and Hengist, Jandra was by far the most beautiful of all of them.

And those eyes of hers!

As she walked up, Karan saw her approach. She knelt and bowed her head to Sam, "Highest. We have but missed you."

"Rise, Karan. There is no need for this formality between us." Sam smiled to Jandra. Karan rose and saw that Jandra and Sam needed a quiet moment between them.

"I will take my leave, now. Perhaps we can discuss this town session at another moment, Second."

Jandra looked at Karan, "You have saved the turn once again, Karan." She turned to Sam, "I think we should hand this duty over to Karan. She knows everyone and their needs, and does it much better than I can."

Sam nodded and spared only a moment for Karan, "Whatever you two but wish. Karan, we have an advisor's meeting at early midturn next turn. I will see you then."

Jandra said her farewell to Karan and turned back to Sam, knowing that Sam had dismissed Karan, "You have finally returned. You look most beautiful. You must have taken the moment to bathe."

"I had more dirt upon me than there was on the ground. Did you hear of the women that we sent to the infirmary just prior?"

She nodded, "More from Apien. Woden is becoming a shelter of safety. How was their health?"

"The child be fine, as be her Birth-Mother. I think the others will live, also, but am unsure. These women come to us from a long distance, and yet so unprepared for the crossing. If I knew which direction they came from, I would provide provisions along their path, but they come now in all directions."

Jandra wanted to reach for Sam's hand, but didn't, giving Sam the space she so needed. Sam had also wanted to reach for Jandra's, but hadn't for fear Jandra was yet frustrated with her.

"Woden is indeed becoming their shelter. And now with Oisin pursuing battle in Apien, it be a good guess that she brings back many more who seek our shelter. I think they seek a permanent place."

Jandra looked into Sam's eyes and smiled, "Your power grows stronger, does it not?"

"How do you but know of this?"

"The color of your eyes grows more intense with the power. They are strikingly beautiful, Sam, if not a little forbidding."

"Forbidding? How do you mean, Jandra?"

"If one knows you not, they will think you can see through them with such eyes as this."

Sam laughed, "I must speak truly. I looked in the mirror when fixing my hair. As I saw my own eyes, they but frightened me."

"I know not which is more humorous. You frightening yourself or you trying to fix your own hair."

Sam nodded and laughed a little, "It be true. It be a little wild."

"A little wild? You are a master of understatement, Sam." She looked at Sam, "I have missed you and am glad you are back. In our short turns together, I have grown used to you in the bed next to me. It be strange and lonely without you, and I have never been lonely prior."

"I also thought of you during my journey, which is a strange thing for me. I liked my journey much, but it was not the same as prior. I kept thinking of you and wanting to return to you, but not to Woden. You have invaded my thoughts."

"That does not sound good, Sam."

"I think it as good. As I lay by the sea, listening to its sounds, I thought of you and the sound of your voice. The waves made me think of your hair. And as I began to fall to sleep, I thought of you, your smell, and what it feels like to hold you, always next to me in our bed, and I missed all these things."

Jandra's eyes shone, "In truth? You speak these things truly?"

Sam nodded, giving Jandra a long, strong hug, "Most honest truth, Jandra. I cannot make up these things. In truth, I wished that you had come with us, but then I would not have wanted the others. They would have been interruptions to ourselves. But truly, as much as I like my freedom and the sounds and smells of the outside, I missed you. And that but surprised me."

Jandra did something she rarely did, which was kiss Sam. She usually let Sam take the initiative on this since she was The Highest, but couldn't control herself this turn. Sam was pleased and returned the kiss and embrace.

"Thank you, Jandra. It is most pleasant when you do this. I often wonder if I am overly bold in my kissing of you. I have noticed that you do not take this upon yourself to begin. This be a pleasant surprise."

She blushed, "I am glad you have returned. I have come to detest a separation between us."

"Let us go to our dwelling, then. May has our meal prepared, and then we can remedy your loneliness."

Jandra smiled, and they began to walk back to their dwelling, hand-in-hand. They didn't notice, but some of the community's women were watching, and smiling. As they walked back to the dwelling, they spoke of the advisor meeting next turn, Sam's rounds in Hengist, Jandra's stories from the community sessions, and Sam's journey. They walked the long way back to their dwelling, up and down through all the paths of Woden, just enjoying the silence, their leisure, and the quiet moments to speak together.

They arrived to their dwelling at dark, and the eve remained quiet. They ate their meal on their patio, yet talking of their adventures, and occasionally listening to the sounds of the eve. Sam enjoyed her first real leisure since her journey, and Jandra saw to it that she ate enough. They spent the eve enjoying their moments, and rushing nothing. They both enjoyed being back together.

The morn was also quiet. May had seen to it that the Sam had some quiet moments prior to her advisor meeting. May continued to worry about Sam even though she appeared to be in good spirits. She well knew the stress for Sam being The Highest, and sought to keep the events back on the advisors whenever possible, for Sam. Sam rose late and found Jandra already risen and gone. She was sorry that she missed Jandra, and went to the kitchen for her early morn meal.

May had heard her rise and prepare for the turn, "Good morn, Highest. Jandra said to tell you that she be at a short meeting in preparation of the festival in but two turns. It is but another glorious turn. It rained a little last eve, for which all the gardens and farms will be most grateful. The community smells clean and fresh this morn. As I walked by the river, I saw the lilies beginning to bloom. They be such a beautiful sight. You would most enjoy them. I have prepared a delicious morn meal for you this turn. And I have all the sweets ready for your advisor meeting. I was wondering, Highest. Since you go to Hengist this turn, would you like a bag of sweets to take over to them, as well? It be no bother. I have also given some to the guards. They but need some tending to. Have you but noticed that you be well guarded these turns? There are many more guards than you are used to. They have been most quiet and discreet, however, so as not to disturb you or make you feel a prisoner."

Sam began to eat what May had given to her and thought it delicious, as May had said. "What be this, May? It be most tasty."

"I call it a baked vegetable egg casserole. I made it up. I but heard you brought back many new women."

Sam nodded as she ate, "And men and children. We found a small group of about nineteen out beyond Nodda and Sumi's dwelling, down near the sea. And at the very end of our journey, we found three women and one child. All from Apien and all trying to escape those evils that occur there. Oisin has left to do battle in Apien and rid the place of Manthar."

"Who is Manthar?"

"A man. A leader. A very corrupt and evil one. It is spoken that he rapes all the women, children and men daily. It is also spoken that he enslaves everyone besides his own guards."

"What makes men do such things, Highest?"

"I think it not just men, May. Josin was also as evil. As was Hern. I know not what makes anyone do evil. I understand it not."

"But Josin could not rape all these people, such as this Manthar seems to do."

"No, Josin could not rape, but I have learned that she gave herself to men in return for power. So it be the same, I think."

"I understand not this usage of sex as a weapon. Since when did it become a power issue? I thought it was to be for pleasure, such as we do in Woden and Hengist."

Sam shook her head, "I know not, May. Rape is a rare event in Hengist, and I cannot recall the last moment it occurred between Woden and Hengist."

"Only men can rape, Highest."

"Perhaps in the physical sense. But what Josin did to gain power is a form of rape."

"I disagree, Highest. Only a man can force his sex into a woman. A woman has no such parts and can do no such thing."

Sam shook her head, "I have heard of such, though, May. Women can arouse a man and then cause pain because of it. That be the same."

"No, Highest. I disagree. A woman when raped is entered by force. It be evil."

Sam saw that May was most disturbed by these thoughts, "May, it be fine. But why does this disturb you so? Was someone you hold close, raped? Be this a personal issue within you?"

"Yes, but I wish not to discuss it, Highest. You will see to it that nothing like this ever occurs in Woden again. I am most comforted that you are now Highest."

"May, I will not press further, but was this you who was raped?"

"As you said, Highest, it be best if you not press further."

"I am sorry, May. I will give you your privacy. If you would ever like to share this with me, though, I will be here to listen."

"Thank you, Highest. It be enough."

May sat down at the table across from Sam, "The women wonder why you do not move into The Highest's dwelling. What be your plans?"

"We remain here. I wish not to live in that massive building. I would but get lost. And it is not a dwelling. Since Jandra and I be together, it saves space in the community to remain here. The community can use the building for a community-gathering place. And besides, May, I cannot give up this dwelling. I love this kitchen and the dwelling. It has all my memories."

May nodded, "I understand, Highest. I will but inform the women of the community. I think they will also understand. Highest, you continue to eat your morn meal. I hear your advisors arriving and I want to give them some sweets. Jandra informed me that she would go directly to the meeting so as to organize the advisors prior to your own arrival."

"Is Lillon able to attend as yet?"

"I know not, Highest."

May left to tend to the arriving advisors while Sam continued to eat. She thought about what new advisors Woden and Hengist would need, but thought it better to let the advisors tend to it. She thought about the bridge and the festival and of perhaps opening the bridge permanently, and she wondered why it had ever been closed. The diaries spoke of the evils the First Women had endured, but many cycles had passed since then. Perhaps it was the moment to begin an opening of the communities. Jandra entered as Sam was eating.

Sam looked up, surprised, "Is all well, Jandra?"

Jandra smiled at her, "Yes, Sam. Why do you ask?"

"May told me that you would not be back until the advisor meeting."

"I finished early and wanted to see you. Did you rest well last eve?"

"I always rest well with you, if that be what you would like to call it."

Jandra blushed, "I always feel like a young girl with you."

"You are. If you be not, you fool me. But you be not silly and ridiculous as that age."

Jandra sat down across from Sam, and they talked while she finished eating her meal.

When all the advisors had finally arrived, May went to retrieve Sam and Jandra, "Highest, they are but ready for you. Do you wish to fix your hair?"

"I did, May. Be it that bad?"

May shook her head, "Highest. It is just wild as is usual for you. On your next rounds, find Imly and get your hair tended to."

Sam nodded. Both she and Jandra rose to go into the meeting room. As Sam entered, she saw that she had forgotten that Briggon and his advisors were also attending, and was pleased. Everyone saw her enter and rose so that they could kneel. They all did, and bowed their heads. Sam couldn't understand why everyone insisted on performing this much needless act.

"Please rise. And please find another way to greet me. It be getting wearisome to see only the tops of everyone's head when I enter a room."

The advisors all laughed and sat back down. They had all been eating May's sweets. This turn, May had provided what looked to Sam to be some type of fruit tarts. She hoped that there would be some spare ones for later.

She sat down at her favorite chair and began to greet everyone, "Good late morn, all. Briggon, it be good of you and your advisors to attend.

Please introduce your advisors to all of us in case we remember not." She saw that Lillon was in attendance.

Briggon rose, "Highest. We are most excited to be here. This is the first moment ever between Hengist and Woden that we share in this meeting. We thank you much for it."

Briggon motioned to his left, "This be Landric, my advisor for all of trade and accounts." He then motioned to his right, "This be Moduin, Hengist's advisor for health and building. And next to him be Gerin, Hengist's advisor for festivals and whatever else needs covering. I oversee security and Woden relations."

Sam had her own advisors introduce themselves and then began the meeting, "I will get straight to my agenda. Due to traitors in Woden, trade and much else was ceased with Hengist. That era is over. What remains, however, is how to put things as correct. We are short some advisors. There is much violence and battle in The Realm. We have many new people seeking refuge in Woden, some of them from mixed communities. We have no spiritual leaders except those from Hengist. Jandra needs an assistant. And the festival approaches amidst all the turmoil. Suggestions?"

Sam sat down and took a fruit tart. She would let the advisors figure out the dilemmas of Woden. She knew that it couldn't be her duty alone.

Karan rose, "Highest. All. We have lost many women of late due to their own accord. That leaves us without an expert to the town's charter, an advisor of future planning in Woden, an assistant for The Second, an advisor in charge of festivals, and an advisor for community management. We are also short Meera's counterpart, but perhaps Meera could be given a title and be in charge of the entire guard unit. Since Second is now Second, we also no longer have a community ambassador for you, Highest."

As Karan sat down, Jandra rose, "Perhaps we could combine some of these duties and do with fewer advisors, since we have but combined the two groups. We now also have the Hengist advisors meeting with us, so we should not need as many. I was the community ambassador to The Highest prior, and I could continue to do that. Prior to the former Highest's illness, the duties of community ambassador did not amount to much."

As Jandra finished, Briggon rose, "Perhaps Hengist could provide a more active role. Until Woden has its own spiritual leaders, ours could do what is needed, as was recently done. Our guards could also serve as counterparts to Meera's units, at her command. We could also provide some sentry duty, which we have not been allowed prior. Gerin would also be able to help on a committee for each of the festivals we presently share with you. And Landric, our trade and accounts advisor would like it much if he could but work with Ghada and Alain. It would keep our accounts more accurate and would help all of us to cease useless growing for that which we might have overly much of. And we would like it much if our health advisor, Moduin, was able to work more closely with Tehna. We have much to offer each other in terms of remedies."

Meera then rose to speak, "Janel, of the fisheries, would be but a good advisor. She knows the community well, and is well liked. She is young, having many cycles ahead of her, and always is thinking of the community. She also keeps her thoughts toward Hengist, making certain that their fishers are also supplying Hengist with enough. And Caitha has indicated to me that she also would be an advisor if but needed. We could allow Hengist to have yet another advisor, making it more equal between us and saving us from using more women that we do not have currently."

Iver rose when Meera finished, "I have been your advisor for outside relations. I could but take on the community ambassador duty, as it is much the same. I have also been long interested in the community's charter."

Ghett spoke from her chair, "As the advisor for commerce and trade, I could work with Landric from Hengist and Ghada and Alain, but I think many of our roles are the same and that my role could be done away with. Then, if you so wish, Highest, I could be made free as advisor for something else of your choice."

No one else spoke up.

Sam got up from her chair, "I thank you for your ideas. I will think on them for a few turns, confer with The Second, and then inform you at the next meeting. I would like the next meeting to occur in three turns. Hengist, you will need to be here, as well. I have another issue before us - should we create a third community? A mixed one? Many people are seeking refuge from Apien and New Harborage now, and some seek to come here. I would like a small group to examine this. Volunteers?"

Landric raised his hand, as did Ghett, Karan, Zan and Sephim.

"Thank you. Please discuss this in the communities and report back at our next meeting. I have a question. What became of those five women that were rescued from Sir Devin's ship?"

Karan rose and smiled, "They would like entrance into Woden, Highest. They want no more of a mixed community. One is a midwife and somewhat healer. One is a glass blower and mirror maker. One is a preparer of stored foods. One is a garment maker, and the last would like to learn the fisheries. We are finding dwellings for them."

Sam addressed the advisors, "Be there any issues from you?"

Sephim rose and looked embarrassed, "Highest, I have no suggestions for you about the festival this meeting. It would appear that our past issues with you having a companion are but over."

Jandra blushed and Sam smiled but said nothing.

Sam looked to Tehna, "Tehna, how be all the women, men and children that arrived in Woden just prior?"

"I am sorry, Highest, but one from the large group but died. She was overly malnourished and we could revive her not. One more seems to be between life and death, but the healers have their hopes for her. The men but survive, as do the children. The last three women and child are all well. They are malnourished as well, but have fared a bit better. The last three women would like to remain in Woden. Two of them are but companions already. A few of the women from the large group would also like to remain in Woden, but there be some that desire a mixed community, but would be willing to separate if it meant they could remain in Woden or Hengist."

Sam nodded, "We will have to see what occurs upon Oisin's return. It could be that we perhaps speak overly soon about a third community. If she rids Apien and New Harborage of these evil leaders, the community may wish to remain and rebuild. If that be the case, even some of our newcomers may wish to return."

Meera added, "Or they may all wish to just come here and close Apien and New Harborage for good. They may not trust any other leader at this point and may just wish to come to Woden where they have heard but good things. Combined, they cannot have more than 500 people, if that many anymore."

Karan nodded, but frowned, "That would be a large increase for us, however, and quite suddenly. But then, Oisin would not be able to bring all of them back at one moment. She would have to make several trips, or they would have to begin a long walking journey. Perhaps we could organize it so that they would remain healthy on that journey, unlike the poor ones we just took in. I could speak to our new people to see what they would do if given the choice to return to a new leader or remain here."

Sam nodded, "It is a good idea and can only provide further information. I wonder who their new leader could be if they chose one. I hope it would be a good one. I fear that King Buron might have designs on both those communities, however. Does anyone else have other issues for this meeting, or should we adjourn until the next?"

Jenna rose, "Highest, if I may?"

Sam nodded, and Jenna continued, "I would like Hengist's help with the animals. We have overly much overlap between us, and if we could move the animals between Hengist and Woden, we would have more help, less overlap, more efficiency and improved organization between us. Also, if we but opened the third community between Hengist and Woden, the animal yards would be located between all three. This would also provide more room in the current location for the gardens."

Ghett asked, "Are you meaning that we should move the structures, as well?"

Jenna nodded, "Yes. We but need larger ones with better air circulation, anyway."

Sam looked to Briggon, "Would this suit your needs as well?"

Briggon turned to his advisors, and they all nodded, "It makes more sense that what we currently do, which is to be independent, making for less efficiency between us."

Jandra rose, "I have been thinking that perhaps, if we should open this third community, that all our shops should be moved to the path between Woden and Hengist. We would cease duplication this way and provide easier access to all our goods."

Ghett added, "If we but did this, then we should build a more direct route to the harbor."

Sam rose, "Hearing nothing negative about this move for Jenna's animals and buildings, then Jenna, please arrange for it. I suspect it will take several moons to complete the task. Briggon, could you or one of your advisors please meet with Jenna and provide some help from your end and perhaps move all your animals at the same moment so that we have but one large animal yard? And Ghett, could you coordinate the building with our builders and those of Hengist? Is this agreeable to all of you? Have I left anything out?"

Everyone nodded their agreement. Sam continued, "Good. Ghett, Jenna and Briggon, please report on this at our next meeting, and keep us informed of the progress. Be there anything else anyone needs to raise this meeting?"

Sephim rose, "One more item, Highest. We would like to know why you have not yet moved into The Highest's dwelling."

Sam nodded, but didn't smile, "I have heard this same question from the community, as well. My response to you is that I am in The Highest's dwelling and will remain here. The community is now able to use the former Highest's dwelling as a community center. I have agreed to find a companion. I have agreed to become Highest. I have given up much of my privacy. But I will not move to that overly large and impersonal dwelling. Besides, all my memories are here. I have spoken with Meera about this and she has no problem in providing the needed guards around this dwelling."

Sephim nodded, "Thank you, Highest. I will but inform the community."

Sam thought: *That was overly easy. I wonder what they have planned?* But she left the thought alone.

Elsewhere, across The Realm

She knelt and bowed her head, "My Queen."

She turned, surprised. "You return quickly, yet again."

"She found some of the green stones."

"Really? Does she know of these?"

"Buron gave her a necklace of them, and four gowns with green stones embedded within some of them."

"He gave her four gowns?"

"Yes, my Queen, from here in the Valley."

The High Queen was amused, "Do the women in Woden wear such as these?"

"No, Highness. They typically dress very simply. Plain and unappealing, keeping their bodies well hidden."

She smiled at her messenger, "An observation? Or judgment?"

"She picked up one of the stones and held it."

The High Queen raised an eyebrow, "And?"

"Her leader of their forces rescued her from its effects, Highness."

"And what does she now do with this necklace?"

"I can no longer find it, my Queen. I think the Sea Captain took it with her on her journey."

"Anything else?"

"They speak of adding yet another community to their town. A third community for those that wish to take companions as woman and man."

"Strange. But I have heard in the storytellers of such a thing occurring. Thank you, My Messenger. You have My leave."

She bowed, "Yes, my Queen."

Chapter VII
Sam and Jandra

No one had anything else to add, so Sam adjourned the meeting and began walking to Hengist with Meera, Jandra, Briggon and his advisors for her first rounds in that community. Sam and Jandra walked together, arms intertwined, but Sam felt just a little uncomfortable doing so. She wondered if she could get used to such things as this. One moment she felt close to Jandra, yet on another moment, she felt chained to her.

"Briggon, how much of Hengist might I be able to cover this turn?"

"Only half or less, Highest. I will but show you what paths you might choose when we arrive. The men are most excited about this, so may detain you longer than normal. As they become used to your rounds, it may become more like Woden for you. And we are only half Woden's size."

"Will I see Tadan this turn, Briggon? It has been long since we have had a chance to communicate."

"He but asked about you this morn and would like much to see you. It is I who have kept him from you for fear that he take up overly much of you."

"Briggon, you guard me overly. I always want to see Tadan. What is he up to these turns? How many cycles has he now, ten?"

"Yes, Highest. He is a full ten cycles. He looks much like her now. You will see the resemblance. He has invented something and will show it to you this turn. Do you mind seeing him, Highest?"

"Seeing him gives me peace, Briggon, now that I don't mind being reminded of her."

Jandra wondered who Tadan was, and in what relation to Sam.

Meera knew about Tadan, "Highest, have you but informed Keddi about Tadan as yet?"

Sam shook her head, and Meera asked nothing further about it. She would let Sam work out her own personal issues.

Sam turned to Meera, "Meera. I would like it much if you would but take over the seeing of all the guards in both Woden and Hengist. Briggon could report to you and we need no other. What say you on this, Briggon?"

Briggon agreed, "I think it but an excellent idea, Highest. She did much of it even while the other was alive."

It was not the custom of Hengist or Woden to mention a traitor's name except on rare occasions, but Sam knew of whom Briggon spoke.

"Prepare yourself, Meera, as you are going to become Second of Defense for all of Woden Falls."

Meera frowned and shook her head, "I need no such title, Highest."

"Meera, I give you no choice on this. You will become Second of Defense for Woden. It makes much sense. Jandra, what do you think of this?"

Jandra nodded, knowing it was her idea, originally, "It makes sense, as you say, Highest. I know little of defense, and Meera need not report to me. In moments of emergency, for Meera to report to me adds wasted moments."

"I will make it so at the next advisor meeting. Briggon, Jandra, please inform all your people of such. Meera will now be known as Second. Given Oisin's title of Second, and Jandra's, this but makes the structure improved and provides Meera the authority she needs to make us safe."

As they neared Hengist's gates, Briggon asked Sam, "Highest, may I but offer you, Jandra and Meera your midturn meal? It would but give you the opportunity to meet with Tadan prior to your rounds. He but misses seeing you."

"I would thank you much, Briggon. If I but continue to miss meals, May will quit on me." She nodded, "Yes, I do need to tend more to Tadan. It be my promise to you and him."

The guards saw Sam and the party approaching and opened the gates. Tadan was just inside the gates and knelt as Sam approached, "Highest Mother. It be good to see you again. May I join you for your midturn meal?"

Sam looked down at Tadan with much tenderness, "Rise, Young Tadan. It be good to see you. Please escort me to our meal. Your father tells me that you have a new invention to share with me."

Sam offered her free hand to Tadan, who took it readily. He began talking endlessly, as was Tadan's way, "Highest Mother, it is a most exciting invention. Be there a moment with you after your rounds that we may try it out together? I have not quite yet perfected the balance of it, but I call it a fishing reel. I have not yet figured out how to develop strong fishing line, but I keep working on that. And how are you these turns, Highest Mother? I have but heard that you go about changing into the Chosen One. What have you learned of this enterprise? Have you met with the Spirits of the Falls as yet? Or is that yet but coming? I am most pleased that you be Highest now, Highest Mother. I most enjoyed the ceremony in which you became Highest. Hengist most needs your leadership ability. I am not pleased to say that the former Highest did us much harm, but the men of Hengist are now most excited. I see the blueness of your eyes increases. That be most intriguing. Perhaps we could speak about it this turn. What plans do you have for us now? I have some ideas that you might be interested in hearing. It could change the way we do our gardens and animals. I have also thought about some wind power and would like to try it for your dwelling . . . "

Meera and Briggon laughed. Jandra looked quizzically at Meera, "Highest Mother?"

"You will have to hear that from Sam. It be not my place."

Briggon continued to laugh, "I will not need to think of conversation for the midturn meal."

Meera asked, "Is it but this way with him all the turn?"

Briggon nodded, "He be a bright one. Much brighter than me, and he thinks and invents but all the turn. His mind is always awhirl with ideas and notions. There be not enough sun in the turn for him, and it frustrates him."

"We have arrived at our midturn meal, Highest Mother. Would you like to sit with me or apart from me? Many tell me that I speak overly much, but there is overly much to tell. I hope you but enjoy this meal. I prepared the menu for you. I hope your favorites are here. It is also nutritionally correct, from what I have but determined. Please excuse me while I run to get the fishing reel so that I may show you."

"I would like it much if you join us quickly, Tadan."

Tadan nodded, and Sam motioned for Jandra to sit next to her. She was unaware that Jandra didn't know about Tadan.

Tadan left for the moment, and Sam looked to Briggon, "He does look like her, does he not? It is most surprising. He has her eyes and face structure. Does he wear you out?"

"He wears all of Hengist out. Each turn, he goes out to the community and but speaks to everyone. He offers good advice and ideas that improve our crafts and labor, so he is most loved. But he does overly speak, does he not? Even when I speak with him about this, he recognizes it but cannot seem to halt. He has turned into our wise old man at the age of ten tender cycles."

"And how is Young Alduth recovering? Who be he with now?"

"He but does well, Highest. He lives with Ivers and Raynod now. He learns the blacksmithing trade, but he wants to be The Knight. You will see him this turn. We also but placed Wigrad with Ivers and Raynod. They wanted a family, and Wigrad took to Ivers right off, so it be a family now."

The meal was brought out to them and they all began to eat. Sam hadn't noticed, but now saw that they were sitting in a covered patio. She found it most pleasant. There were other tables and chairs about, as if for others.

"Is this a place where men but eat?"

Briggon nodded, "One of our food preparers thought of the idea. It be a shop to eat at. You can come here and have a midturn or eve meal. Some turns, there is a choice of menu. These companions do this in trade for other items, and it gives the community the opportunity to enjoy their companionship without the every turn task of creating a meal."

"Like the tea shop we have in Woden, then?"

"Yes. But this is for food. We have another for wine and beer that is more like your tea shop."

Meera nodded, "This be a great idea. Someone should do this in Woden, Highest."

As they were finishing their meal, Tadan returned, pole in hand. "Highest Mother, how was your meal? I have brought the fishing reel for you to see. It would be better if we but tried it out in the river, however. That way you could but see the usefulness of the invention. I see you have completed your midturn meal. Delicious, was it not? I hope you ate it all as you are most thin—"

Sam interrupted him, "Tadan, halt."

"Yes, Highest Mother?"

"Would you like me to try the fishing reel out now or after my rounds? Would you like to attend me in my rounds?"

"Yes, I would most like to direct you around our Hengist. After the rounds would be fine, Highest Mother. The fish will be more likely to bite then. Now is not a good moment. It is overly near the midturn for fish to bite. And I would like a fish to bite so that you may see the benefit of this reel. And—"

"Tadan. I think it the moment I begin my rounds. Do you know Jandra?"

Tadan turned to Jandra and bowed his head, "Good midturn, Second." He then turned to Meera, "Good midturn Meera. I apologize for my lack of manners. It has been long since I have gotten to speak with my Highest Mother and I am most excited about it."

He turned back to Sam, "Highest Mother, do the rumors be truth about Second being of the old ones? Of the ones not of our race? Be the rumors true that you will accept Jandra as your companion at this next festival? It would be good for you to do so. I have thought long that you remain alone overly long. I know that love is a difficult thing to lose, but life is not always kind, and we must try to persevere."

"TADAN."

"Yes, Mother Highest?"

"How do you know of these things of love and love lost at your ten cycles?"

"Why, Highest Mother, I can observe, can I not? And I but lost my Birth-Mother, although I have no recollection of the moment. I have but observed you through the cycles and how it has worn on you, and—"

"Tadan, let us begin my rounds before the eve comes any closer."

Sam put out her hand and Tadan took it, leading her on her rounds. Meera, Jandra and Briggon all followed, laughing quietly about Tadan's incessant talking. They were also amused that Sam didn't seem to mind.

"So tell me, Tadan, what improvements do you think I should but make in Woden now that I am Highest?"

"I am most pleased you asked me such a question, Highest Mother. I have many ideas that I would but like to share with you. First, I think that we should improve the loading and unloading of supplies at the dock. I have a new invention that could be easily made and would hasten the loading and unloading of the ships by over half. We have pulleys, of course, but I have designed a maneuverable one that will lift much weight. And then I believe that we should refine the path between Woden and Hengist. A path made of bricks or stones would provide for easier walking, and we now have some excellent brick makers. And then I have designed a wheel that is thinner, lighter and will be easier to use on the wagons. I am also currently working on storing the sun's energy. I believe that I will be able to turn that into some form of energy or light that we could but use, instead of candles. I have also begun working with herbs and medicines so as to help improve our health care. There is something about mold, but I have not quite figured out what, yet. I will, though. I am trying to find a relief for pain. Something that will mask the pain so that an operation can be done without overly stressing the injured person. I have just recently met Ivers and he showed me how he works the metals to make them stronger. I believe I could make an arrow with such a tip so that they would fly truer and fly stronger through wind."

"Tadan. I would like it much if you would but draw up a new community for me. One that considers water usage, health conditions, community atmosphere, and so on. Would that interest you?"

"I have heard but rumors to a third community. A mixed one, be the rumor. I have also heard that it might be placed west of the path between Woden and Hengist, near the river. Such a task would most excite me, Highest Mother. I will put all my energies into it. How many people be there in this community? Would you like all new shops, or should we begin to connect the shops between the three communities? Will they need their own farm and gardens, or should we simply expand Woden and Hengist's? Would you like cobblestone paths instead our present dirt ones? Ah, Highest Mother, we have arrived to your first companions. You know Ivers and Raynod. And this be their new sons, who you already know."

Amazingly, Tadan stepped out of the way for a moment so that Sam might speak to them. Ivers, Alduth, Wigrad and Raynod knelt before Sam and bowed their heads, "Highest."

"Please rise. Raynod, it be good to see you again. Ivers, you are looking much improved from your long journey. Young Alduth, how be my young champion? And Wigrad, I have but missed you. You took excellent care of Second in my absence, and I thank you much."

They turned to Jandra and Meera, "Seconds", and bowed their heads. Wigrad held on to Sam's garments and wiped his nose on his sleeve. Ivers gave him a cloth, which he promptly took.

Raynod spoke, "Highest, Seconds, it is but good to have you here. Ivers has a present for you."

Ivers came forward with three knives, "I have made these for your belts, Warrior Women of Woden. Your kindness to me has brought me much happiness and I will never be able to repay you for such. Please notice the strength and luster of these knives. You may throw them with a true aim, as their weight is perfect. Young Tadan, please make sure you take them by Kinlan's leather shop. He has made them a sheath for their knives."

Sam took her knife and felt it. It was indeed a most wonderful knife.

Ivers added, "And it will not rust. This be a most refined metal. I have spoken to our miners about the metals we need, and you will find this a stronger and more useful knife than you have had prior."

Meera felt hers, tested the weight, and then threw it, aiming for a nearby tree. It flew fast and landed at her mark.

She was well pleased, "It throws well. Highest, try it out. See if you can hit my mark."

"Daring me, Meera? It has been long since we but competed with knives. But I will give it a try."

Sam tested its weight and threw it. It too landed on its mark, right next to Meera's.

All turned to Jandra, and Sam said, "Your turn, Jandra."

Meera laughed, "There be overly many people around. Perhaps another moment, Jandra."

"Meera is correct, Highest. I know not how to throw a knife such as the two of you. I will learn, though. Thank you, Ivers. It be a most special gift."

Tadan went up to Meera, "Can you but teach me to throw a knife so? Is it just in the wrist motion, or is it in the balance of your stance? What makes the accuracy in your throw? Can you describe the motions you go through so that I may reproduce them?"

Meera put her hand upon Tadan's head, "Shhhhh, little one. You speak overly, and it but makes my head ache. Throwing a knife is in the balance of the knife. It takes practice. When you visit Woden, come to see me and I will give you a lesson."

Sam turned back to Ivers and Raynod, "Is all well with the two of you? I hear rumors about this next festival and the two of you. Be they true? And Ivers, is Hengist all you hoped it would be?"

Raynod blushed, "The rumor be true, Highest. I but lost my companion recently, and am most pleased to have Ivers here. And he be a masterful blacksmith. Far better than me. And now with Alduth and Wigrad, we are a family, and I enjoy it much. Already, Wigrad wants to be a blacksmith."

Ivers added, "Oh, no, Highest. Raynod is a most superb blacksmith. He knows many more things than I. And yes, Hengist is more than I had but hoped for. And Raynod is most pleased by the reopening of Woden and Hengist. We have already spoken and worked with the blacksmiths from Woden, and it makes it better for all of us. We were hoping that some turn, we may have a blacksmith shop on the path between Woden and Hengist so that all the blacksmiths could be in one location, and all the people could come to one spot."

"It be a good idea. We but discussed as much this morn at the advisor's meeting. Make certain to keep your advisors well informed, as they will be meeting with us often, now. And how is Young Alduth fitting into your family?"

Ivers smiled, "He be a pleasure, Highest. I have gained much by coming here. But let us allow Alduth to but speak for himself."

Alduth bowed his head, "My Highest. It be good to see you once again. I but practice to become your champion. Each turn I practice with sword, arrow and knife. Soon I will throw them even better than you. I keep my mission well focused, Highest."

Sam placed her hand upon his shoulder, "It be good to have you with us, Young Knight Alduth. I will see you at festival."

Sam looked down at Wigrad, who was holding tightly onto her garments and looking off into space, "Has he but spoken yet?"

Ivers shook his head, "We have tried everything. But he seems content enough, and but twice, he smiled. Once when we showed him his own bed, and another when he heard you come to visit."

Sam bent down to Wigrad and placed her hands on his head. She sent a message, *If you ever have need of me, Wigrad, I am here for you. I will always be here for you. Woden and Hengist will always be your home.*

Wigrad looked into her eyes, nodded, and wiped his nose with the cloth Ivers had given to him. Sam smiled and began to take her leave.

Raynod responded, "Please come back to visit with us more often."

"I will do so, but you need not provide us with more gifts. We will quite willingly return. Good midturn, Raynod and Ivers. Thank you again. Good midturn Alduth and Wigrad."

She took Tadan's hand and they began walking further into Hengist. "Where do we head now, Tadan?"

"I am but taking you to our paper maker. He has something special for you."

Sam turned to Jandra and Meera, "This is turning more into a gift-giving visit. I did not wish these men to go to such trouble. I just wanted to meet with them."

Briggon responded, "They are just pleased you are here, Highest. It will not occur each moment, but for this once, they are excited and are simply showing off their skills."

"Yes, I can see that. You might tell them to not go to such trouble as this in the next visits. I wish to be here for them, not them for me."

"Oh, but, Highest, you are here for them. This is very special for them. It will take but a while for it to become a routine. Please have patience regarding their excitement."

"It is not a bother for me, Briggon. I am not upset. Do not misunderstand. I just dislike seeing them put out by my visit. But, as you say, it will just take a few visits to make it normal."

They arrived at Ludon's shop, the papermaker.

Tadan presented him, "Highest Mother, this be Ludon. He is very special to me."

Ludon knelt and bowed his head, "Highest. Thank you for coming."

"Rise, Ludon. Show me your paper products. I be most interested in these."

Ludon showed Sam a hand-made book, "This book be for you, Highest. Tadan did the drawings in it. The paper is handmade, and I have done the binding myself. Tadan and I are developing a press so that we can make many duplicates. It be a book of drawings of Hengist and Woden."

Sam examined the pages, "Thank you much, Ludon. This be a most special gift. I very much like the paper. It is thinner than anything I have yet seen. How is it that you make paper and books?"

"It is an art, and I am an artist. I also draw. I call my drawings cuts in wood. I but draw a picture and then carve it backwards into a piece of wood. Here, I will show you."

He got a piece of wood that he had carved a picture of a waterfall on, stamped it into some ink, and then stamped the wood onto a piece of paper.

He then showed the picture to Sam, asking her, "Do you but like it, Highest?"

"It is most detailed and interesting. I have never seen anything like this. It be truly beautiful, Ludon. Such things make our lives feel better, somehow. I love the details of these dwellings. And this picture of the lilies is most astounding. You are indeed an artist, Ludon. I look forward to the presses. Thank you much for this book. I will treasure it. How do you feel about Hengist and Woden now, Ludon?"

"I am most pleased, Highest. My companion, Kohal, is especially pleased. He be a fisher and he has told me that we but duplicate our efforts prior. Now it will be different. And we both know that you will be the best Highest Woden has or will ever see."

"Thank you, Ludon. Do you know Meera and Jandra? Jandra is The Second of Woden and Meera is The Second of Defense."

He bowed his head to them, "Seconds."

Jandra spoke, "Ludon, were you prior aware that The Highest has a fondness for books?"

Ludon nodded and grinned, "I do, Second. Tadan but informed me. But she has a love of the old First Ones' books. Perhaps, Highest, you might let me see your book so that I might examine its paper and binding."

"Come over to Woden, Ludon, and Karan will be pleased to show it to you. Briggon, please make this so any turn he but wishes. Thank you for the book, Ludon. I will visit with you again, soon."

"Highest Mother, did you look at my drawings inside the book Ludon gave to you? They are details of many ideas I have for new inventions. I would most like your opinion on these. Would you but study them and let me know what you think? I am most anxious to hear your opinion in these matters."

"Yes, Tadan. Come to our dwelling in a few turns and we can sit together and discuss your ideas and drawings. Perhaps we can experiment with them in Woden. Where do we head now, Tadan?"

"To the leather maker. He but waits for you." Tadan reached up to take Sam's hand. "Is it but true that you have strange powers now, Highest

Mother? Your eyes have deepened in their color since the prior moment we saw each other. They are like liquid blue, now, of a deep clear pool of water. Does this change in your eye color have anything to do with your new and increasing powers? I would like such eyes. May I speak with the Spirit Mothers of the Falls and ask for such? Your eyes are most interesting and unlike anyone's. What can you do with your new powers?"

Sam placed her hand upon Tadan and sent a message only he could hear, *Silence for but a moment, young Tadan. I have but missed you and be most sorry that I have ignored your presence. I will make up for this. I am most delighted to see what a bright and honorable young man you have but grown into.*

Tadan looked up at Sam and into her eyes and tried to send a message back, *Highest Mother. I have but missed you, too. This be an excellent power. Can I learn to do the same?*

Sam laughed and removed her hand, "No. But have you learned yet to ride a horse?"

Tadan shrunk and looked embarrassed, "No. They are overly big for me."

Meera came forward, "We have a horse you will much like. A horse just for you. The next moment you are in Woden, you find me and I will but give you a lesson you will be most proud of."

Tadan nodded, "I will but try for Highest Mother."

As they arrived at the leather maker's shop, Tadan presented him to Sam, "Highest Mother, this be Hildulf. He is The Realm's best leather maker. And he has made you something you will most enjoy."

Sam smiled at Hildulf, who instantly fell to his knees and bowed his head, "Highest. It is with great honor that I meet you. Thank you much for performing your rounds in Hengist. We are but all excited. I have presents for you and yours."

"Rise, Hildulf. There is no need to kneel before me. Tadan, perhaps you can but tell me why everyone insists of kneeling to me."

"It be a show of respect, Highest Mother."

"Is there no other way than going to one's knees?"

"You should accept this for what it is, Highest Mother. Everyone is most glad that you are now The Highest. They but pay you their most deep respect."

Meera nodded, "He is correct, Highest. I have longed told you that the best Highest will be who wants not to be The Highest. That is but you."

"This kneeling is tedious to me. But please continue, Hildulf. I but interrupt you."

Hildulf brought out leather sheaths for their new knives, "I made these especially for your new knives. I hope you like them. They are hand-sewn, of course, but have been specially tanned so as to last a long while."

He turned and brought out a leather vest, "Highest, this be for you. It is a new warrior vest for you. It is sewn with two hides so as to be thicker and safer. I asked Briggon to get your other one from May so that I may sew the correct size. And I also have this leather arrow pouch for you. I but noticed that your other arrow pouch was old and overly worn. Second, and Second, I have the same for each of you. I had to guess at Second's size, but Caitha gave me one of Second of Defense's leather vest."

Meera looked at her knife sheath, arrow pouch and leather warrior vest, "These be most excellent, Hildulf. You are most correct. Mine and The Highest's are most worn and used. The craftship on these be truly excellent. Strong and sturdy bindings and sewing. And the tanning of these hides is superb. Thank you much, Hildulf."

Sam placed her hand upon Hildulf's shoulder, "I say truly, Hildulf. These mean much to me. Is there but anything that I may do for you?"

"You but do it, Highest, just by being in Hengist with us."

"Thank you, Hildulf. I will take my leave now, but I will return most soon. While I like much this warrior vest, I take it in hopes that I will not need to use it."

Sam let Tadan lead her through half the town. It was a long, slow visit as every man wanted to meet with and give her a present. She knew she would have to return soon so as to make the visits normal. The presents were nice, but it was not the purpose of her rounds, and it bothered her. She accepted it for now in hopes that Tadan and Briggon could explain as much to all. At the end of the rounds, Sam went with Tadan to the river to experiment with his fishing reel, while Jandra, Briggon and Meera went to get drinks prior to their return to Woden. Tadan showed Sam how to cast the line and then how to reel it in slowly so as to catch the fish's attention.

She tried it a couple of casts, and finally, one fish bit the bone hook, "Tadan! Quickly. Now what must I do?"

Tadan was jumping up and down, clapping and laughing, "Oh, Mother. This be wonderful. Now reel it in slowly so as to not lose the fish. Slowly and evenly."

She did as Tadan directed, and soon she landed the fish.

Tadan unhooked it and released the fish, "What do you think of the fishing reel?"

"I must speak truly, Tadan. I had not thought it would be of this importance. This be a most wonderful invention. With it, I could learn to cast the line far and reel it back in without tangling the line. Well done, Tadan. Your Birth-Mother would have been most proud of you. Make certain to share this invention with Janel of the fisheries."

"Yes, Highest Mother." He was beaming with pride.

As Jandra, Meera and Briggon walked up, they saw Sam hugging Tadan, and Tadan hugging Sam in return. Meera halted a moment, as she thought she saw tears in Sam's eyes and wanted to give her but a moment.

"Oh, Mother. I know you but miss her so, as do I. But we have each other, and I can try to be but almost as wonderful as she was for you. You have been overly lonely without her, and you have but carried her longer than anyone."

Sam moved away from Tadan a bit and straightened his hair for him, "How can such a young one understand and know my feelings so? In overly many ways, Tadan, you sound like your Birth-Mother. She was but a bright one, also. I knew of none brighter than her. Have you been told that you have her eyes?"

"I remember her eyes, Mother."

Jandra interrupted, not knowing what was occurring, "Highest, we have brought you drink."

Tadan and Sam turned to Jandra. Each had been startled by her and hadn't realized that the others had returned.

Tadan began speaking, "Father. Second. Second. It be most wonderful. Highest Mother but caught a fish with my fishing reel. She but likes it, Father. It worked perfectly for her. I knew it would work. Now if only I could make a stronger fishing line."

Sam bent down to Tadan, "Tadan. You need to meet someone that I know who will be most special for you. And I bet she will know how to make but a stronger fishing line. She is also most intelligent."

Sam turned to Briggon, "Can you but bring Tadan over to my dwelling soon so that I may introduce him to Keddi?"

"Of course, Highest."

Sam sat down to rest for a bit, and Jandra and Briggon sat next to her while she finished her drink.

Tadan went to Meera, "Second, could you but give me a lesson now on how to throw your knife, so? Also, may I hold your sword? Could you teach me one move with this sword? I would most like to—"

Meera placed her hand over Tadan's mouth, "First rule of defense, Tadan. Do you know what it be?"

Tadan shook his head as Meera's hand was yet over his mouth. Sam was laughing, as were Briggon and Jandra.

Meera looked into his eyes and leered at him, "It be to go quietly. Without a sound. Do you understand?"

She removed her hand and Tadan began to speak, "But Second, I learn from doing and by asking—"

Meera placed her hand back over Tadan's mouth, "Shhhhhh. A warrior listens, but speaks not. A warrior watches and lets the wind send messages. Listen to the wind. Listen to which way it blows. This be important when throwing a knife or shooting an arrow. Observe the leaves of the trees . . . "

Sam shook her head, "Now there be a pair. Briggon, you have raised him well. You should be most proud."

"Not I, Highest. All of Hengist has but raised that young man. He will do great things for all of Woden. He is but the brightest of all of us. And he has a true and loving nature about him, with no show of arrogance. It is his continued innocence that all love."

Jandra had remained quiet all the turn, not wishing to interfere, but guessing about Tadan.

Sam noticed Jandra's quietness, "Jandra, you have spoken but little this turn. Is all well with you?"

"Yes, Highest. I learn to be a warrior as young Tadan, and listen and observe as Meera teaches. That young Tadan most admires you, Highest."

Sam raised her eyebrow and had guessed as to Jandra's quietness, "I am sorry, Jandra. I thought all but knew about Tadan. Briggon, please tell Jandra."

Briggon nodded and turned to Jandra, "Second, it is most likely as you think. Brett was Tadan's Birth-Mother, and I be but his Father. He was two cycles when Brett was but killed. Although it is practice that the sons live with the fathers in Hengist, Tadan was always wanting his Birth-Mother and mother. I would have to take him over for frequent visits. He began speaking at his first cycle and has not halted since, except for one moment. He remembers well his Birth-Mother, and her death most upset him, as it did The Highest. After her death, he moved not for well over two moons. He spoke not for over six moons. I but took him to see The Highest once, and they both cried and held each other for two turns, but would not speak to each other about it. But when he returned to Hengist, he began to speak again. His Mother is most important to him."

Briggon turned to Sam, "Highest, you are planning on introducing young Tadan to Keddi?"

Sam nodded.

Briggon also nodded, "That will be good."

Jandra felt like she had lived in a separate community for all her life. She wondered how all these things had occurred, yet she had known none of it. That Brett had a child had remained unknown to her. That Sam was a Mother was something that had never occurred as a possibility. And to learn that this very special child was of Sam's companionship with Brett just astonished Jandra.

Have I lived in Woden, truly? Where did I come from?

She could stand it no longer and asked, "Why is Keddi important to Tadan, Highest?"

Sam looked at Jandra but tried to refrain from emotion. She took a deep breath, and then sighed. She wondered if these hidden events were always to be so. After a long moment, she responded, "Keddi be Brett's sister."

Jandra gasped, "What? How could that be? How is it I have not known this?"

Sam laughed a little, but only because she understood Jandra's disbelief, "You? How would you but feel if you were me and I but recently learned this, as well?"

Jandra couldn't believe what she had heard, "All these cycles and you knew not that Keddi was Brett's sister?"

"I learned of this only turns prior, upon Keddi's arrival back into Woden. If you look closely at Tadan, you will see a resemblance."

Sam looked at Meera and Tadan. Tadan had thrown Meera's new knife three attempts, and watched Meera throw it the same. Upon each occasion, Tadan observed Meera very carefully and then tried to imitate her style. Sam saw Meera unsheathe her sword and hold it out for Tadan. He smiled but said nothing, and took hold of the hilt. Meera let go, and the sword dropped to the ground. Tadan was surprised at how much the sword weighed. He fought to pick it up and did so, but barely.

Sam turned to Briggon, "Would you ask Ivers a favor for me? Please ask him to make a small sword and a knife for young Tadan from me, unless of course, you wish it not so."

"I will, Highest. All of us must learn to use such in our lives until evil ends in this realm. While it is not Tadan's calling, he should be but prepared."

Sam rose and went over to Meera and Tadan. She looked down at Tadan, "I must take my leave now, Tadan. Festival be in but two turns, and we shall see each other then. I have made arrangements for your Father to bring you to Woden directly after the festival, as there is someone I wish you to meet. If you would but like, you could come to visit me every few turns in Woden and we could discuss your drawings and ideas. Perhaps you would like to do my Woden rounds with me and meet our women. They might also enjoy hearing of your ideas and may give you more."

Tadan gave the knife and sword back to Meera and went to Sam. He held her, "Highest Mother, you have made my cycle. It most pleases me to see you and makes me but calmer. I will come over, on that you can be assured. I hope you invite me in truth, as I will come. I have missed you so, Mother."

"Be strong, Tadan, as there is only cause for joy. A new era has occurred and I have finally let the bonds of prior go. My dwelling is but your dwelling. Come whenever you have the need. Meera will inform the guards of so. And remember, although your Birth-Mother be not with us, her love will always be with us."

They hugged each other and Sam kissed him on his head and sent a message, *I love you much, Young Tadan. You make me most proud. Your Birth-Mother is most pleased by you.*

Tadan smiled and waved his farewell. Briggon went over and placed his arms around Tadan, "Thank you for coming, Highest."

Meera, Jandra and Sam all walked back to Woden, mostly in silence. Briggon had given all the gifts for a guard to take to Sam's dwelling so that she wouldn't have to carry them, so Sam was free to think on the turn. It was mideve by the moment Sam and Jandra had arrived to their dwelling, and Meera took her leave from there. Their eve meal was prepared and ready, and Sam was most hungry, again.

She halted near a guard for a moment first, "Please send a messenger to Keddi. I have need to see her, if she can but come this eve."

The guard nodded and left to find a messenger.

Sam went into the kitchen and found Jandra waiting with their meal on the table. Jandra said, "Sit down and eat, Highest. Even though you are eating these turns, you remain overly thin. It be all this riding and walking that takes away all your size."

Sam and Jandra sat and began to eat. May had prepared a fish dinner, with the entire fish stuffed with rice, vegetables and sauce. She had also baked fresh bread, and Sam thought it a fine meal. She noticed that there were some fruit tarts remaining from the morn. Sam looked at Jandra and saw that she looked overly concerned. Sam didn't know how to begin a conversation about this turn, as she was used to living alone and keeping her thoughts inside.

She fought for conversation and finally decided on just a question, "How did you think of the turn, Jandra?"

Jandra slowly closed and reopened her eyes, sighing slightly, "As like most turns with you, it was ever amazing. I have come to believe that most your turns are filled with surprises and adventures. My life up to you has been one of mostly quiet turn-to-turn living. I feel like I am but a passing friend in your life, like Oisin or Meera, or any other. You know not how to live with the idea of constancy, Sam. I have come to understand that you do not purposefully withhold knowledge from me, but there be so much to tell that you know not where to begin."

Sam raised her eyebrows slightly and thought about that statement. She thought that Jandra was mostly correct in it. Nothing much in her life had been permanent. She had no model for what constancy even looked-like.

Finally, Sam nodded, "I think you speak truthfully and accurately. In reflecting on it, May and this dwelling are the only constants in my life. It be a true but sad statement in that I don't know how to treat you on a turn-to-turn basis. I had Brett for a few cycles, this be most true, but it has been as many cycles since she has but left, and I am well used to lovers entering and exiting my life and dwelling. With each comes excitement, and when they leave, comes a relief of being back to my way of life. I enjoy you here and with me, Jandra, but I do find myself having to think about it and making myself to act differently than my old patterns. I am sorry I am not better for you."

"No, Sam. It be not for you to be sorry about this. Even you were not aware that Keddi was Brett's sister. And when would you have had but the opportunity to inform me about Brett and Tadan? It be all most stunning, and must be so to you as well. I am continually stunned by how much you have held within you all these cycles, especially in regard to Brett. Most women I know speak continually about their complaints and sorrows. You rarely speak at all, let alone about your thoughts and feelings. At the end of this turn, Sam, I find myself simply amazed to learn that you are a mother. A mother to Tadan, the boy-wonder of intellect. I am continually amazed at how revered you are across all of Woden. And I remain but continually amazed at your humbleness. The former Highest was never so humble, Sam. She most enjoyed being adored and recognized. And you never tire of doing your duty. The former Highest would take a cycle or more to do as much as you do in one turn. And I have been continually amazed at how you treat your advisors, and them you. Never was a meeting so cordial with the former Highest. There was always violent arguing and shouting, and she would never halt it. Now I am led to believe that she might have even encouraged it so. And then you arrive at the end of this overly busy turn and blame yourself for not treating me as a newly arrived lover. We have our issues, Sam, and will have to learn to work through them. I think our issues be mostly mine, though. You expect nothing from me and seem delighted for whatever you get from me. It is I with the expectations, and yet you are The Highest. Should I expect more from you at the end of every turn when you have given yourself fully, already?"

Sam laughed, "I would think you have but the right to do so. If we are to become companions, I would think you would want more of me than a tired and worn-out woman at the end of each turn."

"How is it I knew not that Brett but had a child?"

"How is it I knew not that Brett but had a sister?"

Jandra laughed, "It does seem strange, does it not? We number only over 2,000 people in all of Woden. Is it that many that so many facts go unlearned?"

"I know not, but I am stunned that you knew not that Brett had a child. Perhaps because it was but a boy, it became quiet."

Sam got up and went to the counter, "Would you like a fruit tart? These are exceptionally good."

Jandra nodded, "Just one for me. You can eat the extras."

A guard entered and knelt to Sam, "Highest, Keddi has arrived."

"Please send her in, and thank you."

The guard left and Keddi entered and knelt, "Highest." She rose and bowed her head to Jandra, "Second."

Sam smiled at her, "You have arrived at but just the correct moment. Sit and have one of May's delicious fruit tarts. It be one of her best sweets."

Sam put one in front of Keddi as Keddi sat at the long table, next to Jandra.

She took a bite and smiled, "It must be fine to have your own cook. My ability with sweets is if I can pick a fruit fresh from its limb."

"There be more if you would so like. Thank you for coming, Keddi. I have but two issues I need to discuss with you. First, do you think Woden should continue the training and use of Scouts, such as yourself and Brett?"

"I have thought on this issue, Highest, and in truth think the idea needs but refining. It is my suggestion to pick twenty or twenty-five of the best guards and give them specialized training for scout work, but that they go for shortened periods. I was sent for what was to be half my life. I think it would be improved if we trained our guards for scouting duties and then send them on special assignments, say for perhaps two-to-three or four moons, at most. In this fashion, they could lead a more normal life than our scouts do at present, and they would stand less risk of discovery. I think we send our scouts for overly long and discovery is almost guaranteed. By leaving within a moon or so, they are not so involved within the community. The negative to this is that the information will be somewhat more difficult to obtain. But it can be bought. I think it most important that the scouts be able to return home, to a safe place, and to have such to think about. Otherwise, it can be like walking to your own death, and there is little enough motivation in that."

Sam agreed, "It makes but sense, Keddi. Would you be willing, now that you are to remain in Woden, to work with Meera to train our future scouts and organize the scouting patrols?"

"I was hoping something like this would occur so that I would be able to contribute in such a way. I would be most delighted to, Highest. It would be my pleasure."

"But it means that you must ensure that I learn this two-arrow practice of yours. My training is to be but one of your duties too."

She laughed, "That be easy enough, Highest."

"Good. I will inform Meera of this. I have one more item this eve, Keddi. You are aware how surprised I was to learn that you were Brett's sister."

Keddi frowned and shook her head, slightly, "I am sorry that you had to learn of this in that fashion, Highest."

She waved her hand, dismissing the notion, "It be not an issue. There are many things we learn these turns. And now there is something I must share with you that I have but neglected to, but only out of absence of mind on my part. Please know that I have not hidden this from you. The presence of it just struck me this turn, or I would have but informed you sooner. Keddi, were you aware that Brett but had a child?"

Keddi looked shocked, "A child? Brett? Where be this child? A girl?"

Sam shook her head, "No. It be but a boy child."

"Is he well and in Hengist? Who be the Father?"

"He be well. And he is extremely bright. He is of ten cycles, and his father be Briggon."

"Briggon? Brett laid with Briggon? Be there a different Briggon?"

"No. It be the Third of Hengist Briggon. He be the father. Brett's son is named Tadan. And I would like you to but meet him. Briggon would like as much, also. Tadan resembles Brett much in his thinking and in his facial looks."

"A son. I am caught most unaware, Highest."

"I know Keddi, and I am but sorry to have to tell you in such a manner. You should have but known this much sooner. Tadan was but two cycles when Brett was killed. He remembers her well."

"This be foolishness. How could a babe of two cycles remember their Birth-Mother?"

"Tadan was never a baby. He spoke fully at one cycle. He remembers most aspects of Brett. Some clearer than even me. He is even aware which of his features resemble Brett's."

"When might I meet Tadan?"

"At Festival, or directly after. Would that but suit you?"

"Oh, yes, Highest. It be as if a part of Brett yet lives, be it not?"

"It is for me now. For many cycles, I could not think of Tadan as he brought overly much pain just to see him. But now he brings happiness."

"I never would have believed that Brett would have a child. Forgive me for asking, Highest, but why was it not you, instead? I would have guessed that, as Brett was so focused on perfecting her guarding abilities."

Sam smiled slightly, "You will have to forgive me for not answering your question, Keddi. Perhaps another moment. For now, go and think of Brett's son, Tadan. She was his Birth-Mother. And Tadan will be most excited about meeting you."

Keddi rose, "Thank you, Highest. It was a shock, but a good one. May I ask a question of you?"

Sam nodded, so Keddi asked, "I am unsure about who is to ask who to be a companion at Festival."

Jandra nodded, "You mean, do you ask Margeria, or does she but ask you?"

"Yes, you have my meaning."

Sam and Jandra both laughed, and Jandra responded, "The rules and laws be most unclear on this these moments in our community. In truth, since you are residing in Margeria's dwelling, it be more correct for her to ask you. If it be her dwelling and you ask her, you give her no dwelling to go to. You also have the higher status in rank because you are a scout and she but a guard. In this regard, it also be more correct for her to ask you. If you, as the higher rank, asked her, it could be seen as forcing the issue, which be frowned upon. But there are rules in regard to the number of cycles each has, who has seen other companionships, and so on. My best council to you would be for Margeria to do the asking of you to take her as your companion. There would be no argument on this. Does that help, Keddi?"

"Oh, yes, Second. Many, many thanks. Margeria and I have worried about this, and festival is in two turns. This relieves our stress. Good eve, Highest. Second."

Keddi waved and left, and Sam just shook her head and laughed, "That was but a quick decision on their parts. They did not wait but two moments."

"They are so excited and happy. It is good to see such."

Sam looked at Jandra, "Is there such excitement for you, Jandra?"

Jandra blushed lightly, "I think it be more nervousness on my part. I am unsure if you are prepared for companionship. I think you will accept it should I ask it of you, but I remain unconvinced that it is what you desire, fully. I think you be more like Oisin in this regard."

Sam thought about her statement a bit and then replied, "Perhaps we should but wait until festival next, then, do you think? I would like it much if you could be happy about such. And I would like you to rest in the assuredness that it is what I but want. It makes no difference if we but do this now or festival next. The advisors will complain, but I will almost miss their incessant complaining about this should it go away. But know this, Jandra, whether we wait or no, I want you as my companion."

"Perhaps you are correct. It should cause no stress, and yet I feel overly stressed. I will wait until the correct moment and am certain that it will occur. What be your plans for next turn, Sam?"

"Rounds in Woden. Visit the infirmary and all our new guests. Visit the fisheries and the docks. And you?"

* * * *

"Final Festival preparation. We arrange but the last details. It will take up most of the turn. I hope it will go well for all. The bridge be in good order, and we have arranged that Hengist will sound a louder sounding alarm, and arrange for it to be used much so as to ensure return of all the women. The food looks to be excellent, and the entertainment will be more grand than ever prior. And were you aware that there will be a full moon's rise this festival? It be a rare occurrence."

"Do you begin in the early morn?"

"There be no need. By early midturn is soon enough. Do you need me in the morn?"

"Would you like to but escape with me this eve?"

"Escape? How? Where do we head?"

"It be a surprise. Willing to take a risk?"

"No guards, Sam?"

Sam smiled, "No. None. If we can but escape."

Jandra agreed, and Sam enacted her plan. She had Jandra enter the patio and state that she heard a noise off in the trees. When the guards moved in that direction, Jandra and Sam slipped out the front door and moved down to the river and into the shadows. Sam then led Jandra out to the gardens and into the animal farms. She got a horse and bridled it, took a horse blanket, and helped Jandra onto the horse.

Jandra became confused, "Sam, are you not getting a horse for you?"

Sam shook her head and mounted behind Jandra, "Shhh. Only whisper. I have need to be with you without guards surrounding us every moment. I but ride with you. Have you yet been to the hot springs?"

Jandra turned and smiled, "Long prior as a young girl. Is that where we head?"

Sam smiled, placed her arms around Jandra, took the reins and moved the horse off quietly. After a short while and once they were well away from Woden's gates, Sam relaxed.

"I think we managed to escape, Sam."

"And Meera will be at our door upon our return. I will catch it for this, and it will be but a long while before I will be able to make another such escape."

"Will Meera be very angry with you?"

"Oh, she will, but I will but tell her that I help to train her guards. Poor guards. Meera will be all over them for this. I will but have to set it correct, somehow, for them. But enough of worrying. We are to have some fun this eve."

Sam nudged the horse into a slow run. As they came closer to the springs, Sam slowed the horse to a walk. She then began to move her hands to Jandra's breasts and between her legs. Jandra moaned at the sudden and unexpected feeling, the motion of the horse adding to her pleasure. Sam kissed the back of Jandra's neck while removing Jandra's shirt. She moved one hand back between Jandra's legs, into the warm and moist spot, and the other onto her breasts. The horse kept moving slowly, and Sam held tightly with her arms around Jandra as Jandra drifted off into total sensual awareness. Sam could hear and feel Jandra breathing heavier and becoming totally unaware as to her surroundings. Sam forced Jandra to take it slowly.

She whispered into Jandra's ear, "Make it last."

Sam kept the horse moving slowly by nudging it every now and then with her legs. It was a more difficult thing to keep Jandra moving slowly.

She whispered again, "Make it last."

Jandra moaned loudly, "I cannot. I have never felt this way."

Sam moved her hand away for but a moment, and Jandra moaned again. She moved both hands to Jandra's breasts. Jandra took one of Sam's hands and placed it back between her legs and Sam began to fulfill Jandra's pleasure. Slowly, Jandra came to a total consuming release, and then drooped into Sam's arms, leaning back onto her.

Sam laughed softly, "Yet with me?"

"Barely. I cannot move. I think my body died. It has never felt this way, prior."

Jandra rested her hands and arms on Sam's legs as Sam picked up the reins again and trotted the horse to the springs. Jandra just relaxed onto Sam the rest of the way. When they got to the springs, Sam helped Jandra down, they undressed, and entered the hot springs.

"How long prior since you came here, Sam?"

"A while prior. A cycle or more. I brought us a flask of wine, but no glasses. Do you mind drinking from the flask?"

"Look, Sam. The moon. It be almost full."

She looked at Sam as if an idea finally came, "That be why you brought me here this eve. The moon is almost full. It be beautiful, Sam.

Thank you. This be most wonderful. I can see why you like to but escape. It is so peaceful here, and the hot water feels so good on my old bones."

"You are not old. You are beautiful. You are truly the most beautiful woman in all of Woden."

"Come over here and lean against me while we share the wine and gaze at the moon."

She did, her back leaning against the front of Jandra while they drank the wine, watched the moon move slightly, and felt the hot water pass their bodies.

"Sam, I think you are a romantic, but have never shared that with anyone. Except probably for Brett."

Sam just smiled, "I like the outside and nature. I find the moon upon the water mesmerizing. And I but wanted to see your body with the moon upon it. I speak truly, Jandra. You are a most stunningly beautiful woman. I have never prior seen such as you. Never. Did your mother ever say where you came from?"

"No. I wonder, though. I wondered about it just recently. I be not certain I am from here."

Jandra placed the wine flask upon the bank and wrapped her arms around Sam. They sat there like that for quite a while until Jandra thought that Sam had fallen asleep. Gently, she began rubbing Sam's breasts and slowly moved one hand down between her legs. As she did so, Sam moaned softly. Jandra kept her motions slow and soft for a long, long moment until she could feel Sam moving into her. Slowly, Jandra increased the pressure until after many long moments, Sam shivered and moaned, and then relaxed onto Jandra. Jandra continued to just hold Sam for a long while.

Finally, Sam sat up and moved into deeper water, "Look at the stars. Are they not beautiful? Upon many occasions I would but come here when there be no moon, and the stars shone almost as bright. On one occasion, I but came here and saw an entire eve of shooting stars. I counted well over 300 and halted there, but watched them through the entire eve. It was a most wondrous sight."

"I do not think I have ever had the occasion to halt and watch the moon or stars much. They have been but passing things to me. This moon is most beautiful. And as you say, it is beautiful against the water. I have seen shooting stars once, and only just a few then. I love the stars, but they seem overly far away."

As the moon's setting began to occur, Sam rose and put out her hand so as to help Jandra do the same, "We must leave as it will be morn overly soon. It is why I but asked you if you had an early morn meeting."

They dressed back into their garments, Sam helped Jandra back upon the horse, Sam mounted, and they began their journey back to Woden.

As they returned to the animal farm, Sam said, "I hope you but had a good eve, Jandra. If the guards found out we were but gone, they will be here waiting."

"I had a most wonderful eve, Sam. Thank you much. I think it was the best eve of my life. What a wonderful gift you gave me."

As they approached the farm, Sam noticed no guards around. She silently jumped down from the horse, helped Jandra down, and returned the horse to its stall. She brushed the horse and unbridled it, and found some extra feed for it.

Then she turned to Jandra and whispered, "Let us see if we can sneak in as well as we snuck out. We will go silently to the river, and then walk up from there as if we had gone nowhere at all."

Jandra nodded and laughed quietly. They snuck down to the river and followed it until they were near their dwelling.

Sam began to speak as if she were not hiding, "The birds at the river are most funny, are they not Jandra?"

"Yes, Sam. I am glad that we were able to help the babies to find their Birth-Mother."

Jandra couldn't help but laugh, but it didn't matter. The guards heard Sam and Jandra and looked at each other, wondering how they had gotten out of the house without any of the guards seeing them. The main guard felt lucky in that The Highest and The Second had just gone to the river and no where else.

As Sam approached the guard, she nodded, "Nice eve, is it not? We heard the birds and went to check on them by the river. We return inside now. Thank you for keeping watch."

The guard nodded, but said nothing. Jandra put her hand over her mouth to keep from laughing. She had never done such, prior, and it had most pleased her.

* * * *

They had gone to bed in the early morn, having spent most the eve at the hot springs. Jandra had risen and left for her meeting prior to Sam rising. After eating her morn meal, Sam readied herself and walked over to the infirmary.

As Sam entered, Anselet greeted her, and knelt before her, "Highest."

"Please rise. How be you this turn, Anselet?"

"I am well, Highest. It is good to see you. I assume you have come to see all the ones you have rescued."

"Be they well and improved?"

"One has but lost her unborn child. Another is dying. We cannot save her, Highest. She became overly weak from starvation. Another is borderline, but I think she will live. All the children seem to be doing well. We will be providing families for a few of the children soon. And for those women who wish to remain in Woden, Karan has but given her permission for them to be housed. Be that correct, Highest?"

"If Karan wishes it to be so, then so it be."

Anselet nodded, "I will escort you around to the ones you wish to see."

"The five women from the ship. Be they yet here?"

"They are, Highest. Would you like to begin with them?"

Sam nodded, and Anselet led the way. It seemed that the infirmary was filled this turn. Sam noticed that Patrice was no longer in the bed she had occupied and thought she had but returned to her own dwelling.

"Can we get some of the stronger ones to the festival for at least a small part of it?"

"As you wish, Highest. I will see to it."

Anselet led Sam into one of the smaller of the infirmary's rooms. As they entered, Sam saw that all five women from the ship were in the one room.

Anselet walked in and introduced Sam, "This be Woden's Highest. She has come to meet with you this turn."

All the women looked wide-eyed, and all got up from their beds and knelt down to Sam, and bowed their heads.

Sam turned to Anselet, "Where might I find you when I am but finished here?"

Anselet had thought she would be staying, but simply nodded and said, "I will wait for you outside the door, Highest." She left and closed the door.

The women were yet kneeling, "Please rise and make yourselves comfortable."

As they went back to their beds, Sam said, "Perhaps you could provide your names to me. I know you not, but welcome you to Woden."

"I be Noirin, Highest. Thank you for rescuing us from that ship and those men. We are most grateful for your intervention. I know not if you have been informed, but we would like to remain and live our lives in Woden."

Sam nodded and went and opened the door, "Anselet, would you please send a messenger to Karan. I have need of her assistance, if she but free to come."

Sam closed the door again, "You know of Woden and our laws?"

"Yes, Highest. Karan has informed us."

"Tell me of yourselves and your crafts. Where were you kidnapped you from?"

Sam sat on the edge of one of the beds. Noirin began, "I am a glass blower and mirror maker."

She motioned over to another woman, "This be Immolet."

Immolet rose, "I be but a midwife and learning-to-be healer."

She sat and another rose, "Highest, I be Caitlin. I would like to learn the fisheries."

Gaoth rose, "I be Gaoth, Highest. I am a garment maker and maker of thread."

Neilla rose, "I prepare foods for long storage, Highest. I can also sew. I am called Neilla."

Noirin spoke again, "We were taken from New Harborage, Highest. We overheard that we were being taken to Fornaith, in the far northern regions, to a ruler named King Buron. It mattered not to us, though, as we were but prisoners in New Harborage, as well. All the men be evil in our realm, although we have but heard that the men of Hengist do not treat women badly. I am sure that be because of Woden. None of us wish to ever live out in The Realm again. We wish to remain here and live the Woden way, with you, Highest. There are reports of you throughout The Realm, and anyone that can but escapes to come here now. We have good skills for Woden, Highest. And if they be not sufficient, we are but willing to learn whatever you need of us. We have heard the rumors and know you to be kind and fair. We know that all are expected to share the work of Woden, and that all live in peace here."

Sam looked around at the others, "Does she speak for all of you?"

Neilla spoke, "We have had many turns now to discuss our lucky turn of events. We were being taken to Fornaith, as they have not enough women of breeding age. The men be afraid that there will not be enough children left in The Realm, so rape women two or three moments each turn just to ensure that they become with child. We have but heard that the women of Woden are warriors and are well able to defend their community. We wish to be in Woden, live peacefully, perform our trades, and learn to become warriors. We have heard that you are the greatest of them all and can throw a knife at hundreds of paces, shoot three arrows accurately at one moment, and wield the heaviest sword of all."

Sam laughed, "I but sound like I am an overly strong and large woman." She shook her head, "I am not these things. Yes, I can but throw a knife, shoot an arrow, and wield a sword, but there are others far more skilled than myself."

Gaoth spoke up, "Nay, Highest. We have heard that you are the bravest of them all and lead all directly into battle with no fear. I can see this be in you, Highest. The women of Woden have also said this to be so. We hear much while we wait in the infirmary."

"Tell me of New Harborage. What goes on there, now?"

Caitlin spat out her words, "Evil! Wickedness! It is not but a breeding ground of hatred, greed and sickness. There is no peace and there is no safety. We were but guarded turn-in and turn-out. When we were allowed to sleep, we would be awakened so as to be raped. I believe the women's wombs go dry now, younger and younger, from these punishments and evils. I hate these men, Highest. If you but give me a sword and teach me to use it, I will wield it mightily against them. More blood will flow from my sword than all the blood they made run from women."

Gaoth said, softly, "Some women kill their own babies when they are born so as to prevent them from coming into such an existence."

Sam looked at each of them, "Are any of you with child?"

Neilla shook her head, "We all were. We have all but lost our children. None of us be with child now, Highest. That be both good and bad. Prior, we desired not these children, but now as we are in Woden, we are saddened by their loss."

The door to their room opened. Karan peeked into the room, "Highest? You sent for me?"

Sam turned to Karan, "Please come in. I need your advice and assistance."

Karan knelt and bowed her head as she came into the room, "I am here for you, Highest."

"Rise, Karan. Tell me, do we have but dwellings ready for these women?"

"We do, Highest, but there is a dilemma that needs your decision. These women would like to but take each other as companions. Caitlin and Gaoth will be making their companionship at the festival this next turn."

"And there is a dwelling for them?"

"Yes, Highest. But that be not the issue."

Karan paused, and Sam looked at her, wondering what the problem could be.

Karan continued, "I have looked into the laws of Woden on this and have found nothing for or against."

Karan paused, but Sam out-waited her. Karan continued, "Immolet, Neilla, and Noirin all want to be companions and live in one dwelling."

Sam looked at Karan and smiled, "That certainly is a new one, is it not? And you say that the laws say nothing on this?"

"Nothing, Highest."

"As companions?"

"It is my understanding of such."

Sam looked at Noirin, "Can you explain this to me?"

Noirin blushed but stood steadfast, "When women be shackled together for cycles, strange patterns occur. We are all three but as one."

Sam provided an argument, "Three can be a difficult number, Noirin. Often, the third but can feel left out."

Immolet nodded, "Perhaps if that comes to be, Highest, then one of us may choose to take their own companion. In the meanwhile, it is but our way and would hope to not be separated."

Sam looked to Neilla, "Neilla, you seem to be the quiet one. Do you ever feel left out in this triad?"

"No, Highest. Never. This is truth."

Sam nodded and looked to Karan, "Karan, what do you think of this?"

"There is no law, so it be not against the law. The women will all have something to say about it, but they also know it is not against the law. It is new and so will face the tongues of new things. In moments to come, it would be accepted, if these three make it so. Their mannerisms within the community will make all the difference."

Sam looked to Noirin, "This makes much sense to me. The community will expect much of you, and being a companionship of three might make it overly easy to avoid the community."

"Highest, we would but vow to make it good in the community. We would work to have them embrace us."

Sam frowned a bit at Noirin, "And if I but made that a condition? And if it should not occur, as you say it would, then I would but split the triad. What say you to this?"

Immolet, Neilla and Noirin all nodded. Neilla responded, "It is as we have but heard. You are the most fair and kind in all The Realm. Highest, please place any condition on us you wish. We will vow and live up to the conditions. We pledge you our lives and support. They are but yours to command."

Sam looked at Karan. Both were startled at the statement. Sam asked, "How did you come to use those words?"

Neilla looked embarrassed, "But, Highest, those are the most famous of all words throughout The Realm. They are but the words you spoke when you took your oath. All know of such. It rings throughout the land. Every other ruler demands allegiance except you. You give yours to your people. It is why all women seek to come here."

Sam was dazed. She wondered how word of such could have spread so quickly throughout The Realm. It was a large realm and mostly unexplored, yet all seemed to know of Woden. Sam thought Woden to be a quietly unknown community. She was beginning to understand that it was the most talked of community in The Realm.

"Karan, let this unusual companionship occur, but under these conditions: They are to be accepted by the community within two moons. They are to serve as a model of companionship. I want no ill-will between these three."

"Yes, Highest."

Noirin smiled, "Thank you, Highest. You will not regret this decision."

Sam frowned, "I hope not."

She took her leave and left the room. Anselet waited outside. Karan followed Sam.

Sam turned to Karan, "Do you have the moments to tend to me while I do rounds in the infirmary? I suspect many issues will arise and I would most like your council."

Karan bowed her head, "I am at your command, Highest and am pleased to be here for you."

"Anselet, can you take me to some of the members of the larger group? I wish to see how they fare now."

Anselet led them to the main room in the infirmary, and also its largest. Most of the group from Apien was housed here. The children that were able and well enough had already been placed in dwellings with others. As The Highest, Karan and Anselet walked in, the nursing ones saw her, knelt and bowed their heads.

Anselet told The Highest, "They speak very little. I think they were punished prior if they spoke. We have obtained very little information from them."

"Please sit."

Sam sat in one of the chairs and looked about them. They were now clean, fed and nursed back to some health.

Karan began the introductions, "Highest. You already know Tedra and Bolden. They will be seeking a mixed community if one can be provided."

Sam acknowledged them by bowing her head to them, a formal custom of Woden. They returned the bow, but said nothing.

"These companions be Antherna and Laval. They would also like a mixed community if possible. And these be Gein and Reims, two single men that would like a mixed community, along with Neillen and Crecy."

Sam nodded her head to them and said, "Woden presently thinks about the idea of a third community. While you are welcomed here to rest and heal, I can make no vows that this will occur. If it does not, you will have but a decision to make regarding your future, as without a third community, there will be no available way for you to follow your practice."

Gein rose, "We understand, Highest, and thank you for this safe refuge."

Karan continued, "The remainder all wish to remain in Woden or Hengist. Over here is Boltar. He be a horn carver. This be Lourtides. She be a cheese maker, and is with child. This be Lanceten and is a trained guard. And this be Nolsteney. She is a spiritual woman, Highest, and is also a midwife. The children are the ones not here, but you are already acquainted with them. They have all determined to remain in Woden or Hengist."

Reims rose, "Highest, I object. Jemera is overly young to make this decision. I would most welcome her into my dwelling until she be old enough to do so. I think it not correct that she remain in Woden."

Sam turned to Karan, "Karan, please send a guard to get Jemera. Let us see what young Jemera has to say to this. And please bring whoever she is dwelling with, also."

Karan nodded and left the room to send the guard.

Reims responded, "This be not fair, Highest. Jemera knows not what she wants."

Sam looked at Reims, eyebrow raised, and frowned, "And why do you think you should be the one to make this decision for her, Reims?"

"I am her father, and I have that right, by law."

Sam suddenly recalled that Sansa had told her Jemera had a father, but that Jemera had first presented herself to Sam as an orphan on their first meeting. While alert to the potential issue, Sam remained calm, "Not by Woden laws, you do not. Why did Jemera not mention this to me prior when I but spoke with her? And why did you not mention that you were her father?"

Reims was nervous and was fidgeting. He was unable to look The Highest in her eyes, "She will lie when you speak to her. She is but a liar, Highest. She will say that I beat her and raped her. This be not truth."

Karan re-entered during Reims statement. She looked at Sam quizzically.

Sam looked at Karan, "Be there a guard outside the door?"

Karan nodded.

Sam turned back to Reims, "It would seem you give me a dilemma. Please wait outside with the guard for but a moment, Reims. I would like to speak with these others."

Reims shook his head and began to look defiant, "I have the right to remain."

Sam saw that he looked like he was ready to fight. She rose and motioned for Karan to get the guard. Karan opened the door and asked the guard to enter.

Sam looked at the guard, "Do you have a knife on you?"

The guard nodded and handed The Highest her knife, handle first.

Sam took the knife and aimed to the left of Reims, and threw it directly into the wall, as she had aimed.

"Would you like to fight me, Reims? I could make certain that the fight be fair and that we both have swords. Would that be what you desire?"

Reims looked at the thrown knife. He began to make a move for it, as Sam had suspected he would. She pulled the sword out of the guard's sheath before the guard could even react. Sam moved over to Reims and placed the sword at his throat.

"Woden has no room for the likes of you, but I will make certain of your story prior to pronouncing your sentence. I hope for your sake you do not lie, as you said of Jemera. On your knees."

Reims was surprised at the quickness of The Highest, and of her skill with the knife and sword. He fell to his knees and began to sob.

Sam sighed and turned to the guard, "Have another get Meera for me, or Keddi if Meera be not available."

Sam looked around the room at the others. She wondered if Reims had been controlling the group. The others were frightened, but she saw that Tedra was smiling.

Karan looked at The Highest, surprised, "I am sorry, Highest. I knew not."

Sam held the sword to Reims' throat, but answered, "You could not have, Karan. He has masked his evilness well. It would seem that he be one of the evil ones from Apien."

Reims, yet sobbing, shook his head, "Jemera is my daughter, Highest. She belongs with me. She will not follow the ways of the High Mother without me. She but fights me on this even now and will not permit me to teach her."

Sam looked down at Reims. She held her disgust within her, "So you be a follower and a believer of this High Spirit Mother and King Buron?"

He nodded, "I am."

"Then why have you come here to Woden and Hengist? Why do you bring this belief with you?"

"Woden and Hengist need someone to set them free from their ways."

Sam spoke so softly and low that it made everyone in the room gasp. "Speak no more, Reims. You but slit your own throat."

Meera walked into the room and saw Sam holding a sword to a man's throat. She then saw a knife in the wall. She looked at Sam, and Sam shrugged.

She removed her own sword and took the one from Sam, handing it back to the guard, "Does this one give you trouble, Highest?"

Sam filled her in on the story. As she did so, Jemera came in with Ceamach, companion of Lorin, one of Meera's guards. As they entered, Ceamach and Jemera knelt and bowed their heads to The Highest. They rose and Ceamach nodded to Meera. Meera had the infirmary guard remove Reims from the room so that Sam could speak with Jemera without him present. He sobbed and kept saying that Jemera would lie.

"Ceamach, thank you for bringing Jemera here this turn. It would seem that Reims be her father. Do you know of this?"

Ceamach looked to Jemera and placed her hands on Jemera's shoulders, "She has told us of this, but would say no more. Jemera, The Highest would like to speak to you and ask you some questions. You know what I have told you of her and of Woden. Do you think you can answer her questions truthfully?"

Jemera nodded and looked at Sam.

"Jemera, did you live with your father while in Apien?"

Jemera nodded her head.

"Did your Birth-Mother live with you?"

She shook her head and said, "She died."

"Were you there when she died?"

She nodded again, "She died having a baby."

"I did not think women could live with a husband in Apien. I thought Manthar kept all the women in one location, and he was the father of all the children."

"Manthar allowed Father to keep a wife. He had special privileges."

Sam looked at Meera, but said nothing.

Meera asked, "Jemera, your father says you be overly young to make a decision about remaining in Woden. He but wants you to remain with him. Which would you prefer?"

"I want to remain here, with Ceamach and Lorin. I like them, and they are good to me. They do not beat me."

"Do you understand the laws of Woden, little one?"

Jemera looked at Meera, "Ceamach has explained them to me. And I know that I never want to be with men. They hurt me and they are mean. They do things I don't like."

Sam placed a hand on Jemera's head. She sent a message of safety and love from the community, and looked into Jemera's past. She did not like what she saw, "They are not all like this, Jemera. You will find Hengist to be as kind as Woden."

Sam bent down to Jemera, "Jemera, if you would like, you may remain here. Ceamach and Lorin would be delighted if you decided to remain with them. There are many others your age in Woden for you to play with, and no harm will come to you from anyone in Woden. Is that what you would like?"

Jemera nodded and placed her hand into Ceamach's, "Can I go now? I want not to be near him anymore."

Sam stood and nodded to Ceamach, "Thank you. She will remain with you now. Take good care of her. She has been through much."

Meera nodded to Ceamach as they left, then looked at Sam, "What will you have me do?"

"Let me make certain the others do no such harm."

Sam went from one person to the next, placing a hand on their head and reading their past. She no longer trusted any of this group to speak truth. What she learned was as she had guessed. Reims had controlled the group, as he had been the most knowledgeable of the journey. They all knew the same story - Reims came to Woden to win it over for Manthar. Sam knew that if Oisin didn't win her battle, he would be the first of many to try as such. She would have to be more careful of new ones into Woden.

To the ones who wanted a mixed community, she said, "This will be your dwelling until Woden decides what to do regarding a third community. For the rest of you, when you feel improved, we have dwellings waiting for you. Karan will help you become located into Woden or Hengist. If you have any needs, please see her and she will do what she can. I welcome you to Woden Falls."

Nolsteney came forward, "Thank you, Highest. I hope I can serve Woden well as a spiritual woman. When you have need of me, Highest, I am now here to serve you."

She knelt before Sam and bowed her head, "I have long wanted to be here in Woden. Thank you for taking me in."

"Thank you, Nolsteney. We have much need of a spiritual woman. Your kind and gentle ways will be most welcomed in Woden. I hope you are able to find a companion soon. I am also glad that you are here."

Nolsteney looked up into Sam's eyes. Sam held out her hands to Nolsteney. She took them, and Sam made her rise. They looked at each other, and Sam told her truth, "We want nothing of this belief of Reims. We have much need of a spiritual healer as we have had much death lately. If you are able to provide spiritual guidance and healing, you are most welcomed in Woden. Prior to these events, our children had no concept of betrayal and execution, such as this. Help me to rid them of this concept and you will indeed be a most honored woman of Woden."

Nolsteney looked straight into Sam's eyes, kindly, "It was the same in Apien and New Harborage. Most all our women in The Realm have been abused and suffer terribly. I will work hard to make it better for all the women, Highest. I have longed to be here for most my life. While there was great need of me in other places, I now need a home to live out the last part of my life."

Sam nodded and let go Nolsteney's hands. She then turned to Meera, and they both left, with Karan following.

As they got outside the door, Meera turned to Sam, "Is he as evil as you first thought?"

Sam frowned and glared, "No. He be far worse. He was a follower of Manthar and but raped that little child every turn. Take him away and kill him. He came here to enslave us all. Make it quick and short."

Meera nodded, "It will be done directly. I will report back to you."

She turned and left. Sam looked at Karan, "It now seems I need be more careful with all our new arrivals. Thank you, Karan. Please make sure that those who wish to remain in Woden are placed quickly. Nolsteney could use a dwelling this eve, if one be but ready. And you might introduce her to some of the single women more her cycles. She be but gentle and kind and will serve Woden well. Please make certain that she but attends festival. We could use a woman spiritual leader.

* * * *

After leaving the infirmary, Sam walked down to the fisheries, guards-in-tow. She hadn't had the spare moments to get to the fisheries for over a moon, and was feeling somewhat guilty. The fishers were an integral part of Woden, and much of their food source relied upon these women who braved the currents every morn. Except for domesticated birds, Woden relied little upon animal production from the farms. Some sheep were used mostly for their wool and for special occasions, and cows were primarily only used for milk and cheese production. So Sam was well aware of the importance of the fisheries to all of Woden. Given the distance from the community, the fishers mostly dwelt near the docks in near-shore dwellings, as did the net makers and the boat and shipmakers. Sam knew that the fishers would be well back from their morn runs, and would be at the docks cleaning and repairing.

As she approached the fisher docks, Janel saw her coming, "Look sharp, The Highest comes."

All the women gathered around Janel to greet Sam, "Highest. How goes it? Should we kneel to you, Highest?"

Sam laughed, "No. I tire of seeing the tops of women's heads. Just show me your catch of the turn."

"We had a good haul this morn. We have enough to but smoke and dry much of our catch. Except for May. She but requested one of the large red fish for your late eve meal. Lucky you. We caught many red fish this morn, and they be but good size, too."

Tiada put out a stool for Sam. The rest of the women just sat around on floats and such.

"When will you be able to get more of those little white muscles of fish?"

"You mean the scallops, Highest?"

"I think so. I know not the name."

"Karan found such a name in Woden's dictionary. We know not if it be correct, but that is now the name for them. Soon, Highest. Another moon."

"We have some new women coming into Woden. One of them but wants to be a fisher. Have you need of another?"

"Sure we do. Does she know fishing or must she be trained?"

"She must be trained, but it is her choice alone."

Eile looked at Sam, "Highest, why be your eyes so blue these turns? Be it because you are The Chosen One?"

Sam nodded, then shook her head, "It is but strange, is it not? It even frightened me when I looked into a mirror."

Eile laughed, "When are you going fishing with us, Highest?"

"When might I catch a large fish? One worth fighting?"

Brid smiled and nodded, "Aye, you refer to the big ones. They be in two more moons, Highest, and are but worth the wait."

Wida came over and offered Sam some fried fish, "We just prepared these fish cakes for our meal. Have some, Highest. This be good fresh fish, and you will like the coating. We also have some new fresh beer just made."

Sam ate her midturn meal with the fishers. She much enjoyed the fishcakes and had never had them quite like they had been prepared.

She especially enjoyed the beer, "How did you come by the beer so fresh?"

Emma pointed to Muirgel, "Murigel's companion, Harva, brought it by just prior. It is luck that her companion is but our best beer maker."

Janel added, "And seeks to spoil us upon our returns from the sea."

"So what think you of all the changes occurring of late?"

Wida shook her head, "We but heard from Oisin's crews. New Harborage and Apien need to be demolished, from what we hear."

Brid got up, as if angered, "Aye, and all those evil men need to be killed. We but heard what they do to the women and young ones. Oisin's crew will get them, though."

Emma asked, "What be this we hear of a third community, Highest? We have heard that Woden will have but a mixed community. Be this so?"

Sam nodded, "It is a discussion only, Emma. But, as you have all said, New Harborage and Apien should be dismantled. Where would all those people go?"

Sam told them of the large and small group that just walked over from Apien. She told them of Manthar and of all the events she had heard regarding Fornaith.

Emma nodded, "It is but a dilemma, Highest. We leave it to you and trust your vision for Woden. You are the best Woden will ever see. We know you will do well by us. By the way, Highest, do we but hear you will accept as a companion this festival? You have but remained alone for a long while. Be this report but truth?"

Sam smiled, "Perhaps. I have not yet been asked. I have yet to inform Oisin, though. She has been gone the entire moment of this. She will understand, but I wish not to surprise her, so."

Brid responded, "She has her own mate, Highest. Oisin will manage. She be but a strong one and will want you to do what is best for you and Woden."

"You speak truly. I am grateful for the reminder."

"We are just about to go out to pull up a few catches, Highest. Do you wish to join us? We vow you a short adventure. I do not think you have seen our new fishing beds. We will not take overly long, and we could use but more strong arms as yours."

"Under one condition."

Janel looked surprised, "A condition, Highest? Whatever you wish, but what could this be?"

Sam smiled mischievously, "Make my guards come. It will make me laugh, plus give you a few more strong arms. If they but wish to follow me everywhere, then they should be made to go on the fishing boats."

Sam went in Emma, Evergren, and Janel's boat, while the two guards each went in one of the two other boats. They rowed out to where they had placed the pots at the bottom of the sea. Each pot weighed a great deal, so the fishers were glad to have the extra hands to lift them. Sam noticed that the two guards each looked rather pale and sickly from the waves, but they said nothing and continued to help.

Janel's boat raised the first pot. Sam had seen these types of fish but rarely. They were also red but with long arms that could snap.

Sam looked to Janel, "Why does May not cook these for me?"

Janel laughed, "These be bottom feeders, Highest. And May thinks that bottom feeders are not good enough for you. When we return, allow us to steam one of these for you. You will most enjoy it. I cook these with corn, and have some corn bread with it, and it makes but a fine meal."

Emma added, "I put the meat in a stew with other fish and vegetables. This is but a great bottom feeder, but May does have her desires."

Sam laughed, "What else am I not getting that I would but enjoy?"

Evergren said, "We will make it point to but expand her thinking for you, Highest."

Finally, all the pots were pulled up, emptied, and then returned with some bait placed inside. It was hard and difficult work, especially in the cold winds and water, and Sam fully appreciated the abilities of these women. She thought that the guards would now appreciate these fishers much more than prior and thought it a good lesson for them. When they arrived back at the docks, they all helped to unload. Janel went about preparing the bottom feeders for Sam and the guards. When the work was done, and the nets had been hung, Janel fed Sam and the guards the bottom feeders.

Sam was delighted, "These are wonderful, Janel. I need all of you to make May taste these. I like these much. Either that, or just invite me down when you but have them." She laughed and ate.

Brid said, "We could but do that, Highest. We often have bakes of such on the beach. It be most fun. We do it in the early eve, in fair weather."

The guards also liked the taste, but ate little. Janel and Sam both saw that the guards looked a little ill from their sea outing. Sam waved her farewells and began her walk back to Woden.

She waited for the guards and walked alongside them, "Well, Eabha. Cranait. How did you but enjoy your sea adventure?"

Eabha spoke first, "It was an adventure I will not soon forget, Highest. They but have most difficult and wavy work. The motion of the sea seems quite constant to me. I but like the land."

Cranait nodded, "I hope I have to never but sail on the sea. These small boats and that short journey were enough for me. But I most enjoyed the fish."

* * * *

Sam walked back to her dwelling in silence for the rest of the way, as the guards needed to be more watchful. She decided to pass by some of the shops on her way back. She was hoping that Imly could do something with her hair so that others would stop talking about it. She passed by the shop and saw some light, so she knocked and went in.

"Imly? Are you in?"

Imly came out from the back of the shop, "Oh, Highest. You surprise me. What can I do for you?"

"Well, Imly, many are—"

"I can see, Highest. Your hair. May has but sent you over, has she not?"

Sam nodded.

"Sit. Let us see what I can do with this. How long has it but been since your last visit with me, Highest?"

"I know not, Imly. I care little about appearances. And this hair is such a bother. It is always flying about."

Imly began to cut and trim, "I will fix it so that when it flies, it will look wonderful. You have beautiful hair, Highest. It just needs a bit of taming. I hear that your turns of dwelling alone are almost over, Highest. Be that true? If so, it be a wonderful report for you. It was a hard loss on you. I also hear that Woden is but considering a third community, one of mixed believers. Be this true, Highest?"

"Possibly, for both, Imly. It is true that I have settled down to one woman currently, but I have not yet been asked to be a companion. And yes, we are but a third community because of all the men and women coming over from Apien and New Harborage. Life be dangerous in The Realm now. What think you of this?"

"Well, Highest. Since you ask my opinion, I am happy to provide it. I hear that Second would like us to move our shops between Woden and Hengist. To this, I object not. It would increase our abilities to trade better, but I like not the idea of a mixed community. Those people think overly strangely for me. I but like our life in Woden. It be safe and peaceful. If we bring in a third community of mixed people, how can you assure me that they will not try to force us into their ways?"

Sam told Imly of the diaries, of Manthar, and of King Buron. She told the stories of the women who were seeking refuge in Woden. And she told Imly of how the women and men were arriving in Woden, all but dead from starvation.

"Can we read from these diaries, Highest? They sound most fascinating. I would like it much to hear more from them. Where did the First Ones come from?"

Sam explained about the lost diaries, of the experiment, and of the men and women, and how Hengist must have been first formed.

Imly gave Sam a hand-mirror, "There, Highest. That be much improved. Look at you. You be most stunning, now. You were prior, but now the hair is a bit more tamed. I think we should try to recover the lost diaries, Highest. Do you not?"

"I do as well. As soon as we can spare a moment, we will do so. Thank you much for the hair fixing, Imly. I will send over two flasks of wine in appreciation of this most difficult task."

Imly laughed, "It be not as hard as that, Highest. Your hair is wild, but beautiful, so a pleasure to work with. Take care, Highest. We need you. Eat more. Your face be but overly thin these turns."

As Sam exited, she noticed that there had been a change in her guard duty. Two new guards were now waiting. She walked back to her dwelling, seeing that most of the shops were now closed. She knew that May and Jandra would be waiting and wondered if she would ever be free from commitment again.

Sam abruptly halted, realizing she was unsure of what she wanted.

I have never thought about this issue. After Brett, I have merely gone along all these cycles, free from the burdens and worries of commitment. What do I want? Perhaps I am more like Sumi and Nodda. Perhaps I want commitment as from Jandra. I don't know.

She shook her head, dismayed at her own lack of knowing, *What is it I truly want? Have I been so free that I now fear this commitment? Can I live with but one woman now? I have had many lovers in these past cycles, and enjoyed them all. Can I but commit to Jandra as I had to Brett?*

Suddenly, a guard came up to her, "Highest, be all well with you?"

She had startled Sam from her thinking, "Oh. I am but thinking. I am sorry to have startled you."

She went on walking to her dwelling. *What makes me feel as if I should get on the back of a horse and take off to nowhere as fast as I can? I cannot make such a commitment to Jandra if I have not these answers. What be wrong with me? I should but halt this foolishness. Women and men but rely on my sensibilities. How can a Highest have such doubts as these? This be foolishness. One eve prior to festival and I act as a spoiled child. But why do I want to run away? Perhaps I don't wish this companionship. I do not love Jandra, but do care deeply for her, and she be most excellent in sex. Truly, she be the best partner on a turn-to-turn basis, ever. But be sex more important than love? She truly be the most beautiful woman I have ever seen, so it be not the issue of her appeal. I just need more freedom. I need not more nagging, certainly, as I have that in May.*

Sam reached her dwelling and halted to look at it. There it was, as it had always been. Familiar. Brown. One story. With a full bank of windows and glass on the back side. The door on the front that Brett had made for her. Flowers, trees and shrubs of all types surrounded it. She felt frozen, unable to move or go in. She walked around it, instead, looking at it from all angles. She knew the guards thought she had gone crazy.

Sam walked by a guard, taking quick notice that the guard wasn't paying any attention to the weapons she carried. Sam walked close by, wondering if she could steal the guard's sword. She made a quick decision and suddenly unsheathed the guard's sword without her awareness.

"Nice sword. Find another, and we but practice."

The guard was stunned but ran over to another guard and borrowed her sword. As she returned, Sam lunged at her. The guard was barely able to counter. Sam was far away the better swordswoman, but enjoyed the practice.

Another guard came near, and Sam said, "Join in. Two against one. It will but even the odds."

The other guards were confused, but watched carefully. Sam held her own against the two guards, and although they tried, they couldn't match her moves. Sam's moves became stronger and stronger against the guards, and they began to worry. It wasn't like The Highest to make such moves in practice.

One guard had gone to get Meera. Meera walked up casually, studied Sam carefully, unsheathed her sword and said loudly so Sam would take notice, "HIGHEST. If you want to but practice, then practice with someone who is better than you."

Sam looked at her, non-smiling, "We shall see, Meera. Make your best moves, as I will not soften mine."

Meera nodded and the practice began. The guards watched intently as these two women, leaders of Woden, practiced as if in real fight. The force of their blows against one another sounded loudly, and in truth, neither woman held back. Sam moved her sword with all her might against Meera, but Meera was able to counter and move Sam back.

In a final and frustrated move, Sam raised her sword and came down with every ounce of her strength left, yelling out as she did, "NOOOOOO!"

Meera held her sword true with both hands, saw Sam drop her sword, and then re-sheathed her own, "Highest, let us but take a walk."

Meera picked up the guard's sword and returned it to her. Sam nodded at Meera. She hadn't noticed that Jandra and May had been watching the moment. As Sam and Meera walked away together, Meera motioned for the guards to remain near the dwelling. Jandra and May were worried but had decided not to interfere.

As they got down to the river, away from everyone else, Meera asked Sam, "Would you care to talk about it, Sam?"

Sam sat down at the river's bank, "There be this uncertainty and rage within me, Meera, which I can't explain. I know not where it comes from. I was walking to the dwelling from the fisheries, and I suddenly realized that I know not what it be I truly want. I know not if I can make such a commitment."

Meera nodded, but said nothing.

"I suddenly realized that I have had many lovers these cycles, but have remained free of commitment. Now that I but face it, it frightens me. I feel like running away as fast as I can. Away from Woden. Away from being The Highest. Away from companionships. Away from demands. I feel but a prisoner in Woden."

She looked at Meera, "I am angry, and I know not why. I came up to the dwelling, and could not go inside. I feel rage. Where is that coming from, Meera? What be wrong with me?"

"What is it you need, Sam?"

"Release. Freedom. Moments alone. I know not. I think I am but as a spoiled child. I had but a commitment prior, so what is so different about this one? You have made but a commitment and seem to enjoy it. You are a Second of Woden and it seems not to bother you. How is Second so much different than being Highest? Why does it but bother me? And how can I be The Highest every turn and then return to my dwelling to face more issues and problems? I used to be able to return to my dwelling in quiet and solitude. Now I face the same lover but every eve. How do you do it, Meera? Who I am to be Highest?"

"Hold, Sam. You are overloaded. It but sounds like becoming The Highest and taking a companion are but overly close together. Perhaps you should not take a companion at this festival, but let the issue settle itself by the next festival. You move, by necessity, overly quickly, but it does not need to be so. You are The Highest, and that is difficult to change, but you need not rush into a companionship if the commitment but frightens you so. I would place wagers that Jandra agrees with me on this."

"I feel invaded, Meera. And that seems so very unfair to Jandra. It be not of her doing. I like her ways fine and she but well pleases me as a lover. Another would make it even worse. Jandra is most patient and understanding. And she be most beautiful to look at. She complains not about remaining in my dwelling, with the spirit of Brett. I would not be so giving or understanding. Perhaps it is as you say. Perhaps it is overly much at one moment."

"Do you need her, Sam?"

"I need you, and you have always been there for me."

Meera shook her head, "No, Sam. It be different. I need Caitha at the end of the turn. I like to go to my dwelling and listen to Caitha tell me of her turn, and feel her wrap her arms around me. I need her, Sam. I need her to soften me and to help me through my life. I hope I do the same for her."

"But I have needed both you and Caitha in this way. You but do that for me, except for the physical side, which I have but taken care of with lovers, such as Oisin."

"No, Sam. It be not the same. Do you think of Jandra when you be not with her?"

"Yes. I think of her. But not always as I should."

"In what ways?"

"I think of her beauty. I think of her inner strength. I think of her leadership abilities and how they but please and surprise me. I think of her stance as a Second and how it but grows. I think of her eyes and how they but look at me at special moments. I think of her honesty and directness with me. I think of her gentleness when we are but alone. And she but worries overly, which I don't need. But I also think of Oisin overly much."

"If Jandra but left you this turn, Sam, and moved back to her own dwelling, how would that but make you feel?"

"I know not. Perhaps empty for a moment. Quiet. I would miss her touching. I would not miss being controlled or being told what to do. I would feel but sadness."

"Would you want her back?"

"As a lover? Yes. As a continual companion? I know not. But it must be so. It but frightens me. Someone there all the moments. How do you but do it?"

"I am not there except in the eves, mostly. And I need Caitha."

"Did you at first?"

"I think it more like you describe. It was but frightening at first."

"I was not frightened with Brett."

"You were younger and not so set in your ways, you old woman."

Sam laughed, "Perhaps you be correct, Meera. I am feeling better. What would I but do without you?"

"And I cannot do without you, you crazy old woman, who also happens to be the leader of all of Woden. But it somehow adds a certain distinction to Woden to have but a crazy old woman of a leader, think you not?"

Sam laughed again, "Thank you, Meera. I especially like being called the old woman. That is very comforting for me. What is your parting piece of advice?"

Meera laughed, "First, never raise your sword above your head with your weaker arm in control."

Sam laughed at that, "And you used to tell me over and over again, 'Second, never raise your sword in anger. You will but lose your fight.' I remember your words well, but not well enough to heed them, I guess."

"You are just overly loaded with responsibility. My Second and last piece of advice is to speak with Jandra about this. Work through a solution together. She has more understanding than you but give her credit for."

Sam nodded and rose, "Walk me back, Meera, and then return home to your dwelling and Caitha. You are more to Woden than Second of all her defenses. You are but my healer."

"I have to but admit, Highest. That last sword move nearly made me lose my sword. That was a most powerful blow. You get stronger."

"I hope I didn't hurt you or the guards. I am but embarrassed."

"No need. They should be but embarrassed for their weak display of practice. They will hear from me on this. And it would appear that you but stole one of their swords while they but looked."

"So it would seem." Sam turned and gave Meera a hug, "Thank you, my friend."

Meera hugged her back, then turned and walked toward her own dwelling. Sam looked once more to her own dwelling, paused a moment, then walked up to the patio, to Jandra. Jandra waited on the patio, looking very concerned.

Sam went up to her and saw that May was yet present, "May, we will take our meal inside. There be no need for you here. Please go to your dwelling and enjoy your companion. We will see you next turn at festival. We will manage our own morn meal. Thank you much."

May had lived through many of Sam's moods and recognized this one well. She knew that Sam needed solitude and quiet, "I will inform the guards to make themselves hidden, Highest. I will see you at festival."

May left and Sam guided Jandra inside to the kitchen area. Jandra sat down while Sam placed the meal on the table, and then she also sat down.

Sam placed some food onto her plate and some onto Jandra's as well. "Jandra, be you nervous about the festival?"

Jandra nodded, but didn't take the meaning as Sam had intended, "I am, but I think it will go well. Hengist and Briggon have planned it with much attention."

Sam shook her head, "This pleases me, but is not my meaning." Sam took Jandra's hand and held it, and looked into her eyes, "Tell me truly, Jandra. Does taking a companion but make you nervous?"

Jandra eyes opened wide at the question, and a single tear dropped from Jandra's eyes, "How did you but know of this, Sam?"

"That is unimportant. Tell me, Jandra. Tell me what makes you nervous. Be not afraid of this."

Another tear slipped from Jandra's eyes, "I know not, and it confuses me most. I know I want you, but I am afraid of disappointing you and of being a burden to you."

Sam looked at her and simply said, "And . . .?"

"Oh, Sam. This be most difficult. But I am afraid of commitment. I have been free of it for the past cycles, and now I feel like I will not be worthy. That you will tire of me. That you facing me at the end of every turn will bore you and unexcite you."

"But what of your needs, Jandra? What do you need?"

"I love you as a lover, Sam. You are the best I have ever had. But I need to feel needed and loved, and you do neither. You are most independent and remain that way. I have little impact on your life, but you have turned mine upside down. I cannot halt in my thinking of you. Your touch. Your eyes. The way you hold me. The things you say to me."

"I do need you, Jandra. But I don't want to need you. I don't want to hurt like I did when I lost Brett. It be overly painful. But I do need you. I just don't want to admit to it, so I but hide and deny it."

Sam took Jandra's hand, "I have thought as you have. Can I make this commitment but to one lover for the rest of my life? I have never truly thought about what it is I want. I know not. When I had but lovers and no companion, I but wanted a companion. Now that I face a companion, I but worry about wanting many lovers, instead. It confuses me. It would seem I always want what I don't have."

"Sam. Halt a moment. What is this word you use, 'don't'?"

Sam laughed, "I think I but get used to these words from the diaries. I find them creeping into my thoughts. I but like the sound of them. They sound so old and formal. Don't you think so?"

"I do, but they will take some getting used to. I wonder why they used them, so. I but interrupt you, and do not, no, *don't* mean to."

Sam thought a moment, and then said, "You mentioned that I don't make you feel needed."

Jandra moved her hand away, "You don't *need* anyone, Sam. You are a free spirit. You like me here when it is convenient. But this eve, for example, you could not face coming inside to me. I made it impossible for you to enter your own dwelling. It be overly much for you. And it be embarrassing for me. And, Sam, you yet love Oisin. I can see this as so."

Sam saw the look in Jandra's eyes, and felt saddened by it, "You but think of moving back to your own dwelling?"

Jandra's eyes let loose more tears, "Our companionship be not working. And you truly need me not. I be in the way in your dwelling. I will have my items moved back to my dwelling in the morn. You need fewer moments together, and I need more."

Sam turned her back to Jandra, as she didn't wish Jandra to see her face. Sam was deeply upset and tears were beginning to form. She didn't wish Jandra to see her cry. Jandra looked with amazement at Sam, as she hadn't understood how deeply Sam had hidden away her need.

Sam lowered her head and defeatedly said, "I know not what to do."

Sam began to leave the room, having committed her heart overly already, but turned back to look at Jandra.

She smiled a difficult smile, one with a heavy weight, "It be but funny, Jandra. The moment you decide to not make this commitment, I but learn how much you mean to me. I am sorry for any hurt or pain I have but given."

Sam started to leave the room. Jandra went to her, desperately, "Sam. Hold."

Sam turned around and saw Jandra's hand held out to her. Jandra saw tears running down Sam's face, "I should not have entered such a relationship unless I could have left my prior sadness apart from us. I knew not the extent to my feelings. I am but sorry I made you live in our, no, my dwelling. I see now that I was but selfish."

She turned and began walking out of the room once again.

Jandra began to cry and fell to her knees. She lowered her head into her hands and wept. Sam turned around, once more, and saw Jandra crying, wholly consumed with despair. She stood, not knowing what to do.

How did this happen?

She couldn't take more hurt, but wanted desperately to go to Jandra. She briefly hoped. But she hoped with despair. Fear consumed and paralyzed her. Fear, a feeling Sam knew little of in battle, had taken over. Sam looked at her fear and felt it, and began to recognize what it was doing to her. She remembered something her Birth-Mother had told her: *If you can know and face your fear, you will but defeat it. If you cannot, it will defeat you.*

Sam thought quickly. *If I but go to Jandra this moment, it will mean that . . .* She suddenly halted thinking, faced her fear directly, and conquered it. She went to the now-shattered Jandra and knelt down to her, with her.

She moved Jandra's hands away from her face and gently moved her head up so she could look into Jandra's eyes.

"Jandra. It is my own fear of commitment that has but created this moment. Know that it has been many cycles since I have spoken these words, but know that I speak them truly as I could not say them if they be not so. Jandra, I—"

* * * *

A guard and a messenger had entered the kitchen suddenly, and interrupted Sam. Both she and Jandra rose and faced the intruders to their privacy.

The guard and messenger had knelt and bowed their heads.

"Rise. What is the cause of this interruption?"

Sam was not pleased by the interruption, and Jandra looked dazed, but tried to pull herself together.

The messenger stood and said, "I am sorry, Highest. Two ships arrive. One ours. One of another's place. Both are loaded with women, men and children wanting to seek refuge in Woden. Oisin has sent these two ships back to us. There is a message from Sea-Duty Second, for your ears only."

Sam nodded to the guard, who turned and left the room. Sam looked at the messenger, "Tell me the message."

The messenger looked at Jandra and back to Sam, "Highest. Sea Duty Second said for your ears only. I am sorry, Second."

Sam began to protest, but Jandra turned to her, "I will wait in the sitting room," and turned and left.

The messenger began, "Oisin has met up with what she called a little old person of dirt and earth. This sage, as Second has also referred to her, demanded the necklace that King Buron had given to you. The sage has sent me with the necklace back to you. The sage tells me to inform you to have one of these green stones placed into the handle of your sword and another into your knife. The sage has sent back a knife that she but wants you to have and carry with you at all moments. The sage also said to tell you that she has sent a message to you that abides within me, but I know not how. She has informed me that you would but know what to do to retrieve it."

Sam nodded and moved toward the messenger. She placed her both her hands on top of the messenger's head and mentally searched for the message. Finally, she found it and heard the Old Raggedy One.

Your moment is coming soon, but danger first approaches. You and Woden must be ready. Have the green stones embedded into your sword and knife, and but carry your knife with you always. Heed the warning well. Buron but gains strength from the Spirits of the Valley.

You have less than one moon to but prepare for Buron's first advance. Prepare what powers you now have. I will return soon and give you what you will need to overcome him, but be warned: He is strong and he but builds his forces. Buron and the Spirits of the Valley must not win this battle, but the battle just begins. Guard yourself well. Meera is your best ally, but lose not Jandra. You have her embedded within you now, through her tear. She is now a part of you and will bear your line. She now carries The Promised One. Buron also knows of this. Lose her not. If need be, take her to the Spirits of the Falls for protection. They will tend to her and the child."

The message was stunning, and confused Sam, but she tried not to show it. She removed her hands and spoke to the messenger, "Who but meets the ships?"

The messenger bowed her head, "Karan and Meera were called. They are at the harbor port now, Highest."

"Bring me Meera. And hurry. Run. Then get Keddi and Margeria. Then, as quickly as you can, bring me Ivers from Hengist. Waste no moment. Halt for no one. Guard these secrets well. And return with Meera. You will but give her the green stones then. Leave the knife with me."

The messenger gave Sam the knife, turned and left. Sam retrieved one of the guards and together, they went to the sitting room where Jandra had been waiting.

Sam looked at the guard, "I want the guard doubled on Jandra from here on. There are to be no errors about this. Two eves prior, we but escaped from this dwelling. No guards were aware. That cannot occur again, or at the next moment, those guards will but feel my wrath. Jandra is to be the most guarded and protected person in all of Woden. Be this clear?"

The guard nodded, "Yes, Highest. I will inform all the guards and make it so. Would you like me to inform Second of Defense?"

"I will do so. Leave, and from this moment, prepare Woden for battle. Under all circumstances, Jandra must be guarded. We must remain vigilant. Within one moon, we will be attacked."

The guard left. Sam noticed that Jandra looked surprised and frightened. She sat down next to her.

"I will be leaving to the harbor in but a few moments. We have two ships just arrived from Oisin, filled with women, men and children who wish to be in Woden."

"But, Sam, you mentioned that we will be attacked and that I am to be the most guarded in all of Woden. Why be this so? How do you know of this?"

"A messenger but arrived from Oisin. And Oisin was but met by the Old Raggedy One who sent me a private message."

Sam knelt down in front of Jandra and looked up at her, "Jandra. We have but a few quiet moments left before many arrive. You must know this prior. I need you, Jandra. I may not now or in the future say enough of this, but know it to be true. I want you here with me, as my companion. I vow I will never again act as I did. I know I am not a perfect companion, and I know we have overly many issues to work out between us. But you are a part of me. Jandra, I have not spoken these words since Brett, so know them to be true and for you only. I need you. You and I are now connected in ways you don't yet know or understand, but Woden needs you. You and I must live together, not for us, Jandra, but for the future of this realm, as what comes from us will ensure peace. It be not correct for me to ask this of you, as I am Highest, but I must ask it. Jandra, will you accept me as your companion?"

Jandra's eyes were wide-open in surprise. As had become typical in their brief relationship, events became overly consuming and continually interfered with their personal issues, but Jandra had come to accept this. And as Sam had said, it was considered most inappropriate for The Highest to ask anyone to be her companion.

Jandra looked into Sam's eyes and saw them steady and true. She looked deeper into their blueness and saw that Sam's power was strong. She leaned forward and placed her arms around Sam.

She laid her head down on Sam's shoulder, moved a hand to Sam's head, held it gently, and softly said, "I love you, Sam, but our relationship be not working between us. Why do you now say these things?"

Sam moved her arms around Jandra and rocked her gently. She knew not how long they remained that way, but were once again interrupted.

Meera had arrived, out-of-breath from running, "Highest. I am here."

Sam turned and looked, "Wait outside for but a moment. I will come and get you."

Meera left and Sam turned back to Jandra, "Jandra?"

Jandra had sat up when Meera arrived, but now moved her forehead to meet Sam's, "I know not, Sam. You push overly hard at overly quick a moment. Our relationship is not working. It would be best if we parted now prior to it getting worse for you. And for me. I cannot take this as it is, Sam. Please place no more pressure on me. Our relationship has but gone overly far already."

"I need you."

"You do not love me, Sam, and that will make all the difference. But why do you guard me? And why do you but make Meera wait? This is not as I am used to from you."

Sam looked at her and frowned, "Then it should be. You are the most important to me and all The Realm now, Jandra. You must know and carry that with you." Sam moved back a bit and looked at Jandra. "Be strong for what I am about to tell you. We have few moments to discuss this, but you must know so that you will but accept the guards and know of the reason for them."

Jandra nodded.

"I took one of your tears and made it mine. Are you aware of this moment?"

Jandra nodded again, "I recall the moment. I know not why you did as such. It was the moment after you returned from your death. What of it?"

Sam closed her eyes for a moment, then reopened them, "I be only half human. The other half belongs and is of the Spirits of the Falls. My mothers." Sam closed her eyes again and waited a moment, then resumed, "As The Chosen One, my child will be the ruler of all The Realm. the Spirits of the Falls would like it so."

Jandra thought, *What child? Tadan?* But waited Sam's answers.

"But we must first win peace. And the battle begins. Buron but gains his strength from the Spirits of the Valley. They be but controlling spirits and fight against the Spirit Mothers of the Falls. We battle for them, and I am to be the one with the power against Buron."

"But, Sam—"

Sam placed a finger against Jandra's lips, "Shhhh. The story is yet to come. Although you didn't know of it, when I but took your tear and mingled it with my own tear, we became much more than companions. We joined, as a man from Hengist and a woman from Woden do at Festival. You became a part of me, in ways even I understand not. I know not how to tell you this. It is not the moment in which I wanted to inform you, Jandra. This should have been told in private, and at a special moment. I am but sorry."

Jandra raised Sam's head with her fingers under Sam's chin, "Tell me what you must, Sam. I am strong enough to bear it."

Sam didn't think anyone was strong enough for the story she was about to tell. She placed her hand on Jandra's stomach, "You but carry our child, Jandra. I know not how this be so, but the Spirits of the Falls have made it thus. Yours and mine. It be inconceivable, but it be so. It grows within you."

As Jandra gasped, her eyes opened in wide-disbelief, "A child? Our child? How be this possible? I be far overly old for this. This cannot be so, Sam. It be impossible. I want no child. We do not even have a relationship. This is most bold untruth."

Sam shook her head, "Our child, Jandra."

Jandra stood up and held her stomach; her womb, "A child. Yours and mine, Sam?"

Sam nodded, "The Spirits of the Falls have made it so. I know not how."

Jandra looked at Sam and softly asked, "Do we want a child? I wish not to carry a child at my cycles, Sam. I want not this child. Should I have not been consulted prior about this? How DARE you do this to me!" She was becoming well angered.

"I am sorry, Jandra, to have gotten you involved in all this, but it is out of our hands. The Spirits of the Falls have insisted, for the future of all The Realm and the future of Woden."

"Yours and mine, Sam? They insisted? But this is my life, not theirs."

"Yes. Ours, Jandra."

"What if I decide to move back to my old dwelling and not be your companion? How fair is this to me?"

"I know not. All I know is that you now but carry the future of all of Woden and the entire realm. You and I are as one."

"This is why I must be protected so?"

Sam nodded, "Buron knows of such. The Spirits of the Valley, or someone must have discovered this and informed him. He will now seek you out to prevent this. But worry not, Jandra. We will keep you safe."

Jandra sat back down, frustrated and angry, "Finish with your messages, Sam. Meera but waits for you. I know not what to think of this. You should have told me of this."

Sam got Meera and came back in. She informed Meera of the message from the Old Raggedy One, the approaching battle with Buron and Oisin's messages.

"Meera, prior eve, Jandra and I but escaped from this dwelling so as to have some private moments. The guards noticed not. I would not normally tell you of this, but I have something you must now hear, and must now guard to the death."

"Tell me how you but escaped without notice." Meera wasn't pleased at the report.

"I will, but first hear this. Jandra carries my child."

Meera shook her head as if to clear her ears, "WHAT? This be not possible."

"Yes, Meera. It is. The Spirit Mothers of the Falls have but made this so. I will tell you more later, but know this. This child is from our Spirit Mothers and is to be the future of all of Woden and the entire realm. This child is brought by our Spirit Mothers to provide a leader for all the realm, Meera. Jandra must be protected."

Meera turned to Jandra, "Do you but want this child, Jandra? Did you but know of this?"

"No. But what choice have I been given in this? It is but new to me as well. I know not if I even remain with Sam past this eve. I know not if I can even have a child." She sounded more than well angered.

Sam tried to ignore her anger, "The Spirit Mothers will provide for this, Jandra."

Jandra narrowed her eyes, "You trust overly these Spirit Mothers, Sam."

Meera was astonished that Jandra had said she might be moving back to her own dwelling.

Sam turned back to Meera, "I have informed the guards that if they become negligent once again as the eve prior, they will but face my anger. I will have them put to death, Meera."

Meera sat down, "A child, Sam?"

Sam also sat down and showed Meera the knife, "It would seem there is more to this realm than our small ways and being. But Meera, there be much more. The Old Raggedy one has sent me this knife. I am to have a stone from the necklace embedded into the handle. The same is to be done with my sword."

Meera nodded, "A stone. Into your weapons. And it will provide you gained strength without touching the stones. That is why you have but called for Ivers. He awaits outside. Oisin but has the necklace though, Sam."

Sam shook her head, "No. That is but why the Old One went to Oisin. It has been returned with the messenger."

Meera exited and returned with the messenger and Ivers. She put out her hand out to the messenger, "Give me the necklace."

The messenger did so, and Meera looked at it, then at the messenger, "You have done well. Keep your messages private. You may leave."

She turned to Ivers, "Take this necklace. Tell no one of it. Do you understand?"

Ivers nodded and took the necklace. Meera turned to Sam, "Give me the knife sent to you, and then get your sword."

Sam gave Meera the knife from the Old One, and then left to retrieve it. Meera said to Ivers, "This knife is extremely important. Take one of the stones from the necklace and embed it into the handle. Can you do this?"

Ivers nodded as he examined the knife, "I can. Why is this important?"

Sam returned with her sword and gave it to Meera. Meera handed it to Ivers, "Take this sword and do the same."

Ivers took the sword, "It can be done."

Meera asked, "How long?"

"Two turns."

"Make it one. Do you but like it in Hengist, Ivers?"

Ivers looked shocked, "Of course, Second. It has made my heart happy. I can't imagine losing this life. I would fight to the death for Woden and you, Second."

"Good. Then know this. This work you do helps to save Woden now. We are about to face battle, and these stones are most important to Woden and Hengist. They must be secure and never fall from this knife and sword. Our very existence will depend on your work. Can you but do this, Ivers?"

He knelt and bowed his head, "Thank you for this opportunity to but show my allegiance and gratefulness. I am indebted to you. I will do this work by two morn's hence. It will be without exception."

"Go now, and get this done. Have them returned immediately when you are but done. Thank you, Ivers. Inform no one of this work."

He rose, nodded, and left. Meera turned to Sam, "I but assume that you have called Keddi and Margeria here to be personal guards to Jandra."

"When the battle begins, I want Jandra taken to our Spirit Mothers, without delay. They will tend to her and make her safe. Until then, Jandra must be safe and well guarded. I want no mistakes."

"I do not suppose my voice counts, any longer."

They both ignored her.

"How long did the Old One say until we do battle?"

"Within one moon."

"How did you but escape from this dwelling without the guards noticing?"

Sam told the story of how they left the dwelling, where they went, and how they returned. "And I but stole a sword from one of the guards, as you have already guessed. That be not as important, however. The guard knew me and was not looking for me to steal their weapon. It is prior eve that concerns me most. This must not occur again. Their vigilance must be guaranteed."

Meera nodded and went to get Keddi and Margeria. She brought them back inside and told them the story Sam had told her. They both listened without comment, but Sam could see their eyes widen when Meera told of the child, as well as when Meera told them of the guards not knowing of Sam's and Jandra's escape from the dwelling.

When Meera mentioned that they would need to take Jandra to the Spirit Mothers of the Falls, Keddi asked, "Where be our Spirit Mothers? I know not."

Sam and Meera told Keddi and Margeria the location of the Spirit Mothers, and then Margeria asked, "You would like us to be Jandra's guards until the battle begins?"

Meera nodded, "I need our best here with her. You could but teach and practice with the other guards at the same moment."

"Why do we not take Second to the Spirit Mothers now, Highest?"

"We will soon. I but await the Old One now. We will directly after, unless an urgency occurs prior."

All looked down at Jandra. Meera asked Sam, "What will this child be like, Sam?"

"I know not, Meera. I know not if Jandra and I but want a child. We have had but little moments to ourselves. A child will be most demanding."

Jandra rose, "Enough of this. The ships need seeing to. I would like to go, but fear you will not allow me. I would like to see the women, men and children that have but come so far to hope to live in Woden."

Keddi said, "Wherever Second goes, Margeria and I will be there. Second of Defense, will you do something about the guards?"

Meera nodded her head, frowned and lowered her brows, "You may count on this. I will also see that Anicia and Anyst guard Jandra. Woden, Hengist and their guards will be on full alert by very early morn. It will be but a long eve for all the guards. For you and Margeria, it will be less than one moon prior to Buron's battle."

Meera left to send a message to Briggon. Upon her return, she looked at Sam, "Will Jandra be coming with us to the ships?"

Sam looked at Jandra and then at Meera, "We will all be there, so that might be the safest of locations. Let us go. There be much to attend to."

"By the way, Highest, Reims has been but attended to. He is no more. I saw to this personally."

Sam nodded. They all walked to the docks. Sam walked with Jandra, behind Meera and Keddi. Margeria and a few guards brought up the rear.

Jandra asked Sam, as they walked, "What be these green stones, Sam?"

"They are stones the Spirit Mothers would have me use to increase my power. I know not how."

"Who be this Reims? Is he not one of those from the Apien group?"

"He was. He be but another traitor. He was the father of Jemera, but was a follower of Manthar. He but raped his child each turn, and beat her. I asked Meera to rid Woden of him."

Jandra just looked at Sam, wondering how she dealt with so much, but was also well angered at her. She said nothing, yet not knowing what to do regarding their companionship, but had decided to not take it out on Sam this moment.

The group had to exit the community's eastern-most gates and then walk down to the harbor's docks. They were shocked at the numbers of women, men and children that they saw as they approached. Karan had wisely called for all the advisors to help, and all were there trying to provide some order. As Sam and Jandra approached, Karan and all the advisors knelt.

The newly arrived watched and guessed that someone of importance had just arrived, and followed Karan's example. As Sam neared, the advisors all said, "Highest."

Sam heard murmurs from the crowd, as if they had not expected to meet or see The Highest of Woden. Meera let Sam through her guard, but held Jandra back.

"Second, please take what I tell you well. I mean no disrespect. I was there protecting Sam when Brett was but killed. Sam has now provided that I guard you. I will not allow you to be killed, as was Brett. You but asked to come with us. You are here. While you be here, though, you will be where I can but protect you. You will do what I say, when I say it. Do you understand me?"

Jandra was beginning to feel as a prisoner and began to know how Sam felt when she said the same, "I can help organize this group, Meera."

"I know you are able to do this, Second. But it will not be so. I know not these newly arrived and will not place you in any jeopardy. It be The Highest's command. And it will be so."

"At least, Meera, I will expect my orders to be carried out, then."

"It is no problem to but provide your orders for others to follow."

"I am your prisoner, it would seem."

Meera looked at her, not smiling, "Better me than Buron, Jandra. Of this I am certain."

"I will abide by your commands of me, as what choice do I have in this?"

Sam looked to the group, including her advisors. She guessed there to be about 150 new arrivals, "Please rise."

She said to the group, "Welcome to Woden. We will care for you until we can decide what it is you hope for and require. Until Woden makes some decisions of itself, you are but guests in Woden and Hengist. You will be made comfortable, and we will but care to your needs. Please know that you will all be confined to the dwellings you are provided until we can make further arrangements. There will be no exceptions to this rule. No harm in any fashion will happen to you unless you disobey this rule. Woden wants to embrace our newly arrived, but we now face a battle in The Realm and must maintain order in our community. We but need your cooperation and understanding if we are to win our battle. We will not ask you to take part in our battles, but if there be trained guards and fighters who volunteer, we will not turn you away."

Sam turned to Meera, "I would like Briggon and Hengist here, as soon as possible."

"Yes, Highest."

Sam saw movement behind Margeria, looked over Meera's shoulder and saw Briggon already arriving with his guards and advisors.

Sam looked back to Meera, "You have already made that so?"

"I but follow your command, Highest."

Sam leaned closer to Meera, "You always try to make me look more intelligent than I am."

Meera smiled, but said nothing.

"Thank you," then she turned to Karan, "What arrangements have been organized?"

Karan looked overwhelmed at the numbers, "We but try, Highest. There be many arrivals here and we have barely the space. But I see Briggon has arrived, so perhaps Hengist will relieve the stress. Not to worry, Highest. All will be housed by late eve."

"Karan. Meera. I want not these arrivals at Festival next turn. We know not these arrivals and cannot trust them."

Karan and Meera nodded. Briggon had come up and overheard Sam's orders, "It will interfere with festival only slightly, Highest. All of us, your advisors, will make it so that the guards take turns guarding and attending festival. Between Woden and Hengist, there be enough dwellings."

Karan nodded, "And there be extra rooms in the Community Dwelling, Highest, since you decide not to move there. That will provide for at least 30 of these arrivals."

Jandra moved forward enough to ask, "Are our food supplies adequate for all these arrivals?"

Karan went to Liley and brought her over, "Liley, Second would like to know if we have adequate food supplies for all these?" Karan moved her hand to show all the new arrivals.

Liley shrugged, "Is there a choice in this? I have spoken with Janel and she has informed me that they will provide more fish in the interim. And we have but eight moons of storage. A little over our requirement. So we should be fine. Hengist?"

Landric responded, "We also have a little spare this moment, so between us, there will be but enough."

Liley nodded and turned to Jandra, "We will provide enough for all, Second."

Sam looked to Meera, "Who is in charge of the Sea-Duty while Oisin gone?"

Meera looked by the docks and found who she but searched for. She motioned to a guard to bring Grian over to The Highest.

"Grian is Oisin's assistant while she be out of Woden. She is most capable and will patrol and protect the harbor and Woden well. Senan is Hengist's." She turned to Briggon, "Is Senan patrolling the waters?"

Briggon nodded, "All ships are presently on full alert, with full crews and weapons. We are ready, Second of defense."

Grian arrived, knelt and bowed her head to Sam, "Highest. How may I serve you?"

"We need your strength and full protection. We will be but attacked within the moon. Are you prepared to defend all of Woden from the sea, without Oisin?"

"I am fully prepared. Our ships hide our weapons, but they are present and prepared. We can overtake five ships, if need be, at the same moment, with Hengist's assistance. Oisin has but prepared me well, Highest. We have also prepared a trap, if needed. Have no fear. Oisin relies on me with much reason. I will fight to the death for you, Highest."

"Thank you, Grian. Take orders from only me or Meera. Do you understand what this means, Grian?"

Grian nodded, "I be Oisin until her return. I but command the waters until then. And Senan takes orders from me."

"It is an overly large responsibility, Grian."

"I will protect Woden's shoreline with my life, Highest. You may count on me and my crew."

Sam nodded, hoping it was truth, "May the Spirit Mothers be with us all."

Sam turned to Meera once again, "Send a messenger around to the sentries, or have you already seen to that as well?"

Meera nodded but didn't confirm Sam's statement, "It will be done as commanded, Highest."

"I am not needed here any further. Karan, if you need any further assistance, Janel is but a fine organizer. She can help. Caitha will also be another you can but call on. Meet with me in the morn and bring me up-to-date on this progress."

Karan nodded, "Now that Briggon and Hengist are here, we will be completed in but a short moment. The Community Dwelling provides much space. Thank you for your statement to these arrivals. They but needed to hear those words."

Sam turned to Briggon, "Thank you, Briggon. I will see you in the morn."

Sam turned to Jandra, took her arm and began to walk back to their dwelling. Keddi and Margeria led the way while six other guards followed closely.

As they walked back to their dwelling, Sam was feeling slightly pleased and smiled to Jandra, "Jandra, I think I like this idea of companionship. I feel most comfortable this eve with the idea."

"Now is a fine moment for this, Highest, as now I am not sure. And I know not about this baby. I would like a few moments to think on all this, prior to festival."

Sam hadn't thought of the possibility of Jandra yet being upset, "But Jandra, I heard you say that you love me. Does that not mean that we can becom—"

She couldn't hold her anger in any further, so interrupted Sam, "I don't know, Sam. I am confused. I want not this baby. Not at my cycles. I don't even know if we should be companions. We have overly many issues to think on. And now you force the issue, and imprison me over some stupid story about The Realm and this child. About how the Spirit Mothers have made this baby. What am I supposed to think on all this, Sam? This makes no sense to me. What does make sense to me is that this eve, you could not even return into your dwelling because I was there. BECAUSE I WAS THERE, SAM! You don't want me. You but want a lover. You want some vessel to carry your child. Find another, Sam, as I cannot do this thing between us any longer. All that you want is sex."

Sam halted, staring blankly at Jandra. She hadn't even noticed that Jandra was so angry with her, "I am stunned. And you be correct. I am a terrible, lousy companion. I know not why this child must be, but the Spirit Mothers have made it so. They say it so to save The Realm. I know what imprisonment feels like, so I now apologize for this."

She knelt before Jandra, "But I say this to you. I need you, Jandra. I truly need you. I have many issues, I know, but I am willing to try. I want this to happen between us. It feels good. It feels but the correct thing to do. I am sorry I have been such a worthless companion to you. I know I am but selfish and act as a child in this regard, but give me a chance, Jandra. I vow to give you my very best. I need you, Jandra. Please, remain with me."

Just the sight of Sam falling on her knees to her softened Jandra's heart. She felt that she would most likely be sorry for this, but had decided to forgive Sam, and give their relationship another chance. Jandra rolled her head and eyes, then laughed. She said softly, "If others were not watching, Highest, I would but kick you at this moment." Sam laughed, rose and held tightly onto Jandra.

Jandra said softly, "I know I will come to regret this decision, Sam of Woden."

As they arrived to the dwelling, Keddi said to Sam, but so that all the guards could hear, "Highest, you and Second may try to escape, but your turns of escaping be over now that I and Margeria be here. We are not as easy as what occurred prior eve. You may rest quietly knowing of this. We remain on full alert."

The guards winced at hearing this. They knew that what had occurred was going to come back to them. Meera hadn't yet spoken of it, but they knew she would, soon. In the meanwhile, they would try to make amends by being less naïve and more alert. Sam smiled and nodded at Keddi's words, and she and Jandra went inside.

"I have but a short message to have delivered, Jandra. Wait here. I will return quickly."

Sam went to a guard and asked for a message to be delivered this eve. The guard nodded and went to have it sent.

Sam returned to Jandra, and they both went to the bedroom, Sam holding on to Jandra's hand on the way. They prepared themselves for sleep and got into bed.

Sam moved close to Jandra and held her, "I am but relieved that we have this companionship issue finally concluded. It has but driven me crazy."

Jandra looked up into Sam's face and moved some of the hair away from it, "I had not noticed until this moment, Sam. You but tended to your hair. It has been well cut and looks much improved."

"How is it that just looking at you makes my blood move so? If you were but a lover, I would have tired of you by now. Instead, just the idea of coming into the bed with you excites me and makes me feel as a younger one. I cannot get enough of you, Jandra, and now I can but admit it."

"You just love sex, Sam of Woden, but I do love you."

She moved up to Sam's face, and kissed her. The kiss was so passionate and consuming that it caught Sam unprepared for its intensity. Jandra put her hand on the back of Sam's head to bring it closer. Her kiss strengthened in its overwhelming impatience and demands. Jandra had also been relieved to be rid of the anxiety of thinking about the companionship issue. After the turn's overly emotional events, Jandra needed the physical release that she had come to count on with Sam. Although she was astounded at her own self-centered and absorbed desires, she abandoned herself to her own body's cravings. Sam found herself happy in the thought of the eve's pleasures, and she too submitted to her physical yearnings of Jandra.

Sam awoke prior to Jandra after an eve of satisfying their longings and releasing their stress. Sam looked outside and saw that it was late morn. She had been awoken by a soft knocking on the door from the sitting room.

As she opened it, she saw Karan. Sam raised a finger to her lips so that Karan would remain quiet. Sam wanted Jandra to rest.

They walked into the sitting room together. "Karan. This be a pleasant surprise. Be there something wrong?"

Karan yawned, "No, Highest. You but asked for a report. I am here to deliver it. I hope that I did not wake you."

Sam shook her head, sat down, and motioned for Karan to do the same, "No. I was waking. You look but exhausted, Karan. Have you not slept this prior eve?"

Karan yawned again, "Oh, I am so sorry, Highest. Yes. I mean, no. Not really. I went to bed, but could not sleep, so rose and checked in again on all our new arrivals. They are all settled now, Highest. We placed 48 in the former Highest's dwelling, so that helped a great deal. Briggon and Hengist took 41 of the arrivals, all men, and that but left us with 42 more. We had 12 empty dwellings ready for new arrivals, so we placed 31 more in those, and the rest went into the infirmary because they needed care and increased attention. The infirmary is now overly loaded, but the healers offered it and seem to be enjoying the escape from their turn-to-turn experiences."

"Has Ailis not noticed your absence, Karan?"

"She is at the road to Hengist helping to set up the festival."

"Then lay down here on the long chair and rest until we finally get up, Karan. We will take our morn meal together. I will get you a blanket and pillow so that you may finally get some sleep."

Karan looked shocked, "I cannot do that, Highest. I would but interfere with you and Jandra."

"Thank you for your concern, Karan, but I insist. Lay down and rest. I will return."

Sam found an extra blanket and pillow and returned to Karan. She was laying down and already half-asleep. Sam lifted Karan's head and placed the pillow underneath, and then placed the blanket over her.

Karan moved slightly and said, "Thank you Ailis. I love you."

Sam smiled and went back to the bedroom where Jandra was beginning to wake. Jandra opened her eyes and looked sleepily at Sam, "I heard voices. Is all well?"

"Karan came to give her report. All the new arrivals are but in dwellings, thanks to Karan. She is exhausted, so I made her rest in the sitting room. As soon as she laid down, she fell asleep. Ailis is helping to set-up the festival."

"Then you will need to remain quiet as we but finish last eve's urges."

"Be gentle with me, then, Jandra. Your cravings excited me beyond any lover I have had, but I remain slightly sore from your passion."

Jandra grinned roguishly at Sam, "I don't think so, Sam."

When they had rested for a bit after their morn's delights in each other, Sam held Jandra close and whispered, "I need you, Jandra."

Jandra looked at Sam and smiled, then rose and prepared for the turn. She took some extra garments out to Karan, sat down next to the long chair Karan was sleeping in, and shook her slightly, "Karan, it be late morn. We all need to get to festival. Come and eat your morn meal with us."

Karan rolled over, yet sleeping and answered, "In a moment Ailis."

Jandra smiled and tried again, "Karan. Wake up. You need to eat your morn meal with The Highest."

At the mention of Sam's title, Karan jolted awake, "Highest?"

Seeing she was yet dazed, Jandra leaned back and waited, "Karan. Do you recall where you are?"

Karan looked at Jandra quizzically, "Second? Oh, I remember, now. Good morn, Second. I did not mean to waken you."

Jandra laughed, "You have not, Karan. It is late morn, and you but slept a short while. I have brought you some fresh garments. Get yourself prepared and come and join us for our morn meal. We have overly enough."

Karan was a slight woman but with pleasant features. Her soft brown hair reached to her waist that she normally wore in a long braid. Karan was always well contained in her mannerisms and seldom abrupt. Jandra knew that Karan had a rough beginning in her life. Her Birth-Mother and mother had both been killed in battle when Karan was in her sixth cycle. Another family adopted her, but those mothers had too been killed in yet another battle during Karan's ten cycle. From there, she lived mostly on her own, moving from one family to the next, never remaining permanent, and often running away if she felt it necessary. Woden had seen it as a problem until Karan met Ailis during her seventh cycle and Ailis' nineteenth cycle. They had quickly formed a companionship and had been together since that moment. Karan was now in her forty-third cycle, and had never ventured alone again. The Woden community had thought that Karan wouldn't be able to hold a companionship together, but twenty-six cycles later, she had proved all of them wrong.

"It is Festival this turn, Second."

Jandra looked at her in question, "Yes it is, Karan. Has this festival a particular significance for you?"

Karan smiled and blushed, "It is the festival that Ailis and I but became companions, twenty-six cycles prior."

Sam entered the room, "Come, let us eat. I have prepared the meal. Good morn, Karan."

Elsewhere, across The Realm

The Queen looked down upon her, "Rise. Give Me your report."

"Her lover is pregnant with the Promised One, my Queen."

She was fully surprised, "Are you certain of this? Her lover?"

"Yes, Highness. It is so. The Spirits of the Falls' leader has sent her a message telling her to protect her lover."

"So her most beautiful lover must be young then."

"No, my Queen. Not young, but not old. When she was told of such, she became angry with The Highest, as they were in a discussion regarding their companionship. The lover was moving out until this report. She doesn't want to be with child."

"Moving out? Do they not become companions, then?"

"It is reported that they become companions, Highness. But it is a most unstable relationship. I believe The Highest will miss her freedom in such. She seems to like a different lover at all the moments. And she seems quite . . . vigorous in her needs."

"Why did her lover desire to leave her?"

"Her lover finds her overly self-centered and overly independent, Highness. And the lover knows that The Highest loves another."

"Loves another? Then why take this one as a companion?"

"She loves the Sea Captain, who already has a companion, Highness. Woden only requires a companion, but the companion doesn't have to be loved. The Sea Captain doesn't love her companion. They are only companions of convenience."

The Queen shook her head, "They take companions, but they love another? Don't you find this practice rather questionable?"

Her messenger laughed, "Indeed, my Queen. Most. But it seems to be the law, and now she must find a companion, as she is now The Highest."

"Perhaps it might be more sensible to change the law, then. But we digress. What else?"

"The leader of the Spirits of the Falls has lied to her, Highness. She told The Highest that Buron is under your command, and that they now fight you and the Spirit Mothers of the Valley, through Buron."

The Queen became angry, "She lied? Why would she do as such? What would she gain from this lie?"

"I know not, my Queen, but my guess is that this unborn child has something to do with it. Woden now prepares for battle against Buron."

The High Queen paced, "Of course. Far'lin'ter'il wants this child for herself. She must be this mysterious High Spirit Mother." She looked up, deep in thought. "But, hold. You don't think that the Spirit Mothers of the

Valley are involved in the dece. . . . no. This could not be so. Not them. Surely not them." She began pacing again. "And now Far'lin'ter'il wants to keep this child away from The Realm. It all becomes clear now. I will have to interfere, then."

"But your vow, my Queen—"

"—will be broken. It must be so. But not now. Perhaps I make a mistake in My thinking. We will watch carefully. As this unborn moves closer into The Realm, we will make a decision. She must not be born into the hands of those Spirits. She belongs to The Realm. That *also* was vowed."

"Yes, Highness. You speak truth."

"Anything else, as if this were not enough?"

"Yes, my Queen. Her lover forgives easily. I read somewhere, but cannot recall where, that there are those in The Realm that forgive easily, such as this, rather than fight their lovers. It returns not to me at this moment, but makes me think once again that she is different."

"You rely overly on these books. Check with the storytellers. They will know. Have you found out where she comes from?"

"No, my Queen. Even she doesn't know of such."

"This lover of hers sounds most special. Is The Highest as good as this to deserve such a beautiful lover with such a kind nature?"

"And the lover is most intelligent, my Queen. More so than The Highest."

The Queen raised an eyebrow, "Pity. It sounds like this lover is wasted in that small town. The most beautiful in The Realm, you say.

"With no doubt, my Queen. In all The Realm. I exaggerate not."

The Queen was intrigued, but pushed it aside. "Anything else?"

"The leader of her forces is also most special. I much like this warrior woman. She goes by the name of Meera."

"Strange name, but all their names sound strange to Me. But she is only human so has no powers."

"You speak truth, my Queen, but she has an exceptional warrior's heart, and could serve The Realm well."

"Do they have enough forces to beat this miserable and conceited Buron? I am sorry that I brought him here. I have spent many sleepless eves since his visit. The memory of him gives Me chills. I hope I haven't made a mistake."

"You did as such to save her, my Queen. It helped in the only way we could. They do have sufficient forces, but we could secretly help the odds a bit, my Queen, when the moment arrives."

"I will consider such, but find out of Buron's forces, and theirs as well. I don't want to interfere in this battle unless necessary. We seem to have enough of our own."

"Yes, my Queen."

"Anything else?"

"No. That is all for now, Highness, but we continue to observe."

She paced some more, "Tell Me. Does this small town of hers keep her busy?"

"Amazingly so, my Queen. More curious than this, they know not of all else in The Realm."

"Nothing?"

"Only of Apien, New Harborage, Fornaith, and a few other small human settlements, my Queen. This is all."

"They know not of us?"

She shook her head, "No, my Queen. Nothing, except by name. Nor of the Mungardies, or the Dungaras, or any of the Mystics. They think The Realm is all human, except for the Spirit Mothers."

"How can this be so? Are they as innocent as all this?"

"Yes, my Queen."

"And her lover, as well?"

"There is a young lad, her son. Tadan. He is the child of her now-dead companion. He is most intelligent, and seems to know of The Realm. But no one really listens to him."

"Ah, yes. I recall this child."

"And one other thing, my Queen. Her lover? She recalls nothing prior to her seventh cycle. It is as if she has been blocked of such memories, as she is most intelligent. Her eyes shine with such, my Queen."

"So, she has beautiful eyes as well?"

"Unlike any other. Even The Highest's eyes are beautiful, but are not as stunning as her lover's. In all ways, my Queen, this woman is astonishing."

"Such a waste for her to carry this unborn. But at least the Promised One will be beautiful, as she will need be. So be it. Keep Me informed."

Chapter VIII
Festival

Karan had never been with Sam for a meal. She was nervous as they sat to eat. Sam served the meal, and they all liked the egg and potato casserole that May had prepared. Sam noticed that it had cheese and onion in it, also; two of her favorites.

"Did you get enough sleep to make it through the turn now, Karan?"

She looked up, "Oh yes, Highest. Thank you for letting me sleep here. I was ready to fall down I was so tired."

Jandra poured each of them some juice, "Karan, how be our new arrivals? Be they in fair shape?"

"Mostly. There are some with ailments, some with physical wounds, and many with mental wounds. The healers but feel most needed these turns. Almost to a person, all of them seem in shock and overly frightened. They all begged to remain in Woden, and they all vowed to do whatever it be required to be here."

"Are all desiring a mixed community?"

"No, Second. Most of the women and young female children want to remain in Woden community permanently. Many of the men would like to live in Hengist. There be 131 total, Highest. Of those, I would guess that around forty of those would like a mixed community. Highest, be there more of this meal?"

Sam rose and got more of the casserole for all of them, "May be the best cook, is she not?"

Jandra and Karan both nodded in total agreement.

"Sam, this be the festival and turn that Karan and Ailis became companions twenty-six cycles prior."

Sam lifted an eyebrow, "Twenty-six? I remember rumors in Woden that they guessed that Karan would not remain long in the companionship. You were considered but a wild one and untamable. It seems to have worked well enough for you."

Karan nodded, "Yes, Highest. Ailis is my life. I knew it the moment we met."

Jandra asked, "Did you ever want a child?"

"No. All I wanted was Ailis. Thankfully, she accepted my need."

Jandra looked at Sam to see if she had a reaction. Sam showed none, knowing that Jandra would be watching her.

"Karan. Jandra. What should the Highest but wear to the festival this turn?"

Jandra looked surprised, "You attend Festival this turn?"

Sam nodded to her, "Yes. I will spend the turn with you. I have others to tend to the details of Woden Falls." Sam raised her eyebrow and grinned, "I have been told that this be an important turn for Woden Falls, so I must attend."

Jandra lowered her head so that Karan couldn't see her blush and smile.

Karan replied, "I like your white and gold gown, Highest. You be most beautiful in it. It would make all happy to but see their Highest as a Highest."

Sam looked to Jandra, "Jandra?"

"I agree with Karan. This turn you should look more as a regal Highest and less as a warrior. It will help the festival to have a calmer atmosphere. Battle will be here soon enough."

Karan looked startled, "Oh, Highest, I forgot. I meant to inform you that Lillon has finally recovered and will begin attending to you again this turn, at Festival."

Sam looked to Jandra, "And when are we but going to find you an assistant, Jandra?"

Jandra looked at Sam and cocked her head slightly toward Karan. Sam thought about it a moment. She knew that Karan was certainly capable enough, but wondered if Karan could do that plus keep up all the archives and past of Woden.

"Karan, have you ever wanted to do something other than advisor?"

"Highest? What do you mean? Are you displeased with me?"

Sam laughed, "I should be as displeased with all the advisors. No, Karan. I but wonder if you would like to be The Second's assistant. You would work more closely with her. Be this something you might consider?"

"Second, would you but want this as well?"

"I gave Sam the idea, Karan. Would you do it?"

"Oh, yes, Second. I would love this. When do I begin?"

Jandra rose, "How about now? Let us get The Highest prepared for her turn at the festival, then you can tend to me."

Karan got up from the table and knelt before Sam, "Highest."

Sam looked surprised and held her arms up to Jandra as if questioning this, "Karan, there is no need for this. Rise and tend to Jandra."

"But, Highest, there is. You have been so good to us. To all of Woden." She bowed her head, "Thank you, Highest."

"Show me your gratitude some other way, Karan. Kneeling only allows me to see the top of your head."

Karan nodded and went to Jandra. "I can make up your schedule this turn. I will confer with Lillon and we will but ensure that yours and The Highest's schedules but match. I have many ideas, too, Second. I have been but thinking that we could place an addition onto this dwelling since The Highest insists on remaining here. A place where the assistants and you can be when The Highest is in the other portions of the dwelling. More like a formal, but comfortable meeting room. The present sitting and meeting room will not be sufficient with both of you in one dwelling."

As Jandra and Karan were preparing Sam for her turn at the festival, Karan spoke to Sam, "Highest, I would like to suggest that we find the first diaries. I think they hold much information that we have not. It might tell us where the First Ones call home."

Sam stepped out of her own garments so that she could be fitted into her gown. Karan had never seen her naked prior, and while Jandra acted as if nothing were out of the ordinary, Karan gasped.

Sam looked at her, thinking something wrong, "Karan, what is it? Be something wrong?"

Karan blushed and turned away, "No, Highest. I am sorry. I have never seen you this way prior, and your beauty but caught me off-guard."

Jandra laughed, "As it does all. Pay no attention to her, Karan. She knows or cares not. She be blind to this effect on others, as well."

Sam scoffed, "Beauty! What be it but a physical possession. What a waste." She turned to Jandra and grinned mischievously, "But I do so admire yours, my Jandra."

Karan and Jandra helped Sam into her gown and other garments, then Karan asked, "Where be The Highest's pendant, Highest?"

Sam shrugged, "I know not. It probably is yet in the former Highest's dwelling."

Karan went to the patio door and spoke to a guard.

"I am having it retrieved for you. It will look wonderful on this gown. Second, who but fixes The Highest's hair?"

Jandra laughed, "The wind. But you can try while I prepare myself. My gown needs no attending, as does The Highest's."

Karan nodded and motioned for Sam to sit on a chair. She began to try to tame Sam's hair and saw that it was going to take a while.

"Highest? May we place The Highest's hood over your gown?"

Sam nodded wearily. She detested this type of fuss, "Whatever would please you and Jandra."

Jandra nodded to Karan, "A good idea, Karan. Let us make her look like the most regal of all Highests."

Sam looked to Jandra, "Who but tends the bridge this eve and morn?"

"This is getting to be but a barbaric custom, is it not? Briggon and Meera will personally attend to it this festival."

"What of the gates? Who attends to them?"

"Meera and Briggon's guards. Their guards will check all the dwellings mid-morning. There will be no easy passage, Sam. But be this necessary?"

Sam nodded, "I agree with you, Jandra, but it is the law of Woden until it be changed."

"Then let us change it."

"I think it will change by next festival. I see these things changing now. With a mixed community, if we but approve that, this custom will become meaningless. Change must occur, but change needs to go through its process, Jandra. It can't be rushed."

"There, Highest. I have but fixed your hair."

Sam rose, not caring to even look at it.

Jandra looked over and laughed lightly, "It be a miracle, Karan. How did you do it?"

"It be wild, so I made it to look like the wind has blown it into shape. You have most beautiful hair, Highest. You too, Second. Will you allow me to fix yours as well?"

"I would like it much. But mine is not as beautiful as Sam's."

"No Second, you be wrong. Your hair is even more beautiful, but different, which is good."

A guard entered, holding up the pendant, "It has been found."

She gave it to Karan and left.

Karan placed it over Sam's head and stood back to admire it, "It is as if it has always belonged there, Highest. You have a most beautiful chest and the pendant fits well on it."

Sam cared not and went to Jandra. She helped her to prepare and thought her to look stunning.

Sam motioned over to the chair, "Karan, prepare The Second's hair."

When Karan was done, Sam took Jandra's hands and made her rise.

She placed her hands on Jandra's head, gently, "Jandra, look into my eyes."

Karan just stood and watched, not knowing what The Highest was doing. Sam probed into Jandra, using her increasing power, and searched for the unborn child. To Karan, it was as if they both stared into each other's eyes for unmoving long moments.

When she found her, she sent her a message: *My unborn child. Raise your awareness and know who and where you are. You reside in your Birth-Mother's womb. She will care for you until you are but born. Listen to her sounds. Listen to the sounds of Woden. Show your Birth-Mother your love. Grow peacefully and listen well. Love your Birth-Mother. Learn of Woden while you grow.*

The tiny unborn child woke. The movement startled Jandra. She moved her hands to her womb and felt it, whispering, "Sam. What did you do?"

Sam placed her hands on Jandra's, "I didn't hurt her. I but spoke to her."

"Her? Sam . . . oh."

The child had moved again, and Jandra had felt it.

She sat back down, "This be most strange, Sam."

"She but prepares herself."

Karan couldn't hear their conversation but thought that something had happened to Jandra, "Second, be you well?"

Jandra looked over to Karan, "Yes, Karan. I am fine."

When Jandra looked up at Sam, she noticed her eyes, "Sam, look into a mirror. Every moment you use your power, your eyes but change. It is as if they were the color and movement of sun-soaked waves. They shimmer."

Sam ignored the comment and looked to Karan, "Be you ready for festival, Karan?"

"If you mind not, Highest, I will go prepare. I will meet you at the festival."

Jandra waved her off, "We can tend to ourselves. Have fun this turn, Karan. Tend to me later."

Sam went to the door and spoke to Keddi and Margeria, bending down to pet Rundle, "There will be enough guards at Festival, so go and enjoy yourselves. I am certain you have but raised the level of embarrassment in the guards. They will be most watchful."

Keddi nodded, "Thank you Highest. I am going to leave Rundle with you at all moments now. I will but give him a message to watch and guard The Second. Be this fine with you, Highest?"

Sam nodded, "Will you come to feed him, then?"

Keddi also nodded, "You need not worry at all about Rundle. We will all now be most watchful of The Second. May I take Rundle to her and give him his direction, now?"

Sam nodded and they went inside to Jandra. Keddi motioned to Rundle, and then to The Second. Rundle understood the hand motion and went and sat alongside Jandra. He would now follow her wherever she went.

Jandra looked to Sam, unsmiling, "I now have a child and a dog? Be there a bird about that you would but have me take on as well, Sam? Or perhaps a few fish?"

Sam and Keddi both laughed. Sam replied, "He is but your guard so that Keddi and Margeria can enjoy the turn at Festival."

Sam held out her arm to Jandra. Jandra took it and they began walking toward Hengist and the festival. Sam looked behind and saw that Rundle followed, on his best guard. She also noticed that guards were everywhere about them.

"Oh, Sam. This child but makes me know it is there."

Sam halted and placed her hand upon Jandra's womb. She felt the child move slightly.

Jandra looked concerned, "It be overly early for this. I should not feel this child for another two moons."

Sam shook her head, "This be no ordinary child, Jandra. She is but of the Spirits of the Falls even more than I be. And she will be as beautiful as you."

"How do you know of this?"

"I have seen her."

"Now? In my womb? You have seen her?"

Sam shook her head again, "No, Jandra. I have but seen her as The Highest of All The Realm. I have but seen what Woden will be if I can but get us that far. But first, we must win the battles against the Spirits of the Valley and Buron."

Jandra moved into Sam. To Sam, she seemed afraid, "Hold me."

"What is it, Jandra?"

"I but want the child to feel us together. I don't want her to feel my fear, so remove my fear from me, Sam."

Sam placed her arms around Jandra and held her tightly, "Why do you fear, so, Jandra?"

Jandra placed her arms around Sam and held her as tightly, "Why do I fear so? How can you ask this?" Jandra fought against her anger but was surprised at Sam's continued ignorance of her feelings.

"I now have a child that I must protect for the future of all The Realm, and who will but rule the entire realm if I can get this child to the moment of birth. And I have a lover and soon-to-be companion that is the warrior for the Spirits of the Falls, and who must lead us into battle. Sam, all The Realm is going to come to Woden to fight you to prevent this child. And they will seek to kill you. And I have a lover who does not need me or love me. Why should I not be fearful, is the better question."

Sam spoke softly and moved slightly away from Jandra, but took her hands into her own, "Jandra. I know these are fearful moments, but we are well prepared. Oisin but fights off Apien and New Harborage at this moment, and my powers but grow. The Old Raggedy One will return soon and give me increased power to battle Buron, and my Mothers are to provide more preparation for the battle. Meera and Keddi will see to it that our guards are but prepared, and Meera is also beginning training for all our women and men. And you need have no fear for this child. The Spirits of the Falls watch over this child every moment."

Jandra took her hands away from Sam, yet well frustrated with her, "It be useless to fear with you around. You but see everything as an adventure." She thought about it for a moment, "Sam, what makes you so certain that the Spirits of the Valley are truly our enemies, or this queen they mention? Should we believe everything we have been told? We know little of the Spirits of the Falls, and nothing of the Spirits of the Valley. We could be no more than puppets in their battles. Battles that may not even concern us. The Spirits of the Valley and queen could well be our allies for all we know, whoever they be."

Sam was surprised, "What makes you ask such a question, Jandra? This be a most strange question. Be something telling you otherwise?"

"I know not. It be just a thought, perhaps. But we seem overly trusting, at moments. We should not go so naively into believing the Spirits of the Falls. This does not seem as correct, Sam. It is overly convenient."

Suddenly, Jandra laughed, and Sam wondered what was so humorous, "Jandra, now you laugh?"

"Oh, Sam. I thought my life boring and routine. I wished for a little excitement and now look. You are correct. I might as well give in to the moment. Let us take our strange family and go to this festival. I have never prior known such companionship as this, but I now suppose I should learn it well."

She looked at Sam, "I love you, Sam."

"You are the best lover I have ever had."

Jandra turned and began walking again, "Except for Brett."

Sam took Jandra's arm and began walking with her, "No. Even Brett. You are but a wild woman, and I like it much."

"You will seek out other lovers when I get big with this child. It will change my body."

"No, Jandra. I will not. Don't think this truth as it will not be so."

"Sam, have you noticed that our speech changes because of you reading those diaries?"

"I have. We seem to be taking that strange words 'don't' and 'didn't' into our usage. Do you think others will pick this up also?"

"That would be humorous. We begin to speak like the First Ones. Be there another word that I might begin to use?"

"We could try can't for cannot."

"I will try. Where do you head us first during Festival?"

"You are but the arranger of this festival. You take us around. I am but yours for the turn. I know not when the events but occur."

As they crossed the bridge, Sam could begin to see the festival arts and crafts booths. Jesters and mimes were busy running around entertaining all, food was abundant, storytellers were telling their stories, and then Sam saw Tadan introducing his new wind machine. Many of the builders were standing around looking at it.

"Look Sam. Tadan holds court with the builders over there. What be he up to, now?"

"I know not. He is always inventing something new."

Ivers had been looking for The Highest and when he saw her, he came running over and knelt and bowed before her, "Highest. I have completed your knife for you."

He held it out to her.

"Rise, Ivers. Show me how you did this so as to not ruin the balance."

Ivers rose. He bowed his head to Jandra, "Second. Highest, this knife. Where be it from? I know not this craftship. It be most excellent."

"It be from long prior, Ivers."

"This metal is wonderfully strong. Even with the stone, the balance be perfect. Try it out, Highest."

Sam, Ivers and Jandra, with Rundle in tow, all walked over near the forest where few people were.

"Where should I aim, Ivers?"

Ivers pointed to a small tree a good distance away, "Can you but hit that tree, Highest?"

Sam raised her eyebrow, "You but test my skills, Ivers. That be a long distance. But let me try."

She felt the knife and tested it in her hand, readied it, looked at the tree, took her aim and threw the knife. Even from that distance, Jandra could see that the knife was on target. As it hit the tree, the tree cracked in two and fell to the ground.

Sam went to retrieve the knife but Ivers went first, "Allow me, Highest. I will retrieve your knife."

Jandra looked at Sam's eyes and saw as she suspected, "You used your powers to do that, did you not?"

Sam shook her head a bit, looking quite startled at the tree, "No. I did nothing unusual. I but threw the knife to but test it out."

"But your eyes change. They shimmer once again."

Ivers returned with the knife, "Try it on a larger tree, Highest."

Tadan had seen his mother throw the knife and watched as the tree broke in half.

He excused himself from the builders and walked over to watch the next practice. Sam hadn't seen him. She took the knife from Ivers and looked at the stone he had so skillfully embedded into it. It seemed to sparkle with life. She readied herself once again, aimed and then threw the knife to the larger tree Ivers had pointed out. Like before, her aim was perfect, and like before, the tree broke in half. On this throw, however, a slight fire started in the split, but quickly smoldered out in the green wood.

Jandra looked to Sam's eyes and saw that they were intensifying in their blueness. Ivers ran to retrieve the knife.

"Highest. You but draw a small crowd. Be that the knife with the stone in it?"

Sam and Jandra turned to see Meera and Caitha behind them. Tadan was to their side, watching. He said nothing. A small crowd had gathered around, stunned at The Highest's demonstration of her skills.

They all knelt and bowed their heads when she turned, "Highest."

Sam hadn't noticed them. She turned around to get the knife back from Ivers.

Jandra tugged lightly on Sam's sleeves, "Highest."

Jandra nodded her head toward the kneeling crowd.

Sam looked at Jandra and then at them, "Oh, sorry. Please rise. Enjoy the festival."

"Highest Mother, how did you but do that?"

Sam looked at Tadan, yet confused. She shook her head, "I know not, Tadan."

Meera politely dispersed the crowd and returned, "Perhaps we should wait for any further demonstration of your new-found skills, Highest."

Sam was yet looking at the knife, "What good would this but do me, Meera?"

Meera laughed lightly, "It sure is better than chopping the tree down, Highest."

Caitha and Jandra laughed with her, as did Tadan.

Sam turned to Ivers, "The knife has not been weakened by the stone's addition. You did but fine work on this Ivers. I thank you much for this."

Ivers bowed his head, "Thank you, Highest. Your sword will take but another turn."

He turned to Meera, "It be a much larger weapon, her sword, and I but wonder if a stone should be inserted on each side of the sword's hilt. What think you of this, Second of Defense?"

"Can you embed them in such a way so as she will not need to touch them?"

He nodded, "As it be with the knife."

"Then do so."

Sam started to hand the knife back to Ivers but Meera interrupted, "Halt, Highest. The Old One told you to have your knife with you at all moments."

"I did not bring my sheath for it."

Ivers said, "I will get you a temporary one, Highest. You can have a messenger return it when you get back to your dwelling."

Sam nodded. She was yet a bit overwhelmed by the strength of the knife.

"Do you feel any effects from the stone as before, Highest?"

"No. Not as prior when I but touched the stone. This felt no different than usual."

Jandra got frightened, "What is so unusual about touching these stones?"

"I found these stones on a beach when Meera and I but checked the perimeter of Woden. I picked one up and held it tight. When I released it, the stone looked dead, but the power had gone into me. It made me feel strange. And I quickly wanted as many of those stones as I could but find. Meera saved me from them. I feel no such longings from them this way."

Tadan came close, "Highest Mother, may I take a look at that stone?"

Sam handed the knife to Tadan, "Do you know this stone?"

He nodded and looked somber, "I do, but was unaware of what it could provide to you. You think it safe if I but touch the stone?"

Meera nodded, "I have tried it as well. The stone did nothing to me as it does The Highest."

Tadan touched the stone. He felt its smoothness. He looked into its middle. He picked up a rock and hit it lightly against the stone. Nothing happened to the stone. He tried it again a little harder. Again, nothing occurred.

"This stone be harder than this rock. What happens when you but touch it, Highest Mother?"

"It can make me want more power. More than anyone should have. It but makes me want to touch more of the stones."

"Be there extra of these stones?"

Sam nodded.

"Might I try a few experiments with one?"

Meera shook her head, "Be that but a good idea, Highest? We need to take the remainder of the stones and but hide them."

Sam looked to Ivers, "Give one of the stones to Tadan. When you are completed with the sword, give the remainder of the stones back to Second of Defense."

Ivers nodded and left to get Sam's temporary knife sheath.

Caitha interrupted the moment, "Jandra, you are getting as bad as these two. You but work all the moments of the turn. This is festival. Let us go to celebrate. Are you asking Sam to be your companion this festival, Jandra?"

Caitha took hold of Jandra by the arm and began to walk away with her toward the food booths. Meera just shook her head and laughed. Sam laughed lightly, placed her knife in her belt, and began to follow Caitha and Jandra.

"Did you tell Caitha of the child?"

Meera nodded, "I did. She will assist Jandra through this. I was but thinking that Caitha should go with Jandra to the Spirit Mothers to attend her. It would make me feel better, and it will allow Jandra to have a friend with her."

"If the Spirit Mothers but allow it."

"I would bet that you could make this so, Highest."

"It is a good idea, Meera. I will see to it with the Old One when she but arrives."

"Are you aware, Highest, that you accepting Jandra as a companion this turn is but the highlight of all this festival?"

Sam halted, "Huh? Why be this so?"

Meera slapped her on the back and laughed, "I know not, Highest, but prepare yourself. There will be but a crowd to watch the event. They most likely bet you will not, once again."

"I have made this of my own doing by waiting overly long."

"There be sword contests this festival. I would but like to watch them."

"Watch them? Why be you not in them?"

Meera moved quickly away, "Highest, hold where you are while I tell you this."

Sam looked at Meera, and suddenly raised and eyebrow, "Meera, you did not do as I think you did, did you?"

Meera began to walk further away, "It be just for fun, Highest."

Sam kept walking toward her, "Meera, you did not enter us into this contest, did you?"

Meera began to run toward Caitha, "Help, Caitha. Highest is after me."

Jandra turned to Sam, "Sam, behave yourself."

Sam pointed to Meera, "But she started it. Do you know what she did?"

Jandra just looked at Sam, "You are but a child at moments, Sam."

"But, she entered us into the sword contest, and I am not prepared for this."

Jandra looked at Meera, "You are as bad as she is."

Caitha laughed, "Let them play. We will eat the sweets while they but entertain us, Jandra."

Jandra looked to Meera, "And how is she to do this with her gown on, Meera?"

"I have had a changing station arranged for her, and I had one of the guards bring over her fighting garments."

Jandra shook her head and went up to Meera, wagging her finger in Meera's face, "You had better hope that this be the only moment you steal her away from me this turn, Meera or you will face me and Caitha."

Rundle barked at Meera, sensing that she was somehow in trouble with Jandra, and since it was Rundle's duty to protect Jandra, he joined in.

Most would have thought Jandra serious, but Sam, Meera and Caitha knew that Jandra was playing with her, and Meera was most grateful for it. She liked that Jandra could now tease her so. It had been many cycles since they had a good relationship, and now was delighted to be able to play into the game with her.

She fell to her knees in front of Jandra and folded her hands as if in pleading, "Oh kind and good of all Seconds, please be gentle with me. Please hurt me not."

Jandra laughed and slapped her lightly on her head, "Get up, you old woman warrior. You make me but laugh. As if I could injure you."

She turned to Caitha, "Are you certain that these two be old enough to be such leaders? I find it most disturbing, do you not?"

Caitha laughed and grabbed Jandra's arm and began walking off with her yet again.

Sam looked at Meera, "I hope you no other surprises for me or Jandra will but have your head."

"No, none. A sword contest be but enough."

"What be the prize?"

Meera looked at Sam and laughed, "Why, fighting you, of course."

Sam stared at Meera a moment, then laughed loudly, "If I were not in my Highest gown, Meera, I would but tie you to a tree and take target practice on you."

Tadan went to Sam, "I take my leave now, Highest Mother. But I will attend the sword fight to watch yours and Meera's skills. Perhaps later you would be willing to tell me about this child of Jandra's that also seems to be yours. I know not how this could be so, but I would like to hear it."

"These turns, there is much that even I know not, Tadan."

"Don't? What be this word, Highest Mother?"

"I have been reading the diaries of the First Ones. They use words such as this. It is a word that seems to combine two words into one. Don't means do not."

"What other words like this did they use?"

"Can't for cannot is another."

Tadan giggled, "I can't understand this. This be most amusing, Highest Mother. Will you tell me more of these words later?"

"I think another is didn't for did not. Go now, and have fun at festival. Within a moon, Woden will be under attack and our fun moments will be but limited."

Tadan left and the four walked together, with Rundle following. They tried out the food booths, whereupon Jandra had announced that she much liked the cheese breads and crackers. Caitha and Meera liked the sweets, and Sam liked the vegetable rolls. They went to the beer tasting contest and found that they much enjoyed Hengist's beer over Woden's. Eeda of Woden won the wine contest, and the sweets contest was unsurprisingly won by May. Since Sam was present, she was asked to present the prize to May, and she willingly did so.

May smiled sweetly so as to fool all those watching and said very softly to Sam, "You better take good care of Jandra or this will be the last sweet you but have, Highest dear. You actions last eve were but embarrassing to her."

"I know, May. It is good to have you watch over me so. Someone needs to keep me in my place. I am making it up to her."

"I should think it would take you at least a cycle to do so. Thank you for my prize, Highest."

"I will tell Jandra of your pronouncement for my punishment. Congratulations, once again, May. Is this not the fortieth cycle you but win this prize?"

May pushed Sam's shoulder in jest, "Halt with teasing me, Highest. You well know this be only my nineteenth prize in this category. I but think of changing categories next festival."

All four of them watched the play once again, as did all of Woden. The women of Woden loved it and asked for it to be repeated next moon in Woden. The men of Hengist said that they were busy in production with yet another play. Following the play, Ivers came up and delivered the temporary sheath for Sam's knife. It made carrying it far easier.

During the festival, the jesters made all the attendees laugh, the mimes mimed The Highest, The Second, Meera and Briggon, much to the enjoyment of all, including Sam. The puppeteers entertained the children and adults with their funny puppet plays. And all the contests occurred.

Sam excused herself for a moment and went up to one of the craft booths.

"Good midturn, Agga. Did you but receive my message?"

"I did, Highest. It be prepared for you. I know it will fit as she has tried on such prior. The bracelet is most beautiful and matches."

"I will have thirty flasks of wine delivered for this. Will it be enough, Agga?"

"Oh, Highest. It be overly much. Five flasks will be fine. I am most honored to do this for you."

Sam took the items and placed them in a small pocket behind The Highest's hood. She then returned to Jandra, Meera and Caitha.

Meera met Sam, "Highest, it be the moment you must prepare for the sword contest."

"Where must I do this, Meera?"

Meera pointed to a small tent, "Your garments be in there. I will tend you."

Meera showed Jandra and Caitha where to sit and had drinks brought over for them while they waited and watched. Rundle sat close to Jandra and barked at anyone who tried to come near her. He wouldn't rest until they returned to their dwelling. Meera helped Sam change into her fighting garments, and then they both came out.

"Meera, my sword. Is there another I might use?"

"I have one prepared for you."

The sword contest was a longer contest, as men and women fought so that they might fight The Second of Defense and The Highest. Each round brought forth more skilled and tireless fighters. Meera watched well, looking for future guards. Many of these contestants were but young and hadn't yet committed to a profession.

"They look not bad, Meera. In fact, they look like they have more energy than I."

"That they do, Highest. Except that they save not their energy as we have learned. They will tire soon. By the moment they fight us, they will but be exhausted and barely able to lift their sword."

"I hope you be correct, but watching that one over there makes me think of you in your younger turns."

They watched until there were only two left. Two women had won the contest up to this point. One of the women was young Margeria. Anyst had almost been Second, but had been beaten by a younger woman, Kyra. Sam watched intently as young Kyra and Margeria squared off to each other.

The contest between the two lasted a longer while than expected. One, and then the other, would score points, and the contest continued to remain even. Finally, Kyra made a move Margeria hadn't expected, Margeria lost her sword and the contest was over.

"Meera, she needs but a moment to rest. And, by the way, Meera, who do you but fight?"

Meera looked to Sam and smiled, "I fight you, of course. So that young Kyra but has a moment to rest and watch two old warriors and their moves, so that it be more fair for her."

"Ah, and then the winner between us will but fight young Kyra, be that correct?"

"It is, and you are not to give in to me just to avoid having to fight young Kyra. I will know, Highest, and make it told if you do. Are you ready? The judge is ready to announce us."

The judge did announce them, much to the surprise and pleasure of the crowd. This was a main event this festival and had never been done prior. Sam and Meera were known for their sword ability and all wanted to see them.

As Sam and Meera entered the circle, Meera looked at Sam, "I expect you not to hold back this turn, Highest."

"Oh, I am sure you wish to but tire me so that I will fail against Kyra. Do not overly wish for this win, Meera. I feel most lucky this turn."

They met in the middle of the circle, met their swords together as they always did in practice, and then began the fight. Meera circled and moved her sword continuously, trying to distract Sam's focus. Sam also circled, wondering what Meera was doing. She had never seen her do this prior. Sam kept her focus on Meera's eyes and knew that Meera was trying to distract her. Sam moved her sword down, as if to make a move, and hoped that Meera would take the bait. She did, and moved in and lunged. Sam was ready and moved her sword up at an impossible angle, with all her might, so as to try to dislodge Meera's sword from her. Meera was caught in surprise but not enough to lose her sword. She moved back and began circling again. Sam moved in, and for a long moment, they had continual sword play. When neither was making any gain, they moved apart once again. Meera then came at Sam, Sam held tightly onto her sword and held it against Meera's strongest move. Meera had expected Sam to lose her sword in the move, and was once again caught off-guard when Sam suddenly, instead of moving back to rest from Meera's attack, raised her sword and brought it down with all her force. Meera barely held her sword, but the force of Sam's swing made her fall to the ground, and the tip of her sword touched the ground. Sam was uncertain if Meera had done that intentionally, but according to the rules, if a sword touched the ground, the contest ended. Meera rose and smiled, and then went to Sam and placed her arm on Sam's shoulder.

Sam did likewise and whispered, "You let your sword touch the ground on purpose, Meera."

Meera looked at if insulted at the implication, "I would never do so, Highest. You but win fairly."

"You old lying woman. You just want to watch me lose to this young one."

Meera laughed, "In truth, Sam, your strength grows. At least two of your moves but made me wince. The first one made me twist a muscle in my arm, so your last swing I could no longer hold. Your power is beyond mine, now. But it be good to have a partner that can now outdo me. It has been long since that could occur. Do you wish to rest prior to fighting this young one?"

"Meera. You need to but tell me prior to me hurting you. That is not to occur. I know not my power and cannot hold it back. You must but tell me."

"Worry not so, Highest. It is good practice for me and makes me stronger. As I said, it has been long since I have been challenged by anyone in all of Woden. Would you like a drink prior to beginning?"

They unclasped their arms from each other's shoulder, "No. I am ready. I would rather just get this over with and get on with the festival."

Meera nodded and motioned to the judge to have Kyra enter the circle. The crowd was excited and began urging on the contestants. While they were disappointed that Meera had lost, they were pleased that their Highest had won. Meera went and sat down next to Jandra, Caitha and Rundle to watch the contest.

Kyra entered the ring and walked up to The Highest. She knelt and bowed her head, "Highest. It is my deepest pleasure to joust with you this turn."

Sam reached down and took hold of Kyra's arm and guided her to stand, "Rise, Kyra. You are to never bow before an opponent. I may be your Highest, but I fight against you this turn. Be you ready?"

"I am nervous, Highest. I am afraid to hurt you."

"And what if I were to hurt you, young Kyra?"

Kyra looked sideways at Sam and grinned, "You will not find that possible, Highest. I have but practiced to be the best in all of Woden. Even better than you and Second of Defense."

"Then it shall be a fair fight, Kyra."

Sam moved her sword so that their swords met. Kyra didn't know the custom but had watched carefully as Sam and Meera had done it. She held up her sword and met Sam's.

Suddenly, Kyra moved her sword into attack. Sam found herself moving quickly in defense. Kyra came on as if a bull and didn't relent. Blow after blow she wielded against Sam. Each swing and lunge stronger than the prior. Sam had no moment to counter, so decided to just let Kyra wear herself out. Sam focused on Kyra's eyes, watching intently for her next move. Much of Kyra's strength lied in her quickness. Sam watched as she defended herself and began to see Kyra's weaknesses. Sam saw that she favored attacks using her right arm as the strength of the thrust or swing.

Jandra was so frightened she was stiff. Meera looked at her and laughed, "Jandra. You must take your ease. Sam does well."

Jandra looked at Meera briefly, then turned back to watch, "How do you say that? Look at her. She makes no fight. She merely defends herself."

"No, this is not so. Watch Sam closely. She but watches young Kyra. She is looking for her weaknesses. Kyra wastes all her energy on these quick and lengthened attacks rather than place one well-placed swing. Sam will win this but easily unless she becomes overly tired. She saves her energy, while letting young Kyra over use hers."

"How can you see this to be so? Sam looks like she cannot lift her sword."

"That is but a trick. Look at Sam's leg muscles. They will show you that she is about ready to counter. Once she has found Kyra's weakness that Sam will push against, she will make her move. Kyra is a strong fighter, but she has no cunning, which is necessary in sword fighting."

Jandra hoped that Meera was correct. In truth, Sam had been doing two things: defending herself from the overly energetic Kyra, and watching for her weaknesses. Sam used all the ploys of defense Meera had taught her. When she found Kyra's main weakness, Sam moved quickly in. Kyra was caught off-guard and landed on her rear. But her sword didn't touch the ground. Sam waited while Kyra rose, which also caught Kyra off-guard. Kyra came at Sam quickly, but Sam saw the weakness and stepped into it, again delivering a swing that caught Kyra unprepared. This moment, Sam kept coming forward, moving her sword quickly from one of Kyra's weaknesses to the next. She swung, then lunged, then swung again, each one coming into Kyra's left side, her weak side. Sam also swung low, another area of weakness for Kyra. She had good strong swings, but only when the weight of the sword was in a downward thrust. Sam had long practiced to be equally strong on upward swings, which was the move that usually caught her opponent unprepared. It did so again. As Kyra tired, she favored her strong side, as Sam had planned on. Kyra moved so that her sword came down hard against Sam's. Kyra expected Sam to counter from the side, but instead, Sam moved her sword in an upward motion with more force than Kyra could produce for a downward swing. When the swords met with a sound like crashing lightening, the shock of the force rang through Kyra's unprepared hands, and she let go of the sword. It flew away from her, and she fell to her knees, exhausted. The festival crowd roared, and Sam went to Kyra.

"Well done, young Kyra."

She was panting, out of breath, as was Sam, "Not so well, Highest. You be much stronger than I had expected."

"But not as quick as you. You are but a quick one."

"It worked not, though, Highest. I but thought my quickness would but wear you down."

Sam helped Kyra to rise. As she did so, Sam placed her hand on Kyra's shoulder. Kyra, hesitantly, did the same to Sam.

"Your quickness would but wear me down if you didn't favor your right side, so. A swordswoman must be able to fight equally from all angles and sides. You also avoid an upward swing."

Kyra moved her hand and touched Sam's upper arm, "Your arms deceive me, Highest. They feel like bricks, but look not so."

Sam laughed and put her arm around Kyra's shoulders, "You are a good sport, Kyra. Do you wish to be trained as a scout? Our new scouts will but leave for only a moon, and then return to Woden. But they will be the most highly trained guards in all of Woden. And Keddi will but train you, and to use but two arrows at the same moment."

Kyra looked into Sam's eyes, which shimmered with strength, "Oh, yes, Highest. It is my dream. And now the scouts will return within a moon? That be an excellent report. Thank you, Highest. You have made my cycle."

The judge announced Sam the winner, but neither Kyra nor Sam listened or cared.

Sam took Kyra back to Meera, "Meera. This be Kyra. She would like to be the first member of our new scout unit."

Meera placed her hand on Kyra's shoulder. Kyra meekly returned the gesture, "I know I need much training, Second. But it was most fun to watch the two of you fight. Even at your cycles, you be better than all us young ones."

Sam looked at Meera, and they both laughed. Meera said, "Yes, us old graying ones yet have but some worth left. Go and enjoy the remainder of this turn, Kyra. You will be summoned when to report."

Kyra bowed her head, smiled, and left.

Jandra reminded Sam, "Go and change, my old used-up one. It is almost the moment of companionships. I wish not to miss it."

"Who presides over these this festival?"

"Fornan, once again."

"That be a good choice. I will return in a moment. Meera, you old woman, will you tend me?"

Meera nodded and they went to get Sam changed.

Jandra sat back down next to Caitha, "Meera and Sam are strong. I never knew of this."

"Yes. Our former Highest but kept her advisors well away from the women of Woden. Sam and Meera work hard to make themselves a part of Woden. The former Highest worked hard to keep herself apart from the women."

Meera helped Sam change into her festival gown quickly, and then tried to do something with Sam's hair, "How do you but manage this mane of hair, Sam?"

"I should do as you, and make it shorter."

They both laughed and left to find Jandra and Caitha. Sam was getting nervous again, but made an effort to not display this. She wanted Jandra to be happy this turn. When they returned to Jandra and Caitha, Caitha led them to the spot where the asking and accepting would occur.

Caitha and Meera stayed back, "This be a special moment for you, Jandra and Sam. Meera has told the guards to hold off a crowd so you but have some peace."

Sam looked to Meera, "Thank you, friend."

Meera smiled and nodded, but said nothing. Jandra took Sam's arm and they walked off together to the spot designated for this event. Woden had long held this practice of having one woman or one man ask another woman or man to be their companions. Most of the pairs would work this out before festival, but there were always the surprises that at some moments turned out, but mostly didn't. The Spiritual Leader would begin the event by reminding all of the law that everyone must have a companion, and then reminding all of what it meant in all of Woden to have one. Many of Woden were standing singly at this moment, but there were also the pairs that had lived prior together and had waited for this moment. Some of the singles would but ask another single to be their companion. It was always a moment in Woden to see who ended up with who and who was denied, and would be spoken of until the next festival.

Sam led Jandra a little away from the crowd to under a tree. They waited for Fornan to do the usual beginnings. While he spoke, Sam looked at Jandra and thought her to be the most beautiful and kindest woman she had known in a long while. Just looking at Jandra brought peace to Sam, and for that she was most grateful. Even at this moment of nervousness, being with Jandra eased Sam. Jandra hadn't been paying attention to Sam, as she had been listening to and looking at Fornan. Suddenly, she looked into Sam's eyes and saw them shimmering with her power, and staring directly at her. It mesmerized her, and she could almost see Sam's eyes displaying love to her. She hoped for such, but knew better. She put her hand to Sam's cheek and touched it gently. Sam placed her hand on Jandra's womb. They had both quit paying any attention to Fornan, so were unaware when the event was to occur. It mattered not to either of them, though.

"Jandra. I need you."

"Oh, Sam. I need you. I can barely breathe with this knowledge of you now. I had hoped you would learn to accept me, but that we need each other so is most unexpected. And you are kind to me."

Sam look startled, "Was not your first companion kind to you?"

"No. She liked not my ways. We but tolerated each other. I stayed with her for lack of caring to try again with someone else. That, and I try to be but loyal."

"I didn't know of this, Jandra. How could someone not need and care for you?"

Jandra hugged Sam and then moved back to look into her eyes, "You are but a wonder to behold. Your eyes, your body, even your beautiful but wild hair. You are like a constant gift to me."

"I was unaware that my heart could but feel this happy again. I live now, Jandra, because of you. Prior, I but acted alive only."

Jandra moved her hand so as to move some of Sam's hair from her face, "I can't believe you to be this kind and tender one moment, and the next moment you are able to win a sword fight."

"Here. I but have a gift for you."

Sam reached into her inside hood pocket and retrieved the two items. She took Jandra's right hand and placed a ring on one of her fingers.

"I give you this ring so that you can remember that my care and devotion to you are unending, as like the ring's circle."

Sam then took Jandra's other hand and placed the bracelet on it, "I give you this bracelet so that when the ring no longer fits during the moments of this child, the bracelet will serve to remind you of my unending devotion and commitment. Like the ring, it be an unending circle."

Jandra was fully surprised. She hugged Sam and held her tightly, "I never thought I would be lucky, but I am truly lucky in you. Thank you."

Sam kissed Jandra gently, and touched her cheek, "I know not why this made me so nervous. I am but glad it be over."

Sam and Jandra had been unaware that the ceremony had ended some moments prior, and that Fornan had been standing near them throughout most of their conversation. Sam was pleased to see that Nolsteney was standing next to him, learning what to do for the next festival.

He smiled and reminded them, "You two didn't do as required of you. Others listen, Highest. It needs to be made so."

Jandra looked surprised, as did Sam, "Oh, I forgot. I am sorry."

Jandra took Sam's hands and looked into her face. A little nervously, she asked, "Sam, Highest of all of Woden, will you accept me as your companion?"

Sam laughed and then looked into Jandra's eyes once again.

Very seriously, Sam replied so that all could hear, "Yes, Jandra. I be now your companion. In front of all these witnesses, I pledge you my companionship."

Jandra gasped. Never had she heard such a reply and acceptance. It was tradition to simply say 'yes'. Sam had vowed that she would make it up to Jandra for embarrassing her, and now she had, in front of everyone. She yet hadn't said she loved her, but it would do, for now. Jandra hoped it would grow into a better relationship, as it now seemed to be doing.

Fornan turned to the crowd that had gathered, unknown to Sam and Jandra, and said to them, "This is what companionship be about. It be about each other in such a way that no one else even be noticed. Our Highest has but waited overly long, as she but waited for this special union. All of Woden but be blessed from this union this turn. They be a model for all to follow. Go now. This ceremony be concluded."

The crowd first clapped their approvals and then dispersed back to the festival. Fornan turned to Sam and Jandra.

He took their hands in his, "Highest. Second. You have blessed all of us this turn with your commitment to each other. Your love between each other is apparent to all and is but an example for all to follow. Highest, I know how hard it was for you all these prior cycles, but it is in your eyes now that the wait was worth the pain. Second, your first companionship was not as this, and you have not known commitment such as this. I know not which be harder. To have a love as The Highest did and lose it, or to never have felt this type of love prior. In either case, though, you now have found each other and have embraced the commitment, as is Woden's law. With such as this as an example, all the Spiritual Leaders know that Woden Falls will become a more caring and gentle place. The women and men watch and follow what you do, Highest, and this be but an excellent example. I imagine that ring such as you gave to Second will become the norm. Thank you for this most honest and tender display this turn. You bless us all in this union."

Nolsteney went up to The Highest and Jandra, "In all my cycles, I have seldom seen such truthful display of love. This is to be cherished. The Spirit Mothers of the Falls watch over you this turn and are gladdened by your commitment. This is as they would desire for you. Know this,

Sam of Woden: Our Spirit Mothers foretell of this union, as it will be placed into legends far into a future we cannot see or understand. What comes of this union will also be blessed. While both of you have waited long and gone through much heartbreak to arrive at this spot in your lives, celebrate your arrival here, as the future begins this turn. The Spirit Mothers are certainly with you."

Sam was startled but well pleased at Nolsteney's very early, but knowledgeable beginning. She was able to add what Fornan couldn't - the blessing of the Spirit Mothers. Jandra, too, was pleased that on this turn, Woden finally had, once again, a true spiritual leader.

Sam nodded to Nolsteney and squeezed her hand, "You know not how remarkable you have already made this festival. It is a good omen that Woden once again has a true spiritual leader."

Nolsteney laughed and squeezed Sam's hand back, in return, "I know nothing of being a spiritual leader, but I do know much of the Spirit Mothers, your Woman in the Woods, and what you are currently calling the Old Raggedy One."

She winked at Sam, "Do you yet know who she be?"

"I have but an idea. She will tell me when she is ready."

Nolsteney moved to give Jandra a kiss on the cheek as she touched Jandra's other cheek with her hand, "Take care, Second. You are perhaps the most important person in all The Realm. What you now carry is truly Woden's and The Realm's future. But it will be how you raise this gift to The Realm that will make all the difference. Never believe for a moment that you are just a Birth-Mother. It is you, Jandra, that will provide the little one the sensitivities she will need to be a great leader. No Spirit Mother will be able to provide this. Only you."

Fornan and Nolsteney left, and Sam and Jandra were finally alone. Jandra looked at Sam, "I did not get you a gift."

"Thank goodness. The jeweler will be busy enough because of the ring. You gave me you, and more is not needed." She looked seriously at Jandra, "In truth, Jandra, you are my gift. I need no other."

"I have another need, Sam."

"Name it, and it be yours."

"I am hungry."

Sam laughed and they went to Meera and Caitha, and then they all went to eat. Festival food was always fun as it was always just a little different than the everyturn food. There were plates of little fingers food, little fried foods, small cakes, small fried sweets, sweet drinks, special casseroles, and large plates of meat saved just for this occasion. After they ate, they listened to the musicians and the singers. One singer sang a new song of Sam and Jandra's union. Another of Meera's battles and conquests, and another singer, the finest of them all, sang a song of a great love gained and lost. It was a song so filled with beauty and sadness that all those within hearing range halted what they were about and listened.

A large bonfire had been planned to occur this eve, but when it was discovered that a full moon would occur at the season's change, it was decided to dance to the light of the moon rather than the large bonfire. All of Woden gathered around very small fires, and the musicians began to play and sing. Circles formed around the fires, and the dancing began. Caitha loved to dance these dances around the fires, so she dragged Meera off with her. Sam had never participated in them, and Jandra was tired. The child within her was already making some movement, and Jandra didn't feel she could dance at the moment. So they sat and watched and listened to the dancers and music. Some of the food servers continued to bring up samples and drink for them throughout the eve.

The dances were with mixed partners, as this was the moment of finding a mating partner for the eve, if one desired a child. The dancing was traditionally equally mixed into circles of men and women holding each other's hands as they danced around the fires.

In some mysterious ways, the women wanting to become with child all gathered into the same circles along with the men who wished to become fathers. Other circles, like the ones Meera and Caitha danced in, were not of this nature and were simply dancing for entertainment. Sam and Jandra watched the circles of those looking for a mate for the eve. They watched as the women's eyes met the men's eyes.

"Have you ever lain with a man, Sam?"

"No. It be as I told Devin. I have never lain with a man."

"Have you ever wanted to?"

"I came to the fire once, but did not begin the dancing."

"You did? What happened that you halted?"

"Brett. She wanted to be the Birth-Mother, and she wanted to lay with the man I had chosen; Briggon. She didn't want me lying with a man and became jealous of it. It became a loud scene, so I but left."

"I remember not such a thing at festival, but it does not sound like a good moment for you."

"It was not, but it passed after some moons."

"And I thought it was the perfect companionship."

"In most ways, it was. But for some reason I could never understand, Brett became crazily jealous of me when I was being noticed by others."

"I can understand that. You are most beautiful and most talented. Women and men are automatically drawn to you."

"Have you but lain with a man, prior?"

Jandra nodded her head, "I did. Three festivals. But I did not conceive a child. That be when my companion began to distrust me and not like me."

"Another jealous woman."

Jandra laughed, "Some, but there was more to our disagreements."

"What be it like to lay with a man?"

"The first festival I tried, it hurt, as I was not prepared. He was but rough and overly quick. The second and third festivals I tried, I chose a different mate and a more skilled lover. While I thought he grunted overly as a pig during the sex, the feeling was pleasant enough. I guess that since Buron is to attack Woden, you will not be laying with him."

Her answer was short and brief, "You are correct. I will not."

Rundle suddenly got up and began wagging his tail. Sam looked around and saw that Keddi and Margeria were approaching.

They came up to them, knelt and bowed their heads, "Highest. Second."

Sam and Jandra rose, "Rise, Keddi and Margeria. What may I do for you?"

"We became companions this early eve, Highest. But you got me into trouble."

Sam looked surprised, "How could I but do this? I was not even near you."

"We but saw yours and Jandra's vows. They were the most beautiful union I have ever seen. And you gave Jandra a ring and a bracelet as testimony to your love and commitment. Keddi did no such thing."

Keddi shrugged, "You have made trouble for many companions this early eve, Highest."

Sam and Jandra laughed, and Sam responded, "You will have to but make it up to her then, Keddi. Be this why you came to me?"

"No, Highest. I was wondering if you might demonstrate your skills with this new knife and stone. I was wondering if it worked in the dark with your powers, even though you cannot see with your eyes."

"Oh, like you do with your arrows, through sound. I can but try."

Sam removed her knife from the sheath and closed her eyes and focused. She used her powers to see into the forest, to see without sight. She held out her hand and sensed the life.

"It be most difficult. I have not tried this prior, Keddi."

"Try it, Highest. Focus."

Sam nodded and closed her eyes once again. Then she reopened them, keeping her focus. She looked about her, but mostly she sensed the forest.

She pointed, "Over there. Down the hill a bit. There is a small tree. I but aim for it."

Jandra argued, "But, Sam, you can't see the tree."

Sam felt the knife, focused her own powers, and threw it. Her aim was true. Keddi ran down the hill listening for where the knife hit. There was no challenge for Keddi, as when the knife hit the tree, the tree split in two as prior, and once again, a small flame emerged from where the knife entered the tree. Keddi retrieved the knife and ran back.

"You did well, Highest. You must but practice, though. It takes you overly long this way. You must be able to do that in the same quickness in which you wield your sword."

"You are correct, Keddi. I will begin practice in two turns hence."

Margeria took Keddi's arm, "We take our leave now, Highest, Second. We are going to join in the dancing."

Jandra asked, "Will one of you be seeking a mate this eve?"

Margeria blushed, "I think not yet, but we will see. Keddi brought up a flask of wine for you two this eve, so that you may enjoy the ceremonies."

Jandra took the flask, "Thank you. Enjoy the dancing."

Keddi looked at Sam, "I take Rundle now. There be many guards about you, a new set, so they be fresh. And they do not wish to embarrass themselves. I will return in the morn."

After they left, Jandra began to sit once again, but Sam held her up. She moved into Jandra and embraced her tightly. She placed a hand on one of Jandra's breasts and held it firmly, then kissed her. Jandra knew the guards were about them, but if Sam didn't care, she decided not to as well. She melted into Sam's embrace and kiss, and could feel Sam's urgency in her demands.

Sam finally halted, pulled back a little and looked at Jandra, "I but thought when we had sex every turn that my urges would but leave. With you, they have become like wild fire. I can't get enough of you, Jandra, and want you every moment."

Caitha and Meera had come up unnoticed by Jandra and Sam.

Caitha said, "You two are like young ones. Always wanting and desiring each other."

Jandra saw that Sam blushed, and turned to Caitha, "Oh? And Meera does not come back to your dwelling ripping off your clothes on the way to your bed, often?"

Meera looked surprised, "How do you but know of this? Caitha, did you but tell her this?"

Caitha laughed, "I be not ashamed of your desires, M'Love."

Sam laid a hand on Meera's arm and walked her away from Jandra and Caitha for a moment, "I have some Woden affairs to tend to. I think we should increase training to a half-turn each turn beginning in two turns hence. I would like all the guards and sentries there, from Woden and Hengist. The sentries can trade off. And I would like all of Woden and Hengist invited, for those who would like to learn to protect themselves. I also would like Oisin's crews there as well. We have much to get prepared for and are not ready. Our guards, Keets' mostly, look slack and dull. I also need the weapons and leather makers to produce more weapons as quickly as possible."

"I will send a messenger to all the guards and sentries. Will you train with us?"

"I will train every turn with you. I want Keddi and Margeria as teachers to all, plus you, and whoever else is worthy of that. I would like all to know spears, bows and arrows, swords and knives. I would like Oisin's crew to set some traps at the harbor, and perhaps a catapult made that throws balls of fire onto other ships. I also want the guards to learn to ride and fight at the same moment. They are weak. I am weak. I would like to be able to fight for half a turn and not lose my breath. And I want all to be able to fight with a sword with one-hand in case that becomes but necessary. And that both arms be equal in their ability."

"You ask a lot of these guards, but we shall do this, Sam. We will begin a training camp in two turns, beginning at the sun's rise. How do you plan to notify all of Woden Falls?"

"When you send the messenger, also send one to notify all of Woden Falls that next turn hence, there is to be a community meeting at the Stones beginning after midturn. I command that all of Woden Falls attend. All, without exception. The ill, old, young. It matters not. They must all hear what we face. Can you think of anything I have forgotten?"

"When were you planning the advisor meeting?"

"Prior to the community meeting. Midmorn. Please have the messengers inform Briggon of such. I want Hengist there as well."

"The builders will need to be involved in the catapult building. I will meet with them separately and prepare surprises for any intruders. They will much like the change from building dwellings. I will tend to this. Please keep Caitha with you until my return. I will be but a few moments only."

Sam nodded and returned to Caitha and Jandra. They had sat down and Sam saw that Caitha had placed her hand on Jandra's womb.

Caitha looked up at Sam, "How far along be this child, Sam? It moves overly soon, but it moves in a strange way, as if feeling her Birth-Mother, instead of kicking her."

Sam knelt down and placed her hands on Jandra's head, lightly. She looked into Jandra's eyes and focused, trying to find the unborn's energy.

Sam found her and felt her struggling to learn. Sam sensed the little one was tired, *Rest now. There be next turn to learn more. Let your Birth-Mother but rest, too. Listen only, and rest.* She sensed no fear in the little one, but an eagerness to learn. Sam removed her hands from Jandra and kissed her head lightly.

Sam looked at Caitha, "This child be a child of the Spirits of the Falls. She will grow in unexpected manners. Ones that we be not used to. Caitha, I would like it much if you would but agree to deliver this child. I know you are not a midwife, but I also know that you have attended many birthings. If we have but won our battles by then, I will be there also and will assist. You need to get your kit of herbs and ointments prepared. You and Jandra will be moved to the Spirits of the Falls as the battles begin. Jandra and this child must be safe from all harm."

Caitha looked troubled, "The Spirit Mothers? We are to live with the Spirit Mothers? How be this possible?"

Jandra just laughed, "Such a question, Caitha. I have a child in me that be an impossibility. I have lain with no man and yet I am with child. And, while this child moves and I but feel it, I should not yet know I am with child, as it has not been over my blooding phase as yet. And yet you ask if we can live with the Spirit Mothers. It would seem that all we thought impossible, possible."

Caitha held Jandra's hands in her own, "I will go if you would but like me with you. I want not to see you go alone to such a place."

"It would mean much to me, Caitha. Thank you."

Caitha looked up at Sam, "And I expect two rockers to go with us."

Sam rolled her eyes and saw that Jandra was agreeing, "Whatever you wish, we will see it so."

"Sam, the child has halted its moving about. What are you doing to it?"

Sam smiled and sat down next to Caitha, "I merely speak to her. Nothing more."

They all watched the dancers and listened to the musicians while they waited for Meera. They saw that some of the dancers were now beginning to take their eve mates and disappear inside Hengist until the morn. Sam offered wine to Caitha and Jandra, but they declined.

"It was a wonderful Festival, Jandra. You did a magnificent effort on this."

"Thank you, Caitha. Briggon did most of it, though. He and Hengist were so excited about their new openings to Woden that they wanted to make a celebration of it. I thought the food was the best ever for a festival."

"I too thought this. Never prior has it been so fresh and tasty as this turn's." Caitha turned to Jandra, "What will you name this unborn?"

Jandra looked at Sam and Sam nodded, "It be a good question. As we speak to her, we should call her by her name. And I think we should but name this child prior to the Spirit Mothers taking that role."

Jandra simply said, "I will think on this. I am unready for a child, let alone naming one."

Meera returned, and they all sat and watched the dancers leave, two-by-two, into Hengist. The musicians were settling in for a long eve.

"If the alignment of the moon be in alignment with the new season, perhaps it foretells many new births in Woden."

Jandra nodded, "I think you correct in this, Caitha. What we lose in battle, perhaps we become even with new births."

Sam stood, "Let us not be overly concerned about Woden's future. We know of Buron's strength and we but know of ours. He only thinks he knows our weaknesses, but we showed him only a silly side of Woden. One that was all decorative and ridiculous. He knows not our fighting abilities. Even his ships know not our mastery. Trust in our Spirit Mothers and the Woman of the Woods. They watch over us and protect us. Now, come. Let us be off to our dwellings. It is late and we all have but a midmorn advisor meeting."

Jandra looked at Sam, unsmiling, "I hope the trust we place in them is worthy. But I think we place our trust in them blindly."

The four walked back to Woden together. Jandra and Caitha spoke about the festival on their return, and Meera and Sam listened. It had been a wonderful festival and Sam hoped by the next one, the battle with Fornaith and Buron would be completed. Sam and Jandra took their leave of Meera and Caitha once they reached their dwelling.

Sam took Jandra's hand and led her inside. They went into the bedroom and began to change out of their festival garments.

"I can't get out of this gown, Jandra. Can you but help?"

Jandra laughed and helped Sam remove her Highest gown. It was difficult in that it had over twenty buttons on the back, most of which Sam couldn't reach. Sam stepped out of it and threw it over to a nearby chair. She helped Jandra out of her own gown, then each prepared for bed. As Jandra returned, she saw Sam standing next to the bed, waiting.

"Sam, are you not cold? Where is your bedshirt?"

Sam went to Jandra and embraced her as she had prior, at Festival. She then kissed her, Sam's need and intent more than clear to Jandra.

Jandra shoved her gently away and looked serious, "Were you not aware that when I became with child and we became companions, I would not want sex anymore?"

Sam looked at her, astounded, "But—"

Jandra just looked at Sam, and then moved as if to go to the bed. Sam continued to stare at Jandra, not knowing what was occurring.

Suddenly, Jandra turned around, removed her bedshirt, and ran back to Sam, laughing. She embraced her and returned the kiss Sam had given her.

Sam smiled, feeling grateful for the moment.

* * * *

In the morn, after the sun's rise, Jandra awoke and found Sam missing from their bed. She rose and prepared herself for the turn and went into the kitchen.

May was already preparing food for the turn and sweets for the advisors, "Good morn, Second. All seems well in the dwelling. Sam is out on the patio speaking with Ivers about something. Sit and have some fresh mint tea. I just made a large pot and think it especially sweet."

"Good morn, May."

Jandra was yet tired from festival and the eve's pleasures with Sam. Sam entered the kitchen with her sword that Ivers had completed the work on.

"Oh, Jandra. You rise. Good morn. Is it not a most splendid morn, May?"

May looked at Jandra sideways and winked, "It may be for you Highest, but you wear poor Jandra out. And now I hear you have made her with child. What be these rumors, Highest? This be not possible, although I know more than anyone in Woden that to tell you something be impossible is to but make it possible. Yet, you wear poor Jandra out."

Sam looked at Jandra and went to her side, "You do look tired, as May says. Return to our bed and rest more."

Jandra placed her hand on Sam's face, "I am fine. Give me but a moment to wake up. How is it that you are so wide-awake? I thought you the one to sleep in every morn."

"May woke me. Ivers had come with my sword and asked that I but examine it. So it be May's fault. She but missed seeing me prior turn so woke me early to see more of me this turn."

Sam laughed, but May waved her hand as if dismissing her, "Pay no attention to her, Jandra. She be but full of herself. By the way, Highest, Lillon awaits in the sitting room. And Jandra, Karan is also here. She awaits you on the patio."

Jandra put her hand to her forehead and closed her eyes. Her head ached and her stomach felt as if she were aboard a ship.

Sam became worried, "Jandra, what is it? What be wrong?"

May turned and saw Jandra, "Highest, go tell Karan to get Caitha and have Caitha bring her herbs and potions. I am but out. And hurry."

Sam left to tell Karan, and May came over to Jandra, "Let us get you back into bed for now. When Caitha comes, we will fix you right up. Worry not, Second. This will pass soon enough."

Jandra felt overly ill to complain, argue, or even speak. She gratefully laid down and rested. Sam came in to check upon Jandra, but Jandra had returned to sleep. Caitha arrived soon, having run the entire way, and began to prepare her potions. She gave some extra to May so that Jandra could have them when she needed them. Sam paced nervously and didn't know what to do.

Caitha came into the bedroom and began to rub a potion on Jandra's forehead, and another on her stomach. Then she woke Jandra and had her drink another.

"Jandra, it is me, Caitha. Let us sit you up so that you can drink this for me."

Jandra peeked open her eyes at Caitha and nodded, but didn't feel like rising. She did as Caitha asked, though, and drank the potion. While it tasted awful, Jandra began to feel improved almost instantly. Sam looked overly worried.

Caitha got tired of Sam's pacing, "You do much better in battle, Sam. Just because Jandra feels a little morn illness is no reason for you to become a useless wit."

"What is wrong with her? She was fine prior eve. What can I do to but make her well?"

Jandra smiled at Sam, but Caitha snapped at her, "It is your doing that she but feels this way. How be you this stupid, Sam? She is with child, and this be but usual. Poor Jandra be older, though, so it be more difficult. And it is overly soon for this. *Overly soon*! Thank the Spirit Mothers for May. At least she has some sense about her."

Meera walked in and scanned the room, "Be Jandra ill?"

Caitha looked at Jandra and rolled her eyes, "There be another witless one. They are useful in fight but plain dumb in these matters."

Meera looked for help to Sam, but Sam looked helpless and worried, "Will she be fine?"

Jandra raised her arm and hand to Sam, "Come here, and quit worrying so. Caitha has removed the pains and I am but fine. It is normal, these morn pains, when with child. It is as Caitha says. I be overly old for this, but must go through it anyway."

"I am sorry, Jandra. I wish not for you to have to go through this pain. It but drives me crazy and makes me feel useless."

May came in, "Thank the Mothers for Caitha. Meera, you be as useless as The Highest, here. Has no one any wits about them? Leave poor Jandra be so that she can but recover. Get out!"

Sam and Meera lowered their heads as if they had been punished and left the room. They left hearing Caitha and Jandra laughing, so didn't feel overly bad.

"Is this what we must go through the entire birth?"

Meera shrugged, "Why ask me? I know not about these things. I am only a warrior."

They sat on the patio to wait. Shortly, May came out with a morn meal for both of them.

"Caitha will sit with Jandra for a few moments more and then help prepare her for the turn. I have invited Lillon and Karan to eat your morn meal with you, as Jandra has but asked. Highest, you must take better care of poor Jandra. She be a special one and you have but acted poorly up to prior turn. Shame on you."

"You speak truthfully, May. I will make it so."

In truth, May knew that Sam was treating Jandra well, but just reminded her of her place. May wasn't going to allow Sam to become complacent with Jandra. She had seen that occur overly often. She saw that Sam was happy for the first moment since Brett's death, and wanted it to remain as such. But she also knew that Sam had forgotten how to treat a companion, and that she no longer remembered how to love someone.

Caitha and Jandra finally arrived for the morn meal. Jandra spoke to Karan mostly, and Lillon kept Sam busy with what she thought should be Sam's plans. The morn meal finished when May informed them that the advisors awaited them. All the advisors were waiting, including the new ones. Sam didn't want a long meeting but needed to provide the new positions.

After everyone was seated and arranged, she began the meeting, "Good morn, all. Thank you for coming. I have a few agendas items this morn that need attending. First, the issue of an assistant for Second. Karan has agreed to be Jandra's assistant. Lillon will continue as mine. I have decided that instead of replacing our former counterpart to Meera, that we give Meera the title of Second of Defense and let her be in-charge of all our guards and sentries, including Hengist's. Briggon will report and work with Meera concerning Hengist's guards and sentries. As with all Seconds, Meera will report to me. Alain, Ghada and Landric will work together on the trade and accounts, including trade from outside and inside Woden Falls.

"If we but create a third community, we will keep the accounting the same. Janel will become the advisor to the fisheries and work with Liley and Gerin from Hengist on food production. Gerin, that will be an expansion of your role. Tehna and Moduin will oversee all health issues in Woden Falls. I especially would like the healers to push themselves to learn more. Moduin and Ghett will oversee all building. Ghett, that is but a change in roles for you, but you have always been interested in Woden's future expansion planning. Caitha has agreed to be an advisor and I have selected her for our General Advisor. Our new spiritual leader will be Nolsteney. She and Caitha will oversee this group in all of Woden Falls in the future to prevent what occurred just prior, with ours. Zan, you will continue to oversee our education concerns in all of Woden Falls. Sephim, you have overseen our Sea Affairs, but with Oisin and Janel, that seems well covered. I would like you to be the advisor to ensure that all the crafts become as high quality ones, and to prevent over repetition of a single craft. Iver, you will yet oversee Outside Relations, although we tend to have little of this at present. It will be but a challenge. You will need to make trips on Oisin's voyages to but meet with our smaller and isolated communities. Zan, Iver, Ghett, Moduin and Tehna will all need to work closely together when we have new women and men but come into our community, such as two prior eves. The building, health, education, and relations will all need to be considered at the same moment when such people come to Woden. The Seconds will also oversee these increases within Woden and Hengist."

"Jenna, Ghett and Briggon. What is your report on our animal move?"

Jenna rose, "We have decided to have one central site for all our animals. We have selected a site just south of the path between Woden and Hengist. The builders have already begun to dismantle and move some of the buildings. A new larger and better-ventilated barn is also being built. The builders began preparing the site this morn. It will take a moon or more."

Completed with her report, Jenna sat down. Sam asked, "Are there any issues I have left out or concerns you may have?"

Karan rose, "Highest, I have submitted plans to the builders to enlarge this dwelling. It be not suitable with your growing family."

Sam just looked at her, blankly, "Oh?"

Jandra rose, "And I agree. Do you have any issues with this?"

Sam blinked, and shook her head. She wasn't going to take any issue with Jandra, especially since this morn.

Sam said, "Whatever you would like, Jandra."

Everyone in the room laughed a little, but tried to hide it. It was humorous to them that their Highest could be so easily moved.

Karan stated, "Highest, there are rumors in the community about The Second having your child. While I have heard it so from Jandra and May, perhaps you would give your permission so that I might begin to explain it to all so it be clear. It is most confusing to the women, as they know that women cannot conceive with other women."

"It be strange for me and Jandra as well. We are not born in Woden to have a child shared in blood between companions. The Spirit Mothers have many more powers than we can know. Yes, Karan. Do, as you must. The community meeting will occur in a short while. I would like everyone there. I have commanded it so. Also, concerning all of you. I but wish you to begin attending training at the sun's rise next turn with Meera. It will set but a good example for all our guards, sentries, and anyone else who but desires more fighting ability. I would like to add that in all aspects of this soon-to-be battle of Woden, Meera's command will be absolute. Look not to me during battle for approval. Her commands will be final, and fully followed without question. Any further issues or questions?"

Sephim rose and smiled, "How does it feel to have a companion, finally, Highest?"

Sam nodded, smiled, and looked at Jandra. Being a companion one turn was no different in feeling from the prior turn, but Jandra had been there then, as well. Sam gazed at Jandra in amazement and felt contented because of her.

"It has been a very long while since I can recall such a feeling of happiness." Then she looked back at Sephim, "But since it was you who continually pushed me to get a companion, should Jandra become unhappy with me, I will blame you."

Sephim gasped while everyone else laughed, as did Sam and Jandra. Sephim blushed, "You tease, Highest. But in truth, you and Jandra have provided all of Woden a beautiful and most meaningful ceremony, and we thank you much for it. I am pleased to be able to take this item off our agendas from here on."

"This meeting is over. I will see you at the community meeting. Please ensure that everyone is in attendance."

* * * *

As Sam, Jandra, Meera and Caitha approached the Sacred Stones, Sam saw that all of Woden Falls was present, and the arena was crowded.

Just prior to the meeting, Sam met with Lillon, "Report to me of the meeting when it be completed. Karan also."

After she had settled Jandra upon a seat close by to where she must be, Sam stood in the middle and addressed all. She introduced all the new advisor and Second positions. She introduced their new and only woman spiritual leader, Nolsteney. She told of the approaching battle with Buron and Fornaith and of the fight training that would occur beginning next turn. She explained about Oisin in New Harborage and Apien. She had Karan speak about all the refugees from Apien and New Harborage. She spoke of the Woman of the Woods and the Spirit Mothers of the Falls. She spoke of Woden's recent past with its betrayal, and how it had closed down access between Hengist and Woden. She spoke of the *Morte D'Arthur* book and how it had been used to change their ways. She told Woden and Hengist of the diaries. She spoke of the violence across all The Realm. And she spoke of the need to accommodate those that thought differently than Woden or Hengist. She described how they might become more open to the idea of a third community, located somewhere between Hengist and Woden, for those who partnered differently than themselves. She also told them that she, herself, was not yet certain that this should be so, but whether they host a third community or no, she expressed their need to begin to understand such practice.

"The future can be either closed or open in regard to ourselves. It is up to us. We can face the challenges ahead of us openly and embrace the change, or we can seek to hide from it and close our gates forever. We can share our ways and our quest for peace or we can keep it to ourselves. I have been allowed to see a possible future of Woden, if we but fight and allow for it. The Spirit Mothers would have us become a mix between them and us, and our descendants will rule all The Realm. A place where we become part enchanted and part as we are. And a place of peace for all. The decisions be yours to make. But know this: It will become increasingly more difficult to remain as isolated as we have been. The Realm encroaches. Many will continue to seek out our ways and life in Woden.

"As we decide which direction we but head, there will be those of us who we make displeased. We are large enough that we will not be able to please us all. It would be irresponsible to think that this might occur. We must also think of those of us that become so displeased. What can we do for them as well? Can we accommodate all types of thinking and all types of ways? Do we have the largeness of the land to do so? Should we grow more?" Ghett and Moduin, our advisors for growth and building, will lead the remainder of this community meeting. I will depart now so that truthful discussion may occur without fear. All thoughts and ideas are welcomed.

"No matter our decision, though, know this: We face battle. I face a personal battle against Buron, as he has powers such as mine. I must win my battle and Woden must win theirs so that whatever we decide, we can go forward. I am told that we have the strongest guards and sentries in The Realm, but it may not be enough. Whichever lifestyle we wish to fight for, the moment to fight has come. We will be attacked within the moon.

While we work to secure all of Woden, the fight may enter our gates. You must choose whether to go to the caves or to remain and fight. We will most likely lose some of us in this fight, but I pledge to you that I will fight Buron to my last breath.

"I take my leave and hope you the strength and determination of Woden for this discussion. Our future depends on your thoughts this turn. This be a turning point in all of Woden. Consider it well."

Sam departed, which surprised all that attended, including her advisors. Meera motioned for Margeria and Keddi to guard her. They did so from a distance and, in truth, while Sam knew that she must be guarded, she couldn't see the guards. She walked back to the gates and went to the gardens near the former Highest's dwelling. Since the refugees had arrived, not all of Woden could be in attendance at the meeting. Some healers were yet in the infirmary, and some guards were in the former Highest's dwelling, overseeing the arrivals that had been placed there. Sam decided to go visit the new arrivals from Apien and New Harborage while waiting for Karan and Lillon's reports.

She entered and walked through the dwelling. While she was noticed, most didn't know who she was. As they looked at her pass through the dwelling, she noticed how sad and beaten, both emotionally and physically, these people were. Young children sat next to their mothers or Birth-Mothers, but didn't play. Older children sat alone, looking afraid to move. The adults were generally listless, as well. Sam was most displeased.

She turned to one of the guards, "Have all these arrivals come outside to the park. I wish to address them."

"Yes, Highest. At this moment?"

"Yes. Now."

The guards moved into action, and the arrivals all began to move outside. They were afraid, but Sam knew that she would dispel that in a moment.

When they finally all arrived, she introduced herself, "I am known as The Highest of Woden."

Many of the arrivals looked shocked and fell to their knees. The others, upon seeing that, did the same. Most were begging for mercy and kindness.

"Please rise."

They would not, so she just began, "Then please just sit and hear me."

Some arrivals near the front sat on the ground, and the others followed. "I have just walked through your communal dwelling and noticed how sad and depressed you seem. The children be afraid and the adults be listless. You are now safe in Woden, so why be this so?"

No one answered. Sam thought that perhaps they were afraid of her. She walked in-between the people, to the middle of them.

She then sat down, "Please gather around so that you may all hear me speak."

The arrivals did so and formed a circle around her. They were quite afraid of her, and wanted to maintain their distance.

"I know not your past. I know not what you faced in Apien or New Harborage. I have heard the stories and I see the effects upon you. Woden fights now to rid The Realm of such violence, but fighting against such is also violence, is it not?"

It was not a real question, as she was just speaking so that they would get accustomed to her. She planned to speak for a while until they felt comfortable enough to provide some answers.

"Woden faces a battle against a man called King Buron. We will accept the battle and fight for our ways. Do you know of our ways, practices and beliefs?"

Some nodded. Some did nothing but look at her. Some kept their heads bowed to her.

"Woden believes in peace. Woden believes in truthful speech. Woden believes in freedom in thinking and life, to the point possible within a community. We fight for our beliefs. I know not why you seek to come to Woden, but I but think you come here for these reasons. Be that so?"

More nodded. Sam continued, "Peace, in this realm, seems to demand much fighting to protect it. I am but saddened to think of the lives we will but lose in this battle. But that does not concern you at this moment. Your concerns are more immediate, I but think. Be this true?"

Most nodded this moment. One woman spoke, "Highest, how do we but address and speak to you?"

"Such as you do this moment. Speak. It be the way of Woden. The women and men all but speak freely and truthfully to me."

"What if you do not like what they say? Do you not have them beaten?"

"Beaten? Why would I do so to my people? I am but their servant. If I do not have their truth, Woden is but lost. Ask these guards that surround us if you believe me not."

They looked at the guards, but said, "They are at your service. If you beat people for such, you would have them beaten as well."

"With such attitudes, it be useless for me to try to speak with you. Why did you but come to Woden if you fear me and us so?"

A man spoke up, "Highest. We mean no disrespect of you. It is that we have been beaten so often and brutally that we have little trust left. We come to Woden because we have but heard of your kindness and generosity for all. It be but difficult for us to believe in such after what we have been through. All of us have been shackled for most our lives. We know not how to live without them. Tell us what you would like of us, Highest. We will but comply."

Sam motioned for the guards to sit. She stood and began to walk around a bit, so that all could be close enough to her to see she was not evil.

"What would I but like of you? I would like you to become what you would like for yourselves. What trade would you like to provide to Woden? What hobbies might you take up for enjoyment? What friends might you become loyal to? What fun might you take to enjoy? What festivals might you attend? What companionships might you begin, or continue, to provide and embrace of another in a caring manner? What would you do to enhance Woden so that you might live in a better place? I cannot tell you who you are. You must seek that for yourselves. I want you to be productive in Woden, so that Woden is productive in you. It is but a mutual relationship."

Another woman spoke, "How many children must I bear?"

"As many or none, as you wish."

Another man spoke, "What if I wish to leave Woden?"

Sam shrugged, "That be your choice. We will wish you well."

A child stood, "What if I kneel not low enough to you?"

Sam went to the child and lifted her up, "How many cycles have you, little one?"

"I know not."

"What are you called by?"

"Shallan."

"Were you beaten, prior, Shallan, when you did not kneel low enough to someone?"

She nodded, "Manthar made it so because I did not place my forehead on the ground. Would you do the same to me?"

"No. You have my word. I would not or do not do as such. I wish no one to bow or kneel before me. It is something Woden does, but is not required. Why would I wish to see the tops of everyone's heads and not their faces?"

Sam placed a hand on top of Shallan's head and sent a small message of peace in hopes that the child felt somewhat safe. She placed the child down. She moved to a woman-with-child, bent down, took her hand, and bid the woman to rise.

As the woman did so, Sam asked, "I am here for you, young Birth-Mother. What would like from Woden?"

The woman knelt and bowed her head, "Safety for my unborn. To live quietly."

Sam placed her hand on top of the woman's head and sent the same message to her as she had to Shallan. The woman sat back down and smiled up at Sam.

Sam moved to a man, reached her hand out to him, and bid him to rise.

He did so, as she said, "What would you have of me and Woden?"

"A chance to live unafraid, have a family, and enjoy life and others."

She smiled at him and motioned for him to sit.

She remained standing, "I cannot make you trust us. That will come through the moments of observation and experience in Woden. Woden meets at this moment to determine what we should do regarding a third community. One of mixed relationships. All of Woden Falls will make that decision. As for now, I can see that you cannot trust me. Go back to your dwelling, in peace. When the women return to Woden, you have my leave to explore Woden. Please remain within the gates until we can determine where you will be best placed. Thank you for listening to me. I wish you well this turn."

Having released them, Sam began to move out of the circle. Hearing no sound of movement behind her, she turned around and looked at them.

No one was moving.

She saw that they yet looked frightened. "Would you yet like to remain here for a short while longer?"

They nodded.

Sam felt that perhaps she had rushed them. She returned to the middle of the circle and sat, allowing them their pace. She waited. A small child left her mother's arms and went to sit on Sam's lap. Sam just let her and stroked her hair. She yet said nothing. The child rested her head against Sam. Another child moved close to Sam and sat down beside her. Shallan came beside her, along with her Birth-Mother. Both sat close.

Sam smiled at the children, "Have you ever heard the story of the beginning of Woden?"

The children shook their heads. Sam began to tell the story of Woden's early start.

"They were brave women, men and children."

More children moved closer so they could be near her while she told the story. Then she told the story of the Spirits of the Falls.

"A turn's ride from here be a most beautiful waterfall. It be as tall as ten or eleven women, and the water is crystal clear and blue as the sky."

One of the children asked, "As blue as your eyes?"

Sam nodded and laughed, "Even bluer than my eyes. There is a pool at the bottom of the Falls that you can swim safely in. It is not very deep, but you must be careful as the water is cold. In back of the waterfall is a long and large cave. And at the end of the cave, the cave opens to a beautiful but hidden valley, and that is where our Spirit Mothers but live."

Shallan asked, "Do you like them? Are they mean?"

Sam shook her head, "They are not mean. They can be mean if someone is mean to them, but they like to live in quiet and peace. They have been here in this realm for longer than most of these trees."

Sam told stories of Oisin and her sea battles, and of Meera and her fighting abilities. She told stories of all of Woden and Hengist. She told stories of wonderful Jandra and Caitha, of Karan, and all the advisors. As she told these stories, she didn't notice that the women of Woden were returning from the Sacred Stones. The Woden Women heard their Highest telling stories, so they also sat down and listened. More of the new arrival children crowded in to be next to Sam. No one seemed to tire of hearing The Highest tell the stories of Woden's past, present and future. Sam told stories of the best Second in all of Woden's past, Jandra. She told stories of the healers, of May, of the guards, of Keddi, of Margeria, and Rundle, the brave dog. She told stories of evil people but how the good people won over them. She told stories of how people walked here from Apien, and how brave they were. She told stories of Woden's food, their horses, their gardens, their fisheries, their crafts and trades. She told stories of how proud she was of all the women, men and children who lived in Woden Falls, and how brave and selfless they all were.

Jandra, Meera and Caitha had come up after the community meeting. They sat, unnoticed by Sam, for a long while. Finally, when Jandra could see that Sam was tiring, she walked through all the people listening to Sam, which now numbered fifteen-fold the amount that she had begun with, and went up to her. Jandra placed out her hand for Sam to take, as if bidding her to stand.

Sam rose and took Jandra's outstretched hand.

Jandra turned to all the women, men and children, and smiled, "The Highest be overly tired now. She has been telling you stories for the entire after midturn."

Jandra began to pull Sam gently away, but all the people knelt and bowed their heads to Jandra. Then they rose and one-by-one went up to Sam and introduced themselves. They looked much improved from when Sam first went into the former Highest's dwelling, more like a people with hope and dreams. Each bowed their head to her, said 'Highest', told her their name and their craft, and thanked her.

When all were done with giving their respects, Sam took hold of Jandra's arm and began to walk back to their dwelling, while the arrivals went inside their temporary dwelling.

Jandra looked at Sam and could see that she was tired, "What were you doing with them, Sam?"

Sam halted and looked at Jandra, sadly, "They are so beaten. They are afraid of anything that but moves. The poor children were abused so overly young. These evils must be halted, Jandra."

Jandra kept Sam moving and waited a little while to respond. When she did, she measured her words carefully, "Sam, you take on the entire realm's sadness. You can't do this. Woden and I don't want to lose you. We will accept those who come to us, but we can't be sad for all The Realm. All you can do is but try to improve it, as we do. You worry overly at some moments, but worry does nothing. Only action will change it, and sadly, it will cost Woden many lives in this battle."

Sam nodded. While she was sad, she was also contented that perhaps she had eased the new arrivals hearts a little.

"How did the community meeting but go?"

"I will let Karan and Lillon tell you."

Jandra halted and turned Sam to her, "Sam, Highest of all of Woden. I want to tell you how very proud I am of you. You are the best to ever happen to Woden. But I am afraid I will lose you because of your selflessness. I am often grateful that I carry your child, as perhaps that will make you keep your sense of self about you. You know your unborn needs you. She needs you more than she needs me. I can't tell her of her Spirit Mothers. You are more like this child than I can be. When you think you do not enough for Woden, think again of your unborn. But know this Sam, I am proud of whatever you do and am most grateful to be your companion. My heart dances at the sight and sound of you. No other has ever led Woden such as you do. None such as you has but existed. No Highest has ever sat on the ground among their people and told such stories. These things I want you to know."

Sam looked sad, "It must be but a bad report from the community session."

Jandra placed her arm around Sam's shoulders and guided her gently back toward their dwelling, "Allow Lillon and Karan inform you, as you commanded of them."

They walked the remainder of the short way back in silence. When they arrived, Jandra opened the front door and motioned for Sam to go to the meeting room. She did, and saw that in it were all the advisors from Woden and Hengist. None were smiling. Sam now knew the report to be bad. She went and sat down, heavily.

They all knelt and bowed before her, "Highest."

"Please rise."

They did so and sat down.

Karan rose, "Highest, would you but like our report now?"

"Yes. I might as well."

Karan nodded and looked serious, "The community discussed the issues you but presented for a long while. While the discussion was open and with no hostility, as you but wished, there were conflicting ideas across all."

Sam nodded. It was as she hoped it would not be. A divided Woden. Fear had overtaken her people. They would now not move from their own spot of thinking, but chose to become more isolated.

"Many ideas were presented and discussed. The men and women looked at the strong and weak points of each. They were patient and would have made you but proud of them, Highest. They struggled all the midturn and after midturn with them, in order to please you, but I am afraid that there was only one point on which all agreed. Although it be only one point, Highest, it is important to note that every community member, all of Woden Falls, agreed on this one point."

Sam shrugged and wondered what it was, but already felt defeated. She had thought her people more open and accepting than this, but The Realm was a harsh place, so she would have to understand and accept it.

"What be the point they made, Karan?"

"Each woman and man of Woden Falls agreed, after long discussion of all the issues you but raised, that they were able to place their total trust in you to make the correct decisions for the future and peace of Woden Falls. They say to tell you that whatever you wish for Woden, they will support you. They say to tell you that the issues be yours to deal with, and they trust you to be wise and informative. And they say to tell you that they wish you well in your decisions, and they know that you will take care of their safety, peace, and freedom now and in the future."

Sam looked up, fully surprised. Then all the advisors began laughing, smiling and standing, slapping each other on the back for the joke they played on Sam. They had fooled her into thinking she had lost her ideas.

Karan asked, "Be you surprised, Highest?"

Sam stood, and smiled, dumbly, "I am all surprised. It is but a shock. It is but a gift from Woden."

Karan smiled at Sam, "They say to tell you also that they have never trusted a Highest so, but know that their trust be well-placed."

"I am but fortunate."

She turned to Jandra, "You but fooled me as well."

"All I said was how proud of you I am. I spoke truthfully, Sam. I am proud of you. I have never prior witnessed such a demonstration of love and respect as Woden has for you."

Lillon stepped forward and requested silence, "Highest, Karan does not speak entirely truthfully. There was one other item the community but agreed upon. When they reached the agreement on the point Karan made, then they reached one more."

Sam nodded, and waited, and stopped smiling.

"They agreed that this eve will be a celebration inside Woden, at the park for the beginning of a new Woden. They agreed to all bring food and wine, and the musicians and singers will entertain throughout the eve. You be the guest of honor. And they are also currently inviting all the new arrivals, as well. Highest, you need to prepare. Since you be the guest of honor, your presence is requested. As we speak and detain you, the celebration begins."

Lillon looked to Sam for approval, but continued, "Woden would like you to know, though, that they know this may be their last celebration for some moments in Woden, and hope you agree to it. The guards and sentries will trade off throughout the eve so that all can attend. Highest? What say you?"

All the advisors looked to Sam. They hoped her answer would be positive, as all of Woden was excited about their decision and good work this turn.

Sam looked at all her advisors, and then she turned to Jandra. She didn't smile, and her advisors were beginning to think she was upset or angry, "What think you, Jandra?"

Jandra smiled and took Sam's hand. She knew Sam well enough to know she was returning the jest, "I think you should wear your comfort garments this eve, at the celebration."

Sam nodded, yet not smiling, "Good choice. I will change."

Then she finally smiled, and all laughed. She couldn't believe what Karan and Lillon had told her. It was as a gift. The best gift of all.

"Will Hengist be here this eve, as well?"

"All. All will be there, Highest. Woden is now united, because of you, and all are pleased."

* * * *

The advisors left quickly so that Sam could prepare.

Jandra followed Sam to their bedroom to tend to her, "Are you pleased, my Highest?"

Sam held her, and kissed her gently. The kiss turned more passionate and Sam led Jandra to their bed. Jandra gave but a moment's thought to the celebration, and then decided that The Highest could be a few moments late.

After their pleasures, Jandra pulled Sam up out of the bed and got herself and Sam ready. She then pushed Sam out of their dwelling and took her arm. They walked to the celebration in the park, near the former Highest's dwelling. As they were walking, Jandra saw that Sam looked contented and pleased.

"Your training sessions begin in the morn?"

Sam nodded, "Do you but attend?"

"I do."

"What about our unborn?"

"I have worked it out with Caitha and Meera. I will learn basic defense for now, and Caitha will make sure that I do not overdo. I will also well learn the bow and arrow, as that will not be overly hard on this unborn. On the other hand, Meera is going to exhaust you in your preparations."

"This I know. She will make me but run around all of Woden. I need it, though. I be out of shape, and I need much endurance for this battle. Meera will make it so that none us tire during a long battle. It will be hard training so that the battle will be easier."

"It be good, but let us not think of battles this eve. Your people want you to know how much they think of you, Sam. Never prior has Woden trusted their leader so. You should be most proud of yourself."

"It be enough that you are but proud of me."

"This is not the Sam I know. But I thank you for it."

They arrived to the celebration that was already in full loudness and fun. Dancing and music were occurring, and everyone was eating from the long tables on which they had placed their donations. Lillon saw Sam arrive and took her to the place of honor. Some small tables and chairs had been placed near a patio, and Sam and Jandra were to sit there.

May came up, with helpers at her side, and delivered five plates of different types of foods, and two flasks of wine, with cups, "Here, Highest. Enjoy. Some fresh beer is finding its way to you from somewhere. It should be here soon."

Shallan came up to Sam, with her Birth-Mother. Shallan pointed to Meera's stomach, which didn't yet show signs of an unborn child, "Be that where you child is, Highest?"

Sam lifted Shallan into her lap, and laughed, "How do you know of this Shallan?"

"One of the nice guards told me so, Highest." She pointed to Jandra, "Is that the best Second in all of Woden's past?"

Sam nodded, "It be the very Second I spoke of in my story. Introduce yourself to her, Shallan."

Shallan got down off Sam's lap, went to Jandra, and climbed into her lap. She looked at Jandra and said, "I be Shallan. You are Second. Are you going to beat me?"

"Only if you don't have fun this eve. But I jest, Shallan. No one in Woden will beat you. You are to have fun and grow into a healthy member of Woden. Go eat, Shallan, and find some other children your cycle."

"I love you, Second."

Jandra looked at Sam and shrugged, not knowing what brought that on.

Sam looked to Shallan's Birth-Mother, "What are you called?"

The women paled and spoke softly, "I be but Shaland, Highest. Thank you for being kind to my Shallan. I have never known of such kindness from another."

Sam stood and placed her hand upon Shaland's head and sent a message of safety. She hoped it would be enough, "Go and enjoy the eve, Shaland."

Shaland bowed her head, "Thank you, Highest. Second." She turned and left.

Jandra was eating and urged Sam to do the same. They watched the dancing, listened to the musicians as everyone enjoyed the celebration.

When she finished eating, Jandra rose and held out her hand to Sam, "Come, Sam. I wish to dance with you. Drink your wine when we but return."

Most of Woden's dances occurred in small to large circles of dancers, with the dancers holding each other's hands to form a closed circle. As at the festival, they traditionally danced around a fire circle. This eve was no different. In a celebration such as this, most of the dances were quick and lively, with the dancers going round and round. During the dances, though, there were some that required pairs that stood apart from each other in long lines and would come together and separate in various forms. Sam had never danced much during her cycles, but would now gladly do as Jandra wished. All of Woden was pleased to see their Highest dance. Caitha dragged Meera over next to Sam and Jandra, and they all danced together for most the eve. The music was good and the musicians were in fine form. Extra tambourines were passed out to the dancers, and much laughter and merriment occurred. Even the children danced around their own small fire. After Jandra tired, they all returned to the tables and sat the rest of the eve watching, listening, greeting Woden's members, eating and drinking their wine.

As late after-mideve arrived, Meera turned to Sam, "It will be most difficult to rise at sun's rise early next turn. Be you prepared?"

"I am never desirous of such because of its purpose, but I will be there. We must prepare."

Meera and Caitha rose and took their leave.

Jandra looked at Sam and Sam noticed that she looked tired, "Jandra, let us go to our dwelling. It be overly late, and it has been but a busy turn."

"You just want to do as we did prior to this celebration."

"That was but a preparation for the eve."

Elsewhere, across The Realm

The High Queen was in her gardens staring out across her lake, when she heard her messenger arrive, "Give Me a good report. I have heard enough bad reports this turn to last Me a lifespan."

The messenger could tell that her Queen wasn't pleased about something, but knew not at what. "Good morn, my Queen. They become companions."

She sighed, "Pity. I find myself thinking about her lover. I wonder where she was born. Have you found nothing on this as yet?"

"There is nothing in all of Woden. Highness."

"What makes this lover so special?"

"Just looking at her and her beauty makes everyone desire to be near her, and to be loved by her. I have seen many horses come up to her on their own, and many birds and children. It is most unusual. Yet no one seems to notice as such."

"Is such difference so accepted as this in their tiny Woden?"

"It would appear as such, my Queen. Her lover begins her morn illness, now."

"So soon as this? But I forget. This is our Promised One. She will grow quickly. Anything else?"

"No, my Queen."

"Then leave Me, and report back to Me soon."

Chapter IX
Woden Prepares for Battle

The next morn came even prior to early, as Sam and Jandra had to be at the training fields at the sun's rise. After preparing in silence, they left for the training fields, which were just outside the west gates, close to Sam and Jandra's dwelling. The target bales were being placed into position as they arrived. It was an open area just before the farm and gardens, and Meera had already prior sectioned it off into different training areas. Keddi had been placed in-charge of bow and arrow training. Margeria had been placed in-charge of knife training. Meera had assigned herself to sword training. Ahkna had been charged with overseeing spear training. And Briggon was in-charge of slingshot training, all sizes, as well as filling in for Meera as necessary.

Sam had spoken to Jandra and together they had determined that Jandra would train only lightly. She would learn to throw and use a knife, a sword and a bow and arrow. Apart from that, she wouldn't participate. Sam had both her sword and knife with the stones newly embedded, and told herself to remember the strength now a part of the weapons. She didn't want to injure one of Woden's.

Now that Meera was in-charge of all the defense of Woden Falls, she commanded that all the guards and sentries, except for the ones on-duty, be in attendance. She began the training by having everyone run to the western boundary and back. She offered a prize of a new sword, made by Ivers, for the one who first returned. Sam sighed, and took off running with everyone else, including Meera. Jandra remained behind with Caitha, and waited. They were to be the judges of who arrived first.

After a long enough while, the winner returned, easily ahead of the rest. The winner was a young guard from Hengist, in his 17th cycle. The rest arrived in staggered patterns, Sam and Meera near the front.

While running, Sam noticed a woman of middle-cycles, "Who is that near the front, Second? Is that Anchen?"

Meera was panting heavily, as were all of them, "She is truly amazing, this one. And her sword abilities are beyond most of the guards."

Sam glanced over to Meera, "Is she from Woden?"

Meera shrugged as they continued to run, "Not by birth. She but says that she came from New Fornaith. But this was many cycles prior. She would be quite the warrior if she but desired it as so."

As everyone returned, Meera assigned them to groups, and the training began. After some practice and training on a particular weapon, Meera would have the groups shift to another. Sam had practiced with Keddi on bow and arrow, then on knife with Margeria.

She was particularly anxious to begin sword practice with her new stone-enhanced sword. She practiced on basic moves and worked with the stone's power. Meera practiced with her and saw that Sam could now easily swing her sword with much more power than any other. Meera was trying to think of ways that Sam could practice with her sword while not injuring any other, when a horse and rider appeared.

Sam saw that it was the Old One, and she went to her and helped her down from the horse. They greeted each other, and then the Old One told Sam what she must do with her sword.

Meera listened without interrupting until she heard the Old One say, "You must learn to throw this sword as you would your knife."

Meera interrupted, "She can't throw her sword. This be impossible. It weighs an overly amount."

The Old One just looked at Meera, and then replied, "Make it not impossible. She must be able to throw this sword as she would her knife. And at a great distance."

Meera looked surprised, but asked, "How does one throw a sword?"

The Old One nodded, "It is a fair question or I would not bother to answer you. Two ways she must be able to do so. Over her head from her back, straight out, using both hands and arms. And by either hand, by the hilt. Either way, it will turn end-over-end, so she must practice her aim, strength, distance and landing."

The Old One turned back to Sam, "You must learn this quickly as the moments but run out. I am here to teach you the ways you will need in order to defeat Buron. He but grows overly strong. You must gain your powers."

The Old One made a mark on a distant large tree and returned, "You will not halt this turn until your sword enters this tree. You will begin by trying the over-the-head throw. With each throw, you will run to the tree, retrieve your sword, and run to return. When you tire, draw on your inner powers to ignore the pain, and focus. You are to teach yourself to feel no pain. You have been given this ability. You must now learn to use it. I leave to go to your dwelling to eat and drink. I will know when you hit your target."

The Old One left, and Sam sighed to Meera, "Any ideas on how I am supposed to do this?"

Meera shrugged, "I know not of this, but will oversee it. Perhaps I can gain some idea while I but watch. This will be most tiring, Highest. I have never seen nor heard of such a thing, prior."

"Does nothing come easy?"

Meera laughed, "The ones I am about to make run again to the border and back think not. I will return in a while, Highest, to check on you."

"At least I do not run again this turn."

"I would rather run than do what you must learn."

Sam held the sword over her head and down behind her back. She then took what aim she thought she could and threw the sword forward. It was an awful attempt from the beginning. Sam had arched overly backwards and had lost her balance as she threw the sword. The sword left her hands overly early and flew high into the air. As it landed, far from its intended mark, the ground exploded with a small bursting sound, and a small fire began. Sam ran to her sword to recover it and saw that where the sword fell into the ground was now a hole the size of a small child. Sam shook her head, ran back to the start, and tried again. Jandra and Caitha watched from a distance, wondering when Sam would tire. Over and over again, Sam threw the sword. Jandra and Caitha tired of watching after a while and continued with their knife-throwing practice.

Throughout the midturn, Sam continued to practice. Meera watched and made note of some improvement but had need to train the others. Jandra and Caitha moved to training on bow and arrow. Meera had no idea how Sam continued to have the strength to pick up the sword and throw it so. She saw the impact of the sword upon the ground and wondered what would occur when Sam finally did hit her target. By after midturn, when Meera concluded the turn's training by making everyone run once again to the border and back, Sam hadn't yet hit her target. She felt sorry for Sam, but went on the run with the others. Jandra and Caitha continued to practice with the bows and arrows, but took moments to watch Sam. They noticed that her throws were now longer, but yet not close to her target, nor accurate. With each throw, they saw that Sam would stand, stare, as if in thinking, take a stance, and then throw her sword again. With each landing, the ground exploded.

After the runners returned, Meera dismissed them for the turn. They would begin their training again at the next turn's sun's rise. All were exhausted and sore, and all gratefully returned to their dwellings. Meera, Caitha, and Jandra sat together and watched Sam practice. Occasionally,

Meera would go to her and offer some possibilities for improvement, and then return.

Jandra asked Meera, "How does she continue to lift and throw the sword?"

Meera shook her head, confused at Sam's effort, "In truth, I know not. I could not do so. Sam is a driven one. It is like she knows something we know not. It is as if she knows that our success but depends on her, solely. She knows not that life exists at this moment, she be so overly focused."

Caitha asked, "How long will she but practice?"

"The Old One said that she will remain here until she but hits her mark."

Jandra's eyes were narrowed, "I know not why we trust this one so. I, for one, do not."

Caitha rose, "I leave to get us food and drink. I will return. Jandra must eat."

Caitha returned and they ate their meal. Sam wouldn't leave her practice, so Meera but fed her some bites and gave her some drink. The late after midturn turned into early eve. Then into eve. And yet Sam hadn't hit her mark, nor had come close. Sam continued to practice, never halting to rest. As late after-eve began to approach and the sun's setting began, Sam's throw hit the tree. Although none of the three had been watching, they heard the explosion and saw the tree fall over, consumed in flames. Sam just stood in her spot, staring and unbelieving. She had finally done it. She fell on her knees to the ground and continued to stare as the tree burned. She could barely lift her arms further.

Jandra got up and went to her, "Sam, you did it. You must rest now. You have done enough."

Meera and Caitha came over as well, and Meera went to the tree to retrieve the sword. She couldn't get close enough to get it, as the flames were all around the sword.

The Old One had arrived, "It be late enough. What took you overly long?" She looked at the tree and then to Sam, "Go retrieve your sword. Protect yourself with your inner powers."

Sam looked at her, yet on her knees, so about equal to the Old One, "I will but burn."

"Do not speak back. You have the ability to avoid such. Go." The Old One pointed to the tree, "Get your sword. Only you will be able to remove it from there."

Sam struggled to rise, exhausted. She walked to the burning tree, focused and then reached into the flames to remove her sword. She pulled it out easily, and then returned. The sword was almost red hot from the flames, but the Old One smiled, "Finally, you begin to learn. You are a slow one. But worry not; these other humans such as you are even slower. Go rest and eat. You begin again in the morn. You will continue this practice until you can do this upon each throw. I will mark another tree for your next turn's practice. The Spirit Mothers will come soon to help you with but another ability you must have in order to fight Buron. Where do I sleep this eve?"

Caitha placed her arms around the Old One, "Would you like to come with us this eve? I will make you a special meal and give you some fresh beer. I have a nice spare bed you may use. Would that but suit you?"

The Old One considered, and then nodded. She turned to Jandra, "I will spend part of my turn with you in a few turns. I have much to share with you."

Jandra looked at her, frowning, "Forgive me if I anger you, Spirit Mother, but how do we know that the Spirits of the Valley or queen you speak of truly be our enemy?"

The Old One's eyebrows wrinkled into a deep frown, "You do not believe easily, Birth-Mother. And you are intelligent. I will speak to you of this later, and will try to answer your question so that you feel you can trust us. Will that do for now?"

"Until then."

Sam could barely walk to the dwelling. She felt old and tired. Jandra walked beside her, concerned, but knowing she could do nothing except be supportive. When they arrived to the dwelling, Jandra had Sam sit at the kitchen table and made her eat. May had returned so that she could make part of the meal fresh for Sam. Jandra had a hot bath prepared for Sam while she ate. When Sam finished eating, Jandra helped her to remove her garments and helped her into the hot bath. May entered and began massaging Sam's upper arm muscles and back. Jandra brought a plate of food in with her while she sat next to Sam's bath so that she might eat as well.

When her soaking bath and massage were completed, May placed Sam's bedshirt on her, and Sam fell into the bed, asleep as she hit her pillow. The eve flew quickly by, and Sam found herself being awoken by Jandra just prior to the sun's rise. The turn went as it had prior. Meera required that Sam warm up her muscles prior to beginning her sword throwing, and the Old One nodded her consent. After Sam stretched out her muscles, and although Sam could barely move her arms, she practiced throwing her sword over and over again.

The Old One had marked another tree. This tree was smaller and a little further away. Jandra wondered why Sam was so intent and focused in her practice, but had no opportunity to speak with her. When Sam was not practicing, she was eating or sleeping, and was so exhausted while she ate that she was almost sleeping then, as well. The Second turn of practice went the same of the first turn's. All practiced and ran, and Sam spent the turn throwing her sword. Her distance improved, but her aim was yet poor. Throughout the turn, Sam practiced. As everyone else returned to their dwellings at the end of the training, Sam was yet throwing her sword. Once again, Meera, Caitha, and Jandra sat and waited. As prior, Meera offered pointers as she could. As the eve came, Jandra looked up just at the moment Sam's sword found its mark. As the turn prior, the tree fell over in flames. Sam recovered her sword and the eve became yet another repeated pattern.

Sam's arms hung at her sides as if broken. Her back was so sore she could barely rise from her bed the next morn. Yet, the Old One marked another tree. Once again, more distant, and once again, smaller. The turns passed the same, with Sam becoming stronger and more accurate. By the fifth turn, Sam hit her mark just after midturn. The Old One came and marked another tree, and made her continue. By early eve, Sam hit her Second mark of the turn.

The sixth turn showed greater signs of improvement. Sam's back felt stronger and needed less of her inner powers to mask the great pain she felt. She had been in such pain of late that she could barely breathe, let alone speak to her friends and companion. At the sun's rise of the sixth turn, and just after the Old One marked another tree more distant and smaller, Sam threw her sword once, and hit her mark. The Old One continued to mark trees further and smaller all morn, and Sam continued to throw the sword and hit her mark within a few tries. Her stance had improved to the point where her aim, strength and endurance could now be consistent. Yet, the Old One yelled at her whenever she missed.

"You must not miss. EVER! You must not. Each throw must be accurate. You have but one chance. You concentrate not enough. You use not your powers to see. You use your eyes. Each throw much be perfect. You will practice this turn until you are able to hit ten consistent marks."

Sam listened and showed no emotion, although she was overly exhausted. Meera used her as an example whenever her guards and sentries complained. They would look at Sam, shake their heads in disbelief, then remain uncomplaining for the remainder of the training session. Meera had increased their running to longer distances. She made them move quicker in their practice and she made them move heavy objects from one spot to another, and then back again. She also insisted that they strengthen both their arms equally.

Meera's voice was raw and hoarse from shouting her continual demands.

By late midturn, after all the others had completed their practice, Sam had finally hit her mark ten throws in a row. The Old One then made Sam hold heavy rocks in her hands, straight out from her sides. She told Sam to raise and lower them 100 up-and-down moves.

Jandra began to protest, but Meera halted her, "Sam will need this strength, Jandra, if you want her to survive."

"It be overly much, Meera. The Old One is overly hard on her. It is as if she hates her and wants her to fail."

Meera shook her head, "No, Jandra. In truth, the Old One wants Sam to succeed and pushes her so that she will. This will be no easy battle for any of us, but it will be most difficult for Sam. If you want her to live, you must not protest. Sam must become stronger. She must pass the point of pain."

Jandra stood, angry, "Woden seems to overly trust this Old One. I have heard no reason for such trust as this. We have always made our own way. It doesn't seem they do us any favors. But what choice do I have?"

On the seventh turn, Meera began the training session by having all the trainees run the perimeter of all of Woden. It would take the turn, but she cared not. She went with them. Jandra and Caitha continued their knife and bow and arrow practice, and watched Sam as they rested. Woden was quiet these turns, as most were occupied with training for battle. The other women and men worked together to keep the farms and fisheries up so that the stocks of food would be safe. Woden was focused on the upcoming battle, and few new projects were being started.

Soon after Meera's group began their run of the perimeter, four horses arrived, with riders. Sam had few around to help battle them, if necessary, and hoped it would not be needed. As she looked to the horses, she saw that they were not as Woden's horses. These were special horses, almost magical. They ran swiftly, but it was as if their feet didn't touch the ground, and yet they made great sounds as they approached. As they neared, Sam saw who it was, and knelt and bowed her head. She waited in that position until they arrived and dismounted. Her Spirit Mothers had come to Woden to help Sam gain the strength she would need. The Old One also saw them come up and went and stood next to Sam, saying nothing. She waited patiently. The Spirit Mothers dismounted and went to Sam and the Old One. Nothing was said between them that Jandra or Caitha could hear.

Li'el'in'tiln laid her hands gently upon Sam's head, *Our daughter. It has been long since we have met. Rise and meet us.*

Jandra was stunned as she looked at the Spirit Mothers, if indeed they were as such. They were very tall, and flowing. She couldn't understand the flowing part, but it was the only way she could think to describe them. Their garment colors were the colors of water. Their hair was the longest she had ever seen prior. All four of them seemed to have the same height, hair and garments. When they walked, it was as if they floated.

Let us introduce ourselves before we begin providing you with what you will need to win your battle against this Buron. I am Li'el'in'tiln. And these are Suren'tin'dil', Muristil'n', and Fin'nin'don'nil.

Sam bowed her head as each one was introduced. She knew not what to say to each, so said nothing.

We are here to give you the ability to use your eyes as weapons. You may have noticed that your eyes have changed of late. We will provide you with the power to use them as such, but you will need to practice to develop the skill. Unfortunately, we are unable to give you the skill as well.

At one point during the discussion, the Spirit Mothers' four horses all looked at Jandra, then looked back to their Spirit Mothers. Seeing that they were unwatched, they wandered quietly over to her. They came up close, almost scaring her. She rose from where she sat and let them nudge her with their noses. She knew not what they wanted, but patted their noses and scratched their ears a bit, laughing quietly. They were beautiful horses and she thought them very friendly. When Caitha rose and tried to touch them, they moved away.

"Jandra, why do they come to you, such as this?"

"I know not, but are they not most wonderful?"

After a few moments, they each nudged her softly, once again, then left.

Caitha shook her head, fully dismayed at this sight. Jandra didn't think on it much. She and Caitha watched Sam and the Spirit Mothers, but grew impatient. The only thing they were able to see were the group staring at each other. No words were spoken. No movement used. And no practice done. Sam stood with her Spirit Mothers and listened. After a while, Jandra and Caitha saw Sam kneel once again, and bow her head. She remained this way as each Spirit Mother came to her and placed her hands upon Sam's head. With the exception of each Spirit Mother moving their head slightly backward as if in deep thought, nothing occurred that Jandra and Caitha could see. When all four had done the same thing, they each gave Sam a kiss on her cheek, returned to their horses, and left as quickly as they had come. Sam stood as they began to leave.

As soon as they were gone, the Old One began Sam's practice with the weights, "125!"

When Sam finished, and her arms hung limply at her side, the Old One gave Sam her sword, "Throw it with your right arm. You practice until you hit your mark."

The Old One marked a large tree at a middle distance away. Sam practiced, throwing the sword with one-arm over and over again. It felt clumsy and awkward to Sam after having perfected the over-head throw, and she felt frustrated. While all of Woden could run the perimeter, she was stuck throwing the same sword over and over again.

Upon Meera's return from the perimeter run, and unknown to Sam during her training, all the women and men most recently rescued from Apien and New Harborage approached Meera.

One spokeswoman for the group approached Meera, "Woden be our home, now. We wish to fight in this battle to protect her. We ask you to help train us."

Meera shook her head, "You yet be overly weak from your battles."

She lowered her brows, "We forget not the wrongs they have done to us. This cannot happen again. We will fight, either trained or untrained. It be up to you. We will but have our moment with these evil ones. And if that Manthar be with them, he be ours."

Meera considered, "You will train as I but command. I will not have you counter my commands. I will provide you weapons, but not one command may be questioned, or you remain on your own."

"Yes, Second. We understand and will follow your orders. Please make us useful."

The remainder of the runners began to re-enter the training grounds at late after-midturn. Sam had yet to hit her mark. Once again, the familiar pattern continued. Meera, Jandra and Caitha waited until Sam finally hit the tree. She did so by early eve, and as she was preparing for her first early rest in seven turns, the Old One returned and motioned to the rocks, "150, then you can rest."

Sam could barely lift her right arm by itself, but to add the weight of the rock seemed impossible. She focused and centered her breathing. Slowly, she began the movements. One by one, until late eve, she completed the sets.

The eighth turn brought more of the same for all. Meera kept the practice intense and focused, while Sam was ordered to throw using her left arm this turn. This turn, however, just following the Old One marking the tree, she had Sam kneel before her. Sam did so and bowed her head. The Old One placed her grubby small hands upon Sam's head, and Jandra saw that they remained this way for many, many long moments. She wondered what the Old One was giving to Sam, but continued her own knife practice. Margeria had told Jandra that she was becoming a master of knife throwing, and in truth, Jandra could now throw a knife most accurately to far targets. Her bow and arrow practice was also improving.

When Sam rose, no one could see the brightness and clarity of her eyes. They shone as the sun on water. She began her practice with the rocks. These were heavier this turn, and she did 150 sets. When completed, she lifted her sword and threw it with her left arm, her strongest.

On her fourth attempt, she hit her target. Throughout the turn, the Old One would mark a tree, each more distant and smaller than the prior, and Sam would trade between arms. By the end of the turn, at the eve, Sam was able to throw her sword from either arm or from over-head and hit her mark.

Meera, Jandra, and Caitha heard Sam speak for the first in many turns during practice, "Have I but gained the skill you require of me?"

The Old One shook her head and hissed, "No. Next turn is with blinders. You must be able to throw accurately when blind, after only the briefest of glances at your target." She motioned to the rocks, these heavier than even the morn's, "175!"

Sam and Jandra returned late-eve. The routine was set as all those prior. Sam ate while Jandra prepared her bath. Jandra ate while watching Sam soak in the hot water. May continued to massage Sam's arms, shoulders and back.

This turn, May looked at her more carefully, "Highest, your body but looks more, I know not, more angular. You look overly strong. Feel her muscles, Jandra. Her arms are twice their normal size."

Jandra nodded, "I have seen these changes in her. She looks a different person these turns. Look at her eyes, May. They yet change again. They look as if she looks through one, now. It no longer looks like she looks at me. It is a strange feeling."

Sam listened, "I am not yet strong enough. Much relies on my powers and my ability to use them."

May kept massaging her but said, "Are you not exhausted, Highest? Perhaps you should rest but one turn."

"If I but lose this battle, May, I can rest the remainder of all The Realm and eternity. Buron has much strength. The Old One tells me that he be also large of body and has much more the strength than I have. She gives me hope, though. She says that while he has most the same powers as I, he has not developed them as I have been trained, and he has not the endurance."

Jandra and May spoke for a while as Sam soaked in the hot water. They then noticed that Sam's head bent down, and that Sam had fallen asleep in her bath.

The next turn, Meera asked Sam to practice swords with her as a warm-up. The Old One nodded in compliance, "For a short moment, only. You have much to accomplish this turn."

Sam unsheathed her sword and moved it as if it had no weight at all. Meera touched her sword to Sam's, as their tradition, and they began. Meera made as if to take a large swing at Sam, and Sam swung her sword toward Meera's with both hands, the swing at full strength. When it hit

Meera's sword, the power of Sam's swing broke Meera's sword in half. Meera dropped the sword part she was holding, and held her wrist with her other hand.

She looked at Sam, "Your strength is but scary now, Sam."

Sam sheathed her own sword and asked a guard for one of hers. Meera got another sword from a guard, and they began again. Meera lunged toward Sam and Sam brought her sword around with one hand, hit Meera's sword with it, but on this swing, instead of just breaking Meera's sword, both swords broke in half. Meera put down the broken half of her sword and held her wrist tightly. It had twisted badly in the force. The Old One came over and placed her hand to Meera's wrist. When she removed it, the wrist was healed. She looked to Sam and bid her to kneel. Sam did so. The Old One placed her hands upon Sam's head, and the thoughts flew between them with the span of a breath.

Use not your weapons against them. Use your mental powers to halt their attacks.
I will but hurt them.
Do not do so. Halt them without hurting them.
How?
You must learn to do so. Focus. Move their weapons away from them. Trip them. Have their arrows fly somewhere else. It is only with Buron that you now need a weapon. With these humans, you will but kill them in one blow. Halt their feet. Turn them around. Temporarily blind them. You know of your powers. Now look closely at them and use your brain. Do not be a stupid one.

Sam rose. The Old One told Meera, "Have five attack her with their weapons."

Meera shook her head, "It be unfair odds."

"I know it, but she will not hurt them."

Meera looked startled, having the reverse meaning, but chose five guards and motioned for them to attack Sam. They did so only mildly, as they didn't wish to hurt The Highest. Sam made no move until they got close. As they raised their swords, she held out her hand and sent her power to their weapons. Their swords flew from their hands. Meera motioned for some archers to take aim and told them to aim around her. They pulled their bows. As Sam readied to halt their bows as she had done with the swords, she heard the Old One's thoughts race through her mind:

Do not remove their bows. Do it differently. What think you?
I could but try to change the direction of their arrows.
Good. If there were enemies behind you, you could send the arrows toward them. Use the maximum efficiency. Use their own weapons against one another. Where do they but aim? Can you feel the direction of the aim?

Sam nodded and waited until they pulled their arrows. She then forced her power to the arrows and sent all the arrows into a tree directly behind her.

Good. You must be able to direct your sword's aim in the same fashion.

It be overly heavy. My mind can't control it.

It can. It must! Take your sword and throw it backwards to the tree you sent the arrows. Do not look at the tree again. See it in your head and see where you but want it to hit.

This be ridiculous. I but try.

Sam unsheathed her sword and threw it backwards with both hands. She saw the tree in her head as if it were in front of her. The sight amazed her, and the sword hit its mark.

Meera shook her head, "We do not need to train. You will but halt all of them."

The Old One spoke harshly to Meera and to all that would listen, "Woden must tend to Woden. Your Highest's battle will consume all her powers. Her battle is with Buron. Not all of Woden combined will halt Buron. If Sam does not, the battle is lost. If she defeats Buron, she will have few powers left to call upon to help you. Woden must tend to Woden. Sam will tend to Buron."

Meera nodded, "It will be so, then."

The Old One nodded back to her, "Train them harder. There be many more than what you have. Your numbers be low against them. Your odds will be 5:1, but Woden will fight stronger and better. Half their forces are innocents. You should save them if you can. They will be sent first."

She then turned to everyone and yelled at them, "Train harder. Your life will but depend on it."

They trained again. And the next turn, and the next. They all worked harder. Meera began warning sessions. When the enemy approached, she taught them signals to warn Woden. Horns would be used. The signal codes were given, and each turn, they practiced their warnings and attacks. Sam continued to train on her own. The Old One had her train until mideve every turn now. Sam had to run to the border, back to the harbor, return to the border, then back to the training grounds. The Old One now made her throw her sword in an instant's notice, and expected a perfect throw with each. She made Sam practice throwing her knife with a deadly aim. She made Sam practice throwing without seeing. Lifting heavier weights, more sets. On one turn, the Old One set up a dummy near a tree.

"This be Jandra. The tree be Buron. Buron has captured Jandra. You have but one throw to save her before he breaks her neck. Now."

Sam threw her sword. It hit perfectly in the middle of . . . Jandra, the dummy.

The Old One made Sam turn her back, readied a different set up, and then said "Now." She gave Sam an instant to throw a long distance, with perfect accuracy. When Sam failed, the Old One shook her head and looked disappointed. Sam practiced until the moon rose. The Old One then made her throw her knife first, then her sword in an instant after. Then in the reverse. Once, she tripped Sam as she was ready to throw her sword, then yelled at her for not throwing it as she fell. The next moment this occurred, Sam threw the sword in mid-fall.

The practice sessions grew longer and harder. Everyone in Woden was getting stronger, and with improved aim. They learned to fight in teams. In pairs. To attack smart. To think. To be defensive and yet aggressive. Everyone could now use a bow and arrow with good accuracy, throw a knife with good aim, use a sword smartly, and use and throw spears. Defenses were prepared. Traps were set. And everyone kept training. More and more of the community's people began to train with them. Liley laughed and complained that everyone was eating four more the amounts per meal than normal.

By the twenty-third turn, the Old One felt Sam ready as possible. She had fire thrown at her, and Sam repelled it. She made Sam throw her sword from a charging horse. From a tree. Run long whiles. Sam, and all the others, were now stronger looking than they had ever been. They could now fight all turn without tiring. None needed a soaking bath every eve.

Jandra wondered about the Old One, "If she be so all-seeing as this, and with this many powers to her, why does she not but fight this Buron, or just kill him?"

Caitha just shrugged, "I know not, M'Love. Have you asked Sam?"

Jandra nodded, then shook her head in dismay, "I have upon many occasions, but she is not listening. Her devotion to this Old One is without question."

The Old One sat them all down on the twenty-fourth turn, "You are ready. Prepare yourselves as they but come. Be not afraid and have no fear. You have trained well and hard."

She turned to Sam; *I will now take Jandra and Caitha with me to your Spirit Mothers.*

And Tadan.
It cannot be so.
It will be so. He be also the future of Woden.
It be not allowed.
Then make but an exception.
No.
I have no patience for this, Grandmother. It must be so.
Do not show me this disrespect.

Sam turned and stared at a tree, angry. Suddenly, the tree burst into flames. The women and men just stared, wide-eyed, but couldn't know what was occurring. Jandra worried about what was happening between the two.

It will be so or we but pull up the fight and give in to Buron. You have but used me to fight your battle against the Spirits of the Valley. That be what this fight about. You do not fool me, Grandmother. It is you and the Spirit Mothers of the Falls who have but allowed this to occur. You must take Tadan.

Sam softened, knelt and bowed her head, *Please. I need this so, Grandmother of all grandmothers.*

The Old One pursed her lips together, but nodded, *I will do this for you. It is a small enough favor. I will leave with them as soon as they can be but prepared. Buron and his force will arrive by the next turn after. I will see of your battle in the mirror of the water. Lead your people well.*

Sam nodded and rose, "Thank you, Old One. I will have them prepare now."

Sam went to Briggon and told him what she wanted. He agreed and sent a messenger to retrieve Tadan and his supplies. Sam informed Meera to have Caitha prepare for leaving immediately, and had a guard prepare six horses. Then she told Keddi and Margeria to make haste in their travel, but to return more hastily.

The Old One went to Jandra and bid her kneel. Jandra did so, reluctantly. The Spirit Mother placed her hands upon Jandra's head and began her story:

It is the moment that I will now answer your questions. Jandra of Woden, you but carry the future of all The Realm. You must now leave with me to protect you and our unborn. Many come to Woden now to make it fall. Buron comes for you and for Sam. He comes to kill you both. The Spirits of the Valley have prepared him for this battle as I have but prepared Sam. He is of them as Sam is of your Spirit Mothers and me. But he be stupid. Sam will but win because of her intelligence.

Many, many cycles prior, the spirits were the only inhabitants of this realm. When the likes of you came, which was not foretold in the legends, and which was vowed otherwise, the Spirits of the Valley, and their queen, wanted to use you to control The Realm and all the other Spirit Mothers. We wish not to control, but to live together in peace. We foresaw not the evilness of the Spirits of the Valley. In order to prevent your kind from eons of slavery and evil, and ourselves as well, we had to but mix with your kind to give us Sam so that we might win over the Spirits of the Valley and their queen.

I know your thoughts, Jandra, and no. If Sam but wins the battle over Buron, only this battle with him be over. We must then fight the queen and Spirits of the Valley, but that will be across other cycles. Your daughter that is part of you, part of Sam, and part of us, will become the key to peace in all The Realm. But that be far distant from now, Jandra, as Sam and you, if we but win our battles, will live to see The Realm grow and prosper across many, many long cycles from now.

I take you now to what is but a strange place for you. Worry not. You will be well tended. We also take Caitha and Tadan with us. The child you carry will know this place and feel comforted in it. You will come to know your child's ancestors and stories. Go now and prepare. We have a long journey ahead of us. Sam must now focus only on one thing: Buron. It will comfort her to know that you be safe. I will send her a message when we arrive.

Jandra looked up at the Old One but said nothing. She didn't trust these Spirits, but would say nothing to them about it, as she felt it useless. She knew that none of her real questions had been addressed. She then rose and went to Sam, "Come and help me to prepare. We take our leave."

"It is with a mixed heart I let you go."

They went to their dwelling together. When they returned, the rest of the travelers were ready. Tadan was already mounted and looking excited about the trip. Briggon was speaking to him, and Tadan was nodding.

Sam went to Tadan, "You will now see what no man has been allowed. I send you to protect you. In kind, you must tend and protect Jandra and my unborn child. You be the future of Woden as well, Tadan. Do not overtalk to my Spirit Mothers. Learn as much as you can, and take care of my Jandra. The unborn will be but your leader in cycles to come, so learn of her well."

"Yes, Highest Mother. I am most anxious to meet our Spirit Mothers. I will tend to Second and your unborn, as you request. Remember, she be my family, in a sense."

Sam went to Keddi and Margeria and wished them safe and speedy travel. They prepared lightly, and only with weapons. Keddi and Margeria both carried three full bags of arrows.

She then went to Caitha, "Friend. Thank you for going with my Jandra. I know that Meera will miss you, but I also know she wants you safe. It eases my heart to know that you are with Jandra. Take care of yourself and of Jandra. Meera and I will come to retrieve you when the battle be over. Worry not, Caitha."

Caitha just smiled and touched Sam's cheek.

Sam then went to Jandra, who waited by her horse. She hugged and kissed her their farewell.

"Jandra, be safe. If I but know you are safe, my mind can focus more on what I must now do. Take care of yourself and know that I but miss you and think of you. We will come for you and Caitha as soon as the battle be over." Sam laughed, "And Tadan will keep you well entertained."

Jandra smiled and hugged Sam again, "Live, Sam. That be all that matters. As the Old One said, let Woden take care of Woden. You must focus only on Buron."

"I will miss you, Jandra."

"And I you, old warrior woman. Go now, and be not sad. Return to me quickly as I can't wait long without you."

Sam went to the Old One, *Take care of my Jandra, Grandmother.*

I will do as such. Worry not for her. When you kill Buron, you must do as I say, Sam: remove his eyes and his heart and burn them quickly, or he will but return to the Spirits of the Valley. Do not hesitate in this act. Remember that he be far stronger than you, but he be stupid. Fight smart, as Meera has trained Woden to do. Engage him not in swordplay. He is overly strong for you. And know that he can also but throw a sword as you, but not with either his arms, only his right. When you move to kill him, think not him dead overly soon. Kill him twice or more. Use your sword and your knife. And one last item, Granddaughter: He has not the same power of your eyes. Use them. Practice with them these next turns. Your eyes, Sam. Remember to use your eyes not to see, as your mind can now do that for you, but as weapons.

Come to me when you but win. We will tend to your wounds. I have given you all I can for now. It will be enough if you but remember and remain smart. Take good care of Meera, as I have come to like her and that Caitha of hers.

Sam laughed and hugged her, then set her up on her horse. Sam gave a slap to the horse's rump, and Keddi led the others out to their journey. Jandra turned and waved to Sam, and Sam did likewise. As the horses moved off into the forest and out of Sam's eyesight, Sam and Meera walked back to the training grounds to begin again.

"Sam, did you mean to catch that tree on fire when you but looked at it?"

"No. I knew not I could do as such. The Old One but told me just now to practice using my eyes not as sighting agents but as weapons. Buron has no such ability."

"That at least, be a good report."

Sam slapped Meera on the back, "Let us eat our eve meal together this eve."

"Good. Now, get back to your training. Go practice using your eyes as weapons."

"I will do so. At least I don't run this turn."

"Wrong. You run to the border, back to the harbor, back to the border, and return. Practice with your eyes as you but run. And run faster and harder this turn. You but run lazy."

"You are a hard trainer."

"Carry your weapons with you, and carry a heavy rock. Now go. RUN!"

Sam began, and Meera went to her forces, "We prepare this turn. Let us practice our signals and responses. Go! Run softly and swiftly. I want no errors this turn."

Meera hadn't gotten used to the advisors training as hard as all her guards, but she was proud of them. They were now better than her guards had been when they had begun the training. But she wasn't pleased to learn that the odds would be five-to-one. She knew that they would have to equalize it to the better at the very beginning of the battle. At least the Old One had informed her that the beginning forces against them were untrained and innocents who didn't wish to fight. Meera had informed her forces of such, and they had developed plans to merely injure them and then remove them from the battlefield. Meera guessed that this would narrow the odds to four- or three-to-one. Their traps and tricks would narrow it further, but from there, each of hers would have to take out three or four of their forces. Meera knew that this would be a tough battle. But all of Hengist and Woden were now prepared.

As eve came, the training halted and Meera sent everyone to their dwellings, "From the morn on, we all but become on-guard and prepared for battle. This be your last eve in comfort until after the battle."

Elsewhere, across The Realm

Kneeling, with head bowed, she said, "The battle occurs next turn, my Queen."

"Can they win this battle?"

"They can, but with great loss, Highness. We could take out one of Buron's forces prior to its arrival and make it much easier on them, without anyone noticing."

The High Queen thought for a moment, then nodded, "Do as such. But make certain you are unseen, and that there are no survivors, and no remains."

"It will be as such, Highness."

"Has she gained her powers?"

"They are not even close to yours, my Queen, but she has some. The Spirits of the Falls came and told her to use her eyes as weapons."

"Is this all? This miserable little power? Nothing else?"

"The leader of the Spirits has trained her hard, my Queen."

"FOOLS! They cannot be trusted. And why would those Spirit Mothers train her when they have lied to her?"

"I know not, my Queen. I can only guess that they try to hide what they do so we don't find out."

She sighed her displeasure, "Perhaps. But it is most quizzical. Perhaps the deception is greater than I first believed. But what of her lover? She fights in this battle as well? She should be protected now. Can we do so for them?"

"She has gone to the Spirits of the Falls until after the battle."

The High Queen shook her head, "I don't like this, but at least she and the unborn will be safe. And their companionship?"

"It seems to be well, for the moment. My Queen, there is something most interesting about her lover. Her lover questions Woden's absolute obedience to the Spirits."

"Oh?"

"She has asked upon many occasions what proof there is that the queen and Spirits of the Valley are their enemies."

"And the answer she is given?"

"She is given no answer, my Queen. Her challenges go unheeded."

"They are also fools, then. She sounds most intelligent. How goes this pregnancy?"

"She yet has the morn illness, and already feels the unborn move."

The High Queen nodded, but said nothing.

"The Highest has made the Spirits of the Falls take in Tadan, as well."

The High Queen laughed, "She shows some spirit, anyway. That should be amusing for you to watch. Tell Me more of the lover. How does she fare?"

"She grew angry with what they call the Old One, and challenged her directly. I also saw the Spirit Mothers' horses go up to her while they spoke with The Highest. They walked over to her on their own and nuzzled her for many moments. She laughed softly to them, and petted them. Nothing more. And the new children that arrive in Woden from all across their landmass love her even though they know her not."

"What powers does she have?"

"None, my Queen."

The High Queen turned her head slightly to the side, thinking, "This brings forth a memory that I cannot call into place. Something about that story makes Me wonder, though. Have you yet found out where she comes from?"

"No, Highness. No one knows. We even searched the town records. All we know is that she was orphaned at their gates. They raised her, but she is not of them."

"Is she human?"

"I cannot say, Highness. Being in Woden, I would guess as much, and she has no powers that she uses."

"Make certain they win this battle against Fornaith. Have you found who this High Priestess is, as yet?"

"No, my Queen. She remains a mystery. It seems that even Buron knows not of this. She seems to arrive out of nowhere. But Buron knows little of anything, anyway. All he wants is power."

The High Queen waived her hand, dismissing the notion, "I know this already. He is boring and oafish. I should have had him killed. You know that we will have to take this child from the Spirit Mothers."

"Yes, my Queen."

"Then prepare to do so, as it will create more fighting. Much more fighting. All our enemies wish to see this child remain unborn. The Realm will challenge Me on this decision."

"Yes, my Queen. I am preparing your forces as we speak. They will be ready."

The High Queen looked upon her messenger, "I know that Buron will not live, but she must not die. Let her do this battle against him, but ensure that she lives. She will kill him, but I cannot have him kill her. But no one must see you. And help save that little town of hers. Those women need more help."

"And men, Highness."

"Ah, yes. I forget that little men's town. Do they fight as well?"

"Yes, Highness. They joined together in the battle preparations."

"Good. Report to Me immediately of the outcome."

"Yes, my Queen."

Chapter X
Woden's Battle

Sam and Meera ate on the patio. May fed them well and lots. They then slept. Meera slept on the long chair in the meeting room. They both slept fitfully and rose early, struggling against their eve visions. Sam noticed that she now felt odd without Jandra next to her. From the sun's rise on, Woden was on watch. Meera held her control in the north park. From there, she issued all her commands.

The turn moved slowly. Sam used her moments to practice using her eyes as weapons. Once, accidentally, Sam looked at a bird in flight and saw that she had turned it into a ball of fire that plummeted to the ground. She was saddened by such a senseless death and remained angry with herself for her own carelessness. Suddenly, Sam saw movement in her brain. She sent her mind to scan the forests and sea. She saw them coming. Her eyes could see at a distance, and she hadn't known.

"Meera. They but come."

"You have but the same sight as the Old One. From what direction do they come?"

"From our north, along the shore, through the forest. That be one group. Another group comes from the sea. I see four ships."

Meera informed her guards, and the defense was begun.

"Be that all?"

Sam focused. Meera waited. Suddenly, Sam said, "No. A group approaches from our western border, near the river valley. This be a large group. One-hundred, perhaps. On horses. Fully loaded with weapons."

"When do they arrive?"

"It looks as they prepare for a morn attack. It looks well coordinated."

"Keddi and Margeria return soon. I will send them with guards to dispatch the western boundary group. Where be Buron?"

"On the first ship."

"Has he seen you?"

"He doesn't have the same sight. He has learned that Jandra has gone. He no longer senses her. He knows I remain."

"How much can you see, Sam? Can you but find the innocents used in his battle?"

Sam looked. Meera saw that her eyes focused on nothing, but stared.

"The group from our north is but a ragged group. They look not as prepared or brave as the group on our western boundary. But I cannot tell more. There are many on the ships that I think Buron but masks from me."

"How can he do this?"

"Except for my eyes as weapons, he has the same or more power."

"I will have the group on the northern boundary dispatched this turn and be done with them. We can then but concentrate on the other two groups. Be there more?"

Meera spoke to a guard and had a strong unit go to the north, with Ahkna in-charge. They were ordered to determine if this group be the innocents. If not, no prisoners were to be taken.

Meera spoke to Ahkna, "Surprise them this turn, as they settle into their camp. Make short order of them, and then return. The main battle will be from the sea front and from our western boundary. We will need you back quickly."

Ahkna nodded, "We will return after the moon rises. We will gather what information we but can. Worry not, Highest. We will but surprise them."

"Go swiftly, and run softly. Make no noise in this attack."

Ahkna turned and left. Her guards followed silently and quickly with her, all at a slow run, their bows and arrows at the ready.

"Are our ships prepared and safely hidden?"

"The signals are arranged. The attack will be a surprise."

"No, Meera. Buron will already know where the ships but hide. If not, he will feel their movement when they move to attack. For us to win the battle, I must engage Buron away from all the rest. If he be otherwise occupied, he will be unable to attend to his forces. It is up to me to keep him fully busy. I will call to him at the sun's rise and challenge him to step foot onto Woden to engage me in his conquest. As soon as I entertain him away from the rest, that be your moment to take the battle. Not until then. He will undo all your plans. There will be no surprises unless you wait until I engage him. There be nothing you have that will undo Buron. This I must do for us."

Sam turned to Meera and looked at her for the first moment in many turns. Meera looked into Sam's eyes and saw no response. Her eyes were no longer as eyes, but waving pools of water.

"Do you but see as you did prior? Your eyes look not as eyes anymore."

"If I choose them to, they remain the same. Now, they must be used differently or Buron will use them on me. Meera, as I begin this battle with Buron, you can't look back to me. You must win your battle as I must win mine. If you see me falter, know this: There is nothing, nothing, that you can but do to fight and win against Buron. If I but lose, go to Caitha and Jandra and remain with them. For a little while, the Spirits of the Falls will be able to battle against him."

Sam halted for a moment and then looked again at Meera, "Worry not, though, as I have no intention of losing to him. If you see me falter, do not assume me dead. It be best if you don't look to my battle. You will know when I win. You will hear it and know it."

Sam hesitated, and then said, "There be one thing for you to know. If I win but have become overly injured, you must do this for me: When Buron be dead, his eyes and heart must be removed and burned, or he will return."

"I will make it so if the need be there."

They waited throughout the turn. By late midturn, Keddi and Margeria arrived and said that Jandra, Caitha and Tadan had been delivered safely and well received. Meera gave them their orders to take on the battle of the western boundary. She sent 37 guards and people of Woden with them and wished them well.

Keddi knelt to Sam, "Highest. Worry not about the western boundary. Margeria and I will handle them without question. Good luck in your battle, Highest. We all think of you this turn. We will return with good reports by two turns. No one will escape from us."

Sam placed her hand on Keddi's shoulder, "Be swift and safe. Woden needs you, Keddi."

Keddi nodded, and then rose and left with Margeria. They quickly went to their unit and took their departure.

Meera walked to Briggon, "Prepare the sea front. Be well hidden and silent. The attack begins in the morn."

Briggon nodded and left with Janel.

"There be another group, Meera, but you have no need to worry on them. They came through the tides on the southern boundary and but crashed their ship on the rocks."

"A large group?"

"No, forty or fifty at most. They be gone or near dead. They will not bother us."

"I will send five guards to ensure us of them."

Meera spoke to one guard and had it arranged.

She looked to Sam, "Where do you wish to await the sun's rise?"

"At the eastern gate. We can arrive quickly to the docks from there, as needed."

Sam rested while Meera remained on watch, and then they did the reverse. Sam kept focused on Buron. The sun's rise approached and he still hadn't made movement toward the harbor.

As they waited, Ahkna sent an assistant to give Meera a report, "We have overtaken the northern group, Second. We but extract information from some remaining, as we speak. We have found no innocents in this group. There were but 56 poorly trained guards, with miserable weapons. They thought we be weak women. They but thought we would offer no resistance. We have determined that one group comes through our western boundary and another comes by sea along our southern boundary, making their way into Hengist. The ships have weapons that throw attacks in large amounts, like fire and rocks. It sounds like our catapults, but not. We could make no further determination of this by my departure. Ahkna finishes with the remainder. As you commanded, the attack was swift and quiet, as is the clean-up. No sight of this will be left. Their weapons be not worth keeping."

"Have most of the guards returned with you for our sea-side battle?"

"Yes, Second. We are here for the battle. Ahkna says to inform you that she too will be here by the sun's rise or shortly after. We are prepared, and are now resting."

"Well done. Do not expect this next battle to be as easy. Be there any injuries or deaths on our side?"

"One injury only, Second. Our arrows flew in mass, and they dropped their weapons quickly, in fear. In truth, Second, they be cowards. It was a sight I had never imagined as so."

"The innocents will be as such, but the others will not be so for fear of what Buron might do to them."

As the sun's rise occurred, Sam stood.

She looked out toward the sea and held out her arm, sending a message to Buron, *I am here.*

She told Meera, "I have sent my message."

"Has he returned it?"

"Not yet. He will. The ships make ready to move. When we meet in person and pass through Woden's gates, begin your attack at that very moment. Do not hesitate."

Meera nodded.

Suddenly, Sam laughed. Meera looked at her as if she were crazy. Sam looked at Meera, "He sent his message. It but made me laugh. He said, "I come, my betrothed.""

"How can such be humorous to you?"

"The game prior but continues. I now know the rules. Remember, Meera, no matter what you see, remain to the plan. Even if it appear we begin as friends, remain to the plan. Trust not what you see."

"Yes, Highest."

They waited. Sam and Meera began walking to the docks, away from the gates. Sam was fully armed and readied. She knew that Jandra was safe for now, along with Caitha and Tadan, so she moved them from her current thinking. As she walked, she looked along the path to the docks and wondered if it would be as ordered and clean looking after the battle. She couldn't visually see any of Woden's guards about her, but knew them to all be waiting, as were the ships around the next cove. Just prior to reaching the docks, Sam halted. She and Meera saw the ships approach, and then halted by one of Woden's own. All four ships lowered anchor after some discussion between them and Woden's ship. Sam watched as five large rowboats were filled with passengers and then lowered. Meera motioned to one of the guards, a coded signal, and twenty guards appeared, readied.

Sam said nothing. She monitored Buron's thoughts as best she could, but he masked them well. She knew that Buron was in one of the rowboats. She wondered how the battle would begin, but left that reality to Buron. He would have to take the first move. As the boats docked, Sam could see Devin beside Buron. He was pointing toward Sam. Buron looked fixedly on Sam, and smiled.

He was a monster of a man—a human mountain. Sam guessed him to stand three full heads taller than Briggon and weigh at least two normal men's weight. His arm muscles were massive and were fully exposed. Buron wore no shirt, and wore only the tightest of pants. His sword was another half length of Sam's, and she knew this was why the Old One but made her learn to throw her own. She would never be able to match Buron's strength or length in an arm-to-arm fight.

The boats emptied. All the passengers were fully armed guards. While Meera's guards numbered only twenty, she knew the archers to be readied and would adjust the ratio at a moment's notice.

Devin came forward to Sam and knelt. He looked extremely nervous. "My Queen. King Buron wishes your company."

Sam nodded and looked to Buron, "He but has it."

Devin rose and let it be known that Buron could come forward.

He did so with a smile, "It is as Sir Devin hath spoken, Sam of Woden. You are a rare beauty, indeed. It be rumored you a strong and mighty warrior, yet what I see before me but the most beautiful and petite Lady in all The Realm."

Sam smiled at him, "I now know where Sir Devin gets his flattery from."

"I see you wear your weapons, my betrothed. Please feareth me not. Our union will ensure your protection."

"Thank you, Lord Buron. I have no reason to fear you. I have but just returned from practice. If you had sent a messenger, I would have presented myself more appropriately."

Buron waved his hand in dismissal, "And cover up your body more? Then I be glad I did not, as now I seeth your fine, long and slender legs. They are most welcomed sights after my long journey. They make me desire to touch them. Let us take a walk, my fair Queen. We have much to discuss."

Sam nodded and turned away from the docks. As soon as they entered Woden, Meera would begin her attack. Devin looked at Meera with some fear.

He placed his hand on his sword, and she shook her head, "It not be a good idea for you to do as such at this moment, Devin, if you wish to but see your next moment."

Sam walked Buron into Woden. She was trying to move him toward the other side of Woden, past the other gates.

He asked, "Where be your castle, M'Love?"

"We have no such dwellings, Lord Buron. I but live in a simple dwelling."

"I can give you all the castles and fineries you would desire, Sam of Woden, if you but submit to me this turn."

"Submit to you, Lord? What does this mean?"

Sam kept him walking. She was pleased that she had moved him beyond the former Highest's dwelling, but hoped to make it more.

"You must lay down your weapons to me, my Queen, and then you must lay down with me. It be not an unpleasant thought. My loins begin to stir now at the thought of touching you. Do you not find me but handsome, virile and strong? Many others would but throw themselves down for me and let me have my way with them."

"What of our intended wedding, Lord Buron?"

He looked angry, but smiled, "I cannot wait that long, my Queen. I need a well-bred offspring now. I have but saved my seed for this moment for the entire journey here. I need you and I need your holdings. We can but join them together. I can rule and you can but have my children. I will give you whatever you want."

He reached for Sam and pulled her to him. He forced a kiss upon her. A strong and urgent one, but also a violent and demanding one. He held her by both her arms. She thought it best to surrender into the kiss until she could get further away from Woden and him. He mistook her surrender for acquiescence to his will, and began to explore her body.

"I like your garments much. I can feel your breasts much easier through these than those gowns you women wear."

Sam pulled away, "Not here, Lord Buron. Let us but continue our walk past the gates. This be not a good place."

"I cannot wait much longer, M'Love. Look how I am but ready for you."

Sam could hear the beginnings of Meera's battle.

She struggled to divert Buron's attention, "It be not far, Lord Buron, and will be worth your wait and effort."

"I like this in a woman. You tease and play with me, but want me. I can but see it in your face. You desire me within you. I hear you a chaste woman. Be that true, M'Love?"

Sam nodded and remained well in front of him, "I have saved myself for this turn, M'Lord. In truth, I have never laid with a man."

His smile increased in its proportion, and Sam saw that another part of him also increased at the same moment, "Then I will have to be but gentle with you at first. That will take great patience on my part as I but wish to ravish you. But I would have it so, you as chaste. It be worth the need for patience."

"Lord Buron, a question of you. What will you do with Woden after I but submit to you?"

"You need not worry yourself over these trivial matters. Your people be but peasants and need not interfere with your life with me. You will be well protected, so why concern yourself with these matters? These be not women's matters."

Sam nodded to him and passed the western gates of Woden. They were now outside of Woden's wall, and Sam felt free to begin her battle when Buron made his move, which she was certain he would soon.

As he passed the gates, he demanded, "I will go no further. Come to me and submit. Lay down those ridiculous weapons of yours. They be useless against me. You are but small and weak. Come and feel my muscles." He grinned, "All of them."

Sam began to back away carefully, but Buron came at her like a bull. He grabbed her arms and brought her to him, once again, violently kissing her. He removed one his hands, grabbed her hand, and moved it to his enlarged part.

She revolted against him and broke free, running a short distance from him, "I can't submit to you, Buron. Woden doesn't wish to be enslaved to your ways. We will fight this turn."

Buron laughed mightily, "You women are but fools. Look at me. You cannot win against me."

Sam brought up her hand and sent a surge of violent force to him. He staggered, but didn't fall.

"Weakling. Is that the best you can do?"

He began coming toward her, and she moved away. He drew his sword. Sam saw that she had no choice but to engage him in sword fight, at least for the moment until she could move him to the trees. She raised her hand again and mentally tried to remove his weapon from him. She couldn't, and he laughed. He sent his own force against her and tripped her. She fell to the ground, but quickly rose. She focused on his eyes and blinded him for but a moment. In that moment, she moved closer to the trees.

He grew angry, "ARRRRRGGGG! You but blind me. I will kill you for this."

She moved further into the trees, and called to him, "Here I am, Buron."

Sam was being careful. She knew that she had but one try to kill Buron. She would have to wait for the correct moment. After she temporarily blinded him, he was casting off many violent forces that Sam tried to avoid. One aimed right at her and threw her against a tree. The force was stronger than she imagined he could be, but she now knew how strong he was. And she knew she would need to protect herself against it. She sent rocks flying to him, at great speed. Some hit him and he groaned, but none connected to cause great injury. As his sight returned, he halted the rocks in their path and sent them returning back to Sam.

He came closer with his sword readied. Sam readied her sword, but looked around and studied the terrain. He swung. The blow was fierce, well placed and overly strong. Sam's sword matched the blow, but she knew she could take only a few of those swings before yielding. He swung again, and once again, Sam was forced toward the defensive. She watched his moves carefully, looking for any signs of weakness in the huge, tree trunk of a body. He began to swing again, but she ducked behind a tree. His sword hit the tree, and the tree, as they had done during Sam's training, fell to the ground, in flames.

Sam was quick to send some fire onto his body through her powers. He yelled and brushed them off, but it had injured him some. She tried again, but he learned quickly and cast off the fire. She now knew not to try anything twice in a row. She could use the knowledge, she hoped, later. He raised his sword again and she had nothing else to do but meet it. She did so, but then allowed her sword tip to fall toward the ground, trying to move him off-balance. It did slightly, but he recovered quickly. He had a strong balance from his overly muscled legs. Sam saw that he favored his right arm. She tested her guess by moving behind another tree, forcing him to use his left arm swing. It hit the tree mightily, but saw that it didn't knock the tree over. She sent more flames to him, and he cast them off. She sent branches toward him to keep him busy while she moved away.

He came after her and sent flames her way. She turned them around, and as he neared a tree, she used her eyes, caught the tree afire, and made it fall toward him. As he battled against that tree, she instantly did the same with another. Branches and limbs scratched him, and the fire burned through some of his garments. Sam could smell that some of the hair on his chest had been scorched, but Buron came out swinging and hacking the trees apart. At most, Sam tired Buron but a bit, and provided overly small injuries.

Buron neared her and took his swing. Sam caught it at the last moment, unprepared for his quickness, but the edge of his sword had caught the flesh of her upper right arm.

Sam bled freely and Buron smiled, "Give in to me. It be not too late. I yet desire your body, and I yet require your children. You be not strong enough for this battle."

Sam refused to engage Buron in babble. She swung her sword upward with all her might. While he met it, the impact forced him back a bit. She saw that she could move against him. As he stumbled backward some, she swung again from the other direction, against his left arm, with as much force and anger as she could pull into the swing. Once again, he caught it, but the force of the swing jolted through his left arm, and as the swords clashed, a small spark erupted from them that Sam sent flying into his hair. He cried out, and dropped his sword to brush out the fire. Sam swung again, but he used his powers to move the swing of the sword elsewhere. She resisted, but the swing came lightly upon his thigh. It did no great damage, but it did draw blood. Buron angered and picked up his sword. Sam threw another burning tree toward him, and another, and another. With each one, his anger mounted and his strength continued. She moved away, and he came after her. She circled around to the fallen trees, now burning, and made more to fall on him, until she formed enough to encircle him within the flames. Then, using her eyes, she increased the flames.

Enraged at his ineffectiveness to yet kill her, with all his power Buron sent several of the trees flying toward Sam. As one of the trees hit her square in the chest, she saw that he was yet encircled within the flames. She sensed fear of fire from him.

Finally, a weakness.

The force of one of the trees knocked her back onto another, catching her between the two. Her back and head struck solidly and violently against the other tree, and she felt like they had broken. She couldn't catch her breath, but using the only thing she could move, she used her eyes to send even greater heights of fire to the trees that encircled Buron, hoping for a moment to recover. She was seriously injured but couldn't take the moment to assess the damage. Pain was everywhere. She focused and put the pain aside, knowing it would cost her energy soon.

She struggled to stand and move away from the tree on fire. She had to take a moment to find her sword, and reached for it within the flames. As she did so, she finally saw what she had to do. She focused on Buron, safely held within the flames. She couldn't see him, but knew where he stood. He couldn't see her, and was struggling on his own to fight his terror of the fire that surrounded him. Sam gathered all her strength and prepared her sword. She knew she had once chance, and only one chance. Her body was wracked with pain, and her right arm screamed as she raised the sword to behind her head. She ignored her pain. She ignored her burns.

Sam focused on where her mind knew where Buron was. She knew that Buron thought her now dead. The impact of the tree should have killed her. Luckily, the base of the tree hit just above her head. It was the larger branches that hit Sam in the chest. She focused and moved away from her pain. One throw only was she going to get. She remembered in practice the dummy of Jandra that she had hit, but had missed the tree entirely. She couldn't miss as she had done.

Sam couldn't breathe, but paid it no attention. She settled her body, focused again, found Buron, and threw the sword with all the power she could. As the sword flew free away from her, she directed its aim toward Buron as the Old One had taught her. And as soon as the sword left her hands, she reached for her knife and threw it as well, aiming straight for his throat. As the knife flew free, Sam dropped to her knees and then fell to the ground. She could no longer move, and hoped her sword and knife had hit their mark.

Just before her mind went blank, she sent one message: *Meera*.

* * * *

As Keddi and Margeria helped the Old One down from her horse, Jandra saw the falls began to separate and that a path formed between the horses and the cave in back of the falls. Jandra dismounted her horse, as did Caitha and Tadan.

The Old One looked at Keddi, "Your duty is done, and your Highest needs you. Return safely and swiftly. Go."

Keddi nodded, waved farewell to Jandra, and both she and Margeria remounted, took the extra horses and left. Jandra wasn't pleased to be here at this moment but knew there was no other choice. She was grateful to have Caitha with her, but she already missed Sam. Tadan she knew not what to do with. He was overly consuming for her right now. It had been many, many cycles since she had been to this spot. She had never been here to personally meet her Spirit Mothers, and felt afraid and nervous. She wanted Sam, but refused to let any message flow from her to Sam. She didn't want Sam distracted by herself.

Caitha came up to her and put Jandra's arm within her own, while Tadan stood nearby. The Old One motioned for them to follow her. She walked along the path on the river, back toward the falls, and finally into the cave. They followed her. Neither Caitha nor Jandra had ever been past the river. To walk through the falls and into a cave amazed them. They had never known such existed. Tadan had never even been to the Falls.

They walked through the cave for what seemed liked many long moments. The Old One seemed to know her way, easily. The cave had several paths, and Tadan tried to study which way they walked. He worried about how they might find their way back out. Brave as he was, he remained close to Jandra and Caitha. To Caitha, the cave seemed lonely and unused. She noticed few bootprints where they walked.

Jandra wondered how they could see in such a cave. From her experiences, the cave should be wholly dark, but it wasn't so in this one. The Old One continued steadily on her path, switching frequently from one path to another. Tadan gave up trying to remember which path they took at each junction and just followed. After what seemed half a turn or more of walking inside the cave, they saw that they began to emerge from it, near another cave entrance.

Since they saw no bootprints on the floor of the cave, they all assumed that this was another entrance, and not the one they had come through. They emerged into a soft fog and kept walking, the Old One humming to herself along the way. Finally, they came into bright light, near the river that they thought must lead to the Falls. The river was wide, but easy.

Jandra looked across the river and froze. What she saw wasn't possible from her experience. Before her, but yet across the river, were the Spirit Mothers. They were of water, as it seemed to Jandra. They stood twice her height, as she had seen when they had come to Woden. Their hair grew down to the ground and was the color of water. It flowed about them such as water flows. Jandra saw that their hair was wild, like Sam's, with much resemblance between them. Then Jandra saw their eyes and saw that they were Sam's eyes. They were bluer than the sky and shimmered like the sun upon flowing water. Sam truly was of them. She had never doubted it, but now saw how it was so.

Two of the Spirit Mothers moved forward. Caitha watched carefully but couldn't see their legs move, yet they moved. They crossed the river as if it were but a walking path, then stood before them. The Old One began to speak to them in a language Jandra, Tadan or Caitha couldn't understand. There seemed to be some disagreement, but it was finally settled, and the Spirit Mothers came to Jandra, gently. They moved directly in front of her and then reduced their size a little.

You are Jandra, the Birth-Mother of the future ruler of all The Realm, our grand-daughter. We welcome you to our home and are well pleased you remain with us. Please have no fear of us. We will serve you and make you comfortable while you are here. If you would permit while you are here, we would like to speak with your unborn. You may call me Loudrill'n and this is Strada'n'il. I know you to be Jandra, so this must be Caitha, and this young boy must be Tadan.

She moved closer to Tadan and inspected him well. *You are the first of the males to ever step onto our sacred grounds. The Old One tells us that you be smarter than most males. But we welcome you, nevertheless. You are here because your mother desires it so. But we understand you are here to help tend Jandra. Our legends tell us that you are to become the keeper of the unborn in her life, so it may be good that you come and see what lies in her future.*

Jandra noticed that they didn't speak. She saw that they sent their thoughts silently, like Sam was often able to do. Jandra practiced their names upon her tongue. They were strange names to her, and very old sounding. Jandra began to wonder what Sam's real name was, and guessed that it had a much longer version that none in Woden knew. As she thought about Sam, she began to worry and tried to put the battle out of her mind.

Strada'n'il came over and touched Jandra and the shoulder. *Don't be worried, Birth-Mother of our unborn. Sam is well and the battle hasn't yet begun. Come. Allow us to take you to a place more comfortable for you. Food and drink are ready for you, and your Spirit Mothers await you and the child. It is an exciting moment for all us to, if you permit, place our thoughts upon our grandchild. Come, Birth-Mother. Allow me to carry you across the river.*

Jandra knew she had been lifted up, but felt no hands or arms around her. She was carried across the river as if she floated. She looked back to Caitha and Tadan and saw that they too were being carried across. The Old One had changed her form and had become as the others. Her raggedy clothes lay where she shed them, and she was now draped in what looked liked a beautiful flowing gown made of water. When Jandra was able to, she looked at the Old One more carefully and saw the image of Sam upon the Old One's face.

The Spirit Mothers carried their visitors upstream at a swift rate, keeping in close contact with the river. When they reached a fork in the river, they turned toward the forest and followed the smaller river. After a short while, they arrived at a semi-clearing of the trees where a bend in the river occurred. Before them were their rooms. Some were at ground level and others were elevated onto rocks. All the rooms were interconnected in some fashion that Jandra couldn't guess. There were rooms where only what looked to be beds were. Other rooms contained medium-sized round tables. And other rooms contained smaller sized table and chairs, along with all manner of chairs. Vines and branches separated the rooms with the beds, providing some but not total privacy. The place looked to encompass the entire middle of the forest. Jandra could see no beginning and no ending, yet it flowed as if part of the river and forest.

Caitha saw that the river ran through each of the rooms. The room they gave to Jandra and Caitha had two beds and two chairs with a small table. It also had a balcony that overlooked the river, just down two steps from the balcony.

Jandra thought it a most peaceful place and had it not been for her worries about Sam and Meera and all of Woden, she would have felt great contentment here. Strada'n'il placed Jandra upon the ground so gently that Jandra wouldn't have known had her feet not felt the ground. She had been placed onto the balcony.

She looked into Strada'n'il's eyes and thought, *They look like Sam's. Exactly like Sam's.*

Strada'n'il smiled at Jandra, *Of course they do, Jandra of Woden and Jandra of your Highest. They are of our eyes. She is of us. But you know of this, so it must just be the surprise of meeting us.*

"You can hear my thoughts?"

I can. We all can. And while you are here, we are allowing you to hear our thoughts, as well. There be no need of speech here. The noise becomes unbearable for us. We have provided that you can learn to mask your thoughts. It is easy to do as such. Think of your thoughts as you would your speech, and then all your other thoughts will remain behind the mask.

That sounds most confusing.

Strada'n'il laughed softly and gently, and as if water flowed through her, *You will need to practice, but it will become easy for you. In the meanwhile, little Birth-Mother, we have prepared food and drink for you. You must rest while you are here. We want you to feel contentment and peace so that your unborn child may feel those as well.*

Where is Tadan?

He will be here soon, Jandra. Worry not. We will not harm him in any fashion. Your Highest is correct. Tadan does seem to be connected to our unborn in ways we had not seen. When we reexamined the legends, he was mentioned. He will eat with you, and then we will provide much entertainment for him. He is an inquisitive one, so we will show him many wonders of our home. You don't need to become tired by him, Jandra. We will tend to you now. All you must do is let go of your worries, and rest. I see Caitha arriving.

After Caitha was given the same instruction of speech, Jandra and she were left alone for a few moments. They wandered about the room and settled onto the balcony, sitting in the small table and chairs. It was so different than they could have even imagined. They had no idea that their Spirit Mothers actually existed in a realm of the living, let alone live in a real place.

They tried speaking to each other through their thoughts, but their thoughts became muddled into their speech, and they began to laugh. Jandra thought it was good to have Caitha here with her, but it was meant as a passing thought only, yet Caitha heard it. They continued to laugh and suddenly noticed that the laughter became the loudest sound about them. They had never heard a place so quiet where the running of the water was the only sound.

To Jandra, space and the passage of the moments seemed not to affect life in this place. One slept when they were tired, and ate when they were hungry. It seemed overly simple, but Jandra couldn't see anyone working. She saw no gardens being farmed, no buildings being built, no animals being tended, and no trade of any sort. She also didn't see the Spirit Mothers take food and sleep. The normal passing of the sun and the moon had no effect in this land of the Spirit Mothers. The turn remained the same in its half-sun and half-fog state.

Food was brought to them, along with Tadan. Jandra saw that Tadan was quite taken by this place. As was his fashion, he asked questions about everything. The Spirit Mothers answered as they could, patiently, but seemed glad to drop him off for the meal. Even without speaking aloud, Tadan seemed loud.

Good turn, Second and Caitha. This be a wonderful place to expand one's mind. Did you yet but notice the walls of the room, for example? It is not a wall as we know it, but branches and limbs forming a wall as if they have a mind of their own. And their way of speech, without talking, is much more quiet than ours. We should take up this practice.

Jandra laughed, *It might be a good idea, Tadan, but it is not of our possibility. We are able to do it now only because the Spirit Mothers would have it so. Sit, so that we might eat. Even their food looks different than ours.*

Except for a form of flatbread, they didn't know what they ate, except to know that it was not of animals. They thought they could distinguish the fruits, but even their fruits were different than of Woden. They decided among them that whatever it was, it was delicious. When they were done with their meal, the Old One came in with several of the Spirit Mothers. They already knew Strada'n'il and Loud-ill'n, and now they met three more of the Spirit Mothers - Char'neilane, Aluthe'nen, and Sarth'nis.

We would like to speak to our unborn daughter, if this meets with your permission, Jandra of Sam. We will not harm her, but just wish her to know us prior to her birth. It will not cause you any discomfort or pain. Even now, our daughter hears us speak and wishes to know more. We hear her calling but will await your permission before we answer. Perhaps all of you would like to hear what it is we say to her. It is possible, with your permission.

Jandra decided to simply nod her consent, not wanting them to know of her questions about their sincerity. They asked her to stand and then placed their hands upon her womb. The message they sent was, as they had vowed, open for all to hear:

Our granddaughter. We meet you with much excitement. Your beginning has been long in the waiting for us. Now you are with us, in your land. While you are here, you may listen and speak as you please by sending your thoughts. You are yet a young one, but are well on your way in your knowledge. Your mother, The Highest of Woden, has provided much knowledge to you already. We can feel it as so. We will begin your lessons during your short visit with us. We welcome you into your home away from home. Jandra, your Birth-Mother, is most nervous in you. She is worried about being such. While you are here with us, let us all assure her of you and this birth. She is to be the most important person in your life, Sele'm'tinel'ti'non'n. She will provide you with all the lessons we cannot. She alone will provide you the knowledge of these others that even now seem foreign to you. Trust your Birth-Mother as you will trust no one else in all The Realm, including us. And take good care of her. We will allow you free use of your senses while you be here, but be mindful of your Birth-Mother's needs as well. And come to know of your tender watcher, young Tadan. We have allowed him here at your mother's request and have found him mentioned in the legends. Welcome, young Sele'm'tinel'ti'non'n. Hear our songs to you while you be here.

When they were done, they removed their hands from Jandra's womb and looked at Jandra, *Sele'm'tinel'ti'non'n is her name in legend. Fear not, little Birth-Mother, her name will be the one you provide to her. A legend name is different than the names your kind but provide. She already knows her name in the legends, but awaits the name you will but give her.*

They placed their hands lightly upon Jandra's head and sent her great thoughts of their joy and happiness.

After they removed their hands, they stood before Jandra and Caitha, *Rest now, Birth-Mother of Sele'm'tinel'ti'non'n. You might now hear questions from our unborn. She is your Birth-daughter, so you may choose to answer them as you will. She will not be like the ones born to your kind. Although at the very first she will resemble them, within a very short span of life, she will grow more quickly and much differently* than what you know. But enough for now. Feel free to wander about as your desire. And please know that whatever you wish, we will be here to see that it occurs for you.

They bowed their heads to Jandra, turned and left. Even before they were out of the dwelling, Tadan began his questions, *What do they mean that I am, according to the legends, the watcher to, what did they call her, Sele'lr'tinel'ti'non'n?*

No, Tadan, they call her Sele'm'tinel'ti'non'n. I know not the legends. You must ask them of these.

Jandra looked at Caitha, *Sele'm'tinel'ti'non'n be an interesting name. I wonder what Sam's real name is. Sam isn't a name of Woden, so it must be a shortened one. These are very long names. We could but name her Sele'.*

I think you and Sam need to discuss this issue. The naming of this one will be no easy matter. It would seem this unborn has more to her than I had but guessed. Tadan, after you finish eating, why not find out how you can get eyes such as your Highest Mother's?

He nodded, *In truth, I have many questions to ask, and they have but told me that it is fine that I ask them. I hope I will receive the answers, though. They look at me as if I might have a disease. It is most disconcerting. I know I am the first male to ever be in this land, but I am not evil because of it, am I?*

No, young Tadan. You are just an oddity to them. Have patience. Return here as you need.

* * * *

After reporting back to The Highest and Second of Defense, Keddi and Margeria took their unit to the western boundary. They had a small unit, but highly skilled. Keddi knew they would face well-armed and most likely, well-trained guards. She hoped they would have the benefit of surprise. Their arrows would dispatch several prior to their main battle, but the odds were a challenge. And Keddi knew that they had no chance to set up a trap. These invaders would be overly smart to set camp in a closed valley. They took the horses to the boundary, and then tried to locate the invaders. Keddi could see no signs of them. Scouts were dispatched into different areas. They wouldn't be able to have the benefit of surprise if they rode up on their horses, but Keddi needed to know where the invaders formed.

After some wait, overly long for Keddi, a scout returned and pointed off into the distance, "Over there, Keddi. They just remounted and move again. If you look, you can but see their dust they make from their horses. They be well-armed, as The Highest but said."

Keddi decided that they could take their horses down a little further, and then they would have a chance to lay a surprise. They would have to guess as to the direction the invaders took, but Keddi felt comfortable in guessing their path, knowing there only one good way up to Woden from the valley. They hid their horses and prepared, half scattered across the ledges, for a short concentrated distance. They would provide continuous arrow fight from slightly above. A few were stationed so as to come from the rear and take the surprise there. The rest remained hidden at the mouth of the valley, and would fight hand-to-hand with the invaders. They hoped that the arrow fight would take many lives at the start.

Anchen came up to her, "We are ready, Keddi. We will take them most easily. Fear this not."

Keddi looked at Anchen for a moment, "You are a strong and brave fighter, Anchen. Why have you never prior been a warrior? Woden could use your warrior talents."

Anchen frowned and looked out toward the plains, "I was a warrior in a prior life. Hopefully, no more."

Keddi let the remark go unchallenged, but wondered as to Anchen's past, knowing that Anchen was indeed a fine warrior.

As they waited, Keddi hoped the fight in Woden went well. She worried about The Highest and her battle with Buron. She had heard much of Buron and thought it to be an overwhelming battle for The Highest. She knew Buron to be a skilled fighter and very strong. While The Highest was as skilled a fighter, she couldn't have the strength of such a man. Keddi kept her thoughts to herself, though, even as her women and men in the unit asked her many questions of it. She looked at her unit, of those she could yet see that were only partially hidden. These women and men of Woden were brave. None in Apien or New Harborage had the courage or determination of these. She thought that The Highest had much to do with this and felt lucky to have returned home to Woden to such. She knew their pains and fights had been well worth their efforts and losses, even though the loss of Brett was more than she had ever wanted to bear. She hoped that Margeria would remain safe from harm.

But Keddi knew they would face many losses this turn and felt saddened by it. These women and men, all of them from Woden that fought this turn, should live, and it made Keddi angry and sad.

They should live!

It brought back her anger of Manthar and all the others that enslaved and abused those in The Realm. She had hated her moments spent scouting for Woden, but they had been well worth the anguish of what she witnessed. Now the abuses and tortures would end, she hoped.

She was unsure as to the truth in all the statements being given to The Highest by the Spirits in the Falls, but trusted The Highest to know the difference between truth and lie. Yet, she had a sense in her that all was not as they were being told.

Margeria sensed that Keddi was thinking overly of what was about to occur, "Keddi, all of us know we might die this turn. There be no other way, so we will fight bravely. If we die, we die as brave. No one wants to die this turn, but none of us want to be enslaved into the evils of Buron and all the others. We be aware of what may occur. You have trained all of us well."

Keddi touched Margeria's hand, "Remain safe, Margeria. Watch your back."

Margeria placed her hand on Keddi's shoulder, "You as well. We all need you, but I especially need you."

As the group came nearer, Keddi saw that she should have placed more guards in the rear. She motioned to some on top to move to the rear and hold from shooting until after the front guard began. She sent only a few more, but she could tell that it would help. She felt sorry that they hadn't had the opportunity to set a trap such as had been done with The Highest's trip to the Woman in the Woods. As the enemy approached, Keddi saw that they were indeed fully armed. They all carried swords, knives, spears and many bows and arrows. Keddi knew they would be a strong match and offer much resistance. She also knew that they would be caught unprepared for a moment, but it might hopefully be enough.

Margeria had gone on top so as to start the fight. It would be at her command when Woden would let fly their arrows. She watched and waited. She saw that the invaders had no idea they were there, and felt some gladness in it. As they approached, she waited until the best moment. As the front matched her line, she gave the command: a loud shriek. The arrows flew as the invaders wondered what the noise was, and many went down in the first wave. The arrows continued, but the invaders were well-trained, so responded quickly to the attack. They dismounted and hid behind their horses. But the arrows continued. The invaders sent their own arrows back, but blindly so. They couldn't see Keddi's unit, but would soon figure out that they were surrounded. Keddi's rear guards began their attack.

Some of the men from the invaders rounded up a group and ran forward to attack. The hand-to-hand combat began, with Anchen leading a small group of Woden's forces.

As Keddi saw Anchen fighting against the invaders, she found herself amazed at Anchen's warrior abilities, seeing that they clearly shone over most of the others. But having the battle with which to contend, she turned her eyes back to her enemy. She picked her opponents carefully, and let fly her arrows. And with each, she downed one more. The arrows from above kept flying, and the hand-to-hand combat continued. Slowly, the invaders saw that they were surrounded and out-matched, so surrendered. Some begged for mercy, some remained quiet, and some yet resisted. Keddi had the resisters killed instantly, but hesitated with the remainder. She knew that Meera wanted no prisoners, but yet, they had surrendered. She had her guards gather them together, and she began to take stock of all the losses and remainders. Of the approximately one-hundred original invaders, only fourteen survived.

Of the original thirty-seven in her own unit, twenty-two but remained, and several of these were injured, including Margeria. As Keddi saw her being carried down, she saw an arrow sticking out from Margeria's leg. Keddi was grateful, as it hadn't hit her main body. Keddi knew the arrow to be a problem, but was most likely not life threatening. Another injured but yet alive guard had an arrow sticking out from his stomach. Keddi knew this not good and wished for a healer.

Now they numbered twenty-two to fourteen, and Meera wanted no prisoners. Many of the remaining invaders were badly injured. Keddi sighed and moved to follow her orders. Killing prisoners was difficult for Keddi. She didn't like killing the unarmed, but she would do as was commanded of her. She placed them in a line and tried to block out their pleas for mercy. She had her archers prepare, then ordered the arrows released. In a few moments, there were no prisoners, and Keddi went to Margeria. Margeria had been placed on the ground, and was busy trying to remove the arrow. Keddi smiled at her toughness but knew that Margeria wouldn't be able to do it.

"Hold. Let me break off the end only and let the healers do the rest."

Margeria looked up to Keddi, "I know you wanted not to kill those prisoners, but Keddi, Woden will have its hands full with others upon our return. And the enemy would not have spared us."

Keddi nodded, "Yes. It be certain, as you say, but it makes not the task the easier for it."

"We won, Keddi, and that be all that matters. We yet have our majority remaining."

Keddi nodded, but the weight of the losses sat heavily upon her. She began preparing Woden's dead for their last journey home. They would leave the battle scene to rot. She had some guards help her prepare their own dead by placing them on the horses. The remainder of her unit was busy unbridling the invader's horses so that they could be set free to roam. This battle was over, all the invaders were dead, and Keddi began their journey back to Woden, hoping that Woden was yet theirs, and hoping that Sam had won her own battle.

****

Meera had heard Sam call to her. She had only a vague notion of where Sam was, but went to where she thought the call had come from. Sam had told her she would try to move her battle beyond the wall and hoped to see signs of it. As she passed the gates of the western wall, she looked for Buron's bootprints. They were large enough to find easily, and Meera followed them. When she came to the forest, it was obvious that this was where their battle had been. Meera saw hundreds of trees over on their sides, burning. She followed the bootprints inside the forest, and eventually came to the ring of fire. It was massive, and Meera wondered who or what had built it.

She moved urgently, worried about Sam. She had brought ten of her closest guards with her. At her silent command, they fanned out and searched for signs of Sam, or Buron.

By chance, one of the guards looked through the yet hotly burning ring of trees, "Second, someone is in there; inside the ring."

Meera ran over and saw the small opening the guard had peered into.

It wasn't Sam, but Meera could see Buron, "I must get inside the fire ring."

The guards began hacking away at the burning trees so that Meera could get inside. They worked as swiftly as they could, but the trees were yet fully engaged in the fire. They used their swords to break off the big limbs. Piece by piece, they made a path into the ring. As they entered, they couldn't believe what they saw. Buron was dead. While they kept moving to within the enclosed area, Meera and another guard searched for Sam. After searching for long moments, Meera began to think that Sam had gone back to Woden, when the other guard called her over.

"Second, here she is."

There was Sam, lying on the ground, unmoving. Meera couldn't tell if she was alive or dead, but saw much blood.

Anyst came over to Meera, "Second, we have gained entry into the ring of fire. You may enter now. I will look after The Highest and tend to her wounds."

Before she left, Meera gently checked Sam's body for signs of life. Anyst bent down and checked for breathing. Meera began to panic, as she couldn't feel Sam's heart.

Anyst tried to keep Meera calm, in spite of the moment, "She breathes, Second, but barely so. Do not move her yet, Second. Many of her bones look broken to me. If she is moved, we may injure her more."

Meera didn't know whether to be elated that Sam lived, or worried over her condition, *But she lives!*

Meera felt helpless, "But I must tend to her."

"Second, move away and let us take care of The Highest. You are overly close to her, but you have taught us well. We too love The Highest, Second, and will make certain she is not further harmed by any movement."

Meera unwillingly nodded her consent, "I must tend to Buron quickly, as The Highest has requested. I will return directly after."

Meera went through the small entry they had opened into the fire. She saw that it was as hot as walking into a wall of fire. The heat was so intense she could barely breathe. She went to where Buron lay and saw that Sam's sword had hit him so hard that the sword hilt had halted only when it met his chest. The rest of the sword went through him and out his back. Meera wondered at what distance Sam had thrown her sword, as the impact alone could have toppled a tree. The sword had gone straight through his heart, but Meera saw that if that hadn't killed him, Sam had apparently also hit her mark with her knife. It had gone fully into his neck. Meera pulled the knife from Buron's neck, and then removed his eyes and heart as Sam had requested. It was a grisly act, and messy, but Meera gave it no thought, especially after what he had done to Woden and The Realm. She took his eyes and heart and threw them into the fire, where she heard them instantly sizzle. She chopped off his head, and did the same. She then returned to Anyst and Sam.

Anyst had a request of her, "Go get some horses, Second. Make yourself useful. And bring many bandages and blankets. Go quickly, Second. We need you back swiftly with the blankets."

Meera was too worried to know that she had just been issued orders by her own guards. She obeyed instantly, seeing that Sam looked half-broken. Meera ran with all her speed and tried to clear her head. As she entered Woden, she went first to Sam's dwelling in hopes that May was there. She went inside but couldn't find May in the kitchen. She called and called but heard no answer. May had been in the meeting room, busying herself and trying not to worry. Meera told her about Sam, and May raced around, gathering supplies.

Within a few hectic and panicked moments, she had given Meera a basket of all the things she would need, "Go quickly, Meera, and send me word."

Meera ran to the stables, quickly bridled three horses, mounted, and made them run as fast as they could back to Sam. When she returned, she halted the horses well away from the fire, but saw that the guards had cleared the fire away from Sam. The trees surrounding her had also been on fire. Anyst had taken charge of tending to Sam and had discovered the extent of her injuries. When Meera came up, Anyst wasted no moment in her worry, "Second, give me the bandages. Move over to the trees and make a traveler for The Highest. We cannot place her onto a horse."

Anyst motioned for two of the guards to help Meera make what The Highest would be carried on. Anyst began tightly wrapping some of The Highest's wounds. Her right arm had been smashed when the tree hit against it. Anyst could tell that many of her ribs, on both sides, were either broken or cracked. While The Highest's neck seemed fine, Anyst had found a disjointed bone in Sam's back, but couldn't tell the extent of that injury. Since The Highest seemed to have moved slightly away from the fire after her injuries, as Anyst could tell from the prints in the dirt, she guessed that The Highest wasn't paralyzed.

Although they look not like Sam's prints. Given Sam's needy condition, though, she wasted no more thought on the mystery.

Anyst also discovered that Sam's right thigh had been broken or cracked, and worried a great deal about that injury. She would have to splint that leg with a counter-balance so the bone wouldn't rise into the body, if it were broken. Anyst had decided to leave the many minor injuries for the healers. Sam had burns upon her body, cuts across her breasts and stomach, and bruises too numerous to count. And the last injury that Anyst could find was on the back of Sam's head where her skull had been cracked. It was a slight crack, but whatever the size, Anyst knew that a crack in the skull was never good.

Anyst bandaged Sam's ribs first while she waited for the splint one of the guards made. She cut off Sam's outer garments and wound the bandages tightly around her body. She then bandaged her right arm against her body, preventing movement of any kind. The guard had returned with the splints ready. The guard pulled the right leg down gently but firmly while Anyst made the counter-balance splint. A low dreadful moan stirred from Sam. Anyst knew that this bone setting was a most terrible pain, but at least The Highest had responded. She motioned for the guard to continue. The guard pulled down on the leg once again, strongly, firmly, but as gently and quickly as she could. They both had heard the screams from others when they had done this prior. The pain normally pushed the broken one into unconsciousness. Since The Highest was already unconscious, Anyst knew the pain must have been overly unbearable for an unconscious one to moan so. When they had gotten the splint in place so that the broken bone wouldn't ride up into The Highest's body, Anyst looked carefully at it and thought it well done. The leg looked to be straight now. Together, Anyst knew that she and Lorin, the other guard, had set the bone well.

"We must place her on a flat surface. Be there a flat object around? We need a flat board."

"There be panels of buildings in the tool shed, near the gardens. That would work."

"Good. Be swift. Take a horse and get them."

Lorin took off, not halting to explain to Meera. She wouldn't take long. In the meanwhile, Anyst began considering what to do about The Highest's head. The head wound complicated the back injury. While The Highest must lay flat, she wouldn't be able to lay The Highest onto her back, and yet she must. Anyst knew of nothing else, so decided to lay The Highest on her back on the flat boards, but turn her head to the side. She hoped The Highest's neck hadn't been injured, and she hoped this would not further harm the back injury. As she began to bandage The Highest's head, it suddenly came to her to encase The Highest's head in a pillow of bandages. Having come up with a plan, she worked on The Highest's more minor wounds as she waited for Lorin to return. She placed some of the poultice May had sent onto the burns and minor wounds. She also began to wash some of the blood from The Highest.

Lorin returned quickly with the boards. She brought three in case of the need. Anyst motioned to the other guards, and together they all moved the board against Sam's back, secured Sam tightly to the board, and turned the entire matter over. Then Anyst formed a pillow around the sides of Sam's head and toward its back so that it didn't touch the board, but only slightly so. They then wound more bandages around her head and body, and around the entire board so The Highest wouldn't be able to move her head or any part of her body. Anyst then allowed Meera to come to inspect.

"How badly injured is she, Anyst?"

"Most badly, Second. Three of her wounds could be but fatal. We have secured them well."

Meera bent down to Sam, "Be she unconscious?"

"She is Second, but she moaned when we set her leg. It is a painful experience."

"Why have you secured her so to this board?"

"The Highest has injured her head and back, Second. No movement can occur. The back must heal or she may not move her legs again."

"Her arm is most swollen."

"It is, Second. The arm be not good. But be most likely not life threatening. I but hope the ribs touch not her lungs. They do not appear to. Have you made the traveler, Second?"

"It be ready. Can she travel so?"

"Only slowly, Second. But it be only back to Woden, and we have prepared her tightly."

"We must take her to the Spirits of the Falls. They will be able to heal her more than we are able. She be of them."

"It be overly far, Second. I do not think she will make it such a distance."

"It must be so. Can the traveler be fitted across two horses so we do not drag her behind one? The path be far, but wide enough, I think. I can be there by moon rise."

"It be not wise, Second. She needs immediate care."

"Her injuries need greater care than we can give, Anyst. I, more than you, care about The Highest, and would not risk her so if I did not think it her only chance. Help me, Anyst. I need your help, but this must be done. Please come with me and tend to her. I cannot do this without you. I have not these medical skills you seem to have. We must go quickly as I see The Highest begin a fever."

Anyst looked to Sam's forehead and saw that The Highest's face was flushed. She couldn't tell if it was the pain of the movement or a fever beginning, as Meera had said. Either way, she knew The Second to be correct. The Highest needed more care than Woden's healers could provide. She nodded to Meera and motioned for the guards to begin setting the traveler across the two horses. Once secured, one guard placed a pole between the bit of the two horses, and joined them firmly together so they couldn't part, and did the same to their hind ends. The other guards lifted The Highest on her flat board, onto the traveler and across the two horses. It looked awkward, but Anyst thought it would hold.

The battle of Woden had been won, but at high cost of life. Meera gave the guards a message to give to Karan. She wanted Karan informed that The Highest lived, but needed much care and was being taken to the Spirit Mothers of the Falls. She wanted Karan to begin the process of rebuilding Woden's dwellings and lives that had been shattered in the battle. And she told the guards to tell Karan that she would return soon.

The guards left. Meera went to what was left of Buron and pulled Sam's sword and knife from him. She also picked up Buron's sword and placed both upon a sheath on the horses. She resettled her own weapons, as did Anyst, and they began their long walking journey, taking the most gentle path they could. It would take them at least until the moon's rise, but Anyst guessed that it would take longer. She felt some relief that it was near a full moon, so knew that their way would be well lit.

* * * *

On this eve, Jandra had gone to bed early and worried overly about Sam and Woden. She eventually fell asleep, but fitfully so. The turn had been a long one in the wait. The Spirit Mothers had done their best to provide stories of diversion, but even they awaited the battle's outcome. Well after the moon's rise, Jandra and Caitha were both woken by the Spirit Mothers' noticeable agitation. They were fluttering about as if worried. Many departed to the larger river's edge.

The Old One came to Jandra and Caitha, *Sam comes. Meera brings her. But Sam is gravely injured. We bring her in now. We will place her in the room next to this one.*

I want to see her. Take me to her.

The Old One held onto Jandra so that she couldn't run to the river, *We carry her in now. There is no need for you to go to her. Meera and a guard of the name of Anyst have walked a long way to get her here. Jandra, you must tend to your unborn, and you must prepare yourself. Sam is unconscious and is most injured. When you see her, you will be shocked at the extent of her injuries. Prepare yourself, Jandra.*

She turned to Caitha while yet holding Jandra, *Help prepare her, friend. It will be a shock for you as well. Your own companion is ill, also, with fever, but not seriously. Her guard is overly tired. We will tend to them both. Jandra, I need to let you go now. You must be strong.*

I will be. Just let me see her.

As soon as she arrives, you can be in the room as we unload her from her journey.

Loudrill'n carried Sam into the room as if floating. Sam was yet bound to the board Anyst had strapped her to. Loudrill'n placed the board and Sam onto the bed. Some of the other Spirit Mothers began gently unbinding her from the board. Jandra watched and remained quiet. She feared if she made any noises that they would remove her from the room. It was as the Old One had said. Sam was indeed overly injured and wholly unconscious. She looked frail and beaten. She had defeated Buron and saved Woden, but the cost had been high.

Jandra knew that Sam could heal others some from their ailments. She now watched, hoping the Spirit Mothers might be able to do as well. They unbound her arm and felt it, as they did every injured part of her body.

When they looked at her upper thigh, they turned to Meera, *You have tended well to our daughter. We have called for her Grandmother. She will help heal her. Go now and rest. The morning will arrive soon enough for you. We will also tend to you while you rest as you also are in need of healing.*

Meera was overly tired and was, in truth, yet standing only because Caitha held onto her tightly. Caitha had been excited to see Meera, but her joy had been cut short at the sight of Sam. Anyst looked exhausted and began to slump down. Loudrill'n looked at her, caught her, moved her to another room, and placed her gently on the bed. Other Spirit Mothers began to tend to Anyst, silently, as Anyst slept. Loudrill'n motioned to Meera to follow her, and Caitha followed Loudrill'n, leading Meera to her own bed. More Spirit Mothers came and tended to Meera, while Caitha returned to Jandra and Sam.

The Old One had tried to tell Jandra to rest until after the Woman in the Woods came and helped to heal Sam, but Jandra insisted. She wouldn't leave Sam's side. Tadan entered and stood with Jandra and Caitha. Jandra had never seen Tadan looked worried, as he now did.

When the Woman in the Woods arrives, you should leave. While Sam will remember none of the pain, this eve's healing will be most difficult on her. I fear you will think we kill her. I think it not wise you remain for this. And there be no need.

Jandra remained insistent, *There is a need. Sam knows I am here. It will help calm her. And it help calms me to be near her. Worry not about my presence.* She very briefly wondered why the Old One kept trying to remove her from the room, but let it go.

The Woman in the Woods finally appeared and looked upon her granddaughter. She began chanting, but Jandra didn't know the language she spoke. The chanting seemed liked singing to Jandra, and she thought it most beautiful. The Spirit Mothers began unbinding the wrappings from Sam's body. Piece by piece, they removed the bandages until Sam laid upon the bed mostly naked. Her body seemed overly half injured. The bruises went from side to side. There were scratches, deep wounds and burn marks across her entire body. Her head was swollen from its injuries, as were her arm and leg. Blood seeped from several wounds, and Sam's right arm looked crushed.

Loudrill'n received some unheard sound from someone, and moved over to Jandra. Gently, she moved Jandra and Caitha to the opposite side of the room. Jandra and Caitha watched as the Woman in the Woods touched all Sam's injuries. She moved slowly across her body, chanting the whole while. One of the Spirit Mothers turned to Loudrill'n, gave her a look Jandra didn't understand, and then turned back to Sam. Loudrill'n moved so as to surround Jandra and Caitha, but didn't touch them. It was as if she encased them within herself, but without force. Jandra felt comfort from it but knew not why or how it was being done.

The chanting continued for a long while. Suddenly, Sam's body rose slightly off the bed. Her arms hung straight out from their sides, and it was as if her whole body was supported in air. The Woman in the Woods halted her chanting and gave a loud sound that sounded like a shriek to Jandra. Sam's body jerked as if it had been snapped in two, and a scream burst from Sam that sounded like she was being tortured by demons. It was a loud, long, wailing scream, full of pain and anguish. To Jandra, it lasted forever. To Caitha, it was the scream of death.

As suddenly, the scream halted. The Woman in the Woods lowered Sam gently down to the bed and began the chanting again. Jandra felt like her own heart had been ripped from her breast when she heard Sam scream. Her skin crawled at the sound, and she unknowingly placed her hand over her ears to make it halt. Caitha would later tell her that she had screamed as well, but Jandra would never remember this to be so.

Sam lay in a bed that stood high from the ground. The Spirit Mothers needed it such due to their own height. As they worked to heal Sam, they stood over her and bent only slightly. All the elements of the healing session became seared into Jandra's memory. She saw that the Woman in the Woods seemed to command all the Spirit Mothers. While they all wore what Jandra thought the same garment, she began to see differences in each. As she watched them heal Sam, she began to see that each garment was of the color of water, but as water colors vary, so did their garments. She also saw that some wore long gowns, some wore pants and shirts, and others wore what looked like capes, and yet she hadn't noticed that difference at first. She also saw that their hair was unique across them. When she first entered their dwelling, all she noticed was that their hair flowed like water and was long enough to reach the ground. In watching them more carefully, she saw that Loudrill'n's hair was wavy and moved like the small ripples in a stream, while Strada'n'il's flowed straight as a waterfall.

She slowly came to realize their intimate connection to water. She thought of Sam's eyes and how they changed when Sam used her powers; the more she used them, the more her eyes shimmered as the sun upon water. She saw how closely the Spirit Mothers remained to the moving waters.

And the tear Sam took from me that formed our child be from water, also.

The Spirit Mothers, the Old One, and the Woman of the Woods all placed their hands upon Sam's body. They now all chanted, but clearly at the direction of the Woman in the Woods. They moved about her, in the same fashion as a dance. Tadan moved closer so that he could see better, but he didn't interfere with the ritual. They circled Sam's body, over and over. The chanting became hypnotic to Jandra, and she began to feel tired. She felt she was floating but was too sleepy to know that Loudrill'n carried her to bed, placed a kiss on her forehead, and touched her womb to send a message of tenderness to the unborn. Tadan watched throughout the entire eve, but finally went to bed in the late after mideve.

Jandra woke, unaware of how long she had slept, or that she had done so. She rose instantly and rushed to Sam's side. No one was in the room with Sam, but Jandra saw a Spirit Mother just outside. Sam looked quieted as if her pains had left her. Jandra held her left hand but saw that Sam slept deeply.

A Spirit Mother came in; one she didn't know, *Sam sleeps deeply in her own realm. We have healed much of her pain and wounds, but cannot wake her. It is* up to her if she will leave her unconsciousness for your realm or remain in the place she now rests in. You can talk to her Jandra. She will hear you and later remember. She can't respond to you, though, so do not become frustrated.

Jandra didn't know whether to be frightened, grateful, or angered. *What have you done to her?*

We have begun her healing and we have placed her into a place where she feels no pain. Her injuries were most severe, but she fought bravely and well. She will take a long while to heal. We have slowed down all the functionings of her body except for the healing process. If and when she wakes, it will have seemed like only a few turns to her body. It is up to her, now, Jandra.

Jandra sat by Sam's side all morn. Meera and Caitha came in, checking in on Sam and Jandra.

Good morn, Jandra. How be Sam?

She sleeps in a deep unconscious sleep. The Spirit Mothers have removed her pain and have begun the healing processes, but they said that it be up to Sam whether she wakes or no.

Meera touched Sam's forehead, *Perhaps it for the best. This one would want to rise the moment she be conscious. Woden has much to do, now, and is able to tend to its re-building without her, for now. She will awaken in her own moment, Jandra. Sam wants to be with you and see her child.*

Caitha moved Sam's hair off her forehead, *She looks much improved from last eve. I have never seen a sight such as that. How is it she lived through such?*

Meera shook her head and frowned, *She has a deep will to live. The injuries I saw were most overwhelming. I am grateful that Anyst was with me to prepare Sam for her journey here. I would not have done as well as Anyst.*

Jandra looked to Meera for the first moment since they arrived, *How is Woden? Am I needed more there than here?*

Meera made a neutral expression so that Jandra could make that decision herself, *Woden won their battle, but lost many lives. We have many buildings that need re-building, including most of the fishery huts and boats. The dock is a mess, most of the shops sustained some type of destruction, many of the paths require rebuilding. Even your dwelling, Jandra. Yours and Sam's, requires rebuilding. And the former Highest's dwelling has been demolished. Woden is missing their Highest now, Jandra, but you are also needed here. The decision is yours alone to make.*

Jandra looked to Caitha, *Help me make this decision, Caitha. I can't. My heart is here, but Woden needs a leader. And their leader lies but here. Can I be this selfish to remain here? But I want Sam to be not alone.*

Caitha looked sadly upon Jandra, *It is a most unfair decision for you. But the Spirit Mothers have told you that Sam will sleep for a long while. If you worry about her being alone, then let me remain with her and you leave with Meera to Woden. When you feel that Woden is settled enough, have Meera return with you. In the meanwhile, send messengers everyturn if that would but help. I can send reports with them and you will not feel so worried for her. If you are needed quickly, you could leave one messenger here for me, just in case. Anyst could use the rest by the looks of her, and she but earned it.*

Jandra knew Woden needed her, but she didn't trust the Spirit Mothers enough to leave Sam. *Allow me a few moments to think on this while Meera prepares to depart.*

Caitha and Meera nodded, and then left.

Jandra asked Li'el'in'tiln if she might speak with the Old One. Within a short while, the Old One came, looking nothing at all as the Old One, but like one of the leaders of the Spirits of the Falls. *What may I do for you, Jandra?*

We have many seriously injured men and women in Woden. The Spirits of the Falls have great healing powers. Woden has much need of these if we are to recover.

The Old One looked at Jandra and smiled patiently, *We do have these powers, as you say, but this be a most unusual request. I will speak of it to the others, and we will do what we can.*

Jandra nodded, *Thank you.*

She looked at Sam, noticing that her swelling had been much relieved, as had her fever. She looked quiet and peaceful. The Spirits had cleaned and clothed her, and placed a soft covering on top of her to prevent chill. Jandra held Sam's hand and spoke to her for a long while. She spoke of her love for Sam, of their unborn child, of Woden, and how proud of Sam she was, and that no one could have done as much for Woden. And then she told her that Woden had won their battle, but much rebuilding was needed, so Jandra was needed. She gently told her that she would return within a small portion of a moon's passage, and to remain peaceful and secure in their love. She also told Sam that she needed to remove herself from this unconsciousness. When Meera and Caitha returned, Jandra was ready to depart with Meera, but was glad to have Caitha remain and tend to Sam as well she could. She kissed Sam gently, then left, her heart breaking more with every step.

* * * *

Caitha remained with Sam so that Jandra could return to Woden to provide the leadership it needed. Tadan went with Meera and Jandra to help in the rebuilding. Anyst remained with Caitha to provide a messenger to Caitha, if one were needed. As much as Jandra knew that Sam would have it so, it made it no easier for Jandra to leave her side. As they returned to Woden, Meera told Jandra about the battle in Woden, what she saw at Sam and Buron's battlefield, how many lives had been lost, the prisoners even Meera decided to let live, and the overall condition of Woden. Jandra listened with half-interest. She was pleased that Woden had won its battle, but also now knew that Fornaith, Apien and New Harborage would all require Woden's assistance to rebuild and reorganize, or others would take over, such as Buron had. She also had begun to suspect that the main battle yet raged between the Woden's Spirit Mothers and the Spirits of the Valley.

Tadan was excited to help rebuild Woden. He knew of his mother's thoughts about relocating the shops, and thought this would be a good moment to unite Hengist and Woden in more beneficial ways and patterns. Throughout the journey back to Woden, Tadan described his plan in detail to Jandra.

As they entered Woden, Meera led Jandra to what had been the former Highest's dwelling. It had been destroyed in the battle, but was now a make-shift camp and the center of Woden's rebuilding. They rode up to the tent and dismounted. The guards had announced her return, so all of Woden had come to greet her.

When she dismounted, all knelt and bowed their heads and said, "Highest."

Jandra hadn't noticed the gathering crowd upon her entrance, so was startled at their welcome. But quickly recognizing what they had called her, she became angry, "I don't care the laws of Woden. I will not have this so. Stand and address me only as Second. The Highest be alive and healing, so there be no need for such as this."

Karen rose and went to her, "But Highest, it be the law."

"NO! No longer. Think of The Highest as visiting elsewhere. I command this and will have it no other way. I will hear no more of this. Everyone, rise."

They did and looked at Jandra, well surprised. They had never heard her so angered, but saw that it was not at them, so returned to their rebuilding of Woden.

She turned back to Karan, "Tell me of what occurs presently."

"The animals and farms were unharmed, so our supplies be safe, except for the fisheries. Janel and Briggon think we can but build some smaller boats quickly to begin the fish trade soon. In the meanwhile, many companions must live with other companions until their dwellings be rebuilt. All help the builders in the after midturns to rebuild. Everyone becomes but a builder now. Hengist was unharmed and not entered, but they lost many lives, as Woden, in the battle. They also help us to rebuild. Every after midturn, all of Hengist comes to Woden to help rebuild. Life continues with the same patterns in the morns with everyone tending to the Woden and Hengist duties in the gardens and farms and such, then in the after midturn, Woden becomes rebuilt."

"Tadan has some ideas about relocating the shops. It is as The Highest wishes. Please make certain this occurs. I would like a meeting with all the advisors this eve. Where can such be held, now? I know not which location remains."

On the turn following Jandra's return, in the late after midturn while she was overseeing the rebuilding from the center tent, a large commotion occurred.

Karan ran over to Jandra, "Riders come, Second."

Jandra turned and saw that Meera and her guards were ready. She stood, just waiting to see who the riders were. As they neared, Jandra saw that it was their Spirit Mothers. The horses came charging up to the tent, creating a cloud of dust and dirt as they halted. As the Spirit Mothers dismounted, all the women of Woden that were near, knelt and bowed their heads, including Jandra.

Li'el'in'tiln came up to Jandra, *Jandra, please rise.*

The Spirit left the others yet kneeling.

Jandra rose, *Thank you for coming. We are in much need of your abilities.*

We are here to help your injured, at your request, and are glad we can serve you. We will remain but a short moment only. We will do our healing in privacy so request that your healers leave your dwelling for the injured. Jandra, please be our guide.

How is Sam?

She heals well but remains unconscious. I have good hopes for her, though. She is Sam and has a stubborn will to live.

Jandra asked Meera to send someone ahead to the infirmary and have the healers wait outside. She guided the Spirit Mothers to the infirmary and then watched as they went from one injured to the next, helping to heal their wounds. As soon as they had finished with their mission, they returned to their horses, who had patiently waited without assistance.

Prior to leaving, Li'el'in'tiln went to Jandra and placed her hand upon Jandra's womb, *Take care of yourself and all The Realm's unborn, Jandra, as we take care of Sam. Know that we think highly of what you do for The Realm and for us, as we have never prior answered such a request as this. You mean much to us, and we will watch over you, as you now watch over Woden. You will find your injured much recovered, for those we could.*

As they spoke to each other, the horses of the Spirit Mothers came up to Jandra, nudging her gently. She scratched their ears without thinking much about it.

Jandra bowed her head slightly, *Thank you. I know this was an overly large and inappropriate request on my part, but we had much need. It does Woden good to see its Spirits Mothers at such moments as these. Please give Sam my love.*

Li'el'in'tiln smiled upon Jandra, placed a light kiss upon her head, then the Spirit Mothers left as the wind.

Turn by turn, Jandra oversaw the rebuilding of Woden. With Tadan's new layout of Woden in-hand, and with everyone working to help rebuild, its new buildings and redesign quickly took shape. The old shops were turned into new companion dwellings. The former Highest's dwelling site was redesigned into a large meetinghouse, all on one-floor, half-enclosed and half-exposed but covered. As had been begun prior to the battle, the animal farms were also relocated just off the path between Woden and Hengist, and nearer to the shops.

What everyone wanted completed prior to Sam's arrival was the new Highest and Second's dwelling. Lillon, Karan and Tadan took over this project and wanted it as a surprise to Second and Highest upon its completion. The Hengist shipmakers began work on a new ship to begin replacing the two ships lost in the battle. One ship had been badly damaged, but hadn't sunk, so they began rebuilding that one first. Janel oversaw the rebuilding of the docks and said that they had needed replacing anyway.

Jandra lived with Meera during these moments of reconstruction, not caring and not really noticing. May had survived the battle, but had sustained a few minor wounds. She insisted on cooking for Jandra, however, saying that Woden's unborn Highest needed her care and nutrition. Hengist had lost 158 men, and Woden had sadly lost 263 women. As Jandra did Sam's rounds for her when she could, she noticed that many lives had been forever altered. As sad as it was, she tried to make the rounds daily, as it helped to present a normal face to Woden and it also helped cheer the women of Woden. They all remarked how Jandra was now beginning to show in her pregnancy. Jandra thought little of the unborn during these turns, but was glad that it helped to cheer the other women. Jandra sent daily messages to Sam and Caitha, and in return, Caitha sent messages back on Sam's recovery. It bothered Jandra to not be with Sam, but the progress reports bothered her even more.

Each turn brought another message the same as the prior turn's, *Sam yet recovering and yet unconscious. The Spirit Mothers tend to her well. There has been no movement yet. No need for you to come.*

So Jandra remained in Woden to direct the rebuilding. Turns turned into a moon, and yet the messages remained the same. Jandra and Sam's unborn grew more. May continued to feed and nurture Jandra as she had done with Sam. Meera gave up her and Caitha's bed to Jandra and took to sleeping on the long chair, instead of the reverse.

Oisin returned a moon after the battle. Her ships were badly damaged, she had lost more than half her crew, but she and her crew had won all their battles. She had also returned with 126 new arrivals to Woden and Hengist. Oisin had returned physically injured, as well. Her crew had to carry her off her ship and into Woden. She refused to go to the infirmary, so Meera had her placed in a dwelling near hers. Oisin's injuries included a broken leg, a long sword gash on her left arm that had become infected, and a smaller gash on her forehead that had begun to heal well. The healers tended to Oisin every moment until the infection had left her.

For one long eve, Meera sat with Oisin and told her all that had occurred while she had been away. Meera didn't want Oisin to learn of Jandra and Sam informally. Since Sam wasn't able to tell Oisin of this, Meera felt it was her place to do so. Oisin wasn't surprised though, and took it well enough. She informed Meera that Sam had prepared her for this prior to her departure.

"Aye, Meera. She never would consider having me. But I do love that one."

"You be overly strong-minded and wavering for Sam. She needed someone to love her at all moments, such as had Brett."

"Ah, but I do. Love is one thing. Sex is yet another. And while there be all those wonderful stories of Brett, she sought to but control Sam overly."

"Oh, and you would not? And you know you would have bored of her, and it would have embarrassed all of Woden."

"Perhaps. I do like to find bluer seas on every journey, so perhaps it be true. Yet, I love her well enough and think of her all my moments. When I lay with another, I think of her, only."

"Yet you need to lay with another."

"You speak truth, and it is for this I am happy for Sam and Jandra. With child, you say. Who did Jandra lie with?"

"No man. It is from magic of the Spirit Mothers. Sam took a tear from Jandra when she once cried and made it of her own. I know not how, but the Spirit Mothers had it formed into their unborn. It be now legend that this unborn is to be the future ruler of all The Realm, and will rule it in peace."

Osisin looked skeptical. "The Spirit Mothers seem overly involved with our affairs for my liking."

With the new arrivals that Oisin had brought back with her, and the new arrivals just prior to the battle, Jandra kept all the advisors busy bringing in the new ones in the Woden and Hengist way. Jandra refused to make a decision regarding a third community, leaving that to Sam upon her return. Instead, she had the mixed companions temporarily separated into Hengist and Woden. Since the new arrivals wanted only peace and a better life, they didn't seem to mind the placements.

The trades and crafts continued their production and under Jandra's and all the advisors' direction and leadership, Woden Falls returned to normal, although the rebuilding and relocations would continue for over a cycle. With Oisin's return, the shipbuilding went into high speed. She was glad that Janel had proceeded quickly with the docks, but Oisin wanted the ships rebuilt sooner than it was taking. She took the remaining of her crews and placed them on shifts so that the ship rebuilding could occur every moment of the turn.

Shortly after Oisin's return, Jandra decided to return to Sam to see if all was the same and asked Meera to accompany her on the return. Meera noticed that Jandra had become even quieter than she had been when she had first left Sam to return to Woden. She saw that the weight of ruling Woden had been a burden to Jandra, who had been acting as its Highest in Sam's absence. Unlike Sam, without Sam or Caitha, who had become a close friend of Jandra's, Jandra had no one in which to confide her problems. Jandra held them inside, waiting for her companion and friend to return.

Meera had taken an easier but longer route to the Spirit Mothers just to keep Jandra safe. When they arrived, the Spirit Mothers were waiting for them. Caitha was also waiting, holding out her arms to both Meera and Jandra.

Meera. Jandra. It be good to see the both of you.

Jandra gave Caitha a long hug and then asked, *Sam?*

She be the same. The Spirit Mothers tend to her continually and say that she be doing well, but she remains fully unconscious. How be Woden?

I will leave you and Meera to discuss this while I look in on Sam.

The Spirit Mothers greeted Jandra and the unborn with much love and over attention. Jandra just wanted to see and speak with Sam. She had become overly lonely since Sam's battle with Buron. She found her life empty without her, and often found herself resenting the unborn within her. She thanked the Spirit Mothers for their attention and healing of Sam and then excused herself, saying that it had been long she had been able to see her. They led Jandra into Sam's room.

Remain as long as you desire, Jandra. She misses you as well.

Jandra entered the room and saw Sam yet laying in the bed, much the same as she had seen Sam prior. She looked upon Sam and studied her features. Softness began to return to Jandra, something she hadn't felt since her departure. She sat next to her on the bed, and held Sam's left hand. She moved her fingers through Sam's hair and spoke to her softly for a long while, telling her of Woden, Tadan, Meera and Oisin. But mostly of how much she missed her. She gently chastised her for not removing herself from her unconscious state. She wanted to cry, but now refused to do so.

After a while, Jandra lay down next to Sam. She was careful not to move the bed or to cause Sam any movement. She lay like that a long while, just basking in the feeling and smell of that which she had come to love. She gently placed Sam's hand on her womb so that Sam could feel her unborn grow within her. She remained all eve in this fashion. When the Spirit Mothers came to check on Sam, they saw Jandra lying next to her, so performed their duties in silence, letting Jandra remain where she slept.

In the morn, Jandra bid Sam farewell once again and departed for Woden. Caitha again volunteered to remain with Sam, so would not be leaving with them. The Spirit Mothers told Jandra that Sam's healing process was proceeding well, but that they were concerned over the unconsciousness. On the return journey, Meera noticed that Jandra was in a slightly better attitude, so spoke to her of Oisin, Apien, New Harborage and Fornaith. Meera informed her that it was the feeling of the advisors that someone should go to remain in the communities to restore order and provide leadership until they could form their own.

"Are there many left in Apien and New Harborage?"

"No. There be none left in New Harborage. Oisin moved all who wanted to remain to Apien, to rebuild there. She says that there be fewer than 200 who remain."

"And Fornaith?"

"Fornaith has many. Only the guards died, here in Woden."

"What became of Manthar and all his followers?"

"Oisin had captured him and found him to be quite insane. But before she could rid The Realm of him, the people of Apien overtook Oisin's guards so that they could have Manthar for themselves. From what Oisin heard, the torture they put upon him was quite long lasting."

Her eyes narrowed at the thought. "I have had enough of war, death and torture. I have had enough of injury and battles. Why do these things be so necessary and common throughout our realm? Why do we not celebrate peace and weakness instead of fighting and strength?"

"Because we must. If we laid down our weapons, we and our ways would but perish. If the quality of our life be not important, then we need no weapons. Being slaves would then be most acceptable. I know not why others can't let us to ourselves. It seems that power is most alluring."

"Why did you let Sir Devin live? It be not like you to take prisoners."

"He amuses me. We can yet learn much from him, and he be such a sniveling weakling. I thought he might be an amusement to Woden and Hengist after all the loss they have faced. It is often good to have a common enemy in sight to gain a sense of purpose and to use as a reminder."

Jandra nodded, but said nothing. She had grown much harder in her interim as Highest. She moved her thoughts to Sam, and then to Woden. There was yet much to oversee and accomplish. Meera missed Caitha as Jandra missed Sam, but was busy rebuilding and retraining the guards of

Woden. Most of the guards from Hengist had perished in the battle. She sat with the remaining guards almost daily to reassess what had occurred.

She often asked, "Why did we lose so many in this battle?"

They studied and restudied the battle, looking at it from many angles so that they could learn from it for the future. They captured all the weapons that Buron had brought with him. And Oisin's crew in harbor had captured one of his ships. Hengist was busy rebuilding that one, too. They had found small iron balls with spikes on them that had killed many of Hengist and Woden. They had found shields of metal that had prevented Woden's arrows from penetrating their lines.

Jandra kept her turns filled from early morn to late eve. May chastised her regularly, but Jandra simply smiled, listening and talking to no one unless it was about the rebuilding. She rose in the early morn, took her meal, and then spent the rest of her turn at the central tent where all reorganization commands were given. In the midturn, she performed her rounds. She would do one-half of Woden one turn, the other half the next turn, and Hengist on the third turn. She then repeated the process. She saw many new couples forming in the moon and a half Sam had been gone. Since many companions had been broken through the deaths of battle, new unions were being formed. The new unions were the essence and rebeginning of Woden. In these unions, the strength and customs would continue. But even Jandra was beginning to wonder why they must have separate communities.

Jandra hadn't been to her and Sam's dwelling since the battle. She had been given a strong but polite request that the communities would like to surprise her and Sam. To that end, the rebuilding of the dwelling was a high priority for the communities as they wanted it done upon Sam's return. Jandra had no idea of what this joint project was to look like. Karan reminded her daily to not visit the site, and daily, Jandra agreed to the request.

Karan had become an excellent assistant. She would usually attend Jandra on the rounds, informing her of all the updates. It was a moment in the turn that Jandra had come to look forward to. While not speaking to Karan of much, Jandra had come to like the pattern and took some relief in its familiarity and Karan's easiness with her. Karan never nagged at her. She never interfered with Jandra's feelings about Sam. And she never pushed Jandra to speak.

For the past few turns, Jandra had come to need some rest in the late after midturn. May would provide her with some tea and light foods, and Jandra would rest for a short while. She guessed that it had something to do with the unborn within her that took so much of her energy. Meera had been so busy rebuilding Woden and Hengist's fortifications that she hadn't noticed Jandra's growing womb. It had grown much, and was now noticeable. As Jandra did her daily rounds, the women would welcome her in their dwellings, such as they were until reconstruction occurred, and offer her tea and sweets or drink and a light meal. The community had embraced Jandra as they had Sam, and made an effort to ensure themselves of Jandra's well being.

And yet the daily messages continued, *All is well with Sam, but there be no change. She yet sleeps in her unconsciousness. I give her your thoughts daily.*

Turn in and turn out, Jandra waited and hoped for a report that would make all the effort worth it. Jandra went from turn to turn in a state of semi-awareness. She provided the leadership Woden needed to rebuild, but found nor sought any personal connection to anyone. She remained politely aloof, wondering what she would do if Sam didn't awaken. Turns turned into moons, and yet Sam hadn't regained consciousness. The unborn continued to grow within Jandra. As comforting as the unborn was at moments, at other moments, Jandra resented the unborn and became angered at her. She also became angered at Sam. Jandra knew these feelings of anger and resentment were out of self pity only, so worked to rid herself of them. She engaged herself in the rebuilding of Woden from early morn to late-eve so as to keep herself busy. Almost three moons had come and passed, and Jandra rose to face the turn. As she did every morn, she shut off all her emotions, refusing to allow herself the pleasure of missing and loving Sam.

On this after midturn, while she was resting, Jandra was woken by a large commotion.

May came running in, "Second, come quickly. You are needed."

Jandra rose, running to the outside of the dwelling, her mind racing in thoughts of battle, "What is it, May? Who but attacks us?"

But May was overly far ahead of her to respond. When Jandra got outside, she saw everyone kneeling and with heads bowed, but not in her direction. She looked in the direction of where they bowed, but couldn't make out the figure. She kept looking and then saw the smile on May's face.

Jandra screamed to herself, *SAM!*

Sam had entered Woden upon a horse from the Spirit Mothers. It was not a horse of Woden. It was of the rivers and waters, as Jandra had seen of the Spirit Mothers. Sam used no bridle to ride this horse, and it was if the horse knew where Sam wanted it to go without the need of reins. When the horse came near, it knelt down onto its front legs so that Sam could get off of easily. Jandra saw that Sam's stance had changed. She no longer seemed as Sam, and Jandra became nervous.

What if she has no further need of me? Have her Spirit Mothers taken her from us? From me? Has this battle with Buron changed her so?

Sam dismounted just in front of all those now kneeling. More of the community had heard of The Highest's return and continued to come over. All knelt, and all bowed their heads. And they all waited for a word from their now-returned Highest. Sam saw a guard move to take the horse, but waved her off.

She turned to the horse, "I will call you when I need you."

As the horse turned and left, Sam walked toward those now awaiting her. Jandra was the only one standing, and the only one looking at Sam. She saw that Sam walked with a limp, using a cane to do so. Sam said nothing to those who knelt, but made her way slowly toward Jandra, limping badly.

When she was close, she held out her arm, *Jandra. I have missed you.*

Jandra slowly, and slightly hesitantly, moved into her embrace. As Sam closed her arms around her, Jandra felt embraced into a sense of relief she hadn't felt for what seemed a lifespan. Sam continued to embrace Jandra, and all Jandra could see was Sam. There was no Woden, and there was no life. There was only Sam and Jandra in all The Realm.

It is because of you I lived. I return for you, Jandra.

Jandra noticed that Sam spoke through her thoughts, as she had done while with the Spirit Mothers. But having so overly much to say, Jandra said nothing at all. She allowed her emotions to say it for her.

Jandra held Sam, fearing that if she let her go, she would disappear. Sam returned the embrace, patiently letting Jandra move away from her fears.

"Jandra, speak to me. Are you well? You do not speak."

Jandra simply nodded her head into Sam's shoulders, and cried.

Sam turned to look at all those who waited and saw that they did so patiently. Sam placed her hand gently on Jandra's head, holding it lightly, "All is well, now."

Jandra touched Sam. She felt her cheeks, her hair and her arms. She needed to touch Sam to ensure herself that Sam had really returned, and that she was whole.

Sam gently let go of Jandra and spoke softly, "I will return in but a moment. Wait here."

Jandra finally found her voice, "Where be Caitha?"

"She and Anyst come. My horse, a gift from the Spirit Mothers, is much quicker."

"Your leg. Why do you yet limp? I thought you would be healed."

"I will be. Worry not. I awoke just prior to my healing being complete. I be out of danger now. My back is yet sore as be my leg and arm, but now it be not so serious if I move. I am unable to do any fighting for a long while with these breaks, though. I be your invalid."

"Good."

She spoke even more softly, "What of our dwelling?'

"They rebuild it. It is to be a surprise to us. Karan, Tadan and Lillon all schemed on it." She smiled her first real smile in many moons, her heart finally relieved, "Oh, Sam. You are finally home."

They held each other once more, then Sam turned to Woden, "I am returned. Where do we begin?"

Elsewhere, across The Realm

The High Queen paced, "So, she has finally awoken?"
"Yes, my Queen."
"But she remained with the Spirits for three moons."
"Yes, Highness."
"They tried to find out how she survived the battle?"
"So it would seem, Highness. I don't believe they could though, so finally allowed her back into The Realm."
"They used her to rid themselves of Buron?"
"So it would seem, my Queen."
"She has returned to Woden?"
"Yes, Highness."
"And her lover? She is well?"
"She will have this child soon, my Queen."

The High Queen frowned, "Our moment begins, then. We must bring this child here so as to protect it from those Spirit Mothers. They have lied to her, to Me, and to The Realm. And now they lie to our unborn that has been vowed to us. Does the lover know of this?"

"She has never trusted them, my Queen, even when she was with them. She hid her thoughts well from them, frustrating them."

The High Queen laughed lightly, "She is a bright one, as you have stated. How fares her pregnancy?"

"She loves The Highest well, so her three moons away fell heavily upon her. But she bears up well, and is strong. In truth, Highness, I have never prior seen such a strong one. She faces any challenge straight on with no fear."

"She sounds most interesting."
"She is a most excellent Highest, my Queen."
"Highest? Ah, yes. I recall this. She was The Second. So when The Highest was injured, she must have become acting Highest. How good is she?"

"The Highest is not as good as her lover, my Queen."
"Why do you say this?"

"The Highest is excellent as a Highest, my Queen, and is most attentive of her town, but her lover makes better and stronger decisions. She is more like you, my Queen."

"How fare her looks during this pregnancy?"

"If it were possible, I would say she is now even more beautiful."

"It would seem we will meet her soon enough."

"Yes, my Queen, but there may be a small issue."

"Tell Me."

"They may wish for her to have the unborn with the Spirits of the Falls."

"Then we must intercept her as they travel to them. Make this occur, Force Leader."

"Yes, my Queen. You may count on this. I will inform you when I leave."

"I will go with you. My powers may be needed."

"Yes, my Queen."

~ ~ ~

About the Author

Robbie Collins lives with her High Queen and menagerie near a small town and a very large lake. She has a rather unbelievable background in a preponderous of esoteric knowledge. Upon occasion, she dabbles in Celtic folk music, hiking, snowshoeing, writing, kayaking and gardening. She has always followed the road north.

Printed in the United States
101307LV00008B/34/A